VIRAGO
MODERN CLASSICS
438

Naomi Mitchison

Novelist, poet, passionate Scottish politician, campaigner for sexual freedom, and farmer, Naomi Mitchison has lived through nearly the entire twentieth century. She was born in 1897 in Edinburgh to Louise Kathleen Trotter and the physiologist John Scott Haldane. She cut short studies at Oxford to enlist as a VAD nurse and in 1916 she married G. R. Mitchison, who became a Labour MP. Her adventurous life has included travel in five continents, political skirmishes, vivid friendships and commitment to communities in the Scottish Highlands and in Botswana. Her literary career began with poems and plays but she soon proved herself to be a prolific and varied novelist. She has written over seventy books that include the novels *The Corn King and Spring Queen* (1931) and the controversial *We Have Been Warned* (1935) that dealt openly with seduction, rape and abortion. She has written three volumes of autobiography and Virago publish her biography, *The Nine Lives of Naomi Mitchison*, by Jenni Calder in 1997. Naomi Mitchison lives in Scotland.

THE BULL CALVES

Naomi Mitchson

A *Virago* Book

Published by Virago Press 1997

First published by Jonathan Cape 1947

ISBN 1 86049 374 2

Printed and bound in Great Britain by
Clays Ltd, St Ives plc

07250878

Virago
A Division of
Little, Brown and Company (UK)
Brettenham House
Lancaster Place

CONTENTS

PART ONE	THE SMOOTH MID-CENTURY	21
PART TWO	YE HIGHLANDS AND YE LOWLANDS	151
PART THREE	ILL FISHING IN DRUMLIE WATERS	247
PART FOUR	THE KINDLY HOUSE	337

NOTES ON PART ONE ... 407

    THE QUESTION OF LANGUAGE ... 407

    THE VARIOUS FAMILIES ... 412

    AGRICULTURE ... 419

    GLENEAGLES ... 425

    PRICES ... 428

    GENERAL NOTES ... 429

NOTES ON PART TWO ... 455

    THE HISTORICAL USE OF WORDS ... 455

    GENERAL NOTES ... 466

NOTES ON PART THREE ... 493

    THE JACOBITES AND THE CAMPBELLS ... 493

    GENERAL NOTES ... 496

NOTES ON PART FOUR ... 519

    SCOTLAND — THE UNION ... 519

    GENERAL NOTES ... 524

*Dedicated to the other Bull Calves, living and dead, and
to the Highlanders they may have loved. But
most of all to those who are only
names in a family tree,
and, of those,
my one*

CLEMENCY EALASAID

JULY 1940

Mi Ritrovai in una selva oscura
  Blindly, gingerly, beginning to grope through the prickly
                                            future,

With only thorns left on my white rose
To jag and tear at the heart suddenly,
Hands out, I move.
Knowing that inside those shut drawers, the woolly coats and
                                            the vests,
The cuddly shawls and the flannels, all, all, wait cold and
                                            folded.
When I go down to the room I left last, in pain and happy,
They will come and put them away, sorry for me, hoping I
                                            may have forgotten,
As though forgetting were possible.
Having imagined beforehand, very precisely and very gently,
The white cot by my bed, the old cot with the new green
                                            blankets,
The new dark soft head, the faint breathing, the warmth
                                            and love,
The ghost of the cot is still there when I turn to my right.
And when I turn to my left, there is the sea, there is Carradale
                                            Bay, and sea-deep,
Dark and alone where the Cluaran dropped her, my dear,
                                            my daughter,
Not in my arms, not in my womb: in the box Angus made, a
                                            small weight.

Round about, says the Boyg
  Thinking of these things, wrongly, archaically, personally,
I must retract, I must say to myself
She was not yet human, not individual, cannot be lonely,
It is only my projection of love onto her,
Only the months of bearing, the pains of labour interpreted,

And interpreted wrongly.
Because I had touched her, kissed her, been happy for a few
hours,
I had built up a structure of love and vanity, my pride, my
youngest.
That was irrational, and, because irrational, wrong.
Peer Gynt, for ever projecting and protruding his self onto
the world,
Symbol of the individual, of capitalism, of commercial
progress,
He is finished.   But the Boyg in the Dovrefeld
Still remains above half-starved, half-beaten Norway,
And will remain.

You said to me: Come back, come back, mother — knowing
That I was not wholly here, but half pulled down, half
drowned in the sea tangle,
Beside my baby, where the waves covered, in the wake of the
Cluaran.
I must, I will, come back.

These twenty centuries of bourgeois bargaining,
Since Jesus, himself a Jew, saw through it, saw there must be
No scales of corn-growing justice, but only love,
Have left their mark on me.
Now I am trying to bargain, to say take her death, my grief,
But save me the others, from bombs, shells, from pandemic
Disease, save me children and husband, save Ruth, Dick,
Taggy and all of them,
Clutching out for lives on the spread bargain counter,
clutching them to my heart,
But looking up I see
No bargainer on the far side of the counter, nothing: only
another projection:
Round about, says the Boyg.

CLEMENCY EALASAID

Roll up the map of Europe

Should we try to make sense of a senseless situation?
Over-simplifying, after the habit of the orthodox,
Catholic or Marxist. Shall we try to make sense of Oran?
Try to make sense of inevitable hatred
From mothers of French sailors, babies who had lived
Through the years of hope and pride and delight, boyhood
and manhood,
Now murdered by the Ally, perfide Albion?
How make a bargain on that? Roll up the map of Europe.
The lights have gone out: the concentration camps are full:
the men and women
Who thought themselves safe have been betrayed to the
vultures,
To Himmler, Goering, Franco, to those whose faces
Express Satanic possession. Paris is dead.
Only the bones remain. Paris of the Commune
Dead as the sailors at Oran. This winter we hope to starve
France, Belgium, Holland, Denmark, Norway, Poland:
Harvest of dead babies, disease, hatred: no sense.
My breasts tingle and stab with milk that no one wants,
Surplus as American wheat, surplus and senseless.
Not her soft kind mouth groping for me. Useless, senseless.
If my baby had been starved by England, would I ever
forgive?
Roll up the map of Europe.

Carradale

This was to have been a binding between me and Carradale.
Weeper of Carradale Glen, fairy hare, cleft rock, did none of
you speak?
How shall I stay here, how go on with the little things,
How not hate Carradale, the flowery betrayer,
Dagger in fist?
How be crushed into such humility as can continue
The daily work, alleviation of meals and sleep and slight
laughter?

How, having known happiness, not see it anywhere?
I should have been happy before, in Highland May
Of blossom and bird-song.   Ah, how not be happy
When one could not foresee?

Time and the hour runs through the roughest day
The roughest day is not yet.   This was a rough day
For me and perhaps for Carradale. But the roughest day,
The day lived through by Macbeth who had been king,
Some say a good king, and by Gruach, my ancestors,
Hangs now in the future, the unturned page, the history book
So far unwritten, and we, single-sighted,
Not having seen the ghost funeral nor identified the bearers,
Imagine it next week or next month, Ragnarok, the doomday.
Who knows what each shall lose? Who knows the issue?
Will there be another birth, a fair one, or is West Europe
Too old, too old for that, as I shall be too old
For another bearing
Before the roughest day is past: as I am now
Unable to imagine the new times, because of the blackness
Steadily ahead of me, the still curtain
Over my dancing daughter, my innocent, my small one.
Ah darkness of the spirit, lift, lift, let the hour run through
you!

The roughest day is to come.   We shall perhaps
Live through it, or others will.   In a hundred years
Things may be seen in order, making sense, drawing a new
map:
Human endeavour going roundabout, unselfishly,
May, arriving suddenly on the Dovrefeld, see ahead, make
fresh ski-tracks.
In a hundred years
The French sailors at Oran, the Scottish dead at Abbeville,
The tortured in the concentration camps and all the leaders,
The ones who thought themselves godlike, forgetting the
Boyg,
And I, and my children, and all the people of Carradale,

We shall be dead, at last out of the running of events and
hours. The page will have been turned,
The history written, and we, anonymous,
Shall be condemned or not condemned, gently upbraided
For folly of not foreseeing, for dithered watching of hours
While the roughest day runs by.

But the trees I planted in the heavy months, carrying you,
Thinking you would see them grown, they will be tall and
lovely:
Red oak and beech and tsuga, grey alder and douglas:
But not for you or your children. What will it matter then,
forgotten daughter,
Forgotten as I shall be forgotten in the running of time,
Maybe a name in an index, but not me, not remembered
As I alone remember, with what tears yet, the first kiss, the
faint warmth and stirring?
The waves will cover us all diving into darkness out of the
bodies of death,
Vanishing as the wake of a boat in a strong current.
The hot tears will be cooled and the despair of the middle-
aged, rolling up their map,
Will be forgotten, with other evil things, will be interpreted,
Will be forgiven at last.

NOTES ON THE ILLUSTRATIONS

THE HILT OF CAPTAIN ROBERT'S SWORD: MAKER JOHN
SIMPSON OF GLASGOW, SIGNING I.S.   35
A MINISTER'S HAND   87
GLENEAGLES: THE HOUSE STANDING IN THE MOUTH OF
THE GLEN   133
WILLIAM'S PLAID BROOCH: SILVER WITH INCISED DESIGN
AND NIELLO, JEWEL SETTINGS ROUND THE EDGE   147
SOMETHING KIRSTIE COULD HAVE SEEN   161
LACHLAN'S PISTOL: MAKER MICLEOD, PROBABLY GLASGOW   230
MUNGO'S TABLE SNUFF MULL: RAM'S HORN   244
PATRICK'S INKSTAND: SILVER   268
PLASTER DECORATIONS FROM A ROOM IN THE OLDER PART
OF GLENEAGLES   334
A GLENEAGLES KEY   366
THE CUAICH FROM WHICH FORBES SUPPED HIS RHUBARB:
POLISHED WOOD, DOVETAILED TOGETHER   378

THE originals of most of the objects drawn here come from the Art Galleries in Glasgow, and Miss Annand and I wish to thank Dr. Honeyman and Dr. Henderson for their help. Two of the portraits are from contemporary paintings at Gleneagles, and we also wish to thank the elder branch of the family at Gleneagles for all their help. The portrait of Forbes is derived from the Roubilliac statue in the Parliament House in Edinburgh.

The action of this book takes place on June 16th and 17th, 1747, in and about the house of Gleneagles, on the northern slopes of the Ochils.

Readers unfamiliar with the history of the times, should bear the following dates in mind: (Ⅲ)

1702   Death of William II. Accession of Anne. Union between England and Scotland proposed.

1707   Act of Union passed.

1714   Death of Queen Anne.

1715   Jacobite rising: James VIII proclaimed. Mar at Perth. Macintosh of Borlum invades England, is defeated at Preston. Battle of Sheriffmuir. Defeat of the Jacobites; in the course of their retreat they burn the villages between Stirling and Perth.

1719   Jacobite landing. Jacobites beaten at Glenshiel.

1736   Wade's roads through the Highlands begun, finished eleven years later.

1739   Hume publishes his *Treatise on Human Nature*.

1745   Battle of Fontenoy. Charles Edward lands. The gathering of the clans and march south. Prestonpans. Charles Edward at Holyrood. They march into England. At Derby they turn back.

1746   January: Battle of Falkirk. Jacobites take Inverness. Cumberland waits. April 16th: Battle of Culloden. Charles Edward a fugitive until September. Cumberland's 'pacification' of the Highlands. Penal Laws against the Highlands.

A Ancestors of Helen Erskine, second wife of John Haldane, M.P., of Gleneagles.

Duke of Lennox ═ Katherine de Balsac
|
Earl of Mar ═ Mary Stewart

etc.

John Earl of Mar

John Earl of Mar
(Bobbing John)

B Ancestors of Mary Drummond, first wife of John Haldane, M.P., of Gleneagles.

C Ancestors of Katherine Fraser, the wife of William Murray of Ochtertyre, and Mother of Patrick

D Andrew Shaw of Bargarran

Rev. Andrew Shaw of Bargarran
first husband of Christian Haldane

E Ancestors of William Macintosh of Borlum second husband of Christian Haldane, otherwise known as Black William

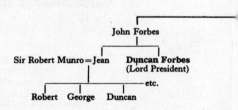

John Forbes

Sir Robert Munro ═ Jean **Duncan Forbes**
(Lord President)

- - etc.

Robert George Duncan

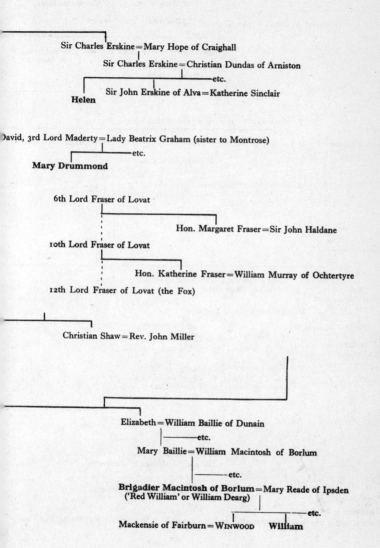

Sir Charles Erskine = Mary Hope of Craighall
  |
  Sir Charles Erskine = Christian Dundas of Arniston
    |
    — etc.
  Sir John Erskine of Alva = Katherine Sinclair
  Helen

David, 3rd Lord Maderty = Lady Beatrix Graham (sister to Montrose)
  |
  — etc.
  Mary Drummond

6th Lord Fraser of Lovat
  ⋮
    Hon. Margaret Fraser = Sir John Haldane
  10th Lord Fraser of Lovat
  ⋮
    Hon. Katherine Fraser = William Murray of Ochtertyre
  12th Lord Fraser of Lovat (the Fox)

Christian Shaw = Rev. John Miller

Elizabeth = William Baillie of Dunain
  |
  — etc.
  Mary Baillie = William Macintosh of Borlum
    |
    — etc.
    Brigadier Macintosh of Borlum = Mary Reade of Ipsden
    ('Red William' or William Dearg)
      | — etc.
    Mackensie of Fairburn = WINWOOD   **William**

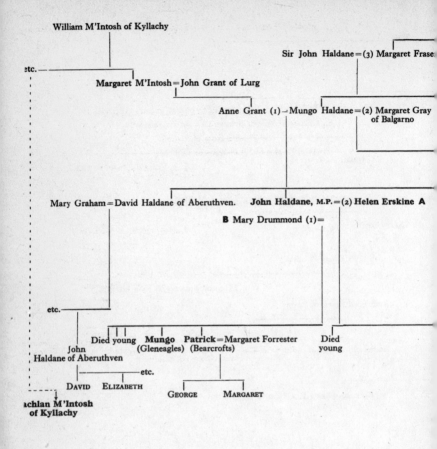

William M'Intosh of Kyllachy

Sir John Haldane = (3) Margaret Frase

etc. —

Margaret M'Intosh = John Grant of Lurg

Anne Grant (1) — Mungo Haldane = (2) Margaret Gray of Balgarno

Mary Graham = David Haldane of Aberuthven.   **John Haldane**, M.P. = (2) Helen Erskine **A**

B Mary Drummond (1) =

etc. —

Died young   **Mungo** (Gleneagles)   **Patrick** = Margaret Forrester (Bearcrofts)   Died young

John Haldane of Aberuthven

— etc. —

DAVID   ELIZABETH   GEORGE   MARGARET

achlan M'Intosh of Kyllachy

Chinnery-Haldanes of Gleneagles

Key characters in **bold type**
Characters living at the time of the narrative and mentioned in it, in CAPITALS AND SMALL CAPITALS

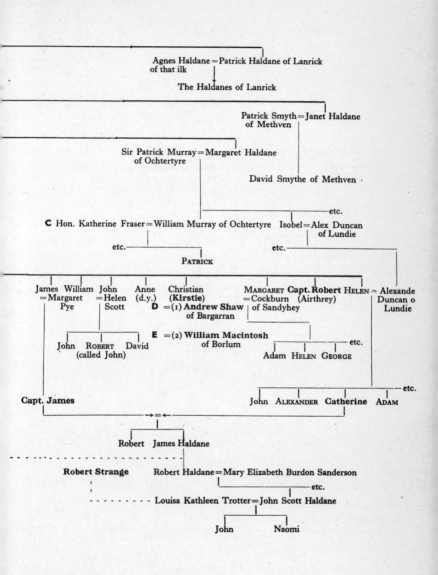

6th Lord Fraser of Lovat = Jean Stewart (sister to the Bonny Earl of Moray)

Agnes Haldane = Patrick Haldane of Lanrick
of that ilk

The Haldanes of Lanrick

Patrick Smyth = Janet Haldane
of Methven

Sir Patrick Murray = Margaret Haldane
of Ochtertyre

David Smythe of Methven

etc.

C Hon. Katherine Fraser = William Murray of Ochtertyre   Isobel = Alex Duncan
of Lundie

etc.   etc.

PATRICK

James   William   John   Anne   Christian   MARGARET **Capt. Robert** HELEN = Alexander
= Margaret = Helen   (d.y.) (**Kirstie**)   = Cockburn (Airthrey)   Duncan o
Pye   Scott   **D** = (1) **Andrew Shaw** of Sandyhey   Lundie
                                   of Bargarran

                           E = (2) **William Macintosh**
John   ROBERT   David   of Borlum
(called John)   Adam HELEN GEORGE   etc.

                                                                                etc.

Capt. James   John ALEXANDER **Catherine** ADAM

→ = ←

Robert   James Haldane

Robert Strange   Robert Haldane = Mary Elizabeth Burdon Sanderson

                                    etc.

- - - - - - - Louisa Kathleen Trotter = John Scott Haldane

                           John   Naomi

PART ONE

THE SMOOTH MID-CENTURY

LIME AVENUE AT GLENEAGLES

CHAPTER I

THEY were walking up and down on the bowling green, elderly
folk, all the lot of them; yet they looked happy. And how
could one be happy at all, she thought, if one was not young?
She looked up and the sky was clear blue and the steep slopes
of the Ochils came down to meet the crops, and beyond at the
crook of the loaning, Janet Mailor was scrubbing the wooden
milk pails and singing Corn Rigs and Barley Rigs: Are bonny,
thought Catherine Duncan, are brushing and alive with leaves
and sweet corn in the mouth, and the lads stand back in the
narrow path to let the Gleneagles lasses pass with their proud,
full skirts, and all of a lad would be respectful and decent
forby his eyes that would be straight in your own for a moment.
Bonny and sweet the long light days of the Scottish summer, and
knee deep along Ruthven water all the sharp-scented things,
crane's-bill and musk, blue spikes and balls of bog mint: moon
daisies and the thousand feather-headed summer weeds, sweet
Cicely, hedge parsley, earth-nuts: green, dew-full crinkled
leaves of lady's mantle: and there the shallocks islanded and
reflected, the fleurs de lys, the curly hooped ones.

On the bowling-green, her Aunt Kirstie had tucked back the
lace from her wrist and stooped to pick up one of the bowls and
sent it down the lawn; but it had the wrong bias on it, and was
away into the rosemary hedge, and Kirstie laughing as though
she had done something clever, and Black William — though
he was grey enough now, where his own hair showed under the
tie-wig — laughing with her. But Captain Robert frowned and
took his sister's arm; he did not like to be scolding Kirstie and
she near fifty, as he had seen that morning when he took a keek
into their father's Book and there was her name and the birth
date 1699, aye, that took you back. Yet it was an intolerable
thing to the Captain, who had been so often in danger of his
life through sea perils half a world away from Scotland, that
any Haldane, man or woman, should not take life seriously,

and Kirstie close enough on an age when a rational person should be thinking on their Maker and not on any Highland husband! But Kirstie laughed again and took a dancing step on the fine, rolled grass of the bowling-green.

Catherine Duncan picked up her needlework from the bank beside her and let on she was taking a stitch or two, for there was Gleneagles himself, Mungo Haldane, coming down from the old castle with his farm account books under his arm. He was talking to Patrick Murray of Ochtertyre, her second cousin; he went with a limp yet, that he had got at Falkirk, and he seemed to be nodding and agreeing in a daft-like way with everything Gleneagles was saying to him. And what would that be, she thought, except this planting of trees, for her uncle was laying out a lime avenue between the house and the chapel, and was for ever writing to nurserymen for foreign seeds, silver fir, sweet chestnut, cedars and mulberries that were well kennt never to do so far to the north. And Ochtertyre would no doubt be saying that he would try the same things, and would ask his cousin's advice with all the gravity and deference in the world! For, up till lately, the Haldanes of Gleneagles had been holding no kind of communication with the Murrays of Ochtertyre; and indeed it had been no comfortable thing for Mungo to have his young cousin with the rebels. He had always seemed a decent enough young man, but there had been his father before him in the '15, and only got out of prison by his uncle John Haldane, the Member, Mungo's father, taking every kind of trouble over it. But maybe now folks took politics more seriously and kinships less so. Catherine had heard Bearcrofts saying hard things enough about young Ochtertyre, whose mother was a Lovat, making him cousin to Simon Fraser, the Fox — not to be trusted a yard, none of that blood! Aye, and adding that there was such a stupidity and short-sightedness about the rebellion as should have kept any honest and reasonable man out of it! But, the Bear would have you think there was a downright wickedness about the Jacobites. When he began to talk that way, everyone else at the table fell silent, and there would be a kind of discomfort all through the room, the way the young folk would make haste to get away from it. And the rebellion was over surely, the last of it had died out almost a year ago, nobody at all talked of it, no need to mind on it now. There would be balls and dinner parties again in Edinburgh and Perth, and she herself would go to Paris and Naples yet!

And meantime it was gay enough at Gleneagles, with this gathering of cousins, and the days they had rambling and laughing, or the boys would be away up shooting moorfowl and the girls playing cards and forfeits, or visiting, and music in the long evenings, and the crowded, gossiping nights, with a sharing of beds and candle-sticks, and unpinning of petticoats and curls, and giggling about brothers — and who was to know what the brothers would be saying about sisters! Only young James Haldane, Captain Robert's nephew and heir to Airthrey, had no sister of his own, could not be teased the same way as the rest. A bonny lad and a good match. But then there was Ochtertyre himself, for all he was a Jacobite, and David Haldane of Aberuthven, and young Captain John who had acted so dashingly in the rebellion, bringing up the pay for the King's troops in his sloop the *Tryal*, and handing it over safely to Forbes at Inverness. Not to speak of George Cockburn, her Aunt Margaret's spoilt boy, but she would never marry the likes of him, a babbler and a boaster. There was a shyness about James Haldane, a dark seriousness — But ach, she need not be thinking of yon kinds of things yet! Soon enough she would be old. Old as her Aunt Kirstie.

Kirstie came over and sat by her niece and picked up a corner of the embroidery. 'Did you have the pattern of that from Edinburgh?' she asked.

'Indeed no!' said Catherine. 'It is from London. Can you not see, Aunt Kirstie, it is away more modish?'

'London,' said Kirstie, puckering her eyes. 'Do you ken this, Catherine, I have never in my whole life been in London. Though I have been farther than I ever thought to go when I was a lassie. And fared worse. I am thinking you will take more than your needlework patterns from London, Catherine?'

'Surely, Aunt Kirstie,' said Catherine, a wee thing uneasy at that, 'but you are never saying to me that you are a Jacobite!'

'Ach no!' said Kirstie, 'but maybe I am more of a Scot than you are. Likely it will be the way we were living in my time. London was scarcely so near.'

The others were coming across the bowling-green now. Mungo Haldane was telling young Ochtertyre how much his seedling trees had cost that year. He had a plan for the afforestation of a piece of moorland beyond Auchterarder. He was in treaty now with James Murray of Abercairney for the lands of Muiralehouse. There was old pasture there which was in bad heart; it had not been limed these twenty years. He would be able to get marl from the small loch. His voice sounded satisfied and comfortable, planning so busily, thinking outward towards crops and trees.

Captain Robert joined them; he was thick-set and red-cheeked, his eyes wrinkled against sun and wind: a dependable and resolute man, as the East India Company knew well. They sat on the seat beside Catherine, and Black William sat himself down at his wife's feet, his head against her knee, with that kind of grace that a Highlander could have so lightly, but that none of the Haldanes had. None of the bull calves.

Catherine Duncan would have liked fine to get away from the company of her elders, and so indeed would Ochtertyre have liked. But they were hemmed in; courtesy and prudence forbade. Aunt Kirstie would begin to talk, to ramble and remember, and all the older ones would join in and there they would be blethering away about what had nothing at all to do with nowadays or the things the young ones were after, whether grave or gay. For Catherine had partly this feeling of being young, of being fit to leap out of her body, almost, with the delight of all one might be seeing and doing on a summer's day; but also thoughts would be coming to her about some later day when she would be a wife and a mother, ordering her household and bringing up her bairns in fear and love of the Lord, for she had strict and certain ideas about some things, and this was how her life was to be when she was rightly a

24

woman. But not yet. Nor was the face of her husband clear to her.

But Ochtertyre was thinking back, as he always did, towards Falkirk and the sudden dunt and pain that had rolled him over and a horse's hoof within an inch of his face: the end of the retreat from the south, the end of the promises, not that it had seemed like that at Falkirk, they had not known till Culloden, and he was out of it then. And how at all could he have been such a fool, how gone off so gaily, liker a schoolboy than a grown man, with the white knot on his coat? And he was suddenly hating the Prince and all his Highlanders, and the pain still in his leg that stopped him from dancing with his cousins, Helen and Margaret and Catherine.

'Can you mind now, Robert?' asked Kirstie, 'the look of the house as it was before the improvements were made?'

'I mind it better than you, Kirstie,' he said, 'for I myself was up and down the ladders with the masons and you in your long skirts, clucking away below, holding on to them in the cold wind there was, and your nose running on you!'

'Ah, mo bhràthair beag, it is up and down the ladders with the big sailors you are now!' said Kirstie, teasing him, for she knew he hated to be spoken to in the Highland speech, and she herself with the queer happy feeling to be back at home, and Black William with her for the first time, and her hand went down, feeling for Black William's hand to reach up and meet her own, as it did. It did.

Captain Robert snorted and shook his head and took a pinch of snuff. It had been a cold spring when the improvements were made and indeed, her nose had run — there were no handkerchiefs for bairns in those days! Mungo looked proudly and affectionately at the family house. He had no children of his own, but he had ceased to care about that now; the house would go to Bearcrofts his brother. It was the Haldane house, they were welcome, all the lot of them. His father had made the first of the improvements, but since then he himself had made more, especially after his tour on the Continent. There was the water closet itself, in the centre, the first in all that district of Scotland, much admired and visited, though he himself preferred the old ways, and if these things became too popular or in use amongst any but the gentry, how would the farmers and market-gardeners do for their night soil?

'I mind it well,' said Kirstie, half to herself, 'and a gean tree there was used to be by yon corner. It was so bonny in the spring, but in winter it would be tapping against the windows and I was feared of it. Helen and Ann and myself, we were mightily scared of ghosts and witches.'

'It was the nurse you had,' said Mungo, 'she was one of the Reid lasses, and her head full of nothing but ghosts and fairies and superstitions. But our Mother liked her, for she was clean and kindly enough, and would sew away at your coaties and sing, and she had you aye well sorted up for the Kirk on a Sabbath, with your shoes blacked and your faces scrubbed and a wee posy for each one of you.'

'Aye,' said Robert, 'she near had me frighted as a wee lad, with her stories and all she would be at on Hallowe'en. But I never let on or screeched about it the way you lassies did. And I mind she would be at me on the Sabbath morn, seeing I had my catechism answers by heart. But what she herself could be thinking on in Kirk, and her head stuffed with charms and nonsense, aye, that has me beat still!'

'She would have her week-day thoughts and her Sabbath thoughts, as indeed many of us have,' said Mungo, 'poor Phemie Reid! You mind, Jamie, she was married on one of yon Morrison lads; he had some trade, aye, he was a weaver, and then her first bairn died and she crying out it had been bewitched.' He chuckled. 'Aye, and then Patrick comes back from Leyden, and nothing would suit but he must go storming down to Phemie's cottage, and there was the poor thing skirling and moaning away and the toom cradle beside her, and she in no mood to take a lesson in reason and natural science from Patrick! She said —' He broke off: 'What ails you, Kirstie lass?'

'I hate you to be speaking of witchcraft,' said Kirstie, low and violently.

'But I wasna speaking of it seriously!' said Mungo, surprised. 'Phemie's bairn had just died of a hoast, the way bairnies do, or maybe young Morrison came home with the drink on him — for they were all sore on the drink, yon weaver lads — and gie'd the bairn a bit bash!'

He laughed; but Kirstie said again: 'I hate you to be speaking of bairns dying!'

Mungo patted her shoulder; he minded then on Kirstie's own bairn, or was it two of them, that had died. That was the way things were, but the women aye took it hard, poor bitches. And now she had the other bairn by her second man, and that when she was nearer fifty than forty. Dod aye, they were wild stots, the Highlanders, getting bairns on women in their old age, as it might have been in the Book! And he looked benevolently at his brother-in-law, wishing he'd had poor Kirstie at the start.

But she was speaking again, half to herself, and Mungo settled himself back, gazing at the hills behind the house, the steep grass slopes and sudden screes of Gleneagles, dotted with the grazing of the new flock of black-faced sheep that he had brought from the south. It was fine just to have Kirstie by them again. 'It is the difference between then and now,' she said, 'it is everywhere. We lived on our own food mostly. I mind the tenants coming in at the term with their rents in meal and grain, and the bustle of weighing it out and heaving it into the great kists, and the sweet smell in the air and the meal dust dancing in the sun-shafts, and our mother with the heavy iron keys and the account books bound in our own sheep skins! There would be a fine dinner for the tenants and toasts all round, but the food would be our own growing and killing, every dish of it. And no tea for the servant lassies!'

Captain Robert interrupted — this was one of his subjects, as Kirstie should have remembered: 'Aye, Kirstie, and it is those same ones are for ever wanting their cup tea and thus depriving the Revenue of the duty on beer and our own spirits. I would allow no man nor woman with an income of less than £50 sterling a year to buy this tea except under special licence from the Revenue. As it is, they will buy maybe a pound, and it will last them a month, and the half of it smuggled, since it goes into smaller bulk than the spirits. The Government should take it in hand!'

Black William looked up, the dark, thick lashes lifting from his eyes that were the very same red-brown colour as a stag's eyes. 'That is my Lord President's scheme, I believe,' he said.

There was a slight silence, then Captain Robert laughed: 'You will not know, Borlum, but Duncan Forbes should not be spoken of so lightly here! Mind you, I am for him myself and so would any man of sense be, as far as his ideas go, aye and his loyalty to the Government and the King's Army, in spite of the hard way that he was treated by some of them.'

'Some of them, indeed!' said Kirstie. 'It is a queer thing altogether how there is not one of you men that will call Cumberland by his right name.'

Mungo spoke across her seriously: 'There is a greatness about the Lord President, but it did not show itself in the dealings he had with our brother Bearcrofts.'

'He was near as wee as a louse yon time, was Dunky Forbes,' said Kirstie, 'though indeed the man has done better since.'

Robert laughed again: 'You will aye be taking the Bear's part, Kirstie! Did she never tell you, Borlum, of the quarrel between her brother and the Lord President?'

'She did not,' said Black William, and looked at her half reproachfully.

She shook her head at him and gave a bit frown, so flat a lie it was and not over creditable to her own good sense! But he gave her the wee boy's look out of the corners of his eyes that meant she was not to breathe a word, and, as always, she gave in. For it could be nothing bad but only a spark of devilment and with it the deep and sweet trust in Kirstie that was at once wife and playmate, and there was the way she never could feel her age now she was married on her black fellow.

'Maybe she was in the right not to speak,' said Robert thoughtfully. 'Duncan Forbes will doubtless be related to yourself, and it was no very creditable thing.'

'To neither of them,' said Mungo gravely. 'Nay, Kirstie, you cannot have it that Patrick was blameless; no man can lose his neighbour's esteem for nothing. I had forgotten that the Forbes's of Culloden were cousins of your's, Borlum.'

'Aye,' said William, 'Duncan Forbes' father's sister Elizabeth, who was married with William Baillie of Dunain, was grand-mother to my father William Dearg. The strange it is,' he went on gently, his head against his wife's knee, 'that the man who almost won England for James VIII was cousin to the man who lost Scotland for that King's son.'

The Haldanes looked embarrassed, as indeed it was likely that the Highlander had meant them to be, for these rebellions had seemed to them folly and worse, yet they could not help having a certain admiration for Black William's father, the Brigadier, Red William Macintosh of Borlum, who had been not only an able and gallant soldier, but a true lover of his country and its agriculture; and there was something of the same gallantry about this son of his who had married their sister, though none of them knew him well as yet. Mungo said: 'Then you will be a cousin to the Munros of Foulis?'

'Aye,' said William, 'I knew Duncan, the Doctor, well enough.'

'Ah, poor Duncan, he was a well-liked man, a kindly one. When I heard how he had been killed at Falkirk, he and his brother . . . They were not the only friends of mine I had cause to hate the Highlanders for.'

'It was a sorrow on me too,' said William, and pulled up his right sleeve. There was a scar on his forearm. 'That cut was sewed up by Duncan Munro, who was himself a Highlander. He had the neatest fingers for it. He will be in heaven now, I'm thinking.'

The hate that had come on Mungo for a moment, thinking of Falkirk, an almost visible anger that had made young Ochtertyre duck his head and shift uneasily, had subsided as quickly as it came. 'I would have my doubts but heaven would be a dull place for a doctor!' he said.

'Ach well,' said William, 'you will mind that Duncan cared for the music too!'

Captain Robert leant forward a little: 'You will doubtless be related to our own cousins of Kyllachy?'

Black William stiffened, no longer leaning at all against his Haldane wife. 'They are in the Clan Chattan,' he said.

'Kyllachy was out in the '15, and his old father with him,' said Robert amiably.

'That did not stop him from being the worst kind of a laird,' Black William said.

'Aye,' said Mungo, 'I mind he was for ever trying to raise money on his lands.'

'You do not raise money out of lands,' Black William said, 'but out of men and women, out of their sore labour and pain, out of driving them from their own harvests to carry your's, out of short leases and rent raising! His tenants were in my clan too. I have seen some of them. Landless like the Gregarach and through no fault of their own!'

Again there was a little awkwardness, again some fierce thing had come on them. Again Catherine Duncan looked across at Murray of Ochtertyre, who shuffled with his well foot. 'Do you mind this, Mungo,' said Kirstie, 'Lachlan Macintosh of Kyllachy asking our father could he get courting myself? And our father, having the sense to trust his own flesh and blood, even though it stood up in a petticoat, came to ask my mind on it. And I said no, I would not marry him though he were my cousin twice over and ten times as handsome — for he wasna so bad to look at: in those days when a man could still wear the kilt! Indeed I am thinking I told my father I would never marry a Highlander!' She laughed low and sweetly, because now her own Highlander was leaning back again against her knee, was looking up at her with the wrinkles of laughter and admiration round his eyes and mouth.

'Now there is a thing you never told me, Kirstie Haldane!' he said, and she felt herself even with him in the game, whatever it was.

'Ach,' said she, 'how would I tell you when you were never asking me?'

He laughed: 'It seems to me that there is mostly plenty that no one has told me. I am not yet understanding all this about the Lord President and your good brother.' He pressed his hand against her foot to stop her speaking, and looked solemnly at Mungo.

'It all goes back a great way,' Mungo said. 'You will not be unaware, Borlum, that the Bear was one of the Commissioners for the Forfeited Estates after the '15? Aye, I can see you ken that! Well, a man cannot help to take away his neighbours' property, in whatever cause, and still be as well thought of as he was. It is — usual — to be a wee bit lighter on those you have known all your life than on those who are strangers. My brother set his face against that.'

'Aye,' said Kirstie, 'Patrick did a queer thing yon time not to feather his own nest, but maybe a right thing.'

'Maybe,' said Mungo, 'though I still think that a present from a friend is no' exactly the same as a bribe from a stranger. How did it look to you, Ochtertyre?'

Murray of Ochtertyre answered uneasily, 'Indeed, sir, I only had my father's word for it all. As you know, he was out of his estates until ten years ago. It gave me, as a laddie, the opportunity to acquire a passable French accent. My father would always speak well of your father, sir, since it was he who helped him to get free of an English prison. He did not speak so well of Bearcrofts.'

'Nay, it would have been more than human nature to speak well of him!' Mungo answered, heavily and passionately. 'Do you ken this, Borlum, there was a time when two gentlemen would be playing at the cards and when the nine of diamonds came up, it was not Stair they would name. It was my own brother was the Curse of Scotland! Was yon no' a hard thing to thole, Borlum?'

'It would have been harder for himself,' said William, 'but I know well that your motto is Suffer.'

'Well then,' said Mungo, 'it was this gait. My brother Patrick was Member for the Cupar Boroughs, as you will maybe have heard. Added to that he was Provost of St. Andrew's. But that wasna the trouble. Aye, he shouldna have taken the appointment as Commissioner for the Forfeited Estates, for all there was so muckle siller in the salary, full more than the thirty pieces of Judas!'

'He betrayed no man!' said Kirstie sharply.

'Och!' said Captain Robert, 'there is no such great temptation to that on a thousand pounds sterling a year! But he was harsh, even to women and bairns. Folk could forget his justice, for there had been no mercy with it that they could be minding on.'

'I heard,' said Black William, a hand on Kirstie, quieting her, 'that he was seeking to be made a Lord of the Court of Sessions?'

'Aye,' said Gleneagles, 'when Fountainhall died and there was a judgeship to be filled, Patrick got the King's letter. But the Faculty of Advocates and Clerks petitioned against him. It was partly that they were angry at his going that way about it, and an English King having the appointing of a Scots Judge; but forby that, there was pure enmity against my brother. That went back to the time he was Commissioner and accusing the Court of Sessions of prolonging the creditors' lawsuits and they in their turn accusing him of wanting to have it all in his own hands, power and pickings! And he and they each writing and publishing against one another and accusations of disloyalty and Jacobitism flying all ways at once like a covey of wildfowl! And the leader of the Faculty was your cousin, Duncan Forbes of Culloden; he was Deputy Advocate in those days, so, in a way, it was to be expected. They petitioned against Patrick first, that he had only practised thirty months in the five years he had been called to the Bar and then, when that appeal was reversed by the English, nothing would serve but an attack on his person and character. There was much that could have been said, Borlum, not without justice, but they went beyond what was decent, aye, they did that. And they brought false witness against him, ach, one can laugh at it now, but it was no laughing matter at yon time. They accused him of Jacobitism, which was a thing that couldna be, Borlum, as you will doubtless understand: aye, and of bribery and evil living. Half the Lords of Session were against him; there was Lord Dun, that was David Erskine and a far-out cousin through Kirstie's mother, and Lord Kimmerhame and Lord Polton and all the Dalrymples. Ach, they were like hounds after him. Ormiston, the Justice Clerk, that was father-in-law to our sister Margaret, he would have made the peace between them; but Forbes would have none of it. He was wild and wud after my brother. So he never got his judgeship, poor Pate!'

'It was a wonder the English were not helping him,' William said.

'He had quarrelled with Walpole by then,' Gleneagles answered. 'He was no respecter of persons, neither in his own land nor yet in London. And it was a bitter tongue he had, aye, and a clever one. Indeed, he may have used it on the Lord President!   I wouldna wonder.'

'Have none of you had occasion to have dealings with Culloden since then?' William asked again.

'I have tried to avoid them,' Mungo said. 'Maybe yon thing was mostly my brother's fault, but one must stick by one's own flesh and blood.'

'I have needed to see Culloden officially,' Captain Robert said, 'on East India Company business, ships' papers, licences and the like. And for that matter the Bear is my — and Kirstie's — half brother, no' our full brother! Duncan Forbes did right in his affair with the Glasgow magistrates and little thanks for it from England. And indeed Gleneagles is too soft altogether with yon brother of his, the way he is telling it.' He half shook his head at Mungo. 'He and poor James, they were wild lads together. Aye, rough and ill-mannered. Foul tongued too, and I cannot abide that, even at sea. You'll mind, Mungo?'

Gleneagles nodded: 'Aye, I mind well. It was as though the Bear had a kind of contempt for the gentry and for decent honest folk. He was that way from the time he became a Professor at St. Andrew's. He would be setting up his new knowledge against our father, even. And worse yet after he came back from Leyden with a pack of foreign notions. The Lord kens what he may not have found there. Anabaptists maybe.'

'He would speak of religion,' Robert said, 'but not in a right way. It was as though he were too familiar with Church history. As a man might be with his own family. He will have lectured upon it over much at St. Andrew's.'

'Aye,' said Mungo, 'he has said those kind of things to me about the Kirk that I would not care to repeat. Though I will say this for him, he never said them outwith the house nor in hearing of the servants.'

'It is certain,' said Black William, 'that there are other truths beyond what we know of in Scotland.'

Captain Robert looked hard at his brother-in-law. 'How is it, William Macintosh, that you are defending Bearcrofts, and he against all that yourself and your father stood for?'

'Not all,' Black William said. 'You will remember that my father, in the pamphlets that he published from prison, was aye thinking of the people of Scotland, the people who work with the plough and the spade and the dung-cart. Could one not suppose that he and Bearcrofts might have been at one mind on that?'

'Aye,' said Kirstie, 'do you mind what the common people said of him?

    ' "Forth of the fiery furnace, hot and scalden,
      "Pure as the gold, proceeded Peter Halden!" '

'That was the Edinburgh mob, the worst rascals unhung. I am ashamed that you know of it, Kirstie!' said Captain Robert.

'But I do,' she said, 'and more.'

'And forby that,' said Black William all too gently and clearly, 'there was not one else of you at our wedding. I am not blaming you, far from it, the way things were. We could not hope that any of Kirstie's folk would stand by her in the Church. But Bearcrofts did.'

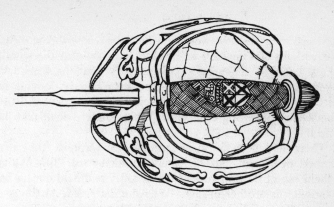

CHAPTER II

MURRAY of Ochtertyre had escaped at last; when Borlum had said that thing so quietly about Bearcrofts, Captain Robert had jumped up, swearing under his breath, and Gleneagles himself was on his feet. It had seemed to be so purely a family matter that he had made his excuses hastily, bowed himself away. And for that matter he had heard a voice he knew fully too well: another cousin of his own and theirs, George Cockburn, Margaret Haldane's spoilt boy, drunk already. When they were speaking of bad landlords he had thought of George, who was going the sure way to spoil all that his uncle, Cockburn of Ormiston, had been doing to improve the estate, grant long leases and encourage good and thrifty tenants. George cared for nothing at all but cities, the things you would get there for money, the pleasure a rich young bachelor could have — before he gets caught, thought Ochtertyre bitterly, wishing George something worse than his own lameness. As for himself, if he got out of this without attainder — as he might if he was careful — he would never want to live forth of his own lands again. It had been two tenants' sons of his own that had got him away after Falkirk. If he had been taken prisoner — Cumberland and the English had burnt alive some of the Culloden prisoners. He had not believed it at first, but it was hell's own truth. George Cockburn would never have had the main guts to be in the thing at all! And of a sudden he was remembering the few words he had spoken with the Prince, Thriepland of Fingask had brought him in, past the sentries, easily enough. They had spoken in French; the Prince had liked that, had taken his hand, speaking eagerly, looking him in the eyes: *angoisse de cœur se souvenant d'amour passé* and there was George bawling one of his Whig songs — devil take him and it!

There had been a queer moment, for Captain Robert had flushed deep and had his hand on his sword. But William Macintosh of Borlum got to his feet softly and held out his bare hands to his brother-in-law. 'We were disarmed, Airthrey,' he said, 'I have neither the kilt nor the claymore.'

For a small time Robert said nothing, only stared at the crested and silver-mounted sword-belt that Black William still wore, broader and stronger than his own belt, since it was meant to buckle over a kilted plaid. Sometimes the disarmed, the clansmen, had used such gear for cart straps or harness, or hid them deep out of sight, at the bottom of the meal-kist or over a rafter. Those who went to the cities had mostly thrown them clean away; if they could afford it they would get gentlemen's gear, light dress-swords and that. But those who needed to stay at home among their own folk, where there was no forgetting of what had passed, where the men in the bothy and the girls at the sheiling went about dour and sad now, in the harsh hodden grey of the English labourer, those would wear their sword-belts, empty, as a sign of what had been done, a sharing of what once was pride but had been turned to a shame, only to be borne by all together. Black William had accustomed himself by this to a different and cannier set of gestures, never laying his hand where the hilt of his sword, the claymore he had worn as a lad in the '15, should have been. Captain Robert still stood, red and resolute, breathing hard, his hand on his own sword that he had used more than once against privateers and Chinese pirates. A different pattern and weight from the Highland sword. Catherine was watching her aunt, and Kirstie had her two hands up at her neck, the way she might be quieting and keeping in its place an over-leaping heart.

'Come, come,' said Mungo, 'you will not be quarrelling over what was never meant ill. You were in Java at the time, Robert, and it was my own place to have gone to my sister's wedding, and I didna, and indeed I am fair delighted that my brother Pate had the grace to be there for me. The marriage will have been in an Episcopalian meeting-house, I am thinking?'

'Aye,' said Kirstie. 'And not over-legally, since there were more than five persons there, Patrick included. But you will mind I have had enough of the Ministers.'

'Well, well,' said Mungo, 'I am not fashing myself at my age over place or sermon, gold ring or rush ring. It is the giving of the heart that's a' there is to it, and I see fine you have that.'

But Black William was looking at Airthrey yet. And all of a sudden Captain Robert gave a twitch, as it might have been someone standing on a ship's bridge who sees the hurricane coming and must give his orders quick. For quick as that his hands went to the sword's buckle and slipped the sneck out of the leather, and he handed the sword to Black William with a stiff bow. But where was the use? Black William bowed in turn, but put his hands behind his back. 'No,' he said, 'that is against your own law, Airthrey. Forby I will not take an English sword — even from yourself.'

But Mungo had an arm of each of them; his voice was kindly, fatherly, with an increasing burr to it. 'We will walk as far as the Castle mound, will we no', Robbie? And this new brother of ours that has never seen the way that his wifie's forebears lived when we were a' savages, Highland and Lowland alike! Come your ways, Willie lad, and I will even show you where I am planning to have my lime avenue. Aye, and the new dyke and the stone gateway.'

They were walking away now, and off the bowling-green. The two women looked after them. 'Were you frightened, Aunt Kirstie?' Catherine asked.

Kirstie nodded. 'But there's nought to fear now. Men, ach! They're but bairns. Good bairns, aye surely, and who's to say that a bairnie's no' away better than a grown woman? More douce-like and forgiving when the anger is past. And with a better idea of heaven and more will to get there.' She was watching the backs of the three men, who did not once look behind them. 'We women are for ever needing to take thought for the morrow, aye and the morrow's morn. We canna afford to be generous and daft the way the men are, more's the pity.'

Catherine was not understanding. She said: 'But it is always the ladies of a household that will be taking care of the charities, Aunt Kirstie!'

'There's a muckle great difference between charity and generosity, Catherine!' said her aunt, and laughed. 'The one is the money in the plate at the Kirk door, put by cannily each week against the Sabbath, and clipped placks at that, most like, and the other is — ach, throwing away one's life or one's love and never thinking twice on it.' She fell silent, sad-looking now, one hand on the farm account book that Gleneagles had left on the seat. 'If a' the governing of the world were left to the women of it, they would never do the daft-like things the men do, throwing away their own lives, aye and others'. The world could surely be managed the way a household is, cannily. Aye, a good household under a good and careful woman. And the men and the bairns would be free to dream and to have their adventures.'

'Yet our own Mary Stuart was for ever throwing away men's loves!' protested Catherine.

'Ach-och!' said Kirstie frivolously, 'maybe she was half a bairn and half a man, for a Queen can never be a right woman, for a' the men and a' the Ministers that write and preach of her as the De'il's own daughter! But this is a' blethers, Catherine Duncan. For indeed, the older I get the less I am knowing.'

'You will have had your own adventures, Aunt Kirstie,' the girl said.

'Aye,' she said, 'I had.' And she looked in a sad and steady way ahead of her, but syne she smiled.

Catherine moved nearer; she was wanting to stay now,

hoping her Aunt Kirstie would speak; when George Cockburn was behaving the way he sounded to be, it was spoiling everyone's pleasure! She picked up her embroidery again. 'Please to be telling me them, Aunt Kirstie.'

'Well,' said Kirstie, 'it is a simple enough story. You will be wanting to hear which lads were courting me, Catherine. And I think I will even tell you the truth, for it will be more instructive for you that way.' Catherine settled herself back down to listen, and Kirstie went on: 'Now you will know that my father, your own grandfather, John Haldane of Gleneagles, was a Member, first, of the Scots Parliament, and then, after the Act of Union, of the English Parliament. And he was that kind of a man that took his duties with the greatest seriousness, and if he had sworn an oath, he kept it, even though it might have been better unkept. We Haldanes had aye stood for liberty of conscience and against the Bishops and the great nobles and any kind of divine or unreasonable rights, either of kings or others. There was to be no going back, in Scotland at least, on the great over-setting of John Knox; we were brought up, Catherine, to think with pride and determination on that, although we did not hold with the extremists nor the wild goings-on there had been but lately in the south-west. I can mind my father arguing with a Cameronian preacher, aye and getting the best of it, for he knew his Scriptures. But that time of religious anger and intolerance was nigh past, amongst the gentry at least; as past, almost, as the light world of corruption before John Knox.'

Kirstie sat quiet for a moment, as though she were looking deeply back. And Catherine said, hesitating: 'Yet, Aunt Kirstie, was it not vastly romantic and sublime in the old days? Whenever I read in the old songs and ballads, I am seeing it full of knights in armour and distressed ladies and poetry and enchantments. . . .'

'You will need to be making up songs about it yourself and set up as rival to Lady Wardlaw and Lady Grizell Baillie!' said Kirstie. 'But those days did not seem in any way romantic to us; we were over near. Though maybe we will have thought over much of the wickedness of the Bishops and the Papists, and that at an age when we knew nought at all about it, nought but the names of the sins but never how folk could come to be sinning them, nor how it might seem like the workings of Free Will. Ach, it was no kind of good, yon, to a bairn, and we were for ever getting it hindside foremost, listening to the argy-bargying of our elders; for there would be the ugsome black shape of the De'il behind it a', and the muckle lonely fear of Predestination that would set us greeting into our pillows night after night, not knowing how it would be with ourselves, and minding on such bits of the sermon or the Sabbath readings as had caught our minds, the roaring lions and the flames and worms of the Pit! We were aye thinking on the anger of the Lord, since we had no right understanding of His Love. And indeed I am thinking that is aye the hardest thing for a young lad or lassie to understand. Excepting there was something in it of the sweet herb posies and the clean Sabbath claes — for we werena so thrang to change our body linen as folks are these days, and if the fires were needed for our own meat and broth and the servants' porridge and the muckle pot of meal or mashlum for the beasts, then there'd be no washing done from one month's end to another. Aye, and we didna cover up what shouldna be there with a parcel of court scents from London!'

She laughed to herself a little, but Catherine blushed, for indeed there were times when scent was easier come by and used than soap and water! Gleneagles was an older and less convenient house than Lundie and you could not be always after the servant lassies. She picked a new strand of embroidery wool out of the hank, and Kirstie went on: 'But dearie me, here am I havering away and my story getting no forrarder. You ken, Catherine, there was a wild lot of us wee ones, and our mother couldna keep her eye on us more than the half of the time. When she was brought to bed she wouldna be lying long, and all the gossips would be in, as the custom was, drinking their toasts to herself and the baby, and giving luck money to the nurse, and there would be sweeties and sillabubs and hatted kit and maybe oranges for the lave of us. When we grew older we were with her oftener. She taught us our reading and writing and catechism. Phemie taught us plain sewing, spinning and weaving, but our mother taught us embroidery, straw-work and the making of preserves and medicines for man and beast. When we were older we went to the Minister at Blackford twice or three times a week for our Latin and ancient history — and many a rap of our fingers we had from him when we didna mind the Kings of Israel! In summer we would walk there, and in winter we would ride through snow and myre with our cloaks and plaids happed about us, and tie our ponies up at the wall of the Kirk yard.

'The time came when the boys went to school, and, if they did not aye learn plenty, at least they would be sitting next to the sons of the miller and the weaver and the poor tenant, and they would be speaking together and maybe making friendships that would stand them in good stead all their days. We lassies had each a term or two at the young ladies' academy at Perth, but indeed, Catherine, I canna mind one thing that I learnt at yon place!

'Or, odd times, we would be riding over to the public library at Innerpeffray; our father was a trustee, for it had been founded by his father-in-law, Lord Maderty, Mungo's mother's father. There were plenty old books there, Cicero and Demosthenes and all of them, and Testaments with parallel translations into every kind of language. And the relics of the great Marquis, who was brother-in-law to Maderty, that the boys used to have out and handle, aye, many's the time I have caught Jamie and Johnnie letting on to themselves that they were Montrose — and forcing Anne and myself and wee Rob to play Campbell to them and be well beaten! And that in spite that we were a' good Whigs when it came to the voting, and you might think we would be friends of the Campbells. But there is a thing about gallantry and a noble presence, aye, and a generosity of the spirit and a single-heartedness against odds, that gets under the skin of every one of us. Maybe we are not that kind of family ourselves, but decent ordinary folk, by and large, yet there is this romantic thing, as you will likely find for yourself, Catherine Duncan, that is more than what's in the songs and ballads, and it will come down like a storm upon us douce Haldanes, and then we will be like the bull calves and butt our way through dykes and thorn hedges, and many a knock will we get on our soft, silly noses, and fine and grateful will we be to any that are kind to us then. That's no' clear. But it will be, lassie, it will be.

'And so our lives went on, here at Gleneagles and round about, knowing our neighbours, even though we didna aye love them as we should. But it wasna till I was fourteen years past that I made the journey to Edinburgh. I doubt that would have seemed to you an unco tedious kind of life, Catherine?'

Kirstie had spoken with a feel of apology in her voice, as of one girl to another, and Catherine grew of a sudden generous and warm towards her. 'Ach,' she said, 'what's Edinburgh, Aunt Kirstie! It isna that. One could be going to the grandest balls every night and yet not be happy. But you — you were young the same way we are young, feeling the same thoughts in you, here on this very same bowling-green!'

'Aye, the very same,' said Kirstie. 'For the grass is trodden and rolled, but it rises again with the May weather, year by year, thirty-two years between then and now. For I am minding on the summer that I was sixteen years old, Catherine, for that was the first year that the lads were coming in earnest. A fine time for any lassie if she can but be sensible and keep it ever before her that it's not the eye and the ear alone that need to be convinced.

'I had been in Edinburgh twice, then. Queen Anne had died the year before, poor body, and everyone worrying themselves daft in case the Jacobites and Papists would take this chance and attempt a revolution. But the Lowlands and the Kirk were firm against that; there was a tightening of feeling, even for the Union and all it was bringing with it — for the folk who had been most eager for it at the first had not found it all they were letting on it would be — and in the Elections at the beginning of 1715, the Whigs had swept the country and our father and my two stepbrothers, Mungo and Patrick, back in

Parliament, and all going well. He had been busy enough before that, for he was Commissioner of Police and there was plenty law-breaking and difficult cases, and appointments to be made, and folk would be appealing to him, by letter or by word of mouth, and he aye listened to them, more especially if they had any kind of commendation from a Minister. Forby that, he had the estate at Gleneagles to see to; there was not so muckle planting of foreign trees in those days, but he did plant Scotch fir and beech and ash, and he was experimenting with the land, and with new breeds of sheep and cattle. It was mostly held on run-rig in those days, with the wee township in the middle and the infield all round it, mostly over-cropped, so there would be constant difficulties there; and when he was at home my father would be striding round with his great stick or his broadsword, dinging it into the tenants that there was to be no offcropping of the infield — that's to say, Catherine, two crops running of oats or bere, but no dunging of the land in between, ach, you would scarcely hear of such a thing now! And no fourth-cropping of the outfield, for they would take crop after crop from there, after the cattle had been folded on it, leaving it in bad heart when the time came for it to go back to pasture. You will understand, Catherine, they would have short leases then, and each trying to get what he could while the lease held, and not caring what happened after, let alone never thinking of making any improvements. And one canna wonder at that, either, seeing that if they did, the most of the lairds would raise their rents on them. That way each household would have a wee, small part of the infield, changing it about year to year, which didna make for improvements either, and the herds in common in the outfield, and a nasty lot of wee brown hens that made little more than a mouthful apiece and that were mostly used to pay the rent. Dinner after dinner of boiled hen did we have! Aye, there was a different face altogether on the land then, more tenants maybe, but worse, more beasts but far worse, these, and the half of them having to be killed at the back-end and scarce worth salting for winter.

'But I am away from my story again! I had come to that spring when we were in Edinburgh, in lodgings up a stair off the High Street, and Kyllachy came courting me. I had a new dress that my father had bought me in London when he went south for the opening of Parliament. Hoops were narrower in those days. It was a green and white striped armozeen over an Indian quilted petticoat. I wore my hair far simpler than we do now, in long curls and a green ribbon snood over it, aye, a maiden snood. My hair was pure straw-gold in those days, and the candle lights used to blink bonnily into it; but it broke out of the great curls that we favoured in those days into a daft lot of wee curls that my mother and her woman could not control, neither with butter nor bear's grease.'

'Your hair is bonny yet, Aunt Kirstie,' said Catherine.

'Ach no, it is all speckled with white the like of a hen!' said Kirstie.

'But,' said Catherine, suddenly fond and daring, 'I have seen a certain new uncle of my own touch it with his fingers the way it could be the finest gold.'

Kirstie stiffened a wee bit, then laughed. 'Any black Highlander will aye be thinking wonders of our light hair in the Lowlands! For that matter, Lachlan Macintosh of Kyllachy would be praising my looks to me. Indeed he would be praising everything about me. I had been learning music in Edinburgh; I could play the spinet, and the great harp forby that, but eh, Catherine, I was playing no better than a performing dog and there's the truth of it! And fine I knew in my own heart that I had no feeling at all for the music, and whenever my cousin of Kyllachy would be leaning over the harp and praising me, I thought he was none of the wisest.'

'Do you never play now, Aunt Kirstie?' Catherine said, and remembered how the great harp in the music-room at Gleneagles had a string broken, as though no one cared for it much in the family.

'Na, na,' Kirstie said. 'I have my William to sing to me these days, and when I can be listening to songs from France and England and Spain and the Americas, and more Highland songs than I had thought ever could have túnes put to them how would I be tinkling away?' She laughed. 'But Kyllachy was a braw gallant, if you look mostly at the outside, and flaunted about the streets of Edinburgh in his Highland gear, the red tartan and the eagle feathers and a'. But on the Sabbath he went decently in black Presbyterian trews, the way my father would think well of him, and he would come with us to the Kirk and have on that he was mightily interested in Kirk matters.

'There were a two-three other gallants I had, Catherine. My tocher wasna so muckle, but indeed it was something, and I was a bird from a good nest. There was young David Oliphant, the same that married one of the Maxwell lassies later; there was one of the Hays, a younger son of Kinnoul's and a senseless kind of a laddie; there was Sandy Erskine, that was a cousin on my mother's side, for, you ken, Catherine, my mother was Helen Erskine, and her brother, Sir John Erskine of Alva, married into the Sinclairs, and indeed I am thinking that all the families in Scotland are related some way! But I got a queer kind of a scunner against the Erskines myself, and this was the way of it.

'There was a man condemned to the gallows at Perth for sheep-stealing, and for all I know of him he might have deserved hanging as well as another. But instead, my uncle, Sir John Erskine, bought him off and held him as his slave. He was a tall, ugly, thrawn devil of a Highlander, with no English at all; he was working in my uncle's silver mines, the far side of the Ochils, till he got to be too ill for it; everyone was laughing at him and giving him the worst things to do, and never a penny for himself. In those days I had no great principles about such things, for I had seen little of them; but now I am certain that it is a terrible, unchristian thing for one Scot to be slave or serf to another, as I have seen in the Ayrshire coal mines and as my William saw in America on the plantations done to his own men — you will need to ask himself about that, Catherine, and times he cannot bear to speak about it — and I am against it altogether. But this man of my uncle's, Alec Steuart, I mind his name was, he was rowing a ferry-boat across the Firth of

Forth one time when my uncle was crossing, and when they were an hour out from Leith all of a sudden he jumped overboard and drowned himself. Well, I heard that from Sandy Erskine, and he laughing fit to burst, thinking it the finest joke, and there came a dark flash in my mind, and I saw this Alec Steuart as a lost soul that should have been saved, and I thought if only I had once cast him a kind look or word, maybe he wouldna have done this awful thing, and syne I thought of the brass collar welded on his neck, weighing him down into the cold waters of the Firth, and, though it was no business of mine, yet it seemed some way to be my business, and I quarrelled with Sandy over it, and off he went with his head in the air, saying I was a wee fool.

'The one I liked the best was David Oliphant; he was reading for the Bar, and with plenty of conversation and a serious wit. The worst of it was, he was no great Church-goer; he never sat under any one Minister, but would be now at one Church and now at another, and making a mock of the sermons among his friends on the Monday, or so I heard. He would even go to the Quaker meetings with Patrick; they would have some fine cracks together, having their bets on when the spirit would move some poor Quaker body to rise in the meeting and discourse. Patrick was just then back from Leyden; he brought me a watch, oh, the bonniest wee watch you can conceive of, Catherine, with a branch of cherries in enamel on the back of it. I lost it, many years later, at an ill time for myself.

'There was a doctor in Edinburgh that had a notion for me too; he was a Hume and some kind of relation to Davie Hume the philosopher. I liked him well enough, but I couldna abide the thought of his cutting up dead corpses, and they procured for him the way most doctors' are. Sometimes he would be looking at me, studying for something to say that would please me, maybe, and I would be near screeching wud, with the thought that he could be looking just the same on a woman that was an unburied corpse. There were mostly plenty doctors in Edinburgh in those days, for there was the best of teaching at the University; the great part of them might be younger sons;

my William's friend Duncan Munro was that—he was in India when I was a lassie, or maybe he would have been after me himself, for his brother Robert, the Member for Wick Burghs, was often at the house. There were University lecturers too, in medicine and theology and jurisprudence, the worst drinkers of the lot mostly, and merchants and bankers, aye and merchants in a gey small way, who would be selling you a pair shoes or two yards cambrick or towelling in the forenoon, though he might be taking his glass of wine with you at night. Indeed, as I mind, there were not many gentlemen in Scotland that only minded their estates. And the reason for that is not far to seek; excepting for the great Dukes and that, we had gey little siller! A man can live on his estates by thrifty management, but no' unless he will give his full time to it, and, even so, he will be needing to drink ale rather than claret and his wife to wear linsey-woolsies and no' be hankering after silk. And that is scarcely human nature, most of all when our neighbour is a rich country, the like of England.

'There were plenty Ensigns and Captains in the English Army, and officers and troopers of the Black Watch. Indeed old Kyllachy, Lachlan's father, was an officer in that, and there were men of family who enlisted in the ranks; for a good family name and fame will not by itself pay a man's debts to his tailor even! Many an evening would Ann and myself stand in the windows of our lodging that looked on the gay, crowded, shouting High Street, daffing away with an officer on one side of us and a private soldier on the other. Aye, aye, the heavy brush of the kilt against one's muslin skirts. The pure English, of whom we saw a few, would never understand how it was my sisters and I could stand up for a reel with a corporal or a private man.

'There was one Englishman that I was taken with for a time; his father was at the King's Court, with some kind of handle to his name, and this laddie was none so bad, yet I didna like the flat round face of him nor yet the way he spoke, quacking and lisping the way a high-bred duck might do. My father had a kind of ettle that I should marry into England. Aye, Union

Jack they called him. But none of us did, not one of the lasses. It was only Jamie that married bonny Margaret Pye and he carried her off from school! I have wondered, odd times, what she will have thought of the family she married into. We lasses all married into the old country, as our mothers did before us. And our father would not force us against our own inclination. He aye said that a marriage should be a matter of prudence and foresight and religion, but the heart should be in it too, most of all for a lassie.

'Ach aye, he was a kind man, John Haldane, my father and your own grandfather.'

She dropped her head in her hand. Another of the cousins came running out of the house, tall Margaret, her striped chintz dress kilted up over her petticoats. But now, some way, Catherine Duncan did not want to leave her aunt or the story. She said quickly: 'But — did you never meet Uncle William at that time?'

'More's the pity,' said Kirstie, 'no. Though even if I had — ach, Catherine, I doubt I would never have seen in those days what like of man he was. He would have been — just one other Highlander. With as bad prospects as the rest. Let alone that he and his folk were Episcopalians. But he saw me once. Aye, he saw me walking down the High Street with my sisters. And he asked who were the lassies.'

Margaret, Bearcroft's daughter, looked curiously over at Catherine, half-beckoning her to come; there had been a quarrel among the lads, but the lasses were planning a game of cards and then after supper to dance on the lawn; the fiddler was drinking in the kitchen now. But Catherine never looked up until her younger brother, Adam, a midshipman on leave, came running and calling: 'Sister! George Cockburn has been drunk and fighting again!'

'With Ochtertyre?' asked Kirstie quickly.

'Yes, to be sure, Aunt Kirstie,' said Adam, 'and Ochtertyre has blooded his nose!'

'I hope this will be an example to yourself, Adam, against drinking to excess,' said Kirstie.

'The Navy need to drink,' said Adam, but added, 'and the Navy rum is the horridest stuff in the world, Aunt Kirstie, so for myself I am under no temptations, or not until I am at least a Captain, when my pay will allow me claret! But George is behaving worse than a fool now, for he is threatening that he will tell all the authorities that Ochtertyre was out last year.'

'Ach, never heed,' said Kirstie, 'for all of them know. Indeed, I heard one of the magistrates asking poor Patrick Murray was he better of his riding accident, and the both of them letting on to the other that was all it was.'

'But,' said Adam, 'if they are informed officially, it will be harder just to make a mystification of it.'

'George will think nothing of the kind when he is sober again,' said Kirstie, 'even George Cockburn! Give him credit at least for being a gentleman when he is out of his cups, Adam.'

'If he were in the Navy I would take your word for it,' Adam answered judicially, 'but the Army is different.' He frowned at Catherine who was laughing at him. 'And Ochtertyre is vastly distressed,' he added.

'Who else is by?' Kirstie asked. 'Have some of you taken him in hand or must we send for his uncles?'

'Johnnie is there with George,' said Margaret, 'and David and your brother Alec, Catherine. They are walking him up the Glen. And James is with Ochtertyre.'

'What are those two doing?' Kirstie asked.

'I think they might be saying a prayer,' said Margaret, 'but ach, it will be nothing at all. Come away, Catherine, we will have a set of loo, and then, when the lads are back, we will just stand up for a dance under the trees. You'll be there, Aunt Kirstie?'

'Well, if my own lad is back!' she said. 'Does your father ever dance these days, Margaret?'

Margaret shook her head. 'He hasna the figure for it, Aunt Kirstie! Used he to dance?'

'Ach yes!' said Kirstie. 'Patrick could stand up for a reel, and so could Gleneagles. And indeed Mungo had an eye for the lasses, though he was too canny to marry when he was young and too bashful when he was old! But that's past. Go you to your card game, Catherine.'

But Catherine said: 'I'm no' for the cards if Aunt Kirstie will go on telling me this story of hers. For I doubt we were coming near the best part. Were we no', Aunt Kirstie?'

Kirstie smiled. 'Ach away, I'm nothing but an old wife, blethering about past times. But I'll even tell you more if you care to be listening, Catherine, my soul.'

Tall Margaret dropped a half-curtsy and turned back to the house with Adam. As the afternoon wore on, every flower became sweeter, and there was a loud and constant humming of bees going steadily backwards and forwards to the hives. The damask roses by the door, small, clustered roses, deep almost to purple, smelled vastly, headily sweet. They should be picked and dried now for rose candy and rose water. Margaret often did such things at Gleneagles for her uncle, just as she would have at Bearcrofts, her father's house. She began to pick off the heads of the roses into her skirt, her cousin Adam Duncan helping her.

'WE came back from Edinburgh in the early summer,' said Kirstie abruptly, 'for indeed the cities were no' very healthy in the warm weather, and my brother Willie had died of some kind of an unchancy fever the year before. Our father came back after we did, for it was no light matter travelling from London to Gleneagles in those days. He was gey and anxious, we could all of us see that; and he would be for ever fidgeting and alarming our poor mother, walking up and down in her room and telling her all his thoughts, which is no' a very fair thing for any husband or wife to do.

'Rob Roy had come down out of the hills as far as Crieff, and drinking the Pretender's health at the Cross, with all the bare-foot, filthy rabble of the town after him cheering and screeching and rolling drunk in the gutters, for none of the inn-keepers dared refuse a free barrel to that lot — and the half of them Highland Jacobites themselves; and all the decent folks quiet as death behind their shutters, and dead scared, too, lest one of the Gregarach would take it into his head to set light to a roof or a stack by way of devilment and revenge. There was not more than half a troop of the Black Watch in Crieff then, and they lay low, for what was the use of starting the killings with themselves? But the Highlanders went off again and nobody hurt that time; yet for long enough afterwards we lasses were in the house before dusk, with the shutters barred early and the honest candles lit.

'You will have no idea, Catherine, the terror we would be in those days of the Gregarach and the lave of the landless Highlanders. There was nothing at all to bind them, see you, and, though they might call themselves Christians, it was a different thing from ourselves, and indeed half of them were Papists. They would do anything, anything at all, and laugh and sing like the devils out of hell while they were doing it. You will scarcely see a wild Highlander these days, Catherine, only the tamed ones — the like of my William! — and maybe they will seem to you romantic, for that is a way rarety has of changing the nature of a thing or a person. But that was not the way of it then.

The queerest thing is, Catherine, that, to-day, gin I met the whole clan of the Gregarach, with Rob Oig and Hamish Mor or whoever at all is leading them now, I would be a wee bit uneasy, maybe, but not scared down to my bones, the way I would have been. For now I have a kind of understanding of them, and that goes far to take away fear. And I know that the half of them are neither brave nor cruel, but sick scared themselves, and doing wicked and daring things because of it. You will understand, Catherine lassie, that they were sinned against in the beginning, and that is the simple enough start of an ill matter. If evil is done to one man or woman, they may be able to do this great thing and forgive their enemies, taking example of our Lord Jesus Christ, and then, in a matter of years, all will be well. But if evil is done to a whole race of folk, then they will be bound to do evil again. For, instead of going through with their wrongs, of letting themselves become soc-riven and harrowed by them, ripe for the seed, they will stand against it — aye, they will kick against the pricks — one speaking to another, keeping the thing aye in mind, and their days will be full of hate and destruction and their nights will be dreams of murder and triumph, the way it was with the Gregarach then, and is now for ower many Highland folk in this land of ours. And the reckoning is not yet.

'How will I make it plain? You see, Catherine, we in the Lowlands have been steady and settled and secure. We have things sorted up, the way every thing and every person has a place fixed. Each ox will go to his own stall in the byre, the sowing corn will be here and the meal corn there, the soc of the plough will be greased and wrapped after the spring, the sheep will be smeared one by one with tar and butter, one year in twenty-five the oak woods will be cut. There will be peats and coal, there will be stores against the winter, cheeses and hams and sugar loaves, salt herring and kippered salmon, pears and currants in syrup, tea and oranges, sauces and pickles with the date writ on them in ink by the mistress of the house, wines and beer and the great crocks of butter. There will be books in the study, knowledge of what has passed and thoughts for what is to come. There will be the Kirk Sessions and the heritors to take care of worship and morality; the Universities will press forward with learning and medicine; the Merchant companies and gilds, the City Fathers and the Magistrates, they will take care of property. The Army and the police are there for our protection. There is an abundance of trades, and the polite arts have their place in the capital; both in the clubs and in the drawing-rooms, will be found correctness of taste, boldness of disquisition and liberality of sentiment. An honest man has the world before him; though he start as a herd-boy or a journeyman, his son may be a banker or a general or famous as a wit. Morality is the muse of the north. Tell me now, Catherine, does that seem right to you?'

'That will be progress,' said Catherine Duncan, a wee thing awed by the thought of it, 'under the Lord's providence. That will be the way things are. Indeed, I have never heard it expressed with nobler sentiments, Aunt Kirstie.'

'Aye,' said Kirstie. 'But it's no' true.'

Catherine sat back, shocked, letting the embroidery slip from her knee to the ground. 'But — ' she said, and could get no farther. A fine sentiment carries its own truth surely! How could her auntie be saying such things?

'That is the idea we have of ourselves, we Lowland Scots,' said Kirstie, 'and there is a part of it that's no' lies. Indeed it could all be true. If the lairds thought first of their tenants or their land itself and only second of their own pride and idleness, if the burgesses and the bailies thought first of the labouring men and women whose rights they have in their charge, if the lawyers and the physicians thought more of their clients and less of their fees, if the ladies thought more of their households and less of their vanities, if the ministers thought more and deeper on God and His Son and never at all on braw new ways to hurt poor sinners, then all would be well. But it isna so

Yet we have aye got at the back of our minds, we honest folk, the thought of how things should be, and each individual man and woman secure in the possession of his own soul and his own bit property, gin it is only the lad's strength of arm or the lassie's maidenhead, and a wee cot with a kailyard for the old folk at the end of their days. Everything redded up and the slow, steady righting of wrongs and betterment of life.

'But I have seen the colliers in Ayr and Lanark and the salt-pan workers along the Firth, so poor, Catherine, that they couldna hardly be said to be living at all. Aye, arled to their masters, slaves with no hopes of betterment. And I have seen the free workers the same way, the Paisley weavers when trade was bad and the fishermen when the fishings were slack, aye, in yon year the English Parliament put the tax on the salt and spoilt the curing, and this good Scots security of ours nothing but idle words to them, an evil mocking that their Ministers and their masters had put on them for their own ends. I will even go so far as this, Catherine: those who are making the best living out of a country, they will be expressing their fine moral sentiments, even the way I was doing myself, and you believing every word of it, my soul, and they will aye be saying that the way things are must be the best, since that is the best for themselves.

'But they will not be seeing the kind of a lie they are telling themselves, oh, not at all. They will say, and they will believe, that the present ordering of life was ordained of the Lord. Which is a far worser blasphemy than any wee thing the Papists will be saying about saints and the like.

'So what I was giving you was just our own idea of ourselves, Catherine. But it was not the same idea they have in the Highlands. Though it was long enough before I understood their idea, and indeed I am scarcely understanding it yet, and times they will have me flummoxed altogether by some queer way of doing or thinking. But I would say the root of the matter might be that they have not the same idea of property as ourselves. The laird is no' exactly the laird, he is still the chief one of a great kind of family, and, just the same as you canna

54

have ilk bairn in a family sorted up, the way you can with every hand in a farm or a manufactory, so there is a kind of disorder and equality about the Highlands, the way it will fair break the heart of a Lowland housewife, until she sees, aye, she sees there is a thing at the back of it all. And, just the same, they will not think of the land as belonging to or vested in any one man, no more than the sea itself or the salmon rivers. And that is the reason why it is a worse thing for Macintosh of Kyllachy, say, to treat his estates as strictly his own property, than it would be for your own father at Lundie. That is the way, too, you will never get a right Highlander to live in an orderly way in a town and take his wages year by year and do as he is bid by a master. The Highlanders will do best when they are sharing, the way the fishermen mostly do, and it was the same with their farming, even; they do best with everything held in common, the old way. Indeed they are altogether against progress, as we see it in the Lowlands.

'But it is no' easy understood, yon, and, until it is understood, there will be hate and fear between the two nations of Scotland, ach, a kind of unreasoning thing, the way we ourselves felt about the Gregarach who were more disordered even than the lave of the Highlands, and hated us orderly folk all the more. They turned our own worst thing against us, the town mob, the ones that had no possessions nor security any more than the Gregarach had, and were half of them Highlanders without even the same speech as ourselves. Aye, yon Crieff mob were Highlanders surely, that had lost the clan thing that could have held them together and made them gentle, since in it they must be the equals of gentlemen. And they had it lost through the bad faith of their own chiefs and cousins, often enough.

'I can see it now, fine. But I didna see it when I was a lassie, and ach-och, the wild scared I was of these savages with their short, ragged kilts and the red, hairy legs they would have, and the black, greasy long tags of hair, for not many of them would have a decent wig or a tailor's coat, but only the plaids wrapped round them, and a fierce and fearsome array of dirks and pistols, and the sgian dubh in the top of the stocking, that would do as well for a man's throat as for a deer's. And, though I liked the pipes well enough, yet they could be a gey nasty, hellish laughing kind of sound, as though the men that blew them didna care the weight of a straw for life nor honour, neither their own nor another's.

'And there was a kind of smell of this about the Highland gentlemen we would be meeting, and we lassies would let the fear and the hate into our tongues and out with some bitter kind of a text or a Latin tag — I had that on my tongue's tip then, though it is mostly all gone now — or we could just be turning our backs and dancing with a Whig gallant and never a Tory. Indeed I am clean ashamed of the way we were behaving, although it is so long syne and every word of it forgotten.'

'But one must have one's principles, Aunt Kirstie,' Catherine said. 'I would not wish, myself, to be over friendly with a Jacobite. A true Jacobite, that is to say,' she added hastily, for indeed she could not see that she had to keep from speaking to Ochtertyre!

'It is a gey useful word, the principles,' said Kirstie, 'but the older one gets, the less principles one has, and the more practice. It is the other way when one is young. And indeed I had mostly plenty principles myself. I mind one time that summer, we had ridden over to Duncrub, one of the plough-boys following after with our saddle-bags, so that we could titivate ourselves up before the dancing. Lord Rollo was a Tory, but he had the best piper in Strathearn!

'Well, we were in fine trim, we lasses, and I was wild for a strathspey those days. We understood it was a Jacobite house mostly, but we werena fashing ourselves over much, and indeed I liked my cousins of Lanrick well enough and they were there. So was young Ochtertyre's father, and his wife, Katherine Fraser, Lovat's kinswoman, a clever and a stately one, yon, in a gown of stiff satin and her long ringlets bound back with ribbons and rose-buds. Not one of us was so braw. Lady Lanrick — for you didna call the laird's wife Mistress Haldane, those days! — she was just a wee dump, I mind, her dress just nothing ava, and her plaid aye huddled round her. For indeed they had fully as many bairns as they could do with, mostly lassies needing tochers, for the lad bairns died young, a' but three of them, and her husband a poor manager, that would be thinking he could mend his fortunes if the Stuarts came back. But they were none of them Papists at least. That wouldna ha' done. Did you ever meet with any of your Lanrick cousins, Catherine?'

'Poor Isobel came over to Lundie once,' said Catherine, 'but I have scarcely a recollection of her, Aunt Kirstie. I heard she was in trouble last year. What came of her in the end?'

'You will mind she was married on Stewart of Ardsheal, that was one of the commanders on the unlucky side at Culloden? He was skulking all last year. The English took their opportunity of burning Ardsheal House, and Isobel herself near her time. For wars will take no count of the reasonable things of life, such as the getting and bearing of bairns. She needed to escape with no more than what she had on and a wee bundle of swaddling clothes for yon bairn that wasna born; the redcoats are ill enough to face for a hale woman, let alone one that's ailing and in fear lest her big belly might offer too pretty a chance to a dragoon's bayonet. She had her bairn that night in a turf hut, biting on a cloth to stop any screeching that might get the best of her and let them know where she was. And the next day on again through the snow, for it was a cold, late year. And maybe that was away better than a prison in London. And the bairn lived. Aye, the bairn lived.'

'Did you see her afterwards, Aunt Kirstie? Yourself?'

'Aye, aye. She came to Borlum. Poor Isobel, I scarcely knew her, the grey look there was about her then! Her plaid that she had lain on — a fine Inverness wool with a scarlet lining — it was a' stiff with blood and muck. I put her in claes of my own and the most of hers fit for nothing but the fire. She stayed with me a matter of weeks.'

'But you were harbouring a rebel, Aunt Kirstie!'

'What's about it? She was my own cousin, gif her man was twenty times a Jacobite. And who was to ken?'

'You will trust your own folk that much, Aunt Kirstie?'

'There would be no question of sic a thing. More especially after me and himself having the wee lassie. There has been a warmth and kindliness for me at Borlum ever since that, a look in the eyes — ach, well. But Isobel went back and lived in a part of the Mains that had not been burned. Ardsheal is in France, and her father and her two elder brothers forby. There is a younger brother, she was after telling me—a doctor in England some place. Aye, Taunton in Somerset, wherever that may be. Somewhere the far side of Bath, I am thinking.

'But in the year of the first troubles, Isobel Haldane was not born nor yet begotten, aye that very summer, that June when my sisters and myself were setting to our partners on the close-scythed grass in front of Duncrub. My first partner was David Smythe of Methven; his mother was a half-sister of my father's. He was another Jacobite; yet none of us knew then how far they would be carrying it, and indeed, while the dancing was on, we lasses were not fashing ourselves over much.

'You ken, Catherine, minding on a thing that's far back, the like of yon, you will not have it clear, only maybe here and there, a dress or a bit tune, or a thing you had to your dinner that wasna just broth and salt meat and the kain hens the tenants were bringing in for their rent, nothing more than crows! But what you mind right is the feel of a day or an hour, the love or anger in your own heart or the things pulling it all ways at once that you canna put a name to, and the feel you had towards your own folks or others. That way, I mind all being well yon day for the first of the dancing, and the light look of the trees and the green corn beyond, and the gaiety of the ladies' plaids; for in yon time, Catherine, there wasna a lady, Highland or Lowland, that didna wear the plaid. We would draw the edge with the fine fringe of it drooping, across our faces and keek over, the way you will do with masks these days. Well, we had been at the country dances, Flowers of Edinburgh, Monymusk, and Torryburn Lasses, and syne Lady Rollo called us out for a minuet.

'Now there is a dance that goes so slow that you and your

partner have time to speak to one another, and I was dancing with Lachlan Macintosh of Kyllachy. And what I mind is a sudden kind of rage in myself, spoiling the dance, choking me; you canna dance right if you are in a rage, and whenever I turned to meet my partner there was nothing in me but a wild seeking for some hurting, fierce thing I could say to him. Yet I was not old enough to have any such thing at my tongue's end.

'But what I canna mind, Catherine, is how it was that Kyllachy had angered me so, whether he had let out some scornful kind of half compliment, half jibe at me and my folk, some arrogance, something that sounded the way he was already treating me as a loser and himself as a winner. No, I canna mind it ava. Yet it must have been that kind of a thing. For the Jacobites and Tories were raising their heads then, were starting to boast, to invent the most fantastical tales of the money and men they had, and the fine strength and support they would get in England or Ireland, with a great naming of titles and lands and an air of familiarity with men whom they had neither seen nor spoken to, who might not indeed exist at all beyond their own imaginings. For, as there is no truth that goes so deep as a Highlander's truth, so there is equally no lying to match theirs, for they will even believe it themselves, and it was maybe that which had me so wild yon day. For I have a great regard for the truth, Catherine, and so, I am hoping, have you.

'And now I will tell you a thing, my soul, that I have not told to your own mother, even, though she was my own wee sister Helen. Kyllachy and his brothers had another young man with them at yon time; it seemed he was an acquaintance of theirs. And nothing would suit them but he must be presented to myself. And when I saw the red tartan he had on him, the same as on them, I fell into such a rage against the Highlanders — aye, a bull calf I was to yon red! — that I turned my back and I wouldna speak to him. My mother chid me for my unmannerliness, since she was half a Tory herself, as almost all the Erskines were; but I let on that my stays were over-tight on

59

me, and I missed a dance. Aye, I missed my first dance with William Macintosh of Borlum.'

Catherine Duncan did not know at all what to say, for a shadow had come on her aunt and on the story. 'But suppose you hadna been angry, Aunt Kirstie,' she said, hesitating, 'maybe nothing at all would have come out of it. Oh, I am sure it was not any kind of a Judgment on you!'

'Na, na,' said Kirstie, 'I wouldna care to think that the Lord would play such a mean wee trick on a lassie — and indeed according to many folks it was a righteous anger I had!' She laughed again. 'Ach, there was nothing of the kind in it, and if I had danced with him thon time, my life would still have been set to the same tune and not a new one. For it was going the way it needed to go, and me driving myself along with my principles and the things happening in the world outside to point them the way they did. For in August that year came the Earl of Mar's hunting party on Braemar, and ten days later the raising of poor King Jamie's standard, when the golden ball dropped from the top of it and put a cold feeling into the minds of those that were watching and not altogether certain, and the King they had been drinking to and making their songs and pictures about, not there at all, but in France yet, working away to get over on to his own side the new Regent of France, who was as canny a man as ever gave promises to his right and left and never letting the tae ken what was doing with t'ither!

'There were two white ribands hanging from the standard, Catherine, and the one of them was lettered "For Our Wronged King and Country", but the other read "For Ourselves and Liberties". It is a queer thing how both sides in a political quarrel will each of them aye be speaking of liberties and that with as much truth and honour as any politician can have — mind you, Catherine, the most of my folk have been politicians! — and yet they mean an entirely opposite thing. And our father would say to us that the Jacobites would enslave our country to a Stuart papist who would bring his Inquisition with him, as we could read in *Foxe's Book of Martyrs*, and to the nobles and clan chiefs and the great landowners that would be suppressing trade and the cities and the good understanding with England.

'But I mind our mother suddenly on her feet, speaking in an over-clear and loud voice, and that at the table before all of us bairns, asking her husband how could he be saying such things and he knew that this was the chance for Scotland, and let him mind how, whenever he went south to the London Parliament, the English mocked at him and his Scots speech and the little siller he had to spend compared with themselves, and his insistence on keeping the Sabbath! And she turned on Patrick, who had been elected for the Cupar Boroughs in the General Election and who had ridden north, as Mungo, who sat for Stirlingshire, had also done, the same day that he heard Mar had sailed from London; for indeed nobody was taken by surprise who had any knowledge of the inward of events in Scotland. And she said: "They will even be laughing at you, Patrick, for all you tried so hard to shed your Scots coat and your Scots tongue at Leyden!"

'I mind that I went hot to my hair, and looked down at my plate expecting I didna ken what. But the two Haldanes — Mungo was in Stirling speaking with the burgesses who had elected him — were so dumbfoundered at this from Helen Erskine that was wife to the one and stepmother to the other, that they couldna answer. And she went on at Patrick: "You are a Commissioner for the Equivalent, Patrick," she said, "and that is mostly a bribe to the Darien Company sharcholders, that are three-quarters of them Whigs, to let the lave of Scotland be eaten up by England and pay all manner of taxes for an English National Debt, whilk was money borrowed to pay for an English war that was no affair of Scotland's! But I never thought you would be so easy bought, Patrick." And syne she turned to our father: "You will have had your Darien money paid back, have you not, Gleneagles? I doubt it will not be taken from you even if King James comes into his own!" And she spoke with that kind of a scorn that went through the lot of us like an east wind and met its answer in ourselves, for I knew I had the same thing in my own heart against the Tories and my cousin Kyllachy, and ach-och, Catherine, it gave me the most awful kind of mixed feeling about my father and mother, and how could I act as a good child should do, and I prayed in a loud whisper for Guidance, and poor Ann doing the same thing.

'But Patrick stood up and banged his fist on the table and he said: "You are no mother of mine, Helen Erskine, though you have never been an ill step-mother. But I am telling you this. You would have it that your own lot are the only ones that care for Scotland. That is a lie. You would turn the clock back, Helen Erskine, to land-owning and a King's Court and easy-oozy ways and no questions asked of the gentry and no justice for the poor, and with that poverty and hunger as they were in the bad years and no chance at all for the common folk to leave the land and their ill crops and go to the cities and the trades and freedom."

' "Shame on you, Patrick!" said our mother. "You would be blaming me and the Opposition for the bad years, most of which you were over young to mind for yourself, but they were sent by the Lord as a warning to Scotland! You would have it that everyone should live by the trades and professions, since that means more work for lawyers such as yourself, but you know fine that the best days for Scotland were never the trading days!"

'Again Patrick would have answered back, but this time our father stopped them both and with these words: "There is no set of ideas in the world that is worth a civil war, and between us all we have done harm enough to Scotland!"

'But I saw how he was hurt by the things his wife and his son had said, and, gin I'd had as much boldness then as I have now, I would have run and kissed him. But I was feared of my father, the way my own wee lassie is never to be of hers. Ach, Catherine, I was that fond of all of them, and all with some kind of right on their side, and Patrick the most far-seeing maybe; for Scotland was so sunk in poverty thirty years back that she could scarcely have stood on her own feet, let alone borne the expense of yet another Court at Holyrood, and the only way out seemed to be to keep in with England, at whatever cost to ourselves.

'Ann and Margaret and I, we talked it over in our bed that night, lying with nothing but the linen sheet over us, for it was close weather and poor Ann in one of the sweats she used to go into. Aye, she died the next year, soon after she was betrothed. But that is the way I am minding the very words they said, and times I have asked myself, since, who was in the right and, if poor King James had been less used to misfortunes, or if he'd had my William's father, the Brigadier, in command of his armies in the stead of Bobbing John — for that was how we aye thought of Mar — if the Rebels had won, in which case they wouldna have been Rebels but Restorers, would that have been better or worse for Scotland?

'Howsoever, there was worse to come than quarrelling. Less than a month after the setting up of the standard, we had General Gordon of Auchintoul in command of the clans, here at Auchterarder. During almost a month, there was one lot of them or another quartered too close for comfort, and for all our mother's favouring the Jacobites, she kept us lassies within the house. Even so, we had officers quartered on us that paid in little but promises. They killed a thousand of our sheep for the army, and drove nearly as many more, with cattle and horses to match. They'd had plenty practice in rieving and droving, those ones! Our poor mother thought she should have had better treatment, but it wasna till her brother's wife got through a letter to Mar — and that with main difficulty — that any check was put on them. It was the same or worse for my uncle, David's father, at Aberuthven.

'When they took the laird's gear they werena like to spare the tenants'. We tried to drive our beasts up into Glen Devon, but they chased them into Frandie and got them there. Chrystie of Glenhead, Anderson of Craigbeckie, and Paton of the Three Catters, all well-doing tenants, they came to us greeting, the three big men, the best of their beasts gone and no winter keep for the rest, for the Highlanders had requisitioned hay, straw and oats. It was not so much the value of the things that was breaking their hearts, but the labour they had put into it; they had thought the year's work was over and all safe harvested, they had got the best of poor cuttings and bad weather, the way we need to in the north, and then — ach, it was no use at all our mother saying that all would be put right when the King came into his own, they answered her with hard words, for all she was Lady Gleneagles; Paton was an elder of the Kirk. Nannie Cairns from the Fisher Lands, over by Aberuthven, she had her teeth knocked out by a MacLean who was taking off her milk cow. And they took the sheaves out of the barns and threshed the grain out themselves, with the pipers skirling up and down while they did it, or else they made the tenants do it for them and syne they burnt the empty barns for payment! Aye, they did that at Crosshouse and Hill of Broich. We just daredna ask what next.

'The Highlanders would be doing it with all the politeness and fair speech in the world, but you learnt in time, the better the sentiments, the worse the act that would follow them. Aye, they would murder and thieve and rape like gentlemen! Rob Roy was at Auchterarder then, and little enough control of him General Gordon or Mar himself had. The officers could often have some decency, but they were a feckless lot of courtiers and idle lairds, the half of them, and when they needed to give orders to their men they had not the Gaelic, while the men had no word of English. Ach, it was the worst kind of confusion and stupidity, and although Mar sent word that all this was to be stopped, nothing came of it, but the restoring of a dozen sheep, maybe, and plenty fine words. But when you have an Army raised and eager to be doing something, and you give them nothing to do, not so much as a sight of their enemy, then you will get the worst out of them.

'So it went on for a month. And after Sheriffmuir they put the sheep they had taken for the Army, from half over Perthshire, into our parks, where there was still some winter feed. There was such a terrible wild bleating of the poor beasties, night and day, that I cannot hear a sheep now without thinking on yon times. But worse was to come.

'It was a hard, bad winter; drifts of snow, I mind, up against the house. The most of our coals had been taken for the Army, and we hadna plenty peats; so it was cold in the house, forby we were needing to give cooked dinners to half our tenants and their wives and weans, the way things were, and our own girnals three-quarters empty! There could be no visiting about, but we heard how things were the same everywhere, and little news even from Edinburgh, all posts held up. Our father used to ride over to the Headquarters at Auchterarder or Braco, through the dirtied, horse-trodden ruts between the snow-banks. There were always some troops lying there or at Gleneagles, though the main body of the Jacobite Army was quartered at Perth. Our mother had a mind to ride there herself, but our father wouldna let her, and indeed the horses we had left were scarcely fit for the journey.

'He would get the Jacobite side of the news, the invasion of England by Macintosh's Brigade and then the falling back for yet another plan, so they said. On the Sabbath, too, we heard news at the Kirk at Blackford; when it became clear that the Jacobites were at least not winning straight off, and, later, that Preston had been as complete a defeat as you could have; then there was a suppressed kind of rejoicing amongst the most of the congregation, and the Minister preached off his Ordinar' on to more heartening texts; for indeed the Old Testament is gey and full of texts about the down-setting of enemies, so that we could get much consolation that way, and it wasna till I was far, far older, Catherine, that I ever jaloused that the same set of texts would do for the other side, gin ourselves were the enemies!

'The Auchterarder Minister was a poor timorous old body, but Mr. Reid from Dunning exchanged pulpits with him and preached on a Sabbath with the loaded pistol hanging down over his black coat. To be sure, there would, times, be officers from the Highland Army amongst the congregation, or even men from the ranks. That would mean a greater need for ingenuity in prayer and discourses. But they would aye be the decenter sort, sometimes men who had been forced into the thing against their wills, tenants of Jacobite lairds, maybe. The worst would be having their Sabbath services in the Gaelic, and the most of them either Episcopalians or even Papists.

'It seemed queer to my father and brothers that the Jacobites were making so little of their own opportunities, and times he thanked the Lord it was his wife's cousin, Bobbing John the politician, that was leading the Armies and no' a professional soldier, the like of Borlum. And fine and glad we were to hear that Borlum had been taken prisoner at Preston, and we hoped he would pay for it with his head. But syne we heard that young Ochtertyre — that is this one's father — was taken; his own father, Sir Patrick Murray of Ochtertyre, who was sixty past, had surrendered already, after the proclamation, and was held at Edinburgh Castle. So if anything was to be done for young Murray, it was the Haldanes of Gleneagles who would need to do it. Then came Janet Smythe, Lady Methven, our father's half-sister, to say that her boy David was taken too. Poor Janet, her man was terrible old then, and little help to her, and she would come to our father for everything. She had seen David last riding off on the Kinbuck road; he had waved his bonnet to her. She kept on repeating that, and then she would fall to greeting, and our mother giving her spirits of hartshorn and aquavite and the elixir salutis that she had from Edinburgh every year and that would make you vomit with the very smell of it.

'We knew that our Lanrick cousins were sure to be in it, though we had no news of them for a time; and thus we, as a family, were all in a conflict, and times I was half longing to go with my mother to Perth and the Jacobite Headquarters and maybe make my curtsy to King James, though indeed he was nothing to turn the head of any leddy, young or old, poor Mr. Melancholy! But the Duncrub lasses were there and the half of our friends and neighbours; you ken, we were that close to the Highland line, and Strathearn divided and jumbled about, and not even my father utterly whole-hearted on the one side. For he didna want what you might call an English victory, only some kind of compromise reached in Scotland and between Scots; and indeed he was not the only one, for before the end of the year Sinclair, who was another cousin, for Katherine Sinclair was married on our uncle, Sir John Erskine of Alva, and Lord Rollo himself, had sent private letters to Argyll.

'Times it had seemed almost like the old wars of the chiefs, but this time between Mar and Argyll. Yet this Argyll was no' a wee cross Archie, but Red John of the Battles, no more pleasant and likeable than the most of the Campbells, but a General and statesman that knew his business as both. And the clans were aye quarrelling among themselves, MacLeans and Gordons and Frasers and MacDonalds, and Mar would be demanding money from the Perth merchants or from the well-doing lairds, and then giving it to some feckless Highland gentleman that would come to him with some fine story of his own distresses and nobility!

'And then, in the later end of January, on the coldest night of the year, the MacDonalds and MacLeans and Camerons burnt the villages on the Stirling road. Aye, they burnt Auchterarder, Blackford, Dunning, Muthill and Aberuthven. They were saying it was to stop Argyll coming forward to take Perth. Maybe such things are a military necessity. But we were wakened out of our beds before it was light to sort up the house against the coming back of the men with the poor bodies who were homeless and hurt. Our father and the boys were away down with what horses we had, and blankets, and their flasks full of brandy and whisky. Ann and our mother were in the kitchen, stirring the broth. Mungo had shot a stag that had come down off the hills and was the makings of it. Myself and the lave of us, we had blankets and straw laid in the hall and a good fire. When we looked out into the dark we could see the nasty, red, wee glows here and there, a wicked, wavering light out of the moonless black, and by and bye the tail of morning coming over the hills, and our father's and Mungo's voices, calling cheerfully enough, for they were aye happiest when they were busy.

'But then there was greeting and moaning and I ran out to the door and helped the poor bodies into the house, Patrick looking grim and quiet with a sore burnt lad-bairn in his arms.

There was poor Jane Eadie and the Brices from Blackford, and from Auchterarder Phemie Reid and her man, the Donaldsons, the schoolmaster's wife, near her time and bleeding from her mouth and nose where they had knocked her down, the wee Graemes, and Andrew Mailor the joiner, who was father to Janet that is dairymaid here the now, but she was a wee, naked, crying bairn that night, and her mother sobbing her heart out over her. My sisters and the lasses served them broth to their breakfast and blankets to their shoulders. Later that day we had the Hallys from Muthill and old Mistress Clow and her grandchildren from the house at Damside, and later the Pernies and others of our own tenants from Dalreoch and the Four Quarters of Aberuthven; it was they that told us how Aberuthven house itself had been burnt for pure spite and devilment; but my cousins had escaped to Stirling.

'And all these poor folk and plenty more, with every bit thing they had burnt over their heads and that in January. The seed-corn had been burnt with the meal. The bairnie's cradle, the weaver's loom, the joiner's and mason's tools, the surgeon's instruments, the Minister's books, the wee things the lassie had put by against her wedding, all gone. It had come on them worse than sudden, too, for the Highlanders had seemed friendly enough, and Clanranald had been to the Davidsons' house where he had been quartered before Sheriffmuir, and had kissed all the family and promised that no harm would come, and then he had given orders for the burning. But I doubt he was coldly revenging himself for the death of his brother, the Captain of Clanranald, and I am thinking that most of the MacDonalds would be the same. I mind Phemie telling me of her own wee house burning and one very tall Highlandman standing with the plaid drooping from his shoulder and watching the flames with a wee smile and his eyes only half open as though he might be seeing far out, and she tried to creep in past him to gather up some bits of her things that were lying scattered, but of a sudden the still eyes and mouth that had seemed almost gentle went twisted and savage and he pounced on her the like of a wild cat and she ran, screaming. Ach, it was a wild cruel thing and it was terrible to see all those poor souls. There were a few killed at the time and more died later on of cold and hunger.

'Yet it was the end of the rebellion. By February it was all over — bar the trials, and our father, with Mungo and Patrick, off to London and the sitting of Parliament, that was no' a very pleasant sitting for any of the Scots Members. They took with them a schedule of the damages which themselves and the people of Auchterarder, Dunning and Blackford, had suffered, and in time the English Government gave them debentures against it, or some of it. Our own damages were reckoned at seven thousand pounds sterling, and the debentures were for the half of it, and it was the same for everyone. And they are not paid to this day. You see, Catherine, the English put it all into the hands of a private company, aye, the York Building Company, and when their affairs got into a bad way, and by and bye they went into liquidation, we in Scotland just lost our money. But whether or no we got compensation, the beasts had been killed, the meal eaten or squandered, and the houses and byres burnt, aye and the hearts broken. For ourselves, we got no rents from our tenants for two or three years after that.

'Yet the first thing that our father and Mungo did when they got to London, was to make interest for our two cousins who were prisoners.'

Kirstie fell silent, looking at the house. It did not seem now as though there could ever have been so much misery in it. The three men were coming back across Cairnquarters, the field between the bowling-green and the old castle; she could see that Captain Robert had his arm about his brother-in-law's shoulders. Suddenly Kirstie spoke again: 'There was just one other thing, Catherine, my heart of the corn. When Argyll's men were chasing the Jacobite Army back into the north, they burnt Ardoch House, where Mar had his headquarters. It had the finest collection in Scotland of Roman antiquities from the camp at Ardoch; they were all scattered and broken up. These things are maybe nothing as compared with human lives. Yet I could wish that hadna happened.'

CHAPTER IV

THE three men crossed the wee stone bridge between Cairn-quarters and the bowling-green. This was a part of Mungo's enclosure scheme. The thorns on the dyke had been quickset, the same way he had seen them in the south—in the market gardens round London, for example; but these had been cut with less skill, and some were blackthorn instead of the haw-thorn. In the garden at the back, he had a nursery of young trees that Black William was to see; he would let his good tenants have them at cost price for their enclosing. There would be thorns and crabs and hollies, and maybe a few beech trees. But he had ten or twenty thousand seedlings, grown under his own eye and from his own seeds, Scots pine, silver fir and spruce. Black William spoke of larch, which he had seen growing in France, high enough up, but the Haldanes were certain that they would be over-tender. Gleneagles heard that Atholl had a few: 'Duke's trees, Duke's siller!' he said. 'Atholl can keep himself out of mischief with yon kind of follies. I am for trees I can be sure of.'

There was a thing Gleneagles himself had in mind, a scheme for the land beyond Muiralehouse, waste moor, the most of it, forby one or two plantations. He and the lave of the heritors would be at the joint expense of a bounding fence, and would make a great plantation of the whole thing, aye a forest! You could not suppose that the grown trees could be worth less than five shillings sterling, each one, and say you plant three thou-sand, four hundred and twenty-two trees to the acre, and thin them early — six men could plant an acre a day between them, at a shilling a day, and syne you would need your skilled foresters, family men that could bring up a son to the same trade, for it would be an eighty years' job! Well then, the moor of Orchill would be a safe and steady investment so long as Scottish ships — or what was to hinder selling the timber into England? — were sailing the high seas.

70

Captain Robert agreed; he could see the thing opening up a future for Scotland; now that one benefit at least of the Union was being felt, with the lifting of the embargo on Scottish ships trading across the Atlantic to the English colonies, Glasgow might soon be building a fleet of her own. There might even come a time when the Virginia trade might be centred there; already the Glasgow merchants were doing well out of tobacco, though it was a thing he himself scarcely used, nor did he encourage it on his own ship. That was a far-enough cry from the wee trees, all the same! It was fine for them to have this new brother to talk it over with, a knowledgeable one surely. You would see that by the way he handled the growing seedlings, not over tenderly, yet with a kind of sympathy towards them. He himself had brought over seeds from America and tried them out at Borlum. But he was hardly sure yet of what would do.

On their way, the men would have a word with the two ladies, let them see that yon thing which had leapt and flashed, was by as though it had never been, that Kirstie's man was as welcome as herself to the Haldane house. 'And what like of a gab have the two of you been having?' Gleneagles asked. 'Were you speaking of the London fashions, Kirstie? Will we be seeing you in a monstrous great wig with feathers in't?'

She shook her head. 'You ken fine, Mungo, that I will keep to my tartan screen and my own hair, that's at least clean, under it!'

'Your tartan screen is not lawful wearing these days, Kirstie!' said Robert.

'What's the law for if it's no' to be broken, Robbie?' she said. 'Gif my own man cannot get wearing his kilt, at least he will see his tartan on myself.'

'Aye, you suit the red, Kirstie,' said Rob, and laid his hand softly on the edge of the Macintosh tartan, and looked across at Black William the way the thing would not only be healed, but would lead to a new understanding.

'I was telling the lassie here about the '15 and our own part in it,' Kirstie said.

The men were silent for a moment. 'It seems far enough back, yon,' Captain Robert said. 'It was all over before I myself was old enough to think.' And then he suddenly turned to his brother-in-law: 'What did you think of it then, Borlum? And what did your father think?' The Highlander did not answer at once; he seemed to have withdrawn himself, sinking down as a man might behind a rock on a braeside, his gun at his knee, watching. 'Do you know that about your man, Kirstie?' Robert asked, suddenly impatient. The Haldanes had been the first to offer friendship, wanting to be open, wanting forgiveness, co-operation and kindliness, or whatever way you might see the thing; but Black William was still not quite giving himself, was still unwilling to put himself into their hands. They had suffered so little, the men. Kirstie, though, had suffered; Kirstie his wife. She smiled from her brother to her husband, telling him with her eyes that there was no trap.

'It seemed to us,' said Black William, 'that the Union with England was destroying Scotland. It had been bad enough with Queen Anne, but the new lot had no interest at all in Scotland; we were thought of as a kind of county of England.'

'Ach, yes,' said Mungo, 'we found thon down at Westminster: "Have we not bought the Scots and the right to tax them?" Aye, that was said to the Scots Members. Yet what else could be done? Given what had passed. You couldna just repeal the Union.'

'That was so,' said Black William, 'but if we could have had the other dynasty, the Stuarts would have seen Scotland righted.'

'But at what a cost,' said Mungo. 'We would have had the wars of religion again. And they were the worst. They had torn us from top to tail. We needed to get breath, to think on other things but religion, and, ach, all that wildness and passion and prophesying!'

'Aye,' said Captain Robert, 'we needed reason and tolerance, and beyond all, capital.'

'That has had its cost also,' said Black William; and again Captain Robert had to look at his empty sword-belt. 'But I agree with you, Airthrey,' Black William went on, 'the way things were, it would have been civil war in Scotland. If only King James had been a different man, with fewer principles and a better heart, he might have carried all before him. But he was not.'

'Maybe the other one had that,' Mungo said, 'last year.'

'The Prince,' Captain Robert said with an effort of good will, since it would have come far easier to his tongue to say The Pretender.

'But it was too late,' Black William said. 'Our country had begun to save herself other ways. We had seen beyond the Stuarts. The things I was trying to do at Borlum last year and the year before — Kirstie and I together — they were small things, but if I had gone out at the head of my folk, the way Lady Anne Macintosh asked me to do, aye and more than her, I would not have got my turnips sown and harvested, nor got my tenants persuaded to try them; I would not have got them to bring the best of their kye to be served by my prize bull, nor to thresh their grain at the new Dutch mill that some of us have built — to thresh it there not as a servitude and due to the laird, but of their free will, because it was better and cleaner threshing. When the Prince landed at Moidart, my potatoes, the first I had tried out in an open field, forth of the walled garden, were in full leaf: folk coming out from Inverness even, to look at them and tell me they would never do, and I wondering if I had been right to try them in light soil or if I should have put more dung to them. While he was in Holyrood and some at least of my clan going there — and there were those who missed the fighting but didna care to miss the dinners and Assemblies! — I was working myself with the graips, getting my potatoes up. If I had left them and gone off, they might have been pulling them up by the shores and missing half of them and then telling me my crop was a failure. Ach, I know what my own Highlanders are like. I pitted the potatoes myself, some under oat straw and some under rashes; by the end of the winter some of my neighbours were coming over to ask about them, and might they have a boll or so to try! You will know yourself, Gleneagles, the wild lot of persuading it takes to turn a farmer into new ways, however good they may be. I needed to show them with my own work of my own hands. Did I no', Kirstie?'

'Aye,' she said, 'and the correspondence you had with the Society of Improvers in Agriculture — nights you would be writing and making tables of costs and drawings of the fields, and the candles burning down beside you. Ach well, the posts went on running between Inverness and Edinburgh while the Prince was in Scotland. It was only Cumberland that stopped them for a time, thinking that we barbarians had no need of sic a thing!'

But Captain Robert was flicking with one finger at the seal on his watch chain, the way he did when he had something on his mind. At last he said: 'Yet for all that — I am thinking I know you that much by now, Borlum — when you were asked to raise your men for the Stuarts — '

'I wanted to do it,' Black William answered. 'Aye, you know me that far, Airthrey. Lady Anne came over herself, that one of whom the French Ambassador said: "Rien n'est si beau que cette femme". I said no to her, I thought of the other things that Forbes of Culloden had said to me, of another kind of duty. Some of my men came to me asking me should they go, ready and willing for me to lead them. How could we all not want to go after the '15, after the way we were looked on in the south, after my poor father dead in prison, after all that had been done to my clan? But I studied the thing, Airthrey, asking myself what would be best for Scotland, speaking about it with my Kirstie. We prayed over it, the two of us, seeking most painfully for guidance. You will believe that, Airthrey?' His face had gone pale and old-looking now, his lips lifted away from his teeth.

Captain Robert said, 'I wasna thinking to doubt you, Willie, and I am certain it was a hard thing you did, and a right thing. You were looking to the future that no man can be right sure of, and turning your back on the past that you knew.'

'Aye,' said Black William, 'on the dead. Nos in aeturnum exilium impositura cymbae.'

'Then you will have been on the march to Preston with your father, yon other time?' Mungo asked. He was partly wanting to get on to his trees — he had picked up the account books again and was glancing between the pages, aye there it was, ninepence for a lb. of acorns the winter before the landing at Moidart, and now, see, the bonny they were! Ships in four score of years, only a lifetime more. But partly, too, he was wanting to be friendly to Kirstie's man, the new brother to the bull calves.

He answered: 'I was on that march, and you ken, Gleneagles, we had near-hand got the Castle at Edinburgh. If we had done that — things would have been away different. If we had even known how few men the Duke had with him, my father might have done it. Though maybe if he had, Mar would have said it was against orders! But all went wrong from the time we joined up with the English. Forster and Derwentwater and all of them, they were not soldiers at all, they were — ach, English gentlemen for ever thinking of what they should do and what forms of speech they should use according to the pattern and picture they had made of themselves! They and their duelling-swords with the gold-plated mounts and all, and their men with the dung-forks and sickles! My father could have held Preston with another five hundred well-armed Scots if he had been in command right himself — for that matter he would never have let himself be surrounded there. But the English were jealous of him; he was over rough for them; he was — a professional, and they, ach, they were schoolboys, dandys, playing at the thing. They didna like his voice, they didna like the way he would be breakfasting quick off a sup of porridge and then out into the field; they didna like the easy way he was talking with his men. They were wanting the polish and he was wanting the cold steel under it. Ach well, he could shrug his shoulders and go on, and he hadna been two days in Newgate Prison before he was scheming to get out of it, himself and me — and I took it hard enough, being only a lad myself — and my half-brother Benjie, that was kindly and stupid and above all sweet-natured, the same way as his mother that had been kitchen-maid at Borlum when my father was a wild lad, and now was married on the head ploughman — she is living yet, but gey old and bent and for ever grieving for poor Benjie, for she thought more on him than on the rest of her bairns. Aye speaking of him, is she no', Kirstie? Father was fond enough of Benjie, and Benjie would have died for father any day, aye, a likeable man, my father — but the English didna think so!'

'Was your mother dead at that time?' Captain Robert asked gently.

'Aye. She was dead three years back. She died in his arms. And she, the Lord knows, was English of the English, Mary Reade of Ipsden in Oxfordshire. And she followed him through danger and pain and poverty, and aye with a wee laugh or a bit song. The English are either one thing or the other.'

'You yourself are half English, Willie lad!' Gleneagles said.

'Aye,' said Black William, 'but surely, surely, it is not that which matters. My mother Mary Reade gave up everything which mostly counts with the English, money and ease and respectability — she was a Maid of Honour to Queen Mary of Modena at King James's Court in London — and academic learning — her father was a friend of Boyle the philosopher, who was a kind of Socrates to my father, and indeed that was the way he got to know her — and a comfortable and pleasant home: I myself have stayed at Ipsden. She gave that up to follow a Highlander, a rough Highland bull, who had neither house nor home for her half the time. So I am thinking she would have her place where her heart was.' He stumbled a wee bit over his words and then said, 'But why am I speaking of all this? It will be of no interest to your good selves.'

'But it is,' said Gleneagles, 'we are wanting to know what like of man our Kirstie chose.'

'You will be beginning to think not so ill of us, for all we are Whig Lowlanders?' Captain Robert said.

'Ach, ach!' said Kirstie, 'when the laddies get together they are away softer than the lasses!' She laughed at the three of them, while Catherine Duncan looked down at her embroidery,

embarrassed and puzzled. 'Will the post horses from Edinburgh no' be into Blackford the now?' she asked.

'They could be,' Gleneagles said, 'we will ride over in the
evening and see.'

'You will not be off for the dancing!' Kirstie said.

'Ach, I am twenty years too old for thon!' her elder brother
answered her, but Black William gave her half a grin; he still
had a mind for the dancing, with her anyway. They moved off
towards the nursery of trees, Mungo speaking of the depth of
peat on the moor of Orchill, and then about the Muiralehouse
lands close by there, and the great field with the southerly
slope in the which, once it was drained and brought into order,
he purposed to grow flax. There could be a steeping pond at the
foot of the slope, and the same water would furnish power for
the lint mill he purposed setting up. And had Willie here seen
the lint mill that Mr. Hope of Rankeiller had built over by in
Fife?

But the minds of the two women were again on people and
not on things. 'It is easy enough,' Kirstie said abruptly to
Catherine, 'to say afterwards what should or should not have
happened. It would be fine to live in a book and be able to
turn the page, and times in my life I have been ettling to do
that same thing. Yet mostly I thought I saw where my duty
was, and I would go for it blind, and then it would turn out to
have been no such thing. Yet at the time I had been as certain
as though the Lord Himself had been at my elbow. I would
have convinced myself and my elders that I was in the right.
Now that I have lived the most of my life and have learnt
humility, I am neither so certain of myself nor so willing to
make judgments, and I am beginning to see why it is the worst
thing of all to say Thou Fool to a brother. Tell me, Catherine
lassie, have you ever had a right conviction of sin?'

'I — I think so, Aunt Kirstie,' Catherine said, for indeed she
knew fine when she set her mind to it, as she had done only
this week at family worship, that we were all children of sin.

Kirstie cocked an eyebrow at her, all the same: 'I doubt you
will no' have had it right, for it is a gey nasty thing and it

tears and rives you like a muckle great purging. And it leaves
no sense at all in your whole life before it, and it shows you that
all your judgments were vain, and all that you did for the
sake of principle, hurting yourself and others, most like, was
worthless, aye, was never in God's sight at all. And you think
you might have done no worse and not hurt yourself nor yon
others. But even that isna true. But the truth lies far, far
down, beyond explanations, and you are needing even to strip
yourself of your principles, since they are mostly a kind of
weapon or armour. It may be good and well to have such
things at times, or to arm a young lass or lad going forth into
the world and needing protection. But you must leave them
by when it comes to facing your Maker and the universe He
has made. You must be innocent, not able nor willing to hurt
— you will mind the Latin derivation of yon word, innocent,
Catherine! — and then maybe you'll be fit to take to yourself
a small part of God's love. But ach, none of yon words are
making my meaning right, none ava! And every generation
has its own words, new minted, and the old words must be cast
out onto the midden of past thought that's ever growing at the
door of human experience. It is only actions that show.

'Well then, the summer after that, in the year 1716, we held
Communion at Blackford. By June the most of the houses
which had been burnt were building again, though we were
scarce of timber always — there had not been so many plantings
done these days. So much straw had been burnt that none
could be had for the thatching; it was all turfs, rashes or
heather; but my father wouldna let any of his tenants skin their
fields, which were poor enough, for house turfs, and bog rashes
or heather make an ill roof unless there is good sarking below
them. Just the same, we were scarce of straw or hay for the
folk that would come in for the Communion to lie on, and of
meal for their eating. The Kirk Sessions debated the putting
off of the Occasion until another year, but my father for one,
was strong for it, and in the end and after much prayer it was
thought we should go on: the Lord would provide. And so
indeed He did, in the matter of weather; for we got the hay in

early that year, and what better bedding for man or woman than the fresh meadow hay? And all the days of the Occasion there was good weather, and full moon on the nights. Full many slept in our own barns and stables, that were empty enough that year, but every household would have their guests, some coming from across the Ochils and others from all parts of Strathearn. There were twenty trestle tables set in the Church yard and around. Ilk housewife that had a fine linen cloth of her own or her mammie's or grannie's weaving, would lend it, and you would see the carlin wives going round from one table to another, feeling at a corner here and there, and would it be Meggie's or Peggy's was the better washed and ironed? Ach, the gabble of talk there was, and the half of it no' very Christian!

'But my own mind wasna light yon summer, Catherine, for poor Ann had died in the beginning of it, in the bonny Maytime, with the piercing and wanton singing of the birds all day and half the night. Aye coming through into the shut room where she lay weak and coughing. She had all the assurances of heaven that the Ministers could give her, but what's that to a lassie dying in the first of summer? She should have been sewing her wedding dress; indeed she would be at it till she lost heart and the needle would drop out of her hand and she bade us shut it away. After it was all over, Margaret and Helen and myself, we were dowie and sore-hearted; for grief comes more naturally in the winter. In the summer you are worse torn by it. It was above all paining us to think of our sister shut away under the cold earth when all above was lightness and flowers and the summer singing and nesting of birds. So I made up my own mind that I wouldna listen to merle or mavie, goldie nor laverock. I would listen only to the voice of heaven and seek an assurance that some way Ann and myself would be together again.

'So the thing pressed on me and pressed on me, and an evening came that was so soft and so bonny, my heart almost lap out of me; so I took my ways up into the hills. I mind, Catherine, walking up the steep brae and on, the feel of the grass under my feet — I was carrying my shoes and stockings to save them — first warm and dry from the heat of the day and then gey wet, cold and drenching with the night dew, forby the wet edge of my kilted skirts against my knee. And I mind the orra grief in my heart turning to a more general thing, to a conviction of vanity and time passing and the folly of all human hopes and loves. I had left the late bird-song as I came up out of the glen, and for a time I was strongly comforted by the mere silence and strength and comeliness of the Ochils under and around me in the dusk and moon-rising; but I was needing to shatter even that, to remind myself that they too would vanish like shapes of smoke on the Last Day. Thus I tore from myself all that appeared to come between me and my Lord. Only I couldna think that my religious principles themselves might be some kind of barrier, though I have thought it syne.

'So I walked and I further walked, and of a sudden I began to feel that all could be made well, that an atonement and covenant could be arrived at, and that, some way, myself and Ann could be covenanted together. But the Lord, on His side, was a hard bargainer and He could see through any shift of mine; nor would He be content with less than my whole body and soul. And there came through my mind a quick sight of the lads who had courted me; I thought of Lachlan Macintosh and the red tartan and the wild jut of the eagle feathers he had worn in his bonnet yon day at Duncrub, and hard I put him from me, and the rest with him, and I swore to myself I would take no bridegroom except direct from the Lord's hand and as a kind of earthly substitute for Himself. And I made out in my head a deed and covenant with the Lord, which I wrote out the next day, and I took as my witness the Ochils and the stars above them, and the angels that were beyond the stars and yet as close as my elbow, and suddenly I was filled with a muckle great pride and excitement, knowing that Christ's blood was shed for me, and that by this, having been less than myself, having been sunk and logged in natural sin, I was now become more, I had a grip of righteousness! And I came back down the brae soberly and sweetly, and it was dawn, and the mad birds singing again, but they didna rive me. They were apart from me now, in the natural world of sin and carelessness, whilst I had made my bargain and sealed myself to Christ. Yet they seemed gentle and they had my blessing.

'I told my father where I had been and asked his pardon for any anxiety he might have had on my account, and syne I showed him my Covenant. He could see fine it hadna been with any lad I had gone that night, and he gave his approval to what I had done on condition that I would keep to my bargain with the Lord. But times, now, I am thinking I might have done better to have been with a lad, gif it had been the right lad. But there was a thing that couldna have been — given the principles I had.

'I had the paper on which I had writ my Covenant in under my shift, and the edges of it fretted me as I breathed, and I had no difficulty in bearing it in mind, and it was a kind of uplifting thing throughout the Communion sermons on the Thursday and Saturday; for I had no doubts at all but that I was saved, and I caught a kind of scared look from my two sisters and a kind of proud look from my father. He himself and Mungo had come north from London for the Occasion. But Patrick was yet there, and busying himself about his cousins who were still in prison, and in great fear of being removed from Edinburgh castle to Carlisle and into English jurisdiction. David Smythe was released in the back-end of the year, but Ochtertyre was in prison until the latter part of the winter following.

'Yet that was not the only iron that Patrick had in the fire. He was going about to get Jamie appointed Resident in Moscow to the Czar Peter. Jamie was twenty-four then; he had several languages, and a reputation for courage and good looks and a certain wildness that would suit well with a wild place the like of Russia. But I mind now, he never got to Moscow, nor to St. Petersburg; indeed he got no farther than Heidelburg and the Court there; there was some kind of quarrel between King George and yon Czar. But that will have been later. Patrick was having his fine games at yon time, playing with power and money and aye seeing the worst side of folk and how easy they could be turned and twisted by money and privilege. He came to despise the most of them that way, and the ones he despised the worst were his friends and neighbours that had their good names and reputations, but maybe hid behind all that a kind of easy ordinariness, that could turn to sheer dishonesty and baseness under temptations, as quickly as a wet stack will blacken and heat. Aye, that was why he chose to accept office as one of the Commissioners for the Forfeited Estates, with all the difficulties and hate that it brought him later — as he might have foreseen. It gave him a wild kind of pleasure to be over-setting the respectable and godly and those that had been on the top, able to do what they chose, and to see them at his mercy, aye, Patrick would laugh about it and use his power on them. It wasna until later on that he began to see another side of it, how the over-setting of one lot could mean the freeing of another. At the time I am thinking on he had the same scorn of the common people and of the lairds: of anyone less clever and lucky than himself. Yet for a' that he did what he could for Ochtertyre; he aye had a kind of feeling for the family.

'But I am wandering far, my soul, from the Communion at Blackford, the crowds all in their best going from one preacher to another, responding with groans and cries, but not a few thinking more of the ale-barrels and the girls from other parishes than of the Word. The tenants' wives would have their hair braided and pinned back and the white linen toys over their heads, and the shoes and stockings on their feet that made them walk in a mincing way, for at that time the commonalty went bare-foot mostly. And my father and Mungo and the heritors generally, in their sky-blue and red and tawny coats, and laced hats and swords and high boots, and the sun high and the ground trodden and the chapmen and tinkers crying their wares, or fighting and swearing between times. And each table with its own preacher, and the heaped slices of bread, and the claret in the wide silver cups: the bonny oaken claret barrels with the French brand mark on them. There was always a queer and a tense time on the Sabbath itself, when it came to the fencing of the tables, and some would come that shouldna have come, but others through terror of the Lord and ower much thinking on their own frailty, dared not come though they might have a great longing for the tables and the douce companionship and the Body of God. And times there would be, at one table or another, sudden sobbings and lively prayer and uprisings of the spirit. Folk are not taking the Occasions so hard now, and indeed they are commonly held twice or thrice in a year, so you will not have people so desperately put about to get to them, nor coming in from so far.'

'I cannot like it myself,' said Catherine, shy and yet wanting to say it, 'when the preachers are over-enthusiastic. They take away all dignity, Aunt Kirstie. Our Minister at Lundie will go quietly and thoroughly to his text, and no politics. My father cannot abide the other sort.'

'It all depends,' said Kirstie. 'You will get over the queerest things if your heart is set one way. At Culloden before the battle, the Prince's men took the Sacraments in whisky and oat-cake, thick oat bannocks hot from the girdle. I am thinking it will have been Forbes's own Ferintosh whisky they drank! And they will have been Episcopalians no doubt, but for a' that, neither the belief in the bishops, nor yet the queerness of yon Elements, will have hindered the thing from being a right Last Supper; and that in very truth for many of them. Moreover, my soul, you get what you expect in the bottom of your heart, or you get what you think is that. But maybe it is bad coin you get, but you dinna know till the time comes to spend it.

'Ach, ach, Catherine, the thing I am trying to say, and the thing I am dodging saying, is that one of the visiting Ministers, and the one who took the table where the Gleneagles family were sitting, was Andrew Shaw of Bargarran. And I thought he was sent of the Lord and intended for myself, and the long and the short was that we were married within two months after.'

After a time Catherine asked: 'What like was he, Aunt Kirstie?'

'What like?' repeated her aunt in a queer, dumb kind of voice.

'Aye!' said Catherine. 'Was he dark or fair? Was he tall or short, Aunt Kirstie? You promised you would tell me about all the lads that came courting you!'

Kirstie looked round, all round and up and down, as though house or hills or bowling-green might have some answer to the question. At last she said: 'I cannot mind that Andrew Shaw ever courted me, either before or after our marriage. It seems to me now that he was courting his own idea of salvation, and it must have seemed to him that I was part of it, the same way as it seemed to me that he was part of my own, that he was on the credit side of my bargain and covenant with the Lord. Aye, Catherine lassie, I thought he was sent. There is an arrogance about the way I looked at it and the interest I thought the Lord was taking in myself, that leaves me dumbfoundered now. He was a tremendous preacher, was Andrew; even Patrick allowed that. He had the Scriptures on his tongue tip, he knew them the way another man might know the face of a woman he loved.

'When I come to add up the Sabbaths that I have sat under him — but I canna do that, I canna! Aye, Andrew Shaw in his black coat, with his face white and drawn with passion and argument, and the congregation intent and drawn, too, by his passion, the grown folk hearing him out hour after hour and only a bairn here and there girning at it, and I myself wondering, wondering, if this was rightly himself; if this was my husband, or if it was a spirit that took possession of him in the pulpit, or how at all to put together the two halves of him, or if they were the same and not opposite, then maybe God and the devil were also the same person, only looking on different things. Oh, the Sabbaths I have swithered with such thoughts, Catherine, and far enough from God's love, and lonely, for the congregation was taking it the one way, but I couldna, for at the solid back of it was the knowledge that I was Mistress Andrew Shaw and like to be for all the days of my life, and this was the answer to my Covenant and my principles. Yon were the times when another kind of thought would come creeping in on me, from away back, from Phemie — No, yon's past. I'm never speaking on it again. No, Catherine!

'But I would mind on my Covenant and what I had thought was the seal on it, and I would ask myself, was I clean deceived, was it of God? And syne I would rebuke myself for thinking in an earthly way of my marriage with so muckle a preacher and wrestler for Salvation and bringer of souls to the Lord, and for a time I could beat my soul down into submission. But a day would come when the bull calf would lift its head out of the thorns and myre. And I would say: at least yon thing was never sent nor meant, Kirstie Haldane: it wasna the good Lord and you canna blame Him. It was your own mistake and your own vanity, and you will remember that the Haldanes have aye had Suffer as their text and motto, and it must have been given to them for such times as this. And, gif the old ones could suffer in the old days when it was first written down, so can yourself. For there is nothing at all that canna be tholed and that the human spirit canna get the better of. And so I would resolve. And at least it would ease me to take the blame off the Lord and lay it at my own door. Yon were the times I would be writing to Patrick. You see, Catherine, I couldna be writing to my mother nor yet my sisters; I had too muckle pride.

Twenty-six years, yon thing took, aye, more than the half of my own lifetime. And I knew, almost as soon as it had happened, that there had been a mistake. Either a mistake or a fault. And mostly all the time I was far from my own home and my own folk, away in the south-west. Dreich, long years and broken by little enough except sorrow. For I had two bairnies and the both of them died. But I winna think — aye, for all their father said yon time, I canna think! — either that yon bairns died as a punishment from God for my own sins or any other person's sins, or that they are anywhere but in heaven where bairnies should be!'

'What were they called, Aunt Kirstie?' Catherine asked.

'One of them was called John for my own father,' said Kirstie, 'and the other was called Simon for the other grandfather.

As was right. And neither of the two of them was like his father, nor would have been if he had lived!'

'Was he bad to you, Aunt Kirstie?' Catherine asked timidly, for she had never known the truth of it; there had been stories about her auntie, but she had taken little heed. It had not seemed to matter to her then; but it did now.

'Aye,' said Kirstie, her voice sad and even: 'He was bad.'

'But he died in the end?'

'Aye,' said Kirstie. 'He died.'

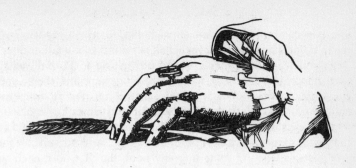

CHAPTER V

'WHERE did you live, Aunt Kirstie?' Catherine asked.

'At Paisley the first years,' Kirstie said. 'A lively, friendly kind of a town, where a newcomer might have been welcome. Indeed there were that many newcomers that they werena talked over and glowered on, the way they might be in Auchterarder or Blackford; they were welcome for the news and life they brought with them. Aye, and the trade. But it is an orra thing, being the Minister's wife, and it was not to wonder at if they would be a wee thing standoffish with myself.

'It wasna the best of marriages, in a worldly way. But my tocher was a bittie diminished after the burnings and stealings of the '15, and, though my mother was put about at me marrying the son of a bonnet laird and a high-flying Minister at that, my father was not ill pleased. You ken, he had thought well of the preaching, and many a fine discussion and argument did he and Mungo have with Andrew over some matter of doctrine. It was so even after we were married, whenever they would meet, and I sitting in the corner or seeing to the laying of the table and that, and feeling sick affronted that my father and Mungo could not see what was doing with their own flesh and blood: that they could become so friendly with Andrew Shaw over these matters of Church organization and the management of folk through fear and bedazzlement by heaven or hell — aye, Catherine, I was thinking on it yon cold way, the Lord

87

forgive me, and indeed I am sure He has, for the thing was half true! That way I could never speak my mind to my father after. Aye, yon were the times I would be writing to Patrick, witty and sharp kind of letters, with a Latin tag here and there, and the anger in them clamped down, a wee hot low at my pen's end. And times Patrick would answer and times he would be sending me something from Edinburgh or the south: a pound of the best Hyson tea, it might be, or a length of satin not suitable for a Minister's wife, or some ungodly book that I would need to read by stealth and then maybe throw away, aye, to leave in the hollow of a dead tree where no Minister could get seeing it.

'But that was later on. At the beginning, Catherine, the whole thing was that strange I couldna get it straight in my mind. We had a stone-built and slated but-and-ben house in the Main Street, with a loft above it and a closet at the head of the stairs to the loft where he shut himself away with his books. For a month, for two months maybe, I could go my ways in a kind of elation, I could over persuade myself, that this was how things should be and my own marriage was something bi-ordinar: the kind that was away beyond the loose, fleshly dreaming of the commonalty. I took a terrible pride, too, in the black and grey linsey-woolsey gowns and the black kerchief over my hair. For now I might wear neither the maiden snood nor yet the tartan screen. It is likely enough that I was high and mighty with my neighbours. If things are couthy and kindly at board and bed, then wives will be neighbourly and kindly in their dealings one with another. But if things are no' right in the house, they willna be right forth of the house. And I made no friends. I was the Minister's woman and they would drop their curtsys to my face, but behind my back it would be snickering and gossip. There were some that tried to be kindly at the time of my first lying-in, but the thing didna work right.

'And at first I had a kind of horror of the Paisley weavers, their pale faces and their clipped way of speaking and the close air and stink of their houses and the lice in their weans' heads. Ach, Catherine, it wasna like my father's house, and I didna connect it in my mind with the house of my other Father.

Though the time came when I did, not maybe with them, but with others of the poor folk of Scotland.

'It wasna till we had been married six months that I met my good-sister, Mistress Christian Shaw. She was older than her brother, my husband; and almost twice as old as myself. I was half feared of her, since by then I had begun to fear most things that had to do with Andrew, thinking they were bound to be against myself some way. Yet, after she had been in the house for only a short while, I began to think that maybe she had a good enough notion of what was happening to myself, and she was not wholly on her brother's side. A queer, tall, thin woman with a quick eye and a clever hand. Aye, Catherine, I mind well of my good-sister's hands, her first finger tapping and creeping like a wee clever thing of its own under the black lace of her cuff and mitten. She had been in England and France, and she spoke to me of foreign places, with an exact recollection of buildings and furnishings and ladies' gowns, and above all of the prices she had been charged here and there, reckoning it up quick into Scots money, the way I would understand it at once. She could tell me to a bawbee the difference between the prices of coach hire, say, or a packet of pins, in Paris or Dieppe or Bath. I would say to myself that yon was but worldly trash, yet against my will I would have a sore interest in it.

'You will recollect, Catherine, my dear lassie, that Patrick would whiles be sending me something, and once it was a piece of Brussels lace, the same you would be making pinners with — they are out of fashion now, but they set off a glossy, well-combed head of hair — and Andrew Shaw seized on it with a great spate of texts raging out of him, and tore it across and said to me that such things were only fit for — ach, it was a gey nasty thing that he said and thought, and he had no right to treat my brother's gift that way, and indeed I had not intended to be flaunting abroad in it, I was only thinking to wear it at home and flat down in a douce-like way! But he never gave me time, aye, he seized on my bonny bit lace, the same over-quick, hurting way he would seize on myself; and often I have thought, gin he could have torn me the way he tore my lace, he might have eased himself somehow, and he couldna have hurt me more than he did. But he left me sitting on the creepie-stool by the hearth, greeting and yowling like a bairn, the way I would be, times, in the bed, after he had left me and gone to his study to write about hell-fire. I was choking with my need to answer him back, to justify myself against him, but I knew by then it was no use, the words wouldna come rightly, but all twisted and senseless with anger, and he could aye make me feel the worse for having spoken, and after, maybe, he would not speak to me at all from one Sabbath to the next, and that in front of my two servant lassies, and it is a terrible ugly thing, thon, from a man, and most of all if he is the father of your bairn.

Then in came my good-sister, Mistress Christian Shaw, and before I knew I had told her, and I mind she stooped and picked up the soiled and scrumpled pieces of the lace, and she smoothed them on her knee, picking out wee scraps of fluff or dirt from the peats, and she began to speak, half in French, of the making of lace, of the delicate work that goes into it, of the fineness of the thread, and the working out of the design, and I listened and gave over my greeting, and she smoothed and she better smoothed and syne she came to the torn, pulled edge and the mark of my husband's grip and she put her hand on my head and she said — '

'What did she say, Aunt Kirstie?' said Catherine Duncan after a moment. 'What at all did she say?'

'Ach, how can I mind on what she said, and it so long past?' Kirstie answered unexpectedly, in a different voice, a light and flittering one, and her head lifted and she looked across to the house: 'Can you feel the smell of the gillyflowers against the wall, Catherine? I had a breath of them the now!'

'But what did she say?' Catherine asked reproachfully. 'You were just after telling me, Aunt Kirstie!'

'Is't me?' said Kirstie in mock surprise, and then: 'Ach well, Catherine, she only said she could show me a way of dealing with a man.'

'But did she?'

'Ach no. I wasna asking her. No' then. It was kind of frightsome, the way she looked. But she was kind to me.'

'Aunt Kirstie.'

'Aye, my dear?'

'There is a recollection comes into my head — indeed, I almost have it — was it not your good-sister, Mistress Christian Shaw of Bargarran, that started the linen thread manufactory at Paisley later? Aye, I thought I had heard that! Then, was it not herself who was tormented by witches, and she a young girl, and she accused them and there was a great trial and preachings, and the witches were questioned and the witch marks found on them and the most of them were burnt?'

'Aye,' said Kirstie, 'that was herself. But we didna speak of it in the family.'

'Did *she* speak of it?'

'Whiles.'

'Was it dreadful? The first time you heard, and you far from home—Was there something fearsome about her when she spoke of it? Aunt Kirstie, do you believe at all in witches and that?'

'Ach no, it is the evil in folks turning against themselves and others. Whether it is there by original sin or put there by the De'il when folks' lives get so that he can edge himself among them and spoil the good that should be there. And dinna you get believing in witches, Catherine, even if you must have your castles and enchantments and knights in armour! Witchcraft was a gey ugly thing, whatever made it. And it is over and done with in Scotland for ever. I winna even think, Catherine, that one old carlin wife has a lucky look and another an unlucky one, and if we sow our turnips with prayer at Borlum, that is no' to keep off the evil eye, or for any kind of superstition, but for the sole reason that if you mean to live kindly and decently in God's grace and love, then you should do it as much outwith the house as in, at work and at play as well as at meat and at divine worship; nor do we expect that the prayers will make the turnips grow unless we ourselves bend our backs to them!'

Another thing came into Catherine Duncan's mind now and she asked, 'Do you yourself go out into the fields, Aunt Kirstie?

And in winter? I am sure I should never be able to bear it for a day! There can be nothing more tedious than sowing turnips!'

'It is away worse, thinning them!' said Kirstie, laughing, 'but indeed I am scarcely ever working in the fields, Catherine, except maybe at har'st. It is only that I go there with my William, and times two heads can be better than one, most of all when you are trying out a new crop or some new way of doing. We would go to the turnip field, wherever it would be, most days; this is the first year we have dared to leave Borlum for a wee while in the growing season.'

'But what do you think of all the time, Aunt Kirstie?'

'The turnips, surely, my soul!'

'But I am sure a person of culture cannot think about turnips, Aunt Kirstie. Turnips havena to do with the mind and the soul. If one sets one's face to the earth, one becomes like the things of the earth, the way the cottars and their wives do!'

'Well, well, if yon's no' the first time that the Haldane nose has been compared with a turnip!'

'No, truly, Aunt Kirstie!'

'Truly, my dear, one is thinking about the men that are working, and one's own man most, and the weather and the wee looks of growth or of shrivelling, and the great plans we have, and a time coming, maybe, when we will keep our kye on neeps in the winter, even in the Highlands, and have our eating beef between October and July, and early-calving cows, and all the bairnies throughout the length of Scotland the better of the good milk. Of the value of such things, in pounds sterling that mean prosperity, that mean an easing of the hard yoke on the backs of countless men and women. Of better ways of feeding and droving. Or I could be thinking of the plans I myself have for the setting up of schools that will be part for reading and writing and part for spinning and weaving, both of lint and of wool. I am hoping your own mother will think of setting up such a school at Lundie, my dear! And forby that, one will be thinking of wee, near-by plans, something that needs sorted here or there: the fine confused tangle of love and hate and jealousy and resentment that's aye drifting around like the peat reek itself, in any clachan or wee township, and how can one get dealing with it. Or here is a letter from some laddie in the Americas writing home to his folk and I must read it aloud to them. And here is an old wife that they are saying has put the evil eye onto her neighbour's stirks, and I must talk them out of their nasty fright and anger and into ease and confidence and making a joke and a story against themselves out of the whole thing. Or maybe it is a neighbour of our own that's coming to William or myself for a bit word; the planning of the Highlands is not at Borlum alone, but all over, yet there must be a wee kind of centre here and there, and we give them a Scots welcome — a Highland welcome with Lowland cooking, aye and clean sheets!

'Maybe they will be up talking and comparing seeds and roots and leaving their blots of ink on my best linen cloths, and that till half way to morning, and my two inlaid bureaux in the south parlour opened out and covered with potatoes and heads of asparagus and Strasburg or Spanish onions, or papers of seed oats and barley instead of the ladies' gear, the ribbons and scented wax and billets-doux that should by rights be there! And our guests will draw the bed curtains and sleep on to noon, and indeed they'll be in-by snoring whilst I am speaking to Big Mor', the cook, and watching my wee dawtie trying to climb herself up the leg of the table or my own skirts, and himself out in the fields already — for we farmers must be at our work early — ach, there is no grandeur to it, Catherine, I ken fine, and you couldna make up any kind of romance or song about yon kind of life; yet I am thinking that if enough folk would do it, the face of Scotland might be away different in a few years, and folks' lives easier and better. In the landward parts of Scotland at least. It will be a harder job in the towns.'

'The towns are changed already, Aunt Kirstie. They say that Edinburgh is as elegant as any city except London itself and Bath.'

'I wasna thinking so much on the elegance, Catherine. I was thinking more on what lies beneath that. Elegance means money to spend, and where's yon money to come from? Little enough from the land if the land has a good laird, for you need to put in mostly all you have taken out, if you are making improvements and experiments. Some will come from overseas, but full much will come from our own industries and manufactories. And that needs to be looked to.'

'How? If the mechanics are industrious and obedient — '

'They are human souls, lassie. With wives and weans and wants of their own. You canna just sit them down to their looms or stand them in front of the quarry face nor the mine face. My cousin Erskine of Alva will have been learning that from the miners at Leadhills! They have their own laws, Catherine, governing their own savings that they have put by against sickness and old age and funerals, and their own library, for they are the most voracious readers of sixpenny sermons! And they have their own ways of doing and living, and they will not have anyone at all from the Leadhills Mining Company — for it is formed into a Company — mell with them there, although when it comes to the work in the mines they have the Company's manager over them and no choice in their labour and times.'

'But what gars you know about the miners, Aunt Kirstie? Surely they are very low people?'

'Aye, maybe. But mostly all the Erskine money comes from them these days, and if yin's not low, why would the other be? Catherine, my dear, it's no' me you should be asking about the high and the low, for indeed I canna tell excepting by how they act. Although at your age I thought I knew fine. And those I had determined in my mind to be low, I treated as low, more especially in Paisley, where I wasna so sure of myself as I was at home. Yet, the Lord knows, I needed friends those days. The Shaws could feel themselves mightily set up to have a Haldane of Gleneagles married to one of their own family, and Lady Shaw, my husband's mother, was for ever giving herself the most ill-come airs and graces, and speaking in a mincing way that she took to be English; it would have been very enjoyable to laugh at yon if there had been my sisters or any other lassies to laugh with me.

'You ken, Catherine, those years were long enough, eight years in Paisley, though I was nobbut a young woman at the end of them, dreich and ill to fare through, the day's darg and the night's darg, but now when I look back on them they go into a small compass, a wee grey part of my life. Whilst these few years I have spent at Borlum with my William are long and full and bonny, wide as a braeside in May and the clouds and sun sweeping across and the many colours and kinds of flowers and birds, and the leap of lambs. Aye, Borlum is my braeside, is é cho boidheach!—for ever between me and the dark foggy glen I have made my way out of. And the things I remember from yon grey time are wee things. When I think on't I remember over much of the sickness of my two bairnies, and I could neither help nor cure, and all their father could do was to pray over them and fright the poor wee souls, not so much with the words, though he spoke to them of their coming end and of hell-fire, but with the writhings and workings of his cheeks and eyes. I could have — ach, Catherine, you will never need to feel about a man the way I did then, you will marry a good and kindly man, my soul, and, though times things may go ajee between you, yet it will never be the way I was with Andrew, you will never feel the hot, wicked hate rushing in where love should be!'

'You could have killed him, Aunt Kirstie.'

'Did I say that, my soul?'

Catherine shook her head: 'It was in your eyes, Aunt Kirstie. And you so mild. How could he have been bad to you?'

'Maybe I deserved it all. Excepting for the bairnies. It was a year, less three weeks, after that, we left Paisley. He had a call to a bigger parish in Ayr. I mind well making up our baggage, me and the lasses, and they greeting, but myself with a toom and tearless heart, and I bade them to leave both the cradle and the trundle bed; other folk might have need of them — never more myself. And the lasses grat sorer; but Andrew's man, a thin and lanky body with a scrimp of hair tied back into a knot over his collar, who was cording up blankets and bedding with his rump turned my way, he gave a nasty snicker of laughter.

'I hadna many to bid me godspeed forby my good-sister. She was a widow now; she had married Mr. Miller the Minister of Kilmains, but he had died three years after; he had been a cheery wee body, not much to look at, but then she herself was neither young nor well-faured. After he died she was aye fidging and changing, first on one thing, syne on another; but now she had settled down to the spinning of fine thread; she learnt how to bleach it right, which was a thing nobody fashed about in Scotland, and now she was speaking of importing a thread-mill from Holland. She rode with us part of the way, speaking mostly of the thread industry and how her thread had in it the making of finer lace than any that was yet made in this country. Lady Blantyre was taking some papers of it to Bath. My good-sister would sell into England or Scotland, wherever she would get the better price; and so she would fall to figuring it out, half aloud, and I to stare along the southward road ahead of me, wondering what might lie there for me.

I thought less, even, of the place we were in now than of Paisley. Where I'd taken a scunner at the weavers in the beginning, here it seemed to me that the colliers were less than human. I could never understand their speech; it was as though their ill-shaped mouths twisted the Scots words out of all decent sounding, forby their speech was full of queer words and phrases of their own, partly to do with their work, but mostly their by-names and miscallings of ordinary folks' ways and things. I thought the colliers would be bound to hate me, and I them; yet I had no over-great love for the full of the Kirk, the respect-able and well-doing, the Crawfords and Scots, and the Countess of Loudon, who owned the half of the mines. There were great traditions of preaching and of polemical prayer here; of dis-courses that would drive the congregation to stone and spit upon the Episcopalians, or any poor wee Quaker that might come their way, while the mere rumour of Popish doings would set them all on edge the like of cats in a thunderstorm. That suited Andrew fine. Myself, I was past caring. But my mother was ailing and I thought I would go home for a wee while; I could conceive of my duty lying there and no' with my husband, for I was still set on doing my duty; indeed, it was all I had left.

'So I was redding up the house against my going, seeing that there was nothing amiss with the linen, setting the lass her task of spinning against my coming back and bidding her to be aye attentive to her master, when a woman came to the door. I saw she was a collier wife by the coarse, grimed duds she had on her, an unshaped drugget gown tied in with an apron of sacking, her bare feet, splayed with hauling the coal skips, and her hair draggled and coal-smeared, no colour in it. I couldna rightly understand what she was saying at the first, she spoke so broad and coarse, nor could the lassie that was a farmer's daughter from the landward side of the parish. But syne it came to me that she was asking for my husband to come to a death-bed, though I could not at first tell whose. He was off with the Clerk of the Sessions on some business, but I sent his man over for him after I had found from the collier woman that the dying man was in one of the wee huts by the pit and the coal bings.

'Still the poor body stood there in my decent room, and the tears ran down from her swollen eyes that were black rimmed and red veined over the white with the soreness of the coal grit, the way the most of the colliers were, and the blackened, twisted hands of her shook, and sudden I was gey sorry for her, sorrier than I was for myself, and I asked could I help her any? And at that she seized hold on my hand and kissed it and began gabbling to me, and again I couldna understand the half of it, but the lassie let out a skreich and cried that the woman was asking me to come myself, but I shouldna go, it was neither safe nor decent for a lady to be going among the colliers! And maybe there was good sense to it, one way, but there is a thing about being told that this or that is dangerous, you will be scared to your bones and yet you will know straight that you must go and do that dangerous thing, and before you have stopped to think, off you will be, with the yes said, and only if the Lord guides you will good come of it. Though maybe He does that more often than some folks think. Maybe, Catherine, He was guiding me yon time, though indeed I hadna put up even the wee-est prayer for guidance. It was just that I was angry and sorry, and with that I was off, but I took with me one of the old linen sheets for tearing, and some of the balm for wounds that my mother had taught me to make. For it seemed, from what I could make out of the woman's speech, that there might be need of it.

'I bade the lassie bide in-by, for she was good enough in the house, but feckless outwith it, and she grat, for she was feared of what my husband's man might say when he got back. But I went with the collier woman. I was a head taller than she was, and I went upright while she went bowed, muttering to herself and twisting her hands that were wild ugly, not the way any woman's hands should be. She seemed far enough from me and mine, but yet I had a curiosity to see these colliers that were serfs and savages and for whom John Knox had ordained no good Scots schooling, for what use would reading or writing be to a collier? They could sum the corves of coal by tallies, and the bairns went to the pit when they were old enough to know why they were whipped. They were worth something to their fathers and to their father's owners, for they could scratch together the loose coals, crawling and whimpering in the lowest roofed of the seams, where a dog couldna rightly stand; they would get maybe a few pennyworth in the day. Or else they must open and shut the wee dark doors that turn the currents of air, alone in yon close black nightmare for fifteen hours out of the twenty-four. Aye, Catherine, that gars your dinner to rise on you. But scarcely till you have seen them with your own eyes. And I hadna till yon day.

'The way it was, there had been an accident in the pit. They had hewed away too much of the coal from the walls or pillars between the rooms where the coal was got, one collier and his folk working each room; it was aye a kind of temptation to get it the easiest way. But the seam had fallen in with little enough warning. They were yet hauling the bodies up through the shaft; a hale man, riding up with his foot in the loop of the rope, could hold himself off the side of the shaft, but these poor battered things would twirl round and bash themselves again. You could hear the echoes of the shouts from below, a terrible eery sound, and up at the pit-head the voices echoed, too, between the coal bings on the steep side of the brae.

'There were maybe a dozen crushed to death in the fall, and one was a woman and two were bairns. One does what lies to one's hand, Catherine; the manager of the pit was there and had things in hand right; there was a second horse harnessed to the gin; the colliers went by me, set and grim-looking, smeared with blood and coal dust, speaking low and in words whose meaning I did not know; the manager made them go down without their candles, for he was feared of fire-damp coming out on them; syne he himself went down, to grope about for the rest, calling till they heard an answer of any kind, though it might be only a wee groaning. But up at the pit-head I found myself, some way, looking after the hurt ones and the dead. It wasna that I knew more than the collier women, but they were some of them running hither and yon, skreiching and keening and making an occasion of it, and some were struck dumb and needing to be told what to do. There were two of the girl bearers that were sore hurt; one of them had the spokes of her coal corve rammed into her flesh, and I didna even know it was a lassie till we came to cut away her clothing at the front. But I kept telling the women what they should do, and it gave them some queer kind of comfort to be told; they could shift something of the horror and helplessness off their own shoulders on to mine.

'We lifted the ones that were living into the huts, and there I was scunnered with the poverty and dirt of the plenishings, although there would mostly be food enough, and drink too; maybe they needed it. There would mostly be nothing but the old straw for the hurt ones to lie on, and times they would be lying next some sick old granny that looked on them with cold eyes, never budging, having seen the like of this often enough through her four-score years. There was little we could do, and a terrible groaning and stench, for some had their chests and bellies crushed. Yet what could be done I was doing. And then came my husband in his black coat with the horn buttons and the least good of his wigs, and before he had even looked at the colliers, living or dead, or given a kind word to man or woman, and in front of them all, he ordered me home.

'Aye, I was wild at that. But where was the use? I began to tie the kerchief that had slipped from my head, and I was going without a word, but three or four of the collier women clung to me, and so, to make the thing easier and more courteous, I kissed them, not even holding back my breath from the reek of theirs. And three days later I found my own hair and my own linen alive and crawling with what they had left there, the poor bodies! I got rid of that with plenty soap and water and the lassie combing my head with an oiled comb, and neither she nor I ever let on to my husband that there was aught amiss. And I went to see the collier women again before I went home to Gleneagles. He hadna forbidden me, indeed he had never thought to. He was thinking of his pulpit and his Kirk session, but he had forgotten the colliers; and I hadna. Some of the hurt ones were dead by then, but others mended up, well enough to go back to the pits anyway.'

CHAPTER VI

'THE strange it was, Catherine, going home yon time! Ille terrarum mihi praeter omnes angulus ridet. Aye, it seemed to smile on me, from all the wee corners and nooks, from the burnie's babble and the light seuch of the wind in the aspen tops at evening. Even my mother's smile, for all I knew it was the smile of mortal sickness. Yet it was deep down kindly, and I needing kindness so sore. Aye, aye.' And again Kirstie sat looking at the grey house of Gleneagles, that was indeed no very special kind of a house, but long and plain and only just so broad as could be spanned by such beams as her grandfather could have cut out of his own woods. There was a wee kind of tower at one end, but again nothing much, no match in size or solidity with the old castle on the castle mound that was now crumbling down and used only for the housing of beasts in winter; it had been a keep in the old days, and had held the Haldanes safe against every kind of Highlander; and here it was that Kirstie's back-back-mother, Marjorie Lawson, whose Haldane husband had been killed on her at Flodden, had welcomed Squire Meldrum with a great and notable kindness, as Lindsay of the Mount tells in his poem. And maybe it is from her that many of us she-Haldanes have taken a part of our nature, and so it was for Kirstie, who had at last got the kindness she needed, and she listened for her man's voice but did not hear it, yet she was not uneasy, for she knew fine he would not be far; he was with her brothers now, and syne he would be back with her, for the long summer evening with the music and the dancing, and, beyond that, the night they would be together and the dulce morning.

She turned back to Catherine and the story again. 'I had been home the last time for my father's funeral. A right gathering of the clans was there and queer to see this or that one married and settled down, and none of us any younger. Mostly all the women folk were some way happy and comfortable, with this and that to brag about, and the long life they could see before them and it full of hopes and enjoyments. I felt myself terrible lonely, my dear, and I couldna get into words what way I was myself, nor would Margaret or Helen have understood. Margaret was newly married on Cockburn of Sandybeg and it was in every way a suitable match, and our father had spoken on it with pious and agreeable words only the day before he died. Wee Helen, your own mother, wasna yet even spoken for, though it was certain enough that she would make as good a match as Margaret, so long, that is, as all would go well and she would not have the same kind of thoughts as her other sister: myself.

'For indeed, my own life was beyond their experience, as I am hoping it will be for ever beyond your own, Catherine. And so I would brag about what I had least heart for—my husband's preaching and the power and nobility of a Minister, and this or that reform and tightening of doctrine and practice in the Kirk. Or else I would fall as quiet as a frozen burn and inside me there would be jealousy and sorrow and a wild spite against my own life when I saw it next to the others, and at such times I would be missing my father sore, with a kind of deep and jaggy soreness that the most of the mourners did not have, and that although I knew he would no more have understood than the lave of them.

'For there was Mungo in his great wig and talk of Parliament and the Whig policies and some braw new lawsuit he was contemplating over his shares in the South Sea Company, and the great confabulations that would be going on over his heirship of Gleneagles, and a signing and witnessing of documents and a spilling of good red wax. Or else he would be speaking about the disturbance that had been made by the Glenshiel affair, and the way the English were looking on the whole of Scotland as a nest of rebels that would turn on them at any moment, and the Highlanders to blame for it all! Yet when he said that, there might be a wink or a whisper here and there, as who would say that just this was what we ought to do in Scotland if we could see our way clear to it. For indeed the Union was turning out a poor bargain for ourselves. Our old trade had been ruined during the times of the religious troubles, yet to trade with the Americas and Africa — though that was mainly the slave trade, and I wouldna care to have any of my own folk in it — and even with India itself, the Scots merchants needed to join the English companies, and they werena welcome. The English at the Court and the landed folk were friendly enough, but the English Parliament was mostly pulled hither and yon by the merchants that were newly into power and jealous lest Scotland should try to take over some of it. Our fisheries had to face the competition of the bigger and better equipped Dutch boats; they might have pulled themselves together and done that, but the new salt tax ruined them. Our coal trade with Ireland suffered from a duty that was not put on to English coal. Our linen trade was attacked, for all it was our staple, just as much as wool was the English one. Forby that, they wouldna even buy our timber if it would mean spending money on roads. Aye, it was bad, and even Patrick would speak bitterly of the betrayal, though he got on well enough with the English members of the Board of Commissioners for the Forfeited Estates; being conversant with Scots law, he was the leader there. Aye, he liked to lead, did Patrick.

'All of my brothers were at their father's funeral. Mungo was never heavy on the drink, but he liked to have things as they always had been, so there had been both bottles and barrels at the coffining of our father, and few that went to bed their lane after it, and one gentleman helping another out into the night to see the stars go swinking around and to make their profound observations on the phenomenon and to speak of poor John Haldane and the good-living, honest man he had been. All of our cousins had come, amongst them Lachlan Macintosh. He and his folk had been engaged in the '15, but not so deep they couldna make shift to swim out, although with encumbered estates. His father, the old man, whom I liked better than any of his sons, had been a Captain in the Macintosh Regiment; he hadna thought plenty on politics or soldiering, but the boys had him persuaded. Lachlan had been a Captain and Sandy was an Ensign, but Hamish was left at home with the estates of Kyllachy, Moril and Ardersier, in case there might be trouble; that would be the way in any canny family.

'As luck would have it the bodach, their father, was the only one taken prisoner at Preston; maybe he couldna run so fast as the young ones! Howsoever, he and his neighbour, MacQueen of Corribroigh, escaped in woman's dress. After that they were for ever at it, the lot of them, thinking that Kyllachy would never beat the rest unless King James came home. Ach, maybe they had a better notion of it than that, and indeed they suffered for their politics; but they made others suffer worse. It was about then they started raising money on the lands. Aye, after Glenshiel. Though I never knew right which of them was in it; and William doesna know right either; he only knows what Lachlan would be saying afterwards! Ach, you shouldna listen to anything I say about my cousins, Catherine, for indeed I am devilish uncharitable to the poor souls.

'When our father died, Lachlan had some hopes of a small legacy, though anyone with a spark of sense could have told him there was no reason he would get one; and nor he did, but he had himself worked up over it, and the next thing he would be blaming the heirs and anyone to whom my father had left so much as a cast pair of breeks. And the more drink he had in him, the worse it would be. And he would aye be showing off to myself and taking too much opportunity of getting a cousinly buss. For in those days, Catherine, a kiss was the common greeting amongst gentlefolk, though indeed there were times it went against the grain. The worst was, Lachlan had a kind of feel of how things were with me, and he would be pressing my hand with the great sympathy he had, and, some way, however angry I was, I knew it might be half real but nothing at all to trust in.

'On the evening of the funeral itself, the men walked back from Blackford, speaking of who had been there and how this or that one had looked or spoken, and of the funeral sermon, comparing it with others they had heard. Then there were refreshments sent for, and maybe it was a certain satisfaction to

Mungo to be Laird of Gleneagles. But I was over-tired and no wish in me but to be saying my prayers and fall on sleep. Yet I didna think I could sleep till the others came, for I was sharing a bed with Helen, your mother, and one of the Erskine girls at t'other side. Aye, it was the same spare bed in the library where William and myself are sleeping, but at that time the bed curtains were dark green and the moths had been at them here and there. Just the same as now, the library was a passage room and the bed back against the wall beside the great press, and folk would go by without looking too much. The shutters were up on the windows yon evening, and candles lit in the two iron sconces on either side.

'I sat on the bed's edge—the mattress wasna too grand those days! — and my mourning clothes seemed heavy on me some way, and I wanted either to be deep asleep or else out in the soft evening, and my face will have been white in the small light of the candles, over against the black of my duds, and the twist of a scowl on it, and my hair about my shoulders. And of a sudden there was Kyllachy and with him another Highlander of his own clan. Aye, it was William, though I didna know that. He was wearing the close-fitting tartan breeches and short coat, as the Inverness fashion was then, high boots and the claymore and pistols at his sides, and his own black hair tied back and clubbed with a red cord. It is that kind of dress a man needs to be young for, aye, and well made, and the belt on him well polished and well pulled in, and the ruffles white and well starched, and a bonny leg under the tight tartan, or any orra thing — and then indeed he's a sight for a lassie's een.

'Kyllachy stopped dead in front of the candles and I could see he had the drink in him, and he wheeled the other round by his sleeve and pointed at me and said: "Yonder, now, is the wee Whiggie that would have none of myself, but married a black crow of a preacher and is repenting it this day!" And he took a step or two my way, and he went on: — ach well, he said a thing that wasna very nice at all about my husband Andrew and himself, and the contrast they could be making, and I jumped to my feet and called him a drunken, foul-tongued

Jacobite, and I might have begun to sob, for sudden he went soft, saying, "Ah, poor lassie, poor wee lassie," and then: "She is fast in her trap as poor Scotland herself, and as fully eager to bide there". And then he said: "Mistress Shaw, if you are set on miscalling myself, let me present to you my kinsman, William Macintosh of — "

'But the other one put a hand on his mouth and said: "Have a little sense, Kyllachy," and then he whispered something in French that I did not hear, and then he bowed to me, and his hair rippling black in the candle light. There was something terribly bold in a gentleman wearing his own hair those days; the most of the bare heads one saw had never seen the back of a comb, but this was beautiful, aye, the black hair and the red-brown eyes and the red tartan, and for a moment I could not get my breath right.

' "Ah, try you now," Kyllachy crowed to the other, and pushed him my way, "for I can see she will not be angry!" And again I was held breathless with a kind of shock and trembling and a queer feel that this had all come of my father dying and leaving me.

'But the other one took my hand that was limp as a dead thing in his, and kissed it, and then he touched my eyelid softly with the tip of his forefinger and he said something to himself in the Gaelic, and then he stood upright and said: "Forget this night, Mistress Shaw. And, if there is any small thing to forgive, then forgive it."

'And I looked slow at him and nodded and said: "Aye, I'll never speak of it". And by then it was as though Kyllachy was not in the room at all. And so they went out and, I mind, I drew the curtains and slipped out of my black clothes, and in a short time was so deep asleep that I never heeded when the other two lasses came into the bed.

'Kyllachy never mentioned the matter again, nor did I. It seemed to me likely that the politics were in it, but there had been a kindliness about it that I didna care to think too much on. Once or twice in the year, maybe, it would come up in my thought again, a clear image, and so pass. And now it was four years on, and I was sleeping in that same bed, though times I would watch all night in the great leather chair in our mother's room.

'Nobody said she was dying, least of all herself, but she knew it. Her brothers would ride over to sit with her, and my first cousin, John Erskine, witty and wild, for ever getting ideas into his head about the lead-mining and improvements that might be made; he was to lose his money on that, later. My brother Jamie, who was now a Major in the Life Guards, came north too, to visit our mother; he was in a great preoccupation with England at that time, for he had one Chancery lawsuit for £6000 against the heirs of Sir Lawrence Anderson of Chalfont, and indeed I am not certain whether yon same lawsuit was ever settled. And there was his petition against the Listers and Curzons for corrupt practices at the Clitheroe Elections, where he himself had stood. Though for myself I cannot see how Elections can ever be anything but corrupt. Patrick used to say it was nothing but stupidity on his part to think of standing there, since Sir Nathaniel Curzon of Kedleston had bought up the burgages or borough houses, and the tenants were bound to vote for his son or whoever else had the interest of the thing. Patrick would say that it was no use at all attacking from the front, the way Jamie was doing; he would need to catch the Curzons and their like on the flank.

'Johnnie was in the Customs at this time; the salt dues at Prestonpans were farmed out to him. But he was no man of business and no judge of men; he left overmuch to be done by his excise officers, with no overseeing, whilst he was making his excuses to get to London and leave his wife at home with the three wee laddies. You will hardly credit it, Catherine, but young Captain John, that we are all so proud of now, was the weakest wee thing and a great anxiety to all of us. Indeed, I did not see either of my two brothers Johnnie or Robbie, yon summer. Robbie was already in the service of the East India Company and away on a voyage. I mind how eager was my poor mother for a letter from him. Once he sent her back some seeds of an Indian plant, and we planted them in pots, but nothing came of it.

'But it was Patrick that I saw the most of at this time. There was a great change on him since the troubles over his Judgeship. It was not only, Catherine, that his hair was grey now and his face deep lined, but it was as though he was more easy hurt, even by wee trifling things, and sometimes he would get wild angry. I mind I told him of the colliers and what I had seen for myself, and he began to speak of the purpose of wickedness where such things were allowed under Scots law, walking up and down the room with his hands twisting behind his back and saying to me that had never denied it, that there must be free competition and how could that be when some men were slaves or serfs? To make them so was to thwart a natural economic law and full as bad as the thwarting of Divine laws! And he spoke bitterly of the heritors at my husband's Church, for he seemed to know, from his law practice, who were the owners of the collieries, and bitterly also of all who would keep up the ancient privileges and servitudes, which mostly went with land-owning, the forced labour at har'st, the carrying of peats, the forced milling and so forth, and the turn-out of the tail of tenants for the laird's hunting or rebelling: above all, the Chief's Courts and powers of pit and gallows, that cut right across the people's law.

'Patrick was passionate on that. Yet, times, it has seemed to me that the common folk want nothing more than to save themselves trouble or any kind of change or new ways of thinking, and if the chief or laird is a good man, just and patient, then his folk will want to take their pleas and quarrels to his court and not to Edinburgh or any strange city, where they will be needing to explain themselves in precise words of a kind they are not handy with, and pay their way in money that maybe they havena got. But I would scarcely expect Patrick to see it yon way, nor any other lawyer! Ach well, if things have turned out bad, it was the fault of the chiefs and lairds who were neither wise nor patient, but the most of them liker a lot of schoolboys, showing off their powers and privileges and nonsense, and, worse, wanting to crow on other dung-hills than their own. A tenant will put up with plenty if he can see the show at the end and feel he has helped in it and is a part of it, but when the show is in London, and a mean wee show at that beside the riches of the English, then the tenants are right to be angry. Aye, and to think of a new order of things and to turn to the trades and the way money and burgess freedom and that have been working out in the cities.

'In the few years he had been laird of Gleneagles, Mungo, with Patrick's advice, had altered the tenancies almost completely from how they were twenty years before. There was no more runrig at Gleneagles, nor the wee starved cattle, nor the raw ditches, down to the rock itself, between the rigs in the infield, where each man had taken the turfs for his own strip. They had mostly been plowed over and filled in and the cross ploughing itself had done all the good in the world to the fields, as stands to reason. The tenants now had long leases, with plenty conditions as to cropping and even enclosing, though not all the tenants cared to take on the extra labour for that, with all my brother's persuading, but no more servitudes, except that all must help with the making of roads. Yet that was for the common good, since with roads, the tenants could have carts, though these would be mostly tumblers at the first, with solid wheels cut from the tree boles; but even so they were away better than creels or wee sledges. I hear that all the gentlemen are getting together now for the betterment of the roads throughout Perthshire, and Athol and Breadalbane at the head of it!

'Mungo was asking money rents of his tenants now instead of the old rents in kind, and our girnals were the emptier and our rats the hungrier, which wasna to say we did not have plenty. But there was far more stuff from abroad than when I was a lassie and always a loaf of wheaten bread to eat in slices with our tea, which we mostly drank up in my mother's room.

'Your mother Helen had been married the year before to her cousin, your father. She was near to the time of her first lying-in, so she could not come to Gleneagles. But Margaret came, and ach, it hurt, when she spoke so comfortably of her bairns. But it was I who stayed with our mother most. She used to

speak often of Ann, her bonny Ann; it was easy seen the hope
she had to meet with her soon. But I myself was aye wondering
whether would we meet, Ann and myself, and if so, how and
where and in what bodies of Life. But I couldna think of Ann
without thinking on my covenant, nor of that without thinking
on all that had followed and all that I would be needing to go
back to gey soon. For my husband Andrew would write,
accusing me of an unsanctified ettling and lust for the flesh-
pots of Egypt or Strathearn, and they simmering on the flames
of the pit. And it was only because of my brothers writing back
to him of what case our mother was in, that I dared to stay at
all: for all it would be more, almost, than I could bear, to go
back, aye, back for the rest of my mortal life. And my mother
would be dead then as Ann my sister was dead, and no way
now to have any certainty of a sweet fellowship with them in
the next world. Love would not do it, nor yet prayer. For
maybe all had been wrong from the beginning and no atonement was possible. And I thought till I shook of predestination,
but I daredna speak to my mother and her so near to the
parting. Oh, Catherine, I minded on the old days and our
family worship, and on the tables of the Communion and
ourselves sitting together in a love that had no ache in it, that
could remember pain or foresee disaster and yet remain unshaken
and constant, since it was all one with the Lord's love.

'But these last nine years the Lord's Supper had meant less
and less to me and I was almost afraid to partake, though that
would have been most terrible notorious in a Minister's wife,
and indeed I could scarcely have held up my head again: yet
I never had the old longing to be at the tables, for all I was not
aware of sin, nor of any special shortcomings, but mostly a
dreadful hurting and striving towards a light that I couldna see
and a goodness that seemed farther from me for all my striving.
I knew now that works alone would never bring me to
Salvation, but what at all had I done that Grace should be
taken from me? Yet here at home I would sometimes have
a whisper of Grace and I would wake at night with a feel
of things being somehow well, yet when I thought on such

moments afterwards I could not see at all what had given me any hope.

'There came a day, Catherine, when my mother had a sudden longing for a drink of the fresh buttermilk, and so I rode up to the sheiling at the back of Frandie where the kye were at summer pasture on the green hill grass. I rode down on to the coal road with the buttermilk in a wooden cogie by my saddle; my head would be bare and the wind off the Ochils cool in my hair, and nothing sore in mind, only the kindly flow of things. I had a knot of flowers at my breast that I had picked at the sheiling while the lasses found me the buttermilk and a new cheese. And there was a man sitting on the dyke-side, a Highlander with his plaid over his head and his feet bare on the grass, but I had no reason to think twice on him, when of a sudden he rose at my pony's head and said, "Good day, Mistress Shaw."

'I mind I gave such a start that my pony shied across the road, for who at all was this kern? And then I saw it was no kern, but yon cousin of Lachlan Macintosh, and his brogues were in his hand, and when the plaid dropped from his head he looked weary as death, and he said in a quick precise manner of speech, and not looking at me over much, that he was on his way over the Glen Devon coal road; he had needed to keep in hiding for a day or two and now he had no food and little money. I said he should have gone to Duncrub or Ochtertyre and not have asked a good Whig like myself; yet for all that I was a wee bittie pleased and maybe it will have showed in my voice, for he answered that a man was loath to go where he was not welcome and there were those that did not care to remember which side they had been on in the '15.

'I said to him lightly, leaning down from my pony, that was now quietted: "So you thought you would be welcome with myself! And that after bidding me forget everything!"

'He said: "I asked you to forgive, Mistress Shaw."

'Now there a thing came like a shadow and I cried at him: "You will call me Kirstie Haldane, for yon's my name here, you night-bird without a name to your face!"

He said: "Will I give you my name? I am not ashamed of it. It is only a thought dangerous, these days."

I looked at him standing there in the green edge of summer grass and sudden I liked the droop of the plaid and the kilt itself, in a way I had never thought to like them, and they seemed to be neither arrogant nor yet beggarly and savage on this one, but some way right, as a bright and tossing florrish on a branch against the April sky. And I said: "I see you are in the Clan Chattan and I think you are a Tory and a rebel, but gin you will tell me of what ilk you are, then I will forget it before ever I meet with a magistrate!"

He said: "I am from Borlum by Inverness. You will have heard tell of my father, Mistress Kirstie."

I knew indeed. I mind I stared at him and said: "There is a thousand pounds on your father's head."

"There is that," he said, and smiled.

"Well," said I, "rebel or not, you had best have a bite of my cheese, and if you will come to the plantation at the back of Gleneagles before night I'll maybe give you a bannock to your cheese and a pair of hose, though they will be a decent grey and none of your red tartans." I unwrapped the fresh cheese, but I had no knife to cut it with and I mind he took the sgian dubh out of his ragged hose-top and put it into my hand. It was warm from there and I got a queer, half kindly, half shuddering feel, as though, straying through leaves my fingers had touched a nest of young warm birds, aye, I could scarcely hold the sgian firm for my cut on the cheese, and I said, to hide it: "You will be on some rebel ploy the now?"

But he shook his head and said: "I am going to America, Mistress Kirstie."

I handed him back the knife with a slice of cheese on it, and it seemed a final kind of thing. I said, again lightly: "Have you money to get to America? It is a far cry from Frandie."

He said, with his head down, looking at the cheese in his hand, that he hoped to raise money from a firm of Writers in Edinburgh. I thought plenty but I said nothing except that he should have a bundle of food if he came to the plantation, or maybe I would send one of the lasses over with it. And he thanked me, and I gave my pony a bit kick and off we went and I didna look back. He could have felt affronted, eating the cheese, and he so hungry.

'I took the buttermilk up to my mother and some of the wild flowers with it, wee white roses, sweet and terrible thorny. I leant over her and I mind she patted my cheek and looked at me happily, and syne she asked what had I seen the day? So after a while I told her and she said in yon weak voice she had that went to my heart: "You will give him two-three eggs, boiled hard, and a slice of the wheaten bread, Kirstie, forby the bannocks, and you will take a bottle of your father's claret. And you will go to my bureau—" and here she fumbled at her neck for a key, yet I needed to find it for her in the end, her fingers had so little strength in them, "—and in the long drawer at the back you will see a China silk square and in that a box of pear wood, and take you from it four gold pieces. They will not be Scots money, nor yet English, but sequins from Rome and Venice and Milan. And you will give them to this man of yours from Helen Erskine that has lived all her life in a Whig house of Haldanes and loved them everyone, yet never saw just the same way they did, and never quite had her will." And syne she laughed a little and said: "But they never knew it, none of them! And they trusted me, aye and I was never false to their trust. But for a' that, what's left of my tocher is my own to spend, and if I dinna do it now, it will be too late." And she pulled me down to her with her weak hands and she said: "Dinna greet now, Kirstie, my doo, but go fetch me the gold money. For soon I will be in heaven amongst the douce Haldanes and there will be neither getting nor spending of money, and I am certain that neither my Saviour nor yet my own man John, will bear this against me."

'So I went to the bureau and I found the money that I had never suspicioned was there and I brought it back to her bed and I said: "What will I say to him, Mother?"

' "Ach," said she, "just say it is from Helen Erskine and that I am giving it to the man that's a barefoot rebel, but has brought the red back to my Kirstie's cheeks." But I didna ken how to answer her, Catherine, for it seemed to have made the thing some way serious and true. And I wish now I could have answered her right, and I wish she knew about William and myself — though maybe she does know, aye, maybe she does — and I wish I hadna just walked out the room. Only I couldna have answered without suddenly speaking of all I had been silent about for long enough.

'So at nightfall I took the things out behind the dairy and into the plantation by the coal road. I had the food and drink, and a pair of plaiden hose made from our own sheep's wool, the same that Mungo would wear about the farm. I'd had half a mind to wear a light dress I had with me, Catherine, a fine white cambrick with an edging of blue, but I put the thought from me as sinful. And I gave him the basket at arm's length and said he would find in it some money from my mother, Helen Erskine. And he said to me, why? And I answered short and quick that she had her political sympathies that were not the same as the rest of the family.

'He looked long on me at that, and sudden I turned to go, but he caught my hand and said would I thank her deeply and could he write to her from wherever he found himself at the end of six months. But I said no, she would be in her grave by then and it would be better for none of her heirs to read any such letter.

'And syne he asked could he not write to myself. But I said, no, no! And my voice rose almost to crying, for it would have been terrible if a letter had come to me from a Highland rebel in America, and yet I knew down to my heart how sore I wanted it. But he still held my hand and he began to draw me close to him, and for a moment I gave in, Catherine, my principles let go of me and I was wild happy from top to toe. I was free, my soul, and his mouth on my own.

'And then I knew, I knew, the thing couldna be, and I took myself out of his arms, with sorrow, even as one leaves the Communion table and the immediate presence of the Lord. Aye, so it seemed to me in the images I knew, in the thought of

the other things I was wanting. And I went back to Gleneagles and he south-west under the shoulder of Ben Cleugh,
and so to Stirling and Leith and the Americas. Tell me,
Catherine, was I a wicked woman?'

'I cannot tell at all!' said Catherine quickly, with a scared
look, for it was all beyond her experience, and yet not like the
old romances. 'But he was to be your husband later. Will it not
have been predestined?'

'It felt all too like free will, Catherine. Though I was for ever
forcing myself not to mind on it. Until the time came that I
could. But there were seventeen years yet to go. All the years
of your own life, my dear.'

'Oh, poor Aunt Kirstie!'

'Well, the thing happened that was bound to and after the
funeral I knew I must go back from Gleneagles to my duty. For
the years of it that lay between this coffining and my own, when
I might be with my folk again. I mind I spoke to Patrick of
predestination, and he said to me that it was a thing that had
come after the wild and dreadful free will of the old days, when
kings and even nobles could think themselves to be out of the
common run and above God's will and laws, acting as though
that Will were not working out as certainly as the following of
summer by winter, but as though their own wills were also
god-like. So in the great revolution of John Knox, and the
century following, the divine right and free will of kings and
such cattle was thrown down and netted into the predestination
of the common people throughout the whole of the world.
And some way he made me feel for the time, at least, as though
it were a noble destiny to be one with the common people, to
have cast off free will and all the wild, kingly and savage
actions and passions that went with it, and to be, as it were,
yoke fellow with labourers and tradesmen and small merchants,
farmers and fishers, and all those that feel themselves, through
their lives, in the grip of predestination, all the poor folk of
Scotland and beyond.'

'Do you still feel that, Aunt Kirstie?'

'Aye, my dear. When I think on it in the same way. But

maybe I mostly see it some other how. And that will be because the yoke is not heavy on me any longer. But the things Patrick said were mightily comforting at yon time, and I could go back to my duty with a strong grip on them and a strong staff to lean upon.'

As she spoke, the men came back from their viewing of the nursery of trees, and in eager conversation, Black William speaking of the easy growing of sycamores from seed and the many farm uses to which they could be put. They had also been through the kitchen garden; there was talk of spinach and carrots, and how to induce not only the tenants, but also, say, the weavers and other mechanics of Auchterarder, who had each his bit garden back of the road and common grazing for a cow or two, to set rows of the new cabbages, and certainly leeks. It had been said for too many generations that only kale would grow in Scotland, and never the bow-kale, as they called the cabbage. It was time to have a new flavouring to the broth! Mungo called to Kirstie that they were away over towards Blackford to meet the post, but her brothers would bring her dance-partner back in good time. She laughed, and William came across from the others and kissed her hand and asked would she wear the flowered satin dress with the wide ribbons?

'Ach,' said she, 'I am too old for yon flimsy dresses!'

'Then how did you come to bring it with you, Kirstie Haldane?' her husband said, and both of them laughed together, and she said in a soft, half-choked voice that indeed she would wear anything at all, even a coat of rushes, if it would please him.

He and the others went off then towards the road and she looked in front of her and said to Catherine: 'You will have no notion, my dear, how pleasing it is to oneself when one can please the man one is married on with a wee thing like the wearing of a dress. I just canna anyhow get used to the pleasure of having such trifles and vanities regarded. It is beyond me still. For I ken fine that, for myself, they are nothing ava, and should scarcely be given a moment's thought in a gey serious world, yet when it is himself asks me — why then, I am the daftest wife in Scotland!'

But Catherine said gravely: 'That is no' daft, Aunt Kirstie. But it is away different from anything in the story, and you will need to tell me how the tune changed, for I cannot understand it yet.'

CHAPTER VII

'I WENT back. If it was no better than I had thought, it was at least no worse. The lass had her task of spinning done. My husband was so full occupied with Church matters that it made but little matter to him whether I was in the house or not. I had full plenty to do, yet it seemed little, since I cared about none of it and had no heart for it. There seemed to be no good end served. And the Sabbath was a burden to me and the Lord far off, and even my own conviction of sin quenched and dead in me. For I could not hear the Word of God except in my husband's voice, and then it twisted away from how it used to be, either as wrath or comfort, in the Kirk at Blackford.

'I began suddenly to see evil in all kinds of places where I had never looked for it, and to think that folk were doing things for reasons that they would not say in the open. When you have seen this in the one place, then you will see it all at once everywhere, like wee nasty weeds rising up all through a garden bed, ettling to choke the right growth. I mind once, I waited on after the service for a two-three christenings there would be. One was a miner's bairn, and the father and mother were there and the lave of the weans, well enough dressed, though in a queer kind of finery, jangling with ill colours. The miners were well paid, for all they were serfs, but they hadna much heart either to save the money or to spend it in decent, canny ways; all went on tawdry clothes and beads or trinkets, and flesh meat and strong ale or spirits.

'When my husband had christened the bairn, he stood back, in his blacks, and out from the front pew stepped Mr. Crawford, that owned the mine and the colliers that were as much part of its working as the gin and the gin horse, the coal corves and the picks. He had a copper pan which he handed to the wife who jouked a curtsy to him, and a pair brogues which he handed to the man, and these were the arles that bound the new-born bairn to be his slave.

'Now, I had seen this before and had thought nothing of it. The parents did it of their own free will. The man collier working at the coal face needed bearers to carry the corves to the pit-head: who else but his own flesh and blood? And the colliery owner was bound to support him in illness, giving him two pecks of meal in the week, and to furnish boards for bed and coffin. Times he would pay head and harigald money to the collier whose wife had borne a live child, a new worker. Had he not, then, some rights over all production of his colliers, whether coal or bairns? And was not this giving of arles at the christening sanctified by the Minister who had bound the child, also, to no less a master than the Lord Himself?

'Aye, there was the bit, Catherine. And, gif the whole thing had something wrong to it, so, more than all, had the Minister that lent his presence to it. And, this coming to me sudden, I asked Andrew at meat that same evening, did he ever ask himself, was it right? But he said most certainly it was right. All mankind was subject in degrees and this immutably, for it was to be found in the Scriptures, and several texts for each degree: as, the children were subject to the parents, the wife to the husband, the servant to the master, the congregation to the Kirk Sessions, and the nation to its lawfully appointed rulers. Even a Minister of the Gospel, even himself, counted himself subject to King George and his Parliament so long as they in their turn were pledged to uphold the Presbyterian Church and to put down all heresies. "But," said I, "yon bairn that was arled at its christening the day, it will grow up to be something worse than a servant. Is it right that the colliers should be subject to punishments more fit for beasts, such as being tied in the gin with the horse or held by the neck in the jougs at the pit bottom for a whole day and night maybe?"

'He bade me remember the Epistle of Philemon and how Paul sent back a run-away slave, indeed asking the master for mercy, but by no means demanding it as a right. "And," said he, "the masters of these colliers are indeed merciful and that in the truest way, since they see to it that, for their souls' sake, all come to the Kirk on a Sabbath, even the young children." And he nodded to himself agreeably, for it was the rule and law in our parish that such children as contumeliously gathered to play pearies or boules on the Sabbath, should be well belted by their fathers, and that in public, on the Monday morning.

'But it seems to me now, Catherine, that yon Epistle of Paul's was writ for another time and place, and it is no guide to ourselves, and it could be that Saint Paul put pen to paper without a thought that it would be used against colliers and salt-pan workers in bonny Scotland. And against other Scots in the plantations who had been christened as free men. Only I wouldna have dared to say yon to Andrew, my husband to whom I was subject, although there is nothing at all I darena say to William. Aye, such is the freedom of his service. Like a wee copy of the Lord's. Showing me, aye, showing me daily, Catherine, that the freedom of God's service is also not of fear, but always of love.

'And, you see, my dear, I wasna convinced by the things Andrew said to me. Whereas, if William and I have any wee difference, it is mostly always myself that is wrong, except in the matter of cooking where he has certain obstinate Highland notions that dinna fit in with the times, nor even with his own ways of doing in the kitchen garden! But I still did not think it was right about the colliers, the more so as I would be going amongst them sometimes, on one excuse or another, and often visiting some reputable member of the congregation on the same day, so that I could be speaking about that, supposing I was questioned as to my day's doings. Yet even so I went mostly when Andrew was in Edinburgh or Glasgow at the Assemblies or on some Church business. I came to dread these visits since he would mostly come back angered with the moderation of the Church leaders, such men as Dr. Wishart, who, said Andrew, was but shaming a noble name by his elegance and fine reasoning and lack of the spirit of wrath and righteousness, and Dr. Leishman of Glasgow, who also allowed politeness to throw a damp on the pit flames that Andrew loved.

'The thing that was most difficult for me, Catherine, was that the colliers had mostly little enough sense that there was aught wrong, and, when that was so, it was surely not for me to raise up notions in them that could have turned them against their masters. Yet here and there they would have the sense of things no' being as they should be and the shame of themselves being serfs bound for ever to one kind of work and it the worst kind, and when a man would be punished or would run away — it was mostly the young ones that did that — and then be hunted and brought back, tied in a cart like a stirk for market, dragged away, maybe, from some honest, decent employment he had found, then there would be anger about. But yet, the men would beat their wives and bairns, aye and the fremit bearers, orphan lasses mostly that were bound to any single man that had no dependent womenfolk of his own to carry the corves for him, and no harm thought of it, although every kind of wrong was done them.

'They didna speak to me easy at the first. Nor at the last, either. For I was wild sorry for them and I wanted to help them. They were in a queer way an interest to me, and I loved them as Christian souls, but I never could like them. And it is gey hard to keep on loving those that you canna like! Although it can be done, and maybe Paul and the rest did it when they were not writing daft epistles the like of yon one to Philemon.

'Times there would be terrible accidents in the mines, and men and women killed sudden, with no possibility of preparing their souls, which were mostly in an ill-enough state, to meet their Maker. And I would ask myself, why did the Lord put yon fire-damp and choke-damp into the mines among the coals, unless maybe He would be thinking ill of the ways we would be getting the coals. A man or woman would drop down sudden with the choke-damp; times they would dig a hole in the ground and put the man's head in and cover it with fresh mould, or else they would fill him full of ale. And if he didna begin to breathe again, why then he would die and the rest would drink themselves full at his wake. In spite of admonitions and punishments they were for ever stopping off work for wakes and holidays, and, for all that such things were preached against by my husband and others, they would even keep the Popish holidays, such as Christmas, to the great prejudice of their masters and maybe to the hurt of their own morals. And yet was it any worse for a man to get wild with the drink on a holiday than to get worse wild with his own bairns on a working day and strap them till they bled? On the holidays at least, the men felt kindlier.

'So it went on. And from year's end to year's end I scarcely took a keek in the glass, myself, to see was I getting older about the face or grey in my hair yet. The place was growing, and from time to time an industry or a manufactory would be set up. They would be mostly to do with weaving and there would be improvements here and there on the looms, so that more work or finer could be done. But in general it was still in folks' houses that weaving went on, the merchants taking round the spun wool, which mostly came from the farms; the lasses still span with a distaff and spindle when they were out in the fields, but within doors the wives would have their wheels, though it was queer how loath they were to have any of an improved kind. Yet maybe they were in the right of it, for, whenever more wool would be spun, so would the price of it come down for the finished cloth! The weavers would make up the wool, sometimes into bonnets and hose or even coats and breeches, and then the merchants would come for them again. So the thing would be kept in families, and at least the women folk would need to stop work in time if the men folk were to have their dinners. The manufactories, where anything from ten to maybe fifty men and women would be working, only started, it seemed to me, after the Galloway enclosures.

'There the outfields and common grazing lands were enclosed with stone dykes, and let to the graziers. And indeed it would improve the land, which, after it was well dunged this way, could be broken for oats. Yet the good of the improvements aye went to the man that had some wee lawyer's paper to prove the land was his own, and the common folk used to break the dykes. Many hundreds of them were driven out from Galloway, and came wandering west and north. Indeed they would be decent folks who came our way after yon Galloway enclosures, not at all the same as the colliers and salt-workers that had been slaves or near it and working in an inhuman kind of way for enough generations to have changed them out of their right shape and ways of thinking. These others from Galloway would be shy country folk, not bold like the colliers, but puzzling themselves, dumbfoundered at the turn things had taken and not able rightly to take to a new place.

'After they had come to the Church and given in their names, I would often times go to visit them, and maybe take a poke of meal and a bit cheese or crowdie with me. My husband approved, yet he would never be speaking to me about it, nor consult me at all on any decision he might make about these folk. The country lasses who came into our wee town were easy taken in and made to think this or that was the way of it, and he would have them on the stool of repentance and preached at three Sabbaths running, which is gey hard on a lassie that can anyway have a sick and dizzy feel on her and the weight in her wame that she doesna ken whether to love or hate. Ach well, maybe I shouldna be speaking of such things.

'My good-sister came over, whiles, from Paisley, and would bide in the house for a matter of a week, maybe, and would speak to the merchants and examine the manufactories and any new improvements, above all those that came from foreign countries where they might be more advanced than we were ourselves. Christian Shaw, for she had been so short a time married that folk seldom thought on calling her Mistress Miller, was living now at Johnstone, an hour's ride from Bargarran House, where her mother and sisters yet stayed. Only one of the sisters married, and she, the same as Christian, married late in life and a school teacher, a decent enough man but one worse than a minister. And Christian had the whole matter in her hands; she had her twisting mills, which would run from ten to twenty bobbins at a time, set up here and there. There was one in Bargarran House itself, in the parlour, and the windows were enlarged to allow more light for the fine spinning;

she near had me persuaded to try one, but somehow I felt I couldna tie myself down, and I could see the way yon machines would get a grip on whoever was working them, and hold them in through a bonny summer's day, even, with the thought both of the fine work and of the money it would be making. Although again, the more thread there was, the less profit to the makers of it. But for all that I have a new twisting mill set up at Borlum, so that we can make our own thread and enough for the neighbourhood, though I have not yet come to selling it in Inverness.

'Christian would get the decent young women from round Paisley and Johnstone to take up the spinning, aye, and the bleaching too; for she knew it all, from flax field to lace. I have seen her turning the lint in the ponds with her own hands, trying whether it was enough watered by breaking and smelling at the stalks, watching it in the washing to see that all the rotted stuff was away from the flax, and then herself spreading it, her hands quick and skilful as a mother's with her bairn. The same with the dressing of the flax, and the bleaching. Although she did not practise the bleaching of linen, she knew well how it should be done, and herself bleached the thread in the windows of her own house and Bargarran House, laying it out on slates, and preparing her own potashes and soaps. She was impatient of any woman that was slower than herself to do a thing, saying, I mind, that she was no better than a man! She had a certain respect for a man's strength of body, but none for his skill of hand and full little for his brains.

'For a time she was troubled with imitations of her own thread, so she drew up and caused to be circulated an advertisement of her own Bargarran thread made by herself and her sisters and such other young women as she had trained to do it. It was sold in papers with the Bargarran arms printed upon them, that was, three covered cups or chalices, and the price was from fivepence to six shillings the ounce, according to the fineness of the spinning. She would either sell it herself or send it in to Edinburgh or Glasgow for sale. It is a queer thing, Catherine, but I am thinking that my good-sister changed the face and shape of Paisley, through yon linen thread, more than ever any Minister could have done. Aye, or any General by the winning of victories. Yon thing that started with a few women in a parlour, working for curiosity and pin-money, has turned itself into rows of wee houses, and the stone spinning sheds at the corners, and a different kind of life, and maybe different thoughts on every subject, for a prodigious number of men and women. Yet she would be pleased enough at what she had done; she aye liked changing things.'

But Catherine Duncan had been thinking along ways of her own. She had never to her knowledge seen a manufactory, still less a colliery. It was altogether too much like talk about savages, and not even the black ones who had at least a different and romantic look on them. 'What,' asked she, 'would Mistress Shaw or Miller have done with all this money she was making out of her linen thread?'

Kirstie did not answer for a moment. At last she said: 'I am thinking she will have left it to charities, Catherine. For indeed she had somewhat to repent.'

'Did she,' asked Catherine, 'did she ever speak of witches again? She was never troubled as she had been as a young girl?'

'She spoke of it,' said Kirstie, 'times. You ken, it is hard to be entangled in yon kind of things and to forget them utterly, even although there was burning for cleansing. And maybe *they* could have been cleansed. Yet not herself.'

'But — did it happen again, ever? *Could* it happen?'

'Truly, my soul,' said Kirstie, 'I dinna like to be speaking of such things. William doesna like me to think on them.'

Catherine was silenced on that from her aunt, yet still curious, for there was something about the way her aunt had spoken. And she herself had gone with the others to wish at St. Mungo's well — ach, there was nothing in it, nor yet in brounies, nor in the Sight. And yet — 'When was it Mistress Christian Shaw died?' she asked at last.

'It was a few years on,' Kirstie said, 'aye, twelve or nearer fifteen years after I went back to my duty as a wife — if yon was what it was. Aye, near fifteen years, for I mind we were still in our deep blacks of mourning when a terrible ugly thing happened. But I will tell it you, Catherine, for I doubt you may find it instructive.

'The wee town was much grown by then; we had our change-house and the merchant shops in the main street, some for the gentry and another new kind of cheap one for the weavers and mechanics and such, that did not even have their own cow or kail-yard, but yet had a pickle silver to spend at the week's end. Already there was a scheme for the regular cleansing of the streets, and householders contributing their pennies. There was a piper and drummer to go round the streets before daylight to waken folks and this again was mostly for the weavers and such, and it would be the better doing of them who would give three coppers and the glass to wet them at the New Year. Then came talk of building a second Church. Andrew did not relish it at the first, for he thought it would take from his own powers, yet later he began to have a notion towards raising himself up a spiritual son, to take the place of the two he had lost by me, aye, a son not born of woman. He would speak of such hopes half aloud at table, and I never knowing whether or no it was meant for me to hear. Together he and this one would combat all kinds of moderation and heresy and London ways of speaking. For he was for ever working himself into a passion over such things. He had himself published a pamphlet at the time of the Marrow controversy, and he was angry because it was never taken up by the Assembly, nor much esteemed. Whiles he would preach of Anti-Christ going about in Ayrshire under the disguise of legalism and good neighbourliness, the publishing of worldly books and a praise of Pagans such as Socrates and Epictetus, and even the setting up of schools for the teaching of non-scriptural subjects. And indeed all such things as could take away from the overweening power of the Presbytery over folks' bodies and minds. Though maybe I shouldna say that. Should I, Catherine?'

'I never looked on it yon way, Aunt Kirstie. But—yourself and Uncle William go to the Presbyterian Church here, and yet

I remember my mother saying a year or two back, you were become an Episcopalian. And Uncle Mungo most terrible angry and affronted at it.'

'Ah lassie, there is a thing will explain itself in my story. There was a certain member of my husband's congregation that was not only a devout and well thought on woman, but also a good Christian, and there is a wee difference, my soul, between the two things. They were the younger branch of the Cunninghams, and her son was a decent, sensible laird, married and with more bairns than tenants. She lived in the old keep that was gey solid, built for a siege, with three rooms all one above the other and a fine dungeon below where she kept pigs that would be making the queerest noises if you happened to be taking tea with her in the upstairs room. She dressed in an old-fashioned way, too, did Lady Cunningham.

'Well, she doesna come into the story right at once. But it was this way. There was an Episcopalian Minister from the north-west that would not take the oath of allegiance and, his name being James Stewart, that was not altogether to be wondered at. Even at that time there were Non-jurors ministering to the half of the Highland parishes whether or not they were Jacobites avowed, and indeed it was hard to find enough respectable Whig Ministers that had the Gaelic, and, gif they were far enough away from the Assembly, they might agree with one another tolerably well, and even arrive at using the same Church if building timber was hard to come by. If there was one good Presbyterian Minister to a northern parish, there might also be a Non-juror, and, even if he were frowned upon and preached against, his congregation was likely to be away bigger, though it might need to meet in sixes or eights in a room or a byre even, to get past the law. But I am thinking that we in Scotland will take a certain romantic and pleasurable feeling out of any kind of secession Church, whatever its doctrines may be, so long as it is held in the kind of secrecy that all the neighbourhood will know about, and an edifying source of disagreement and argument to pass an evening! Catherine, lassie, am I shocking you?'

'Yes, Aunt Kirstie!'

'Ach, never heed. Maybe the whole thing should be taken with a great and mighty seriousness. It is just that I have seen ower much of it. And this poor body, James Stewart, that happened to want to pray for his namesake, had been put out of his parish in case he did it, and the wrong king got the tail end of a blessing through some oversight on the part of Heaven. For a time he had dodged about, hither and yon, taking his services with the readings from his wee Book, and sayings of the Lord's Prayer and such like, and marrying or christening or giving the sacraments when it was asked of him, with a boll of meal here and a dozen of eggs there, and living now in one house and now in another. But his wife was dead and he had a little lassie, round about ten years old, and it didna do, and he was thinking to go away to the Americas, to where folk would be less angry over their politics or religion, since there would be wild beasts and wilder Indians to contend with instead. So he was going about from one parish to another, getting a puckle shillings from the poor-box, or maybe from some kindly, disposed body, and putting them by against the price of his own and his lassie's sailing. Aye, Catherine, and mostly he would get what he was asking, and a friendly word forby that, for folks are good-hearted enough, and maybe they would be thinking that America was the best place for a Non-juror!

'But in our parish he got nothing ava. Yon was my husband's work. It came up before the Kirk Sessions and the Clerk had his book out to write an entry of a shilling or so. But Andrew spoke against it with such vehemence that it was refused. I heard this afterwards from the wife of the Clerk of the Sessions. He was ill enough pleased, for it was he had to turn away the man James Stewart and his lassie, and a decent, kindly-spoken man, for all his Highland accent. The Clerk told his wife, and the same night she had made up a parcel with a pair shoon of her own lassie's and an old plaid, and a wee twist of sugar and tea, and had it over to the Stewarts, and I doubt she will not have hidden it long from her man that she had made the gift, nor would he have been angered at her. It was otherwise with myself.

'But, see you, Catherine, I didna know this at the time, and Lady Cunningham brought in the man, for he had a letter to her from a cousin she had in another parish, in Lanark. So she had bidden him to sup with her, and on her way had brought him round to our house, and it could be she had thought it would be a diversion for myself to speak with a visitor, and this one so suitable, being a Minister, although with the wrong views on earthly kings. And indeed I liked him fine and he was altogether a likeable man, and spoke merrily of his wanderings and the folk he had seen, and of brounies and Beltane cakes; ach, not seriously, but stories he had come on here or there; it was kind of lightsome, and lifted me from a dowie mood I had been in for weeks past.

So, as we sat there, and I had the kettle on for our tea, in came Andrew, and I never suspicioning that he would be angry at me, though gin I had given more thought to it — but ach, Catherine, it was terrible altogether the way he looked and the things he said, and indeed it hurts me yet to mind on it! There was Andrew spitting the words out at us, saying for why he would not help any Non-juror or any Non-juror's child, nay, not if they were in the midst of a burning house or a quick-sand, and the three of us standing against the oak press, and James Stewart, poor decent body, in his old Minister's coat, worn to threads on the elbows and shoulders, and the bonnet crushed in his hands and one of his shoes almost through at the toe. And sudden old Lady Cunningham settled the plaid round her shoulders and took him by the hand and said to him: "Come away now, there is no need for us to be droukit under yon fount of eloquence!" And then to Andrew: "I doubt you should read the Sermon on the Mount again, Andrew Shaw, afore you gie us another of your own!" That angered him so wild he could scarce answer, and she said a thing that wasna meant ill for me, but yet had the illest afterclap: "I am sorry I maun leave you with yon canting Elisha, Kirstie," she said, "and indeed if I could put t'other, that is a better man and a better Christian, into his place, I would fain do it, and I am thinking you would sleep the sounder." And off went old Lady Cunningham with her head in air, and Mr. James Stewart with her. I mind he cast a look at myself as though to say he was gey sorry.

'But there was I left and the drenching, hammering thunder of this husband of mine coming down on me, and indeed I hid my face in my hands, and whilst he miscalled me by the names of all the most notorious whores in the Old Testament, I was clinging to the thin knowledge that I was Kirstie Haldane and no whore, nor ever like to be for all he might shout at me; and indeed I had never looked on this poor Episcopalian Minister with any blink of a carnal liking, and I was thinking mostly on his lass-bairn and how would she fare on the long voyage across the ocean between Port Glasgow and the Plantations.

I tried to think on my Maker; I tried to think on my Saviour. They wouldna come to me, they were held back by this same man that was miscalling me, that ended by slapping me across the cheek. I thought of my father and mother that were dead and couldna help me, and when I thought on my mother I thought for a wee flash on yon Highlander that she had bidden me give the last of her tocher to, yet even yon spark of a thought could be sinful, and I put it by. I was alone then, and, because I couldna get the thoughts of goodness and love to come to me, there was room for every kind of evil thought. Nay, Catherine, I did have evil thoughts! Aye, terribly evil, so that you would be feared of me if you knew of them or if I could tell them now. But I couldna. They are gone, my soul, and they will not come back. And the worst thing I hated my man for — aye, I have said it now — was that he wrote to my brother Mungo accusing me, see you, of harbouring and entertaining a Non-juring Episcopalian Minister against his knowledge and will and my duty and obedience to himself. He didna go so far as to say to my brother that I was an harlot, and indeed he couldna have done it in cold blood, remembering that Lady Cunningham was with us the whole time, but he sprinkled his hints out of Kings and Chronicles, until his letter stank like a midden! Ach, it was wild the spite was in it for him to do the like of thon! I could just scarcely believe it. That he could bring in my own folk against me. And when Mungo wrote to me, not even questioning the thing, but believing ae word that another man wrote against a woman, even although the woman was his own sister, I didna even answer his letter. Instead, I wrote to Patrick.

'At this time Patrick had still a good enough practice, and I would see his name, whiles, in the newspapers. He was one of the Assessors of the city of Edinburgh, and had his lodgings there, but mostly now he lived at Bearcrofts. He wanted me to come and visit him there, but I didna care to some way. I liked his wife well enough, but there was George, a fine serious boy, and our cousin Margaret, both awful fond of their father, and ach, Catherine, I couldna think right about them, nor anyway get eased into some fashion of comfort of my own. Patrick wrote to me not to be so down-hearted, it was better to be miscalled than to be flattered, and he'd had both. Nor was one Church worse than another and Andrew might have been a better man if he had lived through a persecution; he might have had a real enemy then and not need to make the mirror enemy of his wife. But there were things that must just be tholed; there was no remedy for a bad marriage. I mind his quoting from William Shakespeare on that, an English author whom I have never had the time nor the inclination to read. We had best put our minds to the things that were remediable and try to set them to rights. I mind he wrote lengthily then of the wickedness of some landlord, I canna mind on whom. There was little enough to it, yet I felt it was in some way more understanding than Mungo. Patrick had suffered himself.

'So I kept his letter, but Mungo's I burnt. And the Minister James Stewart and his lass-bairn went safely over the great waters. And in America they met with and spoke with William Macintosh, younger, of Borlum. For the ways of Providence are strange.

'And old Lady Cunningham, who had done the harm without thinking, came to ask would I forgive her, and I said I would so and gladly. We spoke on many things, she and I, and together we would visit the houses of the colliers or the carpet weavers. She herself had been but a bairn at the time of the martyrdom of the Cameronians, yet she remembered something of it and had heard tell of more. I would ask her, was it the way Wodrow speaks in his book and did it seem as though the light of this witnessing would shine throughout Scotland? And she said no indeed, most honest, well-doing folk that took the Covenant as maybe the most serious thing in their lives, yet thought these others were going altogether too far; at any moment they might denounce property itself, and all orderly ways; it was an uneasy thing for any man, however good a Whig he might be, if his wife and daughters took to the heather after some Cameronian preacher. And so, although they reprobated Dundee and his thieving Highlanders, yet they were unco relieved when Nisbet and Paton and the lave of them were hangit, more especially when they made edifying ends.

'And she would say this too, that she thought the lives of the Covenanting Saints were no more true than the lives of the Popish Saints, and neither lot had it in them to perform miracles, but only the Lord Jesus Christ. Yet there was something nice about making up stories over the doings of your own side, and maybe Wodrow or Walker or Shields might have believed what they wrote down in their books. And it came to me then that yon Covenanting martyrs were just fine to make up sermons or wee bookies about, and if the cottars that were used to buying the chap-books with fairies and witches in them, were to be got into the way of buying these other books, then the authors would need to put in yon miracles and speeches and bonnie lasses cast into the sea by the bloodthirsty tyrants and a' the lave of it. Yet what would Andrew say gif one of the Saints were to come back on him and ask what was he doing with so muckle power and pride and respectability and being on the right side of the Government? Neither Cargill nor Cameron would be welcome in Scotland as it was now. The Saints are better dead.

'Aye, we had some fine cracks, old Lady Cunningham and myself. But she died. And the time went on, ill followed by worse.' Kirstie stopped speaking suddenly, as though she had come against a stone wall.

After a time Catherine asked: 'And then?'

Kirstie spoke, quietly, the barrier overcome: 'And then, Andrew died and, there being no longer any obstacle between myself and God's mercy, I met with William Macintosh of Borlum, and we were married within a few months after.'

CHAPTER VIII

THERE was a mildness about the evening, as though it would stretch on and on for ever. A Gleneagles lad who had been up cutting peats went by, the peat knife over his shoulder, in his decent servant's grey, tired yet not over-tired. Kirstie and Catherine watched him as far as the corner of the house, their eyes held by his walk, slow as the passing of time. Then Catherine asserted herself again. 'But how,' she said, 'how at all did it happen?'

'Ach,' said Kirstie, 'as for that . . .' and she looked in front of her, past Catherine, past the house, past all that was to be seen with the immediate eye. 'The men will be late for their supper,' said she, 'and that will put the dancing later yet. Here is your cousin Margaret come to tell us that supper is in.'

'But after supper there will be the end of the story?'

'After supper,' said Kirstie, 'there will be the dancing.'

Margaret came over to them, a book in her hand, poetry most like, and she had a striped rose for a book-mark. With her was Adam and her young cousin, Elizabeth of Aberuthven, snub-nosed and red-cheeked, a country lassie that had never yet been the length of Edinburgh, even, and that kicked off her shoes whenever she could, since they irked her still. And indeed she had done that once in the Kirk at the beginning of the sermon and by the end of it the things had got away in behind the back of the pew, and Elizabeth Haldane grovelling for them in the sight of the whole congregation! 'What were the two of you at?' asked Margaret, and bit at the stalk of her rose.

'We were speaking of old times,' Kirstie answered, 'of the Kirk and its Ministers and their over much enthusiasm.'

'You will have had little enough of that, Aunt Kirstie,' Margaret said, 'amongst your Highland Episcopalians with their babbling of the same wee prayers over and over till they end by losing all the sense there ever was in them!'

'Aye,' said Kirstie, 'I felt a thing missing in the Episcopalian

Church at Borlum; indeed it isna there at all. Yet the old Church doesna put so much between you and your God as the new Church and the twist of the discourses can do. It doesna come creeping in on your private prayers. That is, if you make them. But I will admit, Margaret, it is away easier to sleep through an Episcopalian service if you have a mind to!' She got up briskly: 'Come lasses! The midges will have us eaten if we'll not take our ways in to supper.'

She went up the stair to their room, minding a little on William, as she had pictured him yet once again to Catherine, and the look that was between them yon night when he had come with Kyllachy. And when she came in there was himself in the room with his coat off, washing his face. The brothers had gone on to Blackford but he had turned back at the far end of the policies. 'They didna say,' he said, 'but I had it in my mind that maybe they'd had enough of my company and would soonest be speaking with one another. I wouldna want to thrust myself on folk, Curstan m'eudail, and least of all at the first.'

'Well, maybe you are right,' she said, 'and you will get your supper the better!'

'I find myself devilish greedy here,' he said, 'and there's the truth! But your folks must spend a wee fortune in their kitchen.'

She laughed. It was nice, och, terrible nice, to be able to pleasure her man and she was glad the tables were as well set as she minded of them being.

Bearcrofts' Margaret was hostess at Gleneagles, and, her uncles not yet being back from Blackford, they went in to supper —broth, roast goose with beans and artichokes, side dishes of cherries and whipped cream. It was only right and proper that Margaret should ask William Macintosh to say the Grace, seeing he was the only man of her father's generation present. He gave the same he would have given at Borlum; it seemed to Kirstie to have brought her two homes a long step closer together. She looked up from her plate, and saw that her man had been carefully observed, maybe judged. Surely they would not be saying it was an Episcopalian Grace he had used! But now he was sitting by Margaret, next to the empty place which was left for Gleneagles. Young Adam, confident and conscientious, had offered to undertake the carving of the one goose — full easier here on a steady and solid ashet than at sea under the senior midshipman's eye and tongue! — whilst Ochtertyre undertook the other. Margaret had him placed between herself and Kirstie, while George had his sulky elbows on the table at the far end; she looked to her Aunt Kirstie and her older cousins to help her through the supper with no quarrels. But George's elder sister Helen was indignant about her brother, and was speaking in a high, affected voice about fashions and politics, listened to open-mouthed by Elizabeth of Aberuthven.

By and bye James caught her up on a theological matter of which she knew little, and contradicted her. At that, the young Haldanes and half Haldanes all joined in, leaning across the table and talking in loud voices, baying to their own satisfaction and never listening for more than a moment to one another. Kirstie laughed, enjoying it all, for it went away back to her own childhood, the same kind of jokes, it seemed to her, the heavy punning on words and misquotations from the scriptures or Horace, the younger ones picking it up, year after year, trying now to make their own points and snubbed by their slightly elders, Elizabeth rather indelicately scratching her midge-bites. Young Captain John spoke authoritatively of foreign matters, of how Field-Marshal Keith — who was himself a far-out cousin through the Drummonds — was resigning from the service of the Empress Elizabeth; St. Petersburg was no place for a human and rational soldier; what was wanted by the Russians and above all by the Empress was — George made an obvious and indecent interjection which the lasses pretended not to hear, excepting for Elizabeth who was caught with a giggle and a mouthful of goose.

Margaret talked earnestly to Kirstie, about linen bleaching, hemming Ochtertyre between them in case he might be provoked: and would Aunt Kirstie advise her to send this year's sheets from the Bearcrofts weaving into Christy's at Perth for the summer bleach? The fine they were — she could promise that! — it might be from 6d. to 9d. a yard they would charge her. Aye, the coarse linen were down to 2d. Christy's were reliable, honest folk, would not get the Bearcrofts linen melled up with any other. How did Kirstie herself manage? Did she send into Inverness? But Kirstie did her own bleaching, and encouraged her neighbours to use the bleach field at Borlum. Her fine linen was bleached the Dutch way, with buttermilk, forby the potashes and olive oil; some of her materials came from Holland but for one she would send to Danzig, taking a three years' supply. Her coarser linen was bleached in the Irish way. It was cheaper, both in materials and labour, especially for the Highlands where there was no surplus of buttermilk. 'Aye,' said Kirstie, 'I learnt all yon kind of lore from my good-sister.'

They were still on the bleaching and not through with the goose and claret, when Gleneagles and Captain Robert came back. They had both of them had their slice of cheese and glass of strong ale at Blackford, waiting on the mail, and Captain Robert, for his part, would miss the broth and be straight at a goose thigh and stuffings. He settled himself down by young James, his favourite nephew and heir to Airthrey, and Catherine watched, sharp and sensitive to James' manner of affection to his uncle. Captain Robert took the folded newspapers out of his pocket. 'Here, lasses, is the *Mercury* and your Uncle Mungo has the *Scots Magazine*, but the *Courant* has either missed the mail, or else the Tory wretch that is in charge of the bags has thought fit to suppress the good Whig newsprint!'

'Were there no letters?' Kirstie asked anxiously. But all was right, for her man had it and was breaking the seal.

'Aye,' said Black William, 'there it's. And she is well and bonny and has another tooth cut and has walked the length of the lawn before she fell on her back-side!'

'Ian Mor will be making one of his tunes on that!' Kirstie said laughing, for the Borlum piper was a standing joke between them and the half of his tunes not to be distinguished one from another, and she seized on the letter from William's elder sister, Winwood Mackenzie, who was keeping house at Borlum for a few weeks, with her three grandchildren, so that there were plenty wee ones, forby William's own. . . .

'The letters from the south will have missed the mail again!' Gleneagles said.

'Another advantage of the Union!' said Ochtertyre; he could not help himself, the anger against George Cockburn was getting the best of him.

'It will be as bad the other way,' Gleneagles answered, 'London will be cut off from ourselves.'

'And fine London cares if it is!'

'Come, come,' Gleneagles said, 'there will be plenty that do care. There will be Fellows of the Royal Society eager enough for letters from Professor Monro and Dr. Stirling. Aye, and doctors and surgeons crying out for news of the work going on at the Royal Infirmary.'

'What is wrong,' said Captain Robert firmly, 'is that these politics are made the fool's excuse for his stupidity and incompetence. The mails should have been to time, Union or no Union. But one drunken driver or one idle inn-keeper that neglects to see to the right shoeing of a post-horse, will start up these politics that should be dead and done with.'

'How can they be?' Ochtertyre began, 'when — '

But Margaret cut across him: 'Should the foreign mail have come, Uncle Robert?' she asked.

'Aye, there might have been an American mail. You will be interested in the American news, William, I suppose.'

'Yes,' said William.

'You will have friends there yet?' He nodded, his face twisting the wee-est bit.

'You will have seen the Indians, Uncle William!' young David of Aberuthven said, and the younger ones all stopped talking for the moment. 'Did you kill any? What like are they really?'

But David and the rest were something startled when Black William said: 'I did see the Indians in America. And they are not unlike the rest of us Highlanders.' And suddenly it appeared to Catherine, who had turned her over-keen perception away from young James on to her new Highland uncle, that he was, in a way, like the pictures of Indians that she had seen; the dark eyes and brows, the hooked nose, and a thing about the mouth that could be cruel, but was it ever? Could it be to Kirstie? She lost herself in speculation about her elders. And take the decent grey wig from his head and put in the stead of it eagle feathers, aye, the eagle feathers of Indian brave or Highland gentleman ... three for a chief, two for the head of a family. Tory nonsense!

Captain Robert was reading aloud from the *Caledonian Mercury* now: war news from Venice out of the *London Gazette* of the week before. So-called secret intelligence, served up with dotted names and titles modishly southern and sprightly, and funny enough read out in an awful serious, Scottish burr. News of the privateers interested all three sailors at the table. Captain Jekyll of the *Fortune*, protecting the mackerel boats off Yarmouth, had fought five privateers and taken the *Charron*. Captain Combes — and would he be the same Captain Combes who was in trouble with his landlady at Portsmouth two years back? — had taken the *St. Barbara*.

Black William reached across for the copy of June 11th. The Commons had read for the second time the Bill for enlarging the Time for the Use of the Highland Dress with respect to such as are not landed men. To himself and Kirstie that was an immediate and practical matter. If it went through, small sums of hard-earned money, amounts known with some accuracy to Kirstie at least, could be spent in one or another cot or croft, on food for the bairns, on very necessary bedding or such tools as could not be made at home, on enough tea for the winter months, instead of on shoddy and high-priced breeches and coats. Here a cow need not be sold nor a young lassie sent out to service for another year yet. For that matter, his own rents might be paid without overmuch swithering, and the mothers coming to Kirstie behind his back, and the rents in turn would go to improvements. It would not seem like that in London. They would yawn through the speeches of the Scots Members, would have their fixed notions of a kilted rebel. And at

Lima, 30,000 souls had been swallowed up by an earthquake. A horrible catastrophe. Yet you never thought twice on it, Lima being farther from the Ochils than the Highlands from St. James's Park.

The East India Company had received last November's letters from Bombay. All quiet there. The same at Bussora. Names, names to Kirstie. Queer names to William, not like yon other soft Indian names. But to Captain Robert familiar wharves and offices, inns and warehouses. Acquaintances renewed instantly from the last visit. Even the same whores in the same houses. The familiar smell of the streets, the hot, dusty taste of the bazaar sweetmeats.

Two deserters from the Army to be apprehended. Craigie from Perthshire, a wright: Laird, a weaver. And Kirstie thinking immediately not of the King's Army and honour, but of the two decent lads, better surely at their trade than learning murder, however respectable, and the both of them with mothers and sweethearts. Though maybe they were not decent lads at all, but ne'er-do-weels, best run out of their home parish. Why is it then, thought Kirstie, that a body must be, instantly and always, against the law until it can be proved (as it may be, odd times) that the law is also morally right?

Margaret and Helen Cockburn were leaning over their uncle's shoulders, looking at the advertisements. Cargoes of oranges and lemons in to Leith from Lisbon. Tea from 4s. a lb, but that would be only common bohea, not worth buying, up to 24s. for the best Hyson, that only a fool would buy for a show-off. Clean old butter for greasing sheep at 20s. a barrel. Linseed imported from Philadelphia by John Tod: a reliable firm. Those who had furnished forage for Government troops during the last years and had not sent in their accounts, to send them with the corresponding vouchers, to Dundas' Office. The Haldanes had sent in theirs months past. What was more, the accounts, after the usual correspondence, had even been honoured.

'Look, Helen!' said Margaret, 'there is the advertisement of the roup of the lodgings under my father's in St. James Court. A nice enough set of rooms.'

'Is your father much in Edinburgh now?' Helen asked.

'Not so much as formerly. Yet he cannot be happy in the country with nobody to argue with him but myself.'

'When do you expect him here?'

'To-morrow or the day after on his way to Stirling where they are making him a burgess. He has a softness for Aunt Kirstie.' Margaret picked up a bob of cherries and dipped them in the cream bowl. Ochtertyre was looking at the notice of the annual meeting of the Musical Society in Edinburgh. Aye, there was a thing you would miss through not living in cities. How delicious he found Handel, how much he suddenly wanted to hear a concert again!

'There has not been an issue of any newspaper,' said Gleneagles, 'without these notices of land changing hands. And not all since the Rebellion. Forby public advertisements of private shooting rights. Tell me, Willie, what is your mind on this preserving of game?'

'We have never done it at Borlum,' Black William said.

'Nor we at Gleneagles. But there are more guns about than there were, and the sighting of them better!'

'There are fewer guns in the Highlands,' Black William said, 'even for the game.'

'Never tell me,' said Mungo genially, 'that you have no gun hidden up the lum-breast or under the mattresses at Borlum!'

'I do tell you all the same,' Black William answered quietly. 'I gave up every gun there was to my name.'

Mungo was embarrassed at that; he had not meant to be taken so seriously. He poured out a full glass all round and went back a little, asking: 'Would you consider preserving your game?'

'No,' said Black William, 'I would not consider the game to be any more my own than the shadows on the hills or the burn water.'

'Our cousin of Kyllachy had no such scruples,' Mungo said. 'I mind when we spoke ont' he said it would put up the value of his land.'

'Kyllachy can go to the devil his own way,' Black William said.

'And has. Do you ken this? Those who are most set on this preserving will not so much as let their own life tenants shoot moorfowl or the deer that come down to the crops.'

'That is terrible surely,' Mungo said, 'and the thing was not heard of in our father's time.'

'It is an English custom,' said Ochtertyre, 'and came here when the fashions changed. The game laws in England are as strict as the gallows. Here we have had laws these many generations back against killing out of season, either fish or flesh. Aye, and against Sabbath netting, so that the bonny great salmon can take their Sabbath Day's journey up the Tweed to the spawning grounds.'

'And up the Ness,' Black William said, 'many a day I have leant over the bridge at Inverness to watch them, and I a laddie!'

'But the English laws against poaching are for the owners of forest and river. They were a thing brought in by the Normans, and what there is of it in Scotland comes from the Normans; aye, Bruce and Douglas and the lot of them! We need not have let that spread north of Clyde or Forth.'

'We are over-keen on the wee things now,' said Mungo. 'Doubtless we must not neglect the money, but this matter of preserving game shows a mean spirit, as though we were feared of our neighbours. To my mind no gentleman would do such a thing.'

'When an estate changes hands,' said Ochtertyre, 'it is not always the best of a gentleman that comes in. It is those with money in a bank, however they may have come by it.'

'You will not get out of it that way,' said Captain Robert, one hand firm on the neck of a claret bottle, 'for some of those that are keenest on this preserving are the Dukes and such cattle, the worst Tories in Scotland among them.'

'It is the way I said,' Ochtertyre answered. 'Those are the ones with the feudal ideas, that were never native to Scotland!'

'It is the wee ideas of the merchants they will be picking up,' said Gleneagles. 'Profit and interest and all yon things that are well called usury in the Book. There is other five bottles standing on the press, Robbie. Do not be sparing to pour them! Aye, the brandy is with them. But what I am saying is, we need to take the solid and sensible view of these money matters. We have been over niggling in Scotland. I have plenty friends that would take a wee consolation of maybe five pounds sterling in a lawsuit or to help a friend to some office.'

'It is the way they are still thinking in pounds Scots,' said Robert, 'and the money would make a better show that way than with your wee five pounds sterling setting herself up at sixty pounds Scots. But a man that has travelled and seen the muckle great briberies of the Indies or the Barbary Coast or Italy itself, would never touch these paltry cold presents out of Edinburgh High Street.'

'I would not suppose,' Gleneagles said, 'that our brother Patrick had ever taken less than fifty pounds sterling.'

'I thought,' said Black William, 'I thought that you had told me earlier, Patrick was not to be bribed? Indeed, that this was a main difficulty in his life.'

'Aye,' said Gleneagles, 'over the matter of the Forfeited Estates that was so, or in any other thing where his political principles would come in and say yes or no. But in his ordinary law practice it would be otherwise. And I am sure that he never took a present to do a thing that was against his conscience. And indeed I can say the same for myself. But what,' he went on, and suddenly beat his fist on the table, making the glasses jump and ring, 'what, I am asking you, is the value of a moorfowl, or two, or a hundred? A matter of pennies. A bawbee. A plack. A bodle! I will have nothing to do with such trifles!'

'But it might be,' said Captain Robert, 'that we may all need to be considering them. And there is a kind of parallel, though I have not just got it clear in my head for the time being, between the preserving of game and the enclosing of land.'

He began thoughtfully to draw parallels on the table with his fingers out of a wee pool of claret that had got there some way, but Black William said: 'I do not see such a parallel, not at all, Airthrey! For enclosing is for the good of the land and preserving only for the good of the landlord!'

'Aye,' said Captain Robert, 'that is very well so long as you will not be confusing the interests of the two, but how is that possible?'

'It seems to me possible,' said Black William, 'but not if the land is to be bought and sold the way things are these days, and mostly all in the Lowlands.'

'Land,' said George Cockburn, suddenly vivacious, the wine at supper having for the time being dispersed the head-ache left by his earlier bottles, 'land is for its owner's use and pleasure, the same as a woman.' He grinned and began picking his teeth.

'If that is the way you act, cousin George,' said Ochtertyre smoothly, 'your land will play the harlot on you. And if you are thinking to get married — '

'We are not speaking of women!' said Captain Rob, 'and you will hold your tongues, both of you. No, indeed. We were speaking of — aye, birds. Were we no', Borlum, my laddie? And I have seen the most tremendous muckle great peacocks in the marble palaces of the Moguls, and the flights of parrots in the dawn, and the talking mynahs that will be saying the most outrageous things in all languages, and they in cages of gold with the square flash of the bit mirrors set in with garnets and emeralds!'

'There is a bonnier flash,' Black William said decisively, 'to the blue-birds in Virginia, and you will have no conception of the brightness of the red cardinals and the yellow orioles that would make our own goldies look grey, and the winter past and April coming through the wild edges of the American forest.'

'But I,' said George Cockburn, 'I was most definitely and ostentatiously speaking and considering of women — '

'Speaking of women,' said Mungo, 'it seems that the ladies have all left us. And myself not so much as noticing the fact. And they have even taken away the newspapers with them! Ach well, they have left us the claret. Open another bottle, Robbie.'

Young James, who was perfectly sober, having carefully

sipped but the one glass of claret and no drop of brandy from the good Gleneagles cask, got to his feet. 'I am for joining the ladies, Uncle, and so are David and Adam at least. Our cousins will be at the dancing on the grass.'

'Ach,' said Mungo and shook his head, 'you will be at frivolities the like of this dancing, and never wait with your elders and betters for a serious discussion, such as we are having.' He held up his hand, listened and frowned. 'Yonder are the heathen Highland pipes skirling away to lure the lasses and lads from the narrow path. And yourselves will be twinkling along it with your poor burning feet!'

'You are becoming intoxicated, Mungo,' said Robert, 'and that sadly. Indeed I have a feeling of sadness myself. We should do our best to take another stage of the journey away from sobriety to something more cheery.'

But Black William was listening to the pipe music, the summoning urgent thing, the wee sharp waves of the tune beating on his stomach, the buzz of the drone shoving at his feet to come. Aye, to Kirstie. He wiped his forehead with the cool silk handkerchief from his coat pocket, and rose. 'I am for the dancing too,' he said, 'or herself will be wild at me. And I am thinking I will go before my feet become their own masters.'

'There will be Bordeaux wine, aye, and good brandy that has paid the excise, on the table to-morrow,' Mungo said benevolently, 'if the Lord has spared us till then. And you could be trusting to His infinite mercy if you would liefer be dancing with my poor sister Kirstie ·than drinking with her bold brothers; but for myself, I am nearer the three score and ten, so I will even stick to my claret which is a douce benevolent drink and none of your furious hot Highland whiskys. And I will give you a toast before you are away to your frivolities.' He considered seriously, then lifted his glass. 'May the hand of Providence be for ever over us!' He drank off his full glass, and the others finished what was in their own. 'Robbie,' said Mungo, 'we will now discuss the nature of Providence.' And, the ladies being well away now and otherwise occupied, he loosened his breeches a trifle for the more comfort and pleasure of his claret.

Outside on the bowling-green it was a light and lovely evening. The cool of it, breathed in and out, was bringing alertness and a remembered dance pattern into the minds and bodies of the men. Kirstie was wearing the dress of flowered satin. Black William kissed her hands, first the fingers and thumbs and then, turning them over cannily, the tickly soft palms. The piper was wiping the sweat off himself, the fiddler playing over one air after another: The Rock and the Wee Pickle Tow; Hey my Nannie; Bundle and Go; Pease Strae. And here Margaret called the partners out for the dance that was mostly called the Duke of Perth on this side of the Ochils. She led off with David of Aberuthven, turning by the right hand and casting off, herself behind Kirstie, David behind Black William, turning by the left hand, turning corners, setting, the reel of three down the side of the dance, Margaret in the ribbon twist of it with William and young James of Airthrey, David with Kirstie and Catherine, the bonny strict pattern of the thing now across and now up and down, opening and shutting along the line of dancers.

There was a dance to warm you; and after there were more of the hard dances; the Big House ones could have the top of the dance, but below them and in the same pattern the dairy and kitchen lasses danced with the lads from the bothy, the ploughmen, the horsemen and the byremen. There were reels and strathspeys and stripping the willow, Cauld Kail in Aberdeen, Corn Rigs, or Geordie's Byre, and one or another would mind on a dance and call for it or hum a tune till the piper or fiddler had it, and the hotter the dancers the cooler was the evening, and the midges away, and dark enough for a kiss or two not to be that easy seen. Now the newspapers that had come with the mail lay small and neglected on the step of the house. To-morrow would be time enough to read the *Scots Magazine* with its dreich interminable moral couplets in the poetry pages, and the correspondence on electrical phenomena, and the statistics of the Royal Infirmary, and the legal article and the book reviews, and the serial story, sure to be fit for the eyes of the most modest reader, in which the decent loves and adventures of Honesto and Harriet are duly set forth, as little like to life itself as you would think possible. Aye, full little like the flames and screeching and panic of the Lima earthquake, or the miseries of the Jacobite prisoners, yet being tried and transported, and the eight of them from Chester gaol who were drowned accidentally, being hand-cuffed in pairs and so not able to swim, Mackays and MacLeods, never a Macintosh in this lot, away to the plantations, to be indentured servants, ah, that will be one way to set a High-lander to honest work, and in America, in Virginia and Delaware — Turn, turn to the pipe music, the pattern of the dance, the pattern of the cousins, the bull calves, pattern of the Lowlands you are married into, William Macintosh, Uilleam Dubh, forget with your Kirstie, do not be troubled now. If troubles are to come, surely they can wait for the morning.

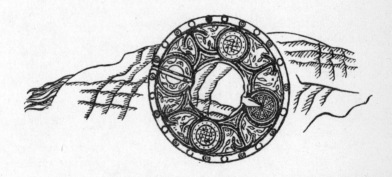

PART TWO

YE HIGHLANDS AND YE LOWLANDS

YOUNG JAMES OF AIRTHREY

CHAPTER I

It was not yet near dark, but the windows of the room were narrow, since window glass had been none so easily come by when they were built. Kirstie leant against the sill of the northern window, watching the light as it went farther and farther back into the colourless profound sky behind the Grampians, a day's ride away across the peaceable strath and beyond Torlum and Crieff Law. She saw no detail now of clefted glen, of near heights nor far and cold ones, only a long darkness, a jagged line lying below the clear twilight, yonder Ben Ledi, made small under the first-created heavens. There were the beginnings of the Highlands, and deep in the north, out of all possible sight, the Speyside and Borlum and the wee lassie Elizabeth. Black William came and stood beside her, closer than in the dancing, his hands caressing, untieing a ribbon, loosing out a brooch from a knot of lace. She turned her eyes back into the room, blinking. The window at the far end, looking up Gleneagles, had darker sky at the back of it, near mountains closing in, and the tops of firs, black and moving like sea beasts in a half-lit pool. There was an eeriness and threat from outby that made her terribly glad of himself at her side and the bed between them and the window. 'Will we have the candles?' she said; and he, also aware of the steep cup of Gleneagles pressing in on them with the fall of light, lifted the shutter bars against it and lit the candles in the well sconces and by the bed.

There were two dressing closets to the room, one with Kirstie's dresses and cloaks, the other with Black William's coats and wigs. Kirstie spoke across from hers, taking the pins out of her petticoats: 'What for were you lying to my brothers, William?'

'Which time?' said William.

'Over the wee matter of guns at Borlum. You need not have denied in yon serious way that you had an odd gun or so hidden. They werena pressing you and you could have spoken the truth and no harm at all in it.'

'Ach,' said William, 'I just didna want, Kirstie, and there it's. They are as nice as can be, your brothers, but they are for ever thinking I am a Highlander and so a double-dealer and a liar and not civilized the way they are. So I just needed to make them think I was as honest as any Edinburgh banker with the one hand on his wee bookie of sermons and the other in his customer's siller, even if it meant a devilish great lie and a scolding from my Kirstie at the end of it!'

'I'm no' scolding you,' said Kirstie, 'but I am asking myself, will I ever get to the bottom of the devilment that's in you.'

'You will not,' said Black William. 'And indeed it is a catching thing and I am not sure that I have not seen it in yourself, odd times! And you know well enough that if we did not go that way about it in the Highlands, we could become as sad and as bad as maggoty sheep. There's mostly plenty to be sad over, mo ghraidh, so we need to allow ourselves laughter and devilment. Yet I can see well, Kirstie, that in a secure and well-doing house, the like of the Haldane house, there could be no need for yon kind of laughter. But if you must needs marry a black Highlander — ' He moved over to the sconces and blew the candles out, leaving only the silver candle-stick by the bed.

She came and stood by his knee, combing down her hair that had less white in it than his, or showed it less. She knew that it was not possible for her, if she found a fault in him, not immediately to find an excuse or opposite for it. All she could do was to think away from him and herself to a Goodness and Love that made the both of them small and bairnlike: that showed no human virtue as of any account save as an effort of free will, but all shrivelled to nothing under the great light of Redemption. And now there was hunger in both of them for a small space of yon light, for a cleansing of their hearts, and they knelt in their white night-shirts with ruffles at the neck, and said the formal prayers of the Episcopalian Church, asking for little things which could surely be God's will, and mostly for health and blessings on their daughter Elizabeth. Each of them named their relations, and Black William did a thing which was only now ceasing to shock his wife. As always, he prayed for the soul of his father, the Brigadier, dead in prison, these four years. Kirstie could no more have prayed for her father — or for her dead children — than she could have stripped herself naked before a congregation. That account was closed. One must, by a constant effort and strengthening of faith, be certain that the separation was not for eternity, but only in the temporal world. She minded on the first nights of her marriage when she had heard her husband doing this terrible wicked and heretical thing, so outlandish that it was scarcely preached against now. Yet some way she did not believe in it being what it seemed, any more than she could believe, for a time, in any other part of her marriage. Such prayers were no more sanctioned by the Episcopalian Church than by the Presbyterians, but William Macintosh had been over much in France and Spain, and had picked up Popish notions, forby he was laird of Borlum and did not consult either the legal Presbyterian or the illegal but condoned Episcopalian Minister on his private devotions.

They ended by saying the Lord's Prayer. It was ill thought of in the Established Presbyterian Church, and Kirstie had never used it through most of her life; there was still an excitement, a newness to it. William knew it well enough. At least he was assured now of his daily bread. Different from yon other times. And sometimes it would be maize-meal bread, dry bannocks, ill to taste, the way the Indians were used to bake it. Ohnawiyo learnt to make it better. He gave a kind of start; it had all come through his mind between the tail of one sentence and the head of the next. A wandering mind makes an ill prayer and an ill husband.

'Amen,' he said, and waited for the feel of the blessing, then: 'Kirstie, I am right sorry I lied to your brothers, but it was only a wee lie.'

'They were wanting to be friends, to heal any hurts you had, my dear. Their hearts were moved towards you.'

'Aye,' he said, 'and there was the thing I needed to keep myself fast against. Oh Kirstie, there's times I feel near trapped here. They'd have the both of us thinking and doing their way, and I can see it on you, the happy you are to be back in your own place, among your own folk and away from the Highlands again!'

Kirstie took his hands in hers. She felt sore and puzzled. It was neither true nor fair, yet he said it the way he was over proud and over open to hurts, touchy as a blood horse in summer. It was the other side of the quality in him which made him also so gentle and kind to herself that she could scarcely breathe for astonishment. Because he could be hurt, so also could he love. Because he had no tough Lowland skin between his heart's blood and the world, he needed to defend his heart all the time, and the kindness of the Bull Calves was no easier for a Highlander to thole than scorn and power of the English. Yet it came of pride; the humble heart could bear to be touched by all. 'Will you never learn humility, William?' she said.

'Only to God,' he answered, 'not to man — nor yet woman.'

'Ach,' said she, 'why will you be saying that to your Kirstie?'

He sat silent with a thrawn look on him and the black lashes drooping over his eyes. 'Uilleam,' she whispered, 'duine mo chridh, mo leannan, mo leannan dileas!'

He turned suddenly: 'Come to bed, ma mie. What was it you were speaking on with Catherine Duncan?'

'I was telling her the story of my own life,' said Kirstie, settling her head on the pillow. The bed curtains were half drawn, for she liked best to fall on sleep to the comforting small blink of the candle, so that by opening an eye she could be assured immediately that it was himself beside her, that it was no dream.

'There will have been mostly plenty that you did not tell her,' Black William said.

'I *could* not tell her the half of it,' Kirstie said. 'And there were things I kept minding on, William, the byous strange look on the face of my good-sister when she lay dying and the

Ministers round her like hoodies. And oh worse, the blood, the blood on the Book, and Andrew fallen over it! Ach William, me knowing it would come, kenning deep in me, and yet the piteous fell thing and no undoing — '

'Hush,' he said, 'hush. You did *not* know, Kirstie. You had no hand in it. Yon thing was all lies!' He spoke fiercely to her, one hand gripping hers. It was not the first time this thing had come up, and mostly at the fall of night and after happiness in the evening. 'What was it you did tell Catherine?' he asked.

She gasped and recovered, glad of the soreness in her gripped hand. 'I told her,' she said, 'about yon time at Duncrub, when I wouldna dance with you.'

'Aye,' he said, 'I mind. You were as cross as a sack of weasels, Kirstie Haldane. And myself little more than a lad. And I vowed vengeance on you.' She moved a thought nearer to him, turning her face on to his shoulder. 'But when the time came to take it, I wasna wanting to. Was that no' a strange thing, Kirstie?' Suddenly he slipped his arm over, holding her to him. 'Unless it is vengeance I am taking now. Kirstie, tell me, is't?' But she only laughed, low, stuffing her laughing mouth into the moving muscles of his shoulder.

And how would two folk, deep in a hard sweet trembling, an overflowing of tenderness, listen to steps outwith the house, on the edge of night? A stone thrown tentatively at shutters? They were not thinking beyond the bed.

It was otherwise in the long attic, the bothy room at the top of the house, where the boy cousins slept, on feather mattresses surely, but under a low roof that caught the sun, not plastered over the sarking, scarcely furnished at all. They had been arguing: some since supper, the rest since the dance. It went on through their slow undressing, politics mostly. Young Captain John laying down the law, saying that everything depended on sea power, speaking of dynastic marriages and exchanges of territory which would take place. The necessity of keeping down the Papists, a general Protestant Alliance. Yet Great Britain must look beyond mere religious differences.

The ultimate significance was with the balance of trade, and, as he saw it, the Navy was the main prop of this balance. All hung on the convoy system and this in turn meant punctuality, common sense, and greater powers to the Naval authorities. He had been thwarted himself, times, by lack of necessary powers. He and Alec Duncan and young James talked wisely about treaties and exports, and the need of an Empire with sufficient well-doing colonists to buy manufacturers' goods from home, and supply raw materials for use and luxury. Yet it was necessary that such colonists should be loyal and obedient and keep to trade within the closed system of the Empire. The American colonists, said Captain John, were trafficking for sugar, rum and molasses with the French West Indies, against all the interests of the mother country. They did not seem to care for what was happening in Europe!

George Cockburn was showing his Venetian lace cravat to his cousin David of Aberuthven, who let on that he took it as a matter of course, but was secretly impressed at the costliness of the thing. If Ochtertyre had been there, he would most like have made some cutting remark, for he knew full more about lace than any of the rest of them; he had seen it at its most luxurious during the time his father had been out of his estates and all of them in Paris. But Ochtertyre was not in the bothy room. He was sharing with Robert Haldane, in the mid-room where the estate documents and the medicines for horses, kye and sheep were mostly kept. They were both asleep, though Mungo, in his own room next to theirs, was sitting up in bed, the curtains half drawn, a woollen night-cap on his head, a glass of brandy in the one hand and a book of pleasantly controversial sermons in the other. He had an ink-well and a quill pen beside him, in the thought that he might be needing them to write down some note about agriculture in the book's margin. It was strange the way these came to him during the reading of theology. Yet indeed they were both of them equally profound subjects when taken with all their implications. Aye, aye, Scotland would rise again like a muckle turnip from the seed.

The pebbles against the shutter gave a wee dunt on Adam's mind; he had the sharp sense at the back of his eye of the furrow cut in the deck by a bullet, a matter of inches from his foot, and he had not thought twice on't until the night after and then it had seemed like something meant for himself, as this tap on the shutter seemed meant. He looked round cautiously and fastened his garters again. Young Captain John was saying that it was mere folly to attempt the conquest of Canada. 'There could never be any great trade that way,' he said, 'and indeed the French have had little out of it beyond a few furs.'

'Might we not develop a Glasgow trade by the northern route?' Alec Duncan suggested.

'Scarcely,' said Captain John, 'and the American colonists have such an overwhelming conceit of themselves that they might become troublesome if Canada were to be added to them, most of all if it was by their own doing. When I was in Boston last year they were neither to hold nor to bind because a certain Massachusetts merchant of the name of Pepperrall had been more fortunate than he deserved as commander of their expedition on Louisburg.'

Through the talk about the Americans, the tap came on the window again. This time Adam found the eye of his cousin James and there was no word spoken, but the two of them slipped away down the stairs, leaving Captain John to emphasize the unimportance of Canada as against India, and the absolute necessity of making sure of the Low Countries. Their stocking feet made little noise and the door bolt slipped back in an oiled and efficient manner, and the young man in the cloak took off his hat to them and asked, in a low, easy voice, with an Edinburgh accent, for Murray of Ochtertyre, who, he understood, was presently at Gleneagles. He himself had missed his way. His name was Davidson, Mr. Hugh Davidson, no, he would not dream of putting them to inconvenience — 'I will find Ochtertyre,' Adam said decidedly.

Young James and the stranger exchanged elaborate politenesses, admitting nothing. Adam came back with Ochtertyre, a riding-coat over his night-shirt and a candle in his hand. 'Bob Strange!' he said, 'what the devil are you doing here?'

'It appears,' said Adam as near giggling as his sister might have been, 'that this gentleman prefers to call himself Davidson, or maybe we misheard one or the other of you! And I jalouse that it would be best to say nothing of the matter to cousin George!'

'Foolery the like of yon,' said Ochtertyre heavily to the lads, 'is nearhand enough to justify George! I thought we were finished with this skulking and running!'

'Indeed I would be more than happy to finish with it,' said the young man, 'and all would be well and I in the embraces of my Isabella, but for some Whig busybody that is needing to make a new proclamation! And indeed, my dear companion in arms — for I take it I may speak with tolerable freedom — I was at Ochtertyre well before this, but discovered that you were from home, and as things look, it would be best for me not to be showing my face for a week or two.'

'A fine Whig house you have chosen to hide yourself in!' observed Ochtertyre.

'Aye,' said the young man, 'I have observed that such houses are the free-est of suspicion. No very profound observation, I fear,' he added, and bowed to the other two.

'You will at least present us to your friend by his right name,' said James Haldane, 'if we are to take the responsibility of sheltering him.' And he looked grave enough, and frowned, for he took the thing more seriously than did his cousin Adam.

'Well then,' said Ochtertyre, 'let me present Mr. Robert Strange: Mr. Haldane: Mr. Duncan. He is a flibberty-gibbet of an artist, and went on the unfortunate side in the late troubles because a romantic young lady bade him do it and because he was thinking to design the Prince's bank notes and so have his name all over Scotland!'

'And indeed there would have been plenty of them printed, and going about the country bringing their troubles with them, but for one thing and another.' He laughed a little, turning to the lads, 'The coppersmith who was making the plates for my rolling press would not work on the Sabbath and besides there were other matters that went wrong. So the poor wee things had not set out on their travels by the time we were defeated.'

'Come ben,' said Ochtertyre abruptly, 'if I know you, Bob, you will not have had a decent meal under your coat for the last month.'

'True enough,' said Mr. Strange and stepped lightly over the threshold.

'Were we wise?' James Haldane asked his cousin, at the turn of the stairs.

'I doubt we were nothing of the kind,' said Adam, 'but what else was to be done?'

'The rebellion is over,' said James. 'How could one gentleman pursue another because of it?'

'George could,' said Adam, 'and indeed there will be a kind of awkwardness over this. Nothing should be said before our elders.'

'William Macintosh would be safe enough.'

'Maybe,' said Adam, 'but he was not in it himself. He has principles — for a Highlander. Indeed he might take the thing harder than some of us.'

'There would have been plenty of his kin killed in the troubles,' young James said, flicking a soot off the wick of his candle. 'But we know full little of him in the family. Were my uncles right in allowing Aunt Kirstie to marry him?'

'Are you so sure she asked leave at them, James?' said Adam.

'Indeed I am not sure at all, and the man has a certain presence and I doubt that women and servants will be taken with him. I cannot help asking myself, was it that way Aunt Kirstie married him? And would not he himself be thinking more of marrying into a good Lowland family? For Kirstie herself is past the age a man could be wanting her for herself alone,' James added, feeling very much of an adult.

'There are those that like their venison well hung,' Adam observed, 'and he has an estate, although he was off on his travels so many years.'

'Aye, if you can call anything by Inverness an estate! His

father was out of it long enough and it cannot be over secure.
It is a canny thing for a Highlander to marry among ourselves
and we will need to watch him.'

'What would make you sure of him, cousin James?' Adam
asked; he did not like to be suspecting folk, though he knew it
might be needful.

'If,' said James at last and slow. 'If he had a true sense of
religion, cousin Adam; if I could think he was serious or had
given thought to the grave questions. We are all over-apt to lay
them aside — I am doing so myself at every turn and to my
shame. Sabbaths when I have thought more on a new coat —
och, Adam, it is a most terrible thing to see the easy root sin has
in oneself, and forby that, an Episcopalian Highlander, who
has had no discipline, no year by year ruling of his life and
searching out of sins, no family worship and close examination,
but every kind of independence and wildness and temptation!
Have you ever thought, Adam, what would the Americans be
like, not in the outward seeming but spiritually?'

'Were not the first colonies founded by men who needed to
flee from the Romish and Anglican Churches?'

'Aye, but since then, Adam, there has been every kind of
schismatist and heretic, all the arrogant who have dared to set
themselves up as spiritual judges, Quakers with friends at Court,
the like of William Penn! Transported felons and idle rogues
that would not work decently for wages, so must needs indenture themselves and go over, and set themselves up in five years
or ten with land they had done nothing to deserve! If you consider it yon way, Adam —'

'Aye,' said Adam gravely, 'it is a wonder Uncle William was
not a rebel two years back after living over yonder half his life!'

'It will have been a different kind of rebellion,' James
Haldane said, worrying it out, 'for the American colonists will
be against all lawful authority (for the which reason I doubt
they will never rebel themselves, for how would they take a
leader?) They will acknowledge no ways but their own:
whereas our own Stuart rebellion had as its aim and goal to
put us all under yet more authority, and that authority an old

and evil one that we had to struggle two centuries to put off. Is that no' right, Adam?'

'That will be so,' Adam assented, 'though I doubt our rebels will not all have looked at it in that same light.'

'There are folks,' James Haldane said, 'who will go into a serious thing, the like of a rebellion or revolution, for the pure pleasure of it, and the thought of a change, and that even in our own family!'

'I would sooner that,' said Adam, 'than to be over-calculating of the profit or loss to oneself.'

'Och yes, *that*,' said James, 'one's own profit shouldna enter into it one way or the other. And one could be headed or hangit at the end, as our cousin Montrose was. That is neither here nor there. It is the principles that count.'

'Well,' said Adam, yawning, 'if we are not up to the bothy in a minute or so, cousin James, they will be asking what did we have for our dinner that we needed to be out so long, and that with our uncles' noble and modern Temple of Cloacina to inspire us! But we will watch our other uncle William Macintosh of Borlum, and see that he is not a Highland tod in the douce Haldane hen-roost, and he away with an old hen maybe, but one that is yet laying!'

CHAPTER 11

KIRSTIE was talking in her sleep, in a hard, harsh whisper, and
the things she was saying were not canny things at all and they
hurt her to say, for she had a wee edge of foam on her lips and
there was a tightening and twisting round her shut eyes, and
William could not bear it at all. He shook and spoke to her
until she woke, with a terrible eery look on her, as though her
inward sight and hearing were yet on some frightsome and
filthy thing which had been driven away only for a time. She
turned quick and held on to William and shook as though she
were in a cold fever; he had not seen her this way since Elizabeth was born. It could be, he thought, with going back to the
Haldane house, out of his own direct protection, back to the
place that did not know, that could not love as he did. 'They
were at me,' said Kirstie suddenly. 'They havena forgotten;
they tell't me so. William, they want me back in the coven!'

He could not bear it, the witch-word, the coven, the word
that pulled at her, whether there had ever been such a thing or
not! The thick, slippery way of her saying it made him feel
sick. Thon time she had been alone, out of his protection, at the
mercy of folk whom he could never now reach and punish. Nor
even forgive. Yet he must meet this nightmare of his wife's
with kindness and sense. 'Well,' he said, and he happed her up
warm in his arms and sudden he was thinking of her, not as his
wife and counsellor, but as his bairn, 'they just canna have you,
Kirstie, not ever any more, for you belong to me now and for all
eternity.'

'Do I?' she said. 'Do I truly? Do you promise me, William?'

'I promised you before God,' he said, 'and you promised me.
You canna go back on your promise, Kirstie.'

'I promised *them*,' she said, 'on the blood. Oh William, it
was blood over all my dream and a terrible sick feel in the back
of my head and it creeping and staining me!'

'Whisht!' he said, and held her close happed and rocked her a

162

little. 'Dinna give way to yon, even in your sleep, my Kirstie. For you are my own right down. Are you no'?'

'Aye,' she said, and breathed deep: 'none other's. But I was so near lost, William, so near! I had ae foot in hell.'

'I mind,' said William, 'you had the look when I came to the house.'

'You took me out of it,' said Kirstie, 'but if you had kennt the deep I was in the black muck, would you have done it, William my husband?'

'I could see you were gey far through, Kirstie,' he said softly, 'and there were plenty to tell me.'

'You didna ken right,' she said. 'Ach, William, will I tell you the now?'

He hesitated. He hated hearing her speak of any of this. It made him feel the very same sick denial of belief that he had felt yon day in the forest when he had come on the half-burnt bodies nailed on to the pines, and the cold ashes all round them, and Tehoragwanegen, his brother-in-law, had smiled in a veiled way and admitted the thing. And the singing of the forest birds had dwindled into a cold itch and tickle in his brain. He had gone away and vomited where the fighting men could not see him. For long afterwards he could not smell wood ash without the thing coming back on him. It was the same now. He wanted to hold it off. Yet she must speak or she would turn it over and over in her mind until it became solid and danger-ous, a malignant growth. If she had been a Catholic, he thought suddenly, and could have confessed it — But he could not bear to think of any man but himself knowing this thing, anyone who loved her less than he did. He leant over and took another candle out of the box and lit it; she wouldna like if the old candle were to burn down or to start to flicker in its last minutes. 'Poor Kirstie,' he said. 'Tell me what you've a mind to and keep looking at me, my dearie, for I'll no' let you go. Not even if it were true. Which it is not.'

She said: 'I told you, William, it was my good-sister, it was Christian Shaw of Bargarran, that brought me to the knowledge of *them* and their doings. Although I would never have known what kind of a thing she was speaking of if it hadna been for the hate and sin in my own heart. And the things I minded that Phemie Reid, my nurse, had frighted me with, long years back: in this same house, William, in this couthy house! And they tell't me what to do, William, and we made the image of wax with the clippings of Andrew's hair in't, and we did what we shouldna do, and he grew ill, and the iller he grew, the worse the passions he would get into and the worse things he would be saying to me, and the more I could feel a kind of justification, and the day came when the heart's blood burst forth of him and over the Book, and he couldna speak, but only made a crawling with his hands and a bubbling with his throat, and syne he died and it was I that killed him!'

'That is a lie,' said Black William, as evenly as he could. He thought he could hear someone speaking beyond by the stair. It must be late, past midnight. The dawn would come before the second candle was burnt down, the slow summer dawn of Scotland.

'Because I killed him,' Kirstie said, 'they were able to sign me to them. On the blood. And syne the appearances began, as they said I should see. I would be sitting alone and a thing would flitter in through a shut window and out through a shut door. And times it would be a thing of lightness, yet no' a right, sunny brightness, but a hot dancing gleid out of hell! And times it would be like a bairn, but aye hell-marked in body or soul. Or with a terrible flickering look of my own sick bairns when they were near to their ends. That was the worst. And times they would be grey kind of wisps and tags with something of corruption about them, like a gnawed sheep on a briar, like the body of a collier licked by a racing mine flame. Oh William, you canna think the nasty they were!'

She sobbed suddenly, burrowing her eyes and face into his neck, so that she did not see his own face stiffening against her visions that were over near to his own. He thought, if one could be shut of the images of corruption for ever, seeing only life — and the words of the burial service came strongly into his mind, as he had heard them at his father's funeral, terrible yet comforting. When this corruption shall put on uncorruptibility. But the grave is victorious over the mourners; it is only those that die that have won the battle. And dizzily he wished that he and his wife were dead together and the battle won for all eternity, and if his hand now were to tighten quick on her throat, over the poor, living, frightened pulse— But then, who would see to thinning the turnips, who build the new barn, who win the Borlum crops in yon other battle, the battle for Scotland and a decent life for all?

'Keep your hand so,' murmured Kirstie, 'over my neck. Your hand is so kind, William, mon ami doux, my sweet friend and comrade.'

One long plait slipped over, pale gold in the candle light, no white showing at all. There was never an Indian yet with soft hair. But the down of the eagle's feather could be gey soft, or the rabbit's foot, or the beaver fur edging the cloak across the brown breast.

Kirstie said: 'The appearances began to come even when there were folk about. I had all the difficulty in the world not to remark on them, whiles, and to keep my eyes from following them about the room, or to keep from starting when one of them would be peeking across my shoulder or whispering the tail of a rhyme into my ear. For they would mostly speak in rhyme and it would seem silly and harmless enough, and for a moment it seemed like company and you would be glad of it — for I was mostly alone in the bit house; I had sent the lassie back home and was doing the work of it myself. But when you took the sense of what had been whispered, there would be somewhere a nasty twist to it, and you would mind on it over well. Whiles it would go to the tune of some wee song or oftener to a psalm tune, and when it did, there, sure as death would come the same tune to the next Sabbath morning's psalm!'

'How at all could you go to the Church, Kirstie, with yon things in your mind?' he asked.

'What would folk have said,' Kirstie answered, 'and I the widow of a Minister? Yet it hurt me wild to be going and I knew fine I shouldna go, and it was the worst kind of blasphemy.

But the time was coming on towards Communion, and that, no, I couldna face it! And, getting myself ready on the Sabbath morning and my black hood and gloves and my white stockings laid out, I hoped that the Lord would strike me soon and sudden. And times, William, I am asking myself, would He do that yet?'

'He could,' said William, 'but in His mercy He has accepted us with all our sins, aye all and worse than your own, for the sake of His Son.'

Kirstie said: 'They would come at night, William, and I would find myself going with them, out beyond the coal bings and up on to the moor. We would strip and dance and the appearances would dance with us and we would be caught in hot gusts and whirled about and up and the feel of a pressing and sweating dance partner against one's belly or a merry hell's riding beast capering between one's thighs. Most of us were widows or other women well on in life, and with our experiences, but there was one young lassie, and some nights she would be terrible frighted and screech, but the next she was bolder than the lot of us and more forward in all kinds of wickedness. For some of what we did was wee kinds of nastiness and harmed nobody but ourselves and that mostly because we were meaning it to. But other times we meant purposely to do wrong, to revenge ourselves on the world or on some one person. Yet times I had a feeling that we were near to understanding in the heart of things that could have been turned to good, yet not good of a kind that would be recognized by the respectable and the members of the congregation. Least of all, maybe, by the men. That could be, could it no', William?'

'Aye,' he said, 'it could.' For he was thinking of rain makers and corn growers and healers, and interpreters of dreams and those that could find the wrongdoer and those that had dealings with the spirits. They were mostly not right men, but some way womanish, and the women not at all the same as the squaws that carried burdens on their backs or sat in a greasy silence beyond the fires.

'But, whatever we might have done, it was evil that we did or tried to do,' Kirstie said. 'And the day came when they told me it was time I should see Himself, the Horny, and he would have his dealings with me. And when that was over there would surely be no more Church membership, since I would be a full member of another body. And I grat wild in my bed, for the thing tore at me, and I was minded to flee away from the west, to sell all the bit things I had, yet where could it be? For I was wild angered yet with my brother Mungo and I would never come here to Gleneagles, yet for all that I couldna thrust myself and the evil that clung to me into Bearcrofts and the life of my brother Pate. And half, too, I was ettling to stay and see the Horny, Nick himself. One or other of the women would half whisper me the beginnings of a thing, till I could almost imagine this or that orra feel or smell of what I was to meet with. Yet maybe it was all lies. Was it all lies, William?'

'Nothing at all but a parcel of women's lies,' said William firmly. He had to believe that, he had to make her believe it!

'So I sat alone in the kitchen, and syne out of the wall came a wee mouse and another after it, and they keeking at me with their sharp een. And I was too feared to move hand or foot, for I thought maybe they were spying on me or maybe they were no right mice ava, but wee devilkins come to live in my house and beguile me and make me say what could betray me to my neighbours. And I thought I must go to my bed and get the blanket between me and the night, but when I was stripped to my shift, there out of the tail of my eye I could see an appearance twisting and winding itself in and out of the bed curtains and I daredna go to my bed and I daredna lift my hand to throw another coal on to the fire and I stared and I listened and it seemed to me I could hear steps outwith the house, heavy and purposed. And it came to me that here at last was the Horny, and I felt as though my body were turning to water under me.

'There came a soft chap on the door and I wanted wild to pray, but no word of it would come. If I could have reached to the shelf and the Book that was on it, I might have kept yon door from opening, but I couldna move, and it came to me that in a short minute I would be saying Yes to my own shame and destruction, to the fire of my own damnation and my eternal separation from all those I had loved. Yet I saw that in a cold way and accepted it, between the first chap and the second. It was no use me thinking the oaken bar would keep out such a One; it might only anger him and then — ach, then he could have slid through in any kind of foul, narrow, slimy shape and I just couldna have borne yon. I went in my bare feet to the door, gey quiet, and I pulled back the bar and went to my place at the hearth side again, and I said Come ben. William, do you forgive me for being yon kind of a coward?'

'Aye,' he said, holding fast against her trembling. 'You are forgiven, my lassie.' He too had known the bitterness of having surrendered, of knowing that something had broken in himself.

'There was little enough light in the kitchen,' she said. 'The cruisie on the wall was almost burnt down, and only a hot glow on the coals, never a bonny flicker of light. I hoped wild that when yon door opened he would show himself man-shaped and not in any of the terrible shapes they told me he might choose. And I forced myself to keep my eyes on the door. I said to myself, Kirstie Haldane, you will at least look this one in the face. And the bar hung loose and the latch made a wee noise of lifting and there was a shape in the dark of the doorway and I neither cried nor moved, only I felt the appearances crowding thick behind me as though they knew there was a welcome coming.

'The shape came walking into the room and it was at least man-shaped and the clothes it wore no very special clothes. It came slowly over to the fire and it didna speak and I didna speak and it sat down opposite me with the width of the hearth between us, and I, a Minister's widow, in my shift only, and my hair over my shoulders. And I thought for a moment on my two dead bairns, of the bonny sons that would have kept me from this, and in my heart I said goodbye to them and to my dead mother and to my dead sister Ann and to my living brother Pate, and I waited for the Horny to open his mouth and to bid me serve him for all eternity, and to have his dealings with me that would bind me to hell, and for myself to say Yes to it all. And I kept my eyes on the Horny, considering the shape he had, for I wanted to keep my own thoughts to the last, before I gave way to a master's!'

Black William shivered and pulled the blanket up round both of them; there are things a man must hate to mind on; even a hunted deer may look on you at the last with eyes that stay too long in your memory. 'Go on,' he said.

Kirstie whispered again: 'And it seemed as though we must have sat there for a matter of minutes, and syne I saw the one opposite me was about to speak. He said: "*You are Mistress Kirstie Shaw?*" And I bent my head in assent and I tried to place the kind of voice that he was wearing for this, since it was none of an Ayrshire voice, and sudden I thought, aye, it is true after all what is said and there is a connection between the Highlands and hell! And syne that one said: "*I have come far to find you.*" And again I assented. And after that he said nothing and I began to feel a wild kind of impatience, for if tonight were to be the night of my damnation, let it come quick, and sudden I cried: "*You have found me now and what are you asking of me?*" And I took three steps across the hearth and I stood there in my short shift, expecting anything, anything at all — wanting it — asking it — ach, William, William!'

'My lassie,' he said, 'my poor mazed lassie, I could see fine that you were looking for evil and hurt from me, though I hadna so clear a notion of why as I have this night, and I knew there could be only one cure for that, so I gave you good. Do you mind yet what I said?'

'Aye,' she said. 'I will mind through all eternity. That one from whom I expected the utmost evil, on whom I could almost smell the Pit-reek, he looked at me and said: "*I am asking you to be my wife in the name of God.*" Could you have said yon, my heart, if you had known how deep in I was?'

'All the more I would have said it,' he answered, 'and that is the plain truth and none of a Highlander's compliments. For I have aye liked danger and I was seeking it that night. And maybe yon was the most risky thing I have ever done.'

'Do you mind,' she said, 'that I seized on your head and felt about it? I am telling you now — and oh the free and light I am feeling, my own true love! — it was looking for wee horns I was!'

He said: 'I didna know that, Kirstie. I only knew you were leaning across me in yon thin shift with no mind of what I could be seeing and feeling. And I but newly on land after a ten weeks' voyage, and long enough since I had even spoken with a woman.'

'Aye,' she said, 'and a lone house and the night far spent. And a woman who was under no protection. Why did you no', William?'

'I had offered the other thing,' he said, 'and, gif you were taking it, I wouldna be the bird to file my own nest. Forby that if I had, you could have looked again the way you had looked at the beginning and I could not have borne it at all. And maybe, lassie, you were like poor Scotland herself, and one more betrayal would have spoilt you clean. But before I had it well sorted out in my body or mind, you cried out: "*If you are not he, who are you?*" And I said: "*I am the one you found on the coal-road up from Gleneagles.*" And syne I said: "*Do you mind on my name?*"'

'What at all did I answer you, William, for all I can think on now was the swirling in my mind like milk in a churn and the butter near to its coming?'

'You said: "*It was a red tartan. It was the Macintosh colour, you were from Borlum on Speyside, your father had a price on his head. But it was grey hose I gave you and my mother died within three months after.*" And I said: "*I do not know if I have either house or land or money, and my father is in prison, but I ask you again if you will be my wife.*"'

Kirstie whispered back to him, her head by his on the pillow: 'I said: "*In the name of God I will so.*" And I took up my woollen petticoat and tied it round me quick, and my bodice and apron, and I said: "*Put you an armful of coals on the fire and we will have on the kettle and make us a cup tea, for I have no spirits in the house.*" And all at once I was caught in a terrible queer burst of laughing, and all because I got thinking on the other kind of spirits, and then — maybe, you'll mind of it, William, you did a wild Popish thing, you made the sign of the cross on me.'

'It got you quiet,' William said, 'the way we could have our cup tea.'

'I had what I thought would do me a month in the press,' Kirstie said, 'and we drank it almost all, between midnight and morning, and we ate bannocks with salt butter and cheese and we talked and we better talked, and by daylight I knew somewhat of the man that was to be my husband.'

'We made up our minds then that, if we had any money at all the day we were married, we would send five pounds to James Stewart, since a Minister's salary was no better in the colonies than in Scotland. And indeed we owed him much.'

'Salvation itself,' said Kirstie. She was not trembling any more now, nor gripping tight on to Black William. In the candle light her eyes were clear of tears. She kissed him lightly and ran a hand down one of her own plaits, unravelling it to plait it smooth again. There was an edge of light under the shutters of the Gleneagles window.

'Will I unbar?' he asked.

'Please to unbar, a charaidh,' she answered gently, able now for him to leave her side, watching him move to the window and reach up. Outside the calm beginnings of the dawn strengthened and widened, though it would be long yet before sun-up. As a young lassie, she had sometimes run up the Glen with her sisters, tearing across pastures and through plantations until they burst full into the golden blink of the sun at last, seen clear of the tops of the hills. But all the time the broad strath had been sunbathed and shadowless. It had only been Gleneagles that had cleft its shadow into the hills at dawn, just as at evening it took the last of the sunset.

CHAPTER III

BLACK WILLIAM turned back from the window and snuffed out the candles. He was tired now. He stretched himself out in the warm bed, his feet slipping down the good linen, his head tucked into the soft of his Kirstie's arm, his mouth nuzzling into her breasts. He shut his eyes, yet could not stop a queer, painful swinging of images across them. By and bye he opened them again. It was lighter already and Kirstie was asleep, breathing softly, at peace. She could tell him everything and set herself free, for the time anyway. If he could only get telling her! It was not fair that she could free herself from her thing, but he not from his. For a moment he wanted wild to tell her, to wake her and make her listen. But if he did — Kirstie Haldane might forgive, but she would surely take herself out of his bed and out of his protection. There was the bit, her thing was not real, but something only in her mind and maybe losing its force there, and, even if she had in truth been a witch in a coven of witches, it was all over and wiped out, as who should know better than himself. Yet his own thing was real, in time and place and free will, and she slept in innocence, half smiling, dulce ridentem dulce loquentem, Curstan his lassie.

He could not help but kiss her, lightly at first, but soon strongly, his lips on hers. She opened her eyes. 'I didna mean to wake you, Kirstie,' he said.

She looked at him. 'You did, so,' she said, then: 'What is it, William? Can I help you?'

'Na, na,' he said, and dropped his head again on to her arm.

She came clear awake, mothering him. 'Tell Kirstie,' she said. 'What is't? Is it the politics? Is it my brothers? William, you have been so terrible good to me, better than ever I thought a man could be. Let me be good to you.'

'Listen, Kirstie,' he said, 'I'm no' good and you shouldna think it. I — I have done the most wicked things. I did them all the years before I knew my Kirstie.'

172

'How was it, then,' she said, 'that the very first thing you did with me before ever you knew me, was pure goodness?'

After a moment he said, 'It could have been otherwise. It near was. I could have been the very De'il you were looking for. Listen, Kirstie, and judge me.'

'I willna judge you,' she said. 'How could I, and the both of us sinners, but myself surely the worst?'

She felt his knee digging painfully against her own; he did not know he was hurting her. He said: 'When I came back from the Americas, I was terrible unhappy. Everything I had been doing there seemed to have gone wrong on me. My father was in prison. I had heard nothing of my sisters. One of my brothers was drowned and nought to hear but ill of the other. I didna know what had come to Borlum, nor whether I would ever see the house again. I hadna more money than would keep me for a month. Yet in a way all that seemed small enough. And all the days of my life, as I looked back on them, and I in Scotland again, small and full of small doings that had left no good behind them, a scatter of wasted years and myself past my mid age. I had been in danger often enough, but that hadna got me what I needed. I wanted — ach, I wanted some muckle great, splendid thing that would catch me up and dash me down and maybe kill me, yet I would ask no better. I wanted to fight all the kings of the sea for the sake of a hopeless love. Ah, Kirstie, I had the death wish on me. James Stewart had spoken to me of Mistress Shaw and I had minded on the lassie of the coal-road, the lassie of Duncrub, and I had thought, here was my hopeless love. But when I came to Ayrshire and began to make my inquiries, it appeared first that you were a widow and syne that there was something queer suspicioned about your husband's death and about yourself. Aye, Kirstie, I heard you spoken of as a witch. We are past the days of the burnings now, but short of that, I doubt your neighbours would have had little mercy, Kirstie. Even the wives of the colliers that you had befriended, my dear. Or so the men said at the inn yon evening. There was wild talk of window breaking and ducking. I thought, poor lassie, this is how folk will be speaking of a lone woman that is maybe dowie and not wanting to be out among her neighbours, but what at all gars the Haldanes let this come to their kinswoman? And I thought it was time I repaid the Haldane money.'

'It was Erskine money, my heart,' Kirstie said, and stroked his cheek. 'But go you on with the story.'

'I let on that I was away to my bed, but instead I went out into the black night, and the thought on me strong of Kirstie at the edge of the young oaks in the plantation behind Gleneagles, and the thing which had separated us and which hung over us yet. Kirstie, I wished in the night that you were not a widow, but married yet on yon man, for then surely I could have carried you off; there could have been killing and rending. I thought of the black dress on the Kirstie lass at Gleneagles, yon time I was foolish enough to conspire with Kyllachy after the Glenshiel affair. It was as though there had been a doom all along and the same doom now maybe, and myself facing it at last.

'There was a moon near to full yon night and the clouds going over her, white at her sides, but black when she swung behind them. For a time, Kirstie, I had a kind of scare on me, coming from no adversary I could see or plan against, but from inside myself. I have had the same scare, alone in the backwoods of Maine or Virginia, and they at their bonniest. I began to sing to check it. I mind I started on the lumber-men's songs that were meant to check just this thing, but I came soon to Indian songs and in a while after to the great music, for it was no night for the little music — aye, even if there might be a lassie at the end of it! I sang the Lament, Kirstie, I needed to, whatever luck it might be bringing. And syne I fell silent, for I was near the house.

'I knocked, Kirstie, and as I knocked I thought I was knocking to my doom; I thought we will die together some way, she and I, and the thing will be fulfilled. There was a feel of danger in the air and my pistols and dirk no use against it. Yet the queer it was, Kirstie, I never had a serious thought of yon witchcraft talk; it had seemed to me a kind of snare laid against a lone and innocent woman by her enemies, who were many, and also mine. I thought right enough, you could have been foolish, you could have hated your husband the way I knew you must from all James Stewart had said, for I had got him to repeat every word of it, aye, in a Boston coffee-house. But I never thought you were a witch, my dearest, and I dinna think it now. Though I am sure you would be the best of story-tellers!

'Yet maybe what I felt at yon door came out of your mind into my own. For there was a moment I could not raise my hand to knock, and syne, after the second knock, came a wee shuffling from within and the eerie soft sound of the bar drawn, whether to let me in or keep me out, I did not rightly know. The moon was behind clouds now and I waited, a dreich cold wait it seemed, though it couldna have been long. And love was at me on the lassie of the coal-road, and a fell knowledge of the years that had passed and the things that had passed in the years, and the wee low housie of my doom. Kirstie,' he said suddenly, half hiding his head in the pillow, 'is this a' Highland blethers?'

'No,' she said, 'but it is like an old pipe-tune and I have not the right knowledge to follow it.'

He went on: 'I came ben to the fireside, and there was a woman in a white shift with her arms and legs bare, and I didna know what at all to make of it, and it was no very welcoming place, and, as she didna speak, I sat me down on the stool at the far side of the hearth, where I could see her. And first I thought could this be a light woman, for how else could she bid me come ben and she in her shift? Whilst I was standing I couldna see her face, but now we were on a level, and I could see into her eyes and they were no' the eyes of a wanton but the eyes of my lassie in bitter trouble. And I could see that her fingers were digging into her palms and her toes into the rush mat at the hearth. And I spoke and still she said nothing and I spoke again and pity was at me so strong that it burned through the feel of doom and it was laid on me that I must, some way, and with all my power, get her clean out of this, into my own hand and God's. For, as the doom broke, I thought sudden of God and His Son and of redemption, either my own or hers, I couldna tell which. And I spoke as you know. But, Kirstie, there seems to be a moment in my mind, a water-shed between two deep glens, and if the runnel in the bog had flowed a different way, I might have killed you and myself.'

'That was your dream,' said Kirstie, 'and it is the same dream that is in half of the stories and the pipe-tunes, and there is why I dinna care too much to hear them nor to let Elizabeth hear them when she is older. It could have been the same dream was on some of the men of Moidart.'

'It was that dream was on the sons of Usna and on plenty of my own clan far back.'

'It is not Scotland's dream,' said Kirstie, 'and I doubt it isna a Christian dream at all. It comes out of the black night at the back of us before we knew of the blessed light. But, William, my dear black Highlander, is this the bad that you said was in you? For it doesna seem bad to me, only a darkness come over you, like the clouds over yon moon.'

William said: 'There was worse to it. Ach, Kirstie, I canna tell you right! But I was all of seventeen years in America, or in France and Spain, and a man will do the most terrible wicked things when he has neither home nor kin to mind him on good and orderly doings. And the most of the folk I was with the same as myself and some of them only wanting to be revenged against whatever Government there might be.'

'I would have liked fine to be with you in America,' she said, sleepily.

'Aye,' he said, 'you could have made it all away different. If you had been there the town we founded might have come to some good. But it needed anyway one besides myself. A woman with courage and sense. I told you, Kirstie, I kept finding indentured men of my own name and clan, men that were transported after the '15, as they are being transported now, God help them! And some had decent and kindly masters and then all could be well enough and at the end of their term they would get land and settle down or move out to some further place; but when they had bad masters, it was nothing but slavery. And you canna stand by and see your own folk half starved and beaten — and the Jacobite prisoners, the same as the Irish, had a bad reputation for working, so they would be cheap cattle and sold to the small men, who are aye the worst masters. So I got things fixed the way that any rebel of the Clan Chattan could come to a room I had in Winchester on the Shenandoah, he or his friends, and they would be safe there and could make their way west from one guide to the other and so to the edge of the frontier and the town we called New Speyside. And indeed it wasna very honest, but mostly they had served the half of their terms at least.

'I am thinking now that if I had got them at the beginning before their hearts were broken, we could have done better. I could make them face danger well enough, I could lead them. Indeed, I led them twice during Indian raids; I kept them steady under the howling and hooting, the creeping up and the unforeseen arrow; there was a thing where they trusted me, in the old way. And I could get them to cut timber or build a stockade or trap and shoot game. But when it came down to ploughing or sowing — Kirstie, I went to New York and Richmond to get us good seed corn, imported poultry, plough socs and harrows, seeds and roots of vegetables; and they ate my seed corn and my hens; they let the new iron socs rust and complained that they couldna manage with the wooden ones, or else they could only work with the foot-ploughs! They wouldna build their houses into an even street, straight with one another, and the gardens fenced against chickens and pigs, but everything was anyhow and no one taking a pride in it. If you had been there, Kirstie — But the few women that came were mostly no better than the men, a feckless lot of lassies that wouldna set to and work. Ach, there were a few good ones, men and women, but just no' enough. And one of the best of the men was an Argyllshire Campbell, Dugal Ban, he wasna a Jacobite at all, but transported for stealing one of the Duke's horses. He and his wife Chrissie, they put their gear on to a cart and went west to break themselves new land; they were sick of the quarrels and complaints and stupidity of the rest. Sad and sorry I was to see them go.

'But, Kirstie, I shouldna have failed. It was my fault and I can see it well. Yon wee town that started in such hopes, it should be there yet! Indeed for all I know it is there yet but under another name and with scarce more than a handful of my folk left, and the rest decent Moravian Germans, the kind that can settle and work. It seems to me now that I should have picked my men better, for the ones that were worst treated were mostly the worst workers. Yet I myself was no good example to them. Times I might work hard, driving myself and them, but other times I would leave one thing by another and all half done, leave them by the quickest way there is, and be drunk for a week at a time on cider brandy and rum and peach brandy from Virginia, drinking healths to the rightful king and singing melancholy songs and playing the pipes till we all wept on one another's necks! We were speaking the Gaelic all the time, and that maybe was not the wisest, for it minded us on what was past and couldna be had again. But if my Kirstie had been there — I doubt you havena given it a thought, Kirstie, but it is a most remarkable thing that I have not once been drunk, not more than a wee thing elevated, ever since we were man and wife. I have never once felt the need of it.'

She laughed gently and said: 'You could be drunk now and then, and neither the Minister nor myself thinking any the worse of you, so long as you didna make a habit of it. But sure, it wasna any badness in you that made things go ill with your town. What can you have done that was bad in any way comparable with my own badness, William?'

He said: 'Ach, so much I dinna ken where to begin! If I start with the breaking of a wee small Commandment, I have stolen bread, aye and eggs and the half of a pound of sausages, when I was hungry. Ah, Kirstie, dinna kiss me as though I were a bairnie! It hurt me wild to do it, I thought what at all would my father say. Forby I half knew I could have earned the money, but at work I didna like. I couldna thole the work at the docks and the over-long hours and the terrible nasty smell there would be from the illtanned hides and the wet tobacco.

But I stole more than that and from folk that trusted me, and you should be angry at me for it and indeed I am sorry! And was when I did the thing. But yet I did it.

'And now I will go on to a bigger sin. Kirstie, my dearie, dinna shut your een on your man! Are you hearing me, Kirstie? This — ach, this is a thing I am terrible shamed and sorry for, and I couldna anyways speak of it to your brothers! It was the time I was up logging in Maine, and the Government Surveyors came round to mark the trees they wanted for Navy masts with the broad arrow — twenty-four inches across or over, one foot from the ground. But we lumber-men were for ever shouting against this, saying it was an infringement of our rights as individuals, and, though I didna think so, I shouted too, for yon English Government men were no favourites of mine, though for another reason. There came a day when we chivvied one of the Surveyors out on to a log raft on the river, and, some way and half on purpose, it tipped him over and he was swept away and drowned, with none of us so much as stretching out a pole to him, but all laughing and pointing and carrying on as though it had been a rat drowning and no' a human soul. Ach, it is a wild nasty thing to be minding on, and never punished, Kirstie, and the guilt of it's on me yet. I am not counting any man I killed in the war, Kirstie, but yon was murder.'

'Aye,' she said, 'and I am thinking by the voice you have, speaking of it, that you have repented it and that bitterly. Yet it was more thoughtlessness. You hadna planned it any.'

'Maybe no,' he said. And syne the thought flitted on him of yon other murders the way it could do whiles at night, the like of Kirstie's appearances, ragged and filthy and unspeakable as hers. But real for all his wild longing to forget it. And not ever to be told! He tried to shove it back, covering it over with the other, which was bad enough. 'And after that the gaffer of my logging gang was fined one hundred and fifty pounds — and had to pay up the most of it — for cutting the King's wood. Nobody found out about the Surveyor, for all that. Maine was mostly against the English or any kind of Government interference. Then, later, after I had been on the Continent, I was in another game that was pure cheating.'

'Aye,' said Kirstie, 'you told me you were an agent for a while with a Scots shipping firm in Boston.'

'But I never told you right the kind of dealings we had.'

'Ach,' she said, half wishing he would stop and let her sleep, 'all trading will have a kind of smell of cheatery about it. You shouldna fash yourself over it, William. You werena in the kidnapping trade, surely?'

'Na, na,' he said, 'nor nearer than the edge of the Guinea slave trade. Yet what we were at was the brawest kind of cheating and no pretence of honest mercantilism, Kirstie. You will need to cast your mind back to how things were before the Act of Union. Until then Scotland was excluded by the English laws from trading with the English plantations or colonies. They had us cut off already from the Old Alliance, from France and the Continent. That was something easier to do, since they sat, as it were, in the gateway. In spite of the Union of Crowns, it was said: The Scots are to us as strangers and prohibited by law. But we were struggling out of bitter poverty and no way to get shut of it but by trade. We had the wits and the timber for the ships. We had our west coast ports and our sailors — amongst them the fishermen who had been put out of their right work by the competition from Holland. Not only that, but enough Scots had been driven into exile across the great waters by hunger or politics, to make another set of traders over in the American coast towns, aye and officials that would maybe wink an eye at a fellow Scot going a wee bit behind the laws. We traded with one another against England, and the same kind of enmity in Glasgow and in Boston, against the English firms that made the English laws through their own folk in Parliament. Nor were any means, fair or foul, ruled out in the kind of money war this was.

'Yet it was gey hard, and they always pressing on us and spoiling any schemes of our own, such as the Darien scheme, and it was mostly that, and the weariness of aye struggling against it and we in the worst position with no King of our own, that made

folk accept the Act of Union and all that went with it, hoping at
least we might be treated as citizens of one country over this
matter of trading. Yet, even with the Act passed, they tried to
check us and to keep their own monopolies and we played the
thing back against their Board of Trade, and there was plenty
of forging of documents and seals and such, and evading the
customs officials — and we Scots getting ourselves the worst of
bad names as traders, and over canny and pinching, selling our
honours for a bawbee. Aye, that will take long enough to live
down. But by and large the colonists, whether Scots or English
by origin, or for that matter Dutch or Irish, were against England and the interference by the Board of Trade, and the
attempts by the English to break down the Charters of the
Colonies, and they would combine with us Scots in these
evasions. And there was the game your Highlander was in,
Kirstie! I have lied with the greatest dexterity and calm, aye,
and muckle great lies, none of your wee ones over a matter of
guns at Borlum! — and that to John Peagrum himself, the
English Surveyor General of the Northern Customs and a nice
enough man at a dinner table, who was fool enough to take my
word as a gentleman. As though such things meant anything
when it comes to money! And I have forged documents,
Kirstie, with my own pen and my own skill of hand.'

'I had no idea you had so much cleverness in you,' said
Kirstie placidly, 'you will need to show me the way to forge a
document, William, for I have not a notion of the way it is
done.'

'Ach!' said William and gave her a wee pinch, 'I did not like
it at all, Kirstie, not after the first few times. Nor would you
have done. It got so that one could have no trust at all in anybody. I just canna do with yon sort of life, Kirstie!'

'What were you at after thon?' she asked. 'Was that when you
went lumbering?'

'Na, na,' he said, 'I was with the Indians.' And fell silent.

'You have never told me much of yon time,' she said. But he
did not answer. It was almost daylight now. Her own sins had
dropped clean off her, they were explained and forgiven away,

they had no more happened than a dream. In the white ease and coolness of heart that she was in, sleep came sliding easily between one breath and the next. If William too could know that none of this mattered now, none ava, if he too could be easy, float into sleep. But he was yet hard, knotted into himself. At last he said: 'Kirstie, you will not suppose that I never looked on a woman until I met with yourself.'

'I did not indeed suppose so!' she said, half waking, and with yon light feel yet to her body and mind, 'and it would have been a most unchancy and peculiar thing if you had not more than looked!'

'But a man can be terrible cruel to a woman,' he said.

'Do I not know it,' she answered, and then: 'Yet I canna see you cruel yon kind of way.'

'I promised,' he said, 'and I neither held to my promises nor ever meant to.'

'But did they even think you meant to?' she asked. 'Was it no' a Highland promise from beginning to end?'

'They could have thought,' he said. 'If one wants to believe, one will believe. And they were mostly foolish.'

'I have felt myself gey light and stripped of all sense and judgment, and you looking into my eyes,' she whispered, blinking at him.

'Maybe you have believed me over much,' he said sombrely.

'I dinna think so,' she said. 'I have thought on that between whiles, and have aye ended by thanking the Lord for the loan of you.'

'May it be so always!' he said, and held her close for a moment.

She asked then, and it was a thing she could have felt it hard enough to say if she had been right waking or even in her day clothes, anything but close and sleepy in the half light: 'Did you leave any bairns that you know of, William?'

After a moment he said 'Aye,' and she woke a little and knew herself holding tight from any movement. He went on: 'There is one I left in the home of the senior partner of the firm I worked for in Boston.'

'Did he know?' she asked.

'Never. He thought it was the bonniest of the lot.'

'It would be that. Was it a lad bairn?'

'No, a lass.'

'Would she be like Elizabeth?'

'Indeed I dinna ken. I was not much caring for wee ones in those days, Kirstie, and there's the truth. But it wouldna have done for anyone at all to know what had passed. For the New England laws were terrible strict and the two of us could have been whipped at the cart tail by all the good-living members of the congregation, likely! A wonderful hypocritical place, Boston. Providence was stricter yet, not only in the outer clothing but in the heart as well. But Boston had its bawdy-houses, and those the worst kind, with the men hating and half feared of the women, feeling it was terrible sinful, and above everything they must never be found out. And I myself, Kirstie, I would come to the senior partner, her husband, in his counting-house, with my hat in my hand, to make my reports, and he in his blacks with his precise manner and coldness, and blaming me if I had the least touch of frivolity on coat or shoes! And he would send me off to the house for some document, maybe, and I up the stairs with the mistress of the house, for her to unlock the great press in their bedroom, and not a look towards myself till we were up there. Then she would fall quick. And I back with the papers and maybe a guinea over for my pains! Ach, I was a wild bad man, Kirstie!

'She wasna the only one. There was an awful nice Highland lassie at Winchester on the Shenandoah. She was from Aberdeen, an indentured lassie — times she said she had been beguiled by the kidnappers, but it could as well have been her own folk that had sold her; they were on a poor croft. She knew mostly all the songs I liked best. But she could neither read nor write, and when I went north we just didna see one another again, and forby her there was Mysie that I would have had maybe if things had been the wee-est bit different. And ach, Kirstie, there will have been women in America and others in France and Spain whilst I was at the wars. And some will be dead and one or two living yet, but with no mind at all on a Highlander that hadna much to spend on them.' He looked at her, searching her face for what she was thinking, wondering how it would seem to a decent woman. And wondering, forby that, supposing he had said the real thing, loosed yon straining beast at the back of his tongue — And had he hidden it from her deep enough? Could she have guessed? Ach, ach, and he wanting so sore to tell it to some living soul! But there was a thing could never be. And she hadna guessed, no, her mind was quiet and mild, and it couldna have been if she had known a spark of what he hadna said. And the wild devil he was, wanting to unquiet her, his own lassie.

She said: 'What more, mon ami? You have only said that you were living as a soldier and an adventurer must needs live. I took you knowing you had been that.'

'You will come into port after a long voyage,' he said, 'or back to Maine or Boston after months in the backwoods, and it is like a sudden wild hunger, and any kind of food will quench it, failing the best.'

'But surely there will be women up on the frontiers too? You have aye told me so.'

'Aye,' he said, 'but that was another thing altogether. A man will bring his wife and daughters or maybe an indentured servant lassie out west to a settlement or a lone house within a stockade. He may be from home, hunting, trapping, lumbering, or rafting, to the town with his furs to sell and his powder and cartridges to buy; he may be fighting the Indians; and if another man, on the same kind of errand, comes to the home and asks peaceably for food and bed, the wife canna turn him back into the forest among wild beasts and Indians. Nor can he in any way abuse his hospitality. I have slept in the one bed with a man's wife, and he far from home, and never so much as thought on her as a woman. She would have shot me with his second shot-gun if I had done so, and rightly, for I would have broken a law that was more binding on all of us than any written laws of the towns.'

'It will have been easy for you, since it is mostly that way in the Highlands, William, but would the town folk and English observe it?'

'Aye,' he said, 'for it was the women themselves that enforced it. They were free women, Kirstie; not kept by a city husband as playthings to be hung about with kerchiefs and necklaces. They were equals, trusted. The frontier has to be that way!' He spoke almost fiercely, not so much to his wife as past her, to the successful men of the Haldanes, the ones that had gone to the cities. And then, softly: 'You would have been one for the frontier, my lassie!'

'Being equals,' she asked, 'did they no' get terrible bold?'

'They will have been as good shots as their men,' he said, 'and the bairns the same. Maybe there is over little reading and music and the like. Yet all the frontier folk are most ingenious with new devices for doing what needs to be done. I am only wishing I could have taken you there, Kirstie.'

. 'Where you would not have needed to hang me with necklaces?' she said.

'Ach!' he said, a wee bit sore and puzzled, 'you know fine that if I'd had the siller you could have had any necklaces you wanted!'

'In the stead of a field of potatoes?' she observed.

'Kirstie!' he said, horrified, and then saw that she was teasing him and bit her ear, and with that they were scrambling and kissing in the big bed, while, outwith the house, birds were starting to sing; the loud, clear mavies, and the wee linties and the like chittering and whistling and stretching their wings among the new-lit bushes. But in the Haldane house all were asleep, and Robert Strange on a heap of cloaks in the long attic of the farther wing of the house, comfortably filled with claret and cold goose, deeper asleep than he had been for this many a day and dreaming that he and his Isabella were in Ramsay's bookshop in Edinburgh, with the folk talking and passing, and he was asked would he engrave the title page for a new edition of Horace; yet he had an uneasy notion that his graving tools were lost at Culloden, so that he was needing to make his excuses and prevarications, but Isabella Lumsden would not understand a thing!

CHAPTER IV

As Margaret Haldane pushed the window back, thinking to herself that the sneck of it would need sorted and she must tell her uncle this very day, the singing of the birds came loud into the room. Catherine Duncan, half waking at the shrill, merry din of them, turned over, saw Margaret's place beside her was empty, and herself slipped out and over to the window, picking up her Indian shawl from the bed foot to throw around both their shoulders. In the other bed young Elizabeth had her head well under the blankets and was curled against Helen Cockburn, asleep too. The cousins at the window leant out, smelling the sweet freshness drifting up from the fields and garden.

Abruptly Margaret said: 'I am in a great distress over my father, Catherine.'

'How?' said Catherine, and pressed a shade closer to her.

Margaret did not speak for a time. Once her eyes filled with tears and she turned her face away from her cousin and dabbed at them. At last she said: 'He has that on his mind that he will not speak on, Catherine, neither to me nor to my brother, and I doubt he will not speak to my Uncle Mungo, for he has this kind of contempt for anyone that has aye lived a respectable and prosperous life, even if they are his own kin. I can see by the look on his face, Catherine, when whatever it may be is in his mind, and it is a bitter, thrawn ugly look, and it must hurt him to be behind the face he has at such times.'

'What kind of thing could it be, Margaret?' Catherine asked.

'Secrets,' said Margaret in a hurt way. 'Bad secrets. Other folks'. But maybe his own forby. Any man who is in the law at all will know more than he should about the worst side of his fellows, and over the Forfeited Estates my father was in connection with informers and traitors and every kind of wee, low, nasty fellow that is out to pull down his betters, and with that he will have seen those same betters cringing and crawling and looking for opportunities of bribery or flattery, and maybe working against one another and denying their convictions! It is terrible to see through the pleasant outside skin of things, the way a lawyer needs to do.'

'Should he not put it all away when he comes out of the Courts?' Catherine said, uncertainly, never having thought of it before.

'It will chase him into his home,' Margaret said, 'and his clerk after him with a set of papers, or a client coming in after supper. Aye, even at Church. Not that I can mind on my father ever getting a right rest and comfort of his Sabbath. He must needs take the sermon as a matter of controversy, whoever has the preaching of it. If it is in any way foolish — and a Minister can whiles make a right hash out of the noblest words — then he will be twisting it round and making a monkey of it till I dinna know which way to look. I would like fine, Catherine, if I could see any fashion of ease for my poor father, but if he will not speak of what ails him, how will he get it at all?'

'Could he speak to Uncle Robert?' Catherine asked, wanting to be helpful. 'It is not as if he had lived in peace and comfort. Though I cannot see why a respectable man should be any the worse for it!'

'I do see — in a way,' Margaret said. 'For they have mostly a touch of the Pharisee. And their hearts are where their treasure is. Any man who is set on his respectability will do the illest secret things to maintain it. But Uncle Robert will be no good to my father. There is only one person in this house could be, and that is not a man. Aye, it's Aunt Kirstie. She was with us, see, Catherine, in the months before she was married to her American Highlander. She and my father, they would walk up and down the policies, having a fine argy-bargy about this and that, and he would be laughing and having his cracks, and the ugly look wiped clean off his face for days at a time.'

Catherine pounced on this: 'Aunt Kirstie never said, Margaret — she was telling me the story of her life, but she left off where yon first man of hers died. But you will know if she was with you after it — ? '

'I know and I dinna know,' Margaret said. 'There were

things said about Andrew Shaw's death, though I never
heeded them, for I knew they werena any way true. But when
Aunt Kirstie came to us she had a hunted look on her. And
there was no part of the family except ourselves that would so
much as speak to her, though you wouldna think it now.
Whether it was on account of some old quarrel or of gossip
over well repeated or because she was for marrying a Highland adventurer without home or prospects, I never rightly
knew. I was sorry for her, the poor woman, but I couldna see
any man wanting her, yet it was partly the widow's weeds she
was wearing, ugly, coarse duds she had cut herself and the
fashions ten years out. Then one day my father took her into
Edinburgh, and me with her, and we fitted her up. Aye, yon
was the first time I met with William Macintosh and I mind
of it well, Catherine, for he came to meet us at my father's
lodgings in St. James's Court, and I had my suspicions of him,
yet when I saw the way he lit up on seeing Aunt Kirstie and
she in the new dress that the woman had just put the last
trimming on to that morning, well, I thought, he has a sincere
love for her. Aye, and she for him. And then he and my father
were at the desk, looking over a document, and sudden I saw
the man put his hands up to his face, and he was weeping.
And Aunt Kirstie whispered that he had newly come from
visiting his father in prison, aye, not half a mile from where we
were sitting, somewhere in the Castle, and his father was old
and seemed near death, but there was no getting him out. He
was terrible fond of his father, was William Macintosh.'

'But he had not seen him all those seventeen years he was in
America!' Catherine said.

'Had he no'? Well, I'm telling you a thing, Catherine, and
it is a secret, but anyone can know it now without harm, though
there was a time when maybe the only good Whig that did
know it was my father. That is, if my father were ever truly
a good Whig. Not that he was ever a Tory, Catherine, you
must not suppose that, but — och, I just canna say right what
he was! Or is. But he knew that young Black William Macintosh was back in Scotland twice at the least and visiting his

father, old Red William, the Brigadier, and helping with the publication and sale of his pamphlets and getting him books. And my father knew for the best of reasons, because this same black one was staying in his lodgings under colour of being an American estate-owner with an interest in modern agriculture, and, as that, my father got him into Edinburgh Castle.'

'But surely,' said Catherine, 'he will have been of the very opposite politics from your father?'

'There is what one would suppose,' Margaret said.

'And would not Borlum have been a forfeited estate after the '15?'

'It was forfeited. It came under the Commissioners to rent or to dispose of in some other way.'

'Yet it has come back to the son of the man that forfeited it.'

'Aye,' said Margaret, 'and his wife a sister to one of the Commissioners. And that could be plain, and to be winked at maybe, but it was before ever Kirstie was a widow that my father befriended the Brigadier and his son.'

'That is not easy seen, not at all,' Catherine said.

'I happened on the Brigadier's books,' said Margaret, 'those ones he wrote in his prison, the *Essay on Ways and Means* especially. They are not my kind of writing, for, as you know, Catherine, I have the most passionate liking for poetry and none at all for economics and such. Yet there was a gentleness about the writing, a fashion of love, oh you would never have guessed that the author was in prison and never like to see a growing tree again in his life! There was no breath nor hint of politics or bitterness. The old man had accepted, in meekness and charity, all that his enemies had done to him, and then had written his books out of pure love for Scotland and the poor folk of Scotland.' Again her eyes filled with tears and she wiped them with a corner of the shawl. 'Amn't I a silly besom to be crying over an old dead Tory, Catherine? But thon books, they were for the same folk that my father is for, also. And there is one knot of the puzzle, it seems to me, Catherine.'

Catherine frowned: 'Why at all should I have heard more talk about the common folk in a matter of a few hours here at

Gleneagles than ever before in my life? For Aunt Kirstie was speaking away about colliers and weavers, and now here is yourself, cousin Margaret, telling me that your father is for the poor folk. And I am asking you, why?' Margaret did not answer at once. Catherine went on: 'There is no merit in poverty, nor no sense in over much thinking about it. For surely we must be charitable, yet it says in the Book: the poor ye have always with you. And indeed a poor person may have the experience of Grace fully as much as a rich one. But for all that it is a queer thing to be thinking so much on them and so little on the folk that are, so to speak, the true community and body of the State, and not the cast-off parings!' She stopped, out of breath with her own effort of thinking and curiosity.

Margaret, older and having had more responsibility, most of all since her mother died, answered as best she could. 'Maybe it is that the others, the good-living ones, have things all their own way, with the world as it is. Either you say that this is God's will and preordained justice, and the pains of the poor at worst a mere flash in eternity; or else you say that it is not God's making nor human justice, and that there should not be oppression of poor by rich, and then you will try to change it, in a human way, and with insistence that your interpretation of God's will is the right one, although it is not the one that most folk use. It could be a kind of presumption, Catherine, yet when my father and Aunt Kirstie feel it so, I cannot be the one to deny their interpretation. Let alone that I have a kind of half feeling of it myself.'

'If there were more people of the same mind,' said Catherine severely, 'it might make a complete upsetting of the rules of society, and none of us knowing our stations in life nor yet our duties and responsibilities towards others. It could be all this which is giving your own father his difficulties and distresses.'

'No,' said Margaret, 'it is more from this that he gets his happiness. He has a kind of belief in the common people that comforts him mightily when his own folk speak ill of him. And indeed he has so many enemies that I myself am never at ease in Edinburgh society. The thing I am feared of, Catherine, is that some of these same enemies may get the wrong end of a secret and use it against my father. He is not so young as he was.' She sighed and leant farther out from the window.

Although the sun was now up and the light clear between the long dewy shadows, the two other girls were yet sleeping. Catherine glanced round at them, then said: 'How does it count, Margaret, this enmity towards your father, when it comes to the lads courting yourself?'

'It does not help any,' Margaret answered, with a short laugh. 'But maybe I am hard to please. I want a man of some sense. And not — och, not sad. There was a Highland lad was courting me once, a son of Robert Munro, and nephew of the doctor's — which would have made him some kin to the Macintoshes of Borlum, not that he ever spoke well of any of the clan — but he was a sad one. Not all the time. Whiles he would be mad gay, doing the most senseless things and I half minded to do them with him, but after a time he would slip down sudden into a fashion of despair, fully as senseless as the other. There is one style for poetry, Catherine, but another altogether for life and I would not want to be mixing them. I like the poetic extravagances so well in books that I just cannot abide them on a lad that would be thinking of a serious thing such as marriage. I doubt a Highland loon would never suit me. But tell me now, which do you like best of our own cousins?'

Catherine, startled, was almost answering, but then tossed her head and cried: 'Och, none of the lads are anything to me!' and sudden gave a rabbit jump back into bed and curled herself up snug.

Margaret stood by the window a while longer. Was it possible that her father could have some other and worse secret? Why exactly had he still so bitter a hate against the ones that had been his enemies in the old quarrel, before ever she was born? He would not even take a glass of Ferintosh whisky in case it could be bringing revenues to Forbes of Culloden! Had there after all been some truth in the accusations they had laid against him? And since then — she did not know what had happened in Edinburgh when the Pretender came to the gates, bidding the Provost open to him. Her father had been the only one of the Assessors who had not run away, and he had been asked whether should the letter from the Pretender be read. But he would give no official opinion, but came home in a state of merriment, and that not of the best kind, at the new fix the respectable had got themselves into! And now Provost Stewart was to be tried for a rebel; and her father as Crown Solicitor acting against him in the case. He had been Sheriff-Deputy for Perthshire, under Atholl, and carrying out the examination of the Jacobite prisoners last summer. They had mostly been the poor or middling sort and would be written down as having been forced out by their lairds. If they were not used to an examination they would mostly agree to everything the Sheriff-Deputy wanted them to. Her father might be kind enough to them, and yet use them to make trouble for any man that he had his knife into. Was that right? If her brother had been home, she could have spoken of it with him, but the Guards were back in Flanders. They had been at home resting after Fontenoy, and her brother Geordie getting well of the wound he had got there. Yet Geordie Haldane would not have known right, although he loved his father. As she did. She sighed, suddenly tired and a thought cold. The sheets were chilly as she slid between them, not waking Catherine. It would be right morning soon and maybe things might come clearer. The milkmaids were up now, Janet Mailor singing away, louder than the birds. This was the time of summer milk, cream, crowdie, and wild strawberries with curds in the Indian and Chinese bowls that Captain Robert had brought back with him, well packed in floss silk and rice paper.

There were breakfasts for all tastes. Gleneagles himself was always up betimes and out to the estate, giving his orders and seeing the work started; or himself transplanting young trees, pruning or thinning. He had a good appetite for porridge, mince collops and broth, to be washed down, naturally and properly, with ale. But others had daintier tastes. The young men and some of the lasses would be for ham or smoked salmon and trout. Margaret and Helen Cockburn were not content without their tea and marmalade. The silver tea urn and its gear stood on the sideboard, with slices of white bread for those that did not care to bite into an oat cake or barley bannock. It was easy enough for Adam and James to get a bowl of porridge and cream away to the further wing of the house and the attic where Bob Strange was yet asleep, and they thought themselves unobserved. Catherine, however, had seen; maybe she was watching James in some particular way. After the breakfast all were out in the policies; Gleneagles was for showing them his spring calves, indeed he had a notion to sell a few of them to his new brother Borlum. Catherine, speaking with James of this or that, waited a moment to tie her shoe, then said: 'What were you after, cousin James, with the porridge bowl?'

James of Airthrey stood in the path, considering, the dark, soft look on him that she liked so well. He was no quick liar; indeed he could think of nothing but the truth in relation with his cousin Catherine. He said: 'Will I have your solemn promise, cousin, that, if I tell you — ' Though, was a man right to trust a woman? Yet Adam's sister, and one he had sat with in the Church at Blackford —

'I have never been held indiscreet,' said Catherine. 'Is it — the politics?'

'Aye,' said James, relieved that she should have guessed so quick, 'a friend of poor Ochtertyre's, and seems a decent body.'

'We will need to keep this from George Cockburn,' Catherine said.

'But,' said James, yet more relieved at the great sense his cousin was showing, 'you do not yourself consider that there is any harm in sheltering a rebel for a matter of a few nights?'

'We are too much mixed up with the thing,' Catherine said, 'to be over particular, and the Pretender will never come back.'

'I have noticed,' said James, looking at her with a great seriousness, 'that you have a particular liking for the old ballads. Does it ever seem to you sad that Scotland will never now have a king of her own?'

'I would not think of it that way,' Catherine said decidedly. 'It might be a romantic thing, but one must keep such thoughts away from one's practical judgments, and it is most certain that kings and courts are no way to bring prosperity to a country.'

'I think we will see Scotland prosperous yet,' said James, and then: 'Have you been to London, cousin Catherine? — how did you think of it?'

'They are cold kind of folk,' said Catherine, and sudden: 'Cousin James, I did not like London near so well as I thought I would! They were looking down on us, for all we had money to spend. We were visiting at houses where we should have been known, but there was never a right welcome; and they were aye speaking in senseless kind of phrases that we could not catch on to, mother and I, for London is as full of gossip as any wee town, and a saying or a joke, most of all if it had a tail of malice or indecency to it, would run through everywhere, and we out of it! But maybe I wasna just used to it, cousin James; Adam tells me the English lads in the Navy are nice enough.'

'England and ourselves,' said James, 'we need to get on with one another.'

They stood by the dike, watching the black calves healthily at play. The rest were within hearing. It was a queer, nice thing, it was kind of warm, to be sharing a secret with James, an honourable secret, for indeed who would betray a poor fugitive gentleman, and stir up the wickedness of the past? But, for all that, a secret, a thing to glance about, a special thing, the same kind their elders might have,

CHAPTER V

Mungo was teasing Black William at having slept in that morning, and indeed there was a joke about cold porridge that went on until Kirstie leapt with a sudden flash of anger; brought her neaf down on the table, and one of the Chinese porcelain cups broken, and she running out of the room in tears, the very same way she used to as a wean and Mungo teasing her. The men looked at one another: 'Who would have thought the poor bitch would take it so hard?' said Mungo, shaking his head over the follies of women.

'We are not so young as we were,' said Black William, 'neither of the three of us. And mostly all the women will fly off at a wee thing where they might suffer a great one.'

'I doubt you will have had practice with the women bodies,' said Mungo, 'did you never think on this marriage that the limmers have aye got at the back of their minds, waiting to pin it on any poor daftie that will give way to them?'

'I have thought on't,' said Black William.

'You could be married twice over in America and ourselves none the wiser,' said Mungo.

'You wouldna think that of me, sure, Mungo?' his brother-in-law said, leaning over the breakfast table.

'I amna thinking it, Willie,' said Mungo, 'for I can see for my ain sel' the love you bear to my sister, but it could have been, and you a Highland chiel. But Patrick would have kennt, and he with his American connections and correspondents.'

'Unless I had made this marriage in the backwoods,' said William.

'Aye, to a wild Indian lassock wi' a scalp in her hand! But you needna look so serious on't, Willie lad.'

'I wouldna hurt Kirstie for a' the gold of the fairies and my own soul in the same balance!' said William with a darkening and reddening of his face.

'Kirstie is doing fine,' pronounced Mungo. He stretched and

pushed back his chair. 'Will we take a bit daunder down by the byres? There is a quey I had from the Perth fair — ' He broke off at a noise from outwith the house, scrunching of hoofs and voices. 'Who the de'il is this ava?' and took himself over to the window and leant against the frame, peering through the unclear old glass that gave the outer world a blueish and wavy look. It is a bonny enough sight, a mounted man and a mettle-some horse, his gillies behind him on the strong brown garrons, and he with the high leather boots and silver spurs, and the eagle feathers in the bonnet over a handsome face, not a lad's face, no, but the years were on them all, though indeed they had dealt lightly with Lachlan Macintosh of Kyllachy. 'It is seldom,' said Mungo, 'that a guest and kinsman should be un-welcome at Gleneagles for so many orra reasons as yon man! For I ken fine that Kirstie canna abide the sight of him and I am thinking that you and he have nothing but the name in common.'

'I have the wit to hold my tongue,' said William shortly.

'Aye, but Kirstie hasna, the tawpie, and if he gets a dram or two under his skin he will say what he shouldna — och, och, I am hoping he is not minded to stay here for more than's dinner!' Gleneagles went out to meet his guest shaking his head, grumbling to himself, his morning spoiled on him.

In a minute, thought William, I will be facing him again, and the queer it is, I like him that much less for Kirstie telling me he had courted her, ach, thirty years back and more, a lifetime, the best of a life: for I mind on me thinking the best was over and myself thirty years old, standing there in the bows of the ship, three weeks out from Port Glasgow, and a stink coming off her, aye the *Fancy*, there was the name she had on her, the stink of our human bodies crossing the clean and lonely seas, and taking our miseries with us. While he — ah, Kyllachy could bide at home and at peace, the worse for nothing but a wee spark less of the siller in's pouch, scarcely even that, for he and his brothers, they made it up out of their tenants and their land, where a good landlord would have gone short himself and his lady the same, if she were a right one — as Kirstie has gone short and myself making up for the bad years at Borlum. A bad lifetime of years, with my father in prison and my brother gallivanting half over Europe and never at any honest ploy, and me wearying, wearying for Borlum and for Kirstie, although I had never thought to see them together. And all this time Kyllachy has been in no hardship, has never needed to work nor to think where his next dinner was to come from, and not troubling himself so much as to answer the letters from his own folk in America, the men his father had raised for King James, and that had got worse luck than their laird! The letters I myself mailed at Richmond, and yon poor lassie — Black William was not seeing the room at all now, the table with the china and silver, the fierce wee eagle of the Haldanes cresting them, a bonny spread and the sunlight soft and crinkled over them through the windows, and sudden clear through the one pane of the new London glass where the window had been broken and mended better than it had use to be. He stood there hunched, whistling slowly, not hearing himself whistle. In America he was used to taking tobacco, but in the Highlands it was hard to come by and gey dear, overdear for a landlord that did his best by his land and his folk and his Kirstie. But the slow whistle changed sudden to the quickening of the tune, the taor-luath, and from a lament to a mocking of enemies, who, in the end, could do nothing to stop the poet's voice, the music and the people.

Mungo was at the door with Margaret, Catherine, David of Aberuthven and young James, all bringing Kyllachy in: Tammie Clow, the butler, with a napkin over his arm and a silver salver of full glasses: William Macintosh of Borlum, who bowed and drank a polite health. The glasses touched with a wee ring, the voices mouthed compliments. It became apparent that their guest was to be at Gleneagles for a night at least. Mungo was whispering to Margaret who would speak to the housekeeper and see that the bed linen was aired: 'The man canna have your father's room,' said Mungo, 'for Patrick himself might be here the day. And I doubt he'll na mix with the lads up by, nor yet with Robert, and, see you, Meggie, I'll no have my own sleep spoiled by siccan a bloutering gomeril in the corner bed. No, you will just have the folding bed brought in here and the man can sleep his lane.'

'And the gillies?' asked Margaret.

'Och, they can lie in the attic of the further wing. There will be straw mattresses in it and I doubt yon'll be better bedding than they twa loons have at Kyllachy!'

Margaret slipped out, to get the things sorted right, and the rest spoke of the weather, the hay harvest and the prospects for the corn, of the news from the Continent, with a snicker of Whig satisfaction, praise of English generals and merchants. And sudden Black William found himself not holding his tongue, but speaking, and it hurt him, it gave him a tight choke in the throat, and yet it was on him wild to speak, and there was no Haldane could be stopping him! 'You will doubtless have the news from Rome, Kyllachy. What will the Prince be thinking of ourselves now?'

Kyllachy gave him a cold look and said: 'Rome is no concern of mine. Nor yet of our Chief. Old acquaintance would lead me to suppose that you yourself might be more like to take your tone on the matter from a female, Borlum.' And he bowed.

'Keep your tongue off Lady Anne Macintosh,' Black William said, gently and insultingly, with a half twirl of the wine glass, the way that, in a moment, the claret might have splashed across the face of the other. And thinking with half his mind, what at all have I to do, provoking the man over our Chief's wife, that is nothing to either of us, for all she came to me and argued, after the Prince landed, and Kirstie and I, we liked her all the better for it; but yet she is nothing, nothing, only a spark of the hate that Kyllachy and I have for one another, a thing apart altogether from the Lowlands and the Haldane house — But, as it went through his thought, young James came between them, saying to Kyllachy: 'It is over early in the day for politics. Come your ways, cousin Lachlan, you must even taste a piece of our new ham. Aye, or a bit salmon. The run has started on the Earn this week, though they will be later here than in the Spey — '

Tammy Clow now brought hot toast on an ashet, and James, carving delicately, produced a curly slice of ham, saw out of the tail of his eye that his Uncle Mungo had hold of Black William, saw a shadow of misery and shame dumbing Kirstie's husband, and all at once felt an unaccountable liking for him and a corresponding dislike of Kyllachy, to whom he said: 'Have you ever considered, cousin, the reasons for the cleanness and uncleanness of animals, as set forth in Leviticus? I have often supposed, in regard to the pig, that, inasmuch as the Hebrews did not use ham — another slice, cousin?' And now Black William was safely out of the room, aye, sent off like a scolded bairn, and he took another bit toast, and adorned it with a fanciful curl of the smoked flesh from off the hurdies of a swine, and oh the mixed feel in his own mind!

Margaret was back and saying to Mungo that the further attic was locked and the housekeeper without the least idea of where the key might be. 'She just tells me the thing was on the bunch with the room keys!' Margaret said, 'as though it could have walked off on its own legs.'

'What key was that, Meg?' asked James quickly.

'The attic of the further wing,' said Margaret, 'for our cousin's gillies to pass the night in.'

'Surely,' said James, 'they would be better in one of the barns with a sonsy bed of new hay, than in yon attic that's a' dust and rattocks and spiders?'

'Maybe,' said Margaret, 'but how comes yon attic to be locked and the key not to be found?'

James gave a look at Catherine; David of Aberuthven had taken on Kyllachy. Catherine said, boldly, but gasping a wee bit: 'It is the most unchancy thing, the way a key will be here one day and there the next. To-morrow it might be — ' and stopped with the sentence dangling.

Mungo, apprised, decided that it must be yon kitchen hizzies, or maybe the auld jade hersel' — for indeed in times gone by there could have been a gay passage or so between himself and the housekeeper at Gleneagles and the both of them past their youth, yet maybe none the waur o' that! And who could she be hiding up yonder, the old randy quean? 'I'll even see for my-sel',' said Mungo, and stumped out.

Catherine and James looked at one another, their wits chasing in silence. 'I would say,' James remarked loudly, 'that our cousin's gillies would do as well in the loft at the stables and not trouble Uncle Mungo over this key.'

Kyllachy heard: 'Ach yes, by all means! They can sleep on the bare ground or anywhere at all! Gleneagles should not fash himself over the like of them.'

'I will tell him,' said James, and dashed out.

But Mungo merely said: 'If Kyllachy canna see to the comfort of his own men, his kin must do the thing for him! And what is more, James, I willna have keys and such gear coming and going in my house.'

'A new key might be made, if need be, Uncle.'

'A key the like of yon would cost me a matter of several shillings Scots at the smiddy,' said Mungo obstinately, 'and another excuse for Jockie smith when he is behind with my shoeing!' And he headed, as thrawn as a starved stot for a hay-rick, towards his housekeeper's room, and James no more use than a wee herdie, his first day out!

Black William went up the glen by the new path along the burn that had been tamed and straightened out with new banking, work that had been undertaken by Mungo's father, the Member, in the times of distress after the '15, when men were gey thankful for any work at all. He had planted groups of birk and alder and flowering crab here and there along the new banks, and now they were grown and bonny, and a scatter of blossom yet on the crab-apples, for spring had been late coming to the Ochils, but the summer all the better for it. Black William never looked at sky nor florrish; all the ease and security had gone from him; it could have been the same way he felt after Glenshiel and never knowing whether man or woman, rock or tree, was to be trusted with its own face. Not that he knew yet, and maybe never would, how much nor for what motives, nor even whether, Kyllachy had betrayed him or his father. All was as secret as the peat hag where horse and man may founder and drown and be lost for ever; as the secret spirits drawn out of air and memories into the shut-eyed dance of a spirit-raiser, and the sacred feather in his hand, and you avoiding, avoiding it. But Kirstie was at the end of the path, he could see the tread of her shoe, here and there, and her brother, Robert, it must be — for the footprint was heavier than a young man's — along with her.

Aye, there they were, on the seat below the plantation of young beech, trees that had never thriven, had been twisted winter after winter by the storms funnelling down the glen. Kirstie was leaning towards her brother, a hand on his knee. And have I the right to disturb them, William thought, and could it not be that Kirstie is happier this way, among her own folks, and what rights have I on her? And he stood and remembered yon thing Mungo had said over the breakfast table about marriage, and if he let himself begin to slither back, if he let himself mind on a certain smell there was to Ohnawiyo's neck and arms, mixing with the heavy smell of the hemlocks, the great dark American spruce that made all these plantations like a child's garden — He stamped and shuddered· and did not know clearly who or where he was, and he wished wild for his sword, for his plaid, for his own tartan, his own manhood, his own Kirstie. And what right, for he had to go back to it, what right had he to Kirstie? Only the right of love maybe. The very same right that God has over oneself. Surely, surely, it was no blasphemy, yon, but truth. If once he were to start in terms of blasphemy and the strict wee words of a thing, in the stead of truth shown by the Inner Light, what could he think? Could he dare to lift his eyes to God, so great a sinner as he was, and the sin continuing and what would be called the worst of it un-repented — aye, known by yon other light to be no sin! And there it was he did most certainly lift his eyes, his heart and his faith, Sursum corda.

Now his thought settled on the folk he had known among the Quakers and on the Inner Light, a thing most ill thought of in Scotland, as how not, since it cut completely across the powers of the Ministers and led in the stead of the Kirk Sessions to the Meeting and the direct guidance of the individual. He had been, odd times, to the Friends' Meeting House in Edinburgh, and once with Patrick. The Edinburgh Quakers knew Patrick of old, and those with most experience and sense greeted him and liked him; he would give them legal advice, roughly, teasing them, and they would answer with the queer, cold water shock of exact truthful speech, unlike any other body of folks in Edinburgh, still less the Highlands. Minding him on the same thing in America, amongst the ugly, plain shacks in Pennsylvania, and Meeting Houses where you might find an Indian in blankets, listening not, maybe, to the thing said, but to the thing behind the words. He could not see Mungo among the Friends! There would not be caution and precedent enough in the Inner Light for him, nor yet for Captain Robert.

But now Captain Robert had seen him, called to him, spoke with the greatest friendliness: 'You'll no' think I was taking your lassie from you?' And then Kirstie crying: 'What at all is it, mon ami?'

Abruptly he said: 'It is Lachlan Macintosh come.'

'You hate him all that, do you?' said Captain Robert. 'Sit you down now, and tell me just why, for I had reckoned him an ordinary enough fool of a kind that — forgive me, Willie — is nothing uncommon in the Highlands.'

Black William sat down between them. They were facing north-west down the glen. There below spread the great strath with the burn winding through it; fallow and grazing, stone dykes and thorn hedges, the blue-green of the unshot oats, the growth coming on them quick with the turn of the year. Aye, some way nice to see land under plough, good land used right, comforting to the spirit. He said: 'Your brother has taken the care and thought that should be taken with his land. Folk will be eager to hold their tenancies from Gleneagles.'

'Surely,' said Robert, puzzled, 'we have been just dealers with men and land. I would not care to think otherwise.'

'It was otherwise, and is, with Lachlan Macintosh,' said William, 'and there is the first reason that I do not like the man.'

'And the second?' asked Robert.

202

'The second is to do with politics,' said William. 'Yet maybe it is all one. For, if you are not just and to be trusted over your own people and over the wee things, you will be less so with strangers and the further kind of things about which one may be in two minds. Yet — when one sees a thing, Airthrey, the way I saw yon kinsman of yours and mine, it makes a jag in the memory that is none so easy healed. Airthrey, I had my reasons for thinking no' so well of the man even before Glenshiel, though it is kind of hard to put a finger on them. Maybe we none of us thought enough on what we were doing nor how it could affect the whole people of Scotland. We looked for the immediate thing and that was mostly power for our cause and glory or revenge or maybe fine feathers for ourselves. We were all of us using our land for that. But my father had lost Borlum, and Raitts was my brother's and mortaged till you could scarce move a stirk from one field to the next. Well then, we took our risk at Glenshiel and we lost. And it seems to me now that one should think twice before bringing any kind of foreign troops into a civil war. I had no land to raise money on, or maybe I would have done the same as the rest. Kyllachy, Moril and Ardersier were still among Lachlan and his brothers, the way they would aye be in the name of the respectable one. But Lachlan had the main hand in it, and the family got raising the rents, putting out old tenants that hadna the silver in the stocking foot and putting in those that could borrow it some gait. Doing no repairs, nor planting. Spending nothing on draining nor liming. Laughing at those who spoke of such matters!'

'It is hard, whiles, knowing what to do for the best,' said Robert, 'and tenants can make more trouble than a right enemy.'

'I ken that,' said William, 'But there is a thing between landlord and tenant, or should be — Airthrey, when I was in America I started a kind of township for the unfortunate Highlanders of my own name, mostly, those that had been transported — after their terms were up, naturally.' Kirstie gave a wee smile at this easing of the truth to her brother and he maybe not always so law-abiding as William might think! — 'And I found more than one of my own father's tenants' sons or grandsons. There was little enough I could do, excepting to share what I had with them. But when it came to Kyllachy's folk, I thought he would be in a position to help. The farm would be his yet, or the wee cot and kailyard, and surely he would be glad to take back a man he had persuaded to go out with him, or whose father he had maybe half forced to send one of the laddies. For those nearest the chief or the head of the family who can share in his honours and drink with him and be named in the songs, they come fast enough, and the same with those that have a strong feel for the politics; but not so much the poor folk.'

'They would have come for you yon last time, William,' said Kirstie.

'They said so,' he answered, 'when they knew I was not going.'

'You are wronging them,' she said.

'Am I? They are overlike to myself. But maybe they would have come. Had the wind blown from some heart-loosening airt! But, Airthrey, I wrote letters for those folk of Kyllachy's and I saw the letters on ship-board, and I kept their spirits high for months speaking of Scotland. But there was never an answer. They werena all transports for the fighting. There were those that had come of their own choice — if you can call it that when there was no other. There was a lassie at my town of New Speyside, a bonny one. Dougal Campbell it was that spoke to me of the lassie, and indeed he was thinking to do a pleasant and friendly thing for both her and me, and I mind I had a spark of drink on me at the time, and speaking of some cailean boidheach out of an old song, although it was the lass of Gleneagles aye at the back of my mind. But this one, Mysie, I mind she came into the room where I was, and her feet bare on the earth floor, and her black hair snooded and soft against the hard split pine of the wall, and she told me how her father was dead, and her grandfather a tenant at Kyllachy, but put out after a bad harvest, and she herself and her minnie and her granny had seen nothing for it but to indenture themselves. It was a sweet, low voice she had on her, and the red coming and going in her cheeks as she spoke of the corn that had sprouted in the stooks with the wet weather they had, the old man and the women folk toiling at it and all to be put out at the term when there was neither meal nor money for the rent. I fear me it wasna long till Mysie was sitting on my knee and dichting her een on the shoulder of my coat, and myself with my hand where maybe it shouldna have been, and, outwith the house, Dugal Ban playing some daft spring on the pipes that he had named after myself. Yet there was all the way I got with the lassie and that is the Lord's truth, Kirstie, though maybe you willna believe me!'

'You will have comforted one another, for all that, yourself and yon poor Highland lassie, away and lone in the Americas,' Kirstie said softly, and indeed she did not believe him at all, but what was about it? 'And I am wishing her well for that.'

'Indeed I was greeting myself, for I got the feel of yon hard har'st away back in the driving wet of the back-end, with no bonny colour of maple leaves, no sweet-scented Indian summer and the lively crisp air of dry days and night frosts, but my own unkind Scotland, and an onding of sleet on storm-blown stooks and hopes. And Mysie Macintosh never to see the smoke rising at evening over her home or the dun cow that was her own cow come lowing for the known milking hand. So there and then I wrote to our kinsman Lachlan and I half promised the lassie that she and her folk would be back within the year, and oh the soft arms and lips of her and the noble feelings that rose through me to be her protector and deliverer! But there was no answer. I could have been speaking to a tree. And Mysie thinking I was no better than the rest of the lairds, plenty fine words but never a deed to match them. Ach, I hated Kyllachy! Indeed, the queerest thing to me was the way that the tenants would still have some habit of affection and loyalty to him or to any other of the lairds and chiefs that used them as though they had less feelings than a poke of money at the Bank! That kind of daft softness at least had been broken in America. Even the poor could be free,'

Robert frowned: 'Such doctrines become dangerous, Borlum. Break one loyalty and all will go. And I wouldna have thought to hear such doctrine from a Tory that fought for his King!'

'You might have a better loyalty between free men,' William said, 'the way we had on the frontier. And maybe it was the same in Scotland in the days of Wallace. There are some kinds of loyalty that are'na worth the breath they are spoken with.' He stopped, frowning, half twisted away from the others, and saw that Ochtertyre was coming down towards them, a gun over his shoulder. 'I have never known for certain,' he said, 'whether or no Kyllachy was the writer of a certain letter which I have reason to know was sent.'

'What was in the letter?' Captain Robert asked.

'It told of my father's whereabouts,' said William, 'and I would not suppose that any gentleman of even moderate fortune would take the price that was on my father's head: yet there are other things besides the money that come in gey handy. I am not dead sure if Kyllachy betrayed my father, but I am glad to my bones that my Kirstie would have nought to do with the man.'

Captain Robert did not like any of this. It jarred against his notions of the right relation between folk of various standings in a society which was, at last, and after centuries, stable and secure and guided by good sense. He did not like to see it broken in upon. And here, now, was Ochtertyre, yet another element of disruption!

Ochtertyre came down the path, limping. But for his wound, he might have been off yet in the hills, shoving away from him all that he did not care to think about, Falkirk and the bad leading of the troops and the Highlanders wanting home, giving way to treacherous despair, the whole great mistake it was, and now Bob Strange come to mind him of it all, Bob Strange so awkward a guest in the Haldane house, and caring nothing for the inconvenience he was putting his friends to! It would serve him right to starve a day or two in the attic, he could make his drawings on the dust of the walls of it!

The Ochils had been heather-hot, heather-sweet. The moorfowl's head peeked over a sprigged ridge, never budging at your canny approach nor the levelling and sighting of the fowling-piece. He had three in the bag over his shoulder.

'Come,' said Kirstie, 'the four of us will be going back to the house, and Margaret will be pleased at a present for her larder.' Then, soft, to William: 'You willna quarrel with yon man, my soul? He isna worth it.'

'I canna promise,' said William, 'but I will do my best.'

'You will most certainly not quarrel,' said Captain Robert, 'this is neither time nor place.'

Ochtertyre said: 'I thought my own was shame enough on the family. I was a fool to let George pick a quarrel with me. You are not that kind of fool, Borlum, I think.'

'I would sooner George Cockburn drunk than Lachlan Macintosh sober,' said William sombrely, 'but maybe the occasion will not arise.'

Kirstie laughed: 'I will do the answering for you, my heart, and indeed it will be a pleasure for me, and a bafflement for Kyllachy. And do you just hold your tongue.' She took one arm of his and another of Ochtertyre's, who shifted the gun on to his shoulder. The stock of it had a solid and pleasant feel; the smell of powder was nice enough. Maybe Bob Strange was mistaken over this matter of a new proclamation; there would be an amnesty surely. It was time for the whole thing to be forgotten. If he could forget it himself, so could anyone!

CHAPTER VI

THE four coming back from the glen, speaking of this and that, passed by the end of the plantation between the house and the coal-road, but the trees had grown from stack props to Navy masts since Kirstie and William had met there, and the thin summer dress caught against the rough plaid. The spruce had been thinned out, but the edging trees, oak and beech mostly, would take another of man's generations to reach any kind of cutting size, another yet for maturity, and some might stand well beyond that. William thought of his young plantations at Borlum, a comforting crop, the trees, tieing you into a rotation away beyond your own temporal life, something nearer eternity. Then, at the corner of the road, they met Kyllachy and George Cockburn. It was necessary for Captain Robert and Kirstie to stop, expressing pleasure at the arrival of their guest, for the cousinly kiss from Lachlan to Kirstie, and George meanwhile making some teasing remark to Ochtertyre who eluded it with forbearance and maybe a certain pride. 'What like of trees have you been planting at Kyllachy, cousin?' asked Captain Robert.

'Och, I am not so industrious as yourselves,' said Kyllachy. 'None of us up in the north can equal you at this side the strath when it comes to the managing of an estate. Let alone, our winters are over cold for the wee trees.'

'We find no difficulty with our seedlings at Borlum,' Kirstie said.

'If I had a Haldane wife,' said Lachlan, 'I might have a plantation on my estate and even an assured seat in my heavenly mansion! But alas, I was never so fortunate.'

'And you cannot manage either of the two of them on your lane!' said Kirstie, daffing, but with a sharp edge to it.

'I am certain you could grow spruce and fir, both,' said Captain Robert seriously.

'If you will give me a lend of your sister, I might attempt it,' Kyllachy said. 'Will you no' grow me a plantation, cousin

Kirstie? Indeed, I would do a man's work towards it!' And he took her hand, with a sheep's eye at her.

But before she had thought on the way to send him off, William had knocked up his hand with the edge of his own under the wrist, saying nothing. 'William!' said Kirstie, 'I can take care of myself!'

And, 'American manners!' Kyllachy said, 'Remember, Borlum, you are considered to be a gentleman now!' And George laughed.

'Come, come,' said Captain Robert, 'No one has intended the least thing to anyone else!'

'Indeed no,' said Kirstie, 'and if George will take cousin Lachlan the other way of the road, he will see some young plantings towards Blackford that will show him exactly how they should be laid out.'

'I am in no need of assistance from the family,' said Kyllachy, 'but yon man of yours, Kirstie, should be looked to, or he may get himself into trouble the same way his brother did over another woman.'

'What do you mean?' William said stiffly.

'I mean,' said Kyllachy, with a hard and formal smile, 'that you of Borlum are much given to the sex and your brother Benjie was hanged over the head of a London street-walker whom any man of the least sense would have left alone.'

Black William began to see patches of purple and red before his eyes, driving him to action of a kind he knew he would regret but was bound to take. He said: 'Benjie never did a wrong thing in his life, for all the English got him, and never betrayed a friend, and that is more than you can say, Kyllachy.'

'That cannot pass,' said Kyllachy; but as he said it, Captain Robert and Ochtertyre were between them, so even was George and Kirstie pulling her husband back. The thing was over in a minute and nobody hurt. Captain Robert, who had drawn his sword, sheathed it again. George bowed and said: 'If this comes to anything, I shall be glad to act as second to my cousin of Kyllachy.'

Captain Robert said angrily: 'It is not coming to anything,

as you put it, George! I will not have these squabblings at Gleneagles. It is a serious enough world without such follies, and if you had seen what I have seen on my travels you would not be such touchy Highland gowks! And as well the English disarmed you! And let there be no breath of this at the dinner table. Nor of any other quarrel!'

George bowed slightly, so did Ochtertyre. Kyllachy raised his eyebrows and smiled: 'I fear that Borlum has overtender feelings over certain matters; my own conscience is clear.'

Kirstie said: 'Then take yourself off, you and your conscience together, for the lave of us are seeing double! We for our part are going down the road.' And she seized on William and turned him round and wheeled him off.

Ochtertyre said suddenly to Captain Robert, watching George and Kyllachy walking off together: 'It is the greatest pity that those two should be getting so friendly and they in the mood they are in.'

'They can do no harm,' Captain Robert said decidedly, 'and you, cousin, have behaved with discretion. Indeed, I can scarcely believe you took the foolish side in the late troubles of your own will, and I am prepared to say so should the occasion arise.'

'I am most happy to hear it,' Ochtertyre said, 'and I fear it is possible that Kyllachy knows more than he should about some matters.'

'About yourself or about yon man of Kirstie's?' Robert asked.

'Both of us, maybe.'

'Well,' said Captain Robert, still with the greatest cheerfulness, 'it is more than likely that Borlum knows as much about Kyllachy, and so between us all we shall keep an even keel in the rough weather of these politics which have drowned so many poor souls. And do you not get fashing yourself, Ochtertyre, but behave in a douce and reasonable manner and all will be well. And now what at all is doing with this Highlander?'

For William had thrown himself down on the steep wee brae at the road's edge and had burrowed his head into the turf where June primroses stayed late and pale in the shadow of a broom bush; his hands gripped at the grass, his back was to Kirstie and the Haldanes. Sudden he twisted round and said: 'I would like fine to kill Kyllachy.'

'Well,' said Robert, 'you will do nothing of the kind here, and I am ashamed of you, Borlum, for it was your own doing.'

'If he had not touched Kirstie,' Black William said, 'nor spoken on Benjie.'

'Who at all was this Benjie?' Captain Robert asked, but half kindly.

William was pulling with his hands at the turf and moss; he let it scatter on the road at his feet. He said: 'Benjie was my half-brother. He was born two years before my father married. Times I ask myself how did it seem to my mother, finding this wee one when she came home to her husband's house. Yet by the time I can remember, all was well, and Benjie would be with us on all our ploys, and, being three years older, he would be half shepherding us and keeping us from a dozen deaths a day in the burns or up on the screes and crags or maybe racing round the lum-heads atop of the house. His mother was married and had other bairns by her man, but she was aye kind of grateful to Borlum for getting the first on her and she a maiden lassie, and father was terrible fond of Benjie and had him taught with the rest of us, and mother would be giving him a sweetie or the half of an orange when there was one. He had the best nature in the world, but he was a wee thing slow in the uptake and my sister Winwood and I, we were for ever teasing him and he aye took it in good part. And the years went by and he wanted nothing but to be under our father's orders, and it came to the '15, and off we went on King James's war, with the gathering, gathering of the pipes ahead of us, and two of Benjie's half-brothers on the mother's side along with us — one of them was wounded later — and an assurance of victory that I have never had since.

'Benjie was taken at Preston with father and myself and grat like a bairn at handing over his sword to the English, and myself comforting him the best I could, and we were handcuffed together and making a joke of it, but I was dowie enough. All the way into London from Highgate they made a show of us, tied or hobbled the like of sheep and cattle, and the Londoners hooting and spitting and making their jokes on us. Only they didna laugh at my father any more than they would have laughed at the herd bull with his horns down. Benjie and I, we comforted ourselves with the look of him, even from the back, and the quieted look of the crowd as he passed; we could say to ourselves that we were his sons and a part of his strength.

'Well, they put the nobles into the Tower of London, a dark and nasty English prison, and there it was they had torn the living guts out of Wallace. But ourselves were put into Newgate, a more cheery kind of prison altogether, at least for those with money and wits. During the daytime, there was a din of argifying and screeching and singing in the passages and common rooms, and here and there a knot of folk praying or drinking, and you rubbing shoulders maybe with a thief or a forger, but often enough with some poor debtor body, forby all manner of folks that happened to hold an unpopular opinion on matters of theology or politics. Indeed, it was a most educative time we had, and father dinging it into Benjie and myself, that were as shy as lasses to start with, that we must hold up our heads in argument. Times Benjie would get himself terrible fankled up, and myself, having more gift of words, would need to get him out of it for the credit of Scotland and our cause. Father never seemed to have much mind of his fetters, though I found them irksome enough myself.

'We were locked in our room at night, but they were a decent lot of folk, our jailers, not wanting to make things worse for us than they were, let alone that my father had a puckle silver hidden in one of his boots that came in handy here. We had been forced to surrender at Preston without making terms, through the stupidity of the English gentry that had no professional knowledge of war, and there was no reason at all why they would not have had our heads off, nor why we might not have been tortured in some way. But the common English are the most decent enemies one can have; enlisted men are bound to be cruel, with the way they are mostly rogues and convicts or else pressed by force away from their homes and families; but any of our wounded men that were left at farms or cottages on the march to Preston, they were treated with the kind of human-ity and civilization that you would find in America, but scarcely at all on the Continent where there have been many wars and over much hate and folks' natural goodness has been killed in them.

'But our jailers in Newgate saw that we got decent food and bedding and our linen washed. One of the lassies who brought in the clean linen got us a broadsheet that was newly published and mostly about my father, and we were all terrible pleased at it, and Benjie gave the lassie a silver button off his coat, and we were all daffing away and laughing at the queer notions each lot of us had on the pronouncing of words, and next time she brought a newspaper, and she sat there mending our hose and Benjie beside her. We were but young, Benjie and I and the London lassies, and after that Benjie and his one, the lassie that had his button, Lizzie Pratt she was called, they would go off into the wee dark closet there was off our own room, and syne there would be laughings and squeakings, and Mistress Lizzie back with her dress rumpled and cap over one ear. He had his hands fettered, the same as we all had, but what was to hinder a lively lassie from squeezing herself between, and if there was any wee thing he couldna do with his hands bound, the like of lifting a petticoat, why, she could even do it for herself. As for myself, I didna like my own lassie so well, for there was an awful towny smell about her, and our father wasna thinking on such matters. These easy wee London hizzies were no more to him than mice or puddocks, he who had been husband to yon other English woman, Mary Reade of Ipsden.

'Maybe you will have heard, Robert, of the way my father escaped, and some of us with him, on the very evening of his trial. He wasna speaking much beforehand, but I can tell you now it was his English brother-in-law, Thomas Reade, that had a file smuggled in to us, and once the fetters were off him, my father knocked down the one jailer and had the other in a corner begging for his life — and indeed we didna want to hurt the creatures any — and we made a charge for the gate, and he came on a soldier and wrestled the man's musket out of his hands and unscrewed the bayonet, and I mind of his saying in the Gaelic that it was a better sgian than none. We used the Gaelic amongst ourselves all the time, the way nobody would be understanding us.

'So we got to the gate of Newgate Prison and my father leaving a trail of bloody heads behind him and folk sprawling half dead in corners, the same way a wild bull might do. We separated, each running a different way, for indeed even my father could scarcely knock down the whole of London! As for myself, I slipped up a side lane, and then another, and along by St. Paul's, and hoping there was nothing to distinguish me from any other lad in yon great city, and I had the nastiest cold feeling in the world. It is a queer thing, but I have never liked to be running away, yet there is what I have needed to do, more than once in my life.

'We were all to meet at a certain inn on the north road, up in the woods beyond Hampstead, a quiet place, known to my father of old. He got there, and so did I, in the back of a country cart, under a cabbage net and between two monstrous great casks of dung. But we waited a night and a day and Benjie never came. It was not till weeks later that we heard what happened. Ach, it was a senseless, cruel thing, and I hate to think on't.' He stopped for a moment and Kirstie put an arm round his neck.

He went on: 'Benjie escaped from Newgate the same way as ourselves, and was making his way to the place that had been decided on, and then he saw this lassie, Lizzie Pratt, with a basket under her arm, and he must needs follow her up a street. And she got talking with some young London sparks and giving them back sharp answers, the bold way they will go at it in the south, and sudden the men set on the lassie and were giving her more than she bargained for, and poor Benjie ran in on them and struck and drew blood. But he wasna armed any, and they got him down and took him off to prison, and there it was clear enough he had a Scots tongue on him. Mistress Lizzie followed and lied all she could to help him, and he never said who he was, but the English had a terrible fear and hate of any Scot at yon time, and they hanged our Benjie and they branded the hand of thon poor lassie on some excuse, for their laws are terrible strict. And there was the end of it. But it hurts me yet to think of yon two poor souls that were kindly and loving, caught in a hellish great rat-trap the like of London, and when I heard Kyllachy speaking of Benjie and the lassie — for she was easy, maybe, but she gave herself, she didna sell, for Benjie's silver button was nought but a love token, she was no street-walker at all, and, ach, Benjie was in the right to strike when he did!'

Kirstie said softly: 'We named our own wee lassie for yon London Lizzie, though folks will not be suspicioning it.'

Captain Robert was embarrassed to find his brother-in-law suddenly with tears streaming down his face. He said: 'Aye, we have mostly all done foolish things; I was near married myself once on a bonny Indian lassie at Madras. It is the soft way they move, it will get into your dreams some way.'

'Aye,' said William, half choked with tears, 'the way they move, like the south wind in April, and you so lonely.' And he was minded again on the thing he had not thought on now for long enough, but that was coming back on him wild the day; Ohnawiyo's first coming and the aloof soft way she walked through the streets of Boston, the deer-step of her moccasined feet through the dirty, melting snow, her brother beside her like a wild king, with the deed in his hand that he had signed without understanding, that had brought him to the Boston office to be beguiled and baffled by the powers and papers of the white men. And he, sick of it all, sick and lonely and half hating yon woman, his master's wife, that had slept with him and yet despised him, and wholly hating the black coats and the Boston Sabbath, had taken the side of the Indians, had answered to the kingliness of Ohnawiyo and Tehoragwenegen — what was yon word, Basileia, the Kingdom — And now Robert was going on, soothingly: 'Och aye, it will have been the same for yourself in the Americas.' But if he told them —

215

And then, there was young James Haldane and Catherine Duncan with him, and a disturbed look on them, and hastily William composed himself, wiping his eyes on the handkerchief that Kirstie passed to him, she and Robert conspiring in a clumsy way, but och, kindly meant! — to help and steady him. As Lowlands and Highlands must aye do good by one another to make a right Scotland.

With the easy sympathy and fondness there was between them, young James and Captain Robert were already walking away from the others, back by the short cut to the house, leaving the rest to follow. And Catherine Duncan said: 'Aunt Kirstie! Do you mind on telling me of cousin Isobel that you sheltered after the troubles?' Kirstie nodded. 'You would do the same again? And you, Uncle William? Well, we are in the same fix now!'

Ochtertyre said quickly: 'Is it — ?'

'Aye,' said Catherine, 'it is your friend, and he in the attic and Gleneagles wanting to put Kyllachy's gillies there to sleep, and the key not to be found, and Gleneagles and Margaret Bearcrofts both in a wild rage over this key and storming round the house like two bulls — '

'Where is the key?' Ochtertyre asked anxiously, having left it in the young men's keeping.

'Indeed,' said Catherine, and patted the lace bosom of her dress, 'I am afraid I have the thing myself, but by the greatest good fortune no one has asked me! But none of us know what to do and it is getting beyond James and myself — ' she caught herself up quickly ' — and — and Adam, who is overlike to laugh about it, so we thought, well, we thought we must just come to you and Uncle William.'

Ochtertyre said wretchedly: 'I should never have let Bob Strange set foot in Gleneagles!'

'You could not have acted otherwise,' said Catherine, 'Cousin James has told me how it was.'

Then all at once the four of them had their heads together, whispering quick, question and answer, and William began to take the lead and get the thing clear. It had been a moment before he was listening right; then Ochtertyre, who had thought him soft, suddenly knew him hard and determined, burn water freezing to bright ice. Catherine handed the bosom key, half wishing it had been to James, over to her uncle. He said: 'It is most certain that you must be out of this, Ochtertyre. The Haldanes have at last begun to think well of you and it willna do, with George the way he is, to risk spoiling their good will. It is also certain that Gleneagles himself must be told and I cannot think he will feel bound to inform his brother magistrates, if it is put to him right. I am not so sure about Bearcrofts' Margaret nor Robert; there could be an awkward matter of principles, and I am very sure that no other of the young ones are as discreet as yourselves. We will get the gillies out of the road easy enough. But it seems to me that the thing will look best if I myself take the blame of this flyaway laddie when it comes to telling Gleneagles.'

'I believe you are right,' said Ochtertyre after a moment, and bowed: 'I thank you.'

They went down quick to the house, noticing that James had got Captain Robert turned away towards the dookit; he was pointing up and the Captain appeared to be observing something among the swirlings and flutterings of the pigeons. 'Yonder the gillies!' said Catherine. William strolled over and spoke to them in the Gaelic, then back to the others: 'That is done. Now for Gleneagles.' 'What did you say, Uncle William?' Catherine asked. 'I told them,' he answered, 'that there was a bocan walking up in yon attic, the same you would be calling a bogle, but Gleneagles himself did not know of it, and I advised them to say nothing at all to anybody, but to sleep in the stables.'

He left the rest and went straight to Mungo who was now looking among his own papers for the key of the attic, having a kind of half idea that he might have been storing seeds up there. 'I am more than sorry,' said Black William, 'that you should have been inconvenienced on my account.'

'On your account, is it?' Gleneagles said. 'Devil a bit! It is this key — ' William held it out, saying nothing. Mungo spluttered. 'My key. Ye Hielan'man!'

William said patiently: 'I had not the least notion yon attic would be needed by the family. So I took riever's leave. I can only say I am sorry, and, forby that, ask you for generosity and help, and I dinna think you will refuse it.'

'What at all have you been up to, Willie, you rieving loon?' asked Mungo, relieved and cross and some way affectionate.

'When a friend comes, needing to be hidden, one canna refuse.'

'It would have been better manners to ask your host,' said Mungo.

'Aye, but you werena alone and I didna like — '

'Willie, I have to suppose that this is some skulking Tory and I am only hoping it isna the Pretender nor yon Flora Mac-Donald hizzie come back wi' a man's trews on her!'

'Och, it is only a poor Edinburgh gentleman that was half beguiled into the thing.'

'So they are a' saying. Well, seeing it is Kirstie's man's doing, we must even let it pass. Though if it had been some folly of Ochtertyre's I would have felt it my bounden duty as a magistrate to allow no sic a thing!'

William bowed: 'I am eternally grateful,' he said, 'and now may I go to yon attic and tell the laddie he needna be feared since he is amongst gey generous and good-hearted folks?'

'He had best stay there,' said Mungo, 'and mind this, Willie, ye skellum, we will need not to tell the young folk, more especially not George Cockburn.'

'Your nephew James knows of it,' said William.

'Does he indeed, the canny chiel, and he saying I must get me a new key from the smiddy! I hadna thought the lad would have so muckle gumption. Go you, then, and mind and dinna be seen.' He gave back the key to William, as Margaret came in, worried, dust on her hands and dress where she had hunted for the key along all the bookshelves. 'I have it, lassie!' said Gleneagles. 'The thing must have got itself among my papers at some orra time when I was maybe taking out the garden seeds I had stored there.'

'Well, well,' said Margaret, 'I am terrible glad the thing is found. But yon gillies have taken their gear over to the stables for to-night and when I was for stopping them I got nothing at all out of them but a gabble of Irish!'

She was still flushed and a thought cross, and Mungo suddenly bethought him of a bit ribbon he had, put by in a drawer, and how would it go on yon French muslin? But William was away to the attic, to make the acquaintance of Mr. Robert Strange and to tell him the lie of the land. 'I have been a thought anxious,' said the young man, 'with all the comings and goings there have been, for I have no desire at all to be tried and transported.'

'America is a mighty fine country,' said Black William.

'The arts have not come to flower there,' said Bob Strange, 'and I am most passionately eager to see the Galleries of Europe. And that in the company of my Isabella.'

Suddenly there was a loud and crashing noise — one of Captain Robert's great Indian gongs — and the young man looked extremely startled. Black William reassured him. 'It is midday,' he said, 'and there is the call to family worship and I must be off to it. You will remember, Mr. Strange, you are in a God-fearing Whig house!'

'Indeed,' said Bob Strange, 'I will not so much as make a profane drawing on the walls for the next half-hour!'

CHAPTER VII

IT would only be in the long days of summer that family worship took place at midday. Other times it would be in the evening, after work and before bed, a settling of the day. But, over the hay-making, for example, work might trail out late into the evening. At any rate, Gleneagles himself had come to a decision on the matter, and it was not questioned. He sat himself down now, adjusting first his chair and then his reading glasses, at the head of the cleared and shining table. The Book was open in front of him. The family all sat round the table, the younger ones nearest the foot. Beyond them were the house servants and farm servants, mostly on benches they had brought in, but Mrs. Grizzie, the housekeeper, with a certain look of indignation about her yet, the butler, the head plough-man, the joiner, the head cattleman and the head dairy woman, on stiff chairs in the front. All had their Books and most their psalm books. The men had their bonnets on their knees or under the benches. The farm servants were in their stocking feet or barefoot, for the sake of the room. The young lassies sat together, their hands doucely under their aprons. One of the horsemen, Tammie Clow's nephew, leant over to show a whitlow he had on one finger to Mrs. Grizzie; she would dress it for him after worship.

'Where is George?' asked Gleneagles, rapping with his fingers on the table. 'He is up the glen with Kyllachy,' said Captain Robert. Gleneagles did not speak his mind on Highland Episcopalians, for he was thinking kindly of Kirstie and William. He opened the Book and began to read aloud. The rest mostly all opened their own and followed him with a finger on the line. It was a terrible dull chapter, nothing to catch on to, no kind of argument. You could slip off it easily into other thoughts, as James was slipping into the thought of Catherine Duncan and then of all the lies he had told, and with such assurance, and speaking to his Uncle Robert of a queerly-marked pigeon among the flock at the dookit! Would he need to lie yet more before he was done with it? But it was Kirstie's man had taken on the most of the lying. Young James watched him, aye, surely, he was serious-minded. Surely he might be counted as one of them!

But the Highlander did not feel himself watched; his eyes were fixed now, cast down, dark among the blue-eyed, brown-lashed Haldanes. And in the dark of his mind the well was troubled, the Inner Light darting, not steadied as it should have been. At Borlum, morning and evening, he would take the family worship, himself reading the chapter and sometimes, sudden, seeing a new meaning on it, an illumination. It was a smaller gathering there, all could be round the one table, no separating off of the gentry. He would be sitting among the men, Kirstie among the women, the wee one on her knee; it was friendlier so. Afterwards they would speak of what was to do on the estate, or more generally, of affairs in Scotland and else-where. Times he would read aloud a piece from the papers. Thus they would come to an understanding of the day's darg and the year's darg. And, because all was open, in the sight of God and the congregation, so it became a right purpose, a Concern, the way the Quakers would put the thing. His thoughts were running over much to the Friends, maybe, though it was the way he had seen the best of the Friends in America at their dealings with the Indians that was aye in his mind, dealing with his own folk in the north. Ah, but his thought was running more than over much on America! He was a heretic, a thief and liar, a murderer, an adulterer. He dropped his head farther towards his hands, tight clasped, twisted together at the table's edge. His eyes shut in a hard, hurting withdrawal. I have left undone those things which I ought to have done and done those things which I ought not to have done and there is no health in me. They would never say so simple and true a thing in the Presbyterian Church. No Minister would ever get thinking it about himself!

Now all stood while Gleneagles took the prayers, lengthily in a kind of discussion with the Almighty, reminding Him of this or that wee thing that could have slipped His notice. The older folk listened critically; Tammie Clow was much given to theological argument with his master, especially in the evenings whilst helping him off with his day-gear and on with his night. Gleneagles was aye ready for a bit argy-bargy, even with his hose down! Auchterarder was a great centre of dissensions and discussions and a working up of small matters into great; there was scarcely a tradesman or farmer that had not his pile of controversial pamphlets and bound sermons. The bonnet lairds discussed theology between their gossip over lawsuits and family connections. Tammie's cousin on the mother's side was clerk to the Auchterarder Sessions and knew of any new movement almost before it was begun. Blackford had a laxer tendency. At one time, indeed, there had been a Sabbath market in the churchyard at Blackford, and the packmen laying out their trinkets on the tombstones as though there would be no such thing as a general resurrection — but Gleneagles had put a stop to all that. When nothing had come of his orders as a Justice of the Peace, he had gone down with his sword drawn and put to flight buyers and sellers alike, and thrown every bit and scrap of the packmen's stuff over the wall in a slow and deliberate way, for the rheumatism was troubling him at the time, and so home. There was no more Sabbath trading at Blackford after thon. Aye, he did things his own way, did Gleneagles, and with a certainty that the ways of the Lord were in some fashion like his own.

They sat again for the singing of the psalm. It was a lovely tune, Desert, one of the nicest, Kirstie thought; she could compass the most of the psalm tunes, though she could never do with the high-up kind of music, the concerts at Edinburgh with the foreign composers and yon orchestras with each instrument playing differently, a bothering kind of thing altogether: nor yet the pibroch that William would listen to for hours on end, finding wee things that caught on his spirits with some definite meaning that was beyond her, but that moved his mind and fancy as no argument could do. And Catherine Duncan, her own voice taking the run up, heard James among the men's voices, heard the two harmonizing and marrying, felt that there was surely a preordained suitability about the whole thing, a security, a hill-side of strength and sense.

The movement of the tune brought an assured cheerfulness with it, thought Captain Robert, as it would have needed to for the Cameronians who made it, three generations back, on the hills. It was one of the psalms he liked best to have on ship-board and especially in times of possible danger. He wished he knew if there was truth or not in Ochtertyre's suspicions over Kyllachy. Or George. It would be a terrible thing if one could not trust one's own kin, and George's uncle, Cockburn of Ormiston, one of the best landlords in it! He would like fine to know what were the two of them speaking on at this moment.

Yet maybe he would not have liked, for none of us care to hear folk speaking ill of ourselves, more especially in a scornful kind of way, and neither George Cockburn nor Lachlan Macintosh had any high opinion of the Haldanes, who appeared to them to have few of the elegant qualities or ambitions that suited a gentleman. George had not much enjoyed his visit to Gleneagles so far, except for two or three cock-fights that some of them had attended at Blackford. But his girl cousins were either not approachable, or else school misses like Elizabeth of Aberuthven that had not even the wits to know when a man was being gallant or witty! Nor were the lads accepting him as their leader or listening to him the way they should have done and he with so much more knowledge of the world than any of them! — even these Naval ones, for they were always kept to their ships or at best in harbours and ports, not free of the Capitals and coffee-houses as he was — and would be yet more after he came of age. Kyllachy, however, could recognize a gentleman when he met one!

Not that Kyllachy was taking George Cockburn at his own valuation. He was too old a fox. But a temporary alliance by all means: nor would it be plain when, or why, or whether it was to come to an end. Certainly at Kyllachy's moment, not at George's. That very morning, when Kyllachy had decided to turn his journey aside and see what sport was to be had at

Gleneagles — and he knew at least that there would be good claret and the very best of brandy — he had forgotten the possibility, even, of meeting Borlum amongst the Haldanes. If he had thought on it, he might not have come: although maybe he would have, but with a different and special edge of malice on his purpose. Indeed he had come with no ill will at all, only a general curiosity, but now he was shot with a pleasantly glowing spark of devilment and power. He knew enough to guess more, or at the very least to have other folks guessing at what he might know. It would be as sweet as honey, as heady as the finest whisky, to put a right fear on Borlum, whether or not there was anything solid to be made on't — maybe the Haldanes would value their brother-in-law's good name at so much down! — above all to humiliate cousin Kirstie, to make her wish she had bitten her tongue out before she had used the sharp edge of it on him! The one that this George was after was Ochtertyre, and if he could be tangled into the same net, so much the greater pleasure. But had George any special knowledge or guesswork that could be used?

The talk, however, only lighted now and then upon what both had so thoroughly in mind. As they walked up the road a spell, George was speaking of the great sense his cousin in the Navy Office had, to sell Ormiston over the head of his old father, John Cockburn the improver, who had, with all his enclosing and planting and building and granting of long leases, brought the estate into such debt that the thing had at last to be cut. Lord Hopetoun had already advanced on it, and was now taking it over. There had been years of unjustified spending, which his own father and mother had done their best to check. It had resulted in nothing but insolence from the long-lease tenants, such as these Wights who considered themselves as good as gentlemen, enclosed gardens, bought fancy stock and new implements, wrote letters to the papers and sent their daughters to Edinburgh!

'Aye,' said Kyllachy, 'these long-lease tenants are no use at all; when money gets cheaper you canna raise their rents on them, and they are for ever demanding this and that and evading their services. One cannot be master in one's own house with that at the door. My people get along well enough without this nonsense. And indeed, one landlord should not be allowed to encourage it in his tenants, for it will infect the rest.'

'There is my advice exactly!' said George, 'but Gleneagles is all for giving long leases, though he has not such wild notions as my uncle of Ormiston, and even Lundie has done the same.'

'And Bearcrofts?'

'You can ask him, yourself, Kyllachy, for I hear he is coming over within a matter of a day or so. I avoid him; he is as disagreeable as a poxy cheek.'

Kyllachy offered his snuff-mull to George, smiling. If the Bear were coming to Gleneagles that would indeed tighten the net. And need careful handling. Better let the boy talk.

For George was still on the happenings at Ormiston, how these tenants had set themselves up, what with market gardening and industries of one kind or another — some of which went right against the interests of the landlord — and his old uncle for ever taking himself off to sit in their houses and argue and drink and eat his dinner with them and grub about in their fields measuring turnips and weighing eggs on his pocket balance, and home smelling of muck! That would be ended now, the old man properly served for his follies. The tenants would find they'd to sing to another tune with the new laird. Hopetoun was not one to encourage any uppishness in his inferiors. George, for himself, was delighted to be rid of Ormiston, and so would his mother be. His cousin, the old man's son, had a pleasant London residence close by the Navy Office in Whitehall, and an elegant circle of English acquaintances.

But while George was holding forth on London, Kyllachy, who considered London an over-rated and expensive city, far less to his taste than either Paris, where a gentleman might do as he pleased with little fear of being recognized, or Inverness, where a gentleman was known everywhere and invited to take his place in every kind of sport or ploy that might be forward, aye, Kyllachy was turning things over in his mind.

Whatever he knew or did not know of Borlum, and his sources
were not to be trusted overmuch, since they were speaking to
please him and get what they could, having come back from the
American plantations without one sixpence to rub against
another, yet he did know certain things about Bearcrofts. The
question was whether Bearcrofts were not so shameless that he
might not shoulder his way through much that should have
incommoded a gentleman of finer spirit. However, the trial
of Provost Stewart was forward now and Bearcrofts' part in it
none too good. There might be sport. And this Ochtertyre a
proved Jacobite. Yet the thing would need neat playing.

George was speaking of a Club which he had newly joined;
there appeared to be some ludicrous ceremonial, and all had
fancy names out of the Greek, though what they did thereafter
beyond drinking was not so clear. Kyllachy passed his snuff-
mull again and thought with some pleasure of a man he had
killed once who was much of George's build and height.

The subject came to the surface slowly in the warm sunshine,
as a corpse might have done. Kyllachy, on his part, left much
unsaid. He could scarcely explain to George about the way he
had got to know a fact here or there, and sometimes in places
where maybe he had no right to be or in ways that could have
looked queer, yet he had got at what he wanted, picking now at
an eye, now at a sore, a hoodie among lambs. And the things
began to show a kind of pattern. For nothing in his life had
gone the way he wanted, every ploy he was on seemed small
and mean before he was through with it, only the satisfying of
curiosity and power had no end. If what yon folk from the
plantations had told him was anyway true — but could there
be any trusting them, either the lassie or the rest? Supposing
now, that the lassie had some kind of grudge against Borlum.
Not that she had said so. But it could be. And Ochtertyre
known to have been in the rebellion, to have had treasonable
correspondence with Fingask and others, not to speak of
Andrew Lumisden, the Pretender's Secretary, and all those
Edinburgh billies that wrote and painted and talked about the
arts and sang treasonable songs. They were used to go to

concerts at the Assembly Rooms. Aye so! Edinburgh was a terrible nest of Tories.

'And the Golfers the worst Tories of the lot,' said George, 'with Rattray of Craighall that gloried in being the Pretender's doctor, for ever winning the silver club! And Ochtertyre would make up a foursome with him often enough.'

'Craighall was as near being hanged by Cumberland as any sheep stealer,' observed Kyllachy.

'Aye, and would have been but for Culloden being Secretary of the Golfers and begging him off!'

'It was mostly all that poor Culloden got out of the Duke,' said Kyllachy, smiling to himself, 'and he so loyal and all! They say he is a sick man now.'

'For that matter it is past time for some of these older men to die off and give us younger ones our say. We have listened over long to the same speeches which have become as tedious as sermons.'

Kyllachy, who was himself not so young as he had been, changed the subject gently. 'It is altogether terrible for a loyal citizen to hear of the evidence that is coming forward at the trial of Provost Stewart. At the very least it shows a lamentable slackness and wavering, and an inability to see where the right interests of Scotland lie, that ill becomes a Lord Provost and his Council, above all in the capital. But I believe that I notice a thing: Gleneagles is not speaking on the matter, although his brother Bearcrofts is Solicitor for the Crown in the case?'

George nodded wisely. 'It may be that Bearcrofts' part is none so good. One cannot but have one's suspicions.'

'Aye, aye,' said Lachlan Macintosh, and wondered quickly whether Margaret Haldane knew anything, say, of her father's letters or visitors, and, if so, would she talk. If he had been twenty years younger — Ach, she could have been as thrawn a wee kirk-pussie as her Aunt Kirstie, as ill for light and gallant pleasing, such as a gentleman might give and ask! Walking the length of the High Street with young Kirstie amongst the looks and nods and compliments, the way a lad could forget even to inquire after a lassie's tocher and she so bonny, she untouched as the first snow on an early morning. And ach, after she was touched, after yon Minister had spoiled her, there was a thing about her yet and if she had answered — He shook his head sharply, as though a cleg had bitten him, and again he offered the snuff-mull, and now there was a thought he was trying to catch on to, some whisper he had heard at the time of the Minister's death. He had not heeded it any at the time. But that was before he had heard of the marriage to Borlum. 'I cannot help asking myself,' he said to George, 'how at all did this marriage between Borlum and your Aunt Kirstie come about. For he must have had bad enough prospects at the time of the marriage, and indeed we were all astonished that he should have got back a forfeited estate so easy, and he in the Glenshiel affair as well as the '15, and his father so notorious a rebel. But I have heard it said that Bearcrofts had more than something to do with that.'

'I would not be surprised,' said George, not that he had ever given a thought to it, but still, one must appear informed.

'Or could it have been,' said Kyllachy, 'that the Haldanes might have had some wish to get their sister married again?'

'Indeed there could not be many would have wanted her,' agreed George.

'I understand that her husband, the Minister, left her nothing. It is said that he gifted everything away for Church purposes. It was thought queer at the time.'

'She might have remained on her brother's hands for the rest of her life,' said George sagely, 'though she could have come back to Gleneagles and made herself useful to them.'

'If they had wanted her,' Kyllachy said. 'But maybe she could be better away.'

George was puzzled. At last he said flatly: 'Why?'

'I have heard a thing,' said Kyllachy with a sort of reluctance. 'But maybe it isna true. No indeed, how would it be true?' He shook his head gravely, would not say another word. Pleasant to tease George, while the thing took shape in his own head. They had turned and were walking back the way. He could see

Gleneagles house below him, small enough, and the young trees the Haldanes had planted, small. Once, just the same, he had seen Borlum house, away below him, wee enough to crush between finger and thumb, had known it was in his power, had known old Red William was on the wander again, with no money, was to be got, could be stopped as a bird on the wing can be tumbled gloriously, from ever setting foot again in Borlum, and that by a touch of the pen, an exercise of power and devilment, a wish put on him. There had been a high, exciting feel to yon day. As now to this. One needed to touch whatever it might be, on the magic spot, the joint, Jacob's sinew: then it would crumble, be at one's mercy. The question was, to find the way to it, to put the touch: to see the change in the face!

'You have missed family worship,' said Bearcrofts' Margaret severely to George.

'You know well enough, Margaret, that I cannot abide your over-Presbyterian forms,' he said, 'and at least I have not missed dinner, for I can smell it on the way!'

'Your Aunt Kirstie and Uncle William are Episcopalians, but they have the common politeness to attend,' said Margaret.

'Politeness of a fawning and insincere kind suits very well for poor relations,' George said. Margaret boxed his ears. It was on the tip of his tongue to say: wait, you, till Kyllachy has done with them! But he avoided it, instead caught and kissed Margaret, much to her annoyance, but maybe one had best say nothing, considering the quarrelsome nature of the lad and so much tindery material for quarrel in these politics!

But now there was a good, rich smell off the dinner in the dining-room, none of your London dinners that are so fine and finicky you can scarcely smell them a room away! In the great silver tureen there was a white soup with herbs and young peas and the bits over from yesterday's lamb. There was a pigeon pie, a broiled eel from the Earn, a pair of young turkies and a great deep ashet of salmagundy; mince with hard-boiled eggs, vinegar and spices, and anchovies laid flat on top of it. There was asparagus, broccoli with black pudding, and on the side table a lemon cream, jellies with thick cream and strawberries.

It seemed to go almost of itself that Black William and Kyllachy were at opposite ends of the table. James sat himself down beside his uncle and Catherine beside her aunt. Some way she felt a nearness to James through doing this, that she could not put into words or thoughts even. Kyllachy, the latest guest, was, naturally, beside his host. While supping the herby soup, with due compliments to Margaret, he asked Gleneagles for advice, not only on the planting of trees — and spoke of what he had observed while walking with George — but in general upon estate management and the conduct of life. And after all, thought Gleneagles, maybe I have been misjudging the man, for he seems sensible enough.

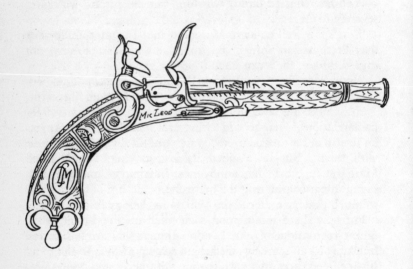

CHAPTER VIII

CAPTAIN ROBERT was looking in the book-case for a work on natural philosophy and wishing that Mrs. Grizzie could forbear rearranging the books during her cleaning. He could not lay hands on the thing, not at all, and he had been wanting to speak on't to William. He himself had seen so many wonders and curiosities on the great seas and in the Indies, full many more than folk in Scotland had ever dreamt on; and some were frightsome and horrible, outwith any decency or orderliness, yet others were bonny beyond all kenning. And, times, when his brother Mungo or Mr. Moncrieff, the Minister at Blackford, would speak of their Creator and the marvels he had wrought, he, Robert Haldane, he would be thinking beyond them to his own notion of a Creator, that was, some way, not man-shaped nor yet spirit-shaped, but without shape nor bounds nor attributes that could be comprehended by the wee brains of mankind that were boxed in so tight and orderly for a short life-time. And it was no manner of use attempting to circumscribe so infinite a being with any words, whether from the Book itself or from the proceedings of the General Assembly at Edinburgh. So, words and speculations could more profitably be spent over exactly-observed natural phenomena, such as he himself had noted down. And it appeared that William Macintosh had done the very same in the Americas.

Failing the book, they spoke on thunderbolts and electrical attraction, on the composition of metals and of soils, and from there to the subject of enclosing and the benefits and changes that came from it, to the soil, the crops and the beasts, and so to the folly of the small tenants and such that were for ever grumbling at it and breaking dykes and uprooting thorns. Yet, said William Macintosh, all could be set to rights with patience and kindliness and maybe a year of explanations, and above all if the poor folk could be made to see that it was not done merely for a putting of money into the laird's private pocket. It was a matter of speaking to folks as man to man, but if you had the tacksmen and even sub-tacksmen between landlord and labouring tenant, and four folk seeking to make their living out of one piece of land and one pair hands on plow stilts or spade, and the ones that didna work thinking they had a right to the best of the living, well then, there was no sense at all to it! But it was half the way farming was not looked upon as a gentleman's pursuit, and that in spite of the pastoral works of Virgil that spoke plenty of sowing and planting and pruning and that in a practical manner. 'My father would repeat me passages from the *Georgics*,' William said, half shy, 'indeed, it was that way we would be passing many a weary morning in Newgate gaol.'

'He approved of long leases, did he not?' asked Captain Robert.

'Aye, surely. If he had been let spend the last twenty years of his life at Borlum and not in the Castle prison, he could have shown it. Aye, he could have shown you all.'

'And your father, now, he would have wished to see a gentleman working on his own land?'

'He aye thought a gentleman could be a man into the bargain,' William said. 'I used to mind on that when I was working as a logger in Maine, and I told him — ' He stopped suddenly, not knowing if Patrick Haldane had ever told his half-brother of certain dealings with those who had been Jacobites, himself among them, then went on: 'His mind was that there should be colleges of farming and the natural sciences that should go with it in the stead of the superstitions that hurt beasts and folk alike, and that all who were to do with the land should go to such colleges and schools, lairds' sons and tenants' sons and poor cottars' sons, and those that could should pay for those that couldna, to make all square. He thought it would be better for Scotland to have a great number of skilful and ingenious ploughmen and smiths and carpenters and such, folk that can wrastle through with hands and wits, as we will all need to if Scotland is to be herself again, and to cut down the dead weight that is on her now, of Masters of Arts that are fit for nothing but arguments on dead philosophies and hold themselves too sacred to handle tool or beast or even to measure cloth on a counter!'

'Aye,' said Captain Robert, 'he was right there. Those are the kind that are worse than sheep when it comes to a storm, and we needing all our sense and strength to get the ship about!' He was thinking on some passengers he had with him once on his East Indiaman, and the trouble and annoyance they had been to him; he had locked them into a cabin at last.

William Macintosh went on, eagerly: 'Forby that he planned that those who were best at the noble art of agriculture and all that arises from it — such as the making of linen and thread, the brewing of ale and distilling of whisky, spinning, weaving and tanning, forestry and the many uses of wood, aye and maybe fishing, mining and quarrying — that those folk, whatever their birth, should come together, in a kind of Kirk Session, only for affairs of matter rather than spirit, and decide from one place to another, how best to use our land of Scotland. They could be working with the colleges, where the thesis for a Degree would not be some academic speculation, but how best to treat a barren acre, and that illustrated, not from dead books, but from live ears of corn or wads of hay! As he saw it, such boards or sessions would be by the district, as, the Mearns, the Lothians, Strathearn and the Ochils, and maybe the islands all together. It wouldna be too much to ask folk to come in to their main market town, twice in the month, say, and to spend a day on business, and appoint committees and decide who was to ride here or there before the next meeting, see the lie of the land, carry orders and get them obeyed, and be faithful to their trust and to some fashion of new times and new duties in Scotland!'

Captain Robert said: 'Such committees or boards would need to be given powers, and that even against Dukes and Lords who are not, most of them, improvers, although Argyll and Islay are none so bad, for all they are Campbells. Did your father contemplate that his boards should have full power over both land and landlord?'

'Aye!' said William, and somehow it was a delight to him

to be speaking of his father again. 'He thought they should be vested with such powers. They would have surveyors and gaugers under them, salaried maybe from the Excise that has aye got money to spare. They would act as judges in all disputes between master and master, or between master and man; they would be managers and owners of the nurseries of young trees for the enclosing and hedging that will be needed, and no estate should be allowed more than its just proportion.'

'But,' said Robert, 'I can see the case where a great land-owner would twist and bribe and force any such committee into his own way. Aye, and the big ones would get together against the small ones and against improvements and modern ways of doing, since all such take from their pride and power.'

'My father thought it was questionable,' said William, 'and I would go further than he did, whether a man's rights over his own property were absolute, when such property could be used against the welfare of another, the way land may be used. The Commons of Scotland have a right to live, surely?'

'I am with you part of the way,' said Captain Robert, 'but I canna just see where the thing ends. There is little property that couldna be used against others. A bank or a business might be used in such a way.'

'That is so,' said William, 'and we would be speaking much of such matters in America, where land is easy come by and easy parted with, but there is, maybe, over much power in the hands of the businesses in the port towns, where goods can be held up and prices raised against the common folk. Where there is usury — which can happen as well in land or goods as in money — then there is no right freedom.'

'Was that your father's mind?' asked Robert.

'He had all thon years of prison to think on these matters,' said William, 'and maybe you get to question things in the long nights when you canna sleep and the long days when you have neither garden nor fields to walk among but only a locked room. And you think mightily of freedom and the many degrees of freedom that are in it.'

Suddenly Captain Robert became aware that his brother-in-law was shaken again, by speaking of his father, just the same way as he had been, earlier in the day, speaking of his half-brother Benjie. It was, he decided, a fashion of pity and loving-kindness, since these two had both of them suffered from injustice, being innocent in all except the political sense. And who was to judge of politics? They were alone in the room now, the others all having gone off after dinner on their several ploys. There was brandy and the fine engraved Dutch glasses that he himself had brought back to Gleneagles, having taken them as part of a bargain over spices at the Hague. He poured a glass for William and a glass for himself. Abruptly he said: 'I am asking myself, William, what will be the outcome of Provost Stewart's trial.'

'It is too in and out for any kind of a true verdict, I would say,' William answered him slowly.

Robert agreed. 'Half of the evidence will come from Professor MacLaurin's diary and he dead and beyond cross-examination. A man will write in anger, maybe, or turn hearsay into fact in a private journal. If the fortification of the walls was not carried out, part of the blame at least must go to the Trades, that were so occupied in electing their Deacons that they hadna so much as time to work on their city walls! And yon hand grenade class, would it be only the Provost that discouraged the thing, or could it have been the wives of over-enthusiastic volunteers?'

'Neither the facts nor the motives are clear,' said William, 'and indeed it is still arguable that the Provost was in the right to capitulate when the Prince sent to him, and not to expose the city to all the cruelties of a siege. He could have been right there even though he was bribed to be. Even though he had plenty Jacobite sympathies.'

'And my brother Patrick?' said Robert Haldane. 'Maybe you see his part in it clearer than I do myself.' He looked aside, towards the book-shelves, deliberately allowing space for William Macintosh to answer, allowing just as deliberately, that someone from outside might know as much about one of the bull calves as they did themselves. It had been an effort to speak as he had done, to be open with one outwith the family over his own secret suspicions: yet at the same time, the casting of a weight off his own mind and conscience. Maybe he couldna have said it without the brandy.

William Macintosh answered, as seriously: 'Patrick Haldane could not have been for either side. How would he be and neither of the two of them the side of Scotland nor the common people?'

'You think that?'

'Aye, how else? The gentlemen that had turned half merchants and so were against the power of kings and courts and the old church, and the merchants that had turned half gentlemen and so had lost the courage and wits that are needed for industrial enterprise and trade, and all of them half hedging, and only Professor MacLaurin whole-hearted in the defence of Edinburgh and that because he was a mathematician and, so, terrible interested in ballistics and eager for an experiment between his walls and the Prince's cannon! It was nothing at all to do with the common people.'

'Yet Patrick, as an assessor of the city, should have been prepared to help. It was his duty to his office.'

'Aye, in a way. Yet I would judge that you Haldanes have whiles had a sense of duty of another kind. One that is not always clear to the rest of the world and that leads you into trouble over the head of it. And I am not saying you would aye be in the right.'

He smiled, meaning it lightly and in a half admiration, and indeed he would defend Patrick and his actions up the brae and down. But Robert felt a kind of rebuke that was maybe not there at all and a terrible wave of discouragement and humility ran over him sudden, as though his Highland brother-in-law were some way older and wiser than himself. Which he wasna! And defence and resentment following on the humility, he said shortly: 'It might seem so.'

And then in came Tammie Clow, with the copper pail for the dead bottles and a request for William Macintosh to step into the upstairs room and speak with Gleneagles. William was more pleased than not; he had begun to feel friendly towards Kirstie's brothers, to tread affectionately and familiarly the stairs and rooms as though he too had been a child in the house. He hoped Gleneagles would speak of Kirstie as she had been before he knew her, and maybe of agriculture.

Gleneagles sat at his desk and he had a sheet of paper in front of him and he was scratching under his wig with his right hand, for he was finding it gey hard to begin and Kirstie's man in front of him with thon open nice look on his face, the way you would say he could be trusted, and yet if all this was true, and it seemed that evidence could be produced — At last he began to speak, and the open smile died away from the other's face, and was followed by yon orra kind of smile that these Highlanders have, and they with their hearts full of mirk guile and deceit!

As the thing unfolded, Black William was taking it in with one part of his mind and considering the immediate steps to be taken to counteract it, but with the other part he was quickly imagining himself a plot for killing Lachlan Macintosh of Kyllachy and fixing the blame of it on the gillies maybe. He shook it off as a childish refuge. The destruction of Kyllachy could bide awhile.

At last he said, gently and scornfully: 'And from what like of folk has Kyllachy heard all this gallimaufry?'

'From some well-doing tenants of his own that have come back from America,' said Gleneagles.

It occurred to Black William that maybe he knew which they were. He asked with a twist of spite on his lips: 'Aye so! Could one of them have been a lassie?'

'She might,' said Gleneagles nervously, and, without noticing what he was doing, handed the snuff-mull across the desk.

Black William took a pinch and said: 'It is remarkable what the lassies will be thinking of.'

'From the way my cousin of Kyllachy spoke of the matter,' said Mungo gravely, 'I doubt the lassie or woman she is now was not lying. He would have kept silent but for the honour of our family. He had — other evidence.'

'Of what kind?'

'I am not saying.'

William thought hard. Again his mind had taken refuge first on agreeable thoughts of what could be done to those that betrayed him, and the lassie worst. Again he shook them off, thinking for Kirstie. 'If there had been any truth at all in this,' he said, 'would not your brother Patrick have known it?'

Mungo wrinkled his face lamentably and said: 'After the things I have heard on my brother, and they more than likely in view of all that has passed and my own suspicions, I would not put it beyond Patrick to have had a hand in any villainies!'

'Could it be,' said William gently, 'that you have over much belief in Kyllachy?'

'He said nothing that did not work in with my own anxieties and with the run of events. He had documents.'

'Not, I think, on this affair of mine?'

'Maybe no. But — ach, William Macintosh, whether the thing is wholly true or not, and maybe it isna, yet there will be something to it, there is aye water where the stink was drowned and it is wicked ungrateful of you to be making me all this trouble and I so good to you over yon chiel in the attic!'

William felt this, but yet he was wondering most what like of documents Kyllachy could have and whether they could be rebutted. And most of all he was thinking on Kirstie and could it be kept from her, and could the crack in the ice be smoothed over. He said: 'It seems, Gleneagles, that I had best be telling you the whole of my life in America.' Mungo made a kind of doubtful noise and twisted the pen in the inkstand and rubbed his hand across his nose and brow, for he was in a wild sweat with annoyance. For a moment William was praying in a tightened, violent way, asking for guidance to a right lie, to what would save Kirstie and himself. Yet he must begin with the truth. Maybe the other thing would be given to him.

He said: 'I left Scotland after the Glenshiel affair, Gleneagles, and I am not hiding from you that I raised some money from the Haldane firm in Edinburgh, and that after being thrown out the door by another firm of Writers, cold Edinburgh folk they were! I wasna looking for it from Patrick and maybe he will tell you his reasons for giving it to me. They were nothing dishonourable, yet I can see he might have hidden them. It was not more than enough for my passage. In America I was about the seaboard mostly, first in the south, in Richmond, a bonny and a merry town, and, later, in Boston, that was neither, yet rich. I started a settlement for the transports of my own name and others who were in trouble. And I will not hide from you, Gleneagles, that it was here I met yon lassie that told the story, full many years after, to Kyllachy. We were young, the two of us, and you will maybe guess how things went. But how, having given my heart to Kirstie Haldane, would I marry this lassie or another? But she was for ever at me to be marrying her and maybe she could be taking her revenge because I didna.' He stopped, watching Gleneagles, who nodded and made sounds of understanding and sympathy with the sins of the flesh. And the queer it is, thought William, that the one of them all that I never went to bed with, was yon same Mysie Macintosh, though it could have been done in a hand's turn and Dugal Ban playing the pipes to us! But I was sorry for the lassie and I would not be taking her maidenhead yon time, though it is a pleasure to be taking her reputation now!

He went on: 'I will not hide from you, Gleneagles, that I was on the Continent or here in Scotland, at one time and another, when I had the money. All these last years there have been folk wandering, exiles from one land or another, over the matter of politics or religion, and making little of crossing the great seas and taking their notions with them. We would meet and discuss, in French mostly, in the ports and capitals of the world, a kind of brotherhood of those that had been forced out of the decent run of things. And in Edinburgh I saw my father, and again I will tell you truly, that it was Patrick helped me over that and from him I had news of Kirstie.'

'In the Lord's name let us leave Patrick out of it!' cried Mungo.

'Later on,' said William, 'I was in Massachusetts and Maine, whiles in a Boston office and whiles working with my hands on the timber. I could fell any of your trees, Gleneagles, in half the time it would take the best of your men. How would Kyllachy know the way I was living?'

'He appears to have run across your tracks. And indeed if a tod stinks he is easy trailed!'

William ignored this. His fingers occupied themselves in softening and pinching the wax of a sealing taper. He had been thinking quick and had concluded that nothing was unlikelier than that Kyllachy could have anything but hearsay of the vaguest kind on the main thing. He could have got evidence, surely, out of the Parish register of the square, wooden Church where they had knelt and he in a whirl of strangeness. He might yet get this evidence if means were not taken to stop him and if he chose to take the greatest trouble over it. But so far there could be no danger of that. The worst could be a mention in a letter from some correspondent who had happened to turn the leaves of the register out of curiosity. Or if the Indians had spoken — But he did not think they would have done so, any more than he would have spoken himself. If *she* had come to Boston — But she hated the white man's town, and he hoped she hated himself enough not to speak of him. Hate was a healthy and decent thing, or indifference, as the Indians practised it. So long as it was not love.

Mungo spoke again: 'You admit that you were in an office in Boston. What was your business there?'

William lifted his head. 'The firm of White and Bradstreet were ship and warehouse owners and brokers, trading with Glasgow and certain English ports. We exported furs, timber and other products of the country. We imported made clothing, paper, wigs, furniture and china, manufactured farm gear and such. There were a certain number of Scots in the firm and we were not always dead honest over the English customs and ships' papers. We are needing to build up Glasgow against Liverpool and Bristol. It was the tail of an old war. Those that can afford honesty, as the English mostly can, will make it into a main virtue and pride. It is not such a great thing to be proud of. There were things to do, all the same, that I didna like doing. It is the same in yon other wars with the cannons and dead men. Only a fool wants to kill.'

'I could accept that,' said Mungo, 'though I dinna like it ava. But — thon other thing! Gin it is true there are no two ways to it. You will have made my sister into a whore. You will have broken God's law and man's. We have taken you as our brother, for all you were half Highland, with little enough of security to give our sister, the way an estate once forfeited can be forfeit again: for all you and your folk were for ever in and out of gaol: for all you were a Papist Episcopalian and dragging our sister after you into yon Babylon! But we never jaloused you were this kind of a stoat, sucking her heart's blood — '

'I'm no' a stoat,' said William, and his voice was shaken now. 'And it was a wee enough tocher I got with Kirstie, though indeed I was asking no more, as you well know, and if you will speak to herself she will tell you if I sucked her heart's blood. And I have been with you to the Kirk at Blackford but it did not strike me as over like to Jerusalem! And — ach, Mungo Haldane, it is all the blackest of lies and if it were anyway true you would have the right to kill me out of hand. But better you will be killing Kyllachy, for it was he that was more of a stoat. And I have never breathed a word of this to a living soul, but listen you, Gleneagles! It was at the time of your father, John Haldane's, funeral, and Kyllachy and his brothers staying here at the house, and I rode over from Ardoch on a ploy I was on with Kyllachy. Aye, I had letters from Spain on me, and one letter had a king's name for the signing of it. Well then, it was near midnight of the day of the funeral and I coming through quietly to find my cousin. There was a bed in the passage room, the same there is now, but darker curtains to it then, and ill to see what might be on it in the small light of the candles. Gleneagles, I heard her cry out and I pulled him off her before she was hurt, but he has hated me and betrayed me ever since then!'

'The Lord preserve us!' said Mungo Haldane. 'Do you tell

me he would do sic like a thing, the villain! And she has never breathed a word o't.'

'And willna,' said William quickly, 'and do you not be speaking to her of it, Gleneagles, not ever, for it is the way a woman body is deep hurt by any kind of sculduddery, and yon could have been the worst. Aye, near was. But you ken fine she has no liking for Kyllachy.'

'Och, och,' said Mungo, 'but I never kennt what for. He will not have been in his right senses, William. I wouldna have been sparing of the drink at my father's funeral and it will take some folks yon way.'

'It was the drink, surely,' said William, 'and he will most likely deny that any such thing ever took place. But it left such a hate at him on myself that he would ruin me with your goodselves if such a thing were possible.' Mungo did not answer, and the story image, that William had made sharp enough in his own mind, began to die out, and the real one to take its place. He said, softly: 'There was she after, the Kirstie lass, and the dead white of her face against the black of the mourning clothes and the tears glinting in her eyes, but not fallen, not ever fallen because of the spirit that was in her, and her pale gold hair, the thin, soft, separate hairs in the shaken curls of it. I have minded on thon all my life, Gleneagles.'

He stopped speaking. It was surprising, some way, that yon thing had never truly happened. He half wished it had, that for once he could have had Kyllachy by the throat. That he could have protected his lassie. That he need not have lied now. For a time neither of the men spoke. The width of the desk was between them and the slow trickle of sunlight across the grain of the leather top and here and there a wee ink splodge or a cut from Mungo's penknife where he had shaped the goose quill to his liking. A terrible black impatience was taking hold on William, a hatred and fear of his new brother and of the Haldanes and the comfortable, couthy house, the solid furnishings that a Lowland house would have, the marks of money power and of the twisting of events that led one family or another to have all the shares in a Bank or to touch this or that

Office of State. Most of the Borlum furniture had been sold and he had bought second-best stuff in Inverness, half ashamed and half laughing, aye, tables and chairs and all, forby Kirstie's own room and it was Captain Robert had given her the embroidered Indian curtains with the braw flash and pride of peacocks that their wee one was aye watching and reaching for. There wasna a carpet in the place, nor yet paper on the walls. Ach well, they had plenty meat and for all comers. If only Mungo would speak!

'I dinna ken what to say,' Mungo began, and William could near have choked him when he stopped there. If the thing had come to a head, could have been ended with some monstrous badness, some lie, some death! But it hung yet in air and he, for Kirstie and the wee one, he must have patience, think with submission on his Maker.

'I am needing to set my mind to it,' Mungo went on, 'but I am sorer fashed over it than over anything that has happened in the family or out! It is gey hard on a body to have sic a burden laid on him and he so near to his parting!'

'I am terrible sorry,' said William gently, 'but it is no fault of mine.'

'Maybe it is our own fault when we let our sister marry a Highland man. And you with your billy in the attic yonder that you would never have spoken on if it hadna been for the key! Who is to know the treacheries you have in your hearts!'

'I am half English, you will remember, Gleneagles, from the honest farm lands of Hertfordshire, and Kyllachy maybe more Highland than myself.'

'English or Highland, what's about it? You canna be trusting either of the two of them, although they have different kinds of villainies.' He stared hard at William, trying to fathom the thing, to get at what was below.

And his eyes were blue like Kirstie's, a candid and childish kind of blue, so that you must be sorry for him and he an old man. And it made the shame rise wild in William, shame of the thing itself, shame of his own body that had acted in this and that way, and shame of the quick lie which yet could not be helped or remedied. He felt the red in his neck and cheeks, but he did not move, neither hand nor lips. And, as they sat, not speaking at all, in, see, the one they were thinking on, aye, there came Kirstie, half running and a light heart in her. And, 'Look!' said she, 'here is Patrick coming and now I have all the folk round me that I love the best!'

PART THREE

ILL FISHING IN DRUMLIE WATERS

PATRICK THE BEAR

CHAPTER I

MR. ROBERT STRANGE was excessively hungry. He was a young man who enjoyed all the immediate pleasures of the senses. A fine day itself and the bonny colours on hill and sky would set him into a kind of ecstasy where he must sit down on the ground and laugh and stare and quote from the Latin poets. Skulking in summer had thus a certain charm for him. But in winter he had been more often to the capital than had been safe for his own head or his friends! Even after Culloden he did not really believe that he himself would be in danger. Not at least till the danger was on him, the soldiers back and front of the house. It was hard for him to learn the lesson that nobody was to be trusted, except maybe a woman. Isabella Lumisden, for all she could not tell a Vandyck from a Corregio, she was to be trusted utterly, as he had known, hiding under her hoop and hearing her composedly answering the English Captain. But once he had been back in his old engraving school and Cooper, whose apprentice and friend he had been, was none too pleased to see him. He was an Englishman of course. But there had been an unpleasant haste and forced cheerfulness, and he had not cared to go back. Not that he admired Cooper's work any the less for it: only the thing had been a disappointment.

He felt as safe as could be here in the attic, but it was as dull as Sunday; he had explored it all over. He had unfastened a bundle of old swords and pikes, tried to use a pikehead to carve himself a gargoyle, but abandoned it as hopelessly clumsy. Next he had tried on the kilts he had found in another bundle, cannily laid away by some Haldane wife against a time they might be needed. They were Graham tartan, come in no doubt with Mungo's mother that had been niece to the great Marquis. But they were musty and heavy and did not show a man's shape the way a pair of well-fitting breeches would do. For a time after that he imagined himself a fencing bout with an

247

opponent who was just a fraction less skilled than himself, and then for a time he watched a bright spot of sunlight, darting in past a broken slate, making a wonderful thing out of an old mat of spider's webs. And at long last in came James Haldane and Ochtertyre with his dinner, and behind them the other laddie and a young lady of reasonable good looks and a stiffish charm, who was presented to him as Adam Duncan's sister, Catherine. He dusted a seat for her, excusing himself for dining alone, and then took the tray on to his knees and his knife and fork out of their case.

The conversation was mostly between the younger ones. Ochtertyre sat silent mostly, his hands nervously round his stiff knee. There was plenty he wanted to talk about, to ask if Bob Strange had a mind of this or that person or event; he wanted above all to speak of the Prince. Yet it hurt to do so; it was like having a wound dressed. Bob could have told him about Culloden, about certain friends who had died there. Bob, who had so clear an eye for a portrait, could have told him of the last days, of the Prince's pain and anxiety and realism, his attempts to get sense into the heads of some of his commanders who were still squabbling and angling for prestige, and the young Stewart aware that their men were not being fed, trying to get at least broth and oatcakes for the Highland troops, that were his own only army· at the end of it. Atqui sciebat! Bob Strange would have seen the Regulus look. But could those things be spoken on, here in the Whig house? They could not be told of lightly, either with mockery or as of mere historical interest. So better not speak at all, better crush them back, into pain, hate of one's own illusions! Let Bob Strange babble away with the lads.

They had begun, casually, to speak of ghosts and such. James had explained how it was his uncle, William Macintosh, had stopped the gillies from any wish to sleep in the attic, and that had put Mr. Strange into mind of other stories of bogles and fairies and appearances of one kind and another. Not that he believed in a word of them, but he had heard plenty in his skulking. They were part of a game for frighting lassies and strangers or folks from the cities that might seem uppish to the landward ones.

'Yet all this must have been gey serious at one time,' said James, 'or we would not have been warned against such in the Scriptures.'

Robert Strange looked down modestly at his plate, as he always did when the Scriptures were mentioned; they were not his subject, oh not at all. He had known providence play some queer tricks which you could not get round by any kind of pious by-road. And there was a quotation this moment burning his tongue from David Hume the philosopher, ah, he was the boy to deal with appearances! Or the modern French writers, whose books you would not find in the Gleneagles library, catch them with a belief in the Sight or any such Highland nonsense! But it would be neither wise nor courteous to shock his hosts.

It was Ochtertyre who answered: 'It is well known that certain houses are haunted, and nothing more likely than that a great pain or a great love might leave its shadow behind it.'

'*Why* likely?' said James, frowning, worrying at it. Ochtertyre shrugged his shoulders. It was likeliness of the heart, not of the reason. He was not called upon to explain such matters to the Haldanes. If they did not see the thing, well then, nobody could point it out to them.

'There are other explanations possible,' said Adam, 'from a white petticoat upward and downward!' He giggled, and his sister near did the like but contrived to stifle it.

'You will get what has no explanation,' said Ochtertyre. 'Do you mind, Bob, on yon thing poor Rattray told us, of the house in Advocate's Close where he cut the judge's clerk for a rupture? Rattray was as clear headed a man as ever held a scalpel and the house within a stone's-throw of the Law Courts.'

'But if,' said James, colouring a little, 'if such things are of the Evil One or of what he has implanted in the human breast, will it matter at all if the house is new or old?'

Adam said: 'Cousin James, can you seriously suppose that the Evil One will be stooping to wee tricks such as the appearance of a fairy host to two old bodies going home sober from the ewe-milking, or the coming and going of shot in a wishing well?'

James fidgeted, for it was that he had in mind. Catherine said, diffidently, being the one woman in a conversation of men: 'Even such matters may distract a person's mind from reason and religion, and a great harm may come from a small and seeming harmless beginning.' And she thought sudden of the education of children — her children — and the bending of a green twig. And it came to her that James Haldane might have had a similar thought.

He looked at her with approval and spoke himself: 'It is certain at least that none of this can be of the Lord, and the likeliest is that these appearances will be pure Highland wickedness put about to keep decent Lowland folk from observing some smuggling or other breach of the law — ' And here he stopped suddenly, because his words had all the look of a rudeness to William Macintosh, or at least Catherine, loving her Aunt Kirstie, might interpret them so! He went on, plunging back, as none of the others had spoken: 'No, what I have in mind is worse things. Though they might start wee enough, as my Cousin Catherine said. The fairy host is uncovenanted. All that we know of comes from one side or the other, from the Lord or from the evil one. There is no middle way.'

Catherine leant forward, saying: 'We must not fall into the Manichean error, cousin James!' And oh the nice wee frown on her, thought Mr. Strange, and all as certain as the saints of getting to heaven by the right Whig road.

James said: 'It is a terrible hard thing to keep straight in one's mind, with the many pitfalls of error to either side. But how I am seeing it is that you may call a thing superstition and laugh at it on the top, but for all that it is the worst kind of danger.'

'A thing cannot be dangerous that has no existence,' said Adam.

'Aye, but see what you are taking for granted, Adam! It could be that most of those who were burnt for witches were nothing but poor, demented, old bodies. Yet there was a black evil at the back of it all, or how else could the Scriptures speak of witchcraft the way they do and how did decent, kindly folks think on it and act as they did, folks that could have no relish of the smell of burnt flesh or the skreiching of a fellow human?'

'I cannot imagine myself at a witch burning,' said Robert Strange in a kind of half anger and half amusement. Yet, he thought, these Haldanes, they would have been there on principle, even if it meant carrying their own coal sacks.

Murray of Ochtertyre spoke abruptly: 'None of you will know of the burnings at the Crook of Devon?'

There was a short silence; Catherine and Adam shook their heads. Then James said: 'Airthrey, my uncle, told me something of it.'

'The thing was away before his time,' Ochtertyre said.

'He told me it was some nursemaid that had spoke of it,' said James.

'Aye, so!' said Adam, 'nursemaid's tales for frighting bairns, and the next, grown men believing them!'

'What was it?' Catherine asked in a half whisper. Crook of Devon was near enough, a few miles ride up the glen and over, and a queer, overgrown, unchancy, midgy kind of place!

'There were thirteen of them tried for witchcraft,' said Ochtertyre slowly, 'twelve witches and a warlock, a de'il's dozen. One of the women died between the trial and the burning. She was old and there might have been rough handling.'

'They would have been strangled before the burning surely?' said Catherine, and felt she could never go past the Crook of Devon again.

'Aye, that was the sentence. They had done hurt to their neighbours. They had put sickness and death on bairn and horse and cow; for some wee spite they would trample down their neighbour's rye or lame his plough oxen; they had all a household in terror if one of them crossed the threshold. The place needed to be utterly rid of them. That was the way the laird of Tullibole, the schoolmaster, the bailie and the Ministers, were all taking on the burden and maybe the danger of the prosecution. All was to be cleansed by wind and rain, aye, down to the last smear of ashes that could have been hell-branded flesh; yet for all that there was no wish to hear a neighbour woman yelling and roasting. Their punishment was hereafter.'

'Aye,' said James, 'yon earthly burning was no more than the beginning of eternity.'

'Yet oh,' said Catherine with a wee gasp, 'we are all in the same peril, any who are outwith Grace! And how can we be sure of that?'

'Aye,' said James soberly, 'but we have our Redemption.'

It was embarrassing to Robert Strange to hear all this between young people spoken so terrible seriously. He could use the phrases himself, indeed he was no unbeliever, and when he and his Isabella were once married and settled they would certainly sit under some intelligent Minister with modern sympathies and an educated taste, such as could be found in the capital. But James Haldane and this lassie who should be speaking of other and more immediate matters, if he could judge by their looks to one another—! Yet maybe this was the Haldane fashion of courting. He broke through to Ochtertyre: 'What is all this bairn's talk of witches?'

'It was a thing that happened eighty years ago and more,' said Ochtertyre, 'and my grandfather knew of it because he was a friend to the laird of Tullibole, and went himself to assist at the trials, with a sprig of rowan under his shirt. For it seems it was a terrifying thing, with the witches that would be whiles grovelling and weeping, and whiles answering out of all order, and other whiles threatening and spitting and clawing, and folk didna like to be handling them. Yet he said that the trial was orderly and the witnesses were all sensible, couthy folk. There was even a certain reluctance here and there, to give evidence, for there was no woman in the coven that was not related in some way with the rest of the place. But it was proved conclusively that they had put charms on their neighbour's children and cattle, that they had met secretly and taken their marks and their devil's by-names, that they had acted with a malice that is of hell only and that they were signed and covenanted to evil in His own person.'

'All that was proved is a folly in the minds of folk who are over canny and strict and narrow in the way Scots landward people mostly are!' said Robert Strange. 'And,' he added, 'if a man thinks that all works of the imagination are evil, all pictures, all stage plays, all music that is neither dancing nor psalms, all that cannot be explained in terms of the kailyard, the byre, the wee shoppie and the Kirk Sessions, all that is forth of his own small experience, then, instead of finding place in his life for the arts, he will get himself bogged in superstition and cruelties and denial of a part of himself that will not be denied, but bursts up again like water compressed in a pump! But forgive me this speechifying.' He bowed to Catherine and the others. 'I fear I have overstepped my licence and said what I shouldna.'

Catherine answered: 'Indeed we would all be partly in agreement with you, Mr. Strange, would we not, Cousin James? I mean, we are not narrow in our views and I am most fond of romantic poetry and music and old stories. Yet they must never overlay one's duty.' Aye, thought James, there's the right of it, the way there must be good bones even under a lassie's soft, smooth skin. She went on: 'And even an enlightened and modern person must admit that terrible things happened in the old days.'

'This wasna that long past,' said Ochtertyre, 'and other things of the like nature have happened since.' And he half wanted to fright the lassie and her with no real knowledge of what could hurt or terrify.

'If you believe in them!' said Adam with a bite of scorn.

'You could ask your Aunt Kirstie about witchcraft,' said Ochtertyre angrily to the two Duncans.

'*Why?*' said Catherine and sudden felt a squeeze of anxiety on her heart, that she could not quite account for.

Ochtertyre did not answer. He had no wish to repeat anything he might have heard about Kirstie Haldane. Whatever there could have been in it at one time, it was now all over, surely. He wished he had not spoken, it was with no ill intent to anyone, only out of annoyance with the younger ones who were so sure of themselves.

'She told me I should not believe in witches nor even think on such subjects,' Catherine persisted.

'Well, maybe she is wise there,' said Ochtertyre disagreeably and cast a look at Bob Strange, wanting him to start a new conversation. But he did not speak and James was worrying at the thing again: 'Yet the power of evil is still working in the world for all the strivings of the godly. And if witchcraft were a manifestation of this —'

'But since there is no such thing!' said Adam, and went on: 'There is plenty of evil without wishing it on to a pack of old women. You will have no notion of the barbarities the French are constantly practising on their prisoners and on the poor Protestants in the galleys!'

But nobody wanted to talk about the French and the foreign situation. It was an awkward subject, with two Jacobites, and Ochtertyre who had been brought up in France. Adam, being in the Navy, felt almost like an Englishman. Mr. Strange asked tentatively about this Mr. Macintosh, who was, he understood, a relative? They had not had much time to make one another's acquaintance. 'Aye,' said James Haldane, 'he is married on one of the family. His father was the old Brigadier, Borlum, whom you will have heard tell of.'

'Was this one involved in the late troubles?' asked Robert Strange.

'No, no, he had sense enough for that!' said James. Ochtertyre coloured at this from the younger man, but Mr. Strange was only amused. 'We think well of him, for all he is a Highlander and has been something of a soldier of fortune,' said James.

Catherine was glad of his speaking so, glad of the family approval on something she approved. But what had her cousin meant, speaking so of Aunt Kirstie and witchcraft? What had the two to do with one another? Again she thought fearfully of the Crook of Devon and down beyond, Rumbling Brig, and the dark gorges and dripping mosses and the powerful hell-dark drowning river, digging among the cliff roots in swelches and whirlpools, out of which could come any kind of shape you could put a name to, any horror you half pictured with the tail of a bairn's memory, kelpies and the like, and oh they couldna be so ugly if they werena sinful! And sudden she knew she must see her Aunt Kirstie and that immediately, must see her cleansed of all dealings with sin and superstition, with things that maybe had no existence, yet could have power! She excused herself to the gentlemen and withdrew quietly and carefully, lest the servants should be making their observations. For a time she did not see Kirstie, then found her in the walled garden, discussing vegetables with the Gleneagles gardener and admiring his new frames and the half-dozen of wee, tough melons that he had contrived to produce from his hotbed. That was more than they could ever hope for at Borlum, but Lundie had its melons and cucumber frames against a south wall. It had been a tolerable year for the apricots, but you could never get vines to grow as they did in the south of England.

They walked down past the herb border and suddenly Catherine said: 'Aunt Kirstie, why did you tell me I should never believe in witches nor even think on them?'

'Did I tell you that, my dearie?' said Kirstie.

'Aye, you did, so! And with a special kind of intent. Now you are looking away from me, Aunt Kirstie. Oh, is there any particular knowledge you have about witches?'

Kirstie bent over, picking quick a mix and melly of sprigs, of the several sorts of thyme, of mint, marjoram and bergamot, sage, balm and parsley. You would not see if her hands were trembling. She said: 'There is nothing romantic or sublime about witchcraft, not at all, Catherine, nothing you could have the least curiosity over.'

'I am not wanting to know for myself, Aunt Kirstie, but — how is it *you* know? Aunt Kirstie, was it your good-sister, was it Mistress Shaw of Bargarran that told you?'

'She told me — somewhat,' said Kirstie stiffly. And then, her voice rising: 'But who has been telling you what of me? Catherine Duncan, were you believing it?'

Catherine threw her arms round her aunt's neck: 'Aunt Kirstie, dinna look so! Dinna be feared! Nobody said a thing, and supposing they did there would be no harm done. Ach, it is nothing but sinful curiosity on my part. Never you greet for me now!' She stroked her own soft cheek down against her auntie's, smelling the bruised herb leaves, holding close this other woman's body and wild, gripping hands.

She heard Kirstie whisper: 'There are those that say I had certain dealings with yon and I thought — I thought maybe Kyllachy had said what he shouldna — what he has no right —'

'And if he had,' said Catherine, 'and if there had even been a wee spark of truth in't you know sure, sure, that I love you!'

Kirstie held on to the young one's hands, lifted them against her neck and said: 'There is a kind of half-truth to it, and I thought some way that you, being a good and gentle lassie, could have felt a shadow on me, though I am aye hoping it isna there, or if someone had spoken, as they could do yet — Aye, Catherine, they could do it. These wild cruel Ayrshire folk, the miners and their masters, the full of the Kirk! They could get telling you that your mother's sister was suspected of witchcraft. And there's the truth of it, Catherine.'

So there was the truth of it, thought Catherine Duncan, and I am not caring. It is neither here nor there between my auntie and myself. And who would have thought of me feeling this way, it is most surprising and yet it is most natural and it has given me a new insight altogether into the nature of good and evil. I must study on this. Aye, and ask for guidance.

But for all that, the curiosity was strong in her. 'There will always be folk making up tales against others that are maybe better than they are themselves. But what at all did they say you did, Aunt Kirstie?'

'They could say the most terrible things with a kind of show of evidence, my dearie. And there is a thing which makes me doubtful of much that is called evidence. And at yon time, when I was so terrible unhappy, I would even have believed the evidence against myself. Yet now I am coming to think it wasna real at all, it was only an evil and unhappiness in myself, making me pictures of a kind that I could seize on. And one picture was of myself as a witch and brewer of malice, the way it goes in the bairns' tales, in yon stories of Phemie Reid's. And that could have been the same with Christian Shaw, my good-sister, who was the centre of a witch trial and all, when she was a child, and maybe a sick and easy frighted child, and so had the images more hardly impressed upon her, and that way her own later unhappiness came out in yon same form and image.'

'What made her so unhappy, then?' asked Catherine, and she knew that, because she had not been shocked by what had been said, but had accepted it with love and even understanding, she had taken a step in growth. And she knew, forby that, she would never speak of it with her mother and father. They would never come near to understanding. When Kirstie did not speak, she asked her question again.

'She hadna found a right man, poor Christian Shaw,' said Kirstie simply.

'If she had, would that have stopped the — images?' asked Catherine.

'Aye,' said Kirstie, 'I am sure of it.' And now she was herself again, now she dabbed her tears dry and smiled a bittie at Catherine. 'For I will tell you a thing. William, my husband, he is healing me of mine. He is aye turning me towards good. Catherine, it is a kind of redemption. There is why marriage has a blessing on it and isna simply a civil contract, the way some folks say. Not that a marriage that has had all the blessings in the Kirk put on it, may not turn out to be unblessed, and maybe another where the two folks were not bothering their heads what was said, may end up among the best. But mine — William and myself were truly joined of God, and it will be more than man can sunder us.'

'I am wondering if most folk feel so about their marriage, Aunt Kirstie,' Catherine said, for she was thinking now, not about witchcraft — and indeed the whole thing seemed simple

and laughable, and the Devon a bonny and friendly salmon
river — but about James Haldane.

'More than would admit it, I'm thinking,' Kirstie said. 'They
are blate at speaking good of marriage, in case other folk would
say they were too much occupied with the bed. Not that this
doesna have its importance, but no woman will want to appear
easy, even to her husband, though I canna just say why, considering the great pleasure, aye, and the great comfort and
good, that it is with the right man.'

'Should we think it a pleasure, Aunt Kirstie?'

'Well, if it is only a duty, they may need to send the press-gang
for some wives, but no' for me, my lassie! Yet for all that it is
not the greatest thing in marriage, Catherine, and if anything
were to take my William from me now, I think I would die just
as though my heart were to be taken from me. But surely the
Lord will be merciful to his two poor bairnies.'

They had come now to the clove-scented square of pinks, and
both knelt by the clipped box edge to pick them together. Then
Kirstie, looking up, saw Patrick Haldane riding slowly up to
the house, his shoulders somewhat bowed, his head dropping,
since he did not care much how he looked. And Patrick was her
own special brother, and Kirstie cried out with happiness, and
picked up her skirts and ran to meet him, down the garden and
over to the house.

CHAPTER II

PATRICK gave his sister an amiable smack, but dodged his head away, since he was kind of blate at being kissed, even by her. 'Give over now!' he said. 'How is your wean, Kirstie?'

'Och, she is getting terrible bonny,' said Kirstie, completely diverted from her purpose. 'And the cleverest wee notions she'll have, you would hardly believe, Pate — '

'She will be taking after her uncle,' he said and chuckled. 'Is your man here?'

'Aye!' she said. 'You'll be wanting to see him, sure, Pate?'

He grunted, with a pleased, warm feeling that he was half afraid of showing or admitting, since if he did, someone could laugh at him, or, worse, he could laugh at himself. He stepped across the threshold and looked round cautiously for whatever was bound to come and spoil him. His man had taken round the horses and baggage without fuss. The house appeared unaltered. At a certain time he himself had been the great one for improvements; it was he had drawn out the plans for the water-closet as he had seen them on the Continent, and had got the lead pipes from Alva's manager. But now he was less sure; a change in a house might be like the ripple of a smile; the mocking change in a face might show a thing behind which maybe should, for truth's sake, be seen, and yet was pain. Mungo at least would not go shifting the furniture about. A woman's trick, yon. He came through to the dining-room and helped himself to a glass of claret, rejected the white bread, and looked in the aumry for an oat bannock, saying to himself that there would be none these days, the women would have hid away such wholesome stuff. However, the things being there, a kindlier feel began to come on him with the wee trustable warmth of the claret. He had not been betrayed, he need not attack, he could be a good Bear.

Kirstie was telling him a hundred things at the once, about the wee lassie, about William, about Borlum, about his own daughter, Margaret. He listened and munched and drank. The scales of justice had been against Kirstie; now all was made up, in human time at least. Eternity was not his affair. His own judgment was valid for this world, he was prepared to stand by it. She was asking now would Tammie Clow bring him dinner? There would be the half of a cold pigeon pie and it would take no time at all to warm up the soup. But Patrick refused, because of his abiding certainty that no one mortal body was ever worth troubling another for. His body could satisfy itself on claret and oatmeal, aye and a wheen cheese. Let alone that he had dined, though badly and early, at Stirling. Supper could be put forward, suggested Kirstie. He shrugged his shoulders, cutting a wedge of the fresh cheese from the sheiling, better than the stuff you got in the Edinburgh taverns where the advocates met when the Courts rose.

Beyond, through the window, Captain Robert was walking the lawn with young James. In the relation between them Patrick was aware of the will, which he knew clause by clause since the firm had drawn it up, in favour of James, the rents of Airthrey, the well-stocked parks and plantations, the modern house. And although yon lad could say to himself, even, that none of this meant more or less affection towards his uncle, yet the buying price was there. It was a human thing to sell oneself. Mostly everyone did it, whether they knew or not. The women most of all; he had drawn up a bing of marriage contracts, one way and the other, and plenty bargaining in them. And Kirstie? Or maybe not Kirstie. It depended on the way you looked on it. But buying and redemption were both the same when you went back to the Latin. 'Come,' said Kirstie, 'we'll away find William and Mungo! I am that happy, Pate!'

'Ye silly wee bitch,' her brother said, following her.

As Kirstie came running in, her skirts caught up in one hand, the stillness between her brother and her husband broke in a half relief that the thing must be dropped for the time being, and half anger that it could not now be worried out to the bitter end. The anger in Mungo, letting Kirstie by, pinned itself on to Patrick, 'So you have found your ways back to your own decent folk, Pate!' he said. 'But you stink wild of the Courts! How many black lies have you whitened up in these last weeks?'

Patrick moved his head irritably as though a cleg had lighted on him. 'There will be as many lies told at Blackford between one sermon and the next as in a year of the Court of Sessions, and full more reputations torn to pieces by the hoodies of the congregation! As you know better than I, Mungo. Well, Borlum, do you see Strathearn and Gleneagles itself as bonny as Paris and Virginia and maybe a suburb of the Holy City, the way your wifie sees it?'

William relaxed a little, feeling that some way things might take a turn for the better; he had breathing space now; his prayer was half answered. He said: 'Your self has spoken of it the same gate as your sister, Patrick!'

'Did I now?' said Patrick. 'Did I speak good? Of Gleneagles and of the family? It is queer the notions a body will take.'

'Ach away!' said Kirstie, 'what will I do with twa sic muckle tumfies for my brothers! William, my soul, what at all have you done to Mungo to put yon thrawn look on him?' She tucked her arm under his, curling her fingers into the palm of his hand, wanting to feel herself little and clasped and secure. He did not fail her there. But for all that he gave no answer.

Mungo pulled himself together. 'Maybe we are too old to quarrel, you and I, Pate,' he said, 'we need to stand by one another, surely.' And sudden he was wanting wild to consult the Bear over this matter of William Macintosh. Who now looked liker Kirstie's true man than her betrayer, and yet — Without noticing what he was doing, he stood rubbing his backside up against the corner of his desk, the way it might have been one of his own stirks under a thorn tree. 'What is the news from Edinburgh?' he asked, and offered a snuff.

Patrick took it slowly. 'Poor Andrew Fletcher is chasing rebels for the Duke of Newcastle,' he said, 'but he hasna caught any.'

'Na, na,' said Mungo, 'he has a sliddery grip that has an eel by the tail! But it is time these Dukes and such gave up the harrying of poor Scotland. Andrew Fletcher, honest man, could be left to the work and it wouldna go so ill for anybody.'

'Albermarle is forth of the country at least,' said William.

'We dinna miss him any!' said Mungo.

'A dog's nae waur than his fleas,' Patrick said, 'and Albermarle has left the most of his fleas behind him. Let alone that a letter will do as much mischief as a tongue, and maybe more. And by the same token,' and he looked clear at William Macintosh, 'the American mails came in an hour before I rode out of the High Street!'

Black William's hand closed over Kirstie's. His mind skidded like a curling stone over dark ice, over monstrous shapes below him. Yet if Patrick had heard, by some illest of ill chances, would he have spoken friendly, at the first? Could it be the Bear was drawing back for a strike of his claws? He must, some way, any way at all, get him alone. Nothing must be said. Not before Kirstie!

And the talk went on, over persons and politics and the clever, unkind gossip of Edinburgh, the way a talk will do, on its own, apart from folks' minds. For there was William in a fine sweat of immediate anxiety and fear of Judgment; and Mungo with his worries and suspicions stounding away at him like maggots at a sheep's neck on a still summer's day; and Patrick trying out a thing with all the interest that Professor MacLaurin, the mathematician, could have had in the shattering dunt of a cannon ball on Edinburgh city walls of a known thickness; and Kirstie aware that something was amiss among the men but she did not rightly know what. It seemed to her mostly to be between Mungo and Patrick, since she had taken the sudden tightening of her man's hand as for herself, for kindness. And so, instead of going out with William and Patrick, she stayed behind, for a coaxing and soothing of Mungo, and indeed it was hardly fair that he, the master of the house and the oldest of the family, should be set agley by the Bear. For there must be the reason he was as cross and uneasy as an old bull in March.

But Patrick and William went along to Patrick's room, the one he always had, where he must see to the unpacking of his papers. He had with him the brief in the case of Provost Stewart, with dispositions from the Deacons of the Trades concerned and a part of Professor MacLaurin's diary. His man had the most of his linen and such laid in the press, the way he was used to having it. His reading spectacles, penknife and quills, ink and sand box, were in order beside the papers. He stood heavily, looking down at them or past them, staring and frowning, yet maybe not at them and not at the knavery of Edinburgh Tories, but at a thing beyond. Black William swallowed and said: 'You were speaking of the American mails, Bearcrofts.'

'Aye,' said Patrick, in a way that gave no help, no clue.

And William saw his sins come black over the face of God, a shadow, a dreadful wing, and something he had known all along. If there had been any drink in yon room he could have done with a dram. Aye, or two. But there was not. Only Bearcrofts with his head hunched and his thick hands stravaiging about amongst the papers. Bearcrofts who had helped him before, who had helped his father, who would maybe never help him again. How could he, how would he, if he knew — what could a brother do but destroy the man who had done that to his sister — 'For the dear Lord's sake,' he said, 'Patrick — '

'Letters from my correspondents in Boston,' Patrick said and nodded his head slowly at William. 'Aye, William Macintosh, you may well have yon look on you. And maybe it is as well we disarmed you all, and it is no kind of use you feeling for a weapon!'

The breath in William's throat broke to a cry and his face darkened and sudden he was on the floor at Patrick's feet, twisted with a blow of pain, a dolour of sin and shame come on him. 'Patrick,' he said, 'dinna tell! Oh, for Jesus' sweet sake dinna tell Kirstie! It will fair kill her, Patrick! Ach, I will go away with no more than the clothes on my back, I will never see her again, so long as she doesna know, her and the wee one!'

Patrick was interested, and then all at once disgusted and abashed with the Highlands, with this kind of naked surrender. It was as though William had stripped himself. 'Stand you on your feet,' he said, 'and face your sins if you have the blood of a mouse in you.'

But the words were not getting to William. There he was, shut in a dropping, closing pit-mirk, and within, as is surely known of Hell, there was no redemption, no forgiveness, only for ever punishment and that no more than he deserved. Yet the heavy swell of his misery broke on a jag of rock, the first, for Patrick had kicked him in the face. He stood up slowly, in the knowledge that, on this, either he must kill Patrick or he must accept everything. His thoughts, that came with pain and difficulty, blood on their edges, made him pictures of men he had known, in exile mostly, that had acted worse than himself and yet had faced it out like gentlemen, getting plenty pleasure out of the world and the flesh, men that would no more have let themselves take a dirty kick from an Edinburgh solicitor than have willingly taken the pox. They were, however, not believers. And he was. And if you were a believer you couldna be a gentleman, not their way of it. There was nothing at all to do but face Patrick and take his punishment.

'You havena speired at me what thing ava I had in my letters,' said Patrick suddenly and with a childish kind of curiosity.

'I ken,' said William.

'You are saying that,' said Patrick.

'How no'?' said William. 'To my sorrow.'

'Would you affirm,' asked Patrick, 'with any truth that is left in you, that you would leave my sister now at once with some kind of a plausible lie, you will know best what, but most likely the politics? And off with you to the Continent, and there make yourself out dead?'

'If thon's your terms,' William answered heavily. 'And you not ever to breathe a word to her of the curse that's in it. But Borlum?' He waited, thinking passionately of Kirstie and his wee one, of his crops and experiments and improvements, his folk at Borlum, the only spark of a straw to grasp on to in all this loss the making of a sufficiently plausible lie. If he could. Lying to her at the last. He would need to say a thing and go quick in the moment of saying — before she touched him — he could not bear it! He heard Patrick saying, 'We will manage Borlum,' and hate of the Haldanes went through him in one fierce wave of the blood. He checked it with all his will, yet his heart went on its pounding. The mark of Patrick's boot on his cheek-bone slowly turned to a bluish-red.

'I am wondering,' said Patrick, 'how Kirstie will fare without a man. She did ill enough yon other time.'

'You could get me killed clean without twisting the knife,' said William, and the tears jumped clear out of his eyes, over his black under lashes, down his cheek and neck.

'Or else,' said Patrick deliberately, 'you could take your ways back to America and see what like of welcome you would get from the children of your loins. Aye, they might have plenty to say to their father, but would it be the most agreeable? A scalping knife, they tell me, gives a better twist than any wee lawyer's paper-knife that I might have.' Again William held himself on his feet into a kind of armour, unaware of his own weeping, knowing only that the worst was yet to come. 'Yet,' said Patrick, 'maybe you might come to an agreement with the Indians. But I fear you would not have the old consolations of the flesh. Since I heard from my correspondents that your wife is dead.'

When that came through to him, William did a terrible shocking thing that made even Patrick blink. He made a Popish sign of the cross and said: 'God rest her soul.'

'Your so-called and denominated marriage to my sister,' said Patrick, 'is legally invalid and the issue of it a bastard.' The words were meant to hurt, but William did not answer. The thought of Ohnawiyo was at him strong, as she had been, a royal one, aye, a mountain lion, a Queen. The one pain might keep him from the other, from the mockery of the bull calves, Patrick's cold Edinburgh voice girding on at him: 'But you will mind that in Scots law there is more than one kind of marriage. Marriage by repute, aye, that is a kind of coarse thing, though it works well enough among the common folk that canna be fashed with the Ministers. It is a thing that takes seven years or thereabouts of faith, and there is something harder than a braw promise in the Kirk and the Minister's fees paid. During the seven years the status of the couple is an interesting and arguable point, whether they are bedding in a state of sin or of provisional grace, but it hasna arisen much in my profession, since the most of those that have practised it havena the siller to back an argification.'

A thing began to strike William through all this. He couldna be sure. He couldna dare to let light the wee low of hope in his breast. Yet he had to speak. 'If she is dead —' And could say no more.

'Aye,' said Patrick, leaning on the desk, 'gin she's in her grave, the poor soul — And how will yon Indians be burying their folk, now?'

'She will be laid in her sleeping mat,' said William slowly, 'and the ones that did it will be unchancy for a time, they will not be hunting nor eating with the rest. And her name — her name will not be spoken, not until the time of mourning is past, not until the raising of the tree.' And he was wondering, did she meekly let death come, as a Christian does, or did she, being royal, go out to meet it, as he had known and seen —

'Aye, so,' said Patrick comfortably. 'Well, well, there is nothing that beats a good-going funeral. Except it could be a wedding. Yet there is never the same gaiety there. For there is a lifetime of trouble ahead and ilka man kens it in his heart, but once a body is waked there are his troubles past.'

'Patrick!' said William, with a harsh swallow in his throat, and could say no more. For now he half thought that there was a plan emerging, a way of escape out of hell. Failing his tongue, his hands turned towards Kirstie's brother, a light and thin-boned hand, of a different race. It was a wonder, thought Patrick, if the man might not have hands as small as Kirstie's own. Himself and Kirstie, they were heavy wristed, a lace cuff did not fall the way it should for them. If a body was caring for such whigmaleeries. He had worn Brussels lace at the wedding, to give her pleasure. Well, well. 'What are you studying on, Patrick?' William was asking, urgently, imploring.

'I am thinking,' said Patrick, 'that there is nothing I did not know at the time of your wedding and myself at it, as you will doubtless have mind on, William Macintosh. I let my sister go to your bed and to your getting of a bastard wean on her, and that because I loved her, and because I like folks better than I like either the laws of God or the laws of Scotland. Or any of your kings and loyalties and oaths, and there's for you and yours, ye Jacobite Highland liar!'

'You knew at yon time — about the other?' asked William in an overpowering astonishment and with a lightening coming on him so quick that he was half dizzy, that his heart was beginning to fill with joy and praise that were beyond words.

'There will be little hidden from a good firm of Writers,' said Patrick.

'I canna begin to understand you,' William said.

'How would you?' said Patrick, with a kind of simple scorn and complacency that must be let go, aye, must be taken as part of his nature, part of the Haldane nature maybe. 'How could you, and you that have no right philosophy, nor the ideas of good and evil well sorted out, the way you can pick and choose, aye and choose evil if there is a sufficient and predestinate reason for it.'

'Did you choose evil when you let sign and seal my marriage contract with your sister?'

'Na, na. It would have been far eviller to go the Ministers' gait and send poor Kirstie back over to the loss of what wits she ever had, poor bitch.'

'When have you chosen evil, Patrick?' William asked again.

Patrick weaved his head about crossly, not wanting William to suppose that he would not be as wicked as the very De'il if he chose, and yet wishing it to be certain that anything of the kind had been done by no Highland accident or impulse, but out of principle and predestination. 'You will speir at them I have overset,' he answered.

'It seems,' said William, 'that I have all the cause in the world to be grateful to you, Patrick Haldane.'

'Aye,' said Patrick, and laughed once, loudly, 'excepting for your face that you will need to be explaining to Kirstie! If I hadna gone about to gie you a wee touch of my boot you would still be crawling your ways down through the floor boards of Gleneagles the like of a louse in a sark. But the thing I canna make head nor tail on, is how in all the world you came to be marrying yon Indian lassie and you so snug in Boston.'

'I am bound to suppose from that,' said William, 'that your correspondents had some word of our firm's dealings in ships' papers and such.' Patrick nodded. 'And I must also suppose you will have heard of my own dealings with Mistress Bradstreet, the wife of the senior partner.'

'Now there,' said Patrick, 'is a thing that had escaped my observations.'

'Thank God there was something!' said William. 'But there was a pure wickedness of the flesh, and I have told it to Kirstie and she didna seem to be fashing any over it.'

'She has a wee spark of sense, the woman,' said Patrick. 'But I see that much less of a reason why you should go with the Indians.'

'It wasna reason,' said Black William, and then he said: 'If you are for my speaking of this, I am thinking I could maybe go fetch the brandy and the glasses from below.'

'Aye, aye,' said Patrick, 'we will be none the worse of a dram, neither of the two of us.'

Young Captain John had been reluctant to walk the garden with Kyllachy. Yet the man appeared sensible enough, was clearly no longer involved in any Jacobitism or such, and had not mentioned a word of money. One could in general be sure that any Highlander would be borrowing if he could get his tongue round you, and then it was goodbye to a month's pay! He had found this when the *Tryall* was lying up in the Firth and the officers of her crew visiting amongst the gentry of Inverness, or what might be supposed to be the gentry. But this Kyllachy fellow was, after all, a relation, although a far-out one. He was knowledgeable on various matters and had some acquaintance with the Continent. The older generation, such as Mungo, had never been forth of the United Kingdom, or not since they had been lads; and plenty waters had flowed under the bridges since then. But Mungo's knowledge of foreign politics seemed to have ended with the Treaty of Utrecht. Scotland had, to his mind, been shrinking since then; had become a paltry, cramped kind of place, unfit for a man of ambition. You felt the intolerable, overbearing pride of the religious, old bones of stupidity calling themselves the Elect and spying upon their neighbours. Not that he himself was in any way free-thinking, but here at Gleneagles you could scarcely speak of politics without someone taking you up religiously!

They were passing the dining-room windows now and sudden Kyllachy stopped, put a finger to his lips and beckoned young Captain John to look in with him. And there, sure, was the droll sight of Borlum on his knees in front of the table and apparently at prayer. It is sufficiently comic to observe your fellow humans when they think themselves alone, their breeches down, engaged in their most private business, and when they are not only naked in the private parts of the body, but in the private parts of the soul, then the comedy, if comedy it is, becomes richer yet. And if in addition you have the strong conviction that religion should be kept in its place and season, which must be at worship, preferably within a suitable building, you will be filled not only with amusement but also with disgust. This surpassed itself when Captain John observed that, at the end of his prayer, which had apparently been of an exhausting kind, Macintosh of Borlum got a good grip of the brandy bottle and glasses and walked out of the room with them!

'Well, well,' said Kyllachy, 'there is a vessel of Grace that will be sufficiently filled!'

'The canting hypocrite!' said young Captain John angrily — he had never liked the man, nor liked the idea of his marrying into the family.

'You might well say so,' said Kyllachy, 'if you knew as much of the man as I know.' And as they walked along, Kyllachy let drop a thing or two.

Black William brought up the brandy bottle and poured it; the dutch glasses were beautiful, clear as air. It was the great pleasure he had now to observe anything beautiful, to be thankful for it. Patrick gave Kirstie as the toast. They touched glasses and nodded. 'Do you mind,' said Patrick, 'when you came to my firm to borrow your passage money, in fear of your life and an old kilt, ready to let on you could speak nothing but the Irish?'

'You were terrible kind to me, Patrick. I knew there were certain notions you had in common with my father, but I never thought they would reach to myself. Indeed at the time I was kind of half ashamed at them; they werena the fashionable wear and I was over full of ambitions.'

'They arena that well thought on now, you will have to dress them up for most folks, even here in the family.'

'Fine I know it,' said William, 'and I am gey careful with all but Kirstie and yourself. Though they will get round it by saying that these are American ideas, when they are good Scots ones all the time! But yon evening I went creeping up the steps to your lodgings, as shy as a wild cat. You hadna any great reputation for kindness.'

'I had taken a kind of scunner at the respectable, and they lying and cheating everyhow to get their estates. You didna ask me for Borlum back, nor even lie to me.'

'I had been so clean affronted by yon other firm that I hadna the heart to lie, Patrick. And, some way, with you that were Kirstie's dearest brother, I didna want. There is a kind of honesty in me at the bottom, Patrick, though maybe now's scarce the moment to speak of it.'

'I ken fine,' said Patrick, 'and if I didna, you would not be standing here the now.' He swirled the brandy glass thoughtfully, smelling at it first with one nostril and syne with the other, and he smiled to himself and at last he said: 'I aye thought you would pay me back this side Doomsday, William.'

'I paid yourself,' said William, thinking back to it, 'though the Erskine money I could never pay. It was out of a present that was given me by a tobacco broker in the port of Richmond whom I did not care for over much, for doing him a favour which I would have done anyway out of pure spite on another man! There was full more good will over my passing on of yon money than there ever was over the getting of it.'

'Now that would have been which year?' Patrick asked casually.

'That would have been in '28, almost a score of years past.'

'You will have sent it as a bill of exchange on an Edinburgh house, I am thinking?'

'Aye,' said William, with a shade of wonder at the question, and then: 'Patrick, you got yon money, surely to the Lord!' Patrick shook his head and William set down his glass and stared and syne coloured up to his eyes: 'And you never said, not even at the time of the drawing up of the marriage contract! Not yon first time I was back, when I was seeing my father in prison!'

'Och,' said Patrick, kind of roughly, 'you had enough on your mind those days, or should have had. You never mentioned the matter yourself, William!'

'There were mostly plenty letters sent me in America that went astray and I was supposing that your own letter of acknowledgment would be one of them. One doesna like to be speaking too much on such things. It will be little use now hoping to find what came to my bill of exchange. But I will pay you when I get my hill cattle sold, Patrick. I am bringing them in to my two parks of sown English grass at the back-end — the hay will be taken off them next month, God willing, and the stirks will have the after growth and foggage, part of the hay itself and a puckle turnips — and the fat they will be for the New Year market at Inverness where mostly there's nothing but skin and bone!' He spoke quickly and stopped as quick, 'Ach, Patrick, you arena believing me, neither on my beasts nor over this money, and how would you? I havena proof. And how will you ever be trusting me?'

'Could you give me the name of the Edinburgh house?'

'Aye, it was Paton and Lindsay; they had a hand in the West India trade and from there to Virginia.'

'They will have been unfriends of mine, even at yon time. Calling themselves Whigs and against the old privilege and thinking out braw new privileges and monopolies for themselves and their English friends! My firm will go into the matter, William Macintosh, and if you are no' lying — But man, this is a pure stupidity. I havena the least doubt you are speaking the truth.' He took another good warming sup of the brandy and pushed the bottle over to William.

But he did not take it. He said: 'I am wild affronted at this, Patrick. You that have been so good — I'll need to tell herself.'

'Kirstie will only be laughing at the two of us. And maybe that's the best. Fill you your glass, William.'

William shook his head. 'Times in my life, Patrick, I have drunk full more than I ought to have, and I willna do that again. I have had enough brandy to speak the truth and no' yet so much as will put an over weight of florrish on the bare boughs of the story.' Patrick grunted, agreeing. William said: 'There are two ways of thinking on the Indians and neither of the two of them right. There is the way that the Coast folk, and the rich Quakers above all, think, which is that the Indians are full of nobility and virtue and truth and maybe one of the lost Ten Tribes on the top of it, and if they are treated right, all is bound to be well. Those that think this way will mostly be living in towns and seeing only tame Indians who will tell them only such tales as they want to hear, and I have known my own Highlanders doing the same; their land will not have been Indian land for a hundred years; they will never have heard the howling of a raid nor the whistle of an arrow at night. But the other kind of folk will say there is no good Indian but a dead Indian, and they are the ones on the frontier who may not have seen any but the same tame Indians, yet they canna get out of their heads the thought of the wife scalped in the kitchen and the bairn in the cradle bleeding to death while the man is away · from the house; they are aye thinking of plain Indian treacheries which are yet maybe no worse than those of our own politicians, only not dressed in the same language of politeness, but altogether naked.'

'And which was your own thought?' asked Patrick.

'I have had them both, according to who I was amongst and the work I was doing. I had mostly the first kind of thoughts when I was with White and Bradstreet in Boston, and anything seemed better than the men of affairs that were my equals or masters there. For all that I am not sure that the American colonists ever got the thing right, except for one or two of another kind of Quaker that were altogether practical in an upside down kind of way, as folk are like to be that are directly led by the Inner Light and not having either their thoughts or their actions pulled one way or another by their own interests. Whiles I have thought that the French were better friends with the Indians, since they were rather explorers and adventurers, a thing understandable to the Indians themselves, and not wanting to take exclusive possession of land and settle and build, the way ourselves do. They could live easily on each other's terms, aye and marry. You will maybe have seen a book called *Mœurs des Sauvages Ameriquains*?' Patrick shook his head. 'Well, maybe I shouldna be speaking of it, since the author is one Père Lafitau, a Jesuit Missionary, and indeed it is a daft kind of book in parts and the pictures made by someone who had as romantical a notion of Indians as — as Catherine Duncan. But Père Lafitau was fond of the Hurons and Iroquois, the man; he just plain liked them and their food and their ways of dressing and hunting and tending their bairns. In yon book he is needing to put in wee bits fornent their conversion and that, though I never knew a pure blood Indian that was converted right, either by Minister or by Priest. My wife wasna, for all we were married in Church and I thinking I had changed the fairy into human flesh.' He walked over to the window and drummed on the pane, wondering how to explain the thing to Patrick Haldane sitting there as non-commital as a sealed packet. He wanted now to get away utterly from the very shadow of a lie. Yet it was no simple thing, even to himself, and gey easy to be wise after the event. And maybe in telling it he might see clearer where it was he had merely lacked judgment and where he had truly sinned. Or whether, since he was a thinking being who had got his share of education in religion and philosophy, the two things were the same and equally punishable.

He said: 'Did you ever see a shape in your dreams and then one day you met it in real life, Patrick?' But Patrick Haldane shook his head; that was not his manner of considering an event. William said thoughtfully: 'There was the way it seemed to me. At the first. They were not tame Indians, thon. Nor were they like the Cherokee that we fought with at New Speyside and beat. They were wearing all their braws, the two of them walking through the bleak Boston streets between the houses of tarred or dark painted wood, going like wolves, staring and listening. And oh, Patrick, I was dead sick and out of heart with Boston, and Mistress Bradstreet at me to be going with her again and half trying to make difficulties with the firm if I didna.

'You will have no notion, Patrick, of the grand yon Indian gear will look on those that wear it right. There is tunic and robe with meaningful and thick embroidery of beads and bears' teeth and moose hair and porcupine quills. They are heavy on one, the same as a plaid is, aye and the same way proud and comforting, and the pattern on them telling as much as the tartan tells. Her robe was of black squirrel fur with the tails fringing it. I had some knowledge of furs by then, and the beauty and costliness of thon great square of picked skins had me by the eyes before ever I thought on the woman that was wearing it about her in precise and queenly folds, and the long plaits of her black, smooth hair losing themselves in it. There was the flash of forest bird colour from her mittens and moccasins — they are like our own brogues only better made and stitched with patterns of brightness. A narrow scarlet line drew down from the parting of her hair to the spot between her eyebrows. He wore his crown of erect feathers and in his pierced ears plumes of pale and quivering swansdown and on one shoulder the brilliant feathers of a jay. They didna speak. There was a tracery of pattern on his face, colours of earth and autumn. He carried a tall bow of hickory wood, and other things, aye, certain other things in a fringed bag of deer-skin, since he supposed that his own magic would still be powerful forth of his own woods. She too had brought magic, and it seems to me now that I had the sense of it even at the first look. Aye, a man and woman of the Sidhe, of the fairy people.

'Patrick, it was borne in on me that I must speak with them, that they were akin to me or my dreams. You will picture me in the decent and somewhat threadbare blacks of my profession, agent in a shipping firm, a kind of uniform that was no pleasure to wear. It was a day of thaw and dampness before the right hard frosts of midwinter, and a salt haar off the sea that minded me terrible of Scotland. There was a smell of cured herring in it, the same you would get in Aberdeen. I had been at accounts and correspondence all morning and I was going back to my dinner and hoping I wouldna meet Mistress Bradstreet, nor need to speak to her in gallantries that were far from my heart and hard to make up day after day. And there was Ohnawiyo the same as the fairy woman that could have been watching among the birches of Knocknasidhe beyond Borlum, in the twilights when Benjie and Lachie and I would dare each other to the widdershins run. There was power of the fairies put upon me as I looked from her fur robe to her face, to her eyes; the trader's thoughts in me withered to nothing and I took my hat from my head and bowed and spoke to them slowly in English, asking what could I do for them.'

'Well, well,' said Patrick, 'we arena so thrang with the fairies in Edinburgh! I am astonished that they didna come riding on two-headed monsters while they were about it. But continue, William.'

'I am trying to say how it seemed,' said William, 'how opposite to all that was irking me most in Boston. Often enough I had cheated the tame Indians who came in with furs, giving them beads and old guns and raw spirits in exchange for the bonny pelts of bear and racoon and squirrel and musquash and, best, beaver. But I had no notion to cheat the two Wolves: Tehoragwanegen, which is in English Two Planets, and Ohnawiyo, which is Good Stream. I turned back with them and gave them dinner in one of the taverns, which they ate shyly and delicately, and a mulled wine which they sipped at and I drank off. I mind I had the dinner put down to the firm's account, and likely enough it was paid some day! In a roundabout way, and as though it were no concern of his, Tehoragwanegen, who spoke and understood English, as most of the Iroquois do, told me of his business in Boston and at last showed me the deed which he had brought with him, and spoke of the circumstances of its signing. I knew well enough the office in Boston that he was bound for, and it looked to me as though yon deed were only too binding by our laws, and sudden I saw the whole thing from the Indian side as I never had before. I had felt, often enough, a spark of compunction at our cheatery, yet it didna do to think over much on't; one needed to be hard and neither give nor expect trust nor faith, and the De'il would see after his own bairns. But now — See you, Pate, the Indians wanted the things we had to sell them, the weapons most of all. Indeed, if one lot had them, the others couldna afford not to. And, once they had bitten, we would carefully raise the price of powder and balls on them, things which they couldna furnish for themselves and without which the muskets were useless. Forby that they wanted spirits and blankets and beads and certain manufactured goods. And the more we sold to them, forever praising up our gear as the best because the white man's, the less they were able to make for themselves and the less trouble they would take to think on new ways of doing in their old crafts and methods. So they were caught in a net, and it pleased us colonists mightily, for we saw an immediate way of profit for ourselves, and certain future destruction of the Indians, leaving the land to us. But now there was a different look to it. The men of the Lodges of the Wolves, Tehoragwanegen's fighters, they needed so many guns and so much ammunition, and their women were at them for mirrors and gewgaws that another set of squaws might have had, and it did not seem to Tehoragwanegen and the elders to make much when the price was a mark on a piece of paper by the chief and war-leader. They did not think of an exact area of land belonging either to them as a tribe or to Tehoragwanegen. Land was not, for the Indians, a thing susceptible of ownership or of exact measurement. Land was all men's; it was only the crops you had cultivated or the game you had killed or the Lodges you had built which could be property.'

'You, being a Highlander, will have had your understanding of that,' observed Patrick. 'For it is the same with you, or was till lately. And trouble enough it had been causing to the rest of us. But your chiefs were cannier and knew fine what they were about when they sold away the birthright of their people.'

'Aye,' said Black William, 'and in my mind I was interpreting the thing into terms of the cheating and bewilderment and hatred that I knew with my own heart and in my own first tongue, so that words of the Gaelic that I had not been using much in the last few years, came back on me in a blinding and bewildering way, and I put my hands over my eyes and when I uncovered them again, Ohnawiyo was looking at me quietly, and as I looked back at her she laid her thin and strong hand on mine, firmly like a strong bird gripping. Nor do I know for certain to-day what she meant by it nor how much. But the thing had me by the throat.'

'And would that thing,' asked Patrick, 'be more accurately termed the power of the fairies or the lust of the flesh?'

'Both the two,' said William. 'You will not be believing me, Patrick, but it was like a part of my soul. I saw myself in her, aye and in him. It was the way a man's own fetch will walk out of a mist on to him and he knows there is a doom coming.'

'Surely you have more sense in you than to believe yon kinds of Highland superstition!' said Patrick.

'It isna superstition,' said William, 'only maybe an over-clear way of saying a thing that we all know. For there are times when one is bound to stand apart from oneself, either in good or in evil. And consider the disquieting shapes of one's dreams, that must be made out of one's own soul and that yet seem utterly separate from oneself. Even Patrick Haldane will have dreamt!'

'Without paying over much heed to it,' said Patrick, and then: 'There are those that say such dreams are sent out of hell by old Nick for his own ends.'

'Even if they are of hell,' said William, 'they speak to a part of us. And that part may not be wholly bad. But of an underworld. Of the hills of the Sidhe. Of the dreams below sleep. Of the spirits of the wild woods.'

'If those are your true opinions,' said Patrick amicably, 'you are a heretic.'

'The same as yourself, Patrick. The truth is not near simple enough to be washed and cleaned and folded away by the Kirk that must have everything in black and white and as precise as a legal document. With heaven of the one part and hell of the other. That may be well enough in an orderly and unchanging place. But it doesna square with the facts of a new world, the like of America.'

'Maybe we are all in a new world,' said Patrick, 'in spite of the continuance of old houses' — and he looked around at the solid, little disguised walls of his own room, a thin plaster over the masonry— 'and old ideas such as your Dynasties of Stewarts and the like. But the Kirk, having made one muckle great change, will not see that there is another — aye, and maybe more — to come. Nevertheless, William, you contradict yourself, speaking with even a half belief in the fairies and such; it doesna go with the kind of sensible actions and speech that you have when it comes to folk. The kind of sense that you have with your tenants. Or with my sister Kirstie.'

'Do you yourself know,' asked William, 'how far bogged she was in yon underworld when I came back from America and asked her to — came to a certain decision in regard to her?'

'Asked her to — be your harlot, you would say, William.'

'You spoke yourself of marriage by repute,' said William, 'and I beg you not to be saying such things, however much pleasure it is giving you, or you will say them when you shouldna.'

'Na, na, I have finished,' Patrick said. 'But as to her — I had more than a suspicion of it when she came to Bearcrofts. If I have the thing guessed right, she had it at the back of her mind that she had killed her man through some kind of spells or other Devil's work.'

'That is so,' said William.

'But there is nothing real to it!' said Patrick violently, 'and you know it and you have her almost persuaded of it, or she wouldna step so lightly this day. I amna such a fool that I canna see that far.'

'There are these contradictions in us,' said William, hesitating, walking about the room, 'and if one refuses to allow for them, then one can see that far less into events and into how folk will act on a given occasion. Which is so with over many of the religious. You are saying that the one side is true and the other utterly false; I wouldna like to say that. But I have a thought that Kirstie's imaginings on the Horny were, some way, yon same part of her soul got loose and become a person on its own. I met this in the flesh with Ohnawiyo and gave it power, and Kirstie met hers for a moment and would have given it power over her, but in the instant of her surrender it became me. But I see you will not credit me with the least sense over this, Patrick! You will have no contradictions in yourself, nor none in the family. Yet I can assure you that they exist. Only maybe there is a kind of direction which one can take in the interpretation of all of them into life.'

'And that direction?' asked Patrick.

'That is of God,' said William, 'and shown by the Inner Light.'

'You speak like a Quaker, William Macintosh, and you are a member of the Episcopalian Church.'

'Aye, and I will go to the Presbyterian Church at Blackford if that is the best way to avoid an unchristian thing such as strife between brothers or between brother and sister. And there is one and the same thing that you do yourself, Patrick.'

Patrick grunted. 'We will get no forrarder this gait. Go you on with your story, William, and with your fairy woman. There is ae thing that you have not mentioned about her, poor soul: was she bonny?'

CHAPTER IV

WILLIAM did not answer for a little time. At last he said: 'You will maybe have noticed, Patrick, that in the songs that are made about the fairy folk, there is seldom any mention of whether they are bonny, and that by such poets as will be extravagantly praising the flax-blue eyes and corn-gold locks of the lassies that were made of mortal flesh. There were things about Ohnawiyo, Patrick — I have no mind of what I thought at the first, only that it became immediately apparent to me that I could not stay a week longer in Boston, and a thought that, by going, all would be solved and set to right.

'I went with them and their deed to yon other office, where, as I had supposed, there was nothing at all to be done. The land had been resold to settlers, passing through two or three hands maybe and something going on to the price at each change. And it was these settlers, who had paid dear enough for their land, who had now been shooting to kill such Indians as had trespassed over their ground, in the ordinary way of hunting or going from place to place, from which in return, vengeance, burning and scalping, as it was like to be almost everywhere along the frontier, for all our treaties with the Five Nations of the Indians.

'There is a kind of daze over it all when I cast my mind back, Patrick. For I was doing this and that in a precise and assured way and with my judgment as sound as it has ever been. Yet my mind and my soul were separate as horse and rider. But the end of it was that the three of us left Boston in the first of the light one winter morning and I had left my blacks behind me for ever, aye, hat and buckled shoes and all. I was wearing my old logging gear and fur cap, Indian moccasins and snow-shoes; but I was out of practice with yon things and it was hard going for me with the other two as used to them as birds to their wings. None of us spoke; we were all bent under packs; each was carrying a gun and a good weight of powder and shot.

They had their bows and ash wood arrows, I pistols, sword and dirk. But the most of my money was spent on a necklace for Ohnawiyo. It was none of my own taste, but those two wanted a great one of gold coins from half the world over. At least I got it cheaper than they would have done. She let me put it on her. She didna kiss as we know it in Europe, but she would hold me close and sudden and I would be overwhelmed by another kind of smell and feel, deep under stars and branches, under berry-bearing bushes and flowering grasses, under hoof and pad printed forest mosses and the sweet unploughed earth.

We were married ten days' journey west from Boston across the Connecticut River by ferry, then up the hill trail south of the Green mountains and down to the Hudson River, a world's width of snow and frost, and a resting of the eyes on the queer, warm beauty of the moving Indians. They were kindly folk at the settlement and the Minister old, a Devonshire man, as I mind, for we spoke a little of Devonshire tillage and the red Devon cattle, before I had him persuaded to marry us without banns. The frost had settled in by then; it was a morning of blinking brightness and good going, after, in the direction they knew and beyond the frontier.'

'How would the Indian not have had you, if she would have at all, without marriage?' asked Patrick. 'I have heard often enough from my correspondents of the other thing, and that honourable. Only last year, for example, there was mention of William Johnson, Admiral Sir Peter Warren's nephew, and the niece of old King Hendrick of the Mohawks. Or was your one looking to bind you, the way women mostly are?'

'Na, na. We were married after, Indian fashion. The other was myself alone. I spoke to them of God as He appeared to me then, and it seemed to me that they accepted. That was the fourth night out from Boston. We might have stopped at a farm-house, but they would have none of it. So we were in under the branches of a thick young spruce. The blown snow had drifted up over them at the one side into a wind-break. Ohnawiyo had cut out the dry dead branches from close to the trunk, making us a hollow, resin-smelling house. Tehoragwanegen and I made our fire, small and hot; we heated the coffee we had brought with us and which the Indians like to drink near boiling, and we poured in syrup to sweeten it. I had lighted the crumbled tinder wood with flint and steel and he had grunted approval, glad not to have the trouble of spinning fire wheel on to tinder for a spark. Under the branches, on cut and springy spruce twigs, we had spread his robe of fringed and embroidered deer-skin and my own plaid that I was aye used to wear over my bear-skin logging coat, since it was handy the same way as an Indian robe, and forby that a man likes, in a strange land, to wear his own gear and to have the chance of being buried in it. And over all we had Ohnawiyo's robe of black squirrel skins, and oh the soft they were! I lay midmost, between the two Indians and with the queer smell there was off the raw fat they would be using on their hair and which would hold in it the smell of wood fires and brushing leaves, a gaist kind of smell and yet one could miss it when one was far from it again.

They were younger than myself, maybe half my own age, though I did not know for certain, the way they do not reckon in our years. I felt terrible kindly towards them and stronger, for all they had me near worn out on the snow shoes. I — I felt father-like speaking to them of the Father, the great spirit, and they answering bairn-like. I spoke to Ohnawiyo, curled against me like a squirrel, of Christian marriage and the Blessing there was in it. I wanted this to be not only honourable but a sacrament, away different from my affair with Mistress Bradstreet or any other woman. I wanted to show the Indians that we colonists could be honourable, aye and to show myself. I wanted to pay them back somewhat. Though, the Lord knows, Patrick, they will have thought as ill of me later as of any other pale-face. And I of them. Maybe there could have been an understanding possible: but not by me; not after what had passed. But it was otherwise yon night under the snow-banked branches, a deep, dark night, and the Queen, the nixie, the woman of the Sidhe asleep on my plaid, and I wanting to be lost in the darkness, in the fairy hill, but yet with a Blessing. And the two things canna be together. No, they canna be.

But there was how I came to be married in Church, Patrick, and it is the truth as near as I can give it to you or to any man.'

'Was she baptized?' asked Patrick.

'Aye, by the same Minister that married us, before the marriage. He gave her a Devonshire name, Marion, on the top of it, his own wife standing godmother, but I never called her by that. And I went on with her to the Lodges of her people and we were married Indian fashion with a cake of maize meal, and I lay with her, and I became a brother to her brothers and to her mother's sisters' sons. For among the Five Nations of the Indians there is much that goes in the woman's line. And I plunged myself, head under, into their life and an understanding of it.

'There was plenty good sense among the Indians, who were for peace amongst one another in the Five Nations. They had come to the conclusion that it was best to keep to their Covenant with ourselves and the Dutch; though whiles the Seneca Indians, who were nearest to the Great Lakes, might be playing off the French against the English with a great sending of embassies and signing of treaties. For the keeping of their own peace, there were the ancestors and the women, that kept the community together. Beyond that were the Three Sisters, that is the cultivated plants that needed peace for their growing; corn, which is to say maize, beans and squash, which is a kind of pumpkin. There was sun and earth also, which hated war. But on the other side were the Thunder Birds and sundry spirits and spirit-animals and ghosts. In a short time I saw that the waters of baptism had washed away nothing of this. At most they had added another kind of spirit or ceremony to a life that was overfull of them. At the beginning I was forever struggling against this, and whiles I would seem to prevail, yet maybe I never did in the least. Maybe I half didna want to. Patrick, I was with them for four years and the last two never so much as back in a settlement. Earlier I had gone whenever they wanted guns or ammunition; I knew I was better at bargaining with the traders than they were, being acquaint with it all. And I took my firstborn back in my arms to be baptized at the same Church where we had been married. I half wish now that I hadna, the way life will be for him. And it was terrible far, and I only did it in a wild kind of passion against the other things. As though baptism, alone, could stand against magic and terror, which we know it canna do, seeing it is but water and gives no Grace of itself. But the way things were I had a kind of Papist feel about it, wanting to do this for my wee fellow, and he soft in my arms, like a March lamb you might be taking in off the hills. But I didna do it with the second. You know, I must suppose, that I had lawful children of my body?'

'Aye', said Patrick, 'I knew as much. Two lads.'

'It is something that they were lad bairns,' William said. 'Some way I canna like the thought of any lassie of mine going with an Indian.'

'You are daft,' said Patrick.

'Maybe. It is since Elizabeth was born. The eldest, who is baptized William but who will be called Oronhyatekha, which is to say Burning Sky after Ohnawiyo's mother's elder brother, he must be going on for ten years old. He will have his own bow and arrows. And doubtless his scalping knife. They will play games, the lad bairns, of putting a live coal between their bare arms and seeing which one can bear it longest. My wee ones didna look anyway other than full-blooded Indians, except maybe there would be a kind of wave in their hair. But, times, folks have taken me for a half-blood, most of all in my Indian gear and with my hair done Indian fashion.' Patrick suddenly leant forward and stared at his ears. 'Aye, I let them pierce my ears, but I never wore a heavy thing in them, only a light plume or so, and the holes have almost closed up. That was late on, when I was deep in and they wanting to get me deeper, when I wouldna even go to the trading posts in case an understanding or sympathy might flicker between me and another white man. For I might have heard a Scots voice and I might have had Scots thoughts. And I was wanting, wanting, to kill any such, seeing they had done me no good. Seeing that both I myself and Kirstie Haldane were married.

'I took part in certain Indian ceremonies, Patrick. It was in one of those that they pierced my ears. I didna know they were preparing to do it. She knew, all the same. It was done by her Lodge. When I came back to her she looked once; her eyes flicked at me the way a snake's tongue flicks. I saw she had known all the time and I accepted it, for there was nothing else to do. I was shivering wild, for it was not the only thing that had been done to my body and I had been shown three terrible things and their hands had been crawling on me during the whole time. I laid my head in her lap and she touched lightly the hot lobes of my ears where the running blood had been plugged with some herb juice that stung. It was a light touch at the first, but syne it became a pulling and a hurting. She had me held against her and she near the time of the birth of the second bairn; I could feel the poor wee soul kicking and struggling with not a thing but the taut smooth skin of her belly between my cheek and it. And as I, not struggling, thought with pity on it and myself, I felt a sharper jag and she had put the copper rings into my pierced ears and I knew she must have had them by her, maybe for months.'

'You will have enough to forget,' said Patrick, 'to last you a lifetime.'

'I have that,' said William. He did not speak for a little time, then said abruptly: 'Will I stop?'

'No,' said Patrick. 'You have yet to tell me how did you escape from the fairy hill.'

After a while William said: 'There would be certain times when all of us who were the fighters in the Lodges of the Wolves would be cast into a deep sleep. We would wake to certain prepared horrors which we must disregard. It was not possible to disregard without worship. Excutior somno simulacraque noctis adoro. I could not go back to the settlements after yon. There are some that can. They are harder men than ever I could be. The hell-mark doesna take on them. And, mind you, I had wanted to get away from Boston and respectability and commerce and progress. And I wouldna have you think it was altogether evil, Patrick. There was a part of the worship that was no' that far from the truth.'

'The same has been said of the fairies,' said Patrick, 'but the Churches have thought otherwise.'

'Aye, aye. And one man's interpretation of good and evil away different from another's, although they may mean the same ends.'

'For the which reason there are Ministers appointed to be our official interpreters at the Court of Heaven.'

'Aye, to come between ourselves and our Word!'

'It is not easy understood how you go to the Episcopalian Church, William. You speak liker an Anabaptist or a Quaker.'

'We find it mightily comforting to have the forms and strength of a deep-rooted Church, Kirstie and I, who have been so terrible tossed in the dark waters. We are less certain of ourselves than the Elect of the Established Presbyterian Church, and when we canna get addressing God ourselves for very shame, when we are most humble, Patrick, then we have the set patterns of prayer to hold on to. They are grand and bonny prayers, yon, like great and ancient trees, like the silvers and hemlocks of the American forests.'

'Well,' said Patrick, 'go on.'

'I canna,' said William. Then: 'Patrick, I did a thing with the Indians. It was thought of otherwise amongst them. But I canna speak on't to you, and you so kind.'

'I so kind, is't!' said Patrick. 'You will not find many folks saying that. I am a lawyer and I have heard plenty wickedness and that calmly. This of yours will be nothing new.' Still William said nothing. He stood in front of the table that was a good and solid one with brass drawer handles, of glowing mahogany wood, Edinburgh made. Patrick had sat so behind a table yon second time William had come, desperate anxious and shy — but oh the shyer he would have been if he had known the money had been lost! And Patrick had spoken easily and firmly of the best way for him to get to see his father in prison. Which was none of an over legal way. And had made some mention of his sister, Kirstie: while he, William, had sat stiff and silent. Geordie had been a wee boy them; he had come running in to his father and knocked his head against the corner of a bookshelf and Patrick had picked him up in his arms and petted him like a woman, so gentle. He could not tell Patrick!

Patrick was saying: 'I will tell you a story, William Macintosh of Borlum, whilst you gather your own courage to speak to me of what has passed. It is the story of a caddie who was working for me when I was a younger man. There was a kind of family or den of them in the cellars below my lodgings in the close where I was living at yon time. As you will know, the Edinburgh caddies are mostly Highland, the same that didna even have the half of a field or the tail of a stirk to inherit. They will run every kind of errand, they know who frequents which tavern or Church or bawdy-house, and what cases are on at the Courts. And they have a muckle Highland pride in that they are to be trusted utterly on their errands, and that, a letter once handed over to them, they will carry it through hell-fire if yon's their commission. And that although they are a set of wild, reckless de'il's bairns in their own lives. My own lad, Donally, had the same name as yourself. He was Donald Macintosh and he came from near your part. At the time of the '15 he was taking letters between the two sides and one of his gentlemen was an officer in your father's brigade. This was mostly night work and poor Donally had the misfortune to be taken by your father's sentries. They started to beat him and all the more because of his red tartan, saying he was a traitor to the best of the clan. And whilst he was yelling on them for his life in came your father, the Brigadier, with his nightcap on his head and his sword in his hand and made them leave off beating the caddie. For all they were threatening him with every kind of thing, the laddie wasna saying who he had been to, but they searched him for a letter. He wouldna have it in his sporran, although he had his pay there — the Brigadier made his sentries give back the money, and that meant plenty to the lad, as poor as the most of these caddies were — and it wouldna be in his shoe soles seeing he went barefoot, but sewn into a fold of his kilt. That way he or his fellow caddies had passed letters under the noses of the sentries, safe enough, but this time the Brigadier looked him up and down and sudden pounced on the sewn fold and slit it up with his sgian point and took the letter and frowned terrible on poor Donally, who fell on his knees crying it was nought but a love letter, but as he said it he knew that the superscription was to none of a lassie, and the Brigadier had seen the same.

'Why were you so careful of it then?' roared the Brigadier, 'and why wouldna ye tell the name?' Donally could scarce speak and at last he said in a daft kind of way, but yet it was true enough, that he did it for the honour of the caddies of Edinburgh. And at that, he said, the Brigadier looked at him without anger and with a face of benevolence that, as he told me, minded him of the Lord (though where he will have been forgathering with the Lord, he didna say!) and gave him back the letter unopened, telling him that he should say to the one that was to get it that he, the Brigadier, had a good idea of who was and was not loyal, and took his dispositions accordingly. 'But,' he said, 'I willna spoil the record of the caddies of Edinburgh and, above all, my own kin.' And he gave a kind of bow to Donally and bade turn him loose and the lad took to his heels and off back to Edinburgh. It was a while later that he told me the thing and added that there was an extra cleverness to it, for he was certain sure that the Brigadier knew the hand-writing and would take his measures accordingly; yon caddies, needing to be on the watch for folks' moods, could aye tell what was passing in a man's mind by the twist of his eyebrows. He had repeated this story of the goodness and cleverness of the Brigadier amongst all the caddies of Edinburgh, until the lot of them had conceived of a reverence and love for yon father of yours which may, likely, have stood him in good stead in the Castle prison at the beginning when he had little money and few friends.'

'Except for yourself, Patrick,' said William.

'Except maybe myself, that was willing to risk a morsel of my good name and that, after all, none so good with most, and converse with a Jacobite prisoner for the sake of the Edinburgh caddies and also for what the Borlum folk said of their landlord when I went there as Commissioner for the Forfeited Estates.'

'Why did you tell me this?' asked William.

'To give you a confidence and courage which maybe you are needing and to tell you that my relation with your family is, as it were, of old days, and it can stand whatever thing you have to tell me.'

'I will try,' said William, 'but if you hate me after — '

'I have the most peculiar and exceptional hatreds,' said Patrick with his sudden childish pride, 'and never for the reasons which are commonly considered adequate or honourable.'

William poured himself a mouthful of brandy and drank it. Then he said: 'It is part of the Indian custom and honour to go on raids, not with the nearer tribes, with whom there are alliances, but beyond. This will be a part of the reason for the sudden and seeming senseless raids upon white settlements, that are thought on as so out of measure cruel and treacherous. They are not the same as the Highland raids of a hundred years back, a matter of taking food and gear or any such ordinary and easily predictable necessity. The time for the Indian raids will be determined partly by the wishes and policy of the ruling women, who keep up the memories of ancient wrongs for the sake of their own power and who will sometimes use wars as a distraction for young warriors who might otherwise fight amongst themselves or with their allies, and partly by the dreams of the chief of the tribe or the elder warriors in each Lodge, though these again will be interpreted by women or by those men who have dealings with the spirit world, and partly by need and hunger for enemy prisoners.

'In these raids the art of killing is practised by those who have imitated it in their hunting and are now tired of the imitation. There is much killing and scalping and burning, and prisoners are brought back, carefully guarded, and at night pegged out by thongs to tree stumps in a way that would be bad enough here, but is pure hell in a country of mosquitoes, such as

America. When they get back to the camp, there are several things which may happen to the prisoners and almost all terrible beyond our notions of cruelty, unless, as sometimes happens, a prisoner is given to a Lodge to take the place of some dead person and that in life, rather than to be killed for him. This would be most likely to happen to women prisoners, and then they would not be slaves nor ill-treated, but held in the same regard as the woman for whom they are substituting. Nor indeed are any of the prisoners treated dishonourably, in a certain sense. But — they are tortured in every conceivable way, Patrick, they are cut into bits, beginning at the fingers and toes, they are hung with necklaces of red hot axes, scalded with boiling water, burnt slowly to death and all with words of a devilish courtesy. Aye, and the prisoners answering in a distant and courteous manner and never asking for mercy. For that is a point of honour and training. When someone, it might be a woman, is so overwhelmed with pity as to stab one of these tortured quivering lumps of flesh in a vital place, so ending an agony that can scarcely be imagined, then the rest are angry, feeling that an attack has been made not only on their own honour and that of the ancestors, but beyond, on that of the prisoner and enemy.

'At first such things were kept from me, Patrick. It would be arranged that I should be sent hurriedly to one of the settlements for fresh ammunition in pretence that all had been exhausted in the raid. Nor was it always immediately after the return of the warriors that such things happened; the prisoner might be kept for a certain number of moons and treated with every kind of hospitality, down to whatever woman he might ask for. Equally, when the thing was done, I would be away hunting. But my wife would be there. The women need not always watch, but she, being royal or what was like to that, would go with her mother and her very old and hideous grandmother.

'I did not suspect at the first. Later I began to. There would be a peculiar look about the camp. There would be a look and smell about my wife that was disquieting beyond all.

Towards the end of the second year I began to know. There were traces of what had passed which they no longer troubled to hide. I tried to speak to her, minding her of what I had told her once of a Loving God. She would agree but as though there were room in another part of her mind for the other thing. Even yet I did not know the worst.

'Whenever there was a raid I would go, dressed Indian fashion, with the rest. If I had been taken I would have been treated as we treated our prisoners and, not having the up-bringing, I would not have died well. But it would have been a terrible affront to my wife and the Lodge if I had not gone. Let alone that I was a far better shot than most of them. And it seemed to me no worse than war in Europe. We Scots have sold ourselves as soldiers of fortune to one nation or another. I gave myself to the Wolves. But I never scalped a living man, though I have scalped the dead. I canna see much harm in that, and indeed folk did much the same in the Old Testament.

'They became less careful as to what they hid from me. It could have been that they were thinking of me less as a stranger, either through familiarity or some fashion of love. I took part in their counsels and it seems to me now that I advised them well. Times I could see a thing fresh and not mixed with dreams and old customs. With the coming of the colonists they had to face an altogether new kind of problem and often it was beyond them.

'There came a day, as it was bound to come, when I saw for myself. I was asleep after a raid. We had been half running or going perilously in husk-light canoes along swift and enor-mous rivers. Honour had been satisfied in blood. I woke before I was meant to wake; I went where they didna mean me to go. I saw Ohnawiyo, my wife, with other women, doing the most hellish things to a bound man. I went back for my gun and shot him through the head and I took Ohnawiyo by the elbow — her hands and wrists and face were blood-stained — and I beat her in a blind and stupid fury, I pulled her hither and yon by the plaits, I tore her tunic and I bruised her back

and shoulders with my gun stock, and she never cried out and
I did no good but only harm. In the end she walked out
through the doorway and I was the one to be left weeping.
My wee lad, who was just able to walk, came in toddling and
bare and I pushed him out roughly and he cried. The Indians
are awful good to bairns and they arena used to any roughness.
I lay on the ground in a passion of horror at what I had seen
and what I had done, all that day and the next night and none
came near me. I slept in the tail of the dark; when I went out
again it was clear I had become unlucky. Folk moved a little
away from me or my shadow. I did not see my wife nor her
sisters. I cooked myself maize-meal porridge and such roots as
I found amongst the cooking pots. It was the same next day.
Nobody spoke. I would hear laughter or singing and go towards
it, but it would have ended before I came. Tehoragwanegen
turned his back on me, speaking on other things. I began to be
frightened. It was as though I had some disease. I wrapped
myself in my plaid to sleep alone. But I could not think right
about Scotland nor anyway dream of my old friends or my old
life. I could not pray, I had no sense of God, I was without
guidance. Syne there was no more maize meal. I went out
into the forest and wished I was dead. I sat me down beside
the edge of a bonny burn in icehard misery, not even pitying
myself. In the stillness a buck came to drink and I shot it. I
carried it back to the camp and skinned it and I was aware that
the folk of the Wolves were watching me. I skewered the meat
and held it in the flames, but my hands shook and it was badly
done. I wanted Ohnawiyo beside me eating the meat of my
buck. And yet I hated her. And yet I wanted her. I had done
what I shouldna to one who was, some way, royal, and she had
taken herself away from me and by her lights she had the right
of it. I cut off the right haunch of the buck and took it over to
her mother's end of the Lodge and laid it by the shut door. And
yet I had the half thought that maybe I was at last rid of her,
escaped, that I might be a free Christian again. Yet, thinking
that, I had carried over the haunch. Nothing happened,
nothing until the middle of the night and I woke and she was

naked beside me and in a while after she had me getting the second bairn on her.

'We did not speak of what had passed, and times I would see it the Indian way. As a matter of custom and continuance and a placation of spirits and ancestors. For a time I was mad keen to beat the rest at hunting and at certain sports and forms of endurance. There was a game with sticks and a ball much like our own shinty, a winter game of throwing wooden snow snakes along runs, canoe racing, wrestling, and always, always the dancing. Because I could never beat them at the things where they had a lifetime of practice, I would think out sports where we would start equal or where I would have some knowledge beforehand. I mind we got tossing the caber and it took on with them fine.

'It was a winter's bairn, the second, and born with a lucky mark on it. We went raiding again with the first of spring, the flowers coming suddenly with the melting of the snow. We brought back our prisoners. I was one of the best of the fighters. Patrick, I dinna know how to tell you. Patrick, I did yon things myself. Patrick, there was maize bread dipped in the blood and fat that was running out of their wounds and we ate that. I was worse than all of them because I was lashing myself on to it all the while. And then — Patrick, it was nothing but the stump of a man, armless, legless and eyeless, and yet living. And the whole thing shifted on me and I saw as a Christian and I killed him and I went away and vomited, ridding myself of the devilish bread, the hell's sacrament, but not of what I had done and seen.

'You will understand, Patrick, that I canna speak on this to Kirstie, no more than I can of Ohnawiyo.'

'That is certain,' said Patrick. 'And then?'

'I began to set more and cunninger traps and snares and to hide away the finest of the small furs that I got, and I began to try and say to myself that in these four years everything could be changed. The Stewarts could be back in Scotland and my father out of prison and into his estates again. Only I daredna say that Kirstie Haldane was unmarried, was waiting for me at the edge of the plantation behind Gleneagles.

'Ohnawiyo was pleased with my good hunting and my skill at sports. But I was feared of her finding my furs. She did once come on some of them. I told her they were to buy us gear, blankets and cooking pots, and, as always, powder and balls. Because I was lying to her and aye feared she would be finding me out, I began to hate her.'

'Do you hate all those you lie to?' asked Patrick. 'You will have lied plenty to Kirstie.'

'Not the same fashion of lies. Not for my own sake. Not to escape. But yon time it was as though my soul were turning to another part of itself, having sickened at the first dream. Yet the folk of the Wolves did not seem to be aware that I was any-ways different. Though maybe they were. I canna be sure. But they trusted me. And I betrayed them. I let on I was going to the trading post. I became in all ways circumstantial. There were some that gave me furs of their own to trade. I half didna want that because it was stealing and what the white men had done to them since the beginning, yet half I did because of the hate that was growing on me at all of them, and because I could sell the furs and buy my passage home. For I was thinking beyond Boston.

'I walked out from the camp and my pack of furs heavy on my back. It was autumn. I had kept saying to myself that I had best wait until after winter, there would be no ships sailing. But I was terrible afraid that if I stayed longer, if I began to lie with my wife again — she was still suckling the second child — I might never go, I might stay all my life in the fairy hill. I went on beyond the trading post till I came to the Hudson River. I sold my furs in Albany at a good price, and from there I went south down the Hudson, working as a logger, until I came to New York. I saw the sea again, grey and cold between me and Scotland. In New York I lived in a household of Quakers, half English and half Dutch, terrible clean folk. And I would help with scrubbing the tile floors and scouring the pots with sand, hoping some way to clean the innocent blood off my own hands. I went with them to Meeting and spoke somewhat of all that had passed, yet never of Ohnawiyo, and I lived a sober and honest and industrious life, and I heard that, after all, there was no single thing changed over Scotland. And at the end of winter I went back to Boston as deckhand on a coasting boat and I heard a Scots voice one day in a coffee house, asking the kind of foolish questions anent the Indians that those newly come to America are like to ask. Because he was a fellow Scot I went over to give him a small spark at least of the truth. He was Mr. James Stewart, the Episcopalian Minister, of whom you know. After I had bought coffee and cakes for the two of us and when he had done speaking to me of Kirstie Haldane, I went to a shipping office and paid over my passage money to Port Glasgow.'

CHAPTER V

'WHAT,' asked Patrick judicially, 'has garred you suppose that you are not eternally damned for yon?'

'I canna say that I am certain,' William said, 'but I believe that our Lord Jesus Christ has died for sinners full as bad as myself and that His death was effective. I am now trying to earn a wee small part of my Redemption.'

'You canna do it by works,' said Patrick. 'You may grow turnips for all Scotland and it will not help you any when it comes to Judgment.'

'I ken fine. Works are for their own sake. I am attempting it by love. Though I have a full understanding that there is nothing any of us can do that is more than the merest crumb set against yon great weight of original sin, which yet melted away to nothing with the act of our Redeeming: as, I think, we both of us believe. But, in a human way — Patrick, can you take me by the hand again after what I have said?' ·

Patrick got up stiffly and deliberately — he had a touch of rheumatism. 'Easy enough,' he said, and shook William Macintosh by the hand.

And sudden William began to laugh, gasping and choking: 'You will have no conception, Patrick,' he said in a daft and breathless way, 'of the easy feel there is on me to have the thing told!' And then: 'One may speak on't to God, truly repenting and asking forgiveness, but one canna be right sure He has heard.' And then: 'It is the forgiveness of the congregation that counts.'

'And I not so much as an Elder!' said Patrick. 'But is this the bottom?'

'Of me, is't?' asked William. 'Aye, you've the onion skinned.' He thought sudden of the Government Surveyor murdered upon Maine, but Patrick needna know since Kirstie knew, and he had forgotten the drowning man's look though Ohnawiyo's he would never forget.

'There is no end to the skinning of onions,' said Patrick, 'as you should know. But I would say that we had come down to the clean flesh of what's fit for using. And now let us consider certain practical aspects of this. It is a remarkable and fortunate thing, William, that none of the story has leaked out before now, although no doubt you would be saying nothing of the worst of it in Boston or elsewhere. But it is a muckle great risk you have been taking.'

William said: 'The thing had slipped clean out of my mind for the moment, Patrick, but I have been accused of a part at least of this to your brother Mungo, and though I have lied somewhat to him and he kind of half believes me, yet I am not sure I have the thing set right to his satisfaction and I am feared you will need to help me again.'

Patrick frowned, his eyebrows crumpling together: 'What evidence has he?'

'Little, and maybe none of it in writing. It will be hearsay and gossip.'

'Who brought it?'

'Some old tenants of Kyllachy's, for the most part. Folk that I knew in America and that had a grudge against me.'

'How would it come to Mungo's ears?'

'From Kyllachy himself. Shortly before you arrived here.'

'Is Lachlan Macintosh of Kyllachy in this house?'

'Aye, surely.'

'Well, well, I was half certain I had smelled a most peculiar and filthy stink on my arriving. But I had put it down to some defect in my brother's famous water-closet. And now I know it is only our cousin, Kyllachy, and we can be rid of it without having in the masons.'

'I doubt he will not be so easy got rid of, Patrick. Unless you know for a certainty more against him than I am guessing.'

'Over the taking of your father?'

'Yes,' said Black William, slowly. 'And the time before when my father was so near taken at Raitts and would have been but for my uncle. Not that any of this is a point against him in law: merely in honour. Other things might be needed.'

'We will go about to consider this matter of rat poison,' said Patrick. 'And meanwhile I will put things straight with my brother. But tell me now, William, how do your wifie's folk seem to you, now that you have met them all together?'

Black William smiled a little, his red-brown eyes in a dance at Patrick. 'I have always liked you terrible well, Patrick, and there's the truth. Having the same thoughts as my father and myself on this matter of the common people of Scotland, and being Kirstie's one. But I havena felt wholly at ease with you until this hour. I thought, you being better than myself — and it is no manner of use you scowling, Patrick, and indeed it doesna suppose any high standard of behaviour! — I thought you would feel the most terrible hate and scorn for me if you knew what was hidden. And now you do know and it appears you arena hating me, although, if all this wickedness of mine had come out in the Courts and appeared in the *Mercury* and the *Courant*, the way they would write about it — But it hasna, thanks to the Lord and yourself, and I can go back with a light heart to Borlum. Well, I like Airthrey fine and we can be having the best of cracks together. But I am a wee bit frighted of Gleneagles and he head of the family.'

'He is a kindly man,' said Patrick, with his sudden leap of anxiety lest one of the family should be misunderstood, as was always likely, aye, next to certain!

'You are kindly, every one of you,' said William. 'And that in a practical way. You will have no conception of the kind Kirstie has been to my poor folk at Borlum, who can be gey tedious with all their wee stories and gossip and melancholies. And to myself, beyond words. She learnt to speak the Gaelic for my sake — or theirs. She has been hospitable to a wild lot of Highland gentry and half gentry that need to be persuaded into better ways of agriculture and managing both of land and of tenants, and that with little enough money to find the hospitality out of and herself needing to turn to in the kitchen or brewhouse. She is aye at her best when there are difficulties to be overcome. Maybe you are all the same there.'

'I amna,' said Patrick, 'as some have a mind of yet!'

'We were speaking of you earlier,' said William, 'and I asking your two brothers to give me the story right of the old quarrel when they wouldna make you a Lord of the Court of Sessions.'

'You will have read my own pamphlet?' asked Patrick, anxiously.

'Aye. It was yourself that sent it to me. But there is a kind of sameness about pamphlets. I let on that I knew less of the matter than I do, Patrick. They didna have much to say that was new to me, only I was ettling to know how did the others in the family feel about you. We spoke also of the Lord President.' Patrick frowned and swore under his breath. 'You have aye got the same sentiments towards him, then. I think you might be mistaken, Patrick.'

'No,' said Patrick, 'I am not so much as arguing over that. It is likely that I will never need to set eyes on Forbes of Culloden again, seeing he is a sick man and not sitting much, and I less in the Courts than I was. This being so, I will keep my own opinions on him and you are at liberty to hold yours.'

'I dinna like to be on the other side from you, Patrick.'

'Well, you must even thole it or take my opinion of Forbes of Culloden. For I am not changing. Come, William, the rest will be asking themselves, what are we doing together this long while, and we with the brandy! Take you down the bottle and glasses, and we will just take a wee bit daunder round the policies and see can we find Kirstie.'

Again it was mid afternoon, and the sun hot. It was on the early side to cut the sown hay, there was growth in it yet, but one could scarcely be sure of the weather later on, and you might have a July without one dry day to it. Gleneagles, however, must needs make up his mind and give his orders. There was another thing to be fashing and fretting himself over. And the sheep must be brought into the fanks and looked over for maggots, the warmth would be bringing them out and then you would have a score of the poor beasties dead on you before you could sneeze twice. And he had not yet broached the matter of Kirstie and yon man to Patrick. As he must do. And gin it were not true but the other thing true which had been said about Kyllachy—? What was a decent man to do between two Highlanders? Aye, and a third in the attic, or at least a Jacobite if he wasna a Highlander! There now was Patrick at last! But the other with him, making the whole thing terrible awkward. And there Kyllachy coming from the garden and two of the lads beside him. He peered ahead to see which of them it was, aye, the muckle great bing of nephews and nieces he had, and no child of his own body that he knew of!

Feeling the hackles rising on Patrick, William made one effort to get him away to some other part of the policies. But the two were bound to meet at supper if they didna meet earlier. He let the thing go. Patrick churned on down the path to meet Kyllachy walking between Captain John and David Haldane of Aberuthven, and Kyllachy smiled and shook out the ruffles round his wrists, and, at the proper moment, bowed and held out his right hand, which Patrick did not take.

Mungo might have his own views on folk, but this was a guest. 'Pate!' he said sharply. 'You will mind on our cousin of Kyllachy!'

'Most certainly I do,' said Patrick, 'and have no wish to be soiling my hands.'

Kyllachy laughed with a hard jerk, throwing his head back, and then he gave a look, not at Patrick but at William Macintosh, and that look none of the best. But young Captain John glared at his uncle, making trouble as usual, the old red-faced, scrub-chinned savage, what did he suppose the rest of the family thought of him and his manners! And he with the other one, this Borlum, this Highlander of the commoner kind of gentleman-rogue, who had lied and cheated his way in amongst the Haldanes, an elegant and amiable pair they made. He put his arm through Kyllachy's and wheeled him away.

'Couldna ye speak decently to the creature, Pate?' said Mungo. 'He is our guest for all he is none of the welcomest, and now I will need to chase after him and burn my tongue with politenesses!' He would not even speak to yon other, only gave him a wild, vexed look that went to William's heart, but which he could do nothing about — not yet.

Patrick bristled against the black looks, which yet he had brought on himself. Which yet hurt him. He was cross now at William as he had not been, earlier, for more cause. He walked off towards the old castle, muttering and humping himself, treading on any wee flowers that were fools enough to stand in his way. William followed, worried over what Kyllachy might do, wishing they could meet with Kirstie. The old castle itself was beginning to fall to bits. The slates were off the roof and most of the floors gone. Mostly always in an autumn gale stones would come crashing down and these would be thriftily removed for the building of walls or steadings. Patrick muttered to himself, wishing the whole thing were down and out of the road.

Once it had been on an island in the midst of a shallow loch where now were good green fields. There were mostly plenty shallow lochans in Scotland that might be drained and the marl bottoms given back to fertility. But there was a thing that could not lightly be undertaken, nor by a private landlord with his own modest means. Though if all could get together — He wondered how things were going now at Borlum. Winwood had said nothing in her letter of crops or stock and there was no one besides who could write, at least not an informative letter with accurate facts of a kind better expressed in the English than in the Gaelic. And then again the whole thought would be blotted out, in an immense thankfulness that the devil that had been locked in the back press in the furthest room of his mind was gone, had left him, and now the room could be swept and the shutters opened to the Light, and after that by fear, all the worse for being unformed and uncertain, of what Kyllachy might do.

Patrick had cast himself down on the castle mound, one leg crossed over the other, his foot twitching with annoyance. Spoken to, he still snapped at William, who left him for a while to go down to one of the enclosed fields and study the method of hedging and the growth of the sown grass, rich looking now under the westering sun, with a good sole of clovers. There was a wee path here, from the farms that lay farther along the Ochils, joining up to the coal-road. For a while William was in conversation with one of the working tenants who had come over to discuss a matter of a mill wheel with Gleneagles and when that was sorted up right to go on to Church matters, since the two of them were Elders of the Congregation. The man had gone straight to the point of asking Black William who he might be, where the Inverness folk could have gone roundabout. It was a pleasant and refreshing talk, with mention of field drains, and the making of drain tiles, and of Kirstie Haldane's wean, and of the best ways of making a turf and boulder dam that would hold water right, and of the best kinds of shafting for a mill wheel. William went back to the castle with a feeling of the solidity of things and there saw Kirstie herself coming, with Margaret Bearcrofts.

'Father!' said Margaret, 'I have only this moment heard that you were come and that from the lads speaking of you!'

Patrick got up stiffly. 'And doubtless they were speaking ill,' he said.

'Aye,' said Margaret, 'they were that, and I told them to think shame of it. But how did you set them off, father?'

'They will be set off by the mere sight of the old Bear's hide,' said Patrick.

'It was more than that,' Margaret answered, a wee thing sadly.

'Poor Margaret is aye coming to your defence, Pate,' said Kirstie. 'It isna all of us have so good a child. And times it has done her little service.'

'Meaning,' said Patrick, 'that she hasna aye a muckle buzz of gallants circling round her in case the honey pot might be opening itself a wee crack! She will do as well without!'

Margaret said nothing, but looked near greeting; she knew her father did not mean it unkindly, but he just had not the least conception of how things might feel to herself. Kirstie took her arm quick, but could not think what to say, seeing the man would never believe his lassie could be hurt any this way. It was William that took her hand and kissed it, saying: 'Whenever I see this lassie I am minded wild of yon princess that stayed in the castle beyond seven bens and seven glens, guarded by a wild black bear, the way only the bravest and best of the lads could be getting to her, for all she was as bonny as a gean tree in April!' Margaret smiled a little, not for a moment taken in by any such Highland flatteries, but all the same soothed by them, as she was meant to be, flattery being as comforting to lassies as the drink to men and no more to be taken over much nor over seriously.

Kirstie said: 'William, my soul, I wish yon Kyllachy were forth of the house!'

'You canna be wishing it more than I do myself,' said William. 'He intends evil to all of us and he will do everything in his power to get us all fankled up and at odds with one another.'

'And neither yourself nor Pate going the best way to put him in a good humour again!' said Kirstie. Then: 'William, what could he say? Which of us all could be in his power?'

They had moved a few steps away, leaving the Bear to speak with his daughter Margaret. William took Kirstie's hands and looked at her deep, asking himself what did she mean, and sudden minded on his punishment by Patrick and how in the worst of it he had promised an impossible thing, to separate himself from his Kirstie, and he took her fiercely in his arms and kissed and kissed her. 'We will deal with yon man!' he said.

She held on to him and whispered into his neck: 'He couldna be making his accusations against me, William?'

'If he were to accuse my wife of witchcraft,' said William, 'for I think that is what you have in mind, m'uan beag boid-heach, it would give me the best of reasons for killing him and think of the great pleasure that would be to me and the great good riddance to Scotland!'

'Ach,' said she, 'it is so terrible nice to be made to feel I am safe that I am aye letting myself get feared of things! William, what at all have you done to your cheek?'

'I knocked it against the edge of the table in Patrick's room, stooping for some papers,' he said, 'and I wish I knew what Kyllachy might know about yon brother of yours.'

'There is what Margaret said,' Kirstie answered him, frowning, 'and spoke of the trial of Provost Stewart and the doubtful seeming part Patrick has played in it. And of other things. Ach, William, we know, you and I, that Patrick has done plenty that wouldna look well to some, and he will have shown folk the way round a law where it was his duty, maybe, to keep the thing tight and strict. But what could Kyllachy know on all this?'

'He might know enough to harm Patrick.'

'And on yourself, my dearest?'

'What are you meaning, Kirstie my lass?'

'I amna speiring on what nor when, William,' she said quick. 'Only — could yon man hurt you?'

He was still holding her to him. He spoke over her shoulder, carefully and lightly; and her head was down on his breast, the way she could be determined not to see, nor try to see, past any look he might choose to be wearing. 'He would know of the dealings my Boston firm had over ships' papers,' William said. 'He could know I had forged a signature or so — and he might guess and truly, that I had learnt yon kind of skill in Newgate gaol. And he might be making up other kinds of stories. But gin you love me, he canna hurt me, my lassie.'

She looked up and laughed suddenly: 'The man supposes he can play De'il among the Tailors and set all Gleneagles by the ears. We will even dance his reel with him but it is he will get the tailor's shears at his dowp in the end!' They turned back towards Patrick and his daughter. 'There now,' said Kirstie, 'is a lassie that will be as loyal as a regiment of soldiers and under the greatest provocations. For the younger ones dinna like my poor brother Pate, and indeed they can scarcely be blamed with the cross he is. He is aye supposing they are against him.'

'And that is just what they mostly all are.'

'Aye, but they wouldna be if he werena so cross and kind of blaming them for having their own ideas, which may be like enough to his own whiles, but not expressed in the same fashion of words. And for a frivolity which is as natural for young folks as the high leap and heather bounce of the deer on the hills. And indeed we were all the same at that age, and Mungo worst of the lot.'

'It will be suppertime soon,' said William hopefully, 'and maybe after the supper we will all be better disposed towards one another.' And then, he thought, will be the time for the Bear to make all right with Gleneagles, touching myself, and if on the top of that, we can get Kyllachy drunk, it will discredit anything he has to say. Best if he could be accused of impolite behaviour towards one of the lasses, for then the story of him and Kirstie could look like the very truth, and these Haldane lasses can take good care of themselves — Or if it were towards Kirstie — Ach, he thought, the dirty devil I am! Maybe we will be able to beat the man clean and I might get clear of this wild nasty snarl of lies I am in. And I dinna like them with the best part of me, and the Friends would say there was another way of doing altogether, and fine I know they are right in the long run, aye and in the short run too, most times, and I should, God help me, act their way and not this roundabout wicked Highland way, and I will try to think with the honest English blood in me and the good American thoughts on freedom and courage that I should come by easy, and so, with my dear Lord and Kirstie and Patrick Haldane forby, I will try and make a shape of being the son my father would have been proud of — and what in all the world is bringing Ochtertyre and young James here in such a commotion and by their looks it is nothing good!

James gave a quick bow to Patrick but came straight at his uncle by marriage and caught him by the sleeve and said breathlessly: 'I have made a most terrible mistake in judgment, Uncle William, and if you cannot help us we are lost!'

William said quickly. 'Is it over Mr. Strange? Does someone know? Who?'

'Young Captain John, my cousin. I thought — och, I thought he would be bound to have the same view on't as myself! And he is against us all on everything! Och, I have never been such a fool in my whole life!' William remembered Captain John's look as he had seen him last, arm in arm with Kyllachy, who could have said — what? 'He is threatening to inform on us. I dared not tell him Gleneagles was involved in this!'

'It is more than Gleneagles will be in it,' said William. 'As the thing is now, Bearcrofts must know.'

'No!' said Ochtertyre, 'he has been the most terrible enemy to our side — to my father — you will get us all into worse trouble if that were possible — '

But Black William had his back to them, had moved with the quick smoothness of a summer adder: was telling Patrick. Kirstie had her protecting arm round frowning, puzzled Margaret, who glanced to and fro between the men, their anxieties and violences seeming to settle on the two quiet women, rooting into them. Patrick Haldane was glaring and fidgeting and throwing off angry interruptions at the young men, but it was William who answered him and calmed him down and at last said: 'We must see who at all is on our side. For the family will be split on this.'

'Our side, is it!' said Patrick. 'You are assuming too much.'

'I am not,' said William, and gave him a wee shake, 'and there has never been a client that needed you so sore.'

Patrick broke angrily from him and walked away for a moment, in a dolour of resentment that his day had, after all, betrayed him, and so back, not to William, but to his daughter and Kirstie. He took Kirstie by the chin and looked her in the eyes and seemed to come to some decision, although his manner was no easier and he stood with his feet apart, not easily balanced but striking his legs heavily down into the turf. 'If I am to be counsel for the defence,' he said, 'I must have my brief with no mitigations nor prevarications. I am supposing, William Macintosh, that you have had the sense to give me the whole truth. Now, what is the worst that you fear?'

'That my cousin should inform in a fit of — of I cannot say what, but something gey unfriendly and uncousinly!' said James.

'In a fit of the principles, I would say,' said Kirstie. 'And I know it on myself and it will over-ride any ordinary decencies, I'm fearing. You are certain sure he has done nothing yet?'

'He kind of half promised he would give me a certain time,' said James. 'And — Aunt Kirstie, I hope I havena done wrong, but I asked my cousin Catherine would she do her best to get arguing with him, maybe, or some way delaying him if things looked to be dangerous.'

'Let us hope she will manage it,' said Patrick. 'I hadna thought of her as a lassie with gumption. But this is by no means all nor the worst that can happen.'

'No,' said Ochtertyre, and gave a kind of sharp tearless sob in his chest.

'Aye,' said Patrick, 'it would seem you are in danger, Ochtertyre, and that for your own evil choice and deliberate folly in wanting to get back the bad old days. I can at least suppose you will have learnt your lesson, whether with or without the taws!' He gave a snicker of crossness and Ochtertyre did not answer him any. 'It is more than likely that young Captain John, who is a worthy and loyal young man, though not acquaint with compromise, will get together over this with George Cockburn, who is neither worthy nor loyal except to his own interests, and has his quarrels set already, and if the two of them think better of mischief-making in the family, then there is one who will shoo them on into any kind of devilment, and that is Lachlan Macintosh of Kyllachy.'

'Kyllachy and George were as thrang as thieves when we met them upby on the coal-road,' said Ochtertyre gloomily.

'Helen Cockburn will be backing her brother out of annoyance at the rest of us,' said Margaret abruptly, as none of the others spoke, 'and David of Aberuthven and his wee sister are aye admiring Captain John and even George, And you have left poor Catherine to deal with the lot of them!'

'Was Adam with her?' Kirstie asked. 'And have you told Alec?' James, standing rebuked, could only say that Alec was at Blackford, and so out of this, and that Adam had not been to be found.

'He will have been over at the stables with the lads,' said Margaret indignantly, half crying, 'and the whole lot of them with their heads full of nothing but cock-fighting and dicing for pennies and telling foolish stories and rhymes, and Cousin Adam, for all his Navy uniform, no better than the worst!'

'The question is,' said Patrick, 'how best to stop them from having their will of us, and that before supper.'

Ochtertyre said: 'Tell me one thing. Am I in danger of my head yet?'

'Scarcely,' said Patrick, 'but of forfeiture of estates, yes. How are you with Atholl?'

'None too good,' Ochtertyre said. 'He would not go out of his ways for me. But Airthrey was saying he would speak for me. Yet that was without his knowing of Mr. Strange. And he might think himself deceived and refuse to help me.'

'Aye,' said William, 'and Gleneagles may think himself deceived over yet another matter and be none too willing for his part. Who has the key of the attic?'

'I have,' said Ochtertyre, 'and if I am taken and searched—'

'Give it to me,' said Margaret decidedly, 'and think shame of yourselves for getting us all into this snarl! No, I will have it!' She stamped and a spark of Patrick's fury went through her face and over-thick eyebrows. 'So this is the key you had me hunting the house for and blaming Mistress Grizzie and the lassies! You are all half traitors to one thing or another and I have no interest in your politics, but I am standing by my father and Aunt Kirstie!'

Patrick nodded at his daughter and took Ochtertyre by the coat lapels, questioning him and cross-questioning him on his doings in the rebellion, and Ochtertyre felt an increasing cold gloom and fear of Patrick and resentment both at him and at Bob Strange. He stammered in his answers, could not even mind of the thing right himself, beyond all, could not imagine why he had ever let himself be mixed up in it! And James, who by his own overweening confidence had brought the whole miserable business less on himself than on others, could only stand by with an acute thought on Catherine, and an attempt at prayer. To assuage the dreadful gap, the anxiety floating between one and another, he asked: 'How did you come by the graze on your cheek, Uncle William?'

'Ach,' said William, not heeding, 'I knocked it on yon stone of the old castle wall.' And sudden noticed a kind of half surprised look on the face of Kirstie his wife.

CHAPTER VI

YOUNG Captain John had taken the other three up to the attic bothy room, where they could discuss in peace, sitting upon his bed. He did not much care for his cousin, George Cockburn, and he distrusted Macintosh of Kyllachy, and yet this was overborne by the hot anger that was drying him up, drying any softness out of him, against this treachery within and towards the Haldane house. He saw himself surrounded by it, a sticky web of treachery, and half made of lies by the elders and half of follies by the young such as James Haldane, who should, as he had told him harshly enough, have known better than to be doing this childish thing. The Jacobite danger was real. Not maybe from such petty skulkers, who in themselves mattered nothing, but in principle. Even though they themselves in the Kingdom of Great Britain were seeming safe, Europe was overrun with kings and popes and their hellish cruelties and plottings. The cause of Protestantism and justice and decency might look secure here in this easy-going back of beyond or to those such as young James who had never so much as exchanged shots with the arrogant, cruel French, nor had the pleasure of clapping one of their over-dressed Captains into honest English irons! But if these Jacobites had won, with a setting up of Courts and Lords and Bishops, and suppression of freedom of speech and worship, and the Churches simmering up with masses like maggots on an August sheep, and in no time at all restraint of trade, aye and a letting loose again of Highlands on to Lowlands, then young James would be singing a different tune! And he himself knew where his duty lay, hateful in a certain way though it might be. But he owed it to Gleneagles, the head of the family, who must be utterly unaware of the serpent in his midst, to take the right course.

'I had determined for the sake of the family,' said George Cockburn, 'not to proceed against Patrick Murray of Ochtertyre, even after the great provocation I received from him yesterday evening. But it will have to be known by what door this skulking Tory was admitted to a Whig house.'

David of Aberuthven looked eagerly from one to the other. Kyllachy offered a pinch of snuff. Suddenly Captain John found himself wishing he had not spoken to the other two, wishing that the indignation he had been thrown into by his cousin James's assumption that he would be agreeable to the turn of events, had not driven him into immediate suspicion of Borlum and immediate speech with Kyllachy, Borlum's enemy, and so to George knowing. Not that George was anything but the most loyal Whig. And political sentiment mattered profoundly. More than any small matter of taste. But the thing was unpleasant. Yet a man of principles must become reconciled with unpleasantness, which would doubtless come his way often enough. Justice must use even such instruments as George Cockburn.

Kyllachy said: 'One must suppose that Ochtertyre is the only certain rebel in the house.'

'There could be none other,' said Captain John decidedly. No need to involve young James. The fright would teach him. But there had been something in the tone that put unease into his decision. After a moment he asked: 'What have you in mind, Kyllachy?'

'You will not have forgotten old Borlum,' Kyllachy said.

'Your own father and yourself were out in the '15,' said Captain John, none too pleasantly.

'But I have proved my loyalty since then, and not by words only,' Kyllachy said. 'Whereas there is no proof of what does or does not take place the far side of the Atlantic.'

'Is this a definite accusation?' Captain John asked, half hoping it would be and yet anxiously considering the worse awkwardness that this would be.

'I would ask you also to consider,' said Kyllachy, 'that at the time of his quarrel with the Lords of Session, Bearcrofts was accused of Jacobitism.'

'That was disproved.'

'Bearcrofts would be no worse an advocate in his own cause

than in other folks', surely. And I know for certain that he visited old Borlum oftener than he would let on to the family.'

'He is the most disagreeable old brute,' said George, 'and it would please me vastly to see him cast down.'

Captain John had been thinking the very same, but disliked hearing it in George's voice. He wanted to do his duty, but by no means to please cousin George who had never so much as faced a musket in his life. David Haldane made as if to say something, then stopped. There were steps on the stair. Borlum came in without ceremony, young James behind him, pale and stiff-looking, glaring at George but not quite able to face Captain John. But Borlum walked straight at Kyllachy and said: 'You have accused me of a thing which is clean against my honour and my wife's honour. I deny it absolutely. You betrayed my father and you have attempted to betray me. You are a rogue and I hope yet to see you hung.'

Ah, thought Kyllachy, he is attacking. That is a sign of weakness. He laughed, flicking his fingers lightly along the ruffle of his shirt. He knew the eyes were on him, and he must above all act as a gentleman. It was David Haldane who watched, with the utmost fascination, the shape of the thing, the buff and blue and tawny coats, the twinkle of belt buckles, the controlled, furious hands and faces. He had not the least idea what the accusation was that Kyllachy had made against Borlum. But young Captain John, putting two by two quickly, had made some kind of guess. Yet this was not his immediate affair; he would not mix in it until he was certain that he was in the right. And suddenly Kyllachy and Borlum began to slip out of gentlemanliness, out of control, were shouting at one another and that with words of the Irish that might mean anything. The others were joining in, George would have his sword out in a moment and someone might be hurt and the thing put on to a wrong footing. He drew his own sword and said with considerable authority: 'Gentlemen, I must ask for silence!' Then, with the very stiffest politeness: 'Borlum, I request that either you withdraw your charge of treachery against our cousin of Kyllachy or that you substantiate it.'

William said, breathing quick and hard: 'I will do the latter.'

'You can do nothing of the kind,' said Kyllachy, 'unless you spin it out of your own head, you sliddery sow-libber!'

'There are others besides yourself that have access to witnesses,' said William, 'and mine might be truthful. Mine might not be a bing of lying mawsies.'

'Keep to the facts,' said Captain John.

'If you can!' added George, but Black William did not so much as look his way. He bowed slightly to the rest and said: 'In the summer of '24 my father was back in Scotland but I myself needing to leave for America.'

'I can believe that!' said Kyllachy and laughed.

William went on: 'I amna going to speak of my own affairs, Kyllachy, but as you know well, my uncle Joseph of Raigmore was tenant of Raitts and my father staying with him under the disguise of being a cousin. He was not there for any politics or such; he was beat and only wanting to come back to Scotland in his old age and maybe try out some farming notions he had, and be with his own folk. He could have been let be. But there was a price on his head. Aye, you will mind of that, Kyllachy. Early one morning, on a pretence of a breakfast before the day's shooting, the English officer in command of the occupying troops at the barracks came to Raitts. My father was in bed, came down in slippers and dressing-gown, lit the fire and had in the breakfast. While they were at it, in came the Government messenger, armed with a warrant, and six soldiers. As it chanced and part through my father's cleverness and part that the thing came at once to the ears of enough decent and kindly folk in the clan and they to the rescue, the thing failed altogether.' William looked round him but could not see behind the faces of the Lowlanders, only that grin he had got to tip off Kyllachy's mouth some way! He spoke with increasing violence: 'But it was a low dirty thing of the man that informed at the barracks and I am glad to my heart he never touched the thousand pounds that was on his kinsman's head!'

'That may be your opinion, Borlum,' said Kyllachy coldly, 'and a rebel's opinion it is!' He turned to Captain John: 'Would you not rather say that such a nest of sedition and treason must be burnt out and that whoever gave his hand to such work would be a loyal citizen to whom the thanks of honest men are due?'

'It must certainly be the part of a loyal citizen to help in the suppression of any Jacobitism,' said Captain John stiffly.

'For a thousand pounds,' said William.

'Rats' tails will fetch a penny the dozen when the corn is in the barn,' observed George, but the remark appeared in equally bad taste to everyone.

'The King's messenger would have been killed,' said William, 'but for my Uncle Joseph defending him from my father's over eager rescuers, and he himself wounded while he was doing it and carried off prisoner to London!'

'There is one of your Borlum lieings and twistings!' said Kyllachy. 'Raigmore was speaking in the Gaelic and who is to suppose he was defending the messenger! He is more likely to have been urging them on against the man and it is the greatest pity the folk in London did not hang him when they had the chance!'

'You know plenty about the thing, do you not, Kyllachy!'

'It was the talk of Inverness. As you would have known yourself if you had not been skulking in America.'

'And not a penny of the money did you touch, Kyllachy, seeing that my father escaped. Ach, ach, that was hard altogether, and you in such need of it! But you got it the next time, when my poor father was alone and that much older and that much more wanting peace. Aye, it was you, you!' James Haldane was shaking him by the elbow now, but he was not heeding at all. David was grinning, young Captain John looked bored and uncomfortable; this dog-fight was nothing to do with his political duty and making it no pleasanter.

But Kyllachy had his temper back, seeing that the other cat of the Clan Chattan had made no impression on the family, having handled the whole thing ill enough when he might have got it all his own way. As might happen if a man had a guilty conscience about another thing. If only he were sure on that! He said to Captain John: 'See now, how wild the man is getting! I am asking myself what will he be saying next. I am sorry for you having let him into the family, and it is a most embarrassing thing for every one of us.'

The shaking of his elbow had got through now to Black William's mind. He saw that things were not better than they had been, but worse, and he knew it had been by his own fault, a mistake of judgment which he must consider morally as a mistake of right and wrong: a sin. Silent as an Indian prisoner he stood in a deep kenning that it had come about because he had acted as a gentleman, not as a Christian. Repenting, he waited for the Inner Light, which did not come. It appeared that he must retrace his steps, follow the trail back through the briar patch of actions to where he had taken the wrong fork, blinded by a mind flap of the thunder birds, the war ones. Kyllachy was now speaking to David, pulling yet another Haldane over into alliance. William stared past them to the attic window, the pupils of his eyes fixed and small, his head dropped a little between his hunched shoulders. The trail had begun in anger and a breaking away from Patrick and the slow deliberation that was giving anger no assuagement. When Patrick had spoken of what he had discovered in Inverness anent Kyllachy's taking of the Government money, a thing had flared in him beyond bearing. He had said to himself that it was anger for what had been done on his father. But now he saw it clearly as a prideful cover to his own guilt. And Kirstie had begged him not to go yet, but he had broken in a fine and refreshing unthought and manly indignation from her and the Haldanes, only James following. He had said he would break up the alliance before it had gone too far, or come to terms. But it was more like that he had drawn it together. Anger and pride had hooded his Light at the fork. The trail went nowhere.

George Cockburn said to his cousin: 'You have taken to keeping peculiar company, James! You that have always been so particular! Perhaps you will have held a prayer meeting in the further attic? And who, pray, has the key?'

'George!' said James in acute discomfort, 'you will surely not take this matter up politically! It is nothing of importance and better not mentioned at all.'

'We will need to see what is said about the importance or un-importance of harbouring rebels, when the fellow himself and Ochtertyre are both under arrest.'

'Surely there is no question of that — George, you cannot —'

But George laughed: 'It is certainly fortunate that there are a few loyal Whigs at Gleneagles!'

Black William suddenly spoke, across them, to Captain John, who stood a little isolated, tapping with his fingers on the gold-plated hilt of his Navy sword, good but chiefly serviceable: 'I fear my anger became too much for me and I have said what could have a wrong appearance, to you most of all. It had but just come to my ears that Kyllachy here had said to Gleneagles that I have a wife in America, with all the consequences that this would have against your aunt Kirstie, who is my wife.'

Kyllachy began to answer, wishing it were a thing he could be right certain of, with written proof, and the young ones, James and David, both flushed with a heat of scandal and excitement and horror for the family, but Captain John held up his hand, sternly, as though it were a court martial, bidding Borlum continue.

'It was more than human nature could put up with. And, next, I had every reason to join in the late rebellion. But I did not do so. As you would be able to hear for yourself from the Lord President, Forbes of Culloden. It was a matter of principle. The same principle led me to condone the sheltering of a rebel here, even to take a hand in his greater safety. I cannot and will not see Scotland, my country, broken to non-sense over the politics. We must have peace and a settlement and look to the future in the stead of tearing up the roots of the past. You will agree with me over that?'

'In a sense, yes,' said young Captain John, uneasily, 'but what was all this gallimaufry about your father?'

'I accused Kyllachy of having attempted to betray him once and having succeeded in doing so another time, and that for money, and I cannot think he is the ally you need in what I must assume is a thing in which your principles are deeply involved, since that is the only reason a man of honour could be in it.' He was beginning to feel a small glow of guidance steadying his voice and temper and affecting his enemies. In his mind he acknowledged it humbly, asking for more.

Kyllachy said scornfully: 'What if I didna refuse the reward that the Government will aye give to its loyal servants! Who thinks the worse of me for that?' But the pains he had taken to keep the thing dark, even from his greatest cronies in Inverness, and now it was out! Patrick Haldane, the snake of an Edinburgh lawyer, getting it maybe in that case about the casks of brandy that had brought him ferreting up north and questioning all the firms where a gentleman might have paid his bills. And he saw a slight movement of repulsion from Captain John. 'I have been an open supporter of the Government,' he said, 'and shall continue so!'

Captain John said: 'It was unfortunate that your father was a rebel, Borlum. You will admit that it is necessary to root out rebellion.'

'By twenty years of prison for an old man that but wanted to stay quiet at home and try out new crops and ways of improvement for Scotland? By dragging out of hiding a young fool that was in the thing by no principle of his own? By ruining a kinsman that has no wish at all to be in the politics and was only there to start with through the over punishment of his father the last time? Think again of your principles, Captain John!'

'That is only one way of putting it,' young Captain John said earnestly, beginning a serious argument in a way he would not possibly have done, earlier, with the Highlander. 'One cannot allow such small matters of maybe one's preference or sentiment to stand in one's way. Justice must be done although it is pleasant for nobody. Ruat coelum. Aye, even if the plaster falls about my own ears!'

'Justice is one word for the judge and another for the condemned,' said Black William. 'You will bundle off a hundred poor tenants and clansmen that were in the rebellion out of sight to the Americas, as it is being done at this very moment of midsummer, and you will not need to think more on't, but they will go on living and suffering. The action is not over with the sentence. And a matter of principle may have consequences that are ill enough to foresee.'

'I am sure,' said George, 'that our Uncle William is so softhearted he cannot nip a louse in his shirt!' David laughed abruptly.

Captain John said nothing for a moment. You could see his principles working within him. Then he said: 'This might be overlooked in itself. But it is part of a great and urgent matter. We have to ask, whether can we set ourselves to uphold natural or sentimental rights as against the rights of the state.'

'Or whether can we set ourselves up as Christians, having mercy.'

'That is only one way of looking at it, Borlum. It involves Europe. Where would you and I and the house of Gleneagles be, but for the delicate and intricate systems of the states, as balanced and fine as a Geneva watch both within and without? The over-great use of mercy has a way of softening what needs to be hard. No, No! Loosen a wee nail here or there, the wheel falls off the coach and all's cowped in the ditch. We canna risk it, Borlum.'

'I have lived forth of this state or any state, forth of its rights or protections. There are other kinds of law possible and folk can behave in a human way, aye, even with nobility, although they are not constrained by laws and sanctions, or by a constitution or the workings of justice as we know it.'

Young Captain John threw his head back, gave an impatient tug to his uniform jacket, made as if to answer, then turned away, saying: 'You will not twist me, Borlum, whatever you may have done to others of the family!'

'I amna twisting,' said William, gently. 'I was laying the beginnings of a proposition in natural philosophy before you.'

'Ah,' said Kyllachy, 'we were thinking you had turned theologian!'

Captain John muttered something, looking at Black William in anger, but yet not, some way, in scorn. With a rough word about seeing what Gleneagles would say to it, he was at the door. Kyllachy began to ask if he should accompany, but got a half shouted No! for his pains. 'Cousin Johnnie!' James said agonizedly, and dashed after him. For a moment Kyllachy was at the door, half barring it to William, then thought better of it, turned his back and walked over to David and George, a hand for each shoulder. William followed the others out and the low western sun was streaming warmly at him at the foot of the bothy stair and his thought was that suppertime must be close and might give them a certain space to work for a new hold, and Patrick might have been weaving a net and all could yet be well. He blinked in the direct stream of light and Catherine Duncan jumped up from the window sill where she had been sitting.

'I couldna follow cousin John into the men's bothy, Uncle William!' she said agitatedly, 'but I waited, och I have never been so embarrassed and affronted in all my life — Mistress Grizzie went by and the look she gave me, och it could have taken the skin off me! And now he and James have gone by me like an east wind off the Castle law and I canna tell whether to follow them!'

'Maybe you should let be now,' said William, 'did he speak to you much on the matter?'

'He was thundering liker one of his own ship's guns and saying that no woman was fit to meddle with the politics, and indeed I was trying to make him suppose I knew even less of them than I do, the way he would get a part of his anger out of himself explaining to me!'

'You are a good lass,' said William, 'and I think you have done enough and plenty for now.' He gave her a sudden look. 'But forby that I think you have another thing in your mind. What is it, lassie?'

Her fingers twisted in the lace at her bosom, over her heart. 'Maybe I shouldna speak.'

'If it is troubling you, say, my lassie! This isna a time for hiding anything from your friends.'

She said: 'Well. It is Aunt Kirstie. I think — Uncle William, she cried out. It was a frightsome kind of cry. I am that fond of her. She cried out when the old wife came in at the door. It made me grue to hear her. Still and all, it could be nothing!'

'What old wife are you speaking on, Catherine?'

'Och well, I believe she used to be a nursemaid here, away back, in Aunt Kirstie's own time. She came hirpling in, the way she was no stranger. Tammie Clow was saying she had come all the way from Auchterarder.'

'That,' said William, 'will be Phemie Reid and I have heard mostly plenty about her. Where's Kirstie, my dear?'

'She is ben, in your room, and the old wife with her. But are you leaving James and myself, Uncle William? What will we do about cousin John?'

'We will trust for the moment to Patrick — and God. For I think it should be near suppertime and I will be back on to the trail, sure, by then. But I just canna leave my own lassie and her in trouble, and there's the truth of it, Catherine.'

'Maybe you are right,' said Catherine, minding on what her auntie had said about the nature of marriage, and watched him go, but herself felt desolate and perplexed. And it seemed to her that her life had been gey easy and without choices and temptations, so that maybe up to now it had been over simple to keep to the right ways. And now she could not be sure, was she still on them or was she astray. Uncertainly she took the stairs down to the dining-room and it was empty, and she put up a prayer for right help and guidance in her difficulties, and someway there was more to it than to any prayer she had ever made before.

CHAPTER VII

PHEMIE REID had a fine puckle tow on her rock, but when the neighbour folks in Auchterarder were saying that Helen Erskine's Kirstie was up-by at Gleneagles and when Providence had seen fit to send her oye off up the glen with empty creels on his beast for a wee load peats, how would she not leave the rock by the reel and the thread no nearer its coming and sit herself up on the sod saddle with her oye walking it at the beast's head? Still and on, thoughts went swithering through her head, that was not all moiled and spoiled with the reading of books. Wee Kirstie that was so awful bonny and cuddlesome, and all the more if you frighted her, for the rose colour would come and go and the wee mou would pucker and the blue een swimming, and there, quick, she'd bury her face in your apron and oh the curly wee pow and the strong and nice feel on yourself to be hurting and healing her, both at the once! Phemie hadna been let skelp the Gleneagles weans the way she had her own, aye, and her oye there forby his minnie! And she let out a screech of laughing that had the laddie turning to glower at her the like of a wild cat and he going with one of the wee Johnson lassies and wouldna like to be minded how she had skelped the bare dowp of him! Na, na, Helen Erskine had been soft with the weans, but she herself had frighted them fine, with kelpies and bogles and casting of devils, aye, wee Kirstie and Rob and Helen and all, her bonny wee toddling bairnies, her very own for all she was a maiden lassie. Some way she didna think so oft nor so fond of the bairns of her body, excepting for the one that was taken early on and the two-three at the end when maybe she was past it but her man wasna. They werena anyways so bonny as the wee Haldanes and they hadna the good claes and she hadna the time to be aye washing them and studying on them and putting the comb through their hair.

As they passed by the crooked thorn she gave her petticoats

a wee hitch and bobbed with her head, the lucky way of it, and saw that her oye touched his hand to his bonnet. She had seen the appearance here, times she hadna done yon thing, after thon terrible powerful sermon by the visiting Minister from Stirling that had left her more feared of hell-fire than of the close kind of fear you got when you kennt a thing wasna canny. Strathearn was full of appearances, grugous or over bonny, and the Terra Navi' housing as muckle Folk as Auchterarder and Blackford. And terrible beasties. The six-legged cattle that pastured under the Ochils. Things that could be set to follow you. And you never kenning. You could maybe be free of them on a Sabbath with the Kirk at your back. But they gathered wild in the week. Lady Gleneagles would be saying there was no sic a thing. But that wasna sense. Where there was any toom place for them, there they would come, and the trees and stones bent to their will and habitation. As could be easy seen. Yon time Bearcrofts had been so terrible cross and said there was no sic a thing as the Eye, hadna his horse lamed yon same day? Och, he was a cross one, the Bear,. a terrible thrawn, camsteerie, carnaptious skellum and no' like her own wee Kirstie.

Och, och, it would be fine seeing Kirstie and she Lady Borlum. And folks saying she had put spells upon her first man, but whatna wifie that willna have thought on that and the man aye blaming and maybe skelping her. The gentry didna do yon. Or there was what they said. She had seen gentry wifies greeting, for a' their silks and satins. When Tullibardine went to his bed roaring fou, a' the house kennt what he would be at. And who was to say what like Athol and Marr could be with the drink in them and their breeks down. Aye and the wee black chaplains ben the house to say their prayers for them! She suddenly asked a question of her oye anent the wee Johnson lassickie and he answered in two words, as cross as a trapped tod, and she laughing till she near fell off the beast.

He stopped a mile from Gleneagles house, for he had his peats cut and stacked and was needing to get them before

night. Old Phemie could walk the lave of it. She was minded
to bed in with the lasses in the bothy — if they werena scunnered with the smell of her, he thought. For the old grannies
willna think on washing from one month's end to the next,
except it will come round to Communion, and they may pin
a clean mutch on their heads but that willna hinder what's
below from crawling its way out. He handed her off the
beast and she hirpled her way on towards Gleneagles. Times
she would laugh and times she would sing away in a half-
cracked voice, bairns' songs mostly, and moments of sweetness
in it. She made her way round by the well that was called
St. Mungo's, though it did not appear to be any saint that she
was speaking to, and preened herself in the water mirror and
studied on the pleasure she would get out of her wish.

Kirstie saw her at the corner of the house. The cry came out
of her. She couldna face this out of the past. Not with all
going agley in the present. For William had gone to the
cousins' bothy in anger and against Pate's advice, and no good
would come of it, and maybe it was all her own fault and she
had brought bad luck on her man and her house was builded
on sand for all she had thought there was a blessing on it,
and here was a thing from the beginning of all come back to
point her sins! Yet she must not let Phemie speak with
Catherine Duncan nor Margaret Bearcrofts, the good lasses,
the ones that hadna been touched, that didna know of evil nor
the things that might come up out of the dark waters. She was
asking herself now, how soon would the servant lassies get
seeing that things were wrong, that there was neither peace
nor security in the house of Gleneagles. Mistress Grizzie would
be making her observations surely!

And now Phemie was kissing her and och the nasty dirt she
had in the wee cracks of her face and neck! And she so clean as
a lassie! Is this over finnicky? But surely to goodness folks
needna stink! There was no harm in an honest working smell
off a decent man or woman, but, but — she hated taking
Phemie up to the room, her and William's room. She seemed
to file the very walls and windows of it and now they were

speaking of this and that and Phemie asking for the wee one, and sudden Kirstie was terrible glad she hadna brought Elizabeth, or Phemie might have touched and filed her daughter into the bargain. And a hope came at her that before next she was here with Elizabeth, whom the others were all now ettling to see, Phemie might be under the earth. And with the hope, a will, an intention that it might be so, a pointing at Phemie, the thought of a waxen image — ach a wild wickedness, a naked sin! And her hate on Phemie for bringing this sin into the house with her. And now Phemie was speaking of the dead lad bairns, and she, as it aye happened, stiffening into hardness against any that spoke of them or pitied herself. And syne Phemie saying with a warm, nasty, sideway look: 'And't wasna to be wondered at, your man gaeing yon gate till's grave, ma doo. Na, na, a mad dog sud be helpit into the rope's end.'

And at that Kirstie had let out one screech, as though she would deafen herself against the voice, against the assumption of kinship, of the same purpose and that not of God. And ah there, for Phemie, there was a win in the game against the Gleneagles weans, against the house and the family, against she couldna tell what, but it was just fine to have power over it yet and over her babsie-ba, and she laughed, sputtering, and Kirstie hated her and longed for William to come and if young James hadna been such an orra fool William would not have left her now! And Phemie at her, asking, asking, what way ava had Andrew Shaw died, and for a moment she felt a terrible ettling to speak of the thing right, of the gushing out of the blood, and of yon awful, feared look in the man's eyes at the last, to one who would understand — as Catherine Duncan couldna — to run to Phemie and hide her guilty head — Phemie would understand, Phemie would comfort — She pulled herself up sharply. 'My husband had a seizure,' she said, 'and folk got spreading the most wicked and unwarrantable stories. These wild Ayrshire folk that canna thole a stranger, and the half of them no better than Cameronians.' She was holding on now, with all her strength, to the orderly and decent

Episcopalian Church. 'You should know better than to give such any belief!'

'Ah!' said the old woman, shuffling herself towards Kirstie over the quilted Indian counterpane of the big bed, 'the douce lying looks she hae till her Phemie, the same as lang syne when she filed her coaties, the wee toddling peerikins. Come, tell Phemie —'

But Kirstie cried out again, and, on the tail of her cry, her husband came into the room and when he looked on Phemie she began to shrink and tremble away and slithered off from the end of the bed, and she seemed to Kirstie to be older and gey shoogly about the hands and head and not frightsome any more, without power and without kinship. 'Kirstie!' said William, 'Curstan m'eudail de'n diabhul tha thu ris? Sguir de'n amaideachd sin agus thig a nall an so air ball!'

'Mercy o' me! said Phemie, 'is't thon the new one? Och, och, he is as big as the Big Man of Craigrossie!' And indeed she herself made a terrible wee seeming now that she was standing before him, or maybe it was he that looked to Kirstie like a strong and noble tree, a deep-rooting beech tree.

'You will have heard tell of poor Phemie, William, my soul,' said Kirstie, in a voice that was some way not wholly her own, 'she that was nursemaid here when we were weans.'

'Aye, and had you and Airthrey frighted out of your wee wits. A wild thing altogether and parents should have more care for their innocent bairnies!'

'Ach, it was all over, long years past, William!' she said.

'The lintie shouldna shield the gowk in her nest, even if the gowk is an old and mangy one. Mistress Reid, if, as I surmise, you are attempting to put the Sight on to me, you will get no satisfaction, because I walk under the Lord's hand and protection and have no fear. And I dinna like to think what fashion of rebuke your Minister will have for you when he is told!'

Up went Phemie's hands, trembling and shaking and dirty as a lum's mouth: 'Och sir, sir, ye winna set the Minister on a puir body that's no' far frae her latter end?'

'And set for hell-fire,' said William. 'Go!'

Phemie gave one more look at Kirstie but nothing passed in it. Hell-fire — och, you would be sorer pained here on mid earth. The gentry and their Ministers had thought on the other thing for a frighting of poor folks, and she had her Friends, aye that she had, with power and dominion, and would stretch their hands over poor Phemie that was aye ready to do Their will. And maybe she would study on a way to get thon big black de'il of a Highlander across Their path. Reiving away wee Kirstie! Aye, aye, she had her frighted fine at the first. Maybe she had best not stay overnight at Gleneagles, with thon man. She was out by the yard door now and keeking round. If she could but see Airthrey. Her own wee Rob. He aye had a crown for her or a pair cast breeks for her oye. She wrinkled her neb at the kitchen corner and smelt the supper on its way. Aye, cockaleekie and plenty to spare surely!

In the room there was silence for a time and Kirstie breathing quick and uneven. William said: 'You lied to me, Kirstie, saying the thing was over, to shield yon de'il's grannie.'

His mouth was fixed, unsmiling, she found it hard to look at him, hard to speak: 'She is nought but a poor creature, William — '

'She isna. She is a wicked woman. You shouldna have let her snatch at you, Curstan beag! You shouldna have lied to your man!' He took her by the shoulders hard and she slid down from his hands like water into the stiff wide foam of her light muslin skirts, on to her knees within them, clinging to him and greeting with her mouth open to running tears, awkward and bairnlike. For a moment he stood over her, black angry like the Father, aye a jealous God, but, as she acknowledged sin and would have welcomed the blow, yet was but a moment off minding on her first husband, Andrew Shaw, and comparing the two men angry, for the first time since her marriage, Black William was kneeling beside her, his arms round her in compassion and understanding, so that all yon comparison was past but another maybe come in its stead.

He said: 'You are in the right of it, lass. We had best be on our knees, the two of us.'

'Put you up a prayer, William my dearest,' said Kirstie in a low and broken voice, 'and maybe — ach maybe the Lord will forgive me if yourself asks it.'

He began to pray in a whisper, haltingly, asking to be shown a way for them both to a new life and a relinquishing and forgiveness of old sins and old mistakes. He asked for grace and to be held in God's love as they were in each other's. They were all unworthy and yet he could not but be aye sure in the deeps of his soul of the fact of Redemption and the love that had made it possible. And, as she listened, Kirstie began to feel an easing of the muckle pain of her guilt, felt herself joined and secure with her man. As she had known it at prayer with her father, but never with Andrew Shaw except at the very beginning and then she had been carried away by something liker spiritual pride than humility. At the end they looked each other in the eyes and kissed and sat themselves down on the edge of the bed, breathing deep and freely like two that have just escaped from a cruel enemy.

William said: 'I have been studying on this matter of yourself and the Horny, my dear one, and I kind of half see how the thing came about. There is a deep part of ourselves that we canna rightly know and that might be some way the natural man and woman before the Fall and also before Redemption. And whiles it is close to God's love and innocent and full of the bonniest colours and sweet sounds and scents. But whiles it is equally close to the Pit and the things of the Pit. Yet we must come to terms with it before we are whole or can be wholly saved. But it will send its messengers in the shape of dreams and visions and if we are feared of them they will become real on us and we will worship them.' He stopped there and it came into his head, first, that the thing might be altogether nonsense, and syne that if it had been sense maybe Kirstie wasna understanding it, for she gave no sign. Maybe it was over much to expect of a woman and he could hardly grasp it right himself even. Yet he was kind of disappointed that she wasna grasping it, that she looked mazed and stupid as a working tenant might do, and you trying to get him to try drilling his seed, say, and he doesna want to understand for it will make him trouble. But Kirstie Haldane — was it true that women were aye the weaker vessels? It was not thought to be so for certain in America nor amongst the Friends, whatever might be said in London or Edinburgh among the bargainers for heiresses. And ach, he had wanted to share this thought with Kirstie, thinking it might have helped her, but she wasna even looking at him! 'Well,' he said, trying to rouse her, 'well, Kirstie?'

And at long last she lifted her eyes and what she said was: 'Could it be this way the coven, thinking and fearing all together — ach, could the coven make themselves an image out of their own souls, something that is orra true for each one of them but maybe not — not — real the same as a chair or a table is real?'

But William did not answer yet. He said: 'Kirstie, you spoke yon word, yon terrible hellish word, the same it might have been a plain daytime word. I havena heard you say it before except in the tail of a nightmare.'

'I thought maybe I could say it — now. I thought maybe I should. But yet could it be possible for the coven to make themselves a hellish dream out of yon hidden inner part of their spirit and the same for each of them? How would all have the same dream?'

'Maybe through over much speaking and brooding on a shape, and the like for their grannies and great grannies, it would come the same way for all. But you said yourself that the thing was thought of under many and foul shapes.'

'Or a shape that was at once foul and surpassing bonny.' She gave a long queer look at him and he knew she must be thinking of him as he had appeared yon midnight. Yet there were other things working in her mind. She said: 'Maybe for the right bad the thing *was* real and no' just a dream. But my own appearances werena dreams, William, excepting my whole life could be a dream, the way it seems now, my dearest, before you came to me. Or is there any way at all to tell what is truly seen or heard from what's but dream and seeming?'

'It would be a wild thing if we couldna know and we gifted with sense. And yet it isna easy at all. But what I am saying is that maybe we have all of us to face what comes from the inner part before we can be our right selves and stand before God. But few enough do and we are mostly unguided, for what I was speaking of is not doctrine of any Church, and it could be the greatest heresy, although I havena heard that it is. But, being unguided, we are easy frighted and let ourselves be overwhelmed.'

'Aye,' said Kirstie, 'we sink in the dark waters in the stead of swimming them.'

'I knew fine you would understand, Kirstie, and better than myself!' he cried. 'Ah, lassie, lassie, now it is all coming clearer to me — '

'What did *you* see, William?' she asked suddenly, and then: 'No, dinna, dinna tell me! You are stronger than I am and your thing will have been stronger than mine, but you dealt with it and overcame it, aye, you did, so! Fine I ken that. And at the end, see you, William, when you can swim the waters and play in them as the Psalms tell us of Leviathan, then you dare to look far down intil the depths, and there is the face of the one you were aye seeking at the bottom of your own spirit, the same as the face in the lassie's glass at Hallowe'en! But it isna common to have the thing pointed out so plain as it was to me, when the bottom of my sin and misery in the moment of my accepting it and drowning, turned to the very fullness of my joy.'

'Aye,' he said, 'and you are the image and opposite and equal in my own dark waters, o m'eudail, Kirstie Haldane, my breath, my soul! Often enough have I called you my soul, and now I know why it was I did it and how the Gaelic is an alto-gether more sensible and accurate language than the English when it comes to dealing with such things.'

'We have found one another again,' said Kirstie, 'but now we canna leave the rest of the family to their troubles, and we will be mightily strengthened by what has passed and we will act right in the Lord's name and all will be well by bedtime.' She got to her feet and dabbled at her eyes from the brown pig full of cold spring water. 'You dinna think we should even try to get the poor silly body out of his hideyhole and away up the hillside maybe?'

'Not by day,' Black William said, frowning a bittie, and again wondering what it was Kyllachy could know against Patrick and whether it was of such a kind as to shock the rest of the family. As it might well be. Kirstie was setting her hair to rights now, peering into the wee gold-framed mirror on the wall. And while she was yet at it, in came her brother Airthrey, who stood in front of William Macintosh and looked at him long enough and at last said: 'I wish to the Lord that I knew what to think of you, Borlum.'

'I dinna always know that myself,' he answered, 'but who has said which?'

'My nephew John, who is as honest as good ships' timber, has told my brother Mungo of a rebel hidden here in the house and mentioned Ochtertyre and yourself. I see this does not surprise you.'

'No,' said William, 'nor will it have surprised Gleneagles.'

Captain Robert gave enough of a start to make it clear that he at least was surprised. 'What did Mungo say to it?' Kirstie asked with a high colour on her cheeks. She had her curling-irons in her hand, for she was minded to go down to the kitchen and get the things heated and her hair in right order, for you aye feel a spark more of confidence when you are back of an outside that is gleg and trim and even maybe bonny to some. But the tongs were now a kind of weapon, the way she had them held.

'Mungo said to me,' said Captain Robert, 'that I would get the key of the attic from you, Borlum, and that I was to bring it to himself. Whatever he may have guessed or heard earlier, he cannot disregard this now, having been officially informed and he a Justice of the Peace.' He held out his hand, but Black William shook his head slowly, giving over no key. 'I am terrible

330

disappointed in you, Borlum,' half shouted Captain Robert.
'And in Ochtertyre, and it shows that once a Jacobite, always
a Jacobite, and none of you to be any more trusted than the
snakes that you are! And I am most of all disappointed in you,
Kirstie, and that shows that there is never a woman with
principle enough to stand up for the right once a man has put
her on to her back.'

He would most surely have got a clip with the curling tongs
but for William snatching down his wife's hand and, though it
was an insult all through to her, yet it was a kind of half compliment to him, the way most folks think of things, and we are
none of us free from that. William said: 'Your brother doesna
mean it, Kirstie. He doesna know the circumstances of the case.
He might think otherwise if he did.'

'I have been lied to and deceived,' said Captain Robert.
'That cannot be gainsaid. And not, I think, on this matter
alone. And as you know, I was gey ready to trust you and be
your friend.'

'Aye,' said William, 'I have hurt the most of you Haldanes
one way or another, and you are easier hurt than you look to be.
I wish it hadna had to be; it was an ill wind blew Kyllachy
here. I believe I know how else you think yourself deceived by
me. But it isna so and Bearcrofts would tell you the truth of it.'

'I am not speaking on this before her,' said Robert, jerking
his head at Kirstie, the same way any brother might do.

'Och,' said Kirstie, 'I am going and I wish you joy of your
laddies' dirtiness!' And she tossed her chin at Robert, the way
of a sister.

Robert seized her by the gathers of her skirt: 'And you with
the key no doubt, ye sneaking hizzie!'

A few stitches went. 'You muckle gowk, Rob you! Search
me if you've a mind, but quit tearing the clothes off me!'

'I have had a wheen women searched in my time,' said
Robert, 'for the stealing of diamonds, and it was more than the
petticoats we had off them. But it would be less trouble and
screeching to break the lock of the door.'

William said quickly: 'Kirstie hasna the key. Nor have I.

But I can get it for you if need be. And will. But I assure you there is an explanation.' Robert looked unbelieving, and it occurred to William that most likely he did not know that young James, his own heir, was in the thing. He went on: 'What does Gleneagles purpose?'

'This man, as I understand, is not protected by the new Act. Whether it will be transportation or gaol, I dinna ken. They'll scarcely shorten him by the head, if, as my nephew says, he is of little importance. But any Justice of the Peace who does not arrest a rebel once he has the official information against him, is liable for assisting him, and a charge of treason would lie against any such man.'

'As no doubt against Ochtertyre and myself,' said William thoughtfully and in a hope that every moment gained might also be gained for Patrick and whatever scheme he might have.

'It is more than likely that it can no longer be hidden where Ochtertyre was in the rebellion. I had meant to speak for him, but seeing he deceived me, I will not do so. As to you, Borlum, if the other thing is anyways true it will be more than the Courts you will have to deal with.' And he shifted his sword a little, as though making it easier to draw.

'Do you suppose it to be true?' William asked.

'I am willing to be convinced that it isna,' Captain Robert said.

Good and well, thought Kirstie, if the men have a thing they want to keep me out of, let them! And indeed it would be queer if it was always that way round. And — and — No, she didna like it ava and yet she had the trust in William that went deeper. She went over to the window and bit at the ends of the silk tartan screen that was over her hair and shoulders, jagging with her teeth at the fringe. And as she stood there she saw a lad on a good horse come up the road from Blackford at a hard trot and turn at the gate and leap off below the window, snatching a bonnet from a curly yellow head, and suddenly she cried out to her husband: 'Here is Wattie Buidh of all the world! What at all is bringing the like of him to Gleneagles?' She lifted the sash and called down in Gaelic and William came hurrying over beside her, and the lad answered and now they were all three at it.

Captain Robert frowned, irritated and disapproving, and at last broke in: 'What is this ploy of yours? Has yon chiel not got any decent English?'

'Och, plenty!' said William, half turning, one knee on the sill, 'but I dinna know if what he has to say will please you. He is the Lord President's man and Kirstie and I know him well enough from two years back when Forbes of Culloden said one thing and my Chief's wife another. But what he says now is that his master is on his way north from Edinburgh and none too well. He had meant to lie the night at Perth but an axle of the coach broke, with the roads the way they are, and it took them a certain time to sort it well enough to finish the day, even, and now he is at Blackford and doesna much care for the look of the beds in the inn, so sent to know could he lie the night at Gleneagles.'

'Now that,' said Captain Robert, 'is devilish awkward altogether and what the Bear will say to it is more than I can guess. But we canna let the Lord President lie at Blackford and he a sick man. I had best speak to Mungo.' He walked up and down. 'Well, if Forbes comes, that settles this matter of treason and I hope you are good enough friends with the man for the blame to be off yourself! The rebel will doubtless be taken to Perth gaol to-morrow under guard of the Lord President's men who have no sentiments about the right way with a Jacobite!' And he walked out, slamming the door and leaving the two in the room to look at one another.

'Is it certain what Duncan Forbes will say?' asked Kirstie anxiously.

William stood by the window, watching Wattie Buidh going his ways into the house. 'Nothing is certain in this world,' he said, 'but young Captain John will lay an official information before the Lord President and he will have George and Kyllachy backing him and insisting and being as legalistic as a pair of inkstands. And it will be gey hard for Forbes to behave in any but the orthodox Whig way — even if he has a mind for any other.'

'What mind could he have?' Kirstie asked.

'He is a humane and reasonable man and he wants the best for poor Scotland. But he is ill, and a sick man is easy tired and mayna have the will to stand for humanity here — if it is that way he sees it, even. And God knows what your Bear will say to him.' William sat down heavily, rubbing his fingers over his temples and under the edge of his wig.

'Couldna you speak to the Bear, William?' Kirstie asked hopefully.

'I have tried but he wouldna listen. Could you try, Kirstie?'

She scarce knew what to answer to that. He might listen. But more likely he would not. And he could be terrible cross. What was he doing all this time? At least, she thought, they will do nothing now until Forbes is here. Which will not be until after our own supper, for we cannot put off eating for another hour and he will be that at the least, and indeed it is time we went down, for I can smell the fish and the cockaleekie. And Margaret will need to keep back enough for the Lord President and his men, though doubtless some of them will stop at Blackford. Mistress Grizzie would have her hands full with the beds to make up and the clean sheets to find and ai∴. And again William said to her: 'Try you, Kirstie.'

PART FOUR

THE KINDLY HOUSE

DUNCAN FORBES OF CULLODEN

CHAPTER I

Mistress Grizzie, the housekeeper, had sent the lasses off with a pair of good plaiden curtains to hang round the spare bed that Tammie and muckle Geordie were setting up for the Lord President in the music-room that was the least used room in the house, kind of wee and musty, but quiet enough for a sick man and handy for the water-closet. She crossed over to the press where the linen sheets lay, pressed and heavy and iron-smooth. It seemed to her, fitting the key into the lock, that the day was going iller and iller, and that through no fault of her own, but by the folly and wanton pride of the gentry, and if they thought that she, Grizzel Pitcathly, could see no farther than her tea caddy and her sugar loaves, then they had made an orra mistake in judgment.

Aye, she had her own mind on the lot of them, Gleneagles himself, the Lord be merciful to him, a fine bonny gentleman and a mighty defender of the people's established Kirk of Scotland, aye and a just man forby, but gey soft-hearted and with over much faith in some. Yon heathen Bearcrofts that hadna so much manners as would cover a sixpence. And now this clanjamphrey of Highland trash with more feathers to their bonnets than pennies to their pouches, and all the lot of them letting on they were cousins, aye, Borlum and Kyllachy and the lave of them, a poor smittry of wee old kailyard castles and not grass enough on the parks to keep the wool on a decent lowland sheep, and queer if they didna leave the Haldane house a poorer place for having them in it! And the whole lot of the young folk talking politics, which was the surest way to sinful anger and letting of blood and breaking of good chairs and glasses, but if folk didna work they must needs wag their jaws over ae thing or another, and the most of it to do with their own stubborn pride over the family and the politics that went with the family! And you could have a decent family pride the like of her own, and her Pitcathlys that were a far-out branch of the

337

other family but hadna just had the same siller, they had been in the same wee place as their forefathers and doing no worse than them, and her youngest brother a Minister. But the great houses of Scotland had a muckle wicked pleasure in being ever at onsetting and strife, and the middle ones such as the Haldanes would cock their bonnets with the rest, and all peace destroyed in Kirk and household. And here now was the Lord President coming and the supper ready and had been this whilie past, and what was she to keep back for him? For the collops of beef would go dry and the cockaleekie was Captain Rob's favourite dish and he was to have it, honest lad, for you will not get a good cockaleekie in the East Indies. But it would be easy enough to keep back a part of the soup that had a rabbit in it for the thickening, and some of the sea fish, though they mightna be healthy eating for the Lord President and his stomach the way it was rumoured to be. Tammie and Geordie had best take the mahogany nightstool with the padded back down from the gentry lasses' room for poor Duncan Forbes; it would do them no harm to go down the stairs the same as their grannies used, though Mistress Helen would be the one to complain, aye, you could lay your life on that! And which ewer and basin, now? Maybe the bonny wee china one with the outlandish flowers and mannikies — And och, here was Phemie Reid come hirpling in ben and Mistress Grizzie could not abide the sight of thon one, but it was best not to anger her, in view of what was said, and Phemie speaking to her in a whining voice as though she was the most hadden-doun body in the world!

'I sall aiblins get a sup o' broth, Grizzie,' said Phemie, 'and maybe a bite o' ma wee Rob's cockaleekie, and syne I'll be making my ways hame.'

'You could bed in with the lasses, Phemie, if you've a mind,' Mistress Grizzie answered coldly, and yet you couldna be turning the woman away! 'You'll no be back at your own fireside till after night.'

'I can gae my lane through a lee-long mirk and my maidenhead gane no faurer than it was at the start!' said Phemie with a wee chuckle, 'forby a bonny midsummer night and the strath

brimming o'er with the flitterings and croodlings of a' the Folk
that will be loosed in it!'

But Grizzie just turned her back and took down a pair of the
best linen sheets for the Lord President's bed, Helen Erskine's
weaving and her initials twined and broidered on them, and
they would sit well over the pillows. A light French bed it was,
that Gleneagles had bought in London one time when he was
down there for the Westminster parliament. The Lord President's
men would need to go in with the lads in the bothy; there were
another two-three feather mattresses from last winter's hens.
She wasna putting them in with Kyllachy's scabby nasty Highlanders! At least if Forbes's men were Highland themselves they
would be decent, civilized Whigs. She called sharply for Peggy
to carry the sheets over. She wasna so much as giving an
answer to Phemie and her nasty heathen talk of midsummer!

Captain Robert came in, worried looking. The feel of the
housekeeper's room changed. Mistress Grizzie turned to him
with a smile; this was one of her favourites and his coming in had
saved her from an answer to Phemie which might have had
consequences of one kind or another. 'Have you seen Patrick at
all, Grizzie?' he asked.

She shook her head. 'Patrick will be after me, all the same,
if the supper is delayed for another ten minutes!'

Captain Robert was going, without seeing Phemie Reid, so
fashed he was with seeking Patrick, when she grabbed him by
the coat: 'Hae ye ne'er a wee word for puir Phemie?'

He gasped with a wild uncomfortable feeling and his hand
went searching down to his breeches pocket; it would be cheap
getting rid of yon feeling at a crown! And he hadna that, but
still and on it was cheap at half a guinea! The feel of guilt that
was yet not his own guilt but for all that filing him, and for all
that taking power from him, making him into a bairn and not
the Captain of an East Indiaman. 'Here's f'ye, Phemie,' he
said, 'and I'll be over at Auchterarder, sure, and see yourself
and your man.' And he hurried out again, pursued by blessings
that he didna want, for some way it was shocking to hear the
Lord's name on Phemie's lips.

'Eh, leeze me on ma wee Rob!' said Phemie, 'ma bonny wee man, aye sae mindful of his puir Phemie!' But Grizzie had locked the press and gone out with a pair of down pillows and their cases, and sudden it came to her that the Haldanes were aye kind, but it was a profane kindness of this world and far enough from the true and godly virtue of mercy. Mercy? What should a merciful man have done? Might he not have destroyed Phemie Reid — aye, long ago! — for the sake of the muckle harm she was doing to others, forby herself?

Mercy, aye, what at all was it? The Lord's mercy could be gey hard to see through. It was never plain simple, the way of human kindness. Mercy could be destruction. The discovery of witchcraft could be a divine mercy and its punishment by men, acting as the Lord's instruments, might also be a manifestation of mercy. Not that she would say that Phemie Reid was a witch, och no, that would be going too far surely, but it was a terrible thing to see the like of her so affecting Captain Rob that he would give her more gold money than honest folks saw in a six-month and all to get shut of her! You would say it was softness in him, yet the Haldanes werena plain soft, they would go through the most peculiar and complicated actions, giving trouble to themselves and others, to do some fashion of kindness that they had set their hearts on. But mercy?

And Captain Robert was still ranging round, seeking for Patrick who was not in his room nor anywhere he could see, and every moment more angry at Patrick, who was being, once again, a cause of discomfort to the rest of the family. And so he came full tilt on Kyllachy who was the last person he wanted, and Kyllachy stopped him with an insistent hand, and, before he could well escape from the glib-gabbit gawkie, was saying things of a disquieting nature anent Patrick. Of whom enough was known to make such things credible, even to his half-brother, but what ill wind had blown Kyllachy in to speak of them! Captain Robert listened with an increasing anger and impatience and wanted his supper forby, and sudden he turned on one foot and said: 'Since I opine that you are selling it, how much do you want for your silence?'

And yet, thought Kyllachy, is this what I want at all? Money, a poor low thing, and this Airthrey no more than a chaffering trader at the end of it all, and he will find it harder dealing with a Highland gentleman than with any sultan of the Indies! Yet it is the things money will get for you, and he smiled a little and his hand went to his waistcoat pocket and played away at the seal that hung there. Horses and velvet coats and good claret, the service of your inferiors and the sly and willing looks of women. But certainly you could be hampered by lack of this same low thing, and more especially in the politics. Not that he had a mind to the old game, since it had become apparent after the Glenshiel affair that no more was to be expected from the Stewarts. But again, if one needs to live on terms with the new Whiggy ways, then this money has to be at one's hand. It will count instead of intolerable attendance at countless sermons. At least with some.

'I observe,' said Captain Robert, 'that you are weighing up this silence of yours nicely, ounce by ounce. And how much will it work out at by the pound?'

'No,' said Kyllachy, 'I am not thinking in this way at all. And what is more, Airthrey, I am not sure that I care so much for the money as yourselves who are in trade and naturally perceive of men and their thoughts in such terms.'

Robert could have drawn his sword on the man for that, since the Honourable East India Company was in no way to be looked down upon by these Highlanders who were too dead-lazy to shift a grain sack or count on their fingers even! But it had to be let go for the sake of the family. Which, once again, was like to suffer for the sins and follies of one of its members! For first it would be the lasses, aye an anxiety to their brothers until such time as they were safe wedded and bedded and another man to fash after them, or it would be Colonel James, young Jamie's father, adventuring off, for all his illness and the concern of the family, and dying at last in Jamaica. And then it was talk of Kirstie and her husband, though maybe there was not a spunk of truth in it, and last year it had been the Jacobite thing setting themselves and Scotland by the ears, and the gleanings of an ill crop yet on hand. But aye and on and ever since he had been a bairn almost, there had been trouble over Patrick! And it was devilish hard and unjust on the decent and honest ones in the family, himself and Mungo most of all! 'Well,' he said, 'if it isna money you are after you will need to enlighten me as to what it is.'

'I might conceive it to be my duty,' Kyllachy said, 'to make it known that one of the pillars of the God-fearing and Whig house of Gleneagles keeps company with notorious atheists and that he is the true author of these rhymes and satires which both yourself and I feel a decent shame in the mere knowledge of and which would most assuredly be held as blasphemous in any court of law.' And he smiled somewhat, having got much satisfaction from the embarrassment of Airthrey.

'Well,' said Captain Robert, 'we have weathered nastier winds, and it might be, och yes, it might easily be that honest folks would give no credence to such a gallimaufry.'

'At the same time,' Kyllachy said, 'it should be mentioned what the Assessor to the City of Edinburgh wrote at the time of the Jacobite siege — '

'In a letter which was steamed open in a thieves' kitchen of Highlanders!'

'Through great zeal for the Government and in a gentleman's library in Inverness. And you will bear in mind, cousin Airthrey, that the main sitting of the trial of Provost Stewart will take place shortly.'

Captain Robert did not like this, not at all; he felt himself terrible cast down and aye at the back of his mind yon other thing anent William Macintosh. Indeed the mere fact of housing a rebel in the attic seemed small in comparison. A man shouldna need to bear all his kin on his back! And so, when Patrick himself came in, Robert could hardly bear to speak to him, even, but the both of them scowling at one another and Kyllachy leaning back, watching as a boy watches two beasties on a stone and maybe he will set his foot on one of them.

'And so?' said Patrick, having listened to what had been said of him with no worse a frown, even with the end of a smile on him. He went on: 'There is aye good fishing in drumlie waters, but the fish may be over big for the line.' He nodded at Kyllachy. 'Take tent of yourself, mannie, or you'll be found in over the lugs, and a cock salmon having the laugh of you!'

'Well, well,' said Kyllachy, 'I see you Haldanes cannot be dealt with as gentlemen. I came to Gleneagles with no intention at all to speak of these matters, but I have been insulted beyond endurance, both by Bearcrofts and Borlum, and I must even give my temper its rein.' He bowed. 'I have no ill will against your good self, Airthrey, nor yet against Gleneagles, but I am not the only one that has been insulted, and we have enough ammunition to sink the worse boats in your convoy — those that any decent family would be glad enough to do without.'

Patrick laughed in a loud, rude and apparently genuine amusement and made a single word remark of the kind that his brother would not have tolerated from one of the crew of his ship. 'That will not help you any,' said Kyllachy, 'and I shall call my men and ride.'

At this Captain Robert was caught in a deep embarrassment between his annoyance at Patrick and his fear of what could happen, not to himself surely, but to the family, and what had Kyllachy meant by this other one, and was it George, and was it possible that they knew of this Jacobite skulker? — for if so, Borlum was involved and through him Kirstie, and all that the wiser part of the family had said at the very beginning, aye, four years past, was proving true and the devil in it that she had ever married a Highlander! It was on the tip of his tongue to say that Kyllachy must at least bide the night with them, for good claret and a soft bed will compose many quarrels, and forby that he would have failed in his duty as a host to let the man go, yet there was this hellish awkward tricky matter of the Lord President, and the Bear yet to be dealt with over it! But maybe if they had supper now at once, the man could be got out the house before ever Forbes came and he could lie the night at Blackford. But och no, he might meet the Lord President on his way, unless indeed he could be induced to take the other road, with all the long summer evening before him and a pleasure to be riding through it, and Kyllachy might do that if he himself rode a mile and a bittock, maybe, out with him, but then who would be at the house to stand between Forbes and the Bear? — unless Kirstie might do it — Och, what a snarl for an honest man to be in and he must speak at once! 'You will have your supper here with ourselves, Kyllachy,' he said, 'and maybe you will think better of the whole thing. Tammie!' he shouted, hearing him at the door, 'Tammie, where is the supper?'

Tammie Clow looked in at the door, carrying a silver ashet with a decanter of rum on it. 'The supper is where you can smell it this hour past and I am just after setting the table,' he said crossly, 'but I canna do more than five things at the once, not for the Lord Almighty Himself, and Gleneagles is after me like a raging Elijah to see to the Lord President's room and that should be Grizzie's work and no' mine!'

Patrick Haldane looked at his brother and Robert went red and nodded. 'It appears you have the two thieves invited,' said Patrick, 'but I am not getting up on my cross for a wee whilie yet!'

'You blasphemous lawyer, Pate, you!' said Robert. 'You might be struck dead for thon!'

'I might indeed, Robbie,' said Patrick, 'and as that might also involve my God-fearing, respectable brother if the Almighty's arm were the wee-est bit shoogly, I will go and get the news from Tammie who is honester with me than my own flesh and blood.'

'I was seeking for you, Patrick — ' Robert began, unfairly put in the the wrong and aware of Kyllachy's smiling.

'Aye, aye,' said Patrick, 'open and eydent like the young quey seeking for the old bull! And see the muckle great heathen mistake you have let poor Tammie make, taking decent rum to Forbes for his nightcap, when the man could be gey easy pleasured by a glass of Ferintosh whisky and the golden thought of the revenue on it!' He went out heavily, shouting for Tammie, and kicked the door to.

'The Haldane house,' said Kyllachy, 'has indeed many mansions, and I will even revoke my decision at your request,

Airthrey, and take my supper with the family, for I opine that the Lord President will take a great and official interest in certain discoveries that I have made.'

'We have not much time left for our bargaining,' said Robert, 'and I ask you again, what is your price?'

'I am in no mood for trading,' Kyllachy said, 'and such things spoil a good supper, such as I am sure will be set before us. Indeed I perceive that I have a better appetite than I have had these twelve months past, and I could not be persuaded to ride before it is satisfied.' And as he spoke there came the thundering of the great gong and steps and laughing from the stairs and hall, that meant the young folk were hungry, but not so sharp-set that they would not sooner be at their daffing with one another than sitting quietly to their meat like decent single-minded Christians. And if Patrick and Kirstie were both late, why, Gleneagles must pronounce the blessing, and the cock-aleekie would be set before Captain Robert and the collops before William, and the great silver serving spoons would lie on the linen cloth beside the silver boats of gravy and a side dish of artichokes for those that cared for such new-fangled garden curiosities, and another side dish of mussels and partan's toes with the shell ready cracked, and beyond on the sideboard jellies and biscuits and sweet almonds, and cherries again, for the south wall apricots were to be kept back for the Lord President.

CHAPTER II

THEY will all be against the Bear, all, all. Because he can see past them, past the comfortable, couthy summer of their prosperity to a stark winter beyond and the bare boughs below the florrish. His father's house is given up to strangers and enemies, the respectable, the treacherous, butterers of their own loaves, Pharisees, turning the Bear's day against him. Let them sit to their supper without him, then, go their own gate out of their own tangles. Kyllachy and Culloden welcomer at Gleneagles than the Bear! He stood by the window, his head sunken between rheumatic shoulders, his years on him. Kirstie put her arm round his neck; he shrugged it away; she kissed his ear, but took the greatest care not to disturb the set of his wig, since she knew of old that here was a thing he could not thole. 'Well,' said she, 'what are you doing for us, Pate?'

He said: 'Forbes of Culloden is the honoured guest to-night. And I heard it from Tammie Clow!'

'He is a sick man,' Kirstie said, 'and there was nothing else for it, and you will be a good Bear — '

'Will not!'

It seemed to her that all this had happened often enough before, but never in such like black earnest, and she must try and put the thing before him in a calm and sensible way and without the flare of temper that she knew was in her too, but which, with God's help, she would dowse before she spoke. 'Pate, none of all this has been done to hurt you,' she said. 'It is just the way the cards have fallen, and indeed, indeed, we must all stand together. The Lord President will have a late supper when he comes and so to his bed, for he will be tired out, the poor soul.'

'He will not be overtired for conversation with young Captain John and your sister's George and this stinking Highlander Kyllachy.'

'Ach away, it is not only the Highland tods that stink! And

346

all the more need for the pair of us to act as reasonable beings. Forbes willna pay much heed to Kyllachy.'

'Will he no'?' said Patrick. 'I'm telling you, Kirstie, there will be plenty said that will please Culloden the King of the respectable. For Kyllachy is going to speak ill of me.'

'It will not be the first time,' said Kirstie, 'and I dinna suppose it will trouble you any, Pate.' He did not answer. 'Could it trouble you, then?' she asked, softly and surprised; she had never before thought of her brother as anyways soft or easy hurt as William was, or equally to be protected by herself if it was somehow possible.

Patrick lifted his head. 'I was maybe not so careful as I might have been over a matter of letters.'

'What's about it?' asked Kirstie. 'Has Kyllachy found them?'

'Aye. Yet I have enough against him to balance the thing. However, it is not only the respectable and successful folk that I have attacked — and laughed at which is a thing they like less — but it is their ways of ruling us and getting the rest of the world to applaud them and to give them an over-ready obedience. Kirstie, I am not sure how you will see it, but it is likely the thing will be out and most of my douce family not knowing which way to look — '

'Sure, you'll have done nothing bad, Pate — '

'Eh well, that's as folks think, and what's bad now mayna be bad at all in fifty years or a hundred. But I will even tell you one of the things that will be said of me to Culloden and with some truth. I have taken certain of the Psalms and have set words to them that are profane, blasphemous and designed to bring the Kirk and its Ministers into mockery and disrepute.'

He stopped speaking and turned away. Kirstie was blushing all over her face and neck. It was like seeing a Book thrown on the floor! Like seeing some filthy nakedness. The thing had shocked her below reason. And yet it was he, Pate, that had done the thing — and och, the hard, cold way he had said it! And now he was looking back at her with a kind of hate, as though she were on the other side from him. And that mustna be. No, she kenned she must be at it quick, must get the feel of forgiveness and sweetness into her heart, the way she could act right by him. No, he couldna have done it, he had said this only to try her! 'You never did it, Pate!' she said.

He gave a nasty cold laugh, and said, 'I did, so.' She had to stay and face it. She had to understand. Maybe if she could some way get at the why of it, the thing would stop hurting. She took a breath and said: 'But what for at all did you do yon, Patrick?'

He said impatiently, harshly: 'To break their rule in men's minds. For it should be plain by now to the biggest gumph in Perthshire, and still more to you, Kirstie, that are no daftie, that the Church of Scotland is the bit and bridle in the torn mouth of the common folk of Scotland that have property and respectability riding them. Break you the bridle and the horsie can get his head free and throw his rider!'

Now at that a thing woke in Kirstie's mind that was more than half in agreement. Yet it did not excuse the means. 'You could have been a shining light in some other Church, Pate,' she said, 'and then you needna have done thon thing. The Psalms dinna belong to the Presbyterian Church. They are far outwith any such bondage.'

'It wouldna have hurt the Church of Scotland any if I had become a Quaker, or a Papist itself, and surely to goodness you wouldna have me shaving wee holes in my head, Kirstie? The things that are half decent and gentlemanly to do are just exactly the harmless things that go nowhere to break the bridle and unseat the rider. If a thing is to be in any way effective then you'll need to make up your mind to it that the decent folks will say it's no' decent! And they have it in them to do you grievous hurt, for all you grow yourself a thick bull's hide over your heart. Yet I wasna doing the decent thing that could have done no harm to my enemies. But instead, I was doing the effective thing: since more can be destroyed by laughter than by argument or blows.'

'Yet werena you bound to be laughing at other things forby the Established Church, its Ministers and congregations? For I have had a half thought myself that all's not well there.'

'Aye. You canna ruin your enemy without ruining wifie and bairns.'

'But, Pate, you will have been laughing at — at — '

'At the Lord Almighty who can take good care of Himself. And maybe He can do with a bit reminder of what His Ministers are saying and doing in His name!'

'Och well — But you arena against the Lord, Pate?'

'That seems to me to be a question without sense, Kirstie. Am I against eating? No. But am I against a rich man eating up a poor man's broth and crowdie? Aye.'

'Och, Pate, I am sure you meant terrible well. But if you are informed against — Did your things get printed? And did folks read them?'

'Aye, more than ever read the pamphlets of mine which you yourself have read and which I kind of jalouse might be thought to be a wee thing dull. And they have started by laughter of an unco' coarse nature. But in a while they have gone on to have serious thoughts on such matters as the place which the respectable have got themselves in the governing of Kirk and law and trade, and the rule of the landed folk and those with handles to their names in this Scotland of ours. Now, I hadna my own name to the things, but I was speaking on them in a letter which came by ill luck to Kyllachy's knowledge, and if they choose to take the thing up there will be enough evidence. Aye, aye, and some in my own profession that would like fine to see Patrick Haldane on his trial for blasphemy.'

'Couldna you have done it any other how, Patrick?'

'Being myself, no.'

'Are they terrible wicked rhymes, Pate?'

'Will I say them to you, Kirstie?'

'Ach, no! I wouldna like. Ach, not at all, Pate! Maybe they arena that bad at all and I would soonest think so, but it would be better if I didna know in case they might be otherwise!'

He laughed and said: 'Are you wanting your supper, lass?'

She said: 'William will be making my excuses. I wanted to speak with you, Pate. Not on this, but on the matter of Culloden. Why must you go on being angry at him all these years?'

'I am not fashing myself at my age to change my mind over this matter of enemies. Maybe he is no worse than the rest now, but he is on the other end of the stick from myself, and he was the worst enemy I had at the time of my old fight for the judge-ship. And neither Forbes nor Munro could ever see a joke that was made by other than themselves or against the side they chose to take over the politics. So Culloden will not like a wee jocose thing there was in a discourse I made, and which will doubtless have been reported to him, anent the Edinburgh Whiggies at the time of the siege.'

'But surely to the Lord you werena a Tory, Patrick?'

'A Tory, is it? Na, na. But I just didna think much of the Whigs nor Provost Stewart nor the plight of the respectable that didna know which way to sell themselves with most profit. Yet I think I have found out enough about Kyllachy to gar him hold his tongue over the Trial, though maybe not over the Psalms.'

'It is certain sure that neither Kyllachy nor George nor Johnnie will hold their tongues over yon poor fellow that is hid. And Johnnie's man that is a Portsmouth sailor with no liking at all for Scotland, has been set to watch the stair.'

'So Margaret told me when she went to open the door of the attic, the poor lassie.'

'Och Pate, she will have been terrible affronted, finding a sailor on the stairs!'

'She was more angry at her own family than abashed for herself,' said Patrick, and chuckled. 'But we may come through the thing yet, though I am less hopeful than I was an hour ago. However, your sister Margaret has writ me — and I needed to go through half my papers before I came on it again — about a particular difficulty that her bonny wee George has been getting himself into. She doesna like me, but she has a good opinion of the firm. I have seen George and told him he is to keep quiet if I am to get him out of his difficulty.'

'What like of a difficulty, Pate?'

'Och, it is the kind of difficulty a man will get into when he mistakes another man's bed for his own. And is discovered while doing so. When a young spunkie the like of George has never a thing to set his mind to but only idle ploys and pleasures, it is not to be wondered at that such things should arise. I have seen plenty of the same in my time and in all families. It is usual for the rich to escape public admonition on the Sabbath, and they do it by keeping the lawyers betwixt themselves and the Kirk Sessions. To the great profit of my own profession! which is another instrument in the hands of property as who should know better than myself.' He scratched his head slowly, feeling up under his wig. 'But Captain John, being a young man of principles, has got into no scrapes that I can lay my hands on to. It is devilish awkward when there is nothing hidden.' He turned towards the window again, looking away up the glen whose one side was now wholly in evening shadow, and suddenly he said to his sister, not looking at her: 'There is a thing, I have asked myself whiles and now I will be asking you: did you have any hand in killing your man, Kirstie?' As nothing happened for a few breaths except for a deeper silence, he added: 'Well, do not be speaking if you would liefer not. I havena got you in the witness box! But there are natural processes which can be helped or hindered, death being one of them. And if I had been so unchancy as to have many dealings with yon first spouse of yours, I would have been sore tempted. Aye, aye, Andrew Shaw was an instrument of tyranny and oppression.'

Kirstie picked up the edge of her gown and dichted her eyes with it, and she spoke in a whisper: 'What were you and the rest doing to let me marry yon man and I so young?'

'You dinna set much store on the advice of others when it comes to the marrying!' he said. 'And our father who had a belief in the rule of the righteous in Israel had nothing against the man as part and parcel of it. I doubt he wouldna have thought so well of an Episcopalian Highlander. You will mind, Kirstie, on our cousin of Methven who bears my own name. He is a Tory, and held notorious office in the Jacobite Army, but it is not that folks have against him. Ach, no, but he is Pate Smythe the atheist all because of his marrying a certain lady that had the imprudence to be a Pole and a Papist. There would not have been a word against him had he taken her as his whore in foreign parts. Not that I have any better liking for old priest than for new presbyter and I would be as well pleased as my neighbour to see the Pope of Rome swinging in ae tow with the King of France — But I perceive you are about to speak, my lass, and you may be sure that what you say will go no farther than myself.'

Kirstie looked at him straight and tearless and said: 'William, my man, has said to me that I am in no way responsible for the death of Andrew Shaw. And I believe him in all he tells me.'

'It is as well you have your belief in him,' said Patrick, 'but mind you this. Supposing the Kirk Sessions had found you guilty of witchcraft and they with all the power and weight of the respectable behind them, then thon would have been the ones you'd be forced to believe, you poor bitch, and to hell you would have gone, on earth and in your own mind and fancy.'

'How did you know?' said Kirstie, staring.

'I have put two and two together and I know the way your man thinks on you.'

'But — oh Pate, it is true what he said to me, surely, surely! I amna a witch! He never said to you that I could be a witch!'

She clutched him by the shoulder and he shook her off with a flick on her cheek: 'Whisht, ye silly tawpie! He thinks the world and all of you, your man, and indeed I canna see why he shouldna. He is as good as you can expect of a Highlander and he thinks you are better than himself, though maybe he expects more sense of a Lowland wife than she rightly has.'

'Ach,' said Kirstie, 'I have full more sense than himself, though I amna near so good. Pate, we are all sinners. You will not have written, surely, that man is sufficient unto himself, that we are not sinners before the Lord?'

'What concerns me is that we should not be sinners before the Elect — neither in our eyes nor theirs. That became clear enough to me through my researches into law and Church history during my Professorship at St. Andrews. Though I hid it in the Latin in those days, having a greater regard for my

skin than I have now, and it was only the students that didna
sleep through my lectures that had any inkling of what I was at.
If you must write in the common tongue you will get enemies,
as poor Davie Hume has found, aye, and has needed to sit
doucely under a respectable Minister Sabbath after Sabbath,
with a look of edification on his face and doubtless a most
fidgety and contumelious backside on the Kirk bench, and all to
undo the effect that his bookie may have had on folks' minds.
But he addressed himself to those with property and learning
and not to the common folk, not to the Grassmarket mob that I
knew—aye, and they knew I would take up their cases although
there was nothing in them for me but the pleasure of winning
them. And look now, Kirstie, what you have got for your
havering with me, here is your man after you to give you a good
skelping!'

For William was with them now, looking from one to the
other. He had left the family in an argument over the ownership of a certain field towards Mill of Gask, the evidence going
back to hearsay of fifty years back, with Mungo and Robert at
it to the neglect of their suppers. George was drinking plenty
and had a sullen look on him, but Kyllachy was not to be
induced to exceed, even though young James had been whispered
to and was giving him toasts across the table. And indeed he
would be the one to be laid out before Kyllachy and that would
be the greatest pity. A wild impatience was at William to know
how Kirstie was faring with the Bear. He had to know. And
both the two of them were looking ruffled and fashed, and
Patrick's brows down like thick untidy wings over his eyes and
Kirstie crumpling her dress in her hand, the poor bull calves
that were mashed in this nasty dark net of difficulties and
obstinacies. 'How has it gone?' asked William of them both.

'Over this matter of Forbes,' said Patrick, 'I have in no way
changed my opinions, but I will meet the man if it is to any
advantage.'

'Well, that is something indeed,' William said, 'and we will
all need to have our wits about us.' He looked at them quickly.
'Is there aught else amiss? Indeed I am hoping there isna!'

'I have been speaking to my sister,' said Patrick stiffly, 'anent certain matters which Kyllachy might have against myself.' And at that Kirstie was seized with a nasty lump of a sob, catching at her between throat and stomach, because while Patrick was putting the thing his way, you might be over persuaded that he was in the right somehow, but syne you thought of what would be said by everyone, and poor Margaret needing to back her father, but herself filed by it, and her own prospects worsened every year! And on top of it all she just couldna bear that William should think ill of her dearest brother, William whom God had joined to her in marriage with manifest grace, William, who was good, whose prayers found blessing like sunshine, William who had saved her from hell itself —

'Is it — a new difficulty?' William asked.

'Aye,' said Patrick, tugging at the edge of his waistcoat, 'it is over certain pamphlets that I have written.'

'What harm could they see in your pamphlets?' asked William, puzzled. 'I have aye thought they were even over circumspect.'

'It wa na yon ones,' said Patrick. 'It was certain others — in rhyme. Upon the metrical versions of the Psalms.' It was more embarrassing for Patrick speaking of these things to William, whom he had so lately got the better of, although in a manner of friendship and teasing, than to his sister.

But William said: 'Do you mean those ones under the imprint of the cock in a bush and sold by Lucky Tibb along by the Netherbow?'

Kirstie stared and Patrick nodded in a fresh embarrassment: 'Aye. Have you seen them then?'

'I was told they were by you, but I didna know for sure, so I didna like to speak.'

'But William,' cried Kirstie, 'were they no' wicked?'

'Och no,' said William, 'they were not wicked at all compared to a real wickedness, and they put me in mind of rhymes that would go the rounds in Boston. Or indeed wherever there is a government that will thole no opposition. But I dinna think Kirstie would like them any, nor yet the rest of the family who

354

are without experience of the lower kind of people, and they will make things no easier. All the same, Patrick, dinna fash yourself on my account. You know fine I am a heretic, although not just the same as yourself, maybe because I was never needing to be angry against just the same folks as you.'

'Then,' said Kirstie, 'if it isna so terrible bad, could we go in to our supper, for I am as hungry as I dinna ken what and I am thinking that Pate will be the same.'

Patrick settled his wig again; he had been sweating. Once at Leyden he and a Dutch student had gone to visit one of the old Anabaptists. After the official extermination, a few had carried the thing on, with the natural heretics of each generation keeping contact, and with correspondence between Holland and America. The two students, the Dutchman and the Scot, had been moved more by curiosity and a natural pleasure in the breaking of laws, yet they had both felt that there was something about the old man which had affected them strongly. And afterwards, being drunk on the Hollands spirits, Patrick Haldane had spoken rashly before his Professor of Law, and syne a terrible scunner had come on him at what harm he might have done. But in a whilie the Professor had said a thing which showed that he too was a condoner of heresy. And Patrick had felt then, as now he felt, that after all the Bear was not alone.

CHAPTER III

THE devil was in the house, surely, and all the folk in it fashing and hashing at their anxieties. For there was Bob Strange in the attic and only too well aware of a stranger clumping on the stair and he with a nasty rough English accent, and as time went by, slow enough, it came to him with an increasing certainty that the Whig Haldanes had allowed their principles to get the better of their humanity and that this time he was in the worst fix of his life. So he cast about in his mind for any way out of it, which meant, to begin with, a way out of the Gleneagles attic. But certainly there appeared to be none at all and he wished with all his heart that he had never set eyes on Ochtertyre or any of the lot of them.

Nor was there a single one at the dining-room table that was not uneasy and agitated. Even wee Elizabeth of Aberuthven, who had been kept out of everything, had got it into her head that this was so, and why, now that she was a lady and dressed by a servant lassie in her best dresses instead of by her nurse in whatever would wash best, why was she never told? She kennt fine that Davie knew by the daft face he was putting on!

Helen Cockburn supposed there was trouble again between her brother and the rest, and shrugged her shoulders, and Margaret Bearcrofts had her sympathy certainly, and she could not abide the smell of vomit which George would have on his clothes sometimes of a morning, and it was high time he went to London and became cultivated. Yet for all that he had more knowledge of the world than any of his cousins, and indeed Margaret's father was insufferable; it was only since his coming in the afternoon that poor Margaret had become so strange in her manner. And there was James, who mostly gave the appearance of having too old a head for his shoulders, and was not one for gallantries and toasts, although Catherine seemed to like him well enough, drinking and clinking with Kyllachy as though the two of them were in a Perth pot-house!

This was distressing Adam as well; he felt there was something going wrong, beyond what he knew, but he could not put a name to it until he could see James or Ochtertyre alone. And if James went on at his present rate, he would get little good of him. James would be walking a good yard off the ground and nearer the lunatic moon by the end of supper and what at all possessed him on this evening of all and he mostly so temperate!

Tammie Clow shrugged his shoulders over the young gentlemen. He had loosed the neckties of over many of them in his time. But he could not but be aware that Gleneagles was sore fashed over some kind of a family trouble, girning away to Tammie over the tieing of his cravat and changing of his wig, anent the follies of women and how the Apostle Paul could have had his share of the feather-pated mawsies, forever taken in by a bonny leg or a braw coat with nothing under it! And which of them all was he thinking on if not Kirstie Borlum? So Tammie kept casting furious glances at Borlum himself, the lying Highlander, and doubtless he had come after some of the Haldane money, might he burn his fingers on it! And indeed, it was Tammie himself that had raised the question of the first ownership of Muckle Neb, the field in the crook of the Earn, and that so as to distract Gleneagles from his melancholy and unease. There was aye the makings of a pleasant and lengthy discussion over the ownership of land or the exact meaning of a text, and both were subjects which could be discussed alike by rich and poor.

The talk had somewhat eased Captain Robert. It was a return to the ordinary family wrangling, friendly and warm as the wrangling of puppies in straw, before these Highlanders had set them all by the ears. And yet there was the black smiling of Kyllachy behind it, and he sipping his claret where young James was drinking the full of his glass. Captain Robert kept trying to signal to the laddie, but he had not seen in time what was wrong, and the brandy had been as handy to James's glass as the claret, so there was little to be done now but hope that some part of discretion was still awake. And meanwhile those wild wicked rhymes, made by Patrick and repeated by Kyllachy, were running through Captain Robert's head. Terrible shocking and blasphemous they were, aye deserving of punishment. But wonderful comic if you put them with the tune, and all he could do not to sing them out loud before the company! Patrick was the clever one, for all he put it to an ill use whiles. But it would never do if the things were to come to Mungo's ears, still less to any of the women folk.

Yet Kyllachy himself was not over satisfied, because of the behaviour of George; maybe, he was thinking, he should do the whole thing himself and not depend at all on this city softie of a Lowlander. If George Cockburn had thought better of it, well, it could be seen to that he would get no credit out of it. Better to trust a kind of kindred hardness in young Captain John. There would be no backing out for that one; his principles would drive him like the muckle De'il.

Margaret Bearcrofts was in a silent angry misery, in which she must blame Tammie for a napkin crookedly folded. Not that he or Gleneagles cared any for such finnicky things; a man's lips could be easy acquaint with his sleeve, it was only the women that were for ever cluttering up a table with what was neither meat nor drink. Mistress Helen there was forever asking for sweet Frenchie desserts and such that nobody would need if they had a right dram in them!

And here at last came Kirstie back, and Margaret gave her a look of anxiety and question, and her heart dunted in her so sore that syne she must glance down at her bosom lace to see was it shaking. But Kirstie's look said no use, and the anxiety must go on. There was a place next to Ochtertyre and Kirstie sat herself there. He could not think of a thing to say to her and it kept on going through his head that he should be doing something of a manly and violent nature, but he could not think what would make matters anything but worse. And the thought of the Prince kept coming at him and had he beguiled them — and himself — or had there ever been a chance of winning? But it was all over and past and not fair that it should be visited on him now! Hard enough to have the pain of the wound with him yet, let alone the bad luck that brought Bob Strange back on him in this house of all houses!

Kirstie was saying: 'When I was a wean it was not often we got partans nor any sea-fish. But the roads are away better these days. Would you have such a dish in France, now?'

'We had écrevisses oftener than I liked,' he answered. They had been cheap and easy come by from the burns in summer and Murray of Ochtertyre had never over much housekeeping money for his lady in those days.

'The same we have scottified to crayfishes,' she said, 'and they will thicken a soup as well as a hen.' And then neither of them had a word more to say, since crayfish soup or potage aux écrevisses was wonderfully far from the inner thoughts of either of them.

James Haldane had now toasted his cousin Catherine three times, and she was feeling that the thing was going too far altogether; even if it was only the family someone would be speaking of it, and wee Elizabeth tittering and covering her mouth with her hands! What had come over James at all! She felt that at any moment he might get starting a song, and he was no better at singing than a sheep — indeed none of the family were gifted in music. He was getting up on his feet again and she shook her head at him. He leant across to her and said in a voice that was both blurred and over-loud: 'You will not be deserting me too, cousin Catherine!'

At that Catherine leapt up with the colour coming quick across the curve of her cheek between the bright falls of her curls, and terrible bonny she seemed to young James and clean as the page of a new psalm book and delicate to the touch as the fur on an otter's belly, and the soft, disturbed, melting look she cast at him as she went, och that was enough to get him to his feet too, to kiss and comfort and doubtless marry the poor lassie! Yet there was a feeling in his legs as though they were not rightly touching the floor and the handle on the door not coming right to his hand, but what of it — and in a moment he would be close and his mistakes and sins that were such pain to him wiped out in forgiveness warm and blinding as the blood of the Lamb, in mutual forgiveness, since she had fled him in his need, in the kiss of peace — But it was Ochtertyre had him by the arm:

'What ails you, man James? Have you not done mischief enough that you must needs follow the dirk with the sword?' He shook him; it was a relief after the wordless misery of supper and the good food that tasted of ashes in his mouth. Ochtertyre had not had the heart to drink!

The walls swung in front of James and as they swung he felt sick and the thought of Catherine Duncan, instead of being a warm pleasure, turned to a horror at what he might have done or said. 'Am I — am I intoxicated?' asked James.

'Drunk as a penny wedding,' said Ochtertyre. 'If you hadna a better head than Kyllachy you should never have drunk with him and he up to your game from the first blink!'

'Och, what will I do?' said James lamentably, 'for I have fallen from Grace and failed all round and every way!'

'You will put your head in the horse trough for a start,' said Ochtertyre.

The light was fading now, up from trees and fields and housen into the still clear sky. From behind in the stable yard came the sound of the pipes and the squealing and laughter of a good reel. But none of the gentry were at the dance this evening; nor yet the ones that were waiting at table, although one of Kyllachy's gillies was distinguishing himself with fine high leaps and neat cutting of steps, though the truth was he would have danced better in a kilt than in breeks. He was keen to get out of his mind yon talk of bocans and frightsome things in the loft, and indeed he would sleep better if there was any way at all to get a lassie to share his blanket.

James Haldane lifted his dripping head out of the horse trough and took such other measures as he could to get the wild stuff out of him. Ochtertyre looked on sardonically and as James finally snecked his buckles again he said: 'You have done us no good and yourself plenty of harm and I will not blame wee Catherine if she never speaks to you again.'

'Was she — was she terrible affronted?' asked James. Ochtertyre nodded. 'Lord help me, I am getting deeper bogged every hour! What ava can I do?'

'I doubt it is not in our power now to do a thing,' said Ochtertyre. 'We can only hope for some help from either Borlum or Bearcrofts.'

'The two that I had supposed to be ungodly,' said James, 'and I judging them out of my own muckle pride and self-righteousness!' He groaned. 'And I have the most terrible headache and I would like nothing except to sleep for a week and the whole thing never to have happened!'

'You can try the horse trough again,' said Ochtertyre without much sympathy. And then: 'I think I can hear Culloden's horses.' And the breath rasped in his throat.

As the horses turned to the left off the coal-road, they could be heard the whole house over from dining-room to attic by all those concerned. Phrases of great politeness, though with the half sad tone due to his age and illness, passed between one and another at the dining-table, speaking of the Lord President. Gleneagles and Airthrey went to the door and Tammie Clow stood behind them with the welcoming glasses ready. Now Wattie Buidh was helping his master down from his horse. It seemed a terrible weight and pain on Duncan Forbes to lift his leg over the saddle. He was speaking in apologies as he did so, but the effort was constantly cutting the words short off his lips; he held to Wattie's shoulder with bloodless knuckles and a grip that trembled, and when Wattie slipped a cane into his hand he leaned hard on to it. Gleneagles and Airthrey were both talking away to lessen any embarrassment there might be, both with a pitiful feeling towards poor Dunky Forbes, in whose office was so muckle power, but who now walked hinkand and shoogly over their threshold and was gey glad of his glass.

Kyllachy was waiting in the dining-room in a pleasant muse. The empty ashets and dirtied plates and glasses were at their clearing; the fresh places were laid. The fish was set to come to the net; patience and canny handling and all would be well.

Young Captain John, after a moment's hesitation, had been

following his uncles to the door. Patrick went after him and laid a finger on his sleeve: 'You will doubtless be speaking to the Lord President of this matter which has become over well kennt in the house?'

'I will do my duty, as I have endeavoured to do at all times,' said Captain John. 'And I canna think that a law officer the like of yourself will attempt to dissuade me.'

'Would this make much to King George, one way or the other,' asked Patrick, 'in comparison with the great embarrassment and distress you will be causing to your uncle Gleneagles?'

'Gleneagles, being a magistrate, would be the first to hand over a rebel to the rightful authorities!' Captain John answered indignantly.

'Are you thinking that?' said Patrick.

And of a sudden Captain John felt a crack opening in the structure of things that had seemed so well builded and reasonable and allowing of no deviation by an honest man. For if Gleneagles, known and respected by three generations throughout the breadth of Scotland, one that feared the Lord and honoured the law and the King, were to know of this and keep quiet, who was he himself to speak? Yet for all that it remained that this Jacobite rebellion was the open sign of an obscene and ancient mass of corruption which still had the most of mankind gripped; but England had freed herself so that folk could deal honestly by one another in open market, going to their own Churches, and speaking their minds without fear of sudden oppression, and if the Scots were not to stand by their neighbours in this matter then they didna deserve the blessings and comforts of civilization and freedom, and if his old uncle were to be a traitor and backslider then to hell with him and his like, for there was no room for them in an honest world! And Captain John, who had stood for a moment's cogitation, his hand clenching and unclenching on the hilt of his sword, turned on his heel and set his back to Patrick Haldane and the treachery of the Scots whom in his soul he disowned!

Patrick watched him go off and syne turned back to the dining-room and shook his head the wee-est bit at Kirstie. William too was watching for a sign, and when it came he made as if to move, but then bethought himself and sat back, waiting, as his kinsman Kyllachy waited, both of them sunk into a kind of Highland daze, letting the minutes float by as mist floats by on the hillside past the shepherd waiting quietly for the break and the sight of his sheep at last.

The ladies had separated themselves slightly from the men and Margaret was directing Geordie, and herself relaying the side table. Elizabeth had a handful of ratafee biscuits and was eating them hastily, since she was not just completely confident that her elders might not rebuke her. Catherine Duncan had come back, her eyes a wee bit red, and now she was turned away from the rest as though to examine a thing on the wall, the tail-end of an old and dirty tapestry hung over a crack in the plaster that should have been sorted this whilie past, half of a tree and a stag's backside, worked long syne in ancient unhappy times by a lady lamenting her knight, Marjorie, Sterne of Strathearn, with her man slain at Flodden, but och, not so unhappy as herself and the white bud of her affections blighted before her eyes! And she could never hold up her head again in front of her cousins — Margaret Bearcrofts was speaking, was saying to her: 'I am thankful to my bones that my father is being at least civil and reasonable anent the Lord President.'

'Aye,' said Catherine in a trembling and uninterested voice, 'Aye.'

'Good sakes!' said Margaret. 'You are never fashing yourself over thon James laddie? He isna worth wasting breath over!'

'He is, so!' said Catherine, 'And, och Margaret, I just canna thole to see him act like a — a — liker a Highlandman than a decent Christian!'

Margaret caught her limp hand and swung it gently.

'My dawtie, he was no more than the wee-est bittie fou, and you'll gar him repent in sackcloth and ashes! I wish that were all that was wrong in this house the night!' She turned sharply:

'Geordie, you muckle sumph, away and find me a clean napkin! And we will need a fresh salad! Is there no sweet oil? This smells liker cart grease! And where are the peas?'

Muckle Geordie trotted off angrily, muttering to himself. He knew his duties fine, without having the lasses on his tail! And now here were voices, and candles in the half light, and the Lord President bowing over Margaret's hand, but greeting Kirstie with an honest neighbourly kiss on each of her cheeks. Liveliness filled the room and the steam of the fresh broth momently softened the glitter of the silver candle branch.

'Sit in!' Gleneagles said, warmly, one hand on the claret bottle.

For a moment all were silent while Duncan Forbes pronounced a blessing and all hoped that the Lord would indeed bless his food to him, the poor soul, since it was well known that most things sat ill on his stomach. As the talk started again the door pushed open and in came Ochtertyre and James and off into the corner of the room farthest from the ladies. James had felt himself gey sober when he was out in the air, but now the heat and smell of the room was making his head swim again. He had a strong feeling that a wee dram would steady him, but Ochtertyre had a tight and warning grip of his arm.

Mistress Grizzie herself brought in the dishes, since she wanted a right sight of the Lord President after all the trouble she had been put to over the head of the man. She had, after all, kept back a part of the bird, with young broad beans to it, forby the sea-fish.

'Ah,' said Forbes, with a smile at his host, 'Facto vocatur laetus opere vicinus!'

'Och aye,' said Mungo, who had left his classics lying for long enough. But Captain Robert, who knew his Martial, having copies of most of the Latin poets at hand in his cabin on ship-board, capped it with the next line: 'Nec avara servat mensa, I'm hoping, at Gleneagles!' he said.

'And they had the same ideas as ourselves on leftovers, yon old Romans!'

'Aye, they had a good idea of the due importance and order

of the things of the body,' said the Lord President, 'although they were far enough astray in other matters. Thank you, I will take an artichoke. I see you have offered acceptable libations to the Garden God, Gleneagles!'

'Garden God, is it! If I didna let my gardener have his will anent the growing of such new-fangled whimsy-whamsies, he would even leave me and go to Atholl, who has a wicked covetous eye on his neighbour's manservant! But we are over far north for the most of yon foreign roots; the first frosts will cut them down.'

'It is wonderful what a south wall will do, even at Inverness. Your good-brother here has had grapes from his vine at Borlum. Though I canna say he has yet set up as my rival with Inverness claret!'

'Yon vine has her roots in a cartload of dung that should better have gone to the turnips!' William said. 'But it was only right that the lady of Borlum should sit under the shade of a bonny vine and pluck a wee cluster, was't no', Kirstie?'

Kirstie smiled. She was most terrible anxious that her William and the Lord President should be the best of friends, this day of all, and forby that, she wanted her brothers to see that it was so. And Patrick had been a good Bear, thus far, and if he would but remain unprovoked — she went and stood beside him in the window, asking him to explain to her just how you would take the measurements of the height of a hill, such as Eastbow Hill that you could see standing against the luminous deep sky where soon a star would show. It would busy and calm him, speaking to her of the mathematics.

The Lord President had eaten now. He had passed the jelly and the syllabub that Mistress Grizzie had whipped freshly for him with her own hands. But any fashion of cream did ill with him. It had been a wearisome day and he would be glad of his bed. But the Gleneagles brandy was pleasant drinking, mild and yet with a great inward warmth, the same as a modest country lassie that will suddenly yield herself whole to the lad she likes. But his mind, distracted a moment, gathered itself up, and it began to seem to Duncan Forbes as though something of a disagreeable nature were about to draw near. For there was a chiel edging towards him, one of the younger Haldanes doubtless, and an orra determined look in his eye, and it was apparent that this was causing discomfort to almost all those present. And now he was about to speak.

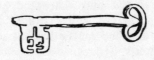

CHAPTER IV

'Sir,' said Captain John with a short bow, and the Lord President stiffened to listen. Black William had sat himself down next to Wattie Buidh at the farther end of the table and was whispering quick in the Gaelic. Wattie listened and times he grinned and nodded, but kept the tail of an eye all the while on his master, who might find himself distressed by all this forced upon him so soon after a meal.

As Captain John made his report, the Lord President, who had at first been looking straight at him, decided that he was speaking the truth and looked instead at the others and saw on their faces various degrees of complicity and distress. They must be considered in due order. Outwith the immediate Haldanes, and one of them the old rascal Patrick, though for once he was keeping a civil tongue in his head, were the two Highlanders, of whom Kyllachy, alone in the room, appeared to be calm and with the smile of one who sees predestinate events in the process of working out. It seemed as though the matter had not come as a surprise, even to the women, for there was a tight-lipped look on Margaret Bearcrofts, although the Cockburn lass was gaping, the way she at least was not involved.

The servants were out of the room, all but Tammie Clow; he stood behind Gleneagles, in a state of loyalty and indignation. So this was what the Highlanders had brought on to a decent house! It was no wonder that his poor master had been so terrible dowie and put about. But if the gentry were to have their pride and politics, then there would aye and on be fashious happenings, and here was the matter of the lost key made clear.

The Lord President lifted his head, worn and dark-shadowed in the candlelight. 'What have you to say to this, Gleneagles?'

'Indeed,' said Mungo, 'I was puzzling my head what ava I should do and I a magistrate.'

'Your duty as such appears to be plain,' said Forbes shortly.

'Och aye. In a sense. But seeing the mannikie was a kind of friend to my good-brother here — '

'This is not like you, William,' Forbes said. 'Who is the man at all? Is he one of your wild cat clan? Has Lady Anne been at you again?'

'Well,' said William, 'it is kind of half that — ' And he glanced at Kirstie for help.

But Ochtertyre made a sudden step out of the corner and he said: 'My Lord President, the blame is on me. I had thought the whole of the unfortunate matters of last year were over, but it seems a man's sins must be duly visited on him.'

'And you hiding it all!' Captain Robert half shouted, and then: 'Culloden, I have been misled — most damnably misled — '

The Lord President held up his hand for silence, and the hand too was thin and over bony. 'Wattie,' he said, 'my pen. You will have paper and ink, Gleneagles. Aye, send for them. I take it there is a secure guard on this rebel? That is your responsibility, Captain Haldane? And your man is English. Good.'

The room had begun to assume another aspect. The food was all away and the glasses, even, pushed to one side for a cold sobriety. More candlesticks were brought in and the Lord President slowly opened his shagreen case and wiped his spectacles. Captain Robert moved to the windows and closed the shutters with a feeling that at least there was to be no over-looking from without. There were only whispers and a wee rustle of papers until suddenly Helen Cockburn gave a half scream: 'This is no place for ourselves! Come, Catherine, come your ways, Margaret, let us withdraw for a game of cards until the gentlemen are through with their business!'

'Aye,' said the Lord President. 'I think we will do as well without the ladies. No — stay, you!' he added quick, jabbing with his pen towards Kirstie.

'I am staying, my Lord,' said Margaret Bearcrofts, and Catherine took her cousin by the arm and stood beside her.

George pushed back his chair: 'I will escort you, sister,' he said, and avoided looking at Kyllachy, who for his part made no move to stop him, but crossed his legs in an unconcerned manner.

'George knows as well as the lave of us!' said Margaret indignantly. 'Why should he be let run from an unpleasantness!'

'Hmm,' said the Lord President, 'this is indeed a family affair. You had best all bide. Guid kens what you Haldane lasses mightna be at! Well, well, I didna think when my coach broke down on me that it was an act of Providence and that I would need to assume my judicial functions so soon.'

'And you so wearied!' Mungo said, in a terrible upset himself. 'Lord preserve us a', I have tried to act for the best and we arena so young as we were, neither of the two of us! And I didna just like to come to an over hasty decision.'

'If you, being a magistrate, were duly informed —'

'Aye, but I wasna. It was just that the wind was in a certain airt and I with my ears cocked. The whole thing could have been kind of exaggerated.'

'If you had any reason for suspicion you could have made inquiry.'

'Aye, aye. But the way it came to me it would have been terrible sore on my mind to have acted officially.'

'Do you tell me that you have an official and an unofficial conscience, Gleneagles? It seems to me that our duties are laid down plain for us and that in writing.'

'Yet we must aye temper the wind to the shorn lamb.'

'And which would your shorn lamb have been out of all this flock of braw hoggies?'

'I had supposed it was Borlum yonder.'

'Well, well, a kind of half black lamb. William Macintosh, what have you to say to all this?' He raised his voice: 'No, I am not to be interrupted! And I will have silence!'

'It is the way I said. You have the facts before you, my Lord President,' said William.

'Indeed I have nothing of the kind, Uilleam Dubh, and I will

369

thank you to behave in a decent and neighbourly fashion, as I know fine you can do when you choose. Who at all is this fugitive?'

'He is only a poor misguided loon that will never do the like again.'

'How do you make that out? Have you known the man long?'

'Aye, aye, for a good wee whilie.'

'Who were his folk? And what occupation did he have?'

'Och well, he is from Edinburgh,' said William, his mind darting all ways to think what else he knew of Mr. Strange. But rescue came.

'He is a painter, my Lord, and most polite and accomplished in all save the politics!' cried out Catherine, knowing fine she would be taken for a daft, fly-away lassie with no principles. Aye, even maybe by James. Although her aunt Kirstie would see farther through at least.

Duncan Forbes raised his eyebrows and the confusion she suffered was real and sore enough, though not for the reasons supposed.

'The matter is becoming a thought clearer, but not yet all I could wish,' the Lord President said. 'It seems I am discovering the ladies' part in this affair, but I have yet to find what this gentleman' — and he pointed his pen at Ochtertyre — 'has to do with it. No! I am asking Airthrey first what is his knowledge of the matter.'

'I didna know a thing until maybe ten minutes before word came that yourself would be here,' said Captain Robert. 'And I was about to inform you in a more private manner, but the zeal of my nephew here became too hot for him to hold.'

'It could easily be that the uniform he has on might have affected him strongly towards loyalty,' observed Forbes.

'The East India Company is no less loyal than King George's Navy and has taken full as many risks against the enemies of order and progress!' said Airthrey.

Kyllachy spoke, softly and precisely, from the far side of the table where he was sitting next to Gleneagles and occasionally taking a snuff with him: 'It might be that I, not being of the immediate family, and knowing all the facts, could give you a fuller explanation, Culloden.'

Gleneagles laid a hand on his arm to stop him, but then withdrew it quickly, for he must not seem to want to twist any evidence. In the hollow of the window Kirstie whispered sharply to Patrick: 'What will he say? Stop him!'

But Patrick whispered back: 'No' yet. Let the snake strike.'

For partly it seemed to him that Kyllachy was bound to speak sooner or later, and better the whole case for the Crown to come out and then, if possible, be discredited; and partly he was finding it gey difficult to speak in an amiable and suitable manner to Culloden, who had greeted him without interest, as though it were a matter of course and not a great and notable condescension and change of mind on the part of Patrick Haldane to meet the man at all.

Forbes himself was gey puzzled, for it was clear that there was more to it than he had supposed, and he took careful notes on what Kyllachy said. It was maybe only natural that the family should have connived, in the way they doubtless had, at sheltering a rebel, who might have been paying court to the wee niece that spoke up. But once the thing was known there was nothing for it but that the law must take its course. Yet it was mostly not the immediate family, but William of Borlum and this young Ochtertyre that were responsible, and how and why were they connected? Kyllachy said categorically that young Ochtertyre had fought in the rebellion last year, and at the same time he was casting suspicions on William Macintosh. Yet Forbes knew for himself that this wasna true. Or did he? Could one be dead sure of any but one's self? Borlum had seemed to behave in a rational and virtuous way over the call that had come to him from the Pretender and Lady Anne. Yet if this had been only a mask to cover a worse intrigue, not even ennobled by the sword? William Macintosh was poor, might have debts left him by his father, had been making improvements on his estate, always an expense, thon, and he would be getting nothing back by growing potatoes and giving his neighbours seed to try. Suppose he had been tempted? Who would be able to hide it better? And what place more seeming secure to meet with a Jacobite agent than at his Whig wife's house? He had been intriguing after the Glenshiel affair, had confessed as much. Why not now? Such things are ill to shake off. They become a habit, an infatuation. And it was too true that there were even yet more than a handful of Jacobite agents in Scotland, the beginnings of trouble that must be stamped out now. Or there would be more follies. And Cumberland again. And hell for Scots folk once more when he himself was in his grave, powerless to stop it, and nothing but a pack of Dundas place hunters in Edinburgh all set to go the way they would think the cat was jumping! And this Ochtertyre duly invited to the Haldane house, to meet with his billies. There was no knowing who might not be involved.

'Stop!' said the Lord President, and then to Ochtertyre: 'Young man, did you fight in the rebellion?'

'I was misled, my Lord,' said Ochtertyre in a deep misery.

'So may the private murderer be misled. Which does not save him from the gallows. Treason is not to be condoned for want of thought. I take it this was well known. Yet I had supposed that the Haldanes of Gleneagles were strong for the Government!'

'Aye, we are, so!' said Mungo, pushing at his wig.

'But not strong enough to do your duty as a magistrate.'

'Would you do it on your own kin? See you, the lad has paid. He will never gang without pain of his leg wound, Culloden. The Almighty has punished him.'

'We canna take on ourselves such personal decisions. The law must be beyond kin or kindness or else we are back in the old days of courts and privileges and the fayour of kings.'

'That may all be so, but what would have been said of me gif I had gone forth like a raging lion after yon poor lad? It would have done good neither to King George, the Lord preserve him, nor yet to Scotland. And there was no need at all for Kyllachy who is my guest to have spoken on it officially!

And it will be queer if a Highlander knows his duty better than one of ourselves!'

'Any and all of you were bound to speak!' said the Lord President angrily. This was going to take till midnight, and maybe he shouldna have touched the sea-fish after all. 'It seems to me that the rest of you were unwilling and Kyllachy has done right in the matter.' He gave him a look. 'Maybe there is more you should say.'

'There is more I could say,' Kyllachy admitted. 'Aye, most certainly. But would it be wise? Might I not be doing a great harm to myself and my kinsmen if I spoke?'

'Less than if you kept silent,' said the Lord President, and syne he shifted uneasily in his chair and a moment later called sharply for Wattie. 'You will come to me in my room, Kyllachy,' he said. 'And the rest will come when they are needed. With your leave, Gleneagles, I will hold the rest of this inquiry in my bed, for I am devilish wearied and I have my medicine to take.'

'Tammie will wait on you with all you need!' said Gleneagles, in such a fash that there were tears standing in his eyes. 'Och, och, that such a thing should have happened in this house!'

The Lord President did not answer. Pain was gripping him, he held to Wattie. How could his mind reason and apprehend when so betrayed by the body? They heard him going up the stair and Wattie comforting him in the pleasant and gentle accent of the north-east. In the room they looked at one another sorely, and all moved a step or two away from Kyllachy. William above all was distressed by this; he had hoped that his neighbour, Dunky Forbes, would maybe take the whole thing in a neighbourly and unofficial way. Most matters had two sides, one laughable and the other terrible serious; it was a question of which side came uppermost. There had been ploys, out there, over which he and the Indians had aye seen opposite sides. And on this, it was a case of turning the thing so that Forbes should see it as in no way serious or legal. But how? He wanted to speak of it in this sense to Patrick, but when he went over to the window, Patrick was frowning and growled at Kirstie that they had brought it on themselves by asking Culloden to the house.

Young Captain John was distressed also and he did not like it that Kyllachy should be bidden to Forbes's room and not himself. Not that Kyllachy could harm him any. His own conduct had been at all points correct. Surely. If the rest had been as well principled none of all this trouble would have come about. Yet he could never be right certain of Kyllachy's principles and he was sorry that his uncle Airthrey was taking it badly. He spoke a word or two to young David of Aberuthven who answered nervously.

'George!' said Margaret, 'how was it you didna speak up with the rest of your billies? I thought you were aye so eident for the London King and Parliament!'

'There was no need for me to speak,' George said sulkily.

'That is mostly always true but it does not stop you speaking,' said Margaret.

George roused himself. 'I perceive you have fallen in love with the rebel and I look forward to seeing you and Catherine scratching each other's faces for his favours!'

'I think,' said Margaret, 'I could try my nails out on you!' And she would have been at him, but Catherine caught her by the sleeve: 'Och, Margaret, dinna notice the silly gawkie! Margaret, what will we do?'

'We could try a prayer, my dear,' said Margaret, and shrugged her shoulders, yet almost wanted to, then and there: 'See, yonder goes Kyllachy.'

Adam came across and joined them. 'I have been speaking with James. He is not unaware that he has made the biggest blunder of his life and followed it with another. I didna know he liked you so well, Catherine. Are you for marrying him? You might do worse.'

'Adam!' said Catherine. 'You are no better than a wee imp of a schoolboy for all your uniform! I amna thinking on marriage.'

'Are you not?' said Adam. 'Well, he is. And he was kind of

wild when he heard you cracking up yon Mr. Strange. How did you do that, Catherine?'

'I will tell you, Adam,' said Catherine, 'when you are older.'

Mungo had his elbows on the table and his head down on his hands. When Robert came and sat down beside him he straightened himself up and his eyes swimming in the candle-light. Robert offered him a snuff and poured out brandy for both of them. 'We have neither of us done wrong,' he said, 'and a good conscience is worth a full barn.'

'A man must act according to his lights,' said Mungo. 'But if he hasna got the first facts right — if he has been beguiled — '

'That goes for both of us. But I canna say I like Kyllachy any the better for it all.'

'I wish he were no kin of ours! The Lord knows what shameful stories he may not be putting out anent ourselves to the Lord President — and will gar him believe them! But what of the other?'

They both looked across to where Black William was standing with one foot upon the window seat and his two hands holding one of Kirstie's on his bent knee and his head down by hers.

'I am thinking there must be some explanation,' Robert said, 'for he has done muckle good to our sister.'

'Aye,' said Mungo, 'a fuller explanation. As there must be for us all.' He sighed and drank and felt the comforting warmth of the dram, and wiped his face carefully on a good linen napkin, the same that were aye set out on the table, his dear stepmother's weaving.

James, too, was staring at his uncle William and his aunt Kirstie, minding sudden on the shocking accusations Kyllachy had made, and how, according to him, they must be living in open sin. And there was a time not so long ago, when he would have believed it, aye, because he would have wanted to. But now it didna make sense. He put it from him easily and it was another count against Kyllachy.

Wattie Buidh came in and over to Captain John and spoke to him softly, and Captain John, pulling his gilt-buttoned coat to a yet straighter fit, followed him out of the room. Airthrey had asked eagerly how the Lord President found himself and was told that he was in bed and the pain abating.

It was late now. The dancing at the back of the house was finished. A lass must get her blink of sleep before the morning's milking. Tammie Clow came in to tell Margaret that the Lord President's men had their supper eaten and were now up in the lads' bothy where doubtless they could be sleeping sound before the young gentlemen were up to bed. Would he give them a salmon to their breakfast? There was another one brought in this evening from the Dalreoch tenant. She asked if the horses were all bedded down and he said aye, Sandy Mailor and the lads had seen to it. The Lord President's roan mare was as bonny a beast as he had seen this twelve months past. He added: 'I havena breathed a wee word, neither to Grizzie Pitcathly nor to any other. But you will mind the way we were a' blamed for thon key!'

'Aye,' said Margaret, 'would you say yon English sailor had it now, Tammie?'

'I would say that,' said Tammie. 'Och, siccan a judgment to come on a decent house!'

Margaret nodded and wiped a stain of cream from off one of the tables. She could feel the hardness of the key between herself and her stays. It couldna slip and it need never be found. She had yet to meet the lad whose hand she would let hunt where the key was gone.

Wattie came back and bowed to Gleneagles: 'Sir, the Lord President wishes the prisoner brought to him for interrogation. Captain Haldane informs us that his man is on guard at the stairhead, but you have the key of the door.'

'Indeed I havena!' said Mungo. 'Robbie, did you get it?'

'I did not,' said Robert. 'But it will be no trouble at all breaking the door. God aye, no trouble! Indeed, a satisfaction. We will go with you.' He went over to William: 'We are about to take this rebel before the Lord President. Are you coming, Borlum?'

After a moment William said, 'Aye!'

It would be a devilish painful thing, but it would need to be done and there was nothing to be gained by putting it off. Indeed it might only anger Forbes and make him see the whole thing blacker. He whispered to Kirstie, and Captain Robert frowned and stamped for he could not bear the sound of the Irish, the tongue of tinkers and sorners and randy pipers and cattle thieves! Ochtertyre made as if to come, but William stopped him.

'Keep you out of it. I will try and say a word to the man.'

At the stairfoot Captain Robert stopped, looking about him for an axe to break the door. It should have been in the bottom of the press along with sickles and snedders and scooching knives and such. But Black William whispered: 'The key will be brought. Though truly she hadna it herself.'

Robert snatched it from Kirstie. It was warm, the key. But he couldna be asking where it had been! They went up the stair. Wattie spoke to the English sailor; the rest tried not to notice the man; it was some way shaming to have him watch them. Below in the dining-room Ochtertyre would have his hands over his ears. William himself had a sick feeling. He had been in hiding more than once and he knew in his bones just how the steps on the stair and the grating of the key would sound to Mr. Strange, who might put a brave face on to it or else might crack — being, after all, no soldier. There could be cries and things said that would hurt for a lifetime. And now, they were at the door. Would Mr. Strange have guessed already? Would he be preparing himself? William shifted his fingers along his empty sword-belt, trying to think how best to say in fewest words that it was not Ochtertyre who had betrayed, but only fate. Mungo was looking away; he put his hands up to his eyes and groaned. Captain Robert turned the key in the lock and threw open the door. Wattie held the candles high. The English sailor came behind them to look, his pistol cocked in his hand.

Mr. Strange was not waiting for them. They stepped in; the candles shone only a little way ahead.

'Surrender in the King's name!' shouted Captain Robert.

He had boarded a ship often enough before. The poor devil must be hiding, uselessly. They clattered through the attic, Captain Robert with his sword drawn, and all together came sudden on a hole in the boards and looked at one another.

The English sailor let slip a large oath and spat. Without a word Wattie handed over the candlesticks and slipped through. It was too narrow a hole for any of the others. He swung by his hands and dropped. Robert and Mungo both knew where he would land, in a small, unplastered store room. After a moment he called up from it: 'The shutters are open.' He leant out and listened. There was always the chance that a man jumping from a height might be lying below with a bone broken on him. But there was no sound. After a while his eyes grew accustomed to the night and he could see down. There was nothing at all.

CHAPTER V

ROBERT and Mungo sat back on their hunkers opposite one another, with the hole in the boards between them: wee boys out of school and what ava will the dominie say? And now William was down beside them: 'I swear it wasna any of us!' he said anxiously.

Neither of the Haldanes answered. Mungo put his hand down to the crumbled edge of the plank, felt about it and smelt at the stuff that came away into his hand.

'It is as well we know there is dry rot in the house before it spreads all over,' he said. It was embarrassing him beyond all to have the English sailor standing about behind him.

Wattie rolled a barrel under the hole, stood on it and got his hands up through the hole. William and Robert taking each a hand, hauled, but in doing it, Robert's foot went through another weak place in the boards. There was a nasty great tear in the good silk hose he was wearing, but at least it made Mr. Strange's escape the more plausible.

'We had best go and tell,' said Mungo uncertainly.

'He canna eat us,' said Robert.

'Na, na,' said Mungo, 'it is yon poor lad Ochtertyre will get etten.'

'There is nothing to be said but the truth. Yet I will not blame the Lord President if he doesna believe a word of it.'

'I am gey an' sure he willna, Robbie.'

'If I had taken the key from Kirstie at the first I might have been in time, but the obstinate quean had it hidden some place.'

'Well, well,' said Mungo, 'we canna stand here colloguing all the night. Let us go to Forbes.'

Up in the music-room Forbes sat up in bed, his woollen night cap on his head and a shawl over his shoulders. There was a harp standing at the foot of his bed and his papers were spread on the top of a partly broken clavichord. And there was a

379

nice wee fire in the grate, since at his age a Scottish summer did not go far to warm the chilling flesh at nights.

Kyllachy sat easy on a stool by the fire. He had witnessed the humiliation of the namely Haldanes who had aye thought of himself as a thigging Highlander. Yet to be pleasantly experienced was power over Kirstie and that might be if he could sufficiently entangle her man. Whether there was money in it or no, he did not care. It was a grand ploy in itself.

Young Captain John was moving about the room restlessly. Once he opened the press in the wall and found an ivory flute and blew on it, softly as he supposed. But the round note came tumbling out into the room, making a wild din in the stillness. He had begun to ask himself whether had he done right; for the truth was always good but yet questionable if it were always good to speak aloud. Wattie had set a stick or two of rhubarb to boil on the fire; he had taken a race over to the garden to find them, earlier on. It was better to mix the imported Turkey rhubarb with this garden stuff when it was to be had. The smell of the cooking rhubarb joined itself to the musty smell of the room and the smell of rum and the smell of illness shadowing the Lord President.

He had decided that this rebel must be carried to Perth and there duly tried and sentenced, most probably to forfeiture of goods or to transportation. It might well appear at his cross-questioning that there was no more to it than met the eye, but if the man were a Jacobite agent, if William Macintosh had been playing the Highland game of dagger behind the back — Yet maybe in the course of the examination he would be cleared. And Forbes had a strong and definite feeling that here was the thing he would far rather happen, seeing the way he liked his kinsman and neighbour, aye and Kirstie Haldane forby. Which made matters all the worse if William had betrayed him. There were also the speeches and writings alleged against Patrick Haldane, devilish altogether from a Law Officer. Yet maybe notice should not be taken of them officially, since the Whig ranks were a bittie ragged as it was, with over much quarrelling on small points and precedence, and they would scarcely stand more depletion, with the trial of Provost Stewart coming on. As to the flytings against himself, it was queer, but some way he wasna caring. Though he would have cared plenty once. He was separate now, not only from the pleasures of the flesh, but from its wee, selfish angers, forby. Maybe Patrick Haldane had been half right to make a mock of the good Edinburgh Whigs that had gained so muckle in goods and gear and public esteem. With it all he had been diligent against the worst of the Tories, the great names especially, and was one of the few that had no fear of them, seemed for that matter to take a certain delight in tearing them down from their high places, though he was fair and careful enough in his examination of witnesses from the trades or towns and those constrained into the thing by their superiors. It would have to be ascertained whether he too had known of this Tory skulker, since if he had it became at once less likely that the man was anyone of consequence. Or — did it? The thing might have yet another twist. The Lord President frowned and fidgeted, seeking to sort it out right in his mind and not wanting to speak again with Kyllachy and thinking his rhubarb had been long enough at its boiling.

When Wattie came in he went straight to it and took it off the fire and knelt on the hearth, half turned, watching his betters having their troubles and embarrassments, and only the flick of a grin when Kirstie Borlum signed to him with her hand. For the rest had brought Patrick and Kirstie with them as their reserves. And indeed there was need, for the Lord President was wild angered at the first, gasping for breath to say what he thought, and so was Captain John who would not even believe his own uncles until he had questioned the sailor and found that the thing was indeed so. Aye, there had been a noise in the attic, but the door locked and so no chance to see what was doing.

'And who of you all had the key?' asked the Lord President.

'Well, my lord,' said Kirstie, 'it was between myself and the lasses. And you willna be saying, Duncan,' she added, 'that we were helping the lad, for we werena out the room, not one of us, and indeed we werena that interested in the poor creature.'

'From my own observation,' said the Lord President, 'I had thought otherwise!'

'Now I canna have you thinking badly of poor Catherine. Indeed she only said what she did out of pure goodness of heart in order to deceive you, Duncan!'

'I see, I see,' said the Lord President, 'and now you will be so good as to hold your own tongue, Kirstie, before I am still more deceived!' Yet for a moment he found it kind of hard to be completely judicial and he had aye had a half liking for women of spirit. Then he said sharply: 'Bearcrofts, what was your part in this?'

It seemed to Patrick most probable that Kyllachy had by now said everything which he had to say against the family and himself. In the which case truth was the best weapon and maybe Culloden would appreciate it. He said: 'When the thing was told me, in the back of the afternoon, it seemed to me that the main concern was not whether or no some wee Jacobite should run or be caught, seeing he was not one of the great nor with power over tenants and such, but who was to be put in the wrong over him. For it had come down to a quarrel between, of the one part, my sister's husband and your kinsman, Borlum, whom I esteem as a good man and one who has the welfare of Scotland at heart, and of the other part, our cousin of Kyllachy, whom I have every reason to think ill of. This being a family matter, my Lord, I was at liberty to choose my side of the case.'

'You call it a family matter, Bearcrofts. Does it not seem to you to be an affair of the State?'

'Not in reality, my Lord. Merely in name.'

'You would put the convenience of your family before your loyalty to the King and Government,' said the Lord President.

'No,' said Patrick, 'I would not say that. I would maybe say that the good of the people of Scotland comes most to my mind.'

'Which is bound up with the good of the Whig rule and cause.'

'And the Presbyterian Church of Scotland,' said Mungo anxiously.

'Most certainly,' said the Lord President and frowned again, remembering what Kyllachy had hinted about the publication by Patrick Haldane of blasphemous libels. 'If we had but the mannie here, you might all be half cleared — or you mightna. Can one of you give me his true name?'

He looked at Captain John who shook his head uneasily, never having known, nor having wished to know, once he had his mind made up that the fellow was a rebel; thereafter at Mungo and Captain Robert who also shook their heads; at last at William, whose eyes slanted away, but in the end were held. He said slowly: 'The man was a certain Mr. Strange of Edinburgh.'

'And how were you acquaint with him?'

After a moment William said: 'Indeed, I was not.'

'How do you make that out, William Macintosh, you wild bad unprincipled man!' said Mungo. 'And you will mind of what you said yourself when yon key was lost!'

'I am terrible sorry, again,' said William, 'and I seem to be aye and always half deceiving you and I know fine you will say it is me being Highland, but thon time I was taking the blame for Ochtertyre and forby that your own nephew, young James, who was in the thing out of a certain generosity of heart, which you will recognize, since you have it yourself.'

'Och, och,' said Mungo, 'I dinna know what ava to think!'

Patrick said: 'Mr. Strange is a portrait painter and engraver, come of decent folk and with no political connections. He was asked to design the Pretender's bank notes and did so with as much gratification as a young lawyer with his first brief, and with full as little thought of any consequence to himself or others. I have one of the notes with me, as it chances — he felt about in his back pockets — 'Aye, here it's. Drawn in haste. And doubtless repented at leisure!' He flipped it into the fire where it burned briefly and was out. 'Mr. Strange and Murray of Ochtertyre had danced with the same partners at the same routs at Edinburgh, and a young man will feel himself bound to stand by his billies. There was all there was to it.'

'Would this tally with any information you have?' the Lord President asked Kyllachy.

He said: 'It might be so. Though what can be worse treachery than to put a second currency into the country, over against the King's own? Is that no' a worse thing altogether than fighting?'

Forbes did not answer. He looked from one to the other. Wattie brought him the bowl of rhubarb to sup, with the powdered Turkey rhubarb mixed in with it and sugar grated over all. It went through Kirstie's mind that they might all be the better of a supper tray, for it must be after midnight. There would be a cold pie below. But she mustna speak again, mustna make a move. Instead she watched her man, standing easily, the weight on the ball of one foot, dark and quiet and observant, not outwardly agitated as her brothers were. It seemed to her that there was a great beauty about him; even the plainness of the plum coloured coat that he had on — and she minded him asking her was it good enough to take to Gleneagles — showed the shape of him through, where the heavy braid and gilt on her brothers' had no meaning at all. Yet maybe it was the way she knew the shape of his body and its movements with all of her own body that was strung to his touch. And sudden she turned her head away, feeling she had over stared, feeling abashed the same as a lassie that has let her lad tumble her before they go to the Church and yet she canna but be glad that she didna hold out against him. Maybe, she thought, he will get another bairn on me yet. But the Lord President lifted his head and Kirstie's imaginings on William fled and she stiffened to attend.

'William,' he said, 'what garred you take the blame of this from Ochtertyre?'

William said: 'I couldna have done otherwise and looked my father in the face when we meet hereafter.'

Kirstie said: 'We had already sheltered my kinswoman Isobel, Ardsheal's wife. I thought you might know of it, Duncan, for it wasna that terrible secret up north.'

'Did you do that now, Kirstie?' said Mungo. 'And how was she at all, the poor bitch?'

'They were gey far through when they came to us, she and the wee one. But the bairn lived. We never told you, Patrick, seeing you would be no friend to Glenshiel and he maybe one that did no good to Scotland. But what else could we do? And the bairn lived.'

'You are soft, Kirstie!' said Patrick.

'Aye,' she said, 'would you have me hard?'

'Well,' said the Lord President, 'it seems that the women are having the say of it and must be let bamboozle and confuse the rest of us. And now, Bearcrofts, I have been hearing certain things on yourself. If they were true they would unfit you for your position as an Officer of the Crown.'

Patrick walked heavily over to the bed and stood, his hands clasped behind him, looking down at Forbes. 'If you choose to take the word of a man who is a known informer, Culloden, you will get whatever you want out of it. You will have heard and believed plenty evil of me twenty-five years back, so doubtless you will have expected and welcomed this.'

'It was not welcome,' said the Lord President shortly. And then: 'You should be beyond the age for any such wicked follies! But you said a thing anent your kinsman Kyllachy which must either be withdrawn or else substantiated.'

Kyllachy spoke quickly: 'He will try and invent any kind of lie about me, my Lord!'

Patrick said, disregarding him: 'It was he that betrayed old Borlum, William here's father, your own second cousin, and got the reward for it.'

'Is that a fact?' said the Lord President, shocked. William nodded gravely. The spoon slid off the bed cover and clattered on the floor.

'My Lord!' said Kyllachy, 'I have ae striven to help the Government in all matters. And that through pure Whig principles!'

'They carried you over far in this matter,' said the Lord President. He thought he could see through it at last, and just what exactly was the quarrel between William Macintosh of Borlum and Lachlan Macintosh of Kyllachy that had involved a whole household, and himself. He had been one of those who, when old Borlum was a prisoner, had seen that he had books and claret, and had even helped over the printing of his own books. You could do no less for a neighbour and kinsman in prison and he an old man.

But young Captain John was angered. He said: 'This is the daftest thing I have ever seen! My Lord President, there are three men here that have acted as traitors and one, besides myself, who has acted loyally, not only in this matter but earlier. And he is the only one who is censured for his actions!'

The Lord President shifted a little under the blankets. He did not relish the rough criticism by the young. Yet it must be met. At last he said: 'Captain Haldane, I am looking beyond the action at the motive behind it.'

'That is the business of theology and not of the law,' said Captain John.

'Aye, but I judge as a Christian and one of a community of Christians, and nothing can get past that.'

Captain John could think of two or three retorts to this, yet he didna like to say them, with Culloden lying there so weak, and it could not be gainsaid that the old man had done justly and wisely by Scotland. Kyllachy kicked a log into the fire and looked at Kirstie. He had not been granted the satisfaction of seeing her blench. Could it be she was some way — protected? He had not found the crack to slip in a wee word over the death of her first husband. Maybe there was nothing to it. He had known smoke without fire before this, and if Gleneagles put so little credit on his accusation against Borlum, for which at least he had some evidence, there would be less credit put on a thing against Kirstie. It seemed there was no more to be got from this. The Lord President wasna taking it the way he should have been. If he had been younger and brisker — aye, and no relation to Borlum forby! It was easy seen Forbes was losing grip. Maybe one should pay one's respects to the Clan Dundas. For it might be soon, the changeover.

For a time there was a stillness in the room. The Lord President lay back, his eyes half closed, making only a slight swallowing motion in his throat that rose, skinny and tough as a stewing hen's, out of the ruffles of his night-shirt. The Haldanes looked respectfully at him or gently at one another. Well, thought Kyllachy, the cow is lost but I needna lose the calf along with her! And if he retired now, in the way of a gentleman, there was nothing could be said and he would still be on speaking terms with the Haldanes and his appearance would cast the greatest embarrassment on to them; which would surely mean that they would be over polite towards him and be at pains to get the brandy out for him, should he come again. Nor would this stop him from making a grand story out of it amongst his own cronies; he could see himself telling it and putting a touch on it here and there where it had not turned out as it should in reality. Aye, it might be possible to drop a word over Borlum and the American marriage contract. Here was a thorn that could be cannily jagged now and again if occasion arose, and best if more evidence could be got. Well, well, that could wait. It seemed as though Ochtertyre were to be let go by default, but he did not care one way or the other. That had been George's bird and if George had deserted, then the bird could fly. He might usefully maintain relations with Captain John; the younger generation should aye be cultivated.

'I perceive,' he said, 'that this is to be a family affair rather than a matter of justice or principle, so good night to you all, for it is late.'

And he bowed himself out, among murmurs of protest or politeness from the others. And Captain Robert above all did not care for someone outwith the circle to speak as though he had principles and they not!

The Lord President said: 'There is a time for everything and this is no time to hark back to the past. I propose, gentlemen, with your consent, to take no official cognizance of the treasonable actions alleged against Murray of Ochtertyre.'

Mungo took a deep breath: 'Amen to that! You are dead right, Culloden, though I say it myself. I could never have sat in Church again with his folk. And I am gey sure he will never be in the politics after this.'

'What do you say, Captain Haldane?' said Forbes to the younger man.

Captain John said awkwardly: 'All this is a matter of principle to me. I cannot see it your way.'

'I have maybe another fashion of principle,' said the Lord President, 'and it is not, as you might suppose, merely the expediency of an old man, although that may have something to say in it. But at least I am of age to be judged by my actions, which have ae been those of an honest Whig. Yet I would say that the fountainhead of my principles had been the good of my poor country, Scotland, which has been so sore torn by the politics. I knew fine that nothing but harm could come to us from the Stewarts, for all we have had so little good of the house of Hanover. But after the troubles were past — gentlemen, you will likely mind of how I counselled mercy to Cumberland and the rest after the battle.'

'And how they would not listen to you, Duncan,' said Kirstie.

'The only life I got was poor Rattray of Craighall, the golfer. I had asked for others, but I was refused in the name of principle. No. There I am wrong. I doubt I was refused mostly because I was a mere Scot, and the Scots to such Englishmen as Cumberland are a despised and worthless and subject race, and why should the conquerors pay attention to what any one of them says.'

'The English arena all of that kind!' said William, 'and it is hardly fair to say that Cumberland and his like are English at all. They are incomers from Germany, and they have a contempt for the true English, since they came by a kind of legal accident to rule over them.'

'Aye, aye,' said Forbes, 'that is true enough. And I found full more decency among the pure English and you have every right to speak up for your mother's folk, William. But I was accused at that time of lack of principle when I asked for mercy; I was told that this was no time for compromise, that the snake's back must be well and truly broken. I, on the contrary, had the opinion that this was the correct moment for both mercy and compromise. These are not virtues at easy times when they come naturally to all of us. But only at difficult times such as the present.'

'You will not get many to agree with you there,' said William thoughtfully.

'Maybe no. But I am in the right of it. We in Scotland have been over much battered to be able to spare any man who will set his hand and mind to the future. Aye, or any woman, Kirstie! We must act together and build ourselves up slowly and surely, by way of the peaceful arts and trades through commerce and agriculture, until we are well of our wounds. Is that plain enough, Bearcrofts?' He turned his head painfully on the pillow till his eyes were on Patrick's, and Patrick's mouth twitched and he gave a quick nod of his head. Forbes went on slowly: 'Aye, Scotland will need all of us. And in a while things will begin to go as they should. But I will not see yon time.'

'Och, och,' said Mungo, 'you shouldna speak so!'

'Well,' said Forbes, and sighed, for he did not want to argue the thing, 'it is true anyway.'

Kirstie said: 'It is late. Will I get us all a bite of supper?'

'Not for me,' said the Lord President. 'I never eat after I have supped my rhubarb. And I am somewhat wearied.'

'Good night then, Duncan,' said Kirstie, 'and sleep sound. See to him well, Wattie, for he has our gratitude.'

'Aye, aye,' said Mungo, 'you could have skinned us all alive, but now the thing has come out as well as it could do. A good night to you, Culloden.'

CHAPTER VI

Margaret and Catherine were waiting for them, each holding a candle, at the foot of the stairs.

'How did it go?' asked Margaret. 'And what is going to happen to poor Ochtertyre?'

'His head is clear of the noose this time,' said her father, 'not that he deserved it.'

'I said it would be so,' said Margaret, 'when you were so long away. Though he is moaning and groaning still. And now' — she dropped her voice a bittie — 'we have left the dining-room to Kyllachy; you'll mind he had his bed made up in there and some way we jaloused he had best be left to his own dreams! Helen and Elizabeth are off to bed in some kind of a vexation that I am hoping they will sleep off. And George has gone mumping up to the bothy and now Alec is back from Blackford having missed everything, but Adam and Davie are telling him. But the rest of us are eager to know just how it all went. Where will we sit?'

William said: 'Let us ask all the world to our room, Kirstie, ma mie, and make it the clearing house.'

'Aye,' said Captain Robert, 'but we will need our night-caps. Get you the brandy, Patrick, and I will find the glasses. And we will have out a bottle of the Madeira for the ladies who have taken so notable a part in our campaign.'

'Aye,' said Margaret, 'the sweet one. That will be just fine.'

'I had best be retiring,' said young Captain John stiffly.

'You will do no such a thing!' said Margaret and caught his hand. 'You are my prisoner, cousin Johnnie! Do you yield?'

Kirstie beckoned to Catherine: 'Come, you and I will get a supper tray, my soul. I must see are the larders so well stocked as they were when we weans would go thieving.'

Margaret Bearcrofts said: 'Aye, I am as hungry as a March ewe. See you bring enough for us all, Aunt Kirstie, for I doubt

390

we mostly had poor appetites earlier on.' And then she called after them: 'You are forgetting the larder will be locked!'

At that all three laughed, but there was a shaken edge to it that was near tears.

'Mrs. Grizzie is aye hiding the key in a different place,' said Margaret, 'but I think you will discover it if you dip your hand into the barley in the blue crock.'

On their way through each took one of the heavy oaken trays from Tammie's pantry. In the blink of the two candles it was all neat and damp; the copper-bound wooden tubs for the washing of glasses were standing bottom up. They left a candle there to light them along the stone passage and lighted others in the kitchen sconces. They both of them felt the need of lights and both of them wondered under what hedge poor Mr. Strange might be sheltering.

There was still a glow of red in the ashes and Catherine threw on some light wood and coals and worked with the bellows till it flared up. Easy enough to heat up the tail of the soup with a measure or so of milk in it and the cooked peas for thickening. Aye, there was the key sure enough and Kirstie went down to the larder on tiptoe, playing robbers and reivers as she used to as a wean with wee Rob, and with Jamie and Ann who were so long dead that now it was no pain to think on them, but rather joy of old happiness remembered. The candle flickered in a cold draught, but she found the pie and a piece of a ham, fresh cheese, butter in a cloth and a batch of scones, as much as she could carry, almost. Beyond, in the corner of the larder, was to-morrow's gigot and a bundle of teals, ready to be plucked and trussed in the forenoon. When they were weans it was always the sweet stuff they were after, raisins best of all when there were any. She could not mind on so muckle fresh meat; when they killed a sheep or a young stot, it would be a day to talk on. Everything needed to go farther and not near the same imported stuff to fall back on.

In the kitchen, Catherine had the broth hotting up over the fire. She had taken a handful of almonds out of a jar and was sitting on the table, nibbling away at them. It was a good high kitchen with plenty head room for the hams and flitches and onions and the bunches of fresh dipped candles hanging butt down.

'When I was a bairn,' said Kirstie, 'there was never the same kind of profusion as here. We werena just so secure over food. If there was a bad har'st we might all begin to fare badly, and worse if it was two years running. Now you will get folks scarcely knowing or caring how the har'st has gone.'

'Nobody goes hungry these days,' said Catherine decidedly, giving the pot a stir, 'unless they are idle.'

Ah lassie, you may believe that, thought Kirstie, but I know otherwise and folks arena always idle of their own free will, nor they canna always sell what they get by their toil. But you will not credit it until you see it with your own eyes, so where is the use of me speaking of it.

She hunted through the kitchen press for horn spoons, since the silver was safe locked away in the plate chest and Tammie with the key, and next she shook out the crisp and sparkling crystals from the Forth salt-pans, and she frowned and screwed her face as she minded that this was all slave work, an ancient privilege and the Whigs thought it none of their business to interfere since the owners of the salt-pan serfs would be supporters of the Government and that with money. Queer, the way all this had come into her mind in the couthy and well-doing kitchen, the very heart of the house, and she hadna meant it to when she thought of the supper tray, and it wasna maybe womanly to think on such things as industries and trade; nor for that matter on imports, and how they are to be paid for by a poor country the like of Scotland: yet there was what she and William would be speaking on, back at Borlum. And forby that, she thought to herself, I could be half jealous, for I dinna like the way we need to be scrimping, whiles, at home. I would like fine to see my own larder so thrang with food. But only if my neighbours' were the same. Aye, and the folk that are working and hungrier than most of us will ever be and a poor dish of sowans or kale to come back to at the end of the day's darg.

Catherine had come on a pot of honey and was dipping her fingers into it. One gets old soon enough and one doesna dip so deep into the honey pot, but neither is one the same way greedy and one can mind of others that are needing a taste. Yet it is kind of nice to see the young ones at it, anyway if they are bonny and cheery and sweet-natured. And now a pleasant steam was rising from the broth. Kirstie dropped in a half-handful of parsley for garnish and piled the bowls on to the tray.

Upstairs the young men had brought in two or three stools; but half the company had sat themselves down on the bed. Captain Robert was handing about the glasses; he had given a short account of what had happened and Ochtertyre leant against the bed post and sobbed with relief, his face buried in a fold of the curtains. Now he would be able to go home, back to the bonny house of Ochtertyre and the friendly folk and a life that would have no politics in it and no wish for change or power, but year by year of home and Kirk and market, fair dealings with neighbours and kinsmen, leniency towards tenants, fulfilment of duties and forgetting of follies. He minded soberly of how he had put up a prayer when the others were with the Lord President and now equally he gave his thanks, muttering the words into the wool of the bed curtain. Bob Strange might go out of his life forever now; he would not write, not even to say that it was none of the ones he had seen who had betrayed him. Bob Strange might go back to the Prince but Murray of Ochtertyre never.

'Poor Duncan Forbes and his rhubarb!' said Mungo, cutting himself a second slice of the pie. 'Praise be, I can still eat.'

'He is mortally sick,' said William, 'and I am mostly sure he knows it.'

'Aye, aye,' said Mungo. 'The very same as ourselves and the thought of the grave ae before us. And he will have the grandest funeral in all Scotland. I wonder now, will he lie with his forefathers or maybe we should take him to Edinburgh, though that wouldna do gif he were to die in the summer.'

Captain Robert, who did not much like thinking of death and its appurtenances, interrupted his brother: 'Duncan

Forbes has had a gey hard time of it between being chased half over Scotland during the Rebellion, and the disappointments and rudenesses he has had from Cumberland since. If he could be easy now and take less burdens on himself—'

'Na,' said Mungo, for he was at the stage of drink when his thoughts turned to his latter end, but most fortunately with a deep assurance that he was a child of Grace, an assurance that could be questioned by his reasonable and sober self, above all on the Sabbath. But now he had escaped from perturbations and could contemplate his immortality and release from troubles, as also the release of the soul of Forbes of Culloden, who would also, doubtless, be in Grace. 'Poor Duncan Forbes has nothing more to get out of life,' he said, 'but muckle purges and gripings of the which he will be freed in the hereafter.'

'Scotland will be the worse for his going, for all that,' said William, and then to Patrick: 'He didna act as your enemy.'

'It will have done the man muckle good,' said Patrick, 'to be cast down and despised and made to feel the same as the common man must the best part of his time, and that in his own town of Inverness. There now, is something that Cumberland and his friends have done for Scotland!'

'If they would all go back to their own places now and leave us to sort ourselves!' said Mungo, 'for there will be no more of the troubles.'

Young Captain John could not help it, he had to burst out: 'You have a poor kind of gratitude to the English Army and Navy that got you out of being over-run by the Tories! When I think of the risks that I ran with my own sloop with twenty thousand pounds aboard of her in pay for the Royal Armies, and now it seems, all against the wishes of the head of the family!'

'Och,' said Mungo, 'you mustna think I am against England in any way, and all the family, including myself, that have been Members of the Westminster Parliament. But the English are terrible dreich to see that there are other ways of doing besides their own.'

'I have heard that said in America as well as in Scotland,' said William. He was sitting on a stool at Kirstie's feet where she was perched up on the end of the bed; they were sharing a glass of the sweet wine — he had drunk enough brandy for the day.

'The Glasgow trade is the greatest bone of contention,' said Patrick, 'and we are bound to build up Glasgow against Liverpool and Bristol. Not that there isna room for all. But you willna get a mannie that has great thoughts for his own trading profits, to see thon.'

But while their elders were discussing, Catherine made as if to carry out the tray with the empty ashets and pie dish to the stairhead, and James had followed her. Kirstie and William both observed, but said not a thing to the company. Catherine laid down the tray and affected surprise but made no immediate move to go back to the room.

James said: 'Have you forgiven me, cousin Catherine?'

'I doubt we are all of us feeling too happy at the outcome of all this to be angry at one another. However much cause we may have.' For she was not going to let him off scot free!

'This is more than I dared to hope,' said James.

'Well,' said Catherine judicially, 'it is not as though you were often intoxicated, cousin James.'

'It was all part of a plot against Kyllachy,' he said, 'that miscarried.'

'I doubt we are none of us unco good at this plotting,' she said, 'maybe we are over honest.' And she flicked a crumb or two of the pie-crust off her skirt with the lacy handkerchief that her father had bought for her in London. She knew that James was staring at her, but in the candle light she needna let on that she was aware. She was wearing a primrose dress with broad stripes of silver over a light green petticoat, and on her hair that was dressed high, yet all her own, primrose ribbons with a heavy Italian lace. It was not in the latest fashion, as she knew well enough, having been told she was over young to wear a great hoop and swinging skirt of flowered brocade, as the London fashions were. Yet she had a strong suspicion that James Haldane did not know much about the fashions himself. But, when her mind turned towards him, there was such a great, blind tossing and tumbling of thoughts and wonders and questionings over him that she felt half dizzy and one hand went to her throat.

Young James reached out towards the other hand and it seemed to her that she could feel it coming as though the dusky candle-flickered air around her were but an extension and continuance of her own body, prickling to the touch as now her skin prickled, and now he was touching her truly, had hold of the hand, was drawing it to him. For a moment she tried to speak, feebly, of the supper tray, of the adventure they had been in together, but none of her sentences ended right and he paying no attention to them, and now she was in his arms and her mouth under his and as the kiss came down on her she could smell the brandy on his breath but it did not seem worth bothering with.

'Good sakes, Catherine,' he murmured, 'good sakes, if I had but you in bed with me!'

She felt she should have protested, have cried out; maybe it was better to let on she hadna heard. It wasna the James she knew and respected, the lad of virtue and principle, walking in the way of the Lord. But it was a lad she liked awful well, that set a warm humming through her body of a kind she had never known. And for an instant her mind went back to her Aunt Kirstie who had met her uncle William in the wood back of the house when the great spruces were only young and feathery. She found herself released, back on her own feet, with her face burning and her knees shaken so that she needed still to be holding on to James.

He said: 'May I speak with your parents anent our marriage, Catherine?'

There, it had come, and she didna know how to answer. 'Och,' she said, 'I dinna know. I am young yet, James — '

He looked at her anxiously: 'Catherine, when you said yon thing to do with Mr. Strange, you werena meaning, surely, surely, that you thought anything of the man?'

'How at all would you believe thon, James?' she said. 'It isna nice of you ava, and someone needed to say something!'

'I was thinking it must be that,' he cried eagerly, 'and you with such courage, lassie! Indeed you did better than us all. When we are married — '

'And who has said?' she cried at him.

'Well, you havena said no!' He was looking close into her eyes now.

'Aye, but I might yet!'

'But you willna, Catherine? Say you willna!'

'We should be going back to the room, James. They will ask what are we doing here on our lone. I would be affronted.'

'We are not going back till you have said you will be my wife, Catherine.'

She stood away from him, taking deep breaths. 'It is a terrible serious decision to take,' she said, 'for all one's natural life. And beyond. Has the Lord indeed joined us, James?'

'We hold the same views on such matters,' said James, 'and I believe that is so. We will make our life together a shining light.'

'Would we do that, James?'

'Aye, my dear lass. And our children will praise the Lord for you.'

She put her hand into his: 'I will be your wife, James.'

They went back doucely into the room. Kirstie's embroidery lay on the chest, beside the door, and Catherine picked it up and began to sew away at it, for she didna want to look up. Slowly her heart quieted and sense began to assert itself, saying she had done well and James was a good match, heir to Airthrey, and her parents would approve; she hadna a very complete idea of her own tocher, but it would be enough and soon the family would be meeting and there would be settlements to be drawn up and clothes and gear and household plenishings to be bought and certain kinds of behaviour expected of herself and of James and an end to one part of her life of which she was not yet tired, for it had gone lightly since childhood, with her brothers and sisters and the cousins here and there, dancing and visiting and snowballing and ploys of all kinds, and the right way easy to ep. Now she must take responsibility; she must have deep thoughts upon virtuous living. And she and James Haldane would be together always.

He was standing over with the rest now, Ochtertyre and her brothers who were just come in. Adam looked at her quizzically, but she wrinkled her nose at him; James would not have spoken. Until to-morrow at least it would be secret for both of them. He brought her a glass of the sweet thick wine with the soft colour of a brown pansy; he had the same himself; she was glad he was keeping off the brandy. He said no word, only their fingers touched and glowed as he bowed and she took the glass. Neither of them named a toast but the glasses rang faintly against each other and their thoughts rang in tune.

Margaret had been daffing with young Captain John who was now cheerier; she came over and sat herself down on the chest beside Catherine. 'I am hoping that Kyllachy will ride early,' she said. 'He has made enough trouble without having his bed cluttering up the dining-room all day. And I dinna somehow think the Lord President will want to see him about the place. I am asking myself,' she added, 'how soon will the whole affair get round to the servants.'

'It will be kept hidden,' said Catherine. 'There are secrets, surely, in every family.'

'Aye, aye, and in every one of us. And the right hand not knowing what the left hand does. And the Lord seeing it all. Aye, even the wee thoughts that seem to come on us from outside ourselves, from the Tempter, so shamed they make us. But maybe you never have such thoughts, Catherine.'

'I think we mostly all have them. And doubts forby. But isna that the way we are all children of sin? Yet if we werena we wouldna have the experience of Grace. But Margaret — would our elders, think you, feel the same as we do, or could it be that when one is old one gets to be wise and equable and the same all through without such thoughts or wishes rising in one?'

'Maybe the Ministers are that way,' said Margaret, 'but somehow I dinna think it. I know fine my own father is not. And every time he gets some kind of praise or pleasure, or more often a hurt or censure, away it will go into his mind which is as full of wee drawers and clips and boxes as an office table, and there it will lie until the time comes for him to pull it out, and some way he will accommodate it all. You canna say it makes for good or evil, Catherine, but it is certain it isna simple or of one kind, the way we are led to suppose the human soul might be, nor can salvation be a simple matter.'

'Yet salvation comes in a single instant of apprehension, Margaret. In the blink of an eye we are changed.'

'Aye, well. It might be so. We havena the words right for such things and I misdoubt they will never be explained. But I dinna think any one of the older folk here is much different from you or I, Catherine, for all their behaviour, except that they have seen and experienced more and so they will have more knowledge on which to base their judgments and choose between one thought or hope and another.'

'Could they be happy the same as we are?'

'Och aye. And so you are the happy one, Catherine? But I willna ask you the how nor the why. But consider, my dawtie, a mother who keeps in her mind the secrets of half a dozen bairns that will be confiding in her, but she mustna tell them to each other nor yet to her man. And if Grace is given to her, it is given to her secrets and all. And indeed the Lord will have his hands gey full with the saving of some!'

'It is beyond our comprehension, Margaret.'

'Aye. And best left there.' She yawned. 'I wish I had asked whether the Lord President takes tea on his waking. But likely someone will know.'

CHAPTER VII

PATRICK signed with his head to William, who slid up from his stool, a dark cat, and quietly over. The candles were burning down; he lifted his hand and snuffed one of them. Patrick said low: 'I will speak to Robert to-morrow anent yourself. It will be best to give him a part of the truth but I will change the date of your fairy's death a bittie, and what is that compared with the great lies that need to be told continually for the well-being and order of the world!'

'You willna mind lying for me, Patrick?'

'Me, is't? Na, na, it will be a pleasure and it will set my two brothers' minds to rest, and there, when it comes to the bit, is the whole reason they and we are going to Church Sabbath after Sabbath to listen to another fashion of lies.'

'I canna just see it like that. There will doubtless be exaggerations and plenty bad discourses, but we dinna need to believe word for word.'

'Aye, but over many do just that, and the Ministers would lose a great part of their power if most thought your way and believed only what they chose — well, what they suppose to be of God, if you must have it your way, William! Your Quakers have found that to their cost, and the Ministers are that angry at an attack on their power that they will ae prefer the worst of sinners to a poor Friend! But maybe at Borlum your Episcopalian Minister is more subservient to his Laird's beliefs!'

'Ach, no!' said William, 'but I would say he liked both myself and Kirstie. So you will put all to rights, Patrick?'

'Aye, in the human way. But that will leave plenty on your mind, William. Can you thole it?'

'It is easier for having been told once, even. But also I dinna think that Redemption is a lie.'

'Unless it is bought or sold.'

'That destroys all. But, Patrick, I will pay you the passage-money when I sell my beasts!'

'Och well, as you like, William. Let us hope the prices hold! Yon graze on your cheek will want a wee explaining to Kirstie. Does it hurt you any?'

'No more than it should. But — I *couldna* have gone from Kirstie, whatever I said to you yon time.'

Patrick laughed: 'I have never seen a man so feared!'

'You would have severed me from my soul. Which is away worse surely than to be severed from the body. For thon I have faced, whiles.'

'Well, well,' said Patrick, 'I will sever you neither from body nor soul, for we will all be going and syne you can take Kirstie to bed with you!' He chuckled and went over to his brothers: 'Here is poor William ettling to get our sister to himself, and she the same, and we had best get off their bed in case we leave it over warm for them!'

'Och aye,' said Captain Robert, 'we will get off and they will get in and we'll even draw the curtains and see which comes over them first, William's breeches or Kirstie's petticoats!'

But Mungo still had his solemn thoughts: 'Gif we are a' spared till the morning we will see whether Kirstie —'

She, however, was not standing a thing more from her brothers: 'Give over,' she said, 'the randy old goats of you, and let decent folks go to their rest! Catherine, my soul, we have had a day of it.'

'Aye,' said Catherine and smiled suddenly, 'a day of days and I will never forget it. Good night, Aunt Kirstie.'

The two girls kissed her and dropped their curtsies to the uncles. Margaret had most of the glasses redded up on to a tray and the empty bottles with them. Her father gave her a rough kiss: 'Y'are a good lassie,' he said.

'You will get Tammie to shave you the first thing to-morrow!' she said, rubbing her cheek: 'Good night to you all!'

The young men took their cousinly kisses, Scots fashion, only for James who was suddenly filled with a great bashfulness and laid his lips lightly on Catherine's hand and neither said a word to the other. Captain John had been somewhat mollified by Alec Duncan who had agreed with him in theory but felt there were practical difficulties. Young Adam tucked his arm through Ochtertyre's, for he had such a daft lost kind of face on him: he might easily go stravaiging into the wrong room or fall asleep on the stairs!

Captain Robert, also, had an arm linked through Mungo's for mutual support and affection. He was telling Mungo of the great pleasure it was to be at home after these many months in the Indies and elsewhere and the hot nights with the over big stars and the queer snufflings and squealings of beasts, whereas here the summer night was cool and the stars of a most reasonable size and brightness and just a decent wee owl to be heard now and again. And Mungo was hoping that poor Forbes would sleep the night through and not be troubled by his medicine.

In the doorway, the Bear turned and grinned at the two who were left: he seemed about to make some remark, but thought better of it. Maybe they had all spoken enough for one day. Kirstie looked at the rumpled bed and stretched and yawned, straightened the cover and turned it back from the pillows. Another candle flickered out. She stood for a moment by the chest where Catherine had left her embroidery with one more wee leaf finished upon it.

'I suppose James has spoken,' she said.

'And she will have accepted him, having gained much in courage over the day, and that through conversation with her Aunt Kirstie,' said William.

'Does it need so muckle courage to take what you are wanting?'

'It needs a spark of courage to say yes to anything,' said William, 'but there is nothing else that gets you any forrarder.'

He took his coat off and hung it up in the dressing-closet; she moved across and stood by his shoulder till he turned and took her in his arms, as she had meant, his long arms hard under the warmth of the linen shirt, squeezing the breath out of her, the lace falling back from his tough brown hands and whiter wrists.

'Wait, you,' he said, 'and I will put you the way your brothers want!'

She laughed: 'I wasna hoping, a few hours back, that we could lie down easy the night.'

She went back to her own dressing-closet and let fall a few drops of rose water into the basin where she was washing. He was whistling slowly to himself, a complicated tune with wee catches in it here and there; she wasna just sure what name there was to it but she had heard it often enough on the pipes. He whistled easily, dead on the note, the way she knew he was happy.

Yet another candle flickered to its end and went out in smoke. 'There is a wild smell of candles and brandy in the room,' she said. 'Will we open the shutters a while?'

'Surely I will, mo ghraidh,' he said, and picked up a brandy glass that had been overlooked at the bed foot. He opened the shutters in the eastern wall and leant out. Already a greying had come into the night sky, the beginnings of morning over the hill. Below them in the barnyard a cock crew. He turned back to her and now again they knelt together by the bed.

He said: 'The Lord has been merciful to us all this day, Kirstie.'

'Aye,' she said, 'put you up a special thanksgiving, William.'

She waited, but for a time he could say nothing. His hand, groping, found hers. He pressed his other hand and his forehead against the mattress. At last he began to whisper and in broken sentences.

But Andrew Shaw had never been at a loss for words: a man of muckle eloquence. And by that far from God and His Son. And far from his wife.

They stood up, having had experience of the Inner Light, having had guilt burnt from them. He still held her hand. 'Come, my soul,' he said, 'let us sleep.'

She put her hand suddenly up to his cheek: 'Is it hurting you?' she asked.

'Ach no!' he answered quick, and blew the last of the candles out.

'A terrible sore bruise to come from a knock on a desk,' she said.

'Aye,' he said, and then: 'Och no, it looks more than it is.'

She laughed a little: 'You needna tell me,' she said, and when he would have protested, kissed him on the mouth. The curtains round the bed were half drawn, but she could see the squared hollow space of the window lighter than the deep shadowed room. The night at its end but no saying yet what kind of day it would be.

It was at such times that the appearances had mostly come, between one light and another, the images of corruption. And maybe they were in everyone, the creatures of the dark sea in which folks must swim or drown until they can find their own image or opposite. The same for everyone but not all allow themselves to perceive them. The same because we are all children of Adam and maybe these appearances come from the first sin, the first taste of death and pain and knowledge that is also fear. She lay silent, considering such matters, thinking also on Phemie Reid who had frighted her as a bairn, and how her own Elizabeth must never be frighted. But William had in an instant put Phemie to flight. Was he asleep? She couldna just tell. His eyes were shut but that didna always signify. Maybe he was hiding himself behind his shut eyes and how would she be unkind to her man and stop him hiding if he had a mind to? Since it wouldna be for any bad reason, only that grown folks, like bairns, will have their own ploys and mustna be forced to speak of them. She herself was gey tired, yet she didna wish to shut her eyes, but only to gaze at the grey window. And as she did so an appearance came floating out of the corner of her sight.

She caught her breath and it floated away, the thing. Had it come from Phemie's frighting of her, Phemie wanting to make her accept — what? Evil, corruption, the rule of fear. But if she did not fear it, she could not be ruled by it. And how would a person of sense fear such things, seeing they needna have power and could only get it gif they were given it. And it was this giving of power to them that was the Evil One's work, and not the things themselves that were neither of Good nor yet of Evil, but like the fairy host, on neither side in the battle.

And now she minded calmly on the appearance that had slid by, and it was a childish kind of thing, a nasty wee face on a kind of bashed and sicklike body. But it was the look, the look saying, 'Wait, you, there is worse coming.' As indeed there might be. If the master of it were to come. She had a very clear and strong idea of what the next move would be, if it came back: if the attempted compulsion to surrender, to do known wrong, even if only a wee dirty thing to start with, if it were submitted to — as how would a poor woman not submit when that compulsion came — better to submit at once and have done with it — She opened her eyes wide, that had begun to blink in the beginnings of the first submission, to darkness. Her heart was beating hard. But William was beside her. And she would continue the argument with evil. Phemie had tried to put compulsion upon her of the same kind. The compulsion of a nursemaid over a bairn. But was it not written: 'When I become a man I put away childish things'? And amongst them fear. And Phemie hadna harmed her; nor could the appearance. The poor wee bit thing, maybe it should be pitied if one regarded it at all. Maybe it would come back and syne she would pity it. She waited, her long plaits clear of her head, her hands loose by her side. It didna come.

After a space of waking and with the room already half light, she looked around and saw that William was regarding her from under his lashes, no more asleep than the bairn you think you have settled into its cradle. She turned herself quick into his arms. 'What is't now?' she asked.

He had been alone, in darkness, thinking on her and she lying quiet. All that had been shut down so long, but had been full awakened by Patrick, as earlier, in the night past, it had been half stirred by her speaking of what had been, making him speak of America, it was leaving him in no peace now! A sudden ache of softness seized on him, a longing to drown in the deep waters.

'Will I tell you,' he said, 'will I tell you, Kirstie — ?'

'No!' she cried. 'No! Dinna tell!'

She clung to him and laid her mouth over the graze in his

cheek. And he checked himself. How could he have dared to do this thing, to risk all their life and happiness? She would have judged and condemned him, must have done. An honest woman could do no less, out of her honesty. He had broken God's law and man's and so now must lie to her still. She must never even know he was lying lest she suspect and question, the way an honest woman was bound to do. There was the price he had to pay, now and for the rest of his life. To deceive his Kirstie. He thought quick of something he could let on had happened, a wee quarrel with Patrick maybe — no, she would speak to Patrick herself — but the passage money, aye that was it, the passage money yet to pay! He would need to tell her of that anyway before the Inverness fair.

'It was a wee thing, Kirstie,' he began.

She said: 'It isna,' and it was more than he could compass to speak the quick and easy words that would set all to rights. But syne she said, settling her head down into his shoulder the same as the wee lassie was used to do, 'I know fine you have secrets, William. And in the goodness of your heart you are lying to keep the thing from me. But you needna lie, mo chridh. Maybe I can guess the kind of thing it would be, and maybe I am better so than knowing it for sure and it would hurt the both of us seeing the thing over plain, and it doesna concern us now. Am I right over this?'

'Aye,' he said, shivering and with little sound to his voice.

'So,' she said, 'there will be nothing that need be said. And you needna lie to your Kirstie. But, my soul, I will ask you to keep silent on the main thing and that willna be hard for you, since it is for your Kirstie's sake. But dinna think you are deceiving me, my love, by keeping silent, and dinna think you are doing wrong. For you arena, whatever you may have done in times past.'

'I might have known, Kirstie Haldane,' he said, 'I might have known that you would see it that way. But I didna. And I do now.'

And after that love and sleep were at them and closed over them, and outwith the house day was breaking over the Ochils.

NOTES

Some of these notes have been published, more or less, in the *S.M.T. Magazine*, *Chambers's Journal*, *The Scots Magazine*, *Today and Tomorrow*, and *Forward*, and I wish to thank the Editors for permission to reprint them.

PART ONE

The Question of Language

The author of a historical novel hopes to be justified, ultimately, by the value of the book as a work of art. Yet there are other qualities involved. Just as a house must be convenient as well as beautiful, so should a historical novel be not only a work of art but also accurate, or rather (since it *is* a work of art and therefore of selection) a historically truthful interpretation of another time which will enable the modern reader to see again and revalue such times with reference to his own.

This part of the book, then, is either for those who are interested in Scottish history or for those who are interested in a writer's credentials. I will say at once that the book is very thoroughly documented and that almost all the characters are real people. But, in real life, Kirstie and Black William, my hero and heroine, are only names in two family trees. They died young. I have given them the lives they might have had, the child they might have had. Andrew Shaw of Bargarran was not, I am glad to say, a real person, though there were plenty like him; but his sister was real.

Some of the people in the book are those about whom a great deal is known, for instance Forbes of Culloden; others are comparatively obscure from the point of view of the history books, yet a great deal can be found out about them from various sources, mostly contemporary. Most of my own Haldane relations are in this category.

But before I go on to discuss the fascinating, intricate detail of sources, I would ask the reader to think for a moment about the question of language. Those who have read this far will have found that the book is written either in words and in a rhythm that is familiar and easy for them, or else that it is slightly unfamiliar, perhaps slightly irritating. Both may be interested to see how it comes about.

Any historical novelist needs to think out a definite convention over the speech of his characters and the language used for descriptive writing between conversations. In my novels of the ancient world I have transcribed Latin, Greek, or whatever it may be, into current English, using slang or debased forms when it seemed as though this was the best way of giving the reader the feel of how people were talking. Sometimes indeed, I overdid this, using a transient slang, which has now dated that bit of the book. While writing, I needed to keep an edge of my thought parallel with the original language, so as to try and get as near as might be to ancient ways of thought, with the deep influence that phrasing and words must have on ways of thinking. For instance, there is no exact translation of such words as nefas or potestas, nor in English (though you would get near it in Highland speech) for aidos. To get the sense of such words, and what they meant to people in terms of action or social organization, one needs to go round.

This book puts a different problem. I am writing about people who lived only two hundred years ago. I know exactly what words they and their friends used in conversation, and in letters and documents. But, because many such words and phrases are not now completely familiar and easy on the ear and eye, because it would mean too much effort and interruption to see the people who spoke and wrote that way as real in the same way as ourselves, I cannot actually use them. Yet I have to give the feel of a colour, a period, above all a country.

First and clearly, I could not translate the spoken Scots of the eighteenth century into current twentieth-century English. It just would not work out right. English was being spoken in the eighteenth century by the English, a different nation from the Scots, building up their ideas partly from other words and another grammar. It was not quite like modern English, but like enough for it to give the wrong feel if I had used something near to it and directly descended from it in the not overlong space of six generations. It would be like making my story people talk a half-foreign language of their own day.

The obvious thing was, then, to base my convention on modern Scots, the spoken language. In the past I have always used spoken, rather than written, English as my standard. The spoken language is a more fluent instrument. Spoken Scots is equally good and lively and, unless it is made needlessly unintelligible by phonetic spelling —

itself a convention and not an accurate one — it need be no strain at all for the English reader. Of course, there are some Lallans versions that are as hard, almost, as another tongue, though with their own interest and savour: the spoken language of the Fife folk, for instance. But remember, we are all of us expected as a matter of course to tackle either, say, American slang or broad Yorkshire (which latter we have not been familiarized with from the movies) and to have no difficulties.

There may be a few words here and there that will be unfamiliar to some readers; some of these are beautiful or in one way or another 'charged' and special, in the full run of the rhythm. But I have often preferred an English word to a Scots one, when the Scots would be really unintelligible to English readers, whilst the Scots readers would be familiar with the English word, and when the English word did not jar with the rhythm or feeling. I would like to remind readers that I happen to be mostly Scottish, born in Edinburgh, and that in my former books I have constantly used such words as burn and glen, redd and sort, daft and douce; I have always interchanged will and shall, Scots fashion. This is only going slightly farther. Yet one must write with the rhythms that are in one's head; and on the whole this book is in current West Coast speech, Kintyre speech — Carradale speech maybe — at any rate the kind of spoken Scots that comes most naturally to me. The descriptions and the talk of the Highlanders in the book are in this, but the Lowlanders speak with a more Lowland rhythm and with more of the special words and wee phrases that occur south and east of the Highland line. I do not think they speak Perthshire Scots, though it is likely enough that I might sometimes slip back to that, when I think in a slightly less West Coast phrasing.

But my current speech is partly, at least, based on Gaelic grammatical structure. It has the kind of thought and ways of reaching a conclusion which go with a language that is in some ways different in social implications from English or even Lowland Scots: in which for instance there is no possessive corresponding to theirs. It is hard to know how far all that goes. Scots is a slightly more elaborate, less clipped, sometimes less compact speech than English. West Coast speech, following Gaelic, uses more auxiliary verbs. I have, I hope, sufficiently indicated the rhythm. Past participles tend even now to be separate syllables: then, it was even more marked. Equally, the name Forbes was pronounced so as to rhyme with corbies. I have not attempted to be consistent in the use of Scots and English words when both are commonly used, and were commonly used then. I have noticed folk here saying ken and know, or greet and cry, in the same sentence, almost. It will just depend on the swing of the thing. A great many agricultural terms are different from one part of the country to another, especially, I think, those connected with ploughing. I do not know either the English or, say, the Fifeshire, equivalents for some of those that I use currently. Just the same, the names of the wild flowers shift from one part of the countryside to another. For scientific accuracy one should use the Latin.

Of course none of this is what people in the eighteenth century actually spoke. If anyone wants to know that, they should read Sir Walter Scott's or Susan Ferrier's eighteenth-century novels, memoirs of the time of which there are plenty, and such collections of documents and conversations as *The Lyon in Mourning*. I could have made my book people talk that way, but, because I was not actually thinking or imagining in it, that would have been artificial, a barrier between myself and them, as also between them and the reader. None of the characters are supposed in any of their reported conversations to be speaking in the Gaelic, though many of my Highlanders were bi-lingual. They would use an occasional Gaelic phrase just as they might a French one, if, as happened with many of the gentry, they were brought up to fluency in French. And now, while I am about it, I want to say a word about the Gaelic phrases which I have actually used. They are mostly phrases which I have heard, maybe said; they come easy to me. But when I find myself spelling them, it is another matter, and I want to protest, formally, against the way Gaelic is spelled and to give it as my opinion that there is no future and little enough present for a language that is written so unphonetically, and I cannot wonder at all that few Gaelic speakers can write the thing, and there is little enough written in it that is of interest to a modern-minded, ordinary man or woman. A real highbrow may get over the spelling because he sees why it has happened, historically and grammatically. But the most of the Gaelic speakers are not highbrow. I have had to keep to the respectable spelling, since those who should have done so, have not had the main guts to propose alterations. I take the word for bonny: boidheach, a lovely word and a familiar one to me, but what will my non-Gaelic speaking readers make of it? They will not know that it is pronounced 'boiach' (or 'voyach' according to the case). That horrible dh in the middle will trip them up, spoil the run of the phrase. And indeed I am hard put to it to think of a single word that is spelled according to its own lovely living sound, so that a page of Gaelic looks crooked and hard instead of soft and running like a peat burn.

In a book which has the social and political implications that this book obviously has, one's motives are not purely artistic — if such a thing is ever possible. My other motive in using the kind of language which I have in this book, is the wish that it may help those who speak and use the current Highland speech to be proud of so notable and bonny a thing — never to think that it is in any way worse than the written English of books and newspapers. I hope it may help those who naturally enliven their speech with Lowland words and phrases, to be equally proud of that, to know it is a living thing, not merely something that died with Burns. I hope that, if this book is taken as seriously by school and University teachers as some of my other historical novels have been (and I believe this one is away better as history!) it may encourage them, and the school inspectors too, to allow the children under their charge in Scotland to express themselves in spoken and written Scots of their own district. Let me remind them that correct 'Kelvinside' English is so deadly dull an instrument of expression, that it has to be enlivened some way. But the way things are, this is done with American words from the movies. I have nothing at all against American as a language, indeed I am often using it, but it is no livelier than Scots and usually less economical and succinct. We should all familiarize ourselves with as large a vocabulary as possible, it will keep our minds supple and alert for the double meanings of things. I am mostly sure that the bi-lingual West Coast children are rather more alive to verbal meanings than those who have no Gaelic.

Yet none of this was there at the beginning. I could never have written this book in the academic English of the literary tradition — Shakespeare to Virginia Woolf. Yet perhaps also if I had not been in constant touch with West Coast speech for the last five years I might not have felt I needed to write this book rather than another. If I had not worked day after day with West Highlanders, danced with them, quarrelled with them, loved them, cheated and been cheated by them, had we not been thirled to one another by common action, by kindness, by violent happiness and unhappiness, then I might have written some other book. If you go back to the why below this — why did my great-grandfather and his brother come west to 'heathen Kintyre' a century ago, to preach on the hill-sides in the teeth of the respectable Ministers and lairds? Why did the folk here listen to them? Why had Gilbert Macallum to take on the preaching after them, in barns or kitchens, Gilbert Macallum whose nephew's grandson, my pupil, should have been a poet of the West, but was killed by a German bomb in Partick? What is the knotting in this net of events between Highlands and Lowlands that has us caught, why should the fresh knot come now, timeously to its place and myself in the centre of it? The whole net is not to be seen; half of it is yet under the waves.

Notes on the various families

The family trees are taken from several family books, memoirs, etc. There are often cross-references in these, so that they can be checked up. Throughout the period of writing this book I have constantly referred to General Aylmer Haldane's book, *The Haldanes of Gleneagles*, and when I was not referring to the book I was often enough referring to him, or to his unpublished notes and family papers. Both he and I being to some extent deviationists from the family flock, we find ourselves with a certain fellow-feeling for the black sheep: Marjorie Lawson, Patrick, and others in more modern times. Nor is Aylmer the only one of my relations with whom I have talked over this book, and who are responsible, whether they know it or not, for this or that bit. Those who have helped me will understand. It is a queer business altogether, this family continuity, in time and place. And it can be used well and ill. If used well, one may perhaps be justified in trimming it into a kind of mythology. I begin to wonder now whether my grandmother, herself a Burdon Sanderson with an accurate and scientific turn of mind,·did not, in her latter years — she lived to be a hundred — amuse herself with seeing how much I, whom she loved, could be made to believe. And indeed I have always been one for believing good stories, whether they were true or not!

When I was pretty far on with this book, another knot came in the net. One of our Free French lads, a Breton, who had come to us by chance as part of the new expressing of the Auld Alliance, was going on to stay with a Miss Smythe. I realized that she was a Miss Smythe of Methven and of course a cousin — see the family tree. We wrote to one another and it turned out that she had family letters of this period which just happened to fit in. The link between us, whom I will call Jean, came of Breton-speaking parents. We were having a wee ceilidh one night·that he was here. There was a *puirt a beul* sung and all at once Jean began to sing the Breton version of it, with the very same kind of feel. I mind we danced a reel after that, and then Jean sang again, and half-way through the tune, which was an old Breton one, Willie Galbraith, fisherman and singer, joined in it, saying this was a song he had known at school. Now, there will have been no direct connection between Paimpol and Carradale, between the fishers of Newfoundland cod and the fishers of Loch Fyne herring, and yet —

But to return to the family trees: I have not indicated any relationship between the Macintoshes of Borlum and Kyllachy, though it existed and can be found in the History of the Macintoshes. It will be plain from these and would be still more so if further relationships were put in, that there was a close net-work of relationships, up from the Lothians through the north-east of Scotland. There were less close relationships between these families, who included most of the Edinburgh Whigs and Tories who held political power in the eighteenth century, and the former power-holders, the great Scoto-Norman families of the Border and south-west Scotland. Quite a number of these had already begun to marry south, into powerful landed English families. There was enough distrust and even warfare between Highlands and Lowlands to have checked intermarriage to some extent. But Gleneagles is only a short ride, even on bad roads, from the Highland line. From the Ochils we see the grand line of the Grampians, the dark clefts of the great glens; on an autumn day we suddenly smell snow and there it is, white on Ben Vorlich or Ben Ledi. We are within touch.

Actually, I have not put in more than a few names in any of the family trees. Many children died young, especially the first and last of a big family; wives died, worn out from what was considered a natural duty; there were many stepfamilies — and many kind and beloved stepmothers.

In all contemporary documents there is every variety of spelling of the surnames. I have standardized this, using the more logical form 'Macintosh' throughout, although the Brigadier, for instance, is usually spelled 'MacKintosh', which is, I think, the present more aristocratic spelling. The name simply means 'son of the leader', not, as in many Highland names, son of a particular person, in which latter case the capital letter seems to be the politer spelling. But two hundred years ago, people were less fussy about spelling, and a great deal of trouble was saved to children, grown-ups and even proof-readers.

At that time, as now in Scotland, a married woman was known as often as not by her maiden name. She was not considered quite so much her husband's property as she was in England; this is reflected in Scottish law. Her children, especially her daughters, might be known by her maiden name too, especially if she was a rather force-ful person.

Also, of course, men and women were known by their place names. And, again as in contemporary working-class Scotland, very often by nick-names. In this book, I have tried not to elaborate this too much. Patrick Haldane quite certainly was called Patrick, Peter, Pate, or Bearcrofts. I also call him by a nick-name, the Bear. This nick-name was also used of himself, by my uncle, Lord Haldane of Cloan, when writing to his mother. What kind of knot these nick-names may be, in the net of a family, is not clear to me, nor is it really my business.

I have taken a few minor liberties over dates and ages. I think I am entitled to do this, and I doubt if anyone would ever find out, but Catherine Duncan, who afterwards married James Haldane (in 1762) was certainly younger than her midshipman brother, Adam, later to become Admiral Duncan. In the interests of the reader, I have called young Captain Robert Haldane, son of John Haldane, not by his proper name, but Captain John. It was actually his elder brother, who had died young, who was called John. But two Captains Robert, even though one was in the King's Navy and the other with the East India Company, would have been too difficult.

Robert Haldane did not buy the estate of Airthrey until 1759, when he had just been elected M.P. for the boroughs of Stirling, Queensferry, etc. He was actually married in 1747, to Elizabeth Oglander, widow of a Captain Robert Holmes of the Royal Navy, but they had no children. He bought the estate of Gleneagles in 1766 from Patrick, an old man by then, and broken by the death of his brilliant son George and his only daughter. But Robert Haldane, called in the family 'The Entailer', left Gleneagles to his sister's children, and left Airthrey, which was a beautiful estate, southward facing and fertile, well planted and bonny, to his favourite nephew James 'the pyatt of Strathearn'. In my book I have imagined that

Robert had already bought Airthrey and made James his heir.

As things fell out, Airthrey was only in the family for forty years. Then the two sons of James Haldane and Catherine Duncan sold Airthrey. Two things were happening: one was the French Revolution, and the other was a corresponding religious revival in Great Britain.

This is not the place to discuss the psychic connection — even identity sometimes — between religion and politics. There are those of us whose hearts choose a certain road, and thereafter they will insist on justification by reason. Others come to their choices through reason and then through their emotions. This happens in an economic and class framework, but not with any kind of clockwork Marxist accuracy in individual cases, whatever may happen statistically. It is known how Robert Haldane came to make his decisions, and this in the main from his own *Address to the Public concerning Political Opinions*. It is fairly clear that a later generation wanted to erase any non-religious ideas which made him what he afterwards became. He had been a midshipman, and had seen something of mutiny in the British Navy, and its very understandable causes. He left the Navy when he was 22, and went to live at Airthrey and be a good husband and good landlord. His account of himself during these years was: 'I endeavoured to be decent', but he had not found that sense of worthwhileness which makes people take action.

As to so many young men in the late eighteenth century, the French Revolution appeared to James Haldane as an answer to all he had hoped for. Bliss was in that dawn to be alive. How well we know that feeling, some of us! But although less than a generation afterwards it appeared to be a false dawn to those who, to their horror, had seen Napoleon rise out of the ashes of liberty, yet we know now that this was not so. The French Revolution had ended a particular kind of privilege in France, and, still more important, the idea and image of it in other countries. It had ended the idea of people as chattels, and had made possible the idea of nationalism as a human and, paradoxically, an international good, which was to be put into words by Mazzinni. It also made inevitable the bad idea which is always the other side of a good one, and by that opened another possible choice and freedom of opinion to mankind.

Yet at the time it was a cruel blow when it became clear that the French Revolution was not all that it had been set up to be, that it was made of fallible human material. At the beginning, said Robert Haldane, 'I exulted in the prospect . . . in any company I delighted in discussing this favourite subject . . . a scene of melioration and improvement in the affairs of mankind seemed to open itself to my mind.' He was still enthusiastic when in 1794 the free holders of Perthshire met to consider the expediency of raising a volunteer corps. He spoke in strong disapproval of the war against France, saying to the Whig and Tory gentry that 'They would have been much better employed had they been meeting to consider how all abuses that were generally allowed to be such might be reformed'. The result of this was — and one wonders whether he realized it was going to be — that he was socially boycotted by all his fellow landowners. His only visitors were a few Evangelical Ministers, with whom he would discuss first politics, and then, gradually, religion. And now the bitter disappointment which came to so many of the early admirers of the Revolution fitted in completely with the doctrine of the total corruption of human nature. Yet, believing this, he was not personally discouraged, and made up his mind to sell Airthrey, and found a Mission to Bengal.

Not unnaturally, a Mission to India led by somebody who had expressed approval of Revolution was not at all a popular idea with the authorities, one of whom said 'he would rather see a band of devils in India than a band of Missionaries'. Robert had to find some other course of action. He was joined by his brother James who, like his great-uncle, was a Captain in the East India Service, and an extremely capable young man. These two at least had the courage of their convictions, and indeed one of their friends, while admiring them, regrets their lack of prudence and meekness; and indeed one sees just how maddening those two bull calves must have been to the rest of the community, butting in all over Scotland.

They set out often on foot to preach the gospel as they saw it, and against the power and privilege of the established Presbyterian Ministers throughout the length and breadth of the land, distributing tracts and setting up tabernacles. And so they came even as far as Kintyre, in a small boat, wet through, to eat ham and eggs in the kitchen of the same inn at Clonnaig, I think, at which the funeral party and I stopped for tea on our walk back through the snowdrifts from Tarbert in the unprecedented winter of 1942. And here they preached to the great-grandfathers of my friends, men who followed the new teaching, and for that were dispossessed of their crofts. Nothing so uncomfortable ever happened to Robert and James, nor to their families. Things may be more equal yet.

To pass to another matter, I have really no historical reason for making Lachlan Macintosh of Kyllachy out as the villain of my book. After the '15 he and his father *did* raise money on the lands of Kyllachy and Moril. But that is all there is to it. He may have been an honest, decent man, not even good-looking for that matter. He died unmarried. But some way he slipped into his present position in this book. Somebody had to bear the burden of a rather typically Highland set-up which had tilted the wrong way.

Another liberty I have taken was to make Murray of Ochtertyre some ten years younger than he actually was.

To show the family ties-up, let me consider the complexities of the Dundas relationships, and let me hope I manage to get them right! In June 1747, there were two powerful men in Edinburgh politics, both being Robert Dundas, though the father would no doubt always be referred to as Arniston. They were both anti-Argyll, Tory in a sense, though not Jacobite. The father had been in political opposition to Forbes of Culloden, who had succeeded him as Lord Advocate in 1725, and also, in common with most other respectable people (but not all) to Patrick Haldane. Not that such political opposition would stop people from drinking at the same taverns or flirting with the same ladies, or perhaps taking bribes from the same clients, in a society as limited and polite as that of eighteenth-century Scotland. Probably father and son had the same office and clerks. The father, Dundas of Arniston, was at this time a Judge of the Court of Session and was made Lord President, in succession to Forbes of Culloden, a year later and against the wishes of the Duke of Argyll.

His son Robert, by his first wife, had been solicitor-general until the year before, had now resigned, but was to be Lord Advocate later. Both were quick, eloquent, ambitious, perhaps fundamentally lazy people, excellent company, but without the sometimes intolerable serious-mindedness of the Haldanes. Both married twice and had numbers of children, though some died young. The father, Arniston, was now married to his second wife, a Gordon. One of the sons of this marriage, only three years old at the time of my book, was to be Lord Melville, Pitt's friend, the most powerful man in Scotland for thirty years, I would not say altogether for Scotland's good, nor even for the good of Europe. One of his daughters, by his first wife, married Bob Strange's son, James — neither born nor begotten at the date of my book — and was grandmother to my mother's father.

Meanwhile, the son, Robert Dundas, was married to his first wife; a daughter of this marriage was, thirty years later, to marry Adam Duncan, then I think, already an Admiral.

The Dundas family were already related to the Haldanes; some hundred years before, James Dundas of Arniston had married Mary Home, daughter of the beautiful Jane Haldane. No doubt they were also related to practically all the other families mentioned in this book!

Just to finish it up nicely, I would mention that, Scotland still being a small place, I discovered lately since that my cousin Philip Dundas was farming within eighteen miles of me, and it is fine to have a cousin as a partner at a ram sale or a reel.

There is one interesting point about the ordinary names. In the *Annals of Auchterarder*, which is my main source for the burning, the lists of people hurt and claiming compensation contains names, most of which can still be found in and around Auchterarder, Blackford, Dunning and so on. They were tradesmen, farmers, Ministers and the like; they do the same kind of things still, though the spelling of their names has settled down. There are very few Highland names amongst them. Probably the same, decent, well-doing, not over-ambitious families settled in these kind of townships, sometimes sending a lad or lass of parts into the more learned professions, sometimes sending a black sheep or more adventurous one to Canada or some far place. But, if you were to take the names in a place in Kintyre, such as Carradale, you would find far less continuity. In the Highlands there has been less settling down, until recently, and a tremendous shifting of population during the nineteenth century, at the times of the clearances. In this village of Carradale, you would no doubt have found MacMillans, MacDonalds, Campbells, probably MacKinnons and MacAlisters, perhaps Macintosh, McDougall, Ferguson and the like. But many are incomers from Ayrshire during the last hundred and fifty years, the farmers especially; there would have been no Clan Paterson then, nor any Semples.

All this, as you see, is very recent history. The families of whom I write were living in the same civilization as that into which we were all born — but not, perhaps, that in which we find ourselves now. A few lifetimes will cover the stretch between now and then. I remember well my old 'cousin Annie', grand-daughter of Mr. Robert Strange in this book. My uncle tells me how, as a wee boy, he was used to go over and visit the elderly wife of one of the estatemen at Cloan — Cloanden in those days. She would give him pieces with brown sugar and tell him stories of her own childhood and how she could mind on an old woman who had been herself a wee lassie at the time of the battle of Sheriffmuir. An English soldier had come to her father's farm to have the wound on his arm dressed, and this man had bidden the wee one to go forth from the kitchen, since it was no sight for a lass bairn. Thus there are three lifetimes only between now and then, and they, some way, seeming shorter and more of a piece than one's own tangled and buffeted lifetime in this century. Or again, my grandmother, as a girl, had walked arm in arm down Prince's Street with a General who had lost the other arm in the Peninsular Wars, and she told me once how she had seen an old lady, who as a young actress had been Goddess of Liberty in revolutionary Paris, wheeled in a bath-chair at some English health resort. But what will be the strangest things which we shall remember and speak of to our grandchildren?

Note on Agriculture

The details of Agriculture in this book come from various sources, and from my own observations. The detailed *1799 Board of Agriculture Report on Perthshire* goes into methods, including those which were practised forty or fifty years earlier. There is a great deal about contemporary agriculture in *Scotland and Scotsmen in the Eighteenth Century*, and of course in many periodicals. The *Essay on Ways and Means of Enclosing* by A Lover of his Country (actually Macintosh of Borlum, William's father) is on and around agriculture; I speak of it in more detail later on in the Notes on Part II. There are other contemporary books or pamphlets, among them the *Letters of John Cockburn of Ormiston to His Gardener 1727-1743*. He was George's uncle and there is some more about him later on. Throughout, the detail on flax-growing and linen-dressing comes from *The Interest of Scotland Considered*, a pamphlet by Patrick Lindsay (though it was published anonymously), dated 1733. There is also much information in such books as Hamilton's *The Industrial Revolution in Scotland*, Graham's *Social Life of Scotland in the Eighteenth Century* and several of Miss Grant's books. One can be checked up from another.

As I show in this book (pages 43 and 109), land was worked on the run-rig system in Scotland up to the early eighteenth century. That is to say, there was a common field. In the middle would be a wee township where the tenants lived, crowded with their beasts into low and miserable buildings of stone and mud. Round this was the infield, almost always over-cropped. It had no dunging at all, and of course there were no artificials, yet it would have to take two crops running of oats or bere. The outfield, beyond it, would have the common herd of cattle folded on it after harvest, but would be made to bear four or five cereal crops running, so that the last one gave back little more than seed. The infield was scored with raw ditches, down to the rock itself between the individual rigs, for each man would dig down to get new turfs for his own strip.

The worse the land, the worse the system of the common field worked. Every man was always trying to steal a piece more of earth to put on to his own strip. The strips would be piled up, so that the ditches between would act as drains, but especially in a dry year, it would be very difficult to get a decent crop off the slopes. Yet it did work fairly well on good deep land, and was practised in some parts of England with fair success up to last century (see Walter Rose's *Good Neighbours*). Quite obviously, it could work, if farmed intelligently by people who were not hard pressed to the point of destroying the fertility of the lands.

With a fair amount of planning by some kind of managing committee, something of the kind could work still over some kinds of farming. In many parts of Scotland, including this, folk who have no land of their own will take a drill or two of potatoes in some farmer's field, in return for help with planting and lifting; the next year their bit of land will be in another field, so that it is a kind of strip system. I myself usually have a few neighbours taking drills of my potato land. In return they help me with planting and lifting, and it suits us all.

One difficulty about the original strip system was that it meant that the land was always ploughed one way. When the system was broken up, the land was cross-ploughed, filling in or partly filling in the ditches, and this in itself was good for the land. Yet one can still see the marks of the old rigs in many fields.

Methods and instruments change together, and it is rather hard to say which change first. It was not possible to have anything but the common field system until fields could be enclosed and fenced in some way. The landlords who cared most for the land and the restoration of its fertility, were, above all, keen on enclosing. Yet that often meant hardship, and the families who had got along somehow on the common field system with a little grain and a cow or two in the common herd, had no place under the new dispensation. As the land grew more fertile, so it produced cash crops as well as subsistence crops, and rents came to be paid in money instead of in kind, as the old way was, when, for instance, the land was often let on steelbow tenure, a kind of share-cropping.

So long as there was one common herd, it was very difficult to improve the breed of cattle — and the same was true of poultry or sheep. But once you had enclosing and, with it, fields put aside for the growing of winter keep, first hay and then turnips, rapid improvement was possible. Yet, after a generation or so, there must have been many fewer owners of cattle, though the new owners had far better herds, and the output of beef was certainly greater and of much better quality. It was, in fact, the age-old problem of efficiency or individualism.

Take, for instance, the methods of agricultural transport. Up to the early eighteenth century most farm carting was done in sledges, then came the solid-wheeled carts. But harness, in common with almost all agricultural implements, was made at home. Horse collars would be straw or rushes as in Uist now. There would be pack saddles, so that horses could carry sacks, but only the rich had riding saddles; country folk would just ride on a sod with a bit of plaid thrown over it.

Now, what happened in Perthshire was this: in 1747 the gentlemen got together to make better roads. The leaders were Smythe of Methven, who was a cousin of the Haldanes, and George Drummond of Blair, a fine, respectable, rather hot-tempered man, but there was a window dressing of Dukes and such. What is not quite clear is whether the better roads were followed by better carts with spoked wheels, or whether it was that the ownership of better carts — probably imported from the south — put the idea of better roads into the lairds' heads. But one result was that the old custom of good neighbouring over the lending of beasts and rough carts, gave place to the hiring of these new good ones that had cost money. The whole thing meant changes and movement and a breaking of the crust of custom.

Another thing which happened in eighteenth-century Scotland was that many of the lairds brought in English farm servants, some of whom got on well enough — for there was no enmity between the two countries unless it was forced from above. They needed to be patient though. The gentleman farmers, such as Lord Kames, took too much out of books, and the books were not written from northern experience. To begin with, they sowed their crops and did every other thing at the English seasons, and their neighbours and tenants thought them daft. But they found after a time that they could not neglect the Tids, the traditional times of ploughing and sowing, nor were their English agricultural implements better than the Scottish ones. They went back to the traditional shapes again, but with the difference that they were well and carefully made instead of being put together somehow out of whatever material could be come by.

For nearly two centuries since then we have gone on with the same type of instrument that was brought in when the run-rig system was broken up and private farming took the place of communal farming. But now we are faced with a different type of instrument, too large for the private farmer. This is going to make changes, in fact it has done so already. Farmers have had to come together to work the Government threshers, which need a team of twelve or fourteen men. And more and more farmers hire the various large-scale tractor outfits either from the Department of Agriculture or from private firms. Hill reclamation and bracken cutting can only be done on a large scale. I believe that grass drying, if it really comes to the Highlands, where we have such superb grass, will also mean communal methods, for it would be fantastic for each farm to have a separate dryer.

Now that the Department of Agriculture provide good bulls, gradually raising the standard of croft cattle, the common grazing of the crofting townships makes sense. Yet crofters still stick to the small strips of corn and potatoes; the tractor outfit is used, but in the most unsuitable and uneconomic way. This is a stupid form of conservatism. Yet sometimes the farmer's conservative ways are due to a lengthy weighing-up process, in which, for instance, a saving of time and heavy labour (as with tractor ploughing) has to be balanced against a loss of skill and the intuitive experience which is really a synthesis, taking place below the level of thought, of a quantity of small facts. It is this local intuition acquired over years, which a newcomer may not have, and which makes him impatient of the old-timer, ruminating at a gate.

It is clear that really good horse-ploughing by a man who has done it all his life, who has perhaps had the pleasure and excitement of the ploughing matches — the poplar twigs for his lucky marks — will always be better than tractor-ploughing. It will look bonnier and it will grow a better and more even crop when the corn is sowed straight on to the ploughed land. But is this enough? In the same time that a skilled man takes to plough one acre with a pair of horses, a semi-skilled man can plough between five and ten times as much with a tractor, and an unskilled man or girl can disc it in a matter of hours. This gives a different type of seed bed for a cereal crop, but the end results are fully as satisfactory, while, for a green crop, it is one stage on beyond ploughing. It means also that it is worth using a tractor on marginal land that would not have been worth slow horse-ploughing. Of course, the initial expense of a tractor and gear is more than that for a good pair and gear. But a tractor is never tired, and never (unfortunately perhaps) in foal. Nor does it produce dung, though paraffin and petrol are as expensive as oats; so a tractor farm must use more artificials. But, by hiring a tractor outfit for his major farm operations, a farmer can save himself the keep of a pair, and probably at least one skilled man.

There, of course, is one of the snags. Saving of time and heavy labour is surely good, but that skill and experience should be wasted is not so good. The MacKinnons up the glen, who used to win the ploughing matches, might say it was bad. It is always possible that we are doing something which will not look so well a couple of centuries on.

At the time of my book, the improvers in Scotland were at least free of the swarm of advertisers buzzing at the farmer out of the pages of his weekly papers, chivvying him, perhaps for his good, but certainly for their own. Other kinds of compulsion were put upon the eighteenth-century farmer and tenant. I am not speaking here of the terrible compulsion of sheep, which destroyed the small arable farming of the crofting glens. That has had its sequel, and all the authorities seem to be agreed that there has been heavy over-grazing by sheep on almost all the hill country in Scotland. Disease is getting too common; so are the worse sort of grasses, which the sheep encourage. So is bracken, which the black cattle used to trample. But, apart from that, there were very real farming improvements, which were meant to help the farmer as much as the landlord. Yet they were not always welcome. Potatoes are grown almost everywhere now, but when seed potatoes were first brought to south Uist in 1743, the crofters refused to plant them until they had been imprisoned by their chief and only let out when they said they would put the things in. When it came to the back-end they brought them to his door, saying he could force them to plant the potatoes, but not to eat them.

Turnips are part of the Scottish landscape now, and that both through sight and smell. But they were only introduced some two centuries ago. I may have slightly ante-dated the introduction of turnips to the Inverness neighbourhood (page 73), but it was about then. Turnip culture was pushed by the Society of Improvers in the knowledge of Agriculture in Scotland. At first they were sown broadcast and hand-hoed, but the Society suggested that it was better to drill and horse-hoe, as is done now except, to be sure, in the most up-to-date farms where horses are outmoded. No doubt they must have been thinned by hand; but I do not think it was realized at first how important they were simply as a cleaning crop. The main thing for Scotland was winter keep for the beasts. In the mid-eighteenth century the cattle had a hard time surviving to spring, when they were taken out to the grass, quite literally lifted, farmers and crofters going round together to lift one another's beasts to their feet. Sown grass for hay started in Scotland at about the same time as turnips, and gradually, as farmers began to count on winter feeding of hay and turnips as well as straw, they gave up feeding on whins, and the stone whin mills which crushed the prickles fell out of use.

The Society of Improvers in the knowledge of Agriculture in Scotland was founded in 1725. In my book, Kirstie speaks as though it were still to the fore, but I think it must have come to an end during the '45, with all the difficulties of communication, and the diversion of energy into politics. Yet one or another of the societies which came after it might have started by then. It had over three hundred members. Gentlemen paid five shillings annually, but farmers and gardeners could join free. The Committee of twenty-five members was divided into reporting sections. There was much correspondence, and members were asked to send up reports of how they managed their own farms. Questions were received and answers sent out, and so were sets of directions on points of husbandry and cattle raising. Much of it seems very sound, though some of it is more appropriate to war than to peace, since at that time, as here during the war years, there were no imported fertilizers or foodstuffs. They were also interested in linen making and fisheries and even in distilleries.

There was a considerable social side to it, meetings and meals and so forth. An Irish Society had been set up soon after. And when it came to an end, other similar societies were set up since they met a real need. Some of them gave prizes. The Highland and Agricultural Society, founded in 1784, had the Duke of Argyll as President. There were two chaplains; one preached in English (his name was Mr. Tough), and the other in Gaelic; but there was only one piper, Mr. John M'Arthur, an Edinburgh grocer. At one of the earliest meetings Duncan Ban M'Intyre sang a song of his own composition about the restitution of the forfeited estates.

There is a great deal of fascinating information about all this in Ramsay's *History of the Highland and Agricultural Society of Scotland*, but the Transactions of the Society are still more interesting. They show that by the mid-nineteenth century, half-way between my book and now, a great deal of good, detailed, semi-scientific research work was being done, for instance on the breeding of wheat. But there was always the difficulty of 'breeding true' at a time when the pure scientists were more interested in physics and chemistry and the general business of making larger guns and faster railway trains, than in biology, still less in plant genetics. So much of the work done by the intelligent farmers, landlords or factors, could not be carried through nor made practical. The theory which would have made sense of it had not yet met the economic conditions and the moment of time when it could come to birth, although the basic facts had been discovered by an Abbé in Bruno in Czechoslovakia. But the Abbé Mendel had been dead for sixteen years when his paper was rediscovered and his original experiments on sweet peas done all over again. For such things will not take effect on society before society is prepared to receive them.

Note on Gleneagles

For all the information about Gleneagles, both house and policies, I would like to thank my cousins, of the elder branch, the Chinnery Haldanes (see Genealogical Table) who are living at Gleneagles now, and who have taken much trouble to help me. I have, of course, wandered round several times since the start of the book, but I have also worked from the drawings which my cousin Katherine made for me. The plan of the house is now somewhat different; originally the rooms all opened into one another, as in a modern Scandinavian house; but passages were made later on.

Again, my cousin Brodrick Chinnery Haldane made some notes about the house and policies in his later years, and his son has very kindly put them at my disposal; we have talked them over together. He says: 'In the grounds to the back of the house there are remains of extensive draining, which from the nature of the ground and its probable value when draining, would not seem to have been a sound commercial proposition. The work looks to me more like work which had been undertaken by idle men, to keep them employed. Possibly in the unsettled times in the early eighteenth century there was at Gleneagles a small number of military, for use in emergency raids by Highlanders, etc. These men would naturally have a good deal of idle time, which was perhaps occupied in such work as draining, which an ordinary proprietor could not have afforded to undertake.' He also says: 'The course of the burn above the house shows signs of having been altered. Probably in old days this burn wandered over the whole of the glen, and later was controlled by having a definite channel made for it.' I refer to this in Chapter v of Part II. None of us are quite certain what the lay-out was in 1747. The lime avenue probably dates back to then, and there is one very old chestnut by the end of the eastern and older half of the house. Certainly the road up Gleneagles to Glen Devon went where the old road is still, to the west of the house. Instead of going on down the main glen of the Devon between the Ochils, it turned into the hills to the west, by Frandie, where the reservoir is now; this would make a much steeper road, presumably connecting the great camp at Ardoch which must have been a headquarters for the Roman Army of occupation, with the south. A short, steep road does for travellers or pack beasts: internal combustion engines and rubber tyres need flatter gradients and don't worry much about mileage: hence increasing expense of modernizing road systems in hilly countries the like of Scotland. Should we try and cut this out and go straight for air and sea transport, concentrating on airports and harbours?

From what remains at present, it is clear that there were extensive schemes of planting, roads, raised ground and so on, all round Gleneagles, especially to the north of the house. There was also a scheme of thorn hedges and sitting out places, from which the view could be enjoyed, whilst those resting under the milk-white thorn were also protected from the cold blasts, thus combining comfort with good taste. Originally the castle mound was an island in a shallow loch which must have been drained, producing good fields and doubtless improved health for everyone. Most likely it was intended to have a front door in the middle section of the house, which was never built, although the two end blocks were; the lime avenue would have been in connection with this, and the two stone pillars, which now stand rather meaninglessly at the entrance to the chapel, were probably meant to head the avenue. Probably Mungo erected them first, and they were moved to the chapel by George Cockburn or some later owner, when the whole centre scheme was abandoned, as it presumably was after Patrick had to sell the place.

One has to think of all this type of work being done by ill-paid and underfed men with home-made and inefficient tools. Some would have been unpaid work, a 'servitude', part of the rent. Although workers were paid so badly, the work went very slowly, and the whole job might be fairly expensive; almost all the Scots lairds, except the greatest, were living from hand to mouth, with very little actual money to come and go on. And in all estate records you will see a great to-do about any kind of improvements. In fact, most of the keenest improvers ran heavily into debt. You will see one instance after another of an estate where in one generation there was a great deal of 'improvement', some strictly practical and agricultural, and others for the sake of the amenities, but in the next generation, there would be heavy debts and perhaps a sale. Scotland, bonny as she is, is an ill land for any single person to wrestle with and to try out improvements on; he will get no quick return, and maybe the weather to ruin all. Nowadays the few landlords who have a great deal of money to spend on something which does not pay, tend to prefer other and more immediately gratifying ways of spending it. This sort of large-scale agricultural improvement, including the draining, ploughing and re-seeding of hill land that has gone back to bracken and rushes, will have to be done through one form or another of public ownership, and with expensive machinery which can only pay for itself if it is being used constantly and methodically over a large area of land.

When I was a child, I was always fascinated by the very odd lay-out of Gleneagles, as well as by the remains of the original water-closet. Those who came to admire and possibly use it, in earlier times, referred to it (and its local imitations) as a 'gleneggies'. Old

Lord Camperdown, the last of that line to own Gleneagles and an immensely staunch Conservative, once gave me, when I was at Cloan recovering from whooping cough, a whole cucumber and, I think, two peaches, only I don't remember them so well. It was the first time I ever had a whole cucumber to myself, and I ate it all: Freudians please note.

Note on Prices

I think what one has to bear in mind when considering eighteenth-century prices, is that by modern notions, home produced things were cheap and imported things were dear, except for wine and spirits, which were somewhat cheaper because of having smaller excise duties on them than they have now. Of course, direct taxation was negligible compared with what it is to-day. Amongst the cheap things were services, whether those of a cook, a ploughman, a dancing master, a doctor or a lawyer. Many people lived comparatively cheaply by not using imported things, or scarcely at all. Most households would use a little sugar, a little tea, and a very little of some of the imported spices. But if they drank ale or whisky, wore wool or linen and ate home-grown meat, cheese, cereals, vegetables and fruit, and home-caught fish, then living was not dear. But you could not export unless you imported, at any rate when the thing was done on at all a large scale. So, if you were going to have export industries, you had also to consume imports. I doubt if people understood that; quite a number of Americans don't seem to even now.

This helps us to understand real prices. (We must of course always be sure whether they are given in sterling or in Scots. To get the value in sterling, divide the apparent Scots value by twelve: that is to say a Scots shilling was worth a penny sterling. But, by the mid-eighteenth century, most prices were written in sterling.) Salaries were anything from a seventh to a tenth of what they are now. With that, however, prices of staple foods, such as mutton, ham, hens, butter, cheese, ale or beer, were lower in about the same proportion. White bread was very expensive, but was still only eaten as a luxury. I cannot find a price for oatmeal, but I think it was always cheap. Everybody took porridge in some form. Wages were rather lower, especially women's wages or those of unskilled rural workers, though not much less in proportion than they were in the 1930s.

However, indoor servants were very heavily tipped; an upper-class servant might expect to get something like a fifth of his or her wages in 'drink-money'. The nurse seems always to have been the main person to be tipped at christenings, and perhaps on other visits between married ladies. Lady Grisell Baillie has constant references to 'drink mony to nurs', 'for nurs and christining', and so on. Most servants, except the casual farm workers, had clothing given to them as well, including shoes. I think this would add up to something very like modern wages, when multiplied by seven.

Some home-grown things were fantastically cheap. Oysters were two shillings a barrel at the beginning of the eighteenth century. Salmon was much cheaper, in proportion, than herrings. Garden fruit was rather dear. The Introduction and Appendices to *The Household Book of Lady Grisell Baillie*, written by Robert Scott-Moncrieff, are extremely interesting and enlightening, and show the proportionate amounts spent on various classes of things by this large but not very extravagant household.

Tobacco at something like 1s. 6d. a lb does not seem expensive, even when multiplied by seven, but the modern price is mostly taxation. Coal was cheaper than it is now if you lived anywhere near the pits, though the London price of £1 10s. to £2 a ton works out very dear when you begin to multiply it.

Some imported things, such as rice or oranges, vary very much from year to year. So do tea and coffee. Game was not very dear, and of course far more plentiful. It is constantly mentioned in the Prince's account books. Three muir fowl (in March) 1s., or a shilling for a pair of partridges.

NOTES ON CHAPTER I

Page 21

Most of the descriptions of clothes are checked up from the dresses in various books, especially *Lady Grisell Baillie's House Book*. Those who like to picture the people in a book should remember that Scottish fashions were several years behind the London ones, especially in country districts where clothes were still made primarily for use and to last.

Page 27

I have ante-dated by about twenty years, the introduction of black-faced sheep. The Ochils were great sheep country. By 1795 (the date of the Board of Agriculture report on Perthshire) it was thought that there were some 50,000 sheep on them. According to this report, one of the Perthshire authorities on sheep was Mr. Haldane of Gleneagles; this was George (Cockburn) Haldane, who would appear from the family records to have been a bad manager, a vain and rather stupid man; for instance he had a claim drawn up to the old earldom of Lennox, so as to increase his prestige in the country. Possibly his imported English and foreign sheep were another bid for local importance, or perhaps he wasn't really as bad as the rest of the family made out. At least he seems to have paid over the compensation money to the heirs of the folk who were killed or had their houses burnt on them, at the time of the burning of Auchterarder, when, some sixty years after it had all happened, the British Government reluctantly admitted that these miserable Scots had some claim on them: though it was heavily contested and considerable parts of the sum involved went to the lawyers.

Page 28

It will be remembered that Forbes of Culloden, the Lord President who was so deeply opposed to tea-drinking amongst the lower classes, was owner of the famous Ferintosh distillery. This had been raided by the Highlanders in 1689, after which the Government — of Scotland — passed a special Act, farming out the yearly Excise of the Ferintosh lands to Forbes for about £22. The years went by, and there came a time when the annual profit was reckoned at about £18,000. After the Union and the establishment of the Board of Excise, there was considerable feeling about this in Treasury circles. But Forbes of Culloden was still the owner in 1747. A pity he did not realize that tea would never get the better of whisky in Scotland: he could have saved himself the worry. See *Culloden Papers*, Menary's *Life of Duncan Forbes of Culloden* and Neil Gunn's *Whisky and Scotland*.

Page 31

The family motto is 'Suffer' not 'Supper' as we all used to think from seeing it on the plates.

Page 32

An English view of the Lords of Session in 1747 might not come amiss here. 'What follows is my opinion in relation to the whole: Erskine of Dun, a Jacobite: Elliott of Minto, a bad man: Dalrymple of Drummore the same: Pringle of Haining remarkable for nothing: Frazier of Shichen a good man but no lawyer: Farqhason of Kileawan the same: Campbell of Monzie a sad fellow in all respects: Grant of Elchies the best lawyer on the bench, but a Grant: Sinclair of Muckle I know nothing of: Robert Dondas of Arniston well spoke of but a violent patriot: Lord Lever a man of fair character: Erskine of Sinwell a Vicar of Bray: Boyle of Showalton, the last made, your Grace must know.' This is in a letter from the second Earl of Albermarle who was Commander-in-Chief in north Britain to the Duke of Newcastle. Albermarle was pure Dutch, his father and mother having come over with William of Orange, so perhaps it was a Dutch view after all.

NOTES ON CHAPTER II

Page 35

Some of the Jacobite prisoners who were wounded and probably in the way, were burnt alive by Cumberland's soldiers. At the time, people were profoundly shocked by this: war was not yet total, but supposed to be still gentlemanly.

Page 36

I very much doubt whether a man in William's position would have had to give up his sword. I am not sure of the property qualifications at this time, but he would probably have been qualified to exercise the parliamentary franchise, and such people were exempt. No doubt he might never have got back the claymore he wore in the '15, and he might have been well advised not to wear a sword when he was first back in Scotland. But once he was into his estate, he would have been beyond the Act, unless he had kept clear of wearing one for some other reason, whether of sense or of sympathy. I am just not sure whether or not he would have had to give up everything in the nature of guns. The Act of 1746 was somewhat stiffer than its predecessor, and more strictly carried out. The provisions against the wearing of tartan would scarcely have been enforced until later in 1747.

Page 37

By this time things bore very hardly on the Episcopal Church in Scotland. Certainly, the clergy were mostly Jacobites; many of them were Gaelic speaking and could genuinely minister to a congregation in the Highlands which might be legally forced to sit under an official Presbyterian preaching in a language they could scarcely understand. No doubt a few Episcopalian clergy were sheltered by Highland families which left them in the rather awkward position of chaplains; but the meeting-houses in Edinburgh were all closed, many others were destroyed, and it was illegal to preach to a public congregation of more than five.

Page 40

Mashlum is a mixture of beans and oats, sown together, and used as feed, sometimes cooked and given hot to the beasts, though this is rare now. It is seldom grown as a crop except by old-fashioned Highland farmers. Most of us use other mixtures for green feed. Hatted kit was made with new milk, butter-milk, cream and sugar.

Page 41

The Innerpeffray public library, the first in Scotland, and now one of the tiniest, is still there. But only relations of the Great Marquis, Montrose, can have out and handle his Bible and sword.

Page 43

Rents, of course, were still paid largely in kind, and the 'kain hens' brought in by the tenants were proverbially tough eating.

Page 45

I came across this story of Sir John Erskine's slave and the brass ring which was caught in a fishing net in the Firth of Forth and brought up many years after, in Tom Johnston's *History of the Working Classes in Scotland*; I did not then know that the slave owner was any relation of my own. The ring is now exhibit No. M R 3 in the National Museum of Antiquities, Edinburgh.

Page 47

For those who are considering the social set-up of Scotland, it is essential to remember that at this time, that is to say at the recognizable dawn of the times we ourselves are living in, there was no class barrier against trade. It came later on, maybe from England, but in the eighteenth century there was no 'leisure class' shame at working with one's hands. Some were very successful, like my own relation, Lindsay the upholsterer, who became Lord Provost of Edinburgh;

his family were good enough and his wife an Earl's daughter. Others, through ill luck or incompetence, dropped in the scale, but this way we are mostly all related in Scotland, whether rich or poor, which is no bad thing. I can't help thinking that when Argyll's brother, Lord Islay, wrote: 'Bread can certainly be made without yeast, I know how to do it myself', he *did* know. Was this un-Greek attitude towards work shared by other European countries? — Holland? Switzerland? It reminds me a little of the social feeling in Czechoslovakia.

Page 47

It is extraordinary how duck-like a cultured English voice sounds, after one has been living for a time among Scottish voices.

Page 48

Adam Duncan grew up to be a great sailor, known to history as Admiral Duncan.

NOTES ON CHAPTER III

Page 55

What I have hinted at here, seems to be worth working out, especially for those who are planning for Scotland. You will find it, somewhat differently expressed, and a stage farther on, in some of Neil Gunn's books, especially *The Serpent*. And in its modern application you will find aspects of it worked out in the chapter on Herring Fishing by D. Macintosh and the chapter on Rural Reconstruction by myself, in *The New Scotland*, and in the Lewis Association Reports. I think it also applies to most crofters' associations.

In this connection, too, it is worth thinking of the Clydeside, and Glasgow itself, not as an industrial centre and port with appropriate industrial tentacles in the directions of coal and shipping, but rather as the edge of the Highlands: the deep, Clyde-filled glen which held up the rush southwards of the dispossessed, piling them up on to one another, body over yet moving body, as stampeded sheep pile up in some far narrower glen, or the mailed knights and horses piled up in the glen of Bannockburn. The Highland dispossessed, with even their religion of origin taken from them, were joined by other Celts, the dispossessed Irish, but these last still with their religion. Such betrayed people will be naturally 'agin the Government'. How at all would the Clyde be anything but Red?

But if the north bank of the Clyde is Highland, the south bank is Lowland, the contact there is with weaving and mines. Keir Hardie was an Ayrshire man; he began and led the I.L.P. whose great days were Glasgow days. The mixture has never quite coalesced, nor has either side made much effort to understand the other. Lack of this understanding has induced the Labour Party in Scotland to behave from time to time with a really remarkable stupidity and tactlessness.

But the hierarchies of Transport House do not really fit into the Clydeside pattern. We still have our anarchists and there are still almost as many minority socialist parties holding meetings and putting out publications as there are minority Protestant Churches. The tradition of both Kirk Sessions and ceilidh lend themselves to doctrinaire arguings. Probably Marxism has found a readier home on Clydeside than anywhere in England (it is arguable that the English feel more deeply and talk less than the Scots). Yes, we like the talk fine; some of the folk who have most notably wasted their own and other people's lives by heady talk, have been from here-abouts. Yet in the end we grow impatient, since, unlike the Irish, the Highland Celts are at bottom disconcertingly, even unpleasantly, practical. The class war in Glasgow was organized in a skilled, practical and even disciplined way. There are plenty on Clydeside to remember John MacLean, though his published speeches read as badly as forgotten sermons. It is at least likely that the organization of Shop Stewards would not have appeared odd to a Highlander of two hundred years before.

I know Edinburgh well enough. I feel easy there in my birthplace, the beautiful northern city, the half alive, emptied capital, the lilac-smelling squares of the New Town, the great amethyst shadow of the Castle Rock. Yet now, surely, I know Glasgow better. And I am always in two minds about this Glasgow. Edinburgh has two faces, one of beauty and order and the possibility of civilization: the other of conservatism and the dead hand — a little enthusiasm over the preservation of past beauty but none over the creation of new beauty along new lines. And Glasgow also has two faces. Neither is of beauty or order. It is a disgustingly ugly town, a huddle of dirty buildings trying to outdo one another and not succeeding, an over-grown village with no decent architecture except Blythwood Square and a few half-forgotten terraces, its ancient buildings hardly to be seen through the mess and squalor that surrounds them. Glasgow, 'the most uniform and prettiest' town that Burt saw on his eighteenth-

434

century tour! The population is as ugly as the buildings. Walk down the Gallowgate; notice how many children you see with obvious rickets, impetigo or heads close clipped for lice, see the wild, slippered sluts, not caring any more to look decent! There is something queerly inappropriate about their bobbed heads, since shortened hair should either be elegantly dressed or else glow and wave with brushing; they have no money for hair-dressing, no energy for brushing; they went down with their men into the hell of unemployment and vile housing. They do not speak any real variety of Scots, but a blurred, debased English, or — since 1942 — American. They lost everything, even the courage and solidarity that stopped London from panicking desperately during the blitzes, as Glasgow panicked in 1942. The other thing that will give you a good scunner in Glasgow is any place where the prosperous Glasgow businessmen congregate to eat — or drink. They have full as little use for beauty as those out of whose bodies the profits were made.

But yet through all one's anger against Glasgow, there is the other side. It is alive, it is full of hope and people wanting to be educated, wanting to try out something new, even though they don't rightly know what it is. And it is friendly — dirty and friendly and hospitable as a great slum tenement building or a Highland clan stronghold two hundred years ago. And it might be great and beautiful.

I think these two faces are the real two faces of Scotland. They have puzzled and bothered and angered observers for some while, and most of all observers who were themselves Scots. As a nation we have been in contact with the main body of European civilization, and have produced our own version of it; for civilization is a general thing, as indivisible as peace — or war — but manifesting itself differently in different nations or groups with varying historical and economic backgrounds. But, while the Lowlands had fairly continuous cultural intercourse with Europe, mainly through France and England, the Highlands, originally part of the first millennium A.D. European civilization, were cut off and had to develop mainly on their own, scarcely feeling the impact of the Renaissance, still less of the French Revolution. The Lowlands, on the other hand, though much more affected by Europe, deliberately cut themselves off from certain forms of cultural expression on religious grounds. Hence a patchiness and narrowness of culture. Add to this poverty and a going-under to poverty which does not always happen; it has not happened in Canada and New Zealand where poor Scots have built up a civilized community. But out there is was possible for man to get the better of his environment, as it has not been possible, so far, either in a Glasgow slum or in a western island with poor soil, difficult weather, and transport if any by MacBrayne. It was possible out there for folk to be proud of being Scots, as it is hard to be proud in many parts of Scotland — so far. The emigrants, for the most part, were newly set free from the tyranny of landowners who had evicted them or their relations; those who remained were either under the same tyranny, though a weakening one, or under a new industrial tyranny, which could even less be struggled against.

Yet the Scots communities in the Dominions, though they have a high standard of living, have produced little in the way of culture. This may be because they come from the Highlands, which, as I have just pointed out, were cut off from Europe, or else because they came from the most strictly Presbyterian parts of the Lowlands, where 'art' was a thing suspect.

Meanwhile we in Scotland are in a pretty bad mess. I would not say this if I did not want so desperately to put it right and if I did not see — or think I see — a way out. I would not hate if I did not love. There are times I find Scotland intolerably savage and mannerless, for all the good manners of the 'old-fashioned' here and there. And even the worse-mannered, the poor or moneyed savages of city or country, have an amazing complacency and self-conceit, a national conceit too that makes one feel God help Scotland if they, as they think, are typical! But the anger one feels is the same anger one might have against one's own family, against oneself in the rare moments when one looks at oneself truthfully. It is, I hope, creative anger and I commend it to other Scots or near-Scots.

Can we, somehow, get the best of Glasgow and the best of Edinburgh and fuse them? Would the half-dead beauty of Edinburgh come alive if it were a capital again? If we could let life and anger loose in the settled dust of the Parliament House? Can the angry and fighting minority in Glasgow break and change and remake it? Can the Highlands break loose from the past and get into contact again with the rest of Europe and make their own statement, in life and in art, of its civilization? Now is the time when everything is changing and being remade.

There could be a Highland contribution. By now the pressure of competition, on the top of continuous betrayal by landowners and leaders whom they trusted, has made the Highlander fully as suspicious and hard and individualist as any other member of capitalist society. And maybe a better liar — this is part of his hardness, protecting a heart that can be over soft. In the country, those that have had initiative have either been heavily suppressed, or else have shot out of their environment and lost touch with it. There is a tradition of timidity and yes-saying, almost as bad as the Irish one, and equally capable of hiding treachery, which may be either to one's own folk and class, or to those — perhaps of real good will although incomers — to whom the yes has been said. Yet such things are temporary. The old qualities have not been killed out; they are in abeyance, waiting for their moment. They are not qualities which fit into a world of hard competition. They might fit well enough into another world; they might be restated in such a world. Even now they come to the surface when there is a chance, when they will be welcomed and not laughed at. There is no reason at all for despair. If people are treated differently, they will be different.

Page 57

There is a fine romantic story about Isobel Haldane and Charles Stewart of Ardsheal, who fell in love with her when she was eighteen. More about Ardsheal is, of course, to be found in *Catriona*. Isobel's father, Lanrick, did not approve of his daughter marrying a wild Highlander. Perhaps he had seen too much of them in the '15 — he had the sense to settle his estates beforehand, so that although he was in both of the risings, the estates escaped forfeiture (one wonders if he had taken good advice from the rest of the family on this). But young Stewart went back north, wild angry and needing to take it out of someone. He got to the inn at Strathyre, which would be small enough, a room and kitchen most like, with beds in the wall. But there was Rob Roy and his gang at the inn, plotting some ploy against decent folks, no doubt. Ardsheal, in the temper he was in, challenged Rob Roy, who was an oldish man but with all the reputation of a successful gangster, and got the advantage of him. Neither was hurt, and Ardsheal got in at the inn, and no doubt the story was all about the border in no time at all. Lanrick thought better of his refusal, and a message came to Ardsheal to say he would be welcome after all.

Isobel seems to have lived somewhere on the estate for three years after the '45 and 'uplifted in money, rents and provisions from the

Tenants £156 Ster'. Later she joined her husband in France; he died at Sens in 1757 'leaving her with eight helpless children'; then she was in Paris with her father, living the wretched life of a political exile, with little money, for the estate was forfeited after the '45. In 1775, she was allowed the lease of a farm and three-fourths of another, but probably never went back to Ardsheal; she came back to England in 1779, with dropsy, a rather usual disease of the period, and died in Northampton. Her second son, Duncan, who put in his claim for the estate about 1782, had been appointed Collector of the Customs at the Port of New London in Connecticut, in 1764, married out there and had eight children. During the troubles, as he says, he 'continued at his post, ran every personal risk, and was at last compelled to leave his station, and lost everything he had acquired in that country'.

So much for the family. But if we consider all this from the point of view of the Ardsheal tenants, it meant that they had to go on paying rents to absentee landlords, although 'on account of their landlord being in the rebellion they had their houses burnt, and their cattle and goods mostly carried off and destroyed'. They might evade a certain amount of rent-paying, though some of those who were actually farming might have other sources of income. It is difficult to be sure what happened when a farm was leased — sometimes the man to whom the lease or tack was granted actually farmed it, at other times he merely lifted the rent, and put someone else in to do the work. But there was certainly no adequate landlord-tenant relationship, in the sense that the landlord was not doing anything about repairs, draining or enclosing and other estate work. Equally, of course, all servitures must have gone by the board, to such an extent that they could never have been started again.

Certain other things with a social importance happened at the same time. A school was started at Ardsheal, with a schoolmaster appointed by the Commissioners for the Forfeited Estates (presumably one of Patrick's jobs), where in 1777 the 29 scholars 'acquitted themselves in reading of English and writing to the satisfaction of the subscribers'. Presumably the schoolmaster, Mr. James M'larene, was paid out of the estate — though that would not have been any great burden to judge by the usual salaries. This school would in itself have been a liberating influence in so far as it gave the children the possibility of another choice of occupation. Of course, schools were started with a definite political intention, to break the old customs and loyalties. That was why it was so firmly insisted upon that English should be learnt. We have seen the tail-end of this Whig policy in our own time, with the final decay of Gaelic. The schoolmasters who strapped the hands of the little girls on the Islands for speaking to one another in Gaelic, not so long ago, were not intentional Whigs. They had no fear of a Jacobite revival — the time for that was long past. But the anti-Gaelic policy was still strong in them. It has been almost completely effective. And that was bad for Scotland, though the original intention had probably been good.

This gives an idea of the shattering of all the personal relationships of the old system on one estate. It would, of course, have been the moment for the application of some new system of landholding which would have freed the tenants economically, as they had — in theory at least — been freed politically. But nobody was thinking along those lines, least of all the tenants themselves. They accepted what was wished upon them by a new set of masters. In the end the new ones seemed worse than the old, just because there was no kind of human relationship left between them. When the new ones, the Whigs (or it might be the next generation of the same family, returning but with the Whig ideas on estate management) chastised them with sheep and clearances, they looked back to a mythical time, the good old days. They became Tories. And many of them are Tories still.

Page 58

It is rather difficult to know which of the country dances date from as far back as the early eighteenth century, nor whether they were danced much as at present. In my book I have chosen the ones with the earliest published tunes, especially the ones I like best dancing myself. Monymusk was composed in 1775, but it is one of my favourites. I am inclined to think that they were danced with rather more careful footwork than we mostly give them; they must have been just as enjoyable. Plenty of the tunes have more than one name to them.

Page 60

The '15 is very fully documented. I think my details are substantially correct. Those about Gleneagles, including Helen Erskine's letter to Mar, are mostly authentic, and come from *The Haldanes of*

Gleneagles. It should be remembered that Scotland had been through desperately hard times; there had been constant civil war, and consequent neglect of progress in industry and agriculture, which had gone ahead in England after their sharp civil war and the subsequent Restoration. The bad years which Patrick and his stepmother speak about on page 62, were seven years of atrociously bad weather from 1696 on. The corn hardly ripened, other crops were as bad, the cattle and sheep died. Bad transport no doubt made things worse; food could not be brought from places where there was enough. But the magistrates enforced maximum prices of the main foodstuffs. People died of hunger all over Scotland; villages disappeared altogether; men and women crawled from place to place, looking for food, died in the kirkyard when they could, in the hopes of a decent burial. A few years later, another year of bad weather destroyed the crops again, the seed corn with the meal corn. Most people in Scotland were desperately poor, living like the peasant Balkans. Though perhaps the computation of the total wealth of Scotland at fifteen shillings a head does not take account of the fact that quite certainly money was not used as much as it is now. People exchanged things, as they often do now in stable country places where they can trust one another, and where they know what they want. Yet I think that Graham's picture of barbarism and poverty in *The Social Life of Scotland* is somewhat exaggerated. As far as the Ochils went, the Haldane tenants certainly paid a good part of their rents in money, though partly, no doubt, in kind.

It will be remembered, of course, that the 'left-winger' of that time, the progressive, the one who thought most in terms of the liberty and prosperity of the human individual, saw this liberty in trade and the cities and the removal of all barriers to competition. That seems rather odd now.

Page 63

These place names are all of actual farms held by Gleneagles tenants. Some are still known by the same names, but I have not found them all, and it may well be that some were not in Perthshire at all, but on the Lennox lands which the Haldanes held, over towards Dumbarton. There is a Haldane's Mill there still.

There is a great deal of detail about the burnings in the *Annals of Auchterarder*, and it was remembered as a terrible thing when I was a child. The thorn tree planted at Dunning to commemorate the burning is still there. Mr. Reid from Dunning, the Minister who had preached against Jacobites, was on his death-bed when the burnings began, but told his wife that the Lord would not suffer a hair of his head to be touched, and bade his coffin to be hastily prepared. He was buried at once, and the manse burnt, the Highland leader much regretting that they had not the old dog's bones to birsle in the flames of the house.

The Haldanes of Aberuthven got their furniture out of the house before it was burnt, but the Highlanders threw it back in, to be destroyed.

If the Jacobites had been successful, the folk of the burnt villages would probably have got some compensation, as this was offered in a proclamation given from Scoon almost immediately afterwards, and caused to be read in the Parish Churches.

Indeed, they might have had their compensation a generation earlier than they got it from England!

NOTES ON CHAPTER IV

Page 70

The story is that the little larches which Atholl planted, shed their leaves in autumn, as their custom is; but, as nobody had heard of conifers doing such an odd thing, they were thrown out on the midden. There, however, they took root, and were in leaf again the next spring. Yet I believe these were not the first larches in Scotland, but that there are older ones at the Botanical Gardens in Edinburgh.

All the prices etc. and the whole scheme for the planting of the muir of Orchil, comes from the *1799 Report on Perthshire*. I believe it has been done on a small scale since. The difficulty is that it is very windy and I doubt if they had thought out the right kinds of shelter belts. I think that nowadays a good deal of the shallow peat could be reclaimed by modern methods (as in Norway), not for forests but for farming.

Page 73

Lady Anne Mackintosh, daughter of Farquharson of Invercauld, married at sixteen to a rather characterless husband, considerably older than herself, was only twenty at the time of the '45. She raised the clan regiment, under Macgillivray of Dunmaglass, who had seen service abroad. For all that Sir Walter Scott, tempering his practical Whig temper with historical romanticism, speaks of her as a gallant Amazon, whilst other writers, nearer to her in time, abused her in the way that men are apt to do when a woman takes it on herself to break through the man-made conventions, she never rode at the head of the regiment. That would probably not have been practical. As it was, Dunmaglass, with all but five of the officers of the Macintosh regiment, was killed at Culloden. So were four hundred out of the seven hundred clansmen, among them Donald Fraser, the blacksmith. He was the one who had been sent out, with four others, each with a loaded musket, to keep an extra guard on Moy Hall when the Prince was there. It was well they did so, for who came marching over from Inverness but Lord Loudon with seventeen hundred men. The blacksmith and his friends all fired and the blacksmith shouted to an imaginary regiment to charge, completely panicking Loudon's men, who bolted for Inverness, some of them even falling into the hands of the sentries at Moy Hall. The flag of Clan Chattan also was saved by Donald Macintosh — Donull na Braiteach — who got away, with the thing wrapped round him, and so saved it from the hangman's bonfire in Edinburgh, where most of the Clan colours were burnt up, to the great edification of the Whigs. Whether such things are worth anything seems doubtful now, but if a piece of coloured cloth means all that to you and your folk, then you are as well to risk your life for it. It is not, maybe, such things that will give us back our honour in Scotland, yet we need to get it back some way and by some risks.

But Lady Anne was in no battles. She received the Prince at Moy Hall after the battle of Falkirk, and entertained him to an 'exceedingly genteel' supper. The main extra items of expense were claret and sherry, sugar, biscuits and coffee. A few days later the Prince went down to Inverness, to stay with the old Dowager Lady Macintosh; it was the only house in Inverness that had a sitting-room that was not a bedroom as well. Cumberland stayed there after Culloden, less welcome and probably far more feared. It was the old lady who said: 'I've had two kings' bairns living with me in my time, and, to tell you the truth, I wish I may never have another.'

I might add here that, both in England and Scotland, the Prince paid for everything that he and his household got, wherever they were; the few occasions on which they were entertained, as at Moy Hall, were put down separately in the account book kept by Mr. James Gib, the Master of the Household. Mr. Gib added that the

Prince always ordered drink-money to be given liberally where he lodged. There would be about seventy persons in his household, and he had his own cooks with him who prepared all the food, baked the bread, etc. In one Scottish billet, however, the hostess, Lady Dalrachny, would not let them bake on the Sabbath. Doubtless it was good policy for the Prince to pay, but — he did so. Cumberland was less particular.

While Lady Anne was raising her regiment and entertaining her Prince, her husband had taken Forbes of Culloden's advice and was circumspection itself. It was likely enough, though, that they were in constant communication of an unofficial kind. She was lovely, fine-boned and delicate-looking with a high, white forehead. She and the Prince no doubt remained on the most formal terms. He was never one for gallantries with the ladies. The Marquis d'Egilles, French Ambassador to the Jacobites, said of him: 'The Scotswomen, who are naturally serious and impassioned, conclude of him that he is really tender and will remain constant. It is a woman who has given me this explanation.'

Lady Anne was taken prisoner after Culloden, and might have been badly treated, but that the Commander of the troop sent to capture her was a former admirer. She only had six weeks' imprisonment. One asks oneself what she was thinking: was it of the regiment she had raised and who were mostly dead, or was she, as she appeared, 'quite undaunted'? Meanwhile some of the Grants managed to destroy a number of Macintosh title-deeds and such papers, during a semi-official raid on Moy Hall. But that was rather for old sake's sake and nothing to do with the '45.

Page 76

This was what her godmother, Mrs. Winwood, wrote about Mary Reade, married at 20—old enough, for those days, to have had other offers and to know her own mind — to a husband eleven years older: 'I fear she will suffer much more daily but tis no more than first I did tell her I feared for her, but I could not persuade her against having him, to her ruin I suppose it will prove to her and her's.' And again: 'She is so fond of her husband as I do not approve of, because he will ruin her as all I have or can do will not help it, so she must smart for her folly.' I take it Mrs. Winwood attempted to make him into a respectable Whig who would settle down, but: 'I think all I can do in vain I fear to make him good for anything at all, but proud and profanish and full of folly and the like things and will at last break his wife's heart.' She had a hard-enough time, chivvied from one place to another, and some of the children dying young, but the one thing he probably didn't do to her was to break her heart. 'She will be still so fond of a Scot Tory as to undo herself altogether.' Mrs. Winwood altered her will accordingly, but left some money and gear to the daughter who was called after herself.

Page 78

English readers should remember that even now it is not the custom to hold Communion in the Scottish Presbyterian churches more often than twice a year. In many churches there is still considerable fencing of the tables; you do not go unless you get a brass communion ticket. The tendency, of course, is for the respectable to go, and for the sinners to stay away, although maybe the thing should be another way round. But the Pharisees are well in control now, just the same as they used to be.

Page 80

Wodrow's *Analecta* is the main authority for these covenants. There is an excellent series of chapters on religious life in Scotland in Graham's book.

Page 81

The Russian Ambassador to London had approved the choice of James Haldane, then a Lieutenant in the Life Guards, to be Resident in Moscow with the Czar Peter the Great. It was intended that he should go with the Russian armies in their invasion of Sweden. But the quarrel between the Czar Peter and our own King George, no genius, stopped all that.

NOTES ON CHAPTER V

Page 89

Pinners were a 'Queen Anne' headgear: a great bow of lace with long tails. A lady of fashion could spend almost more on lace, most of which was imported from the Continent, than on any other luxury. Fashions followed the Continent; there were lace-makers in England, mostly political refugees — it was a group of Mechlin Protestants who started the Buckinghamshire lace industry. But I doubt if there was any indigenous Scottish lace. Hard-wearing peasant lace, made with coarse, sometimes coloured, threads, such as we associate with the Balkans or Greece, seems to be a decoration for Catholic countries, where one can dress up for the festivals of the Church, and where there is enough sun and the leisure that productive land gives, to let the housewives sit on their door-steps lace-making and embroidering. Here in the north we hadn't the weather or the leisure. The women's tartan screens and ribbon snoods were the best we could do, and, since the suppression of the tartans, the Sabbaths became progressively blacker.

I would say that lace was more of a class thing in Great Britain, and especially Scotland, than on the Continent, where there was every variety, between coarse and fine. Here, the wearing of lace would definitely be the mark of a lady or gentleman, someone of leisure and money, surrounded by brittleness and delicacy, who could afford to employ a washer and mender, as well as to buy the flounces and trimmings, cuffs and handkerchiefs. There was money in lace. I doubt if Christian Shaw of Bargarran would have thought of starting her fine thread making if there had not been a demand for strong, delicate and even linen threads for lace-making, and this went with the beginnings of an increase of the leisure class with spare cash to buy it. This was not the same as the landlord class; it might have had more to do with the early tobacco trade.

There was a demand for fine linen cloth but it was hardly so constant. Her Lowland genius for mechanics and money-making might, of course, have turned into some other channel. Paisley might have had other foundations. The thread industry lasted a couple of generations and started Paisley off as an industrial town, with industrial families, who had broken with agriculture, had neither kailyard nor cow, but instead the manual and intellectual skill of the tradesman. Such people could turn their skill to new kinds of machinery, and to new designs; they made the Paisley shawls. It was only a later development of industrialism that thrust a few of them up to become leaders of Clydeside industries, and far more of them down, to become half-skilled or unskilled factory hands.

Page 92

Kirstie was over hopeful about the good that could be done by the setting up of schools of this type. In practice they were largely run by the Ministers, so as to produce the right political and anti-Gaelic principles in the pupils. Nor did the habits of industry, hours at a stretch doing monotonous work with a machine, suit well with the Highland temperament. They are better at doing hard, dangerous or ingenious things than exact and boring ones. The Lowland schoolmistresses complained of their pupils. The schools were usually supposed to pay their way out of their manufactured products, even when a well-meaning laird had contributed a plot of land or the makings of a school house.

Such schools were not confined to Scotland; there were plenty in England at the beginning of the industrial age and equally successful. People were not clear about what they wanted to do, whether they were seeking to serve the God of education or the Mammon of industry. Indeed, the same confused thinking has shown itself since! It was plain that the poor would do better for themselves and not be a burden on the country (but the two ideas were intertwined only too closely) if they had enough education to read the Bible — which would keep them out of mischief, drink, poaching, minor theft and the like, and encourage them in habits of industry and Church-going — and to learn a trade. But there was no question of the education going beyond a suitable point. In Scotland, at least, we had our own revolution, and the theory that the church must come from the people and that the lad of parts must be enabled to reach the Ministry, however poor he might be. To some extent this was so in practice, even two hundred years after the revolution and the Book of Discipline. It was not even a theory in England.

It all hung together with the theory of mercantilism, which meant that every effort must be made to increase exports. Thus every new recruit to the army of workers who could make exportable goods was a national asset. But this was really nothing to do with education itself, and the schools fell between two stools. Charity schools or very cheap schools, with a solely educational (or mixed educational and religious) purpose, were to come in the next century. Though there were still plenty folks to say that the working classes should always be taught to work and that all the reading and writing and whatever else they got in the classes must be directed to that one end. Indeed I find that this idea is still very usual.

Page 94

The evidence about Leadhills comes from Ramsay's *Scotland and Scotsmen in the Eighteenth Century*. James Stirling, the mathematician who managed the Scottish Mining Company, following young

Erskine of Alva, was a practical, decent man, very keen about the welfare of the miners, a Cadbury-ish paternalist. See further notes on him in Chapter VIII.

There is an interesting sideline on the Leadhills mines two generations later in Dorothy Wordsworth's Diary under the date August 19th, 1803. 'Leadhills, another mining village, was the place of our destination for the night . . . We talked with one of the miners, who informed us that the building which we had supposed to be a school was a library belonging to the village. He said they had got a book into it a few weeks ago, which had cost thirty pounds, and that they had all sorts of books. "What! have you Shakespeare?" "Yes, we have that," and we found, on further inquiry, that they had a large library, of long standing, that Lord Hopetoun had subscribed liberally to it, and that gentlemen who came with him were in the habit of making larger or smaller donations. Each man who had the benefit of it paid a small sum monthly — I think about fourpence. The man we talked with spoke much of the comfort and quiet in which they lived one among another; he made use of a noticeable expression, saying that they were "very peaceable people considering they lived so much under-ground"; — wages were about thirty pounds a year; they had land for potatoes, warm houses, plenty of coals, and only six hours' work each day, so that they had leisure for reading if they chose.'

Page 95

I had in mind that they might have moved to Kilmarnock, or some place of that kind of size and history, and I have based the description of the parish on McKay's *History of Kilmarnock*, and Robertson's *Ayrshire*.

Page 96

There is considerable evidence about the coal mines and colliers of Scotland. Legally they were in a rather worse position than their brothers in England. A number of references will be found in Johnston's *History of the Working Classes in Scotland*. I have used Ashton and Sykes' *The Coal Industry of the Eighteenth Century*. Mining is a thing that runs in families, and it is like enough that the grandfathers of men who are working the Ayrshire pits now started work themselves as serfs. It will not be surprising if miners feel ill-disposed to those whose ancestors owned their own, or that they should feel passionately about social justice.

THE BULL CALVES

Page 101

The story of Marjorie Lawson and Squire Meldrum is to be found in *The Historie of Squyer Meldrum* by Sir David Lindsay of the Mount. It is one of the first realistic poems of Great Britain, that is to say, it is about real people and their doings, rather than about personified virtues and vices, trades and professions. It has one of the most beautiful and straightforward romantic love scenes that has ever been written.

> Then in his armis he did her thrist,
> And aither uther sweitlie kist;
> And wame for wame thay uther braissit.
> With that her kirtill was unlaissit:
> Then Cupido with his fyrie dartis,
> Inflammit sa thir luiferis hartis,
> Thay micht na manner of way dissever,
> Nor ane micht not part fra ane uther;
> But like woodbind they were baith wrappit,
> Thair tenderlie he has hir happit,
> Full softlie, up intill his bed,
> Judge je, gif he hir schankis shed.
> Allace! Quod scho, quhat may this mene?
> And with hir hair scho dicht hir ene.
> I cannot tell how thay did play,
> But I believe scho said not nay.
> He pleisit hir sa, as I hard sane,
> That he was welcum ay agane.

They gave one another love tokens after that, rings set with precious stones, for they were young and rich and lusty, both of them come of the best stock in Scotland. They intended marriage as soon as they could get dispensation, for he was nearly related to her late husband, Sir John Haldane. After this early morning encounter, brought about, as Lindsay knew well enough, by Marjorie herself even more than by her lover, she went back to the bower where her maidens were still asleep.

> Quod they, Madame, quhare have ye bene?
> Quod scho, Into my gardine grene,
> To heir thir mirrie birdis sang.
> I lat you wit, I thocht not lang,

448

Thocht I had taryit thair quhile none.
Quod thay, Quhair wes your hois and schone?
Quhy yeid ye with your bellie bair?
Quod scho, The morning wes sa fair,
For be him that deir Jesus sauld,
I felt na wayis ony manner of cauld.
Quod thay, Madame, me think ye sweit.
Quod scho, Ye see I sufferit heit;
The dew did sa on flouris fleit,
That baith my lymmis are maid weit:
Therefore ane quhyle I will heir ly,
Till this dulce dew be fra me dry:
Ryse, and gar mak our denner reddie.
That sall be done, quod thay, my ladie.

Yet things went hard for them in the end, though they had a few
years of love (but the dispensation from the Pope which would have
allowed them to marry had not come through yet) and she bore him
two children. But then he became involved in a dispute over some
of the Haldane lands in the Lennox, and there were years of savage,
though in some ways no doubt, pleasurable, fighting, ending with the
Squire ambushed and terribly wounded, his half recovery but
separation from Marjorie, who was married, perhaps against her
will or perhaps not, at least twice to other people. Courage was a
very necessary virtue in those days; it went with a kind of generous,
half savage kindness, a warmth in action. Her eldest son, Sir James
Haldane, who married an Erskine wife, carried on the Haldane line.

Sterne of Stratherne, O ladie bright,
Marjorie Haldane that was hight,
O back back mither, be kind tae me
Gif I thy dochter sa surely be,
For the faery wolf comes up fra the sea,
And the myrtle tangles the feet of the wolf
But its roots are twined wi the Eildon Tree.

Page 102

I am not sure how much the various measures, mostly fiscal,
which were taken by the English Parliament, were deliberately
meant to ruin Scotland, though there is no doubt that a powerful
section of mercantile opinion was afraid of any possible competition
from the north. There were more of them every generation in the

upper middle class who had, a century earlier, achieved their revolution against the King and the Court. Another King and Court had returned, but no longer with any divinity hedging them. Tney were rather more friendly to the 'loyal' Scots, and of course there was a gieat deal of intermarriage among the highest ranks of the aristocracy. Very large-landed proprietors would have common interests which made nothing of the small matter of a national frontier. The same thing can be observed to-day among a rather different class of owners of the means of production.

Page 107

My feeling is that one of the main intellectual recreations of the upper middle classes at this time, was the perpetual having of lawsuits. This would mean journeys and gossip and business, and delightful wanglings and briberies and gaining of points. Probably the issue was not so important. But I wonder if Curzons and Haldanes would ever have got on very well.

NOTES ON CHAPTER VII

Page 121

This treatment would be worse than useless for poisoning by 'blackdamp' (nitrogen plus carbon dioxide) or by 'firedamp' (methane). It had a certain vogue in England in the treatment of carbon monoxide poisoning, such as occurred after an explosion or from a smouldering fire. It has been suggested by J. S. Haldane in conversation, that the accumulation of carbon dioxide in a hole where a man's face was placed might stimulate his breathing if the respiratory centre had failed, or he had washed out a large amount of carbon dioxide under the stimulus of oxygen want. However, it seems extremely unlikely that the oxygen want resulting from such a treatment would not outweigh the advantage of carbon dioxide as a stimulant. It may be that partial asphyxiation in this way would either kill the victim or cause him to recover normal breathing and some sort of consciousness within a few minutes. If so, it is intelligible that miners should recommend it. But it does not follow that it saved lives.

Page 122

The Galloway enclosures were among the worst in Scotland. I think the landlords here would have been Anglo-Norman by origin, and would have held the land on a regular feudal tenure, and would have considered it their own. Farm workers were badly paid; prices had risen much more than wages. A ploughman, for instance, would have about forty shillings a year, as well as some cloth for a suit, shoes and hose. About the middle of the century some of the farm servants in the Lowlands entered into a combination to raise wages. Their demands were very moderate and they had public opinion on their side. The ringleader was one 'Windy Shaw'. I believe they got something at least of what they were asking.

Page 123

The stool of repentance and the public rebuke were so terrible that many poor lasses even killed their new-born babes, committing what they knew was a worse crime in order to escape the Ministers. The infanticide rate fell when the worst of this public rebuking (scarcely compatible with the Christian doctrine of forgiveness) was stopped. It was mostly the poor that suffered (though Mungo Haldane in his younger days had been rebuked at Blackford for fornication — and that with a woman of his own name, some poor relation, one supposes, who did not come into the family tree! — when 'the wind blew the bonnie lassie's plaidie awa'). As it says in the song:

> Now Jock maun face the Minister
> And Jean maun face the pillar,
> And yon's the way poor sinners fare
> If they hae got na siller.

Page 125

I have wished at St. Mungo's well myself, but not since I was a child. So far I have had little luck with wishing wells; maybe I asked for too much, and those that have experience of these things say that it is better only to ask for less than you want. There is little enough now that I would say I was prepared to disbelieve in utterly. If there had been brounies or fairies or whatever kind of appearances or actualities you might put a name to, would they not have been bound to be driven underground by the jealousy and hate of the Ministers who would not be able to bear anything that took away from their own powers, and would not come to terms with whatever there might have been to come to terms with? Nor would anyone who had any dealings with whatever was uncanny, from the Sight onwards, be at all eager to speak about it. When things are driven to hide themselves they tend to become twisted and anti-social. The one certain conclusion is that it is always the greatest pity to be frightened of anything that is out of the ordinary. Whatever else may or may not be bad, fear most surely is.

Page 126

After the ecclesiastical revolution, the Church of Scotland was rent with floods of controversy. They were much like our own pre-war feuds of the Left, as disruptive of friendships and as dull to read afterwards as Left Book Club favourites have already become. *The Marrow of Modern Divinity*, a tedious dialogue between imaginary persons upon Works, Faith, the Law and the Gospel, and so on, was published in 1646 by an Englishman, a B.A. Oxon (B.N.C.). A generation later it came to the hands of various Lowland Ministers, 'by a merciful and most unexpected disposure of providence'; it was read with great and sweet complacence and occasioned great thoughts of heart. Soon after that the Presbytery of Auchterarder began to require candidates for licence to acknowledge it unsound to teach that men must forsake their sins in order to come to Christ. If you could get rid of your sins by yourself, then how could Christ be acknowledged as the only saviour of sins? One must be logical. . . .

Mr. James Hogg, 'one of the holiest ministers in the kingdom', recommended *The Marrow of Modern Divinity*, which taught the same doctrine. But the Assembly, inclining rather towards Works and the Arminian Errors of Prof. Simpson, fell on Mr. Hogg, saying that believers could and did sin, and were not, by belief, exempt from the moral law. At this Mr. Hogg and twelve others remonstrated to the Assembly on behalf of Grace and against Works. There was considerable controversy for some time, edifying and prolonged sermons and the kind of righteous anger you can only have against those who are near to yourself but yet do not acknowledge what you say as being the only and ultimate truth.

I suppose the alternatives to this kind of thing are toleration, compromise and a kind of half aliveness. But the controversy of one century seems curiously unreal the next. Yet one still has a certain feel of sympathy for the Covenanters, savage and arrogant as they were, because at least they risked their necks. A later generation did not even do that, but lived on the kudos of their forebears.

Page 136

Alexander Christy at Perth advertised his linen bleaching in the *Caledonian Mercury* in early June 1747.

Page 137

I read and took notes on the *Caledonian Mercury* for June 9th, June 11th, and June 15th, 1747. In the book I have assumed that all three issues arrived at once, as sometimes happens with newspapers, even these days, if one lives at all far from the centres. Everything is as it was; the double columns of small print can still be read, for instance, in the National Library at Edinburgh. I also read the number of the *Scots Magazine*, which would have arrived at Gleneagles by the same post. But the *Courant*, the Whig paper, is lost for 1747, and I cannot hear of any library that has a copy.

Page 138

Professor Alexander Monro, the earliest of the Monro family of anatomists, was at this time Professor of Anatomy in Edinburgh; he lectured, presumably in dog Latin, and wrote quantities of papers on various medical subjects. He was a staunch Whig, but attended the wounded of both sides at the Battle of Prestonpans. He did his best to save the life of a fellow physician, Dr. Cameron, younger brother of the Gentle Lochiel: a man who had spent half his life, after studying in Edinburgh and Paris, back in Lochaber among his own folk, doctoring them and looking after them. Dr. Cameron was in the '45, but escaped; he came back to Scotland in 1753, hoping perhaps that the thing would be over, but was arrested, hanged and quartered — an end that did not fit his life. Though we should be used enough to that, these days. To go back to Professor Monro, I should add, perhaps, that his mother was a Forbes of Culloden.

As to Dr. Stirling, he was a greater man, a mathematician, an F.R.S. and friend of Newton, a man of wide erudition and immensely practical; he had discovered the trade secrets of the Venetian glass manufacturers as a young man and, later, became manager of the Leadhills Mining Company for Kirstie's cousin, Erskine of Alva. He would have succeeded Professor McLaurin, another great mathematician, but he was too well known a Jacobite. However, he must have had a lot of fun surveying the Clyde, with a view to making it navigable; this was the first of the series of steps that made the Clyde into what it is now, God help it. He was constantly writing books and papers, several of which were communicated to the Royal Society.

The *Scots Magazine* for April 1747 produced some interesting statistics about the Royal Infirmary. Between 1742 and 1746 there were 317 cured, 108 partly cured, 60 discharged, 146 incurable and 45 dead. Of the patients, these are the larger numbers: 31 amputations, 23 cancers, 21 dropsy, 21 fractures, 15 diarrhoea and dysentery (if it was really dysentery one wonders that there weren't more, but no doubt not all were admitted), 12 anal fistula, 12 epilepsy, 16 hysteric, 6 leprosy, 23 palsy, 15 consumption, 45 rheumatic pains, 37 scurvy (which must have been common in Scotland with the long winter months of salt meat and no vegetables), 29 cut for stone, 21 inflammation of eyes, 153 scorbutic ulcer (do these two last suggest venereal disease?), 10 obstructions (perhaps appendicitis?) and 23 white swelling of joints (tuberculous joints?).

Page 146

I doubt the poor piper will have had a hard time with the midges, as D. will remember he had yon evening we were dancing reels on the grass, I in my bare feet and the most of the men in high boots, for we were going off on some wet and midnight ploy. It is a great question whether the pipes do better on the traditional whisky or not. There was once a pipe band that was started by the Rechabites, and a fine band it was. Well, they were going up one time to play at a competition, and most of them had been buying gear for the band, beyond what the Rechabites had started them with. They did well at the competition, and were getting into the train to take them back to Glasgow. But when it came to one of the Rechabites walking along the station to look for them, there wasn't one in the carriage except for D. 'Ach,' he says, 'the boys are having an ice-cream over at the shop. Away, you, and you'll find them.' But as soon as the mannie's back was turned D. made a dash for the pub where the rest of the boys were and shouted for them to come. But they mostly all had a bottle of beer with them, and, what with getting the first prize, or it might have been the second, they were waving the things about under the noses of the Rechabites. So that was them finished with that lot, but they took another name and did fully as well and I think I am right in saying they most of them were good Trade Unionists and every one voted Labour when it came to the Election.

NOTES ON PART TWO

Note on the historical use of Words

WRITING this book, I keep on asking myself how to get the sense or the eighteenth century, the feel of it as a background? There is any amount of contemporary evidence and plenty of good modern books by historians and sociologists, based on this and other evidence. And it looks as though there was then almost as great a variety of people and ways of living and standards of behaviour, in Great Britain alone, or even in Scotland itself, as there is to-day.

Yet I would suppose that an intelligent reader, two or three hundred years on from now, would place a twentieth-century book, or, to narrow it down, a 'between-wars' book, not by reference to events, famous people or recent inventions, but by a general sense, some kind of background of the meanings of words. Take, in a geographical sweep, E. M. Delafield's *Provincial Diaries* from the west of England, the London-Oxford-Cambridge triangle of a dozen competent novelists, Walter Greenwood's Lancashire, Priestley's Yorkshire, Compton Mackenzie's or Neil Gunn's Highlands: how do they have the same feel of the same land-bloc in the same phase of west European civilization?

There is, first, an extraordinary variety about them, quite apart from their authors' styles or social convictions. Yet they were written about a country with perhaps the best communications in Europe, bound together by daily papers and radio.

How does this compare with the eighteenth century? You might expect yet more variety at a time when news and letters took far longer, when there were marked dialects, and most of the inhabitants never travelled and so the country was divided into quantities of separate little worlds. Yet you might offset this by the similarity of the separate worlds, when all had the same basic trades and occupations, by a much smaller number of literate and consciously-thinking people, and by the non-existence of a number of specialized modern occupations, trades and professions. The eighteenth century, whether of fiction or fact, gives us a predominantly middle and upper class picture. Scotland was in a transition period between a stratified and stable society, semi-feudal in the Lowlands, though differently patterned elsewhere, but at least with a settled kind of structure in

455

which son followed father in the same sort of life, and the later industrialism which was again stratified so that the manual workers were almost another species. In this transition period, following the Knoxian revolution, class barriers were permeable and anyone might be found doing almost anything and nobody very much surprised at it. I doubt if this was so in England. Here the barriers between the original nobility and the successful *bourgeoisie* had largely disappeared following their rather different revolution, yet there is a very complete class stratification in the eighteenth-century set-scene with which we are familiar from books and plays and the lids of chocolate boxes, and which is based on political and literary London. It would be quite inaccurate for my Gleneagles folk. Yet, for all the difference between them, they belong to the same phase of west European civilization and can be easily recognized as doing so. But how?

Let us see what help we get from the modern books which do all convey the sense of their own period. I think we will find that, by and large, certain social relationships are taken for granted and seriously, while certain others are surprising, shocking or in the queer borderland between horror and comedy. There are standards of social decency; when they are broken it is significant. I think one may go so far as to suggest that most of the serious — the significant— talk is about social relationships which are in a state of change. When such relationships are altered or broken it is not accidental, but part of a series of events to which writers should be attending, and out of which they should be fashioning the continuous garb of significant stories, or mythology, with which they must clothe naked historical action. Later on I shall give an example of this, but it is very clear when you come to consider the literary treatment of class and sex relationships. What happens is all expressed in words. Yet there is very little real explaining, or when there is it is usually a bore and embarrassing to the reader. Instead, everything is implicit; it is generally understood that certain words and phrases will convey a complex of social behaviour. One hardly realizes how much this is so until one tries to translate them into another language. Even American is slightly different.

These standards of behaviour and relationship with other persons and institutions vary somewhat according to class and job, but yet they are of the same kind. Assumptions of other, usually tougher, standards, cutting across these, are used in order to bring out the

process of change and are mostly meant to be shocking and to provoke a reaction. This may be a curiosity-horror reaction, inducing
the reader to buy another tough book, or it may be a moral reaction,
sometimes one in which the reader throws the book into the fire, or
else one in which reader and author join in a conspiracy of moral
fervour either to restate the old standards or to affirm a new stopping
place in the process of change — even to the point of Book Club
unity. Author and publisher seldom lose from the reaction. Sometimes we forget that this moral structure of society is temporal in
history, above all in economic history, and held together by words.

It would no doubt be possible to write a complete thesis on this
last tail of a sentence. The first half has been elaborated often
enough and by plenty of the great and small, including Engels and
myself. But I, having only a quarter of a lifetime at most ahead of
me, let alone two pits of potatoes to get in yet, merely propose to
make a few observations on the last five words. I am hoping, through
them, to get some light on the feel of the eighteenth century in Scotland and what were the significant relations and the words with
which they were expressed.

Abstract words, adjectives most of all, may be written and even
pronounced the same, over several centuries. Yet their meanings
quiver and change. One reason for writing this book in Scots, is that
certain words in current Scots speech are somewhere near the same
as they were two hundred years back, although the same words
have become archaic, have stiffened up and lost their meanings in
English. This is so most of all for religious words. Faith and Works
mean something still in Scotland, even for those who are by no means
members of any Presbyterian congregation. When writing with the
feel and sense rhythm of Scots words one does not have to explain
what one's book characters mean by them, as I think one would need
to in the phrasing of the south, for any but a historically-minded
audience. This means that my book is mainly written in the hopes
of being read by the generality of Scots folk, whether or not they
have had a secondary education, but not in hopes of being read by
more than a minority in southern England — folk who happen to
be interested in the kind of problems I write about or who want a
real understanding with Scotland. Maybe it is for these last most of
all that I write. Yet it remains that much of this book is about
problems of thought and conduct which still appear to interest most
Scots, excepting those who, like the most of the city proletariat, have

been ground into a featureless, history-less, culture-less pulp by the international mill of capitalism.

Yet I would be far from saying that the words Faith and Works, for instance, have exactly the same significance now that they had two hundred years ago. We do go through historical change, although it runs slow on the west coast which has given me my phraseology, since the means of production are little altered, or have altered sufficiently gradually for ways of thought to slip over slowly and painlessly. The crofter-weavers of Lewis are more secure and with a higher standard of living than their crofter-fisher forebears, but they are still mostly all Wee Frees. Yet in each succeeding generation the Elect manage to torture their children slightly less with fear of hell-fire.

If a church has hell-fire, or something equally vulnerable by the sceptics, as one of its main foundations and means of keeping its congregation together, it will be against change in methods of production, at least if it has the sense to see that these in their turn produce changed thoughts. But it has not always the sense. The only church that can survive real change in social structure and thought is one that is sensitive to them in a poetic or prophetic way. There are signs of this in some Christian churches, though not, on the whole, in Scotland. Here attention is still directed on personal sins, such as fornication — one of the oldest Scottish customs — drunkenness and the playing of football on Sunday, and not on social sins such as large-scale usury, the forcing of the destructive facts of poverty on to millions of innocent people, or lack of judgment, imagination and intelligence amongst those in authority, which become social sin in them where they might merely be personal mistakes in private persons (a fact half recognized by Black William on page 274). Further: such sin might even be condoned in a person willy-nilly set in authority and perhaps finding it over hard to get out of, as for example a hereditary monarch. This, I think, was recognized by the Catholic Church when they condemned ignorance in leaders. But in a democracy where people deliberately offer themselves as leaders, there can be no condonation.

Now this last paragraph should place my book in time to any critic, for it is typical of the present interweaving of social and religious relationships and words. I am feeling religiously about politics. I am thinking lightly of the breaking of commandments, but with deep seriousness about things which were scarcely reprobated at an earlier time. I use the word sin in a way which someone a few centuries back would hardly recognize. Could we then suggest that one way of getting the feel of a historical period is by the correspondence between society and the words in which the organization of society, in personal and group relationships, is expressed?

Perhaps it will be helpful to put aside one's anti-religious prejudices, useful and necessary as they have been, and to think in terms of the sciences of organization. First in temporal order was religion, which, simply as moral organization, usually means a church (to make it easier, let us consider the Christian church only). Then politics. Then economics. The oldest words with the largest number of meanings and greatest aura of feelings round them, belong to religion or morals. The medium words, but goodness knows some of them are not at all amenable to logic, belong to politics. Whereas economics sometimes claims to be really accurate and to use logical and well-defined words. At which a loud howl of No! goes up from quantities of people, including myself. You cannot, for instance, discuss economics without using such basic words as capital, labour and investment. These are words which immediately provoke passionate, illogical or religious reactions from most of us. So where are you?

In 1747, the period of my book, Scotland was still in the tail end of what had been her revolution. It has been a long tail and we are hardly out of it yet, still less were our nineteenth-century historians. But England's revolution was past. Your typical Londoner of 1747 was not religious; he was sceptical, a compromiser, not over keen to risk his neck. It was less than a century since there had been civil war in England, the first and last large war on English soil for a very long time — far longer than for any Continental country — and correspondingly shocking. Anything to avoid a repetition of that. This passionate desire for political compromise brought a general sympathy with compromise, with bargaining rather than bayoneting. The nation of shopkeepers had begun its existence.

But the Scot of the same epoch was much more serious minded; compromise still shocked him; scepticism had to be as respectable and well argued as Hume's. We too were sick of civil wars and shocked by them, but we were used to war on our own soil — especially to English invasions — and we had not yet joined the shopkeeping racket. In fact we were being kept out of it.

Scottish politics and religion were profoundly entangled; we saw our revolution as primarily religious. Indeed it takes an enthusiastic Marxist to clarify its class structure! It is beyond me, for the cross currents tug all too hard for the thing to stay tidy and amenable. Nowadays we are apt to underestimate John Knox, simply as a reaction from earlier pieties (see for instance Muir's *Life*). By modern standards Knox was cruel, treacherous and cowardly, and bullied the poor young Queen in a way that clashes hopelessly with our social standards. But, at the time, he did not *know* that he was on the winning side, that he could afford to be much braver and nobler and more in the modern tradition of revolutionary leaders. At the time, he was one wee David standing against an immensely powerful and dangerous Goliath; he had to use all means to attain his end. At the time, Queen Mary was not a sensitive and intelligent girl, in an extremely difficult social position, trying to be friendly and generous; she was the embodiment of something that had to be broken, the Divine Right of Kings, their terrible free will against the predestination of the common man. He was actually brave to face her as he did, considering that she still had the magic thing about her, which is now, to us, no more than a fairy tale.

Equally, at the time, his democracy was a new thing, a tremendous experiment: this idea of a nation spiritually fed from its schools, where boys and girls, irrespective of rank, were all to go, and governed through local groups, the Kirk Sessions, equivalent in many ways with Soviets. It was not his fault that the economic basis slipped, when the Lords of the Covenant managed to pull away so much of the money that was needed to sustain the system.

Local theocratic government has had a number of indirect effects on Scottish life. As in some other religions, it is an affair for men only. Women have been excluded or pushed into minor activities. It is even harder in Scotland than in England for a woman to work her way into any kind of administrative or executive position, and she is that much more of an object of suspicion and obloquy: all in the Knoxian manner and tradition. Here is the kind of thing that takes longer to change than the structure of organization because it is unconscious; it has sunk in below the level where an economic change takes immediate effect. The Presbyterian attitude towards the arts, especially the visual arts, is even more marked than the attitude towards women, another hangover from the revolution, when arts belonged in the same place with Queens and Popes and such cattle. Our only beautiful towns are those with a pre-Reformation core, or the 'new town' of Edinburgh, product of a sceptical, anglophil generation, only nominally Presbyterian and allowing much more scope to its women.

Knox's revolution, so-called and thought of at its own time and after, was essentially political and social, though expressed in religious words. It redistributed power and to some extent money. As I have said, it was a class mix-up, made all the more difficult to put into a pattern because the king actually left Scotland for England and the boiling up of another more obviously political and economic revolution, and also because the social structure was very different in Highlands and Lowlands. Yet everything was changed by the end. As in the corresponding English revolution, the extremes were crushed. The English Levellers and Diggers, using biblical terms but taking political action, were suppressed. So were our own Cameronians who also practised community of goods and encouraged the wives and daughters of the respectable to take to the moors and an unseemly freedom. When the hundred years or so of violence were over, the moderates survived to govern and have power, but very different from their grandfathers and with other ideas and words about money, land and the organization of society.

Through all this political change, the terms and words used for arguments and invective, public and private, were always religious, and this went on throughout the further course and settling down of the revolutionary epoch. Of course there can be no permanent settling down, no final and fixed pattern of society, after any revolution — so far. It may be that there will be some final change which will not bear within itself the seeds of its own contradictions. It may be that the time will come for love and joy and generosity and the withering away of the state. The hope of the Kingdom is within all revolutions. But the Reformation was one of the least final and stable changes. Yet, because it was always spoken of in religious words, an increasingly political-minded generation supposed it to be in some way different and gave it, in Scotland above all, a dogmatic and biblical finality instead of a political fluidity, with the certainty of further change.

While the words of this revolution were religious and directly taken from the newly translated Bible, the *Book*, just as much of the wording of modern argument is taken from the works of Marx, Engels and Lenin, or as those of the American and French revolutions were taken from Locke and the Encyclopaedists, yet the people who used these words were feeling in a way which we would call political rather than religious, about matters of the church, matters said to be of the Lord. Sometimes these matters appear to us so fantastically petty that it cannot really have made any difference which way they were settled; I think this might have been so from a religious point of view, but not when playing the political points game. To attain religious ends people were willing to use means which we, again, would call political, and to use political scheming and pressure. They saw nothing inappropriate in this, whereas we now have a feeling that 'moral' behaviour alone is appropriate to religious action. Yet it could be that this is a matter of emphasis: if we saw religion as something really important — in the way many of us see politics — then we might be less fussy.

Here then is the kind of snarl that words will land you in. It is quite obvious that at present a great many people think with a 'religious' passion about politics; politics have a 'religious' importance. Political words are the words charged with a 'religious' emphasis, thought about with belief and as dogma rather than intellectually, dispassionately and with the eighteenth-century spirit of compromise which was then thought appropriate to politics. In my book young Captain John, who is in the English Navy, starts by thinking of politics in such terms and is upset with the Gleneagles lot who take them religiously (actually in a more mixed or twentieth-century way), but by the end his 'principles' are involved and he thinks religiously too. Where the eighteenth-century politicians bargained, bribed and compromised, we try to act in a moral way about politics, that is to say with principle. A good many of us are shocked and uneasy at social intercourse between politicians of opposite parties, just as most of my book people would have been if their Minister had been found hobnobbing with a Roman Catholic priest. But none of them would have thought it odd to see politicians of the 'ins' and 'outs' meeting in the same salon (see also what Swift thought of it), except in so far as politics were also a matter of religion. This is one reason why eighteenth-century politics are so hard for a twentieth-century person to follow. I remember once in Birmingham having to take supper with a prominent Conservative politician, because he and my husband, who was a Labour candidate but had in fact been to the same college as the Conservative, had spoken on a 'non-political' platform together. I experienced the same discomfort, the same sense of my food choking me, and the same longing to be really rude, that my forebears in this book might have had, meeting an Episcopalian or, worse, a Catholic.

Yet we may be wrong. Of course moderation and compromise are the traditional failings of age and I am older now than I was then. But I am inclined to think that there may be more common meeting-ground for politicians than I once supposed was possible. It is not a social meeting-ground. On the contrary it is a meeting-ground of action. This all comes of watching the attempts that our late Secretary of State for Scotland, Tom Johnston, has made to get, first, the Council of State — all the past Secretaries of State for Scotland — and then the main body of Scots M.P.s, and beyond them the various boards and committees which have been set up, to agree on common action in matters connected with Scotland. It is almost as if a new principle — a principle of agreement rather than difference — were beginning to get a moral importance, and that among the same kind of people who, at another time, were proudest of not ever compromising. Further, the politicians who stand unflinchingly against agreement on any subject with their opponents, or — sometimes being still more difficult — with their colleagues who assert the same ends but other means, are beginning to appear old-fashioned, in a slightly different period of civilization. These changing relationships between political opposites are interesting, significant, and worthy of having words used about them. That is, they are a changing relation, of the kind I wrote of earlier, and perhaps they will affect and alter political words and phrases so much that these words in their new connotation will give quite a different and recognizable feel to the books of the next decade.

When considering the emotions of the politically conscious of my own generation, I am bound also to bear in mind the slight hangover of embarrassment that there was in the family when I was a child, over my cousin Alexander Chinnery-Haldane, a most virtuous man but Bishop of Argyll and the Isles, and I see the same thing here when Father Webb a man with whom I have much in common but who happens to be a Roman Catholic priest, comes over to tea. That is to say that the change of significance has been slower in Scotland, owing to a slower rate of economic progress, no doubt. If progress is the word. When Kirstie spoke of 'principles' she used the word for religious principles (though in practice hers were partly, at least, what we would call political), whereas its modern use is mainly for political principles (though sometimes religious ones may come in, and, in any case there is supposed to be a 'moral' atmosphere about the word). But its use may be changing at this moment. What matters in practice is when a verbal hangover begins to affect people's actions: when it goes on too long in some part of the same civilization and becomes laughable and distracts folks' attention from the realities, as the 'religious' hangover does now in rural Scotland and rural America. There is not so much human energy to spare that it can be wasted chasing shadows.

Here, then, is the clue to the feel of the Scottish eighteenth century. It is the way people are looking and the words they are using about the political and religious side of their life, and the corresponding assumptions of standards of conduct and social relationships. In some ways my main people in this book, especially Kirstie and Black William, are behaving socially, in a way which I believe (note this use of the 'religious' verb) was the right way for their time, although their expression of it is not mine or of my time or in any way 'socialist', and although various modern outcomes of their ways of thought and action would certainly have shocked and hurt them. Yet they and I are on the same road. I think I should add that they had both suffered severe social shocks, and those of a religious — and economic — nature.

Once, a good many years ago, I was talking with Auden, then a young schoolmaster, about the future, and he said something to the effect that people in the future would only ask about ourselves: were we happy? And did we help them on towards their goals? I suppose both Auden and I were assuming progress. It must have been in the early nineteen-thirties when that assumption had not been much shaken. But I am still inclined to think it is a good working idea about the future — and about the past. Some at least of my book people were working towards the same green pastures as lie in view for the bull calves of my own and the next generation. Between them and us was a time when, as far as we can judge, there was less sympathy with what we are after in the mid twentieth century. Two hundred years ago, in the mid eighteenth century, Scotland was in a transitional period. There was much questioning, much research and experimentation in science — especially agriculture and medicine — philosophy and literature. I think this makes it more possible to get the feel of eighteenth-century Scotland in words and phrases which come easily now to us in another transitional and experimental period, than it would be to get the feel of the nineteenth century when there was a hardening up into certainties and the uncharitable morality of technical and commercial success wrenched out of poverty, with the corresponding success-image of the dour Scot, almost always an east coast Lowlander. The cultural problem of Highlands and Lowlands and what might come of their fusion was never taken seriously between the eighteenth century, which broke the Highland pattern of development, and now when tentative regionalism and a scunner at the culture of cities has begun to open possibilities even for the remote Islands. By and large the Highlands have suffered two centuries of being looked down upon, oppressed, killed off and at the same time sentimentally exploited. It may be too late now to take them seriously. But I believe — and think — not.

I am wondering if my book people would have understood this distinction I am making between personal and social religion. (Meaning, I suppose, if they were real . . . but some of them *were* real and goodness knows the ones that weren't should be fully as real in the book as the ones that were or I don't know my job.) Not, I think, in the terms I have used, which would certainly have shocked them, as they may still shock some people of whose good will I am very sure but who have never thought in these terms. Or as concepts of the future would no doubt shock ourselves, for all we think ourselves so tough and realist.

But, in Kirstie's time, the personal religion of Christianity had not yet broken down into the present odd form of social religion. To-day, for instance, the king is Defender of the Faith: of the Church of England in England and the Church of Scotland in Scotland. At one time this was very serious. It mattered politically that the king should be a Protestant and a Protestant of the right kind: that is, the Whig kind. He must, that is to say, be the main weight in the pan of the Protestant balance of power in Europe, normally opposed to Roman Catholic France except at rare moments when something else tipped the balance. He must equally hold the balance of internal power steady, never allowing a scramble back by the still powerful Catholic noble houses and their followers. Now the king's official religion is not taken seriously in the same way. The King of England might meet the Pope of Rome without being called upon to defend his faith in any violent way, or even mention it, whereas this would have been profoundly shocking two hundred years ago. Yet there are limitations. The king must be crowned in the traditional manner; it would be ill-thought of if he did not attend church, either at Sandringham or Balmoral; he could not be a professed agnostic. He is still that much the king-archon or *pontifex maximus*. God is called upon to save him after every stage and screen performance, as well as by the B.B.C.

Meanwhile, the avowedly religious part of our social organization is altering. After several generations of increasing formalism and interest in the minutiae of the ecclesiastical framework, the Church of England is beginning to disentangle itself from its class loyalties; its leaders are becoming increasingly conscious of 'political' issues, and a change of relationship between church and society, with corresponding discussion and shock, is going on. Something of the same kind is happening in some of the free churches, but Scotland so far has been little affected. I put this down partly to the religious hangover and the fact that emphasis is still laid on personal rather than on social sin, and partly to the inevitable conservatism, which I have mentioned already, of a hell-fire church. Yet in England, where in the mid eighteenth century you would typically have found polite scepticism, erastianism and place- or fox-hunting parsons, you now have the Malvern Conference, and the very interesting and word-worthy spectacle of an increasing number of ministers of the church, from curates to archbishops, insisting that political issues must be attended to, because they are also moral. This type of relationship between church and people will probably, to the future historian, be one of the determining factors in giving the feel of the mid twentieth century atmosphere.

So, once again, the thing is a net, and the back-rope and sole-rope for ever apart and yet for ever bound to each other by the flow moving and giving and half seen and never letting us go.

NOTES ON CHAPTER I

Page 157

Canada was of course French at this time. But it seems doubtful whether England would have troubled very much about the conquest of such an out of the way bit of the French Empire, if the American colonists had not taken the first steps. To them, Canada must have seemed a perpetual menace, with the French officials stirring up the Indians against them. And they must have felt, too, that it was good land wasted. The French tended to be explorers and missionaries, and to trade with the Indians — perhaps to understand them and be friendly with them, in a way the British and their descendants usually fail to do with 'natives' — but not to settle down and take possession of the land. They were beyond the frontier, rather than frontiersmen.

Page 158

I am not sure that my great-great-great-grandfather, Robert Strange, was actually still in Scotland at this time, though he certainly had some months of skulking after Culloden, during some of which he made his living by making rough sketches, pictures of the Prince, or drawings for fans. It doesn't appear that he was, as we say now, 'politically conscious', and he was always dashing back to Edinburgh to see his betrothed, Isabella Lumisden, who did actually do the traditional thing, and hid him under her hoop, when a sudden searching of the house took place. Which only shows how much more gentlemanly, or less efficient, the soldiers who did the search were in those days.

As to his bank-notes, a very few of which are still in existence, I can do no better than quote from James Dennistoun's *Memoirs of Sir Robert Strange and Andrew Lumisden*. His brother-in-law, Andrew Lumisden, was the Prince's secretary, and with him from the time of his triumphal arrival in Edinburgh until 1768, when the Prince, degenerate from drink and misery, dismissed him. Isabella, too, was one of the most active of the Jacobite ladies in Edinburgh, and insisted on her betrothed taking the same line.

Thus it was that Mr. Strange was given the work of designing and engraving the Prince's bank-notes. Some of them are still extant, and the design is pleasant and elegant, though obviously done in haste. Young as he was, he was a good craftsman. Some of his later portraits are very fine, but the pictures which he chose as originals for his etchings are not in this century's taste. But he was a good craftsman.

This is his own account: 'I was shown into the Prince's bed-chamber. There was this evening a ball. After having waited but a short time, the Prince, accompanied by Sir Thomas Sheridan and Mr. Murray, the Secretary, came into the room . . . His Royal Highness was desirous of taking my opinion, relating to a circulation of . . . money . . . which it had been thought expedient to issue . . . I answered Sir Thomas that the subject was entirely new to me; that so far as regarding my own profession, I thought everything of the kind exceedingly practical, but . . .' He went off to see what could be done in Inverness and came back the next evening; they asked what had been done.

'I answered, that it was just as I had apprehended, for that there was no such thing in the town of Inverness as a rolling press; but, that I had had recommended me a very intelligent man of a carpenter, and an excellent mechanic, who had entered into my ideas.' He then showed them his design of a small compartment, to be filled up by the clerks, with the intended sums, with an ornamental border of a rose and thistle. They were to be printed on the strongest paper and then cut separate.

They now talked of larger sums, and he thought they should do something like bank-notes, and he would need to see such notes, to 'concert a form how they were to be drawn up, by whom paid, or at what period; if at a given time, that of the Restoration I imagined would be the properest. This produced a general smile'. He saw his notes, worried about not having the right kind of paper for printing them, went off to see about his press.

'Next day, being Sunday, my carpenter was early employed in cutting out this wood, in order to begin on Monday. It was not so with a coppersmith whose assistance I more immediately required. He was a good Presbyterian and thought it would be breaking the Lord's Day. But necessity has no law; he turned out even better than his promise, overcame his prejudice, went to work and furnished me with a copper plate on Monday about noon. I had passed the morning in making a composition of etching varnish; but had not perfectly proportioned the materials, for I well recollect the aquafortis playing the devil with it: but which was repaired with some little trouble . . . I lost not a single hour . . . I laboured till late at night . . . Not a fortnight had elapsed when I was ready to begin printing, and had even forwarded the notes for a larger circulation.'

Then the news came to Inverness that the Duke of Cumberland had passed the Spey. 'Nothing was heard but the noise of bagpipes, the beating of the drums, and the clash of arms . . . I went betimes to the secretary's office and delivered over the whole of my charge . . . I told the treasurer that an account would be presented by a carpenter who had been very active in serving me . . . and requested that the whole might be paid: which was accordingly done.'

After his marriage Robert Strange spent a good deal of time abroad with the exiled Jacobites, and of course was much influenced by the artistic fashions of his day, so that many of his very competent etchings are of Italian masters who are out of fashion now and likely, I think, to remain in the aesthetic dustbin. Meanwhile Isabella brought up the children; she had a tough time of it, for they were always short of money, and she would have liked some more fun herself. It is clear enough from her letters that she had admirers who might have given her a happier life. But she too had her principles.

NOTE ON CHAPTER II

Page 171

I think this is how sunrise would come to Gleneagles. It did at Cloan, in the next great cleft of the Ochils, north-east of Gleneagles. The autumn night when I finished *Cloud Cookoo Land*, I could not sleep much, and woke early, and went running up through the plantations, holding the finished typescript, and burst out of the High Summerhouse wood into the golden blaze of the sun, coming up, I suppose, over the shoulder of Craigrossie. And so back to breakfast.

NOTES ON CHAPTER III

Page 173

Black William's elder sister, Winwood, called after her English mother's great-aunt, Mrs. Anne Winwood, had married Roderick Mackenzie of Fairburn in Ross-shire, in 1710. She would no doubt have inherited jewels, linen, furniture, dresses and even horses, which had been left by Mrs. Winwood to her mother, with reversion to herself. Perhaps she remembered a little of England; she was born at Cole Green in Hertfordshire. When it came to the '45, Forbes offered Mackenzie of Fairburn the command of one of the Independent Companies which he was raising against the Rebels, and which were not going well up in Ross as the Lord President's own grand-nephew, young Pitcalnie, had gone off to the Prince. After thinking it over for two days Mackenzie refused the command, but remained loyal. He would not fight against the Stuarts 'as this small mealling I possess was given my predecessor by King James V in free gift . . . the case is conscience with me'.

Lachlan Macintosh, who actually inherited Borlum in real life, was the Brigadier's eldest surviving son; the place was left him by his grandfather, over his father's head — the obvious course when the father was a rebel. The other family place, Raitts, had been settled on his mother, but fell in to him, then a minor, on his mother's death. Shortly after the '15, Lachlan went to Rhode Island, where there were cousins; he married one of them, had two daughters, and was drowned, coming home, in 1723. The next boy, Shaw, who succeeded to the property, was a waster (after all his mother died when he was a lad, and his father was on the run or in prison while he was growing up). The two little American nieces stood between him and his inheritance, and in 1736 he went over to Boston where they lived, and kidnapped them; they were rescued and he nearly lynched. His own son, going from bad to worse, became a highwayman and in the end only escaped hanging by an escape, probably to America. He himself may, at one period, have been in Washington's army.

Pages 173-175

See how much more accurate the Gaelic is when dealing with emotion: the preposition aig: at or on, can be used to express something which can never come naturally into English grammar though it may into English hearts. Love is at me on you. It is the sense of love or hate, or whatever it may be, as something outside, which comes at one: Venus toute entière a sa proie attachée. This is the Celtic thing, in which passion is a fate to which one must submit, as happened to Tristram and Iseult or to Deidre and Naisi the son of Usna. De Rougemont in *Passion and Society* speaks of this, and of the death wish, but he has not considered it in relation to the language. It is always difficult to know which comes first. Just as nowadays, when my Highland friends tell me they have to get drunk at New Year because otherwise the thought is too painful of another year passed and wasted, I wonder which came first, the excuse or the whisky. It is interesting to compare the Highland phrase: *The measles are at him*, with the English: *He caught measles*. But I feel as Kirstie did, about the dangers of the death wish and the submission to the passion or the doom that is at one. Though it was an Edinburgh man, David Hume, who said 'the reason is and ought to be the servant of the passions'. I might also, perhaps, refer readers to a poem by my brother, Prof. J. B. S. Haldane, at the end of my first book, *The Conquered*. But then, I have never said we Haldanes were not at all Highland; the Lowland or the Northumbrian ethos might be the stronger, but the other thing will slip out.

Page 174

The Macintosh lament, even modernized, is a beautiful piece of music, and I have used it constantly throughout the writing of this book when I needed to set myself into a mood. There is a record of it, as a duet (Parlophone E 3550). But the words to that and the story of the carriage accident and the dead bridegroom and the lament of the bride: 'Cold is the day without you, my darling' are probably later than Black William's time. He would have sung the older words, the lament of the whole clan for a chief killed by treachery.

It is seldom enough, now, that most of us get a chance of hearing the real music of the Highlands, the Oran Mor. It is the little music, the music of the working clansmen, that we hear. There is a rowing or a scything rhythm to it, and the words will be mostly of barefoot lassies, kissed in the corn or at the sheiling, or of men working or having to leave home, sadly and because of overwhelming economic pressure. The singers of this music will mostly understand that life, having lived it themselves. They will know the undertone of anxiety and uncertainty that lies at the back of the joy even, of mutual love, that is for ever showing through in the music. They are not so willing to sing the Oran Mor, the great music, whose sadness is not the day to day poor folks' sadness, but the deeper sadness and unease of the highbrow, the professional, the bards of a time when bards were highly thought of. These songs are perhaps more difficult to sing, more difficult to get the right understanding of. Their rhythms also are different; their connection is not with the physical body-rhythms of work but with the less easy rhythms of the Highland landscape, of mountain ranges suddenly blotted out by mists, or the complex pulsations of falling water. Or is this over fanciful? There is certainly a relation with early Church music, and Popish music at that, nothing to do with the workaday, though lovely, music of the metrical versions of the Psalms.

Now the second matter which I am constantly observing, is the relationship between the Highland music and the non-intellectual self. The way I see it is that the music both of the songs and of the bagpipes is so intensely emotional that there is only a narrow watershed in it between tears and laughter. You are constantly brought into a state of almost hysterical tension from which the only relief is action. Hence the use of the pipes for supreme evocation of three main human activities: fighting, dancing and mourning. If they had been attached to religion they might have been highly potent. But they were forbidden by the Church. Indeed they might have evoked another kind of religion. Plenty of folk think of them as the heathen pipes. When a friend of mine was hurt at his work he was told it was a judgment on him for playing the pipes up at the Big House on a Sunday evening. And there is this to it; they do seem to blot out certain mental or moral inhibitions: some violent or criminal actions would undoubtedly be easier to commit with the pipes going at one's ear.

I think I can understand how it is that musical people who do not like to have their emotions attacked, who like to listen to music calmly, with a profound, a mental aesthetic appreciation, can hate the pipes. You have to be overwhelmed by them, to give up, to suffer the death wish. In fact if one is listening to a good piper in a smallish room (such as the usual room at the Highland Institute in Glasgow) the vibration appears to have a direct effect on the nerves, perhaps of a slightly anaesthetizing kind. There is a sad and disquieting thing even about the chanters, which is, I suppose, near enough to the pipes of Pan and the earth-spirits. Most reed instruments have this quality of being heard less by the ear than by the middle of the body, and when you add the drones, the music seems to be directed straight at the stomach and loins. Thus I myself dislike a good deal of Mozart, though not all, just as many of my English friends dislike the pipes, because I hear it only with my head, not with my body, even if it is a lovely tune.

Yet see how quick our Highland music will shift from lament to strathspey! A change in the piper's mind, a slither on the slippery watershed of the emotions, and the laughter and dance follow as the Satyr drama follows the tragedy in the pattern of ancient Greek drama. And, like the Satyr drama, the reel and strathspey are not always polite. Most of them went to Gaelic words and many of these words are lost. The authors of tunes and words may be known but they are not published. Some of them go to English words, which are not written down. But anyone with any sensibility, who is dancing, say, to a perfectly respectable melodeon record of a schottiche or country dance, will suddenly realize that something is being expressed which, if put into words, would be supposed to make her blush. It is veiled, or should we say kilted, in musical decency, but only just. The Greeks, coming from a warmer climate and with a non-Presbyterian background, omitted the kilt.

A very fine pretence is kept up, although only some of the women are deceived by it, that this is not so. We would have it supposed that sculduddery is a Dago thing, far removed from our own kail-yards. Our illegitimacy statistics prove otherwise. So does our great national song, to a strathspey tune, of which not one verse is publishable. This does not mean that a woman may not travel alone with greater safety and comfort in Scotland than elsewhere. On the contrary, she will be treated with politeness and as a fellow human being. But if she chooses to light another flame then there will be a fine crackling of thorns beneath the pot.

I am never sure whether it is good for a society to have all this suppressed and seething below the surface. Some kind of a let-up is necessary. We had, and to some extent still have, seasons at which a certain latitude is allowed; there is Hallowe'en and Hogmanay. But respectability would suppress even these. Respectability is an odd thing altogether. Some people think that country dancing is more decent and respectable than the crawling couples of jazz. To my mind that is not so, and it is just why I like country dancing. A long time ago we were staying in a Spanish seaside resort and I was unhappy. There was some kind of Basque festival and the town people came to the large hotel where we were and the visitors came out to watch them dance. Gradually I became more and more separate in mind and finally in body from my highbrow English friends and soon I was down with the waitresses, and then I had slipped into the ring, and then one of the men had thrown me his cap and was setting to me. I did not know the dance at all, but I knew I was accepted among the unrespectable. I danced through the town with the Basques and when there was a respectable motor-car in the street we danced round it and held it up. I would have liked to go on dancing with them all night, but social ties were too strong. Reluctantly I came back from my happiness and the others seemed to think it very odd of me to have been happy that way.

In a dance with a set, or a set and turn, you and your opposite are two birds showing off. The dancers give the low cries of excite-ment that are like the birds': the cry from the base of the throat, from the body. In a dance like the Dashing White Sergeant, the man in the middle of the reel of three is constantly running up, first to one woman, then to the other, checking at the moment of contact almost, the end of the bar catching his foot lightly back. The dancers are upright, tilted back rather than forward, the body muscles tucked in and tense. It is the music that makes all this tension happen, the music that tosses the laughter and low cries out of the dancers' throats.

If I were a psychologist I would try and find out what exactly happens when you hear doubling on a note, what is the physical basis for the shiver you get out of it. For there is the general shape of the musical phrase which is free as strictly barred music cannot be, even though it is normally written in bars, and then there is the flourish which is put on to it. The first with its relationship, which I am not competent to follow, with Gregorian music, and the second with something in the nature of the Satyr play. And both together shaping us into actions.

Page 177

'Winchester in the Shenandoah valley, built of limestone and slate, inhabited by rather uncultured Scotch-Irish.' But not, I am afraid, founded until 1752.

Most indentured servants sold themselves, or were sold, to the Captain of the ship which brought them over, and were then sold at auction by him. Men of 16 to 40, indentured from 4 to 7 years — though the Jacobite prisoners, for instance, were indentured for longer — brought from £16 to £24, that is to say, about their wages for the same time. Of course if they were skilled, they were much more expensive, and occasionally in the south, where there were big estates, scattered 'big houses' and no general system of education, the family tutor might be an indentured servant; he would be treated very much like a skilled Greek slave in the same position at Rome. Irish Catholics were the cheapest.

Sometimes folk came over expecting to be bought by friends and relations, but these had disappeared or had gone elsewhere; they too would be sold at auction. You would also get boys from Great Britain or native born Americans, bound as apprentices and living much the same kind of life. But, even for the convict or 'transport' bound for fourteen years there was always the possibility of getting land at the end of it and doing well. There was always the chance of the frontier.

Page 178

The German minority religious communities often settled down where the Scots and Irish had first broken the ground and then moved on, as the frontier moved, wanting adventure and the chance of a fortune maybe, but not able to manage the hard grind of clearing and agriculture.

Page 178

There was another town which had better luck. The Brigadier's eldest brother, Lachlan of Knocknagel, had a son, Ian Mor — Big John — who was one of the leaders of some hundred and thirty Inverness Highlanders who left Scotland in the hard times, in 1736. They settled in Georgia, and called their town New Inverness, and things went tolerably well. When the prosperous Governor of Georgia wanted to introduce slavery, John Macintosh and the others wrote and signed a petition against it. In this they say: 'It is shocking to human nature that any race of mankind and their posterity should be sentenced to perpetual slavery, nor in justice can we think otherwise of it than that they are thrown amongst us to be our scourge one day or other for our sins.' They might have been foreseeing the events which lay only another four generations ahead of them, when the slavery issue had indeed scourged America and the northern troops were marching through Georgia.

Ian Mor Macintosh, maybe always a wanderer and adventurer, went further yet: he died at his house, Borlum, near Darien. One of his sons was a General in the War of Independence, well thought on by Washington. It may be of interest if I say that I came across all this in the *History of the Mackintoshes*, after writing this part of my book.

Page 178

Some authorities say that the trees were to be twenty-four inches across, three feet up. Actually, these customs duties were more a matter of government and prestige, an insistence on the superior position of England. The plantation duty never met the cost of collecting.

Page 180

We have to think twice before we quite get the hang of eighteenth-century economic policy. Most people of my generation have been brought up on the economic theory of an age of expansion and free trade, which lies below the Marxism which was the next part of our education. And in middle life we find ourselves back in a position of anything but expansion, in which something like the old mercantilism has become part of current thought.

The original mercantilism was a political rather than an economic theory, based on the supposition that war was probable and that a country going to war should have as much gold as possible, just as a well-provisioned household was best able to stand a famine. The general well-being of people in the country (morale) was not considered important, or, perhaps, it was thought to have a religious rather than an economic basis. Mercantilism had an immediate, logical effect on morals. The Puritan, anti-luxury state of mind was mercantilist, and we should ask ourselves whether the religion was appropriate to the economics, or the economics to the religion, or both to the geographical status of Great Britain. You obviously must not spend the national gold on imports of luxuries; if they could immediately be paid for with exports, well and good, but you must endeavour to have as favourable a balance of trade — exports over imports — as possible. Women tended to want the imported luxuries, especially silk, and some foods and drinks such as tea and chocolate, rather more than the men; so the good mercantilist was anti-feminist. He was also against kings and courts and such spenders: and was himself, typically, in the class which was in more or less open revolution against them. He was anti-aesthetic, feeling that imported works of art were one of the most flagrant forms of luxury. There were plenty of texts to back up the economics.

From the nineteenth-century point of view mutual trade with France would have paid; each country had products needed by the other; the greatest happiness for the greatest number could have been achieved by trading; on orthodox capitalist theory it was obvious sense. But Bentham was three generations ahead. The mercantilists in each country insisted that they must have a heavy balance of trade in their own favour which of course made international nonsense. But nobody had begun to think in terms of international sense. They had not been forced by increasingly unpleasant events to do so.

The only way to keep up the balance of trade in a Europe where every country wanted to increase its trade and where machinery was beginning to force the pace, was by colonial trade. Spain, Britain, France and Holland all wanted empires — and not commonwealths of nations, but colonies whose duty was to produce raw materials to be worked up and exported by the mother country. And so, when this broke down in America, when the colonists decided to start industries on their own, the whole theory was shaken, and the mercantilists shocked into what appeared to later centuries as a completely unjustifiable war.

They were duly beaten and their theory received a shattering blow. In fact a new one had to appear to meet the new facts of the situation. It was ready in *The Wealth of Nations*. Adam Smith was a Scot, himself east coast but with strong connections in Glasgow, which had suffered from English mercantilism, especially in this matter of the colonial trade. He had discussed economic theory with the French 'philosophers' — I don't think the word 'economist' was used in its modern sense until the very end of the eighteenth century, when it came from France. He had also discussed chapters of *The Wealth of Nations* with Franklin and other Americans.

But even before Adam Smith's time, mercantilism was beginning to be criticized. Some people were beginning to want free trade with France, especially in Scotland, since English mercantilists were putting obstacles in the way of their Scottish brethren who had, therefore, to try some other method. But religious or politico-religious hatred of France was whipped up by the orthodox in order to discourage trade. We in our time have seen much the same thing happening over trade with the U.S.S.R. in the inter-war period.

Mercantilists, like later capitalists, were always talking about what a good thing peace was, and indeed they really wanted it on the whole, for war meant that the hard-earned national gold would have to be spent. But two mercantilist countries, each wanting a favourable balance of trade, were likely — unless there was an infinitely expansible colonial market, only possible in theory — to go to war sooner or later. It is odd that the similar modern position is still, apparently, not clear to all capitalist theorists.

The eighteenth-century mercantilist line-up — England against the Colonies and Scotland — is clearer from the American history books than from our own, which are concerned, more or less passionately, to show that Scotland gained from the Union. Indeed, this is completely taken for granted now. One sometimes asks oneself whether, if Scotland had been as far away as America, she might not have broken away from England at the same time as America did and on much the same grounds. The economic quarrel, on this side, is masked by the Stewart-Hanoverian struggle amongst the kings and those who thought in terms of royalty and such. Or again, if Wade's roads had been driven across the Atlantic other things might have been different. . . .

Page 181

The Secretaries to the Board of Trade formed a dynasty; there were three generations of Popples. In 1747 the Secretary was called Alured Popple. Other novelists, please note!

Page 184

The morals of the frontier have had a tremendous effect in making the American woman what she is. But for the frontier women, there would have been no Eleanor Roosevelt, and that would be a pity. Yet there is no frontier now, and has not been for two generations. The sharecroppers and Okies cannot move west any longer, or, if they do, they come to California and are duly knocked on the head by the man in possession. So America must develop another ethos.

I feel that this is the moment to add that later on, at the time of the Boston tea party, one of the mob leaders was a shoemaker called Macintosh. He helped to pillage the house of the Chief Justice. Perhaps he was a relation.

NOTES ON CHAPTER IV

Page 189

No doubt the *Essay on Ways and Means* could never have been published at all if, for instance, it had been avowedly Jacobite or anti-Government, and that might account for the dedication to 'The most noble lords, and honourable Gentlemen of the Scots Nation, in the British Parliament assembled' and the somewhat flowery language that follows. But it would not account for the feel of the writing throughout the rest of the book, nor the loving and practical way in which he speaks of farm and estate matters, and of the common people of Scotland. I first read the book myself, in the Signet Library in Edinburgh, and of a sudden I found myself in tears, thinking of the way it was written, only a few hundred yards away in space, up the High Street to the Castle gates and the prison, but too far off in time for me ever to speak with the man who had written it and tell him how some of us are yet working his way: with new methods, new crops, new stocks and new kinds of machinery and fencing: but with his fashion of love and maybe with a better kind of brotherhood amongst the folk of Scotland. I could have told him how some of the things he spoke of had come to be, how we had our Agricultural Colleges, although we need more of them and more money for research, of Stapledon's work in Skye and all that should come of it, of the War Agricultural Committees and their powers, of the Lewis Planning Association, the Skye Crofters Association, and all our other plans for co-operation: things he would have liked well enough to hear. So I, just the same as Margaret in my book, was crying over an old, dead Tory, and that at a time when there was plenty more to cry about.

Page 191

The whole of the evidence for this comes from *The Trial of Archibald Stewart*. The first sittings of this took place between March and June 1747, though the main one was not until July. He was acquitted and at some later point gave a very large silver teapot to his step-nephew, one of my own back-grandfathers on the distaff side.

Page 192

George Haldane seems to have been a straightforward, decent, likeable man, intelligent and tactful; his mistress was a clergyman's daughter from Yorkshire and they had two sons, both of whom did well. The eldest, who, like several of the rest of his relations, went into the service of the East India Company, left in his will instructions about the monument to his grandfather, Patrick. The family feeling has a queer kind of strength, whether with or without blessing of clergy. But this was later. In 1747 Ensign Haldane was with the Third Regiment of Foot Guards — later, the Scots Guards — who had been on the left of the Guards Brigade in the murderous advance at Fontenoy. He had been at the Battle of Culloden, serving under Cumberland of course. There must have been several Haldane cousins, on both sides at Culloden. It would have been easy enough, in a close and small battle, for men to see one another's faces, to know the by-names of the men they were killing, their tastes in books or wine or music, their libraries and their sisters.

Page 193

I am not sure, for all that, if this marmalade was made of oranges. Probably not. Marmalade is mentioned, for instance, in the

Brigadier's *Essay on Ways and Means* (with some annoyance, as a silly luxury) but it may have been made with quinces or some other fruit. Though it is not like him to disapprove if it were made from Scottish garden products. You certainly get advertisements of marmalade oranges (sometimes a grocer would offer oranges and sugar together) in the late eighteenth century, but not, so far as I can find out, as early as 1747.

NOTES ON CHAPTER V

Page 199

Story about ham: when one of the English Commissioners came to stay with Lord Kennedy, and complained, in a somewhat herrenfolk manner about his food, saying to Mrs. Kennedy, the law-lord's wife: 'Madam, your ham is stinking; order it away!' — Mrs. Kennedy turned to her butler and said: 'Did not I order one of my own hams, made at Dalquharran, and not that nasty, rotten, stinking, English one?'

Page 207

It is a funny thing, the way it has now become 'unsporting' to shoot a sitting bird. With the old-fashioned single barrel flintlocks, which were heavy and took an appreciable time to load, you almost had to take a long and careful aim on a still subject. But one of the early triumphs of nineteenth-century chemistry was the percussion cap cartridge used with a fulminating powder. The modern cartridge came into use about the middle of the nineteenth century, producing an important new industry. Naturally the product of the new industry was more expensive as well as far more efficient than the old-fashioned charge of powder and bullets done up in an envelope. The percussion cartridge immediately made it possible for its users to shoot flying birds, especially when you had a modern double-barrelled gun with an internal firing mechanism and an ejector, choke bored from light, strong steel.

But all this meant paying for patents, profits on industry, as well as wages of skilled men. So the poachers were left with the old flintlocks — or, later, with ejectorless hammer guns — and the rich shot the fast-flying birds with their fifty- and hundred-guinea guns. By the time of the good guns the rich had plenty of leisure for walking — pleasant enough after sitting on your backside in an office arm-chair or on the benches of the Westminster Parliament itself, and when there is a keeper and maybe gillies and ponies to carry the bag — and the ownership and monopoly of all the game on all the hills of Scotland was theirs. Driven grouse fly too fast for a cheap gun. Too fast, whiles, for a dear one! But what is a miss anyway, when you are shooting, not for the pot, but for 'sport', for the pleasure of tumbling a flying thing dead out of the air (which, like stopping a ball, does some queer pleasurable thing to the pit of your stomach and all your emotions, as I know myself) for the pride of regarding the bag? The keepers would make plenty out of it, too, partly on selling, but more on wages and tips and, again, power and pride. They would encourage the same idea.

So it became 'unsporting', in some way shocking, to play the equally skilled but different game of seeing your bird, the wee cocked head of a grouse over a heather clump against the sky, or the dark lump of a blackcock in a birch tree, and stalking and shooting the sitting bird. That way one is more likely to shoot them clean and not let them get away wounded as a fast-flying bird can do, even if well shot, on the mere rocket speed of it. As one of the Cameronian preachers said: 'A fowler, when he shoots a bird, it may rise and fly, but not far, for there is some of the shot in it.' And the sitting bird is more likely to be for the pot of the shooter, though indeed he will have had a great thought for the sport of it forby that.

I am asking myself, how will it seem to the Commandos who were sent out on to the Argyll hills with instructions to look after themselves, and feed themselves for a while? No doubt it was mostly the deer they were after and there were plenty stories coming down our way from Inverary, and the things the Duke would be saying, though maybe half of it would be lies or at least a good flourish on the first story! It is only the cleverest of the Home Guards that can get a bird with a rifle. And in the eighteenth century only the most skilled marksman would try for a flying bird; it is said that the Prince was the first man in Scotland to shoot that way.

The story is that, in the time of his skulking in the Outer Hebrides, he used to whistle and get the green plovers — the peewits — to come flying round him, and then he would shoot them flying. Some of his friends tried to do the same thing, but always failed. In fact, there was a kind of flavour of magic about it. But it was one of the things which folk remembered him by. He certainly had no very special gun; it was just that he was an extra good shot. No doubt he would have made the very best of poachers. And maybe that is yet another thing that the Highlands have in his favour.

Page 211

There is a B. MacKintosh, 'a natural son of the Brigadier' mentioned among the names of the men raised in the '15. Among those who were taken prisoner at Preston and afterwards escaped with the Brigadier, was his younger brother, John, a Major in the Regiment. A reward of £500 was offered for his recapture as well as the £1000 for the Brigadier. The two of them made their way to kindly Oxfordshire and hid in the wild woods of Checkendon Common near Ipsden Bassett manor-house, and no doubt they would have slipped in there an odd time or two for food and drink and talk with Thomas Reade, the Brigadier's brother-in-law. And surely they would have spoken of Mary Reade, dead now these three years past, and of the love that both her husband and her brother had for her.

NOTES ON CHAPTER VI

Page 213

This broadsheet was entitled An Excellent New Song on the Rebellion, and has a nice canty tune. It goes:

> Macintosh was a soldier brave,
> And did most gallantly behave,
> When into Northumberland he came,
> With gallant men of his own name.
> Then Derwentwater he did say,
> That five hundred guineas he would lay,
> To beat the militia man to man;
> But they prov'd cowards, and off they ran.
>
> Then the Earl of Mar did vow and swear,
> That English ground if he came near,
> Ere the right should starve, and the wrong should stand,
> He'd blow them all to some foreign land,
> Lord Derwentwater he rode away,
> Well mounted on his dapple gray;
> But soon he wish'd him home with speed,
> Fearing they were all betray'd indeed.

'Adzounds!' cried Foster, 'never fear,
For Brunswick's army is not near;
And if they dare come, our valour we'll show,
And give them a total overthrow.'
But Derwentwater soon he found
That they were all enclos'd around.
'Alack!' he cried, 'for this cowardly strife,
How many brave men shall lose their life!'

Old Macintosh he shook his head,
When he saw his Highland lads lie dead;
And he wept — not for loss of those,
But for the success of their proud foes.
Then Macintosh unto Will's he came,
Saying 'I have been a soldier in my time,
And ere a Scot of mine shall yield,
We'll all lie dead upon the field.'

'Then go your ways,' he made reply;
'Either surrender, or you shall die.
Go back to your own men in the town:
What can you do when left alone?'
Macintosh is a gallant soldier,
With his musket over his shoulder.
'Every true man point his rapier;
But, damn you, Foster, you are a traitor!'

Lord Derwentwater to Foster said,
'Thou hast ruin'd the cause, and all betray'd;
For thou didst vow to stand our friend,
But hast prov'd traitor in the end.
Thou brought us from our own country;
We left our homes, and came with thee;
But thou art a rogue and a traitor both,
And hast broke thy honour and thy oath.'

Lord Derwentwater to Litchfield did ride,
With armed men on every side;
But still he swore by the point of his sword,
To drink a health to his rightful lord.

Lord Derwentwater he was condemn'd,
And led unto his latter end;
And though his lady did plead full sore,
They took his life, they could get no more

Brave Derwentwater he is dead;
From his fair body they took his head;
But Macintosh and his friends are fled,
And they'll set the hat on another head.
And whether they are gone beyond the sea,
Or if they abide in this country,
Though our king would give ten thousand pounds,
Old Macintosh will scorn to be found.

There were also various songs about the death of Derwentwater, as well as the many on the main fighting and characters of the '45. It is curious how singers always prefer the later and usually obvious bogus Jacobite songs. Some of these earlier ones are lovely. There are some good Whig songs too, mostly to lively airs; there is something Cockney about many of them, and some hard hitting. Occasionally there is a definite hate-song against the Scots, as against the Irish. Both are seen as peat-stinking, ragged, sub-men, to be poked like monkeys: here for instance is a Highland lament as seen by a Whig Pan-Alley-writer and laughed at by his fellows:

I sochte my Tonald and my Shohn,
Paith in ae morning creeting;
I thochte she no pe unco teide,
Put only fa'en to sleeping.
Put my Tonald's head rowed owre te prae,
Him's nersh lay owre anither;
I put my Tonald and my Shohn,
Paith in a hole thegither.

Compare 'The Lovely Lass of Inverness'! Yet maybe the truth of the matter is with neither.

Page 219

In the eighteenth century, Gaelic was always referred to as 'Irish' tying it up to a supposedly inferior race, and of course usually in a slighting way. It was not until it had completely ceased to be dangerous politically or to be taken seriously aesthetically, that it was 're-discovered'. Borlum estate, by the way, was at one time owned by 'Ossian' MacPherson. Curious things have since happened to the Celtic languages; they have largely been used as vehicles for propaganda, especially in Ireland. They are not well adapted for this, as they have none of the technical words which are necessary for a modern revolutionary politician. I don't know how much the Erse enthusiasts are laughed at in Ireland, probably not openly so far. And I know little of the position in Wales where there are certainly far more natural Welsh speakers than there are natural Gaelic speakers now in Scotland, or in Brittany; but it is fairly clear that there were some rather inefficient attempts by Nazi agents to exploit the Nationalist situations there, and perhaps in Scotland, by way of the language split.

Here there appear to be at least three ways of taking the language. It can be, and is in some parts, an honest, currently used, second language, although many of those who speak it normally and know plenty of songs in it, would be hard put to it if they needed to write it correctly. They do not, on the whole, read the classic Gaelic poetry, any more than they read equally difficult poetry in English or even in Lowland Scots or Old Scots. But there are few naturally Gaelic-speaking men and women, beyond the very old, who do not, also, speak a version of English, usually with care and with a delightful intonation; some of the grammar and certain phrases will translate literally, and thus give this spoken language an extra tang. It strikes me personally that bi-lingual school children are particularly intelligent, and indeed it is generally supposed that an extra language is a help in itself — though this is usually said of respectable languages such as Latin or Greek. It is a pity that the number of natural Gaelic speakers is always exaggerated by the enthusiasts. Campbell of Canna, for instance, puts the village of Carradale, where very few people speak Gaelic at all, and none as their ordinary language, down as a Gaelic-speaking area!

Then there is the view expressed by An Comunn Gaidhealach: that it is a noble language, an instrument of culture, and should be encouraged. Now I have considerable sympathy with this, and would have more if there was some sense put into the spelling of the thing, let alone the pronunciation, and if An Comunn did not so consistently look back to the good old days and refuse to take any of the necessary steps which must be taken before Scotland can be a worth-while nation again. But what, I ask you, what at all is the point of people learning the Gaelic songs and singing them at Mods with the correct pronunciation but not really knowing what they mean? — and the half of them secretly preferring the jazz which is put across to them with greater persuasive powers than ever the Gaelic songs have! And what is the point of the Mods and the dressing-up and the fraternizing between those who can well afford the price of a kilt or a silken sash and those who have had to save painfully for the cheapest material, if that fraternizing is not going to go on to fraternal action of a practical kind on less pleasant occasions? This is not to say that An Comunn has not done good and is not still doing so to some extent, but I do believe that it is a pity to divert people's energies at such a critical moment as this, and some of those who occupy themselves with the Celtic past might better consider and act for the future.

Finally, there is the view of Gaelic as a political instrument, which I confess I do not find very convincing. I am not even really certain whether some of its protagonists really know as much about it as they would like the rest of us to suppose. In fact, I think some of them are only pretending to with any success because they are fairly sure not to be caught out. Those who might catch them out are usually too lazy or too diffident to do so. Let me put my foot into it still further by saying that I do not believe that a revolutionary change in Scotland will be worked by these people or in their way.

The new Scotland will be away different from the old Scotland, at least in looks. It may drop everything, the language, the music, the dances, the kilt and the plaid, the memories and stories, the remaining crafts of the countryside, aye and the kirk sessions in with the rest. Yet the soul does not die and it returns in its right shape. It will be well to keep certain traditions of thinking and doing alive, here and there, so that if they are what the soul needs with which to clothe itself newly, they can be brought out and burnished again.

I think this is clear from what has been happening in the U.S.S.R. In 1932 nobody was wearing anything but the plainest clothes; they were poor and half ashamed to be interested in anything but machines and politics. But a few men and women kept alive the old Russian culture, knowing that the new spirit, when taking shape, would need it; I believe Lunacharsky had a good deal to do with this. The museums were full and their curators were respected and valued servants of the State, a little out of the main current, but waiting. Now it seems that their spirit is clothing itself in the ancient songs and embroideries and music, reshaped for modern needs. It may be that we in our own lives will hear the Oran Mor of the Highlands, newly written and newly sung, and about the great doings and hopes and joys of an actual people, no longer out of a shadowy and mocking past. But this we will only get if we deserve it and work for it, if we do not cling blindly to the old things, but welcome the new, whatever strange forms they may come under, if they are for the good of Scotland.

NOTES ON CHAPTER VII

Page 220

Most references to family worship show it occurring at night. But how does that fit in with the undoubted drinking habits of some of the respectable church-going gentry?

Page 222

No Scot who knows the history of his or her country will need to be reminded that Auchterarder was a great theological centre, and it was here that the Disruption began. When I first remember it, there was a fine open sewer running down the middle of the street; then an almost equally fascinating sewage system was put in. Later we got the Gleneagles Hotel.

Page 222

I mind how I asked Ian MacLaren, at a dance in the Hall, what was the nicest Psalm tune, and he said Tune Desert, and hummed it to me outside by the byre in the bright moonshine. And many of us will always remember his singing of the Psalms at Lochend Church.

Page 224

Cockburn's *Letters to his gardener: 1727-1744* are fascinating and instructive reading. It gives a vivid picture of an estate and what went on both in the way of activities and in the mind of the improver. One of the people who comes clear out of the letters is Alexander Wight, Cockburn's tenant, fellow-enthusiast and far-out relation. He and his landlord were in constant correspondence, with arguings going on, and good advice going both ways. They both enclosed, sowed grass, clover and turnips, and planted potatoes. Cockburn was very keen on the market garden side of things, always urging Bell his gardener to grow good quality stuff and rarities or extra early vegetables and fruit. He was also most eager for the good of the Ormiston folk, encouraging building and light industries, not to speak of a good public house instead of the wretched little place 'where nothing is to be gott but nasty Barm which we call Tuppeny and by accident ane Oat or pease Cake'. He and the Wights, between them, started flax growing and malting; they took in other people's horses and stirks for grazing, advertising it; they planted trees, they imported seeds and plants, they were forever thinking out new methods.

Apparently John Cockburn finished up with a debt of ten thousand pounds on his estate. The Wights, on the other hand, did well. I think, but cannot find the reference now, that Alexander Wight became Secretary of one of the Improvers' Societies. His son or grandson edited the first Statistical Survey. Probably Wight, the nineteenth-century botanist, came of the same family. I am happy to be able to say that, after the sale of the estate Hopetoun contested Wight's lease, which was by now a perpetual feu, and lost.

Page 226

These Clubs were very prevalent in Edinburgh, the dying Capital, after the Union. It was as though those who might have been living in a high grade and worth-while way, as adults, had lapsed, with the cutting of a vital nerve, into some fashion of childishness.

Page 227

The Honourable Company of Edinburgh Golfers was founded in 1744. Forbes of Culloden was Secretary. Rattray of Craighall was Captain of the Honourable Company. The balls were made of leather and stuffed with feathers.

NOTES ON CHAPTER VIII

Page 231

I am indebted to the Rev. Peter Milne for the name of his predecessor at the Manse at Blackford. The Rev. Wm. Moncrieff, the

Minister in 1747, succeeded his father and was succeeded by his son, Sir Henry Moncrieff.

Pages 232-234

Here I have worked in close contact with the Brigadier's book, the *Essay on Ways and Means*. At times I have deliberately taken a step further than William Dearg went, interpreting his thought into my own century. I believe I am justified in doing this, but, to balance it, if it needs to be balanced, let me here give some of his own words. On long leases (remember, they were still mostly year to year then) with a clause making it incumbent on the tenant to enclose some of his own fields: 'That a law be made, That every Tenant have, from the Term fix'd to begin inclosing his Farm, 19 Years Lease; it cannot in Reason be shorter, because if it take 16 years to finish inclosing his ground, as it may in the low-valu'd land, and the tenant not much at his ease, he has but 3 years to enjoy the advantage of his labour and charges.

'That, during his lease, he be free of all manner of service to his landlord, whatever name it bears, or whatever former paction, either of promise, lease, or tack he underwent; he always paying full rent, customs, kains, in money, victual, and every species as he formerly used to pay, work, either of his person, servants or cattle, always excepted; only one sort of service must still be continued, because I don't see how it is possible gentlemen can go without it, which is, carrying home their firing.

'For, in Scotland, the Nation being intirely destitute of forest, or indeed any quantity of woods to furnish burnwood, and pit-coal being found but in a little corner of it, both which firing might be carried by a few loads; and a cellar of coals, or a moderate stack of burnwood, will serve for firing to a gentleman's house in England, or the South of Scotland a year; whereas 20, yea 40 that bulk or number of loads will not serve of the dry'd moss they use in the most parts of Scotland: wherefore, I am afraid my farmer must serve his Landlord in firing as formerely.

'And I verily believe, when my farmer compares the number of days he commonly was call'd out to his master's work, in plowing, harrowing, sowing, cutting and leading his corn, and building his corn and hay, his servants sent with letters or errands, he will find, that ditching and hedging the fifteenth part of his ground in a year, will not cost him so much, or more, days or labour; and if it should

a little more, let him remember, he now works for himself: for, tho'
he pays as much rent as he did the year his grounds were opened,
the acre he has enclosed this year is his own; last year, it is a chance
if his neighbours beasts, or his own, it is all equal loss, did not eat
a great part of the corn; if they did not his corn, I am sure they did
his stubble, and not thank him for it: for the remotest neighbour
thinks he has as much right to it, when the corn is carried off, as he
who sows or pays rent for the field. Can that be call'd mine, I have
no property in, but the three or four months it is under barley, oats
or pease; and even that third or fourth part of the year subject, by
cow or sheep-keepers sleeping or playing, to be intirely eat up and
destroyed? Besides, these keepers must have victuals and wages;
which charges, and considerable ones too, is saved, when your
grounds are inclosed.'

On his Agricultural Executives: 'I humbly conceive it proper,
that the honourable board do pitch upon, in every shire, three or
five noblemen and gentlemen, of intire, upright, and impartial
characters, and not confine to quality, so much as to having their
inclinations mostly turn'd to improvements, who should be vested
with a power, to judge and determine all disputes arising betwixt
gentleman and gentleman, or gentleman and tenants, in matter of
inclosing, or any hardship a master may offer his farmer, contrary
to the words or meaning of the Act to be made in their favours.'

On his Agricultural Colleges: 'If such a society was establish'd of
practical Agricules, and not speculative philosophick ones (such as
Marcus Terentius Varro calls *Theophrastus*, a Grecian Philosopher, who
writ Volumes on that subject, and of whom Varro says, *He was a
very good Philosopher, but a very chargeable husbandman*), his experiments
would cost more than would pay the charges when practised; but
such, as experience taught the difference of soils, seasons, grains,
cattles, which was fit for the draught, which for fattening, and which
for the pale? Rather than from the perusal of the best authors, ever
treated on that subject: I affirm, such a College would prove of more
real and solid use to the island, to have it establish'd in some, if
not in all our universities, than many of these the munificence of
several princes have endued with large revenues to teach the other
sciences.

'And how much soever, by the *beaux esprits*, I shall be laugh'd at,
I cannot hinder myself from being of opinion, that if professors
rerum rusticarum would every year emit theses on that science, and

hear problems on it propon'd and answer'd, such as, whether or not the most barren acre of land in Scotland, rocks excepted, is not capable, by denshiring, or some other kind of husbandry, to bear some sort of corns, some of the many sorts of grasses, or some of the various sorts of trees?

'Whether laying down to rest a third, fourth, or fifth part of all our land now plowed, being before well ordered by fallow, and in heart to recieve the proper grass seeds for that soil, by which our stock of cattle will both increase in numbers and goodness; and the three, four, or five parts under tillage better dunged, better laboured, and we being more masters of it, we sow less and reap more, than when it was our master, is more eligible, than continuing our old husbandry of plowing and sowing much, and reaping little?

'Whether of the three, four, or five, parts we do labour, it is better to fallow every year a third part; or, without rest or intermission, to plow all as formerly?

'I ask, whether such queries, reson'd on by students, who will or may bring, by the next appointed day to their hall, ears of corn, or wads of hay, to prove the reasonableness of the affirmative part of the theses, is not of more real intrinsick value to the commonwealth, than the speculative problems of the establish'd learned schools?' Denshiring, by the way, is the practice of burning — presumably old grass and bushes or even peat — as done at that time in Devonshire. I suppose it supplied necessary potash. In North Africa, the wheat stubble is regularly burnt by the best of the French farm-colonists.

On the Galloway enclosures, which had shocked Kirstie too: 'I am sorry to own, that the example of the hardships the commons of some part of Galloway lately suffered, or rumour to have suffer'd, has given too much grounds to the whole commons of the nation against inclosing.

'I shall not enter on the province of the civilian, to enquire, how far a man can exert, or extend to the prejudice of another, his power in managing what is call'd his property? Or, whether the penalties of usury, a traffick, by all laws in all civiliz'd countries, exploded, is incurr'd by raising land, as well as money, to too high a value? But my conscience indites to me, that the commons of Scotland have as much right to live in Scotland and pay rent, as any landlord has to live there, and receive it: and, as God Almightly has destin'd them to earn their bread with the sweat of their brow, he gave them Scotland for their theatre to act their toilsome part on. They are certainly as heritable tenants as we are landlords; and if their charters be narrowly, diligently, and impartially search'd into, it will be found the oldest: a decisive circumstance in law.

'And I think, in justice, should be so here, tho' they cannot show their charters in writ. Their blood oft seal'd them, when then there were no signet-writers in Scotland, no charters for lands, but the swords that purchased and defended them from the enemies of Scotland. Undoubtedly it was their very ancestors, who first, against picts, and other aborigines, conquered the kingdom; as they surely were they that, ever since, against Britons, Romans, Saxons, Danes, and Norwegians, defended it; when a great many now illustrious and powerful Scots families, their Ancestors were then of these Nations fought against her.

'I know, these old tales are of no value, by the laws now of use; but, I can never be of any other opinion, but that justice and gratitude fixes an indelible obligation upon us to use our commons well, and to convince and satisfy them, that we never design any other, than to live and let live.'

I have quoted almost word for word from the book, on schooling. He was highly critical of the academic education of his time — essentially ministers' education for making more ministers — just as I am now of the academic education in Scotland to-day, where boys and girls are still taught to value a smattering of snob-Latin more than the necessary technical education of a modern citizen.

Page 235

Professor MacLaurin, who died only a few months after the siege, was 'Chief Engineer' and obviously passionately interested — he even got the Trades to work on Sunday! One's general impression of the events which led to the surrender of Edinburgh to the Tories is that there was general slackness and muddle, people unable to make up their minds which side to be on, a lot of volunteers rushing round, meetings in churches and taverns, a few devoted Whigs and a general Tory sympathy, while the ordinary citizens were completely split. If the city was defended, they might all be killed. Also they were against the regular army. Nor were they unconcerned that the defence works were very expensive. Patrick Haldane was deliberately unhelpful. But I do not know if my explanation of his conduct is the correct one.

NOTES ON PART THREE

Note on the Jacobites and the Campbells

IT is worth considering what happened to all this Jacobite feeling. Off-hand one would say that the whole thing was dead and buried, that it is as unreal now as the disputes of the early heretics. The basis of the thing has disappeared. It is doubtful, even, whether there is a Jacobite pretender to-day; in any case, if there is, nobody can possibly take him seriously. Enough has happened since the '45 to give even the Highlands other things to think of. It had become remote and unreal even before most of the Jacobite songs were written — ten or twenty years later, when such sentiments could be safely expressed by ladies and gentlemen. But that is not the whole of the story.

For it seems that the Prince has taken on some of the qualities of the Kings who Die for the People, the queer company of those who are thought likely, or worthy, to rise again and come back to their people in times of difficulty and distress either as a divine spirit or as a God or hero; the company which includes Agis and Kleomenes, Spartacus, Cleopatra, Nero (though this has only just come to light past the victorious phalanx of Christian historians), King Arthur, Roland of the Marches, Friedrich Barbarossa and Holge Dansk, the Bruce, Drake, perhaps Parnell or still later Irishmen, and in our own day such people as Koloman Wallisch whose legend I have tried to help to make. Nobody in the Highlands knows or cares how, actually, Charles Edward Stuart died, nor after what degradations, although they know that he, the same as themselves, used the Water of Life wrongly for the little death of forgetting. Nor do they think of him objectively. What they mind of is a relationship, the fact that he learnt their tongue, made friends with them, and did the kind of wild, silly, risky things that they like to speak about still, and that they never betrayed him, not even for thirty thousand pounds and they dead poor. For those whose confidence and moral courage has been undermined, it is well to have such sources of pride and such a standard of loyalty. It is something to hang on to until better times and a real, genuine thing of their own, in thought and action.

Nor is this attitude confined to the old or to those who might be expected, say, to vote Conservative. Your Socialist may be a Jacobite and so, I think, may your Communist, if any complete Highlander can ever be a complete Communist. Further: the contradiction is fairly plain between the oppressed, disreputable, class-conscious and increasingly political Jacobite worker and the respectable, success-ful, Whig laird. In fact, the conscious Whiggism of the laird which was often allied with social and technical progressiveness on his estate — a paying thing up to quite recently — sometimes forced on the underdogs a reactionary Toryism, reactionary because it held on to their own things which they understood and which had served them more or less and also because it looked back to an increasingly blurred and mythical golden age of stability and laziness and even a kind of brotherhood. That is dwindling out, but it has not quite gone yet. Doubtless the workers will find themselves another and newer mythology and transfer their loyalty to other leaders. It may be that international socialism will in time produce a sufficiently potent and valid loyalty to reach to the glens. Such things might run along the new lines of hydro-electric power.

Meantime the other thing has a good historical foundation of which Highlanders are well aware. It was the victorious Whigs, backed in the main by the established, Whig, Presbyterian Church, which took the land, first of the useless ex-fighters, the clansmen, and then of their crofting successors. The clearances were on the whole a Whig misdeed. The typical successful Whig was the MacCailein Mor, the Duke of Argyll, chief of the Campbells. This has led to a situation in which I have been told, perfectly seriously, that no Campbell could be a good Labour Party member.

This is all rather disconcerting. The eighteenth-century Party names have had a different historical fate in England. Both Labour and Liberal parties have used the word 'Tory', quite inaccurately of course, as an abusive synonym for Conservative. Even at election times, when we appear to be able to swallow anything, this always gives me a slight historical belly-ache. But, for England, it was fairly sensible. The Tory Party meant the party of landed privilege. It was in no sense the Jacobite party, the party of the under-dogs, the Highland oppressed.

These historical hang-overs cannot quite be disregarded by the practical. You may consider the whole matter of tartans is a tailors' racket, but yet there are some tartans that will make you feel a wee bit uneasy to wear. If you are a Campbell you will be made exceedingly uncomfortable if you happen to go through Glencoe and that although Glenlyon was only passing on the orders from higher up, and although the massacre itself was negligible by modern standards. If you happen to be a Campbell with an income, say, of under £500 a year and living in or near the Highlands, you will find certain difficulties. The sins of your chiefs will be visited on you. From your childhood you will feel that some people at least distrust you, think of you as a crook-mouth, a deceiver. It will be rare if you do not to some extent react to this, for good or for evil. You may find things weighted against you in other ways, at school or at work or at play. In fact, you will be very slightly in the position of the Jew; the Jews, just the same as the Campbells, were rather more successful and less stupid than their neighbours. Probably the middle class and aristocratic Campbells are not worried in this way; they and their schoolfellows will have forgotten any unpleasant historical passages, although I have heard sweeping statements of a disparaging kind made about the Argyllshire Campbell lairds, and that by those of their own class but another clan. For that matter, I myself would have a slight vestigial hesitation in trusting an upper-class Campbell; I would feel myself minding in my blood and bones of my kinship with Montrose and my enmity with 'the master-fiend Argyll'; but yet I would tend to trust the working-class Campbell. Thus showing that one mythology has overcome another.

To revert to the Jacobites: what is not clear is whether in 1747 a politically intelligent and objective person such as I make out that Patrick Haldane was (and still more supposed himself to be) would have realized that the Jacobites were potentially the party of the under-dogs. He would, I think, realize that the Whigs were the party of new privilege, perhaps the coming danger — it would be plain by then to anyone observing *English* politics, so long as they could do it without too much emotional hang-over from the Glorious Revolution. But it should have been clear by the middle of the century in whose interests that had been.

Nor of course had Jacobitism or Toryism any real hope for the under-dogs. The Stuarts were an attractive and intelligent dynasty when not warped by some terrible pressure as children, in the way that James VI (James I of England) had been. They might conceivably have done something for the Commons of Scotland, their natural allies against both the nobles and the new rich *bourgeoisie*, but I doubt if anything would have got farther than the Statute

Book — where already many admirable and even democratic sentiments and hopes had been duly set out and never carried into action. Quite possibly the development of the Highlands at least might have taken place with less immediate pains. But it would have come to the same thing in the long run. Whigs and Tories alike stood for privilege. The real hope lay with the Sceptics, those who were pulling down the structure of an oppressive society, the Encyclopaedists in France, David Hume in Edinburgh, and soon, in their very different ways of thinking, Tom Paine and Wilkes in England. In Black William's America the thing was now becoming plain which would lead in another thirty years to the Declaration of Independence.

Yet it remained that Jacobitism gave something to the Highlands which has helped to tide them over what we trust has been their worst time. I, speaking bitterly to a Highlander, a member of the Argyll Labour Party, of Highland laziness, lying and double crossing, was answered: 'Well, we didna betray Prince Charlie.' Because Jacobitism gave a legend and a small warm spark of comfort to Highland folk, and not for any false romanticism, not for the swing of the plaid nor the skirl of the pipes, not for the bogus songs nor the coloured postcards, but for the soothing of sore Highland hearts, not into sleep but into bearable absence of pain, let us deal gently with their Prince.

NOTES ON CHAPTER I

It is not quite clear what position the good Marxist takes on this matter of witchcraft and fairies and whatnot. I have known them to get as much annoyed when the subject came up as the Ministers themselves — and by that I do not mean the modern Ministers who never took the thing seriously and so are prepared to be ever so broadminded, but the old school for whom it was something of a menace. I think there are several things to be said about this. In pre-revolutionary Russia the superstitions of the peasants and perhaps of some of the workers, held up the course of change, just as the church did. They were equally enemies. The church is having a come-back (let me risk my neck by saying that I find this rather repugnant), but not, I think, the witches, who were less well organized. The Russian attitude is of course obligatory on Communists elsewhere. Equally, the revolutionary protestant church found its enemies alike amongst the old church and the fairies who, as it says in the song, 'were of the old profession'. Both Catholicism and superstition undermined the power of Protestantism, hence all weapons must be used against them. To be against superstition was not, however, to be rational; although you were a violent Calvinist you were yet of the same pre-scientific flesh and blood as your neighbours who had other beliefs; and you tried and burnt witches and warlocks in a state of unreasoning fear. It was only the new and as yet powerless enemies of the established church — the sceptics — who found the witch trials not only shocking but most unnecessary.

What can we say about this? First, perhaps, that the more you want something to happen, the more likely you are to attack blindly and perhaps to mistake your enemies, and the more impossible it is to do them justice. Justice, like poetry, must be made in tranquillity. Of course, things may be so urgent that justice must be overlooked; that seems to happen in times of war and civil war. Second, that well-rooted things take a long time to kill.

Adam Duncan speaks scornfully, though in the idiom of his period, about the appearance of a fairy host and the coming and going of shot in a wishing well. James Haldane answers that these things, though unimportant, as Adam also considers them, may distract people's minds from 'reason and religion'. At another point of time, two centuries ahead, he might have said 'reason and political consciousness' or even 'reason and revolution'. Yet to-day at the second point of time, six generations on from a society when such things were already being disbelieved in, there is still evidence of the fairy host's recent appearance, in the usual rather accidental way, as though, in two sheets of paper carelessly rubbed together, two pinholes might for a moment coincide and a view might be taken through them. As to the coming and going of shot in a wishing well: in January 1933 six of these shot from the wishing well in question were sent to me by registered post. The story was that they always disappeared within twenty-four hours of being taken out of the water. They were put into a clean handkerchief; when I opened it there were only a few grains of sand, which either were put in with the balls or which the balls had turned into. It was said at the time that the well in question was about to be filled in or in some way destroyed by the owner of the land on which it was. I have not been able to verify this, nor have I had any subsequent dealings with the well. Difficulties appear to be put in one's way when one attempts to deal with such phenomena and I am not myself prepared to say that these difficulties are merely caused by Highlanders wishing to cover their own lies and devilments, though this might have something to do with some of it.

An attitude of scepticism before all phenomena is probably desirable. What gets me down is when people believe any kind of nonsense they see in print so long as it is labelled marvels of modern science or new methods of raising the dead (or whatever you like) in the U.S.S.R. or the U.S.A., as the case may be, but yet disbelieve in all forms of magic. Worse, perhaps, they have a kind of half belief in all sorts of unofficial charms and luck tokens, not to speak of gremlins (I ask anyone who has been in an air raid or series of air raids to answer honestly whether he or she didn't conjure up some image of luck to help him through: some object to touch or wear, some corner to be in, things of the utmost irrationality but yet they worked — that is to say for the survivors who are the only people who can tell about them), but they won't so much as see a genuine fairy walking within a yard of them! And indeed I myself stand half-way between the two attitudes in a state of suspended judgment that swings sometimes to one side and sometimes to the other, according to which I am arguing against.

Most of the people in my book are also in a state of suspended judgment, but are rather readier to believe seriously in certain supernatural manifestations, and especially in witchcraft, because that was still a general social belief and had been approved by the theocracy, at any rate until quite recently.

The witch trial at the Crook of Devon took place in 1662, one generation later than the trial and death of a warlock John Brugh, who had exercised his powers in Glen Devon and Muckhart. Two of the witches were named Brugh and were probably relations of his, for such things tend to go in families: such at any rate was the theory, or how else would my fellow countrymen have been prepared to torture the seven year old child of a witch, as they did at another trial? However, I refer to child witches again in a few pages.

The trials make very queer reading. It does not appear as though the coven — twelve women and one man was usual, the man perhaps acting as substitute for the devil at certain ceremonies — had been tortured to give evidence, though they were no doubt frightened and knocked about. One or two were old, none very intelligent. It appears that there was an orderly fashion of things at the trial, and one of the witches, Agnes Pittendriech, was respited owing to her pregnancy, and perhaps escaped, as there is no record of any sentence on her.

What strikes one at once is that it is all on a very small scale. Even Sathan only appeared 'in likeness of a man with grey cloathes and ane blue bonnet, having ane beard' or 'at the dykes of the muir, in the twilight in the evening, like unto a half-long fellow with an dusti-coloured coat', though once he seemed a bonnie young lad. Another time he was 'riding on ane horse with fulyairt [dirtied] clothes and an spanish cape'.

It is doubtful whether anyone gets from the devil more than they can imagine. To get Helen, Faust must be able to imagine her. These poor folk at Crook of Devon got little. Sathan desired them to be his servants and they seem just to have given in. Robert Wilson, the warlock, said that Sathan promised him both gold and silver, which he never got, and sundry times gave him meat and drink but they did him never good. Agnes Brugh was promised a braw gown, but it was not said whether she got it. And ae and always the mark that was given was a sore one, 'painful two or three days'. Many of them could not remember the 'new name' which was given them when they renounced their baptismal name. But Agnes Murie, who sold herself to Sathan for 'als much silver as will buy you as many corn as will serve you before Lammas' (not a large price for a soul, one would say, but presumably more than could be got by any other means) was called Rossina. Bessie Henderson, who had been 'forty years in the devil's service, since the time she milked the old Baillie of Kinross his kye before the calving', she was named Bessie Iswall, and the devil who gave her this name in the night in her bed, was called Charles. Bessie Neil's new name was Sarah and Sathan's Simon. Janet Paton was called Annas and her Sathan was Thomas Roy. Another, Janet Paton, aged sixty, was more fancifully named Nans Mahoun, while Isabel Rutherford was called Viceroy.

One asks oneself whether some stranger, possibly a wee bit queer himself, but wanting to go to bed with some woman, might not have persuaded and frightened a poor thing here and there to accept him as Satan. Or was the whole thing made up by the women themselves?

What they did was all in a small way, whether killing or curing, but mostly the former. There seem to have been occasional attempts at curing which came to nothing. James Kid of Muirhauch, diseased with 'the trembling feavers the space of twenty-two weeks', was charmed by Isabel Rutherford at the head of the Black Craig, but 'he was not the better nor was never well since syne'. There were small revenges to be taken, as when Agnes Murie said to Henry Anderson, who had apparently been sowing bear for various people: 'My bear land would have been better had ye laid a loak lime upon it as ye did the rest.' Henry rashly said that it needed none and a while after he had a stroke. Bessie Henderson and Janet Paton together tramped down Thomas White's rye, in the beginning of harvest, and Janet who had broad soles 'trampit down more nor any of the rest'.

Margaret Lisster had for a time cured several folk of the falling sickness, once for the price of a stand of clothes for her husband. But the time came when the cure ceased to work. Margaret Lisster can have got no fortune from the devil, for she was going round from house to house selling leeks and begging.

Old Janet Paton did most of her evil for a small matter of vengeance on her neighbours. A young farmer, leading his father's peats, let the cart go through Janet's muck-heap. There was scolding and flyting, the horse brought home that load but was never able to draw another, but dwined away and died. Sixteen years back, the same Janet having 'an lippy [only the fourth of a peck!] of lint seed sawn in the deceased Lawrence Keltie, his yard, two travellers having laid down their loads to bait themselves and their horses, two of the said horses went in and weltered [rolled] on the said lint; the said Janet . . . scolded and flett, and immediately there after the said Janet Mailer's ale went clean back that no man nor woman was able to drink the same the space of half an year thereafter.'

There were midnight meetings and dancings, sometimes with a piper playing, but again all on a small scale. Everyone there was on the edge of extreme poverty and hunger, so that very small things would tip the scale between being able to get along with enough meal in the meal-kist to last till next harvest, and having nothing at all, even for porridge. You might well hate and envy your neighbour who happened to have enough and even a wee bittie over. And everything so cold and uncomfortable, not even the pleasure of going to the cinema once a month and sitting in the warm and seeing the comforts of Hollywood. Anything to escape from the day's darg, anything to get a wee spark of power, anything, even hell!

The warlock who was their predecessor, had at least done things in a bigger way, with much circumstantial casting of spells, and doing impressive things with enchanted stcnes. He and his cronies met sometimes in the kirkyard of Glen Devon, and sometimes with the devil himself at Rumbling Brig. He had done more curing than killing, although, if he thought his pay insufficient, he might revenge himself, as on John Kyd, the maltman, whose 'wort grew thik lyk sowings [sowans — porridge] and stank lyk gutter glaur [slime]'. Brewing is a tricky business, even now, and it would be convenient to put any failures down to witchcraft, and I suggest that some company might try it on their next shareholders' meeting if ever a brewery was to do really badly.

One cannot imagine any of this happening in a reasonably prosperous community, where people have some security, both economic and scientific. As things were then, you probably did just as well to go to a witch as to a doctor. But whenever people feel themselves insecure, they are most easily affected by luck, whether good or bad. Luck comes into it yet, in, we'll say, a fishing community. Equally those who practise the extremely insecure artistic professions, will be affectable. I have been ill-wished myself, and that formally; I was extremely frightened and took various traditional measures against it. Whether it could have had any 'objective' effect or not, is beyond me. Psychologists tell us that we never break a bone nor lose something unless we want to in some subconscious part of ourselves. Well then . . . ?

Now, let me go on another tentative step. Children are often insecure, and that although they live in circumstances of physical security. Small children do not make any clear mental distinction between animate and inanimate objects. They cannot or will not understand the rational explanations of their elders, possibly because these leave out something which should, for full reality, be in. Children are, comparatively speaking, in the insecure position of people in a pre-scientific age.

These children may be attacked by desperate fears. Such have been fairly often described by fiction writers, De La Mare, Compton Mackenzie at the beginning of *Sinister Street*, not to mention Robert Louis Stevenson with 'All the wicked shadows going tramp, tramp, tramp'. Such children, in silent desperation hidden from loving and rational parents, as from school friends who might laugh or betray (though the process is often a pre-school one), will make peculiar bargains with the torturers. If for a night they can be exempted from terror they will knock their heads against the bars of the cot, they will lie rigid, will time their breathing, or worse yet. And they usually make bad bargains and are betrayed by their fundamentally inhuman and implacable masters or mistresses. This is a frightful situation and the bargaining becomes more and more shameful and pitiable — and very like the miserable bargains of the witches. At some point the child may in despair give up and go through some psychic process equivalent (for the moment) to selling the soul.

Now, can we hazard a guess about the entity with whom the bargain is made? I think it may be, to borrow for a moment the Jungian word, a very early matriarchal archetype, savage and implacable as the pre-Hellenic, pre-Edda, and long pre-Christians' Gods were rumoured to be. Such Gods were man-eating and mad-making. The child who has had experience of them may, in the course of a classical education, recognize with a slight shock his old friends, slightly toned down into the Eumenides: 'Parakopai, paraphorai'.

What this comes to is that we in the twentieth century are forced to recognize the existence of Gods, and these not noble and nude and antique nor in any way attractive. Yet if certain entities appear separately in the psychic fields of a number of individuals, they represent something. We can call them archetypes or Gods or what-will-you. We can be saved from them, but probably not by our own efforts, except in so far as we can be integrated away from them. Apollo saved Orestes from the Eumenides. At a time when Western civilization was Christian in a sense which it is not now, those that did not choose their Saviour (or who were not chosen by Him, were not of the Elect) might easily relapse into the power of the other Gods, which, very properly, was taken with great seriousness. All this makes historical sense. Can we now be saved, not necessarily by a Saviour-personality, but by some method more acceptable to our epoch?

It is possible that we have here some hint of what has been happening over part of Europe. It is possible that the inhuman and implacable, sacrificial cruelties of the Nazis are due to a psychic regression. 'Race' may be merely a new name for the Mother Goddess who was before Odin and Thor, who was also the Witch who, inevitably and implacably destroyed Baldur and who was to exist again after Ragnarok. We cannot be certain of this until a number of Nazis have been psychically vivisected, which will be a difficult and unpleasant, but necessary job.

Now let us revert to the bargaining child. The child has done something which appears, on a certain level of consciousness, to have been *absolutely* shameful. On another level of consciousness — the daytime consciousness of twentieth-century urban civilization — it is just dreams and nonsense. But when the level drops, as at night and near sleep, the thing again becomes real somewhere in the psyche; the shame is there, as deep as the shame of betraying comrades, and it lasts throughout life unless subjected to some psychic process which will annul or explain it.

This may not have serious social or even individual consequences now. But what would have happened a few hundred years ago? The person to whom this happened would probably have become a witch or warlock. They might not have wanted to do so. Consciously, they might have struggled against it. But the thing would be too much for them. Finally, they would have confessed. This might partly account for the child witches, though no doubt there could also be a psychotic family tendency. However, it is quite certain from the accounts that only some of the witches could have been psychic cases of this kind. Some of them, as I suggest in a later note, were certainly victims of compulsion neuroses, others may have been members of a kind of political secret society, others were simply healers or extra-sensitive persons trapped into the thing and often the victims of superstition and jealousy. There was also no doubt a direct connection with pre-Christian fertility religions. Such religions were often presided over by a destructive mother-goddess of the type we have considered.

This note should be read in conjunction with the later note on page 328 and the earlier note on page 173, Part II. It may be objected that I have swallowed Jung whole. But I am inclined to think that Freudians might come to more or less the same conclusion by other roads. There is certainly a connection between the mother-goddess archetype (though I don't think 'mother' is quite the word for her except in so far as she is the pig or rabbit mother eating her young in what might be called a markedly absorbent form of love! — no doubt she *is* half animal and often animal masked) and the Celtic death-wish of which I speak in the earlier note. I believe the original

Celtic archetypes or Gods were mostly of this nature, though now they have degenerated into kelpies and such which may be exorcized by the sign of the cross or (as in *We Have Been Warned*) by some other symbol.

Page 262

The second Earl of Albermarle who was completely Dutch by birth, was, at the time of the '45, a middle-aged Colonel. He commanded Cumberland's first line at Culloden and in 1746 he was appointed Commander-in-Chief in Scotland. Both Cope and Hawley, who had held the same rank before him, had been failures and he very much disliked the idea of following them. 'I know the people,' he said, 'I know the country, and that my predecessors have split against a sharp rock.' It was certainly no easy job, especially for a foreigner, and his letters show a thorough dislike of the barbarous country. This is clear from his letter quoted in the notes to Part I. His special instructions were to catch the Pretender, and he was constantly being bedevilled by Highlanders full of incorrect information for which some of them at least were anxious to be rewarded. There are times when one wonders at the patience and general decency of the English army of occupation. But this was before the days of total war, and the standards of civilian decency, built up through centuries, had not yet been thrown to the winds.

He left Scotland in March 1747, when it appeared that there were more urgent matters than the military occupation of Scotland. His successor had a much smaller and less important force of troops under him.

Andrew Fletcher, the Lord Justice Clerk, was a nephew of Fletcher of Saltoun, and in his way he too was a patriot. He stood between the Scots people and the Dutch or English commanders who neither understood them nor wanted to. He was a decent, honest man and as such esteemed by his compatriots.

Page 265

Marriage by repute is no longer legal in Scotland, nor is the old form of marriage before witnesses. In fact, civil marriage has become much harder to contract than it used to be. It seems a pity, though it sometimes led to awkward situations. My own mother was very nearly married by accident during a charade, where one of the audience happened to be a magistrate.

NOTES ON CHAPTERS III AND IV

For these two chapters on the Indians, I am very much indebted to my friend Kenneth Porter of Vassar University. We kept up a correspondence about Indians and such throughout 1943 and 1944, the first draft of my chapters dodging across the grim Atlantic. He advised me on my reading, but some of the books were not to be had this side, and then by chance in the London Library I came across the book Black William mentions: *Mœurs des Sauvages Ameriquains*. This so fascinated me that I had to change the part of the world to which William went. Originally I thought of the Algonquin Indians, but then realized that the Algonquins had been pushed out by the date of my book. I dithered over the Penobscot Indians, but again it seemed that by the time of my book, they had degenerated. There was nothing for it but the full romance of the Five Nations — and a change of names and other detail.

In the course of our correspondence it came out that the Highlanders (and to some extent the French) got on best with the Indians, and intermarried most, though that was usually in the south. Here among the Cherokees and Creeks, there are plenty of Highland names: Macintoshes, MacGillivrays, MacKillops, Rosses and so on. But some of this was due to the adoption of white child captives by Indian tribes. It is interesting that Americans who would be made bitterly uncomfortable by the suggestion of a remote negro ancestor, are yet proud of their authentic Indian blood, so long as it is some little way back. There is an Indian artist to-day, whose real name is Alexander Macintosh, though he finds it commercially better to be known as Blue Eagle. It is thought that the changeover among the Creeks from the matrilineal descent (to sister's son) to the ordinary European father-to-son descent was due to Macintosh influence.

Kenneth Porter also told me of a famous Indian raid on the New Hampshire-Maine border which happened in 1724, a little before Black William's adventures. All this must be familiar to Americars, but for Scottish readers I must quote the lines from the ballad which celebrated it:

They murdered Captain Lovewell and wounded Mr. Frye
Who was our English chaplain. He many Indians slew
And some of them he scalped while bullets round him flew.

Mr. Frye was 'a young Harvard student paying his way through
the college by picking up a little scalp-money, or trying to, just as
his companions of a softer breed were helping earn their way by
teaching a winter term in school'.

About the land-grant: I am afraid a good historian of the period
would query it. The Iroquois had a rule that no land-grant was
legal unless made by the Chiefs in full council. But no doubt that
was because this sort of thing had happened earlier. Also they were
New York Indians, under the protection of the King of England
through the Governor of New York, and nothing to do with Massachusetts. Though of course one wouldn't put it past a Boston man
to go out and try to swindle the Iroquois out of their land. I am
not really sure whether my Indians were Mohawks or Iroquois. It
was all so far from Scotland.

The main town had to be Boston, because of my own remem-
brance of it. The one and only time I ever set eyes on Boston was
in the late winter of 1935. We made our landfall in the afternoon
after a rough and cold ten-day crossing. My friend and I stood on
land at last and smelt again land smells, good and bad, as dusk was
beginning to fall. I can mind yet on the trodden snow and the
black tarred sheds and the American voices and the queerness of
the sea suddenly being stopped by this other land mass. This way
I must always think of Boston in snow and strangeness.

There is something maybe a little doubtful about both the
marriage and the baptism; but Devonshire folk are friendly and
easy-going, and this Minister might have been the same. I'm not
quite sure how William managed about taking the wee boy all that
way for his baptism; perhaps he was on horseback with the baby
slung behind him. But people have done queerer things.

The detail of the treatment of the prisoners is mostly from *Mœurs
des Sauvages Ameriquains*. The camp in the snow under the spruce is
really a memory of Long's *Northern Trails* as dreamt over by a child
in Perthshire, by two children, as witness my cousin Archie
Haldane's *The Path by the Water*, where, separately written about,
though in the same year, you have on page 58 his version of the tree
house.

Page 288

The caddie, or cadie (either from old Gaelic cad, a friend or French cadet, a young son) is really a runner of errands:

> The useful cadie plies in street,
> To bide the profits o' his feet.

NOTES ON CHAPTER V

Page 302

The old castle or keep at Gleneagles is said to have been pulled down late in the eighteenth century. There is very little left of it now. The Office of Works took it in hand, with the family prowling around — I remember my father saying one day that they were unearthing quantities of ancient bottles! It is very much like the usual Highland keep (Castle Campbell for instance on the farther side of the Ochils) with a single room all the way up, and a circular stair mostly in the thickness of the wall. There were huge fireplaces and windows also in the thickness of the walls, where it might just be possible to have a kind of slight privacy, and in the thickness of the bottom walls there were vaulted holes that might do for storage or prisoners. On each floor however there was a privy from which a shaft went down, connecting with the main drain at the bottom, which also took kitchen refuse; this in turn went out by a cesspool to the loch. The castle is said to have been seven stories high. It must have been something of a nightmare to live in it and I don't think any modern writer has quite imagined what that life would be like, nor for that matter what it would be like if you were fighting from floor to floor. I suppose there would come a moment when you could set fire to it and it would roar up like a chimney, roasting the men and women who had been driven up the winding stair on to the top floors.

Yet this was where Marjorie Haldane and Squire Meldrum met and loved and behaved in what seems a civilized, though somewhat unorthodox, way. I should think the ground floor was always the kitchen, and the gentlefolk lived, mostly, on the next two floors. Marjorie's garden would have been on the island, though no doubt there would have been stables and byres on it as well.

Page 303

Water power began to be extensively used in the Ochils in the second half of the eighteenth century. There are mill lades everywhere and mills, mostly decayed, either for threshing or for lint; in the latter case the mill pond would most likely have been the steeping pond for the flax.

At Upper Cloan and at Cloan there are the remains of two ancient mill systems, which must have been worked in series, the Upper Cloan water being dammed back, though the dam is now little more than a small marsh, and then being let go into the Hoodiemart burn. Here it was caught again into a long mill lade which can still be traced here and there all the way down the glen to the old mill wheel at the back of the laundry. Yet, now that I come to think on it closer, it seems to me that there is no longer a mill wheel, nor has been for many years, though I can mind on the leaves of the fern growing on it.

But water power is not very satisfactory, as we know at Carradale. For either it is wet weather and plenty water in the dam but too wet to put in the corn, or else it is dry enough for the corn but not enough water in the dam to get us through the threshing. We know just how it is, when the mill is running well, and then all at once the noise begins to come chunkily and uneven and the rollers slow down and there you are with a sheaf unbound beside you and not enough power to pass it through the mill.

The mill pond at Upper Cloan was smaller than ours at Carradale, and must have been still more unsatisfactory, so, some time towards the middle of last century, my grandfather brought in one of the travelling mill-wrights. By his work, which still stands, we know that he was a great craftsman. He made a round building, slated into a superb cone; below it the roof of radial couples and sarking closing in to the centre, has a Gothic and ecclesiastical beauty. This was a closed horse-gang where a pair of horses going round and round could turn the mill all day. No joiner now would undertake to repair this building, but it still stands firm and the Boy's Brigade who camp at Upper Cloan know it well.

But now we have gone back to water power, and another of the burns, but a bigger one, is harnessed to a turbine, and when the lights burn dim at Cloan we know they are threshing at Eind.

NOTES ON CHAPTER VI

Page 311

The attack on Patrick was really rather odd. He was accused of almost anything that anybody could think of, including bribery and not always wearing a gown in the courts . . . It was said that he had drunk the Pretender's health on his knees, and also that, when Professor of Ecclesiastical History at St. Andrews, he had, 'instead of attending divine worship, several times diverted himself with his companions on the Lord's day by singing to the psalm tunes the arguments of Spencer's Cantos intermixed with much noise and laughter'. This strikes me as a very highbrow thing to do, but one must remember that, when he was Professor, Patrick was about the same age as a fourth year student at Oxford.

Page 313

The evidence for all this, and much of the rest about the Brigadier, including the escape from Newgate in Part II, comes from a rare booklet: *Brigadier MacKintosh of Borlum, Jacobite hero and martyr*, by A. M. Mackintosh, printed in Nairn in 1918. Indeed, when I say 'rare' I know of only one copy, and I need to go to the Signet Library in Edinburgh to read it. Though what pleasanter place could one have for browsing and noting than that warm, airy hall among the smell of book leather and the soft streaming in of sunlight on to white pillars and brown law reports, and Mr. Malcolm piling up one's table with dozens of delightful books, any one of which is enough to start the mind stravaiging away down promising historical by-ways! — oh, see you not yon bonny road that winds about the ferny brae, for the muse of historical research is the Queen of Faery, alas only too ready to leave the solid ground of economics and facts. But a grand change altogether from snedding turnips! (Since writing this I have, in June, '46, just bought an uncut copy for 4s. 6d. from Grant's in Edinburgh. So now there are two anyway.)

However, to return to our Macintoshes (and I will stick to the one spelling): the evidence for the events of 1725 seem to come mostly from the State Papers in the Public Record Office in London. It appears that in '25 the Brigadier was 'up and down the country' and chiefly at the house of his son Shaw, the black sheep of the family — and it is possible that the Brigadier was trying to coerce him into behaving decently. I have left him out of my story because, supposing this William, the eldest son, had lived and been the kind of man I have made him out, then probably Shaw, too, would have been other than he was. So I have put the Brigadier's brother, Joseph of Raigmore, in as host; actually Joseph was tenant of part of Raitts, possibly living in the Mains farm.

Things fell out as I describe them. Lieutenant Harris thought he would surely catch the Brigadier; he arranged for the Government Messenger, armed with a Secretary of State's warrant, to come in. This messenger, Mr. Peter John Du Commun (an odd name — I only point out that *Comunn* is the Gaelic for people or association, but probably this is a mere chance) did so and arrested the Brigadier who only asked to be allowed to go up to his bedroom to dress. Some of the soldiers were searching the house, others guarding the prisoners — the Brigadier, Joseph of Raigmore and a servant. However, the country folk seem to have got wind of what was happening in this Highland way which is so irritating to any administrator! One would have thought that eight armed men might have held the house against a presumably unarmed mob. However, it didn't work out like that. Perhaps Lieutenant Harris was really reluctant to shoot. Anyhow there was a fight, in the course of which Joseph was wounded while defending the messenger and the Brigadier escaped, perhaps still in his dressing-gown.

Poor Joseph was kept a prisoner on a charge of high treason, made all the more complicated because the warrant was made out, not for Joseph but for John — that is, the Brigadier's brother who had escaped with him from Newgate earlier on and for whom there was a fine reward offered. Lieutenant Harris wrote in December: 'I applyed to Mr. Duncan Forbiss for councell who has been ask'd before by the friends of the Prisoner to officiate for him, which he told me he had refus'd to do, and that as McIntosh was a relation of his, he desir'd I woold excuse him if he likewise refus'd to act against him.' Finally Joseph was released on bail, one of the witnesses in his favour being the Messenger Du Commun, who had evidently made good friends with him!

When the Brigadier was finally arrested in 1727, he was completely penniless. But he certainly had friends. In 1740 one of the subscribers to a new and expensive History, in Latin, was 'The Honourable Brigadier General William Mackintosh of Borlum'. But, as I have said before, these were the days before totalitarianism towards enemies.

Page 322

The Terra Navis is a ship-shaped moraine at the foot of the Ochils, dating from the slow falling back of the glacier that planed

the ridges of Craigrossie in the last Glacial Period. I doubt if anyone
has ever put a spade into it; in my childhood, at least, it would have
been commonly supposed that anyone so daring as to attempt it
might have met the owners of the hill coming out of the turf to make
their protest. That side of the Ochils is full of caves and gullies and
entrances, though there are more foxes than fairies living in them
these days, and making full as much trouble for the farmers.

Page 328

This note will refer throughout to Jung's book, *The Integration of
the Personality* (English translation published by Kegan Paul in 1940).
It is probably unintelligible and also uninteresting to those who have
not read the book or who are not to some extent familiar with Jung's
theories and his use of certain words such as shadow and anima,
which have other meanings from the specific and technical ones that
he puts on to them.

I bought *The Integration of the Personality* in 1940 on the strength
of several reviews, but though I started reading it that year or perhaps early in 1941, I was unable to go on. It had no significance for
me, or rather I did not intend to allow it to have significance at that
date. The 'I' of the last sentence being the rather forcible bull calf
'I' which overcame the merely intellectual 'I' which read the
reviews and paid for the book and was correct in supposing that the
book would be important for both the 'I's, but wrong about the
timing. Actually I did read the book when I was more than half-
way through my own, in 1943. My book was by then completely
planned, although none of the details of the last part had been
worked out and I was not at all sure how the balance of personal
relationships would finally swing; nor was I aware that Black
William had been lying quite as completely as I later found out he
had been, in the first chapter; he and Patrick were always the ones
that eluded me.

It then became clear to me that (to vary the phrasing in the hope
of arriving at the meaning) I was not intended to read it until I
had worked out my own version of the integration of a personality
(in other words, again, the saving of a soul). Now, when I write
'intended', it may be asked, intended by whom or what? In another
historical period, I might, without undue arrogance, have answered
'God' or 'The Lord'. In the present period, I do not say so; it would
not be anyways true in the sense most people would take it. At

present I think one can without undue strain conceive of an intention *per se* without a personality of any kind behind it, although this may not be a correct interpretation. Some people may find it easier to think of the force behind the intention as a zeitgeist or as pressures of economic or emotional circumstances. Others may simply say I am talking through my hat. Perhaps I am.

I will not now go into the context of my dreams, which, by 1943, encouraged me to suppose that Jung had the right fish by the tail. A second reading of his book in 1945 confirms this, though it also makes me certain that he had not, at that date, got clear in his own mind what are the limitations of the 'shadow' and the 'animus' or 'anima'. I would like to remind his followers that the Egyptians had a number of different names for clearly-defined parts of the individual in relation to various aspects of psychological knowledge of that epoch (see my own *Corn King and Spring Queen*, Part VIII).

This re-reading confirms me in an earlier opinion that the whole thing is (perhaps inevitably) written so much from the male point of view that it is sometimes quite disconcertingly difficult for a woman to follow it sympathetically. The man is the individual; women are a lump. It is not very pleasant to read a book in which you are considered as part of a lump. It is deplorable that, so far as I know, no woman of genius has written on the psychology of the unconscious from the female point of view: or that it has not been possible for any psychologist to overcome his or her limitations and write about it from a bi-sexual point of view which would be even more valuable. One of the difficulties is that most women psychologists are afraid of being anything but stern and practical. One sympathizes with this point of view, but it is a pity.

There is also the difficulty pointed out by Jung (p. 95) that 'traditional symbolism is chiefly a product of the masculine psyche and is therefore not a suitable object of imitation for women'. (Rather an unfortunate way of putting it, yes, no?) One has only to consider how very different the Doctrine or Symbolism of, say, the Virgin Birth and the Mother and Child is to a man and to a woman. For many men, and some of the really great among the Christians, Mary was their final and stable anima-form. Whereas the woman must tend to identify herself, to insist on Mary stepping down from her pedestal and becoming human (as in the tale of the erring nun). Could it be that Protestant man's Mary-hatred has something to do with his fear of this identification?

To return to 1943. It then became apparent to me that Kirstie in her witch episode (during a psychosis induced by great personal unhappiness combined with the shattering of such religious symbols, especially the Tables of Communion, as Calvinism had left her) had almost drowned in the dark waters of her own unconscious and was about to submit to her animus conceived of as the Devil in his many shapes, some foul and some surpassing bonny. Now submission is an essential part of integration: there appears always to be a period or moment of crisis during which it is disastrous to be proud or to insist on being a wholly conscious individual (a very arrogant as well as false thing to suppose one is). Submission is necessary at this stage, but unfortunately it is not always so clear as it might be whether what-is-submitted-to is of good or of evil, or neutral power, which, afterwards, will be integrated and may be used for great good by that-which-submits. Kirstie then, was about to submit. But at the moment of her crisis, the animus was projected on to a real person, William, who thus became her soul, her breath, and in whom she was bound to have the utmost faith since he represented something stronger than her conscious self, and, as she considered of it, in the idiom of her age, nearer to God.

Jung says (page 23) that no woman has portrayed the animus. That strikes me as questionable. What about Rochester? (I rather think Stella Benson portrays the shadow.) What about my own Tarrik? I don't think the animus need be quite so definitely non-human as the anima is as drawn in *She*, still more as Goethe's Helen or Dorothy la Desirée in Cabell's *Jurgen* (I'm afraid I haven't read Pierre Benoit; he struck me as a second-rate author). But the animus has to be recognizably 'over life-size'. Of course the films allow for far more divine happenings than a mere book or play does. Perhaps the perfect animus or anima image should not be in writing at all but in a cartoon feelie. I ask myself sometimes whether Mickie doesn't represent something below consciousness in most people. I am not at all sure that the dark and light winged horses in Disney's *Fantasia* are not archetypal. They certainly are to me.

Now, what about William? He is not dressed Greek or Egyptian fashion, as Jung suggests is appropriate for the anima, but at some time he does wear what is certainly the most becoming male dress, though no doubt not suitable for a Mediterranean climate. And with that he is a 'noble Huron'. He is many-sided and some of the sides plain bad. In so far as he is the animus, though a Highland version of it, I doubt he is likely to be no more sympathetic to a non-woman (or completely male man) than She or Helen are to a non-man. Yet I would hope that, in so far as he is also a semi-historical human being, he might be liked by some of his fellow men. The breeches-wearing Bull Calves, such as Patrick, Mungo and Robert, ended by liking him; but they all had a kind of she-side to them (their animas?) and I have thought the same of later generations.

In my book the hero also goes down into the dark waters and finds his soul, of the one part in Ohnawiyo and of the other in Kirstie. He puts his dream on to Kirstie at the beginning, but does not come to her in the flesh until one side of this dream has met, and sickened of, itself in the shape of Ohnawiyo, who is pre-Christian and in some way royal. As She and Helen and the rest are always thought of as Queens. I have let William speak of her as the Nixie, though I doubt he would not have used quite that word. But it is the best word for the woman shape in the waters.

Now of course it would never have done for William and Kirstie to know themselves and their problem in terms of analytical psychology. Instead they need to put the thing as it might have appeared to them in the words and ideas of their own time, with the additional help of Gaelic phrasing. But, because the archetypes of the unconscious are no less of the eighteenth century than of the twentieth — or any other fully human century — so some of the images will be the same. The more I read about and consider of witchcraft, the more it strikes me that a good many of them must have had what I suppose are now called compulsion neuroses. An apparently external voice and personality forced them to do what they knew was wrong. One occasionally gets into that situation in a dream; and the resultant misery and guilty feeling, even in this shadow world, is such as to make one realize something of what some witches must have gone through.

I would like to add that the simple and immediate projection and identification by either sex on to a member of the other, of animus or anima, is almost certain to lead to disaster. The man who finds his dream girl behind the tobacconist's counter (or in the Rectory garden for that matter) is set for trouble, as his elders often know; and the girl whose dream hero carries her off would certainly have done better to stick to Gary Cooper or Frankie Sinatra. In fact, if you are going to have the romantic, adolescent conception of love which prevails in the desymbolized and impoverished Protestant world, it is perhaps as well to have it on the screen rather than in real life. But what happened to Kirstie and William, though on the surface almost as simple as that projection, was really much more complicated. So a happy ending is for them permissible and even probable.

With these clues I will leave those interested to work out the Jungian basic plot of my book. But perhaps we might go back to *The Integration of the Personality* and see what else can be wrastled out of it.

Jung says (page 23): 'It may be that a woman's animus writes her novels for her, and thus escapes portrayal.' To which I say yes, very likely, but (*a*) why shouldn't the animus enjoy painting its own portrait? and (*b*) what about the anima — isn't she equally writing the man's novels for him, and that in the respectable Ionic chiton and sandals of a Muse? So much so, in fact, that a man may quite legitimately and without being laughed at refer to his muse? But it is a slightly awkward matter for a woman — unless it is Apollo himself who comes to us: a bitter god to follow, a beautiful god to behold. But I think most authors, man or woman, must know how writing may be either intensely laborious, exhausting and fully conscious, with an accompanying sense of pushing a machine uphill or swinging a cold engine: or else semi-automatic, flowing and with an accompanying sense of running or flying downhill. This second kind does not always last long, but it is very exciting, because one really doesn't know what one is writing until after one has written it. It is usually good and certainly controlled by something other than the ego. However, the ego has to go over it afterwards. I don't know what other writers find, but I know my own animus (if that is what it is) occasionally goes in for gross lapses of taste.

Jung also speaks constantly of the general impoverishment of symbolism, which lays mankind open to 'perils of the soul', not only the too direct prophetic vision which may shatter the soul: 'the voice that blasts the visions of blown glass', but also the danger of other symbols and myths invading the helpless victim, a state of things only too plain in modern Germany (as I have already suggested). Now, we cannot just clean up and re-use symbols or myths which are still in general use but have lost their potency and interest, though this is a mistake which is often made. We have to have mythologies which will be potent and protecting for our own era.

I have already written about this in *The Moral Basis of Politics* and I have tried to use a new set of symbols in fiction in *We Have Been Warned*. But I have thought of the symbols, not merely as protection for the individual, but also as social glue, doubtless another aspect of the same thing.

Of course when I say they are a new set, none of them are really new; they are only symbols which have disappeared for long enough for humanity to have changed in relation to them and for them to be described freshly. This way they become again potent (or looked at in another way, fertile). An example of an old mythology re-made is to be found in Wagner, whose symbols have been perhaps only too effective. Or again in Ibsen's *Peer Gynt*.

Many modern writers are aware of the dangers of insufficient symbolism and are hunting around for something. But, besides satisfying them, it must be reasonably universal. Auden and Eliot both use symbols and redescribe some of the major archetypes. They do not do so, however, for the general reader. But the general reader would probably not read them anyhow, and I think they are justified in making things difficult for the kind of person who does read them; in fact a great deal of the excitement of reading both these poets comes from the sudden realization that one is looking afresh on one of the great symbols.

Olaf Stapledon has attempted an entirely new symbolism or myth, but it is not altogether easy on the mind. It is not quite alive, in the way that the old ones are. And I cannot see how it can be, since it starts outside and they start inside. Yet I believe some elements of his mythology might attach themselves to the old one and have life breathed into them. If once they come alive, they might be the 'Gods of the Stranger' which people have always turned to when their own Gods suddenly ceased to have *mana*.

Not all writers get a direct vision of the archetypes in the way that Yeats, for instance, seems to have done. Is it worth noting that the early Yeats — presumably before he came to the self knowledge and state of relative integration of his later years — was always using images connected with water? — even his beasts were otters and fish-eating stoats. And the water is the inevitable way for the searching soul. (See Jung, pages 65 to 73.) Perhaps somebody should study Blake's Prophetic Books along these lines — a grand idea for a Ph.D.! May I suggest that the chapter on Phoebe's dream or vision, in *We Have Been Warned*, written before I had read any Jung, corresponds quite remarkably in its images to his classical ones. Phoebe starts her *athlon*, her labours of the soul, with an 'unbearable situation' (Jung, page 90). She jumps out of the window. After that her adventures are very largely in water, ending where she goes over the falls, into the whirlpool (Corry-vrechan) and presumably down to the bottom. Erif Der in *The Corn King and the Spring Queen* also starts her process of integration by going down into the waters of Lake Moeris.

Another good subject for a Ph.D. would be a critical examination of *Mein Kampf* to try and spot the point where Hitler met his shadow and his never very strong ego became overwhelmed by the anima. His speech is so often exactly like that of someone possessed and assimilated by the shadow, in the classical way. (See page 92.)

However, none of this is very clear so far. And we can make no end of a mess if we try to see round more than one corner ahead. A great deal of preliminary work remains to be done.

Page 329

William had called Kirstie 'My Soul' often enough, and almost as often I have heard it used here, but when I asked folk why they used it, or how it came into their speech, none of them knew. I am indebted to Douglas Young, who tells me that it is actually a phrase of West Coast Gaelic — M'anam agus mo chridhe -- My soul and my heart.

Page 332

The real name of the Lord President's man was not Wattie Buidh (which means yellow Wattie, and is a very common nickname in the Highlands, to this day, for a real yellow-head), but I wanted a Gaelic-speaking man, and, though John Hay, who was in real life the Lord President's devoted servant, might have been Gaelic speaking, he has not the kind of name which makes it sound inherently probable. And there was another John in the book anyway!

I think John Hay must have been a kind of secretary; he kept his master's accounts, and that even during the flight of the Lord President with many of the leaders of the Independent companies across the moors into Skye, while on the Culloden estate and among the tenants there was raiding and burning and killing, not only from Forbes's old enemies taking Highland revenge, but also from

Cumberland's soldiers acting as an army of occupation. None of that, however, was going to stop John Hay, on his methodical master's account, from putting down such items as: To 2½ lbs of tobacco 2s. 10d., or a pair of second-hand boots 2s. 6d. And, as Wattie does in this book, so in real life John Hay nursed his master. At the end, during the last five weeks of Duncan Forbes's mortal illness, John Hay never even got undressed nor left the sickroom for a moment. At the end he wrote to Grizel Forbes (Mrs. Ross of Kindeace) to tell her of her brother's death: 'Madam, The ever to be lamented, my dear Master, Lord President died this morning at eight of the clock and is to be interred in David Forbe's tomb and in his dear brother's grave; I have not words to express the grief that is among all the people here on account of his death — and as for myself, I believe I shall soon follow him . . . I can write no more from grief but ever am the family of Culloden's and your affectionate servant, John Hay.'

This is quoted from Menary's excellent *Life and Letters of Duncan Forbes of Culloden*. I have used this as a main source for anything I have written about Forbes, though I have also consulted the *Culloden Papers*. But I cannot now remember whether it was from there or from some other of the many books I have looked through that I got the statement that, even during the '45, Duncan Forbes's rhubarb was always given a safe conduct through the rebel lines. It was clearly not for nothing that *The Jacobite Journal*, announcing his death as 'a gentleman of great merit and of an universal good character', says: 'We shall always praise merit, even in a Whig.'

During the four years that I have been at the writing of this book I have read or glanced through a great number of books, papers and so on, and sometimes I have not been so methodical as Forbes — perhaps having no John Hay to help me to it — and have stored some wee fact in the back of my mind with no label attached to it to say where it comes from. I think I usually know when the thing is a pure invention of my own, though, when it is, it may be rather in the nature of a deduction than an invention: for I will have put together snippets of fact from one source and another and perhaps added to them some piece of modern scientific knowledge which binds them together logically, and the result, though it is not to be found just like that in any original source, is yet sufficiently probable to be very nearly an authenticated fact.

Note on Scotland — The Union

PROBABLY most thinking Scots folk have asked themselves at some period in their lives whether the Union with England was or was not a good thing. If it was bad for Scotland, it would probably, sooner or later, be bad for the world in general. It is harder to tell whether it was bad for England, and indeed the discussion of this point would involve a long and probably pointless moral analysis. In this note I am not going to do more than sketch in some of the main features of a problem we ought to consider soon, if we are thinking along the lines of political devolution for Great Britain.

There have been a number of books and pamphlets written on this subject, for the most part either about the time of the Union or else during the second quarter of this century. Ian Finlay's *Scotland* in the *World Today* series may have set a new lot of people to thinking on the matter. The history books on which most children and students are brought up, both north and south of the border, take it for granted that the Union was a good thing, and there is no more to be said about it. History books for young people provide, perhaps rightly, comforting certainties, facts to be learnt by heart. One only begins to question them after a number of counter-facts have thrust themselves up on one's attention. Books which put both sides, such as Mathieson's excellent and detailed *Awakening of Scotland*, are not necessarily the student's choice for exam passing.

I think it is quite plain that, at the time, there was really no alternative to Union with England: that is to say, short of a complete and revolutionary change in social structure, which could not have happened because there was as yet no economic basis for it. The actual ruling classes of Scotland, the nobility and landed gentry — many of whom were also engaged in trade and thus had much the same interests as the ruling class of merchants and industrialists which was soon to succeed them — were for the Union. On the whole the ordinary people were against it, and petitioned against it continually from shires, burghs and parishes; but, although many of them were shopkeepers and traders, few of them were rich enough to be engaged in trade in at all a big way, and I doubt if they realized that Scotland's commercial future, if it was to develop on English lines, was bound up with the Union.

The rulers of Scotland were, as the custom was, partly black-mailed and bribed into acquiescence with the Union, yet I am sure that many of them felt, on what appeared to them to be reasonable grounds of political principle, that Union was the right thing. The few intransigent men of principles, such as Fletcher of Saltoun, were, like most of those in all countries and at all times who have held extreme opinions, somewhat out of touch with the common run of opinion and feeling. Such folk are easier to admire at a distance than at the time, when it seemed likely that their point of view would lead back towards hatred and bloodshed and 'enthusiasm'. Fletcher of Saltoun's suggestions for social and economic reform may have been logical, but scarcely commend themselves to anybody now.

A few voices were raised, at the time, for Federal Union. Ridpath's suggestions seem, now, sensible enough. But this was not what England wanted and was determined to have. The proposal was before its time.

Nor had the Scots Parliament been long enough on its feet to be an effective Anti-Union force. It had consisted of representatives of the various estates, but they had never formed a 'government'. Admirable statutes were voted and put into the statute book, but there was no machinery to get them put into action. There had been for a couple of centuries too many nobles and too little money, and the squabbles of the nobles were reflected in parliament. The English Parliament had, by 1707, had a century and a half of real power. The Scottish Parliament was only just beginning to feel for it. Many of its most prominent debaters saw themselves with a bigger and more profitable London stage. It died easily.

The immediate result of the Union was a relaxing of economic tension, and a fairly immediate lift in the standard of living for the rising class of merchants and their families, whether gentle or simple. This came after some particularly hard years of bad weather and poor harvests, as well as the depression created by the Darien failure. The Union was generally claimed as a success, and on the whole the Church of Scotland was for it, or, if they were against, it was for rather tortuous reasons.

The nobility found themselves agreeably placed in London, and became increasingly Anglicized. After two hundred years this process is singularly complete! The Scots members in both Houses were the respectable supporters of the Government, over-anxious to assert that Scotland was not culturally or economically separate, seeking to prove their steadiness and trustworthiness and culture against a fairly constant stream of anti-Scottish feeling. In many ways they certainly were less civilized. They did not hold with the relatively modern English plumbing; they preferred their dinners heavy and smelly; they spoke in an unintelligible dialect. In fact, they didn't wash and they had no old school ties.

In the early days the anti-Scottish feeling in England nearly ended the Union. The Malt Bill of 1713 was an attempt to shift too heavy a burden of taxation on to Scotland, and the Scottish representatives in both houses indignantly resolved to regain their economic independence. That came to nothing, but there was plenty of bad feeling for another hundred years. Sometimes it has a curiously modern, anti-semite ring: 'Let but the Scotch mingle among us as they ought, and keep no separate interest, and then we should be as little jealous of them as we are of any other of our fellow-subjects; but while they hang together and are partial, they provoke us to do the same.' Where have we heard that lately — ? In the latter part of the century Bute made matters much worse. No progressive person could be anything but anti-Scots.

Yet the respectable Scots themselves did their best, poor dears, to remedy this state of affairs. They learnt English style oratory, and copied the fashions and became deadly ashamed of their wet, cold, barbarous country. In Edinburgh, quantities of imitation London publications were issued. As the eighteenth century went on, one finds more and more *Tatler* style essays and verse some way after Pope. The Edinburgh writers are aggressively apologetic, and wary; they are expressing themselves in a half foreign tongue, and proud of their success in so doing. Allan Ramsay tried from time to time to Anglicize his verse. So, rather disastrously, did Burns. All this set the tone for historians and biographers: the Union was a good thing.

The Anglicizing of language had, I think, something to do with moderation in the pulpit. The Arminians and, finally, the Deists, who were gradually permeating the Church, were careful of their language. It was only the rude and violent, the Marrow men and such, who described hell-fire in braid Scots. Now, moderation and toleration are, in a certain sense, an *absolutely* good thing — Kirstie thought so! Your moderate did not burn witches nor condemn the sins of the flesh with tyrannous inhumanity. But yet that is not the whole story. Moderatism went with a certain gutlessness that was never recovered from except by some of the Evangelicals, and that has left its mark on the Kirk and on the people of Scotland who, when speaking unofficially, sneer at their Ministers as men who 'only work once a week', and who have taken on a soft job with steady pay. Which is, indeed, only too often the whole truth.

The new town of Edinburgh may be cited as an example of successful Anglicization, though the *D.N.B.* thinks badly of Craig's original plan! I have not seen it, and do not know how far it was carried out. He was certainly a thoroughly Anglicized Scot, and the brothers Adam, to whom some of the best of Edinburgh is due, were Anglicized architects. One sometimes wonders whether their artistic expression would have been freer and more original if they had not felt it their duty to follow the best models. I believe that one of the wickedest of all Scots, Lord Braxfield, was responsible for the single-sidedness of Princes Street, which makes it so out of measure beautiful — or would if the built-up side were anything but a row of shops fighting one another for an architectural show-off.

The mid and late eighteenth-century Scots were, as far as we know, almost unanimous in general approval of the Union. After the '45 they became nauseatingly loyal subjects. But we must ask ourselves now, what might reasonably have been expected to happen to Scottish culture if there had been either no Union or a Federal Union.

I am thinking less of direct politics and religion than of general culture. Of course, a war with England, perhaps as a result of the Stewart-Hanoverian opposition, would have been disastrous. But, apart from that, how would things have been?

It looks as though Scotland would have been a poorer country for some time. Yet we must not exaggerate this. It was certainly exaggerated at the time, and Graham has, I believe, over-stated Scottish poverty and over-influenced the many readers of his excellent book. If we consider, for instance, the important account written by Thomas Morer in 1689 (partly reproduced in Hume Brown's delightful *Early Travellers in Scotland*) it does not seem as though Scotland struck the impartial observer as being much poorer than England, except in actual cash. They were certainly short of gold, but Morer thinks very well of the crops and stocks and the larger towns.

And, whatever happened, there would still have been the minerals — iron and coal especially — that were to be Scotland's economic mainstay in the nineteenth century. We would still have had natural harbours, facilities for shipbuilding, and — when the coal age was past, and the hydro-electric age come — ample water force for new industries.

If everything had not been orientated towards London, it seems likely that Scots would have developed a culture which might have been stronger because less imitative and self-conscious. I cannot think that our Scots writers, scientists, painters and inventors would have been crushed out of existence in a Scottish as opposed to an Anglo-Scottish society. Burns would not have died in worse poverty!

This assumes peace between England and Scotland. Why not? Norway and Sweden have survived worse political tension than there was between England and Scotland in the early eighteenth century. One cannot now imagine one of the Scandinavian countries at war with either of the others. By the nineteenth century it would surely have been equally unthinkable between England and Scotland.

It seems likely that, without the political pressure from London the disastrous split between Highlands and Lowlands would probably not have occurred. The smashing of the clan system might have been obviated, and a different and less painful evolution for the Highlands would have been possible. The end result could scarcely have been worse than to-day's, and might have been much better. It is surely not too fanciful to suppose that a purely Scottish development might not have involved forced depopulation of large areas and the skimming off of the cream of young and vigorous life from the Highlands.

Probably the increased economic prosperity during the eighteenth century did make for a higher standard of general culture, and did release social and aesthetic impulses of a civilizing kind, including the tolerance of which I wrote earlier. Yet it was certainly bad for Scotland to be run by Secretaries of State. The Dundas oligarchy kept the peace, just as it kept the places, but it stunted the growth of democracy.

If Scotland had been a real democracy, effectively governing herself, she might have given less martyrs to the cause of liberty, equality and fraternity at the end of the eighteenth century. But Dundas had put his foot down on municipal reform, the one way in which Scottish democracy was attempting to express itself. The reformers became Friends of the People. Muir was arrested, tried, sentenced to fourteen years' transportation. The Scottish Convention of Delegates of the Associated Friends of the People, joined by English delegates, became the British Convention. English and Scots political martyrs went together to Botany Bay.

During the prosperous nineteenth century it was taken for granted, alike by industrialists, technicians, writers and the landed who let their moors, that the Union had been an excellent thing, and that Scotland should not be thought of as a separate national entity. The interest of Great Britain was indivisible. It was only some of the Irish who thought otherwise. Great Britain's wars were largely manned and led by Scots. As the twentieth century dawned, the conscious socialist and organized workers of Scotland thought of themselves not nationally but internationally — and that although they acted often in typically Scottish ways and conditioned by a Scottish upbringing. It has taken a deal of shaking up and of highly necessary restatement of concepts, before people began to realize that nationalism and internationalism are not opposites, but only two sides of the same thing, and to realize, after that, that self-government for Scotland is not a step back to the days of local wars, anger and hatred before the Union, but rather a step forward to added values for several million people contributing their share towards the peace and civilization of the world.

NOTES ON CHAPTER I

Page 341

The only trades which a Highlander who was in any degree approaching a 'gentleman' — that is, someone who lives off rents — would demean himself to undertake, were cattle-droving and inn-keeping. Yet these trades were almost professions, since you did not have a master in either. However, it is very possible to overstate Highland idleness. Those who, for one reason or another, needed to live in a fresh environment, often developed brilliantly. One has only to think of various emigrants. And it seems likely that the eighteenth-century Gregorys, world-famous mathematicians and physicians, were landless Gregarach, driven to use their brains. It may yet be possible to change the social and economic environment, leaving the geographical one where it is.

NOTE ON CHAPTER II

Page 347

'Culloden the King of the Respectable.' A note in *The Lyon in Mourning* explains that Forbes was nicknamed King Duncan. Its use occurs in a memorandum by an Edinburgh writer, a mild Jacobite, who speaks of the Prince as 'The Young Man'.

Page 351

I am indebted to my remote cousin, Miss Smythe, for information about 'Pate the Atheist'. Patrick Smyth or Smythe, step-second-cousin to Mungo and the rest, was Commissary-General to the Prince in the '45. That is to say, he had charge of all the stores, a promising job. What happened in this family was no doubt typical of many. As Miss Smythe writes: 'The laird sat cannily at home while the family were "out" and I imagine burnt all letters, as we have a gap from about 1740 to 1750 in the family papers. There is one, giving an account of Prince Charlie in Perth, and how James Smyth (a doctor) was one of the chief people to welcome him to the city. He got into trouble later.' Another letter from the Prince to Peter Smith (note again how interchangeable Patrick and Peter are, at this time, as names), dated August 1745, requesting him to join him, is now the property of the Stewarts of Kinloch Moidart.

There is a story, which I doubt need not be taken over seriously, about Patrick 'the professed Infidell or Freethinker. After the surrender at Preston in 1715 He with 5 or 6 others made their escape in a ship from Falmouth and meeting with a storm when near the Coast of France, all expected to perish, the saills being reef'd and helm Lash'd, Peter was in such terrors he fell on his knees and in agony fell to prayer, when a fellow passenger came up to him in the cabin and whispered in his ear "By my Saul, Peter, ye're no blate". They got however safe on shore and Peter begged they would not mention his being so weak as to attempt praying or showed fears of death.'

The story goes on to say that after the '45, he 'continued secreted and in bad health' and that he finally 'recanted and retracted and professed himself a sincere Christian and so died'.

This is not unlike the mythical story of Davie Hume stuck in the bog and made to repeat the Lord's Prayer before the old woman would haul him out! It seems to me much more likely that poor Patrick Smyth, who was abroad a great deal of the time, came to have non-Presbyterian views about various matters. His wife, Elizabeth Strasbourgh, who died in Aberdeen in 1774 at the age of ninety (she was thus thirty-nine when she married him, and he a few years her junior — they had three daughters — what was the story?) was born 'of a noble family' in Kiovioe in Poland. I think this is Kiev, which was still in seventeenth-century Poland.

There is a letter from Patrick, dated 1714, from Rotterdam. He was serving in Flanders under the Duke of Marlborough. It sounds as though he had just escaped from an entanglement, for he writes to his brother David (the one who was to get into trouble the next year, as Kirstie remembered): 'I think myself very happy that I find myself in no hazard of so ill a wife as it seems our sweet ... makes, and I believe that will help well to keep me to my resolutions.' He was engaged in rather hazardous trade, having ventured thirty pounds sterling on a pound of cinnamon oil, which no doubt came in to Rotterdam from the Dutch East Indies, and which he proposed to get to France. It looks as though he intended to smuggle it, as he says there is a great risk in carrying it in. If he gets it safe through he will make a thousand livres by it. He adds that the exchange is cursedly dear, for he gets but one hundred guilders for ten pounds sterling. He is discouraged by the smallness of his pay and the general uncertainty of the service. In fact he is wanting to get out of it and asks his brother to 'look out for some heiress or other'. He sends back five different kinds of tea, cinnamon, indigo, breakfast cups and 'lifferbeans'.

Looking through the Smythe papers, one keeps coming on misfortunes which are definitely of their own date. In 1792 three Smyth daughters died of 'complaints in the Breast' — consumption. One of them, only nineteen, died actually at Airthrey, staying presumably with her Haldane cousins. In 1798 a year-old son died of inoculated smallpox.

Miss Smythe tells me of a Barbara who married an Episcopalian parson in the Orkneys and was in a list of proscribed communicants. Earlier on she had flirted with her father's groom, who was sacked!

Scottish family papers are particularly interesting to my mind, because we were a poor country and the younger sons at least went off or were packed off to seek their fortunes, so that you get letters and diaries and accounts which give an idea, not only of the country gentleman's life, but also of the sub-structure on which he — sometimes so precariously — rested. Looking through my own family papers, my mother and I came on the adventures of an eighteenth-century younger son — one of the Dreghorn Trotters, her father's folk — who went out, when he was sixteen years old or so, to manage some kind of store in Virginia. He obviously didn't make his fortune, but it was a lively kind of life. I am always hoping that this type of minor social document is not getting thrown away or given to the waste paper collection to be made into more government forms or Shockers for the Troops or merely burnt in despair by descendants who realize only too well that they themselves will never have time or energy to deal with them. The obvious thing to do is to offer them either to the National Library in Edinburgh or to Mass Observation.

NOTES ON CHAPTER III

Page 365

It would be possible in a really favourable summer to get tiny grapes from a vine even as far north as Inverness, if the soil is 'light, hot and open but with some strength' as Cockburn of Ormiston asked his gardener to make it for his vines. His letters are the first one turns to when considering the Scots garden in the first half of the eighteenth century. At first one is probably surprised at what could be grown, though no doubt some were of poor quality, especially such exotics as melons. He writes: 'I suppose you want Melon Seeds for making presents of, so you shall have to stock the whole Country, but I never saw anything but pickling in Scotld.'

He was very keen about his artichokes — delicious globe artichokes, of course — and wrote about them constantly; I think he started them the right way. They were new, but it looks as though his asparagus was taken as a matter of course as he only mentions it once. But — in a letter of February 12th! I am inclined to think that any vegetables that could be forced were forced by those with glass, in whatever form. Frames and small lights were probably the first kind, and one must remember that there was any amount of manure. A hot bed was no trouble to prepare, with plenty of horse dung to hand; though pigeon's dung was very highly thought of and always used when possible. With a great pigeon-loft it could easily be collected, though one would have thought the pigeons must have done far more harm than good — at any rate, the tenants whose corn they ate would have thought so! Dookits have mostly gone the way of other feudal appanages now.

Perhaps the key to it all was abundant manure and cheap labour. It would be possible to grow things by hand — to hang mats over the apricot trees and so on. And it would be worth taking pains to grow things which are now not commonly grown because they are easily imported. Though we miss them when imports are cut off. A good Scots garden in the eighteenth century would have cobs, filberts and walnuts, though I should think chestnuts must always have been imported. No doubt herbs were used a great deal more, and needed to be, in order to disguise tough, salt meat, braxy mutton and aged hens.

One thing that is not at all clear is whether and how vegetables were preserved. Obviously fruit, especially currants and cherries, were preserved in syrup, probably in jars. But what about vegetables? Lady Grisell Baillie's *Household Book* has a number of 'Bills of Fair', mostly no doubt of meals which were in some way out of the ordinary, and often with notables (such as 'Duck Montrose' or 'At the Princess') who could afford the best. There are usually vegetables and often fruit, whether raw or 'in cyrop'. Obviously it was part of the game to have food as early in the season as possible, such as Lord Anadall's January salmon. But what about the Duke of Roxburgh's asparagus on January 3rd? Possibly forced, but Lord Carlile has it on December 17th and I don't believe anyone can get asparagus to come on by that date. Even the extra eleven days which one should add on for the old calendar would not make any difference to speak of. Could it have been imported? Or could it have been preserved? There were no rubber rings but it can be done in a vacuum with parchment, perhaps in brine, as one preserves tomatoes now.

All this is during the first twenty years of the eighteenth century. Now move on to the *Ochtertyre House Book* and notice that in 1738 there are frequent mentions of 'artichoaks' in January. Of course if these were Jerusalem artichokes that is quite easy; otherwise would they perhaps be 'fonds d'artichaut' in vinegar? I expect the asparagus too might be preserved in vinegar, though I can't say I think they would have been very nice. I wish someone would try when we have nice vegetables to spare again. 'Spinage' was the most usual winter vegetable; but perhaps kale was not always mentioned and no doubt there would be vegetables in the broth, as there certainly were leeks in the frequent cockaleekie. In summer there was very often green broth and 'herb soop', and sometimes salad. But what about 'goossberry Tart' in February? These must have been preserved. 'Pottatoes' only come in once or twice a week, sometimes not so often. At the moment (1945) these old account books show a fantastically lost world of plenty. But, though the Ochtertyre servants fed not so badly, having meat quite often and otherwise fish, herrings, haggis and so on, yet the farm servant and crofter had little but oatmeal in some form, bread, kale, milk in summer and autumn and thin beer, or if he lived anywhere near the sea, a barrel of salt herring to come and go on, with maybe an odd smoked haddock. Probably they had mutton when a sheep died, though it would often be poor stuff. But I doubt if they had bacon in Scotland. Most of the eggs would go to the Big House and were in general part of the rent, but they might have an occasional cheese in summer.

Since writing this note, I have heard from Mrs. Ashton, of Grassthorpe, Newark, that in her seventeenth-century cookery book there is a recipe for keeping asparagus all the year round. This is it:

> Parboil them but a very little and put them into clarified butter, cover them with it, the butter being cold cover it, about a month after refresh them with new butter and bury them underground in a pot covered with leather.

The book includes a list of things which a prudent cook should have pickled or preserved, including a number of vegetables, kidneys, cockscombs, and, of all things, lettuce, which is the one vegetable I can see no method of preserving in the state in which we normally eat it. Possibly at that time it was mainly used cut up as a garnish for soups. There is a delightful recipe for preserving 'flowers of any kind', which must have made delicious sweets.

NOTES ON CHAPTERS IV AND V

It may seem to some that I have exaggerated the expression of love for Scotland in the mouths of some of these characters, above all, perhaps, Duncan Forbes, who is not usually presented in a very favourable light. He did the right thing, almost certainly: but the unromantic one. And, though he suffered for it, he did not suffer dramatically. Indeed, the Tory historians would make out that he did not suffer at all — all the suffering must be reserved for their side, the 'unfortunate' one. But neither will the Whig historians admit his sufferings, for that would be to allow that he was badly treated by the English liberators of Scotland. Perhaps we, at the end of a decade which has seen much civil war and many varieties of intervention and actions which one side or another would call treachery, may have more sympathy with a man who tried to do the right thing by his country and sometimes failed in judgment, and was disappointed often and betrayed in small ways, and at last, perhaps, died of a broken heart. That, at any rate, was said at the time. It is likely that some of his suggestions were really bad for Scotland, for instance, the forcible breaking up of the social structure of the Highlands; yet the alternatives from the English rulers might have been worse.

But he loved Scotland and he expressed this, not only in action, but in the fashion of words which I have put into his mouth. A relation of his, Mr. William Forbes, a Writer to the Signet, was with him on his deathbed and speaking in tears of the great loss Scotland would sustain by his death, but the Lord President answered: 'Were I to live longer, Willie, I could only mourn with you over my country.'

This was at least partly because of his disappointment and grief at not being able to do more for Scotland after the end of the '45. It was due to him rather than to anyone else that the thing had gone the way it had, and yet, when it came to pacification and reconstruction, he was not listened to. No doubt this came very largely because his opposite number on the English side was the coarse and brutish tough, Cumberland, who called him 'that old woman that talked to me about humanity'. Cumberland's own officers often found their commander quite revolting, though some of his generals were much like himself, including the generals who kicked Ex-Provost Hossack of Inverness, a friend and follower of Duncan Forbes, down two flights of stairs in his own town, all for hoping that their excellencies would be so good as to mingle mercy with judgment. And, although Rattray of Craighall and another Jacobite doctor, George Lauder, were with great difficulty begged from immediate hanging by the Lord President, yet they were rearrested later and kept prisoner in London for six months.

In the course of a century or so, patriotism — the patriotism of Forbes or Washington or, for that matter, Pitt — turned into Jingoism and had to go through the fires before it could be reborn into decency. I doubt if any one of these three men was anti-foreign. If you were at war, then you were at war; but you remained a citizen of Europe, or of the world. The narrow nationalism which is the opposite of internationalism was a product of later economic circumstances. But these can be, and partly have been, changed.

In the course of this book the folk at Gleneagles have got through a considerable amount of claret, brandy and other drinks. That would have been so. We meet most of them in the *Letter-Book of Bailie John Steuart of Inverness*. It was he who stocked the Culloden cellars. The Brigadier had a bill with him in 1724, which, not unnaturally, was still unpaid in 1737. Kyllachy's father, the old man who was in the '15, owed Bailie Steuart's father £20 Scots, not a very large sum, about which the Bailie wrote a letter to his son Alexander Mackintosh of Kyllachy, a London merchant and one of his constant correspondents. And now I am afraid I ought to quote the letter which is dated August 20th, 1735: 'Your brother Lachlan was apprised of this small debt and promised me payment, which I made no doubt hade been done or now if God hade spared him some longer time.' So Lachlan was dead ten years before the date of my book and it half looks as though he had been an honest, decent lad after all. Bailie Steuart imported an immense amount of wine; his exports included salmon, but whisky is scarcely mentioned except in one transaction where it is exchanged against herring. A hogshead of whisky 'if really good' costs £12 sterling. Even multiplied by seven, that is a bargain!

Page 380

Medicinal rhubarb is said to have been first used in the third millennium B.C. in China. It was always imported thence, though it was sometimes known as Turkey rhubarb since it came to Europe by the Persia-Aleppo-Smyrna route. Rhubarb is the main ingredient of Gregory's Powder, the beneficent invention, no doubt, of one of the Gregory dynasty of Edinburgh professors of medicine. But I am inclined to think that the Scots kitchen garden rhubarb was thought of not so much as a pleasant semi-fruit, but rather as a needful mild purgative. It must surely have been healthy to sup in early spring, after a winter of salt meat and oatmeal. I do not know whether the two sorts of rhubarb were ever mixed, as I have them in the book, but the pot was on the fire of the Lord President's room before I had time to consider deeply of the matter.

NOTES ON CHAPTER VI

Page 392

At this time the salt-pan workers along the Firth of Forth were serving under much the same conditions as the miners. When I was a child in Edinburgh we used to get our salt in beautiful crystals from Prestonpans, and the biggest, saltiest crystals were the 'Sunday salt' left in the pans over the week-end.

Page 393

The Lord President actually died in December of that year. The Dean and Faculty of Advocates went to the funeral in their gowns: and this although they had resolved, earlier on in 1736, after the death of Pringle of Newhall, a distinguished judge, never to do so, in case an awkward precedent were created. With them went the Keepers of and Writers to the Signet, the Lord Provost of Edinburgh, the Magistrates and Council. The Lords of Session and other persons of distinction went to the Forbes house at nine in the morning. Then many of the others walked from the Parliament Close through the steep and narrow streets, heavily shadowed by the mourning houses, down to the Lawnmarket, the bells tolling all the time. They 'met the corpse' at the entrance to the churchyard, and there, in Greyfriars churchyard, the bones of Duncan Forbes will be lying still. Though when I went there to ask, there was no one who could tell me, but only a man who asked me had he been buried recently.

VIRAGO MODERN CLASSICS
&
CLASSIC NON-FICTION

The first Virago Modern Classic, *Frost in May* by Antonia White, was published in 1978. It launched a list dedicated to the celebration of women writers and to the rediscovery and reprinting of their works. Its aim was, and is, to demonstrate the existence of a female tradition in fiction, and to broaden the sometimes narrow definition of a 'classic' which has often led to the neglect of interesting novels and short stories. Published with new introductions by some of today's best writers, the books are chosen for many reasons: they may be great works of fiction; they may be wonderful period pieces; they may reveal particular aspects of women's lives; they may be classics of comedy or storytelling.

The companion series, Virago Classic Non-Fiction, includes diaries, letters, literary criticism, and biographies – often by and about authors published in the Virago Modern Classics.

'Good news for everyone writing and reading today' – *Hilary Mantel*

'A continuingly magnificent imprint' – *Joanna Trollope*

'The Virago Modern Classics have reshaped literary history and enriched the reading of us all. No library is complete without them' – *Margaret Drabble*

VIRAGO MODERN CLASSICS
&
CLASSIC NON-FICTION

Some of the authors included in these two series –

Elizabeth von Arnim, Dorothy Baker, Pat Barker, Nina Bawden,
Nicola Beauman, Sybille Bedford, Jane Bowles, Kay Boyle,
Vera Brittain, Leonora Carrington, Angela Carter, Willa Cather,
Colette, Ivy Compton-Burnett, E.M. Delafield, Maureen Duffy,
Elaine Dundy, Nell Dunn, Emily Eden, George Egerton,
George Eliot, Miles Franklin, Mrs Gaskell,
Charlotte Perkins Gilman, George Gissing,
Victoria Glendinning, Radclyffe Hall, Shirley Hazzard,
Dorothy Hewett, Mary Hocking, Alice Hoffman,
Winifred Holtby, Janette Turner Hospital, Zora Neale Hurston,
Elizabeth Jenkins, F. Tennyson Jesse, Molly Keane,
Margaret Laurence, Maura Laverty, Rosamond Lehmann,
Rose Macaulay, Shena Mackay, Olivia Manning, Paule Marshall,
F.M. Mayor, Anaïs Nin, Kate O'Brien, Olivia, Grace Paley,
Mollie Panter-Downes, Dawn Powell, Dorothy Richardson,
E. Arnot Robertson, Jacqueline Rose, Vita Sackville-West,
Elaine Showalter, May Sinclair, Agnes Smedley, Dodie Smith,
Stevie Smith, Nancy Spain, Christina Stead, Carolyn Steedman,
Gertrude Stein, Jan Struther, Han Suyin, Elizabeth Taylor,
Sylvia Townsend Warner, Mary Webb, Eudora Welty,
Mae West, Rebecca West, Edith Wharton, Antonia White,
Christa Wolf, Virginia Woolf, E.H. Young

Also of Interest

THE NINE LIVES OF
NAOMI MITCHISON

Jenni Calder

Novelist, poet, passionate Scottish politician, campaigner for
sexual freedom, and farmer, Naomi Mitchison (born 1897)
has lived through nearly the entire twentieth century. *The
Nine Lives of Naomi Mitchison* is both a portrait of an age and a
wonderful tribute to the rich and fascinating life of a woman
who has travelled five continents, experienced two world
wars, written over seventy books – novels, travel, history and
autobiography – and who married and bore seven children.
Always adventurous, always an activist, her life included
friendship with Doris Lessing, Aldous Huxley, Stevie Smith
and E. M. Forster and impassioned campaigning on behalf of
the Fabian Society and a tribe in Botswana. With access to
private papers and rare interviews, Jenni Calder draws an
intimate picture of a truly inspiring life.

INVITATION TO THE WALTZ

Rosamond Lehmann

Introduction by Janet Watts

'Miss Lehmann has always written brilliantly of women in love, of mothers and daughters, of suffering' – *Margaret Drabble*

Groping through thick waves of sleep Olivia Curtis wakes to her seventeenth birthday. Within the bosom of a family at once lovingly familiar yet curiously remote, she stands poised on the brink of womanhood, anticipating her first dance with tremulous uncertainty and excitement. For her poised elder sister Kate the dance will be a triumph, but for Olivia, shy and awkward, what will it be?

First published in 1932, richly evoking the texture of rural middle-class England, in the charm and sensitivity of Olivia's personality Rosamond Lehmann perfectly captures the emotions of all young girls on the threshold of life.

THE PROFESSOR'S HOUSE

Willa Cather

Introduction by A. S. Byatt

'Her prose has a supple, lit-up sensuality that constantly makes the reader stop and read again as in a fine piece of poetry' – **Marina Warner**

Tom Outland, killed in the Great War, seemed an embodiment of the American frontier spirit – explorer, inventor and discoverer of ancient Amerindian culture. But he has left a troubling legacy, inspiring to his former professor, Godfrey St Peter, but bringing betrayal and strife to the professor's two daughters. St Peter has recently achieved worldly success, but it is in the shabby study of his former family home that he spends a summer reflecting on the people he has loved – his wife Lillian and his daughters and, above all, the enigmatic, courageous Outland.

MY ÁNTONIA
Willa Cather

Introduction by A. S. Byatt

'The most sensuous of writers, Willa Cather builds her imagined world almost as solidly as our five senses build the universe around us . . . great is her accomplishment' – **Rebecca West**

Jim Burden tells the story of his beloved childhood friend Ántonia, the immigrant girl and woman whose struggle and splendour represent the source of life itself. Willa Cather sought to recapture the superb vitality of frontier America, nowhere more so than in this magnificent portrait of the pioneer woman, seen through the eyes of the man for whom she can only be a memory, never a possession.

THAT LADY

Kate O'Brien

Introduction by Desmond Hogan

Spain in the years before the Armada, and high passion meets high politics. Ana, Princess of Eboli, heiress of Spain's leading family, widow of Philip II's wisest counsellor and rumoured to be the King's mistress, falls unexpectedly in love with Don Antonio Perez, dandy, adulterer, skilled politician. With her unusual looks, her aristocratic arrogance and the simplicities of her faith, Ana cannot understand why her private life should become entangled with the affairs of state and, finally, incur the terrible vindictiveness of the King himself . . . Kate O'Brien's understanding and love of Spain enhance the beauty of this passionate and intelligent novel.

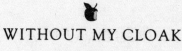

WITHOUT MY CLOAK

Kate O'Brien

Introduction by Desmond Hogan

'A peculiarly beautiful and arresting piece of fiction'
– *J B Priestley*

This stirring family saga opens in 1789 when Anthony
Considine creeps into the town of Mellick with a stolen horse.
By the 1850's, his son Honest John has made the Considines a
leading Mellick family. In turn Anthony builds a fine country
house for his family, little knowing that his son Dennis will
one day threaten the toil of generations with his love for a
peasant girl. This is an enduring portrait of one family's
strengths and weaknesses; of matches made and lost; of
divided loyalties and individual freedom threatened by the
pride of the Mellick name.

Winner of the Hawthornden and James Tait Black Prizes in
1931.

PIRATES AT PLAY

Violet Trefusis

New Introduction by Lisa St Aubin de Teràn

Set in the 1920s, this enchanting romantic comedy shows young aristocrat, Elizabeth Caracole (pronounced 'Crackle'), being 'finished' in Florence with the family of a Papal count – and dentist. All five brothers fall for her, but their beautiful ambitious sister, Vica, has plans of her own.

Violet Trefusis (1894–1972), English novelist, was the lover of Vita Sackville-West, with whom she eloped in 1919. By 1921 the affair was over and Violet returned to her husband in Paris. There she published novels including the well-loved *Hunt the Slipper* (1937) and *Echo* (1931).

A VIEW OF THE HARBOUR

Elizabeth Taylor

New Introduction by Peter Kemp

'Here is a name which stands for something distinctive in novel-writing and which guarantees pleasure'
– *Elizabeth Bowen*

The war is over, and retired naval officer Bertram comes to a quiet fishing village, intending to paint. Inquisitive and capriciously benevolent, he soon interests himself in every aspect of the picturesque backwater. There's a lot going on beneath the quiet surface. Beautiful divorcee, Tory, is painfully involved with the local doctor – her best friend's husband – an affair which deeply disturbs adolescent Prudence. The indomitable invalid, Mrs Bracey, domineers over her two daughters, each gallant in her own fashion. Meanwhile the sad widow, Lily Wilson, pins vain hopes on Bertram's careless kindness. In this witty and compassionate story of illicit love in a quiet coastal town Elizabeth Taylor draws an unforgettable and enchanting picture of love, loss and the keeping up of appearances.

☐	The Nine Lives of Naomi Mitchison	Jenni Calder	£20.00
☐	My Ántonia	Willa Cather	£6.99
☐	The Professor's House	Willa Cather	£6.99
☐	South Riding	Winifred Holtby	£6.99
☐	Invitation to the Waltz	Rosamond Lehmann	£6.99
☐	The Weather in the Streets	Rosamond Lehmann	£6.99
☐	That Lady	Kate O'Brien	£6.99
☐	Without My Cloak	Kate O'Brien	£6.99
☐	A View of the Harbour	Elizabeth Taylor	£6.99
☐	Pirates at Play	Violet Trefusis	£6.99

Virago now offers an exciting range of quality titles by both established and new authors. All of the books in this series are available from:

Little, Brown and Company (UK),
P.O. Box 11,
Falmouth,
Cornwall TR10 9EN.
Telephone No: 01326 372400
Fax No: 01326 317444
E-mail: books@barni.avel.co.uk

Payments can be made as follows: cheque, postal order (payable to Little, Brown and Company) or by credit cards, Visa/Access. Do not send cash or currency. UK customers and B.F.P.O. please allow £1.00 for postage and packing for the first book, plus 50p for the second book, plus 30p for each additional book up to a maximum charge of £3.00 (7 books plus).

Overseas customers including Ireland, please allow £2.00 for the first book plus £1.00 for the second book, plus 50p for each additional book.

NAME (Block Letters) ....

....

ADDRESS ....

....

....

☐ I enclose my remittance for ....
☐ I wish to pay by Access/Visa Card

Number ☐☐☐☐☐☐☐☐☐☐☐☐☐☐☐☐

Card Expiry Date ☐☐☐☐

A VIEW OF THE HARBOUR

Elizabeth Taylor

New Introduction by Peter Kemp

'Here is a name which stands for something distinctive in novel-writing and which guarantees pleasure'
– *Elizabeth Bowen*

The war is over, and retired naval officer Bertram comes to a quiet fishing village, intending to paint. Inquisitive and capriciously benevolent, he soon interests himself in every aspect of the picturesque backwater. There's a lot going on beneath the quiet surface. Beautiful divorcee, Tory, is painfully involved with the local doctor – her best friend's husband – an affair which deeply disturbs adolescent Prudence. The indomitable invalid, Mrs Bracey, domineers over her two daughters, each gallant in her own fashion. Meanwhile the sad widow, Lily Wilson, pins vain hopes on Bertram's careless kindness. In this witty and compassionate story of illicit love in a quiet coastal town Elizabeth Taylor draws an unforgettable and enchanting picture of love, loss and the keeping up of appearances.

☐	The Nine Lives of Naomi Mitchison	Jenni Calder	£20.00
☐	My Ántonia	Willa Cather	£6.99
☐	The Professor's House	Willa Cather	£6.99
☐	South Riding	Winifred Holtby	£6.99
☐	Invitation to the Waltz	Rosamond Lehmann	£6.99
☐	The Weather in the Streets	Rosamond Lehmann	£6.99
☐	That Lady	Kate O'Brien	£6.99
☐	Without My Cloak	Kate O'Brien	£6.99
☐	A View of the Harbour	Elizabeth Taylor	£6.99
☐	Pirates at Play	Violet Trefusis	£6.99

Virago now offers an exciting range of quality titles by both established and new authors. All of the books in this series are available from:

Little, Brown and Company (UK),
P.O. Box 11,
Falmouth,
Cornwall TR10 9EN.
Telephone No: 01326 372400
Fax No: 01326 317444
E-mail: books@barni.avel.co.uk

Payments can be made as follows: cheque, postal order (payable to Little, Brown and Company) or by credit cards, Visa/Access. Do not send cash or currency. UK customers and B.F.P.O. please allow £1.00 for postage and packing for the first book, plus 50p for the second book, plus 30p for each additional book up to a maximum charge of £3.00 (7 books plus).

Overseas customers including Ireland, please allow £2.00 for the first book plus £1.00 for the second book, plus 50p for each additional book.

NAME (Block Letters) ....

....

ADDRESS ....

....

....

☐ I enclose my remittance for ....
☐ I wish to pay by Access/Visa Card

Number ⬜⬜⬜⬜⬜⬜⬜⬜⬜⬜⬜⬜⬜⬜⬜⬜

Card Expiry Date ⬜⬜⬜⬜